history

Unless you feel flattered, in which case, sure, maybe it's you.

Cover art by Tugboat Design
Edited by James Avery Fuchs
Published by One Tall Tree Press

ISBN (digital)
978-0995307032
ISBN (paperback)
978-0995307025

Dedication

For Quinn.
We joked that this book was my mistress, but really it was my love song to you.

PRAISE FOR CHEMISTRY

"Overflowing with wit... Lynch cleverly and dramatically subverts expectations, delivering a fast-moving and very fun zombie blood-fest that challenges ideas about femininity and teenage love."
BookLife Prize in Fiction

"Stella is no Bella... Not your run-of-the-mill zombie book, this title has heart."
School Library Journal

"This was an AMAZING book! I could not put it down. Chemistry by C.L. Lynch is everything Twilight should have been. It is funny, empowering, and still romantic.... do yourself a favor and pick this up."
The Roadside Reader

"Chemistry by C. L. Lynch begins as a humorous take on Stephanie Meyer's Twilight, but quickly turns into a story of a bullied teenager learning to trust others. Stella Blunt is not an easy character to like, which is why it's so great to see her lowering her guard and learning to trust."
IndieReader Discovery Awards - Winner for Humor 2017

"...funny and irreverent... Chemistry is a fun, clever novel that provides a welcome contrast to the more traditional young-adult romances of the genre, even while drawing on their warmth and familiarity."
Foreword Reviews

"Chemistry doesn't just tell a story - it roars it."
The Midwest Book Review

PREFACE

I stood perfectly still. My heart pounded in my chest as I fought back the tears. I must stay calm and collected, keep my dignity, and project as confident an aura as possible.

"Come and find me, my love."

I looked around, scanning the horizon for his shape. Oh, my God. So much humanity, lost.

Hundreds of them swarmed below me, clawing and snarling ghoulishly.

He was out there somewhere. Would he even recognize me? Or would he be too far gone?

If so, I would be the one to end it… and I'd do it with love.

And a meat cleaver.

Act 1

Your spirits kindle to a flame,
Moved by the lightest touch of blame;
And when a friend in kindness tries
To show you where your error lies,
Conviction does but more incense;
Perverseness is your whole defence;
Truth, judgment, wit, give place to spite,
Regardless both of wrong and right;
Your virtues all suspended wait,
Till time has open'd reason's gate;
And, what is worse, your passion bends
Its force against your nearest friends

Jonathan Swift, "To Stella"

1

Howie

I never know when I'm dreaming, which is what makes my dreams so terrifying.

I thought it was a regular day. I was at school, waiting for Stella to get off her bus like I did before I won her over. Nowadays, I picked her up at her house, but today, for some reason, I waited for her bus.

She was getting closer. I felt her mind coming clearer and clearer among the buzz of all the other brainwaves around me. She stood out, like a diamond in a coal mine, like birdsong in the morning, like a beacon in the dark - like a gourmet meal at a hot dog stand.

But she wasn't on the last bus that pulled in. She was coming from another direction. I turned to follow her because everything in me points to her now. My soul is a compass that always leads to Stella. So I turned toward her mind, and I saw her driving a minivan. The back door of the van opened, and a boy my age stepped out. He called, "Bye, Mom!" and took off toward the school. I walked up to the van and knocked on the window. Stella rolled it down. She had changed. Breathtaking as ever, but my heart clenched when I saw fine lines around her eyes, a heaviness to her cheeks, a streak of grey in her hair.

"Howie," she said, "You need to stop this. You need to move on."

"No... Stella..." how could I explain it to her? Her mind... oh... her mind... It was like light, like air, like something electric inside me. And she was still beautiful. What did some crow's feet matter? Some grey? Her brown eyes were still as warm, her lips as luscious...

And I began to beg; I couldn't bear to live without her. She was everything. The next thing I knew I was yanking open the door, embracing her. I meant to kiss her, but I bit down and her flesh was hot and delicious in my mouth. I couldn't stop. I heard the screams from the surrounding people, but Stella wasn't screaming - Stella couldn't scream, she barely had a face. It only took a quick smash of her skull on the windshield to crack it open, and then her brains were in my hands, red as raspberries, and I couldn't get enough. My mind was screaming but my body knew what to do, following its instincts and thrilling to the taste, finally, the taste of what I never let myself even think of longing for. I slurped and exulted in the sheer liberty of finally doing what my body longed to do... and oh, God forgive me, it was so good, so good...

I woke up slowly - at first with reluctance, because I kept thinking, "one more bite, just one more..." and then my consciousness kicked in and I pulled myself awake with horror and disgust. I writhed in my bed, trying to rid myself of the terrible, terrible dream and ended up sobbing into my pillow until morning.

I hated the dreams. They made me feel vile, tainted, evil. I dreaded sleep because I never knew when another one would come to me, and they were coming more and more often lately. Ever since we started talking about the future. Ever since Stella realized that she was leaving me behind.

It was tempting to avoid sleep altogether, avoid the dreams and my bed where they lay, but sleep is vital. Sleep helps restore brain function, and when you're like me, you need all the brain function you can get. Especially if you're dating Stella. Her brain is like a knife. When I wasn't at my best, I felt unworthy of her, no more able to enter her sphere than my dog can enter mine. She tried to be understanding, but she got impatient, and I didn't blame her.

So I forced myself to sleep because sleep helped. So did brains, but brains were hard to get, and my family had to ration them. The first week after I met Stella, I ate three meals a day, sometimes four, just to impress her. My family put a stop to that. We couldn't store enough pig heads in the house to keep up with that kind of demand.

Instead, I started digging into the dog food. We ordered it from the States and stacked it in the pantry - canned brains in milk. I have no idea why normal humans would produce and consume such a thing. It worked for the dog, who would eat anything if we let him, but we found it pretty unappetizing. My family didn't care if I dug into the dog's share. Canned brains were easy to store, and we always ordered in bulk.

I took a can out of the pantry and opened it for Army, who stood next to me with his tail waiving. Then I grabbed another can for myself. I might even eat a second can today, since I had lost two hours of sleep. Otherwise, I might not be able to keep up with Stella, and I loved keeping up with Stella. When I was on, when I was *sharp*, I felt like we could take over the world together. Our banter was on fire. Stella loved to debate, and when I could hold my own against her, I felt her love and respect for me burning hot and bright.

On good days, I thought that maybe this was why everything had happened to me. Maybe she was why I had to lose my parents, and live as a teenager for decades, slurping cold pig brains through a straw: It was all so I could wait for her.

On bad days, I knew that this was a bright spot in an otherwise desolate existence: that one day she would realize that I was too young for her, that I could never get a degree, give her children, earn a pension… could never be the sort of person that she could build a life with. And then she would leave. She'd find someone else, someone who could grow old with her, someone who would still be able to keep up with her even when she had a PhD. Someone who didn't start to drool unless he slurped a can of brains in milk every morning. Someone who didn't carry the most feared disease in the world; a disease widely considered to be fictional because people thought that nothing so nightmarish could truly exist.

So every morning, I woke up determined to make today as perfect for her as possible. Because when that day happened, when Stella outgrew me, I didn't want to have any regrets. But sometimes, before I eat, I'm too stupid for my own good, because I was halfway through my second can of brains before I remembered: Today was Stella's birthday. And I was running late.

Stella's parents were used to their daughter's zombie boyfriend showing up in the mornings. I was eternally grateful for their acceptance. Very few people knew what my family and I really were, and most of those considered us a looming potential health crisis. But Stella's parents always took things in stride, even when they found out that I loved their daughter partly because of her brains.

Usually I just showed up to take Stella to school. Sometimes I'd kill time by washing their dishes or wiping their counters while Stella got ready. But I was early today because I had something a little more elaborate in mind.

I arrived on their doorstep loaded down with bags. Stella was still asleep. I could usually count on Stella staying asleep until some cataclysmic event woke her up. Even her phone, which played *Mars, Bringer of War* at seven every morning, couldn't make her budge.

Mr. Blunt didn't even bother saying hello when I knocked lightly on the door. "Just come in, Howie. Did you think we weren't expecting you? I suppose you've bought Stella a pony or something."

"I wouldn't settle for anything less than a unicorn, and they were fresh out," I said. "How do you think she'll feel about cheesecake?"

"For breakfast?" said Mrs. Blunt from behind her coffee cup.

"And bacon," I said, holding up a bag. "I'm making bacon."

"I don't see how you could go wrong."

Half an hour later I went upstairs with a plate of bacon and eggs and a glass of chilled orange juice, no pulp. Mr. Blunt opened the bedroom door for me. "I'll stand here and watch. You know. To protect her chastity."

I don't think Stella's father actually cared that much about her chastity. He joked about it a lot, but he and Mrs. Blunt gave us our privacy when we want it. He just loved to make me uncomfortable, and I was acutely aware of two things as I stepped into her room that morning: First, that Stella was naked under her cotton nightgown, and second, that her father was standing there, watching us. So I tried to shove my awkward adolescent lust into the corner of my mind that wants to eat people and focused on giving Stella a happy birthday. But it was hard, being this close to Stella. Even in her sleep, her brain waves flickered through me, warming me and filling me with a kind of pleasure that can't be described accurately to those who aren't infected with the Z0381E "reanimation" virus.

I laid the plate on her bedside table and sat on the bed next to her. She didn't budge. I ran my fingers through her sweet-smelling hair and stroked her face gently, lightly touching her fluttering eyelids and kissable lips.

"Stella... Stella.... Beautiful... wake up... it's your birthday."

She opened her lovely chocolate eyes and looked at me. My God. I still got butterflies.

"Fuck off," she said and rolled over. Her brain waves went from that pleasant thrum to a cacophony of irritation. Her covers were half off, and I could see the curve of her hips, the bulge of her breasts under that thin nightshirt. My heart pounded as I imagined running my hands along the warmth of her body, waking her up with caresses. More than caresses; the stuff of fantasies. But I just stroked her hair again.

"Happy birthday," I said, wishing I could put some cheer into the phrase. When the virus started eating my brain, it damaged my processing and language centres first. According to my adoptive father, the centre that translates emotion into speech is one of the first to go. He doesn't know why. So I could never convey my feelings for her the way I wanted to. I was effectively brain damaged. I'm the worst person to wish someone a happy birthday.

I tried again. "Happy birthday." I really tried to put the exclamation mark in.

Stella turned and squinted at me. "Aw. You're trying to sound excited. That's adorable. And pathetic." She buried her face in her pillow.

"Let me show you how it's done, Howie," said Mr. Blunt, coming into the room. He grabbed Stella's shoulders and started to shake her.

"Stella! It's your BIRTHDAY! It's been EIGHTEEN YEARS SINCE YOUR FACE SQUEEZED THROUGH YOUR MOTHER'S VAGINA!"

"Don't you bring my vagina into this, Tim!" shouted Mrs. Blunt from downstairs. "Every year you have to mention my vagina!"

"Let me go back to my dream," said Stella. "It didn't involve my mother's vagina. It was a happier place."

"What did you dream?" I asked. She looked at me, raised her eyebrows slightly and gave a tiny smile. I could feel the arousal in her mind and a corresponding tightening in my groin. Why couldn't I have had *that* dream instead?

"Okay, then, consider this," said Stella's father. "As of today, you are legally entitled to vote…"

"…Goody…" said Stella into her pillow.

"…and look up porn. Just think, Stella, there's a whole world of porn out there, waiting for you, and you don't have to lie when they ask you to check the little box that says you're eighteen."

I hadn't ventured into the world of online pornography. I was afraid that if I did, I might never emerge. After all, I had been a teenage virgin for a lot of decades, and there was no end in sight.

"There's bacon and eggs. And cheesecake," I said.

"Okay, I'm up. Jeez. You know what would be a nice birthday present? Sleeping."

"Sorry, honey," said Mr. Blunt cheerfully. "School trumps birthdays. Just look up porn during lunch."

Stella rolled her eyes at him and started to eat. He chuckled and went back down the stairs, whistling to himself.

We sat in silence while Stella scraped at her plate.

"So, are we going to talk about yesterday?" she said eventually, with a great air of casualness.

A cold wind blew through me. No, I thought. I didn't even want to think about yesterday. I had almost forgotten. I'm good at forgetting.

"If you want to," I said. "It's your birthday." The one good thing about my expressionless voice is that my emotions rarely betray me. Stella was getting pretty good at picking up nuances, but when I wanted to hide my feelings, I usually could.

"I want today to be a wonderful day," I said. "You only turn eighteen once."

"Unless you're you," she said, her voice tinged with bitterness. "Then it's either once or maybe never, depending on how you count things."

"Technically, I turned eighteen a long time ago."

"And yet you plan to be a kid forever..." Her voice started to rise. Then she took a breath. "No. You're right. It's my birthday, and I say that we pretend nothing is wrong. Can you do that?"

"Easily," I said. That was all I did every day. That was all I wanted out of life, forever: to pretend that nothing was wrong. Because when I remembered everything that was wrong, I was overwhelmed by despair.

Stella

I was having an amazing dream. It was the hottest dream I had ever had in my life. Maybe it was the universe's gift to me on my eighteenth birthday, because Howie and I were having steamy, passionate sex. The kind that I really wanted to have. The kind we had never had.

The dream was screaming hot, and Howie kept saying my name every time he entered me.

"Stella… Stella…. Beautiful…" but then he said, "wake up… it's your birthday." I opened my eyes and found myself still in bed with him, but he was fully clothed in his usual prep-school style. I felt a wave of frustration and disappointment. Looking at him in real life only made me want to finish the dream more. With his slim body, tidy blonde hair, shy smile, and oh-so-scholarly looking glasses, Howie is the most adorkable guy in the entire world. I was torn between ordering him away so I could finish the dream, or just grabbing him and taking him right then and there. Except Dad was standing in the doorway, and besides, I might catch Howie's fucking virus - which may or may not be transmissible via fucking.

Then I remembered yesterday, and a flood of anger and hurt poured through me. That fight had been brewing for weeks and weeks - and it had finally erupted in a boil of nastiness after school. I had screamed at him for an hour in the school parking lot before storming out of his car and taking the bus home instead.

Now here he was, giving me breakfast in bed and acting as if nothing had even happened. It drove me crazy, and I itched to pick another fight, because fighting is the only way I know how to deal with emotional discomfort. A good fight is like a good sneeze - it clears things out. But today was my birthday, and he had gone to all this trouble to try and make me happy. It didn't seem like the right time for round two of treating-my-boyfriend-like-an-emotional-Kleenex.

So I took my cue from him and agreed to pretend it hadn't happened. I bottled the hurt and the anger deep inside, ate the delicious breakfast that Howie had cooked for me, and focused on feeling grateful.

He hung over me as I ate, and I felt like a heap of garbage for yelling at him at all, ever. But I couldn't seem to help it sometimes. I breathed in the smell of him. To others, he might smell like the formaldehyde that he injected into his veins on a regular basis to keep his zombie virus at bay. But to me, he smelled like love and trust. I wanted him. I wanted *all* of him, forever. But he kept holding back, and it made me so helplessly furious. He loved me. I *knew* he loved me. So why wouldn't he even *try* to keep me in his life? Why was he giving up on us?

Shit, I was getting worked up again. I sighed heavily and swung my legs off of the bed.

"Did you say there was cheesecake?"

Only Howie would think of serving cheesecake for breakfast. He would get an idea in his head and then do it, without using any kind of social referencing to ask himself, "Is this remotely normal?"

I didn't mind when he did these things in the privacy of my home. My parents, who knew about the virus, got used to his weirdness a long time ago, and it was a perpetual source of amusement for them. But teenagers are rabid about picking out any kind of socially atypical behaviour, so when Howie did this sort of stuff at school, our fellow students acted like sharks who have smelled blood in the water. They didn't know that he was a zombie, but they *did* know that he was fucking weird.

Like, when we had classes together he always tried to get there first and pull out my chair for me to sit down, like I was Audrey Hepburn or something. He never even seemed to notice the titters and eye rolls that we got when he did this sort of thing. I pointed it out bluntly once, and he just gave me a confused glance and said, "What do I care what they think?"

If I told him that it made me truly unhappy, he would stop, but it *didn't* make me unhappy, per se. It was sweet. But it was also a vibrant daily reminder that in many ways, my boyfriend wasn't quite right in the head.

His brother and sister did socially peculiar things, too. Hazel always stood a little too close, Ray never mastered the concept of polite conversation, and Doc Mullins always said completely awkward or terrifying things when trying to reassure you, which left you feeling much less reassured. They were all brain-damaged by their zombie virus and it showed up in the little things, like Howie bringing a birthday cake for breakfast instead of giving it to me at lunch, or dinner.

Howie insisted on lighting candles on the cake - a big one and an eight. Then he *tried* to sing *Happy Birthday*, but he can't sing so he just sort of droned the words. My parents sang too - Dad harmonized because he's a showoff.

"Don't forget to make a wish!" my mother reminded me when I leaned in to blow out the candles.

"What am I, five?" I responded.

"No, you're eighteen," said Howie.

"I was being sarcastic, Howie. Did you have your brains this morning?"

"Yes. Make a wish, Gorgeous."

"Feel free to wish away my receding hairline," encouraged Dad.

"Wish away your hairline, got it."

"REVERSE my receding hairline!"

"Further the receding hairline."

"I don't think we're supposed to know what the wish is," said Howie.

"I'M GOING TO BLOW OUT MY CANDLES NOW."

I leaned forward and blew them out quickly, so they wouldn't think that I had really made a stupid birthday wish.

But I did.

I wish Howie would just fucking try.

2

Stella

The cake was delicious of course, because everything Howie makes is delicious, but by the time I finished eating my second helping we were running late for school. I said goodbye to my parents, grabbed my bag and dragged Howie out the door. The moment we were around the corner from my house Howie took me in his arms and gave me a long tender kiss that melted me into a puddle. There was something about his kisses that softened me. My swear words and general assholery fell away at his touch and for just a few moments, I could act like a real person, instead of a cactus.

"I'm sorry about yesterday," I whispered, leaning into him and taking a deep breath of his smell. God, I wanted him. I wanted him to kiss me all over. I wanted him to spend hours telling me how much he adored me. I wanted him to penetrate me while I screamed his name.

He laid a cool finger on my lips. "I don't know what you're talking about."

But we both knew that he did.

Howie gave me a searching glance with his hazy blue eyes. "Are we… are we still on for tonight?"

"Of course."

"It… I would… You can change your mind if you want. You know, if you decided you'd rather go to a movie or something with the girls."

"No." I was sure about this. "I'm sorry I said such shitty stuff to you. I love you and I want to spend my birthday with you."

"I'm glad." Sometimes Howie sounded like a robot. He unlocked his car door, swung it open and passed me the keys. I liked to be the driver, especially in the morning. He could be a little out-of-it in the morning, and while his driving was always robotically correct, he didn't always spot the people who ran red lights or changed lanes in the middle of intersections and stuff.

"Thank you," I said, getting into the driver's seat. "For the cheesecake. And breakfast. And… generally just being you."

"You're welcome," he said. "I'm sorry I had to wake you up."

"I was having a good dream, that's all. I'm sorry I swore at you."

He cast me a glance that had a hint of a twinkle in it. "How good of a dream? Can I hear it?"

"Why don't you tell me what *you* dream about?" I said irritably. "You're always asking about my dreams and you never return the favour."

"My dreams aren't as good as your dreams."

"Howie, my last dream involved Sponge Bob and a nuclear bomb that I had to diffuse using dental floss."

"My point exactly."

"You don't have Sponge Bob bomb dreams?" I teased.

"I don't even know who Sponge Bob is. I assume he's a sponge named Bob, but he's never visited my dreams."

"So what *do* you dream?"

Howie looked out the window. "I don't want to talk about it."

"If *you* won't tell me *your* dreams, why should you expect *me* to tell you *mine?*"

"I don't expect you to do anything. I just love it when you do." His voice was soft and husky and I felt both caressed by it and wounded by it. I wanted to fight him and kiss him simultaneously. That can't be normal.

Then again, I've never really been normal. I spent my childhood punching kids when they teased me. Nowadays I could usually keep my violent impulses in check, but I still *had* them. I thought terrible violent things on a regular basis. But Howie was always so calm and gentle. He put me to shame.

Maybe he didn't want to talk about his dreams because *he* had sex dreams too, and he didn't want to give me ammunition for a "we should have sex" argument, which we were due to have again soon if my dreams were any indication.

Or maybe he *didn't* have sex dreams. Maybe he had nightmares about his parents turning into zombies. Howie was pretty open with me about most things, except for the part of his life where he got bitten by the undead. He never talked about that and he got *really* quiet if anyone brought it up. His traumatic past always reminded me that there was a giant gulf between him and me.

Then again, there were a lot of those little reminders, and I had become good at ignoring them. Like his music, which ranged from kinda old to really damn old. Or like his car: this crappy Dodge Shadow, which was older than me. Howie bought it new.

I decided to drop the dream thing, in case I was being insensitive, and switched on the radio instead.

"Our first caller this morning is Cindy! Cindy, can you tell us about a time when you ghosted on somebody by mistake?"

I switched the channel.

"So remember, if you hear Dan Mangan playing, call in for a chance to win two tickets to the Commodore Ballroom on March twelfth…"

I switched it again. Stupid morning talk radio.

"They're calling the mystery killer 'The Seattle Zombie' because the skulls of all three victims were empty…"

I looked sharply at Howie, but he was looking out the window in a brooding kind of way and I don't think he was paying attention. I fiddled with the volume knob and accidentally turned it down. I swore and turned it back up again.

"...victims were homeless and one has yet to be identified. Police have not disclosed any further details other than to say that the brains of all three have not yet been found and that they suspect foul play."

"Howie!" I hissed. "Listen to this!"

Howie turned and listened obediently, but the newscaster had moved on.

"...Voted down in Parliament today. The bill would have..."

"You missed it!" I said.

"What did I miss?"

"They said there are people dead in Seattle who are missing their brains. They're calling it 'The Seattle Zombie' killer."

"Oh," said Howie. "That's sad."

"ZOMBIE, Howie."

He gave me a funny look. "I don't think it could be an actual zombie, Beautiful."

"No, I guess not..." I'd seen real zombies in action, and I mean *real* zombies, not just Howie's kind of not-quite-zombie. Zombies didn't just take the brain and leave the rest alone. They ripped whatever they could get their teeth into. I watched them tear Howie's dog into pieces last year, which was a horrifying preview of what could have happened to me or my parents. Luckily the dog turned out to be half-zombie too and he's fine, but I didn't know that at the time and it was upsetting to watch.

"Never mind," I said. "It just... you know. Brains."

Howie looked uncomfortable. "They rarely do eat the brain, Stella. I mean, we're... they're attracted to brains but by the time they've turned... I mean, the skull is..." he paused and looked sickened. Was he thinking about his family? Shit.

"I'm sorry," I said. "I got carried away."

"It's okay," he said faintly, but he seemed to withdraw even more, and I didn't know what to say.

We finished the drive to school in silence.

I parked the car in our high school's parking lot, and we got out of the car without speaking. It was almost time for the bell to ring, so there was no time to try and make Howie talk and find out what was bothering him. Especially since he could just still be upset about our fight yesterday. I know I was. So I just stormed into the school with Howie trailing in my wake.

I was furious with myself the whole way. Furious with myself for reminding Howie of his dead parents by bringing up zombies. Furious with myself for being so upset with Howie over shit he couldn't control. Furious with myself for being unable to discuss it without getting angry. And I was furious at him because I loved him so goddamn much, and I was becoming increasingly aware of the fact that our relationship was on the rocks.

I stopped at my locker and turned around. Howie was right behind me, with that glazed look that he got when I was angry, or determined, or pushing my way through a crowd. There's something about my brain waves that can totally overwhelm zombies. The Canadian government ran an EEG and an MRI and a bunch of other stuff on me. They said I had higher than normal levels of beta and gamma waves, but they weren't sure what this meant. Anyway, Howie seemed to get blissed out on it, and the more emotional I was, the more he loved it. Right now he looked almost dizzy, like he was drunk. And in a way he was. Drunk on me. Would any other person ever look at me in that same way? How could I lose him?

Howie took my hand and my heart fluttered at the cool, gentle touch. "I am desperately in love with you," he said huskily.

I felt a flood of emotion, like a dam bursting. All my pent up rage and love and sexual frustration burst loose. I wanted to just take him and *make* him be mine forever, and fuck his stupid arguments. I dropped my backpack, shoved Howie up against my locker. His lips were soft and his breath was chemically clean. I kissed him deeply, claiming him, trying to make him a part of me. Howie moaned, put his hands on my hips and pulled me tight against his body. He was hard for me and I wished like hell that my dream this morning could be a reality - although *maybe* not right here in the school hall. Maybe. For a minute or so we were holding each other so tight that I thought I might get bruises from Howie's fingers digging into my waist. I didn't even care. But I guess he realized he was being rougher than usual because he let go abruptly and started to pull away. I grabbed his hands and pinned them up over his head against the locker as I pressed myself into his lean, hard body. I swear I felt his knees buckle a bit.

"OH, SICK!" someone shouted.

"Get a room!"

"They don't need a room, they need a CAVERN!"

"Oh, man, he's going to be squashed like a bug."

I held up my middle finger while continuing to eat my boyfriend's face. There was some laughter and the catcalls stopped.

"Okay, but seriously guys, the bell rang a minute ago," said my friend Kate's voice. "Also, you're bracing your left hand on my locker door."

I sighed and pulled away. Howie swung his bag in front of him in the universal code for "I have an erection".

"For Christ's sake, Howie," said Kate. "Be proud. Show your boner."

"No, thank you," said Howie. I knew he was embarrassed, but he looked and sounded as cool as the proverbial cucumber.

"So, you seem to be enjoying your birthday," said Kate to me with a scowl on her thin face. She hated it when Howie and I engaged in public displays of affection, which - in our defence - we rarely did at school. We were the most mocked couple in the school as it was. Between my height and weight and Howie's status as a confirmed loser, everyone was sure that we must be dating each other out of desperation. Howie didn't care. He gave zero fucks about what other people thought. But I preferred my romantic moments to be private. Today was a fluke.

I was already wondering what had come over me.

"I don't know what brought that on, but I hope it happens again," Howie whispered in my ear.

"Go to class," I ordered. He kissed my cheek, nodded awkwardly at Kate, and moved off with his stiff, lurching gait, which was always more pronounced after one of our kissing sessions.

"So, I take it you guys made up," said Kate, yanking open her locker hastily. Her dark bangs, longer than the hair on the rest of her head, fell over her face as she bent over her book bag.

"What do you mean?" I said, bristling.

"I saw you having a massivo argument in his car yesterday."

I didn't say anything. I just stuffed my books into my bag, swung it onto my shoulder, and started marching down the hall toward Biology. We passed a clump of girls standing by the washrooms and something about them triggered my internal emotional-defence alarms. I stopped, turned around, and charged back toward them.

"Where are you going?" Kate called as if she didn't know. I didn't bother to answer as I stormed right into the crowd. They were clustered around a girl with an unfortunate case of acne and a trying-not-to-cry look on her face. When I barged in, everyone jumped aside.

"Is everything okay?" I asked the acne girl. She nodded and took the opportunity to get the hell out of there. I turned to her bullies. I knew them well - they were my bullies, too. The ringleader was Kelly Svancara, who was my arch nemesis before I grew up a bit and started seeing her as the pathetic, socially aggressive, future middle-manager that she really was. Her stunts didn't really bother me anymore, but I couldn't help stepping in when I saw her pulling them on other people.

"Oh, did I barge in on your fun? Sorry about that," I said.

"Wow, you're so brave, Stella," said Kelly, looking up and down at my form-fitting V-neck shirt and ass-hugging jeans. "I wouldn't dare go out in public looking like that."

"You know, it's my birthday and I'm feeling charitable," I said with a smile, "so I *won't* hit you with a comeback that'll go right over your head."

"Your birthday? How does it feel to have your age finally match your dress size?"

"*Almost* as good as it feels to have a soul. You wouldn't understand," I responded before I could stop myself. So much for being charitable. I gave her a little wave and took off, with Kelly and company barking "woof woof!" at me as I walked away.

"Fuck that little ingrown toenail of a human being," I said to Kate, who had been hovering uncomfortably nearby. "How does she know I wear a size eighteen?"

"Lucky guess," said Kate. "She just can't figure out how you manage to be hot in a size eighteen when she can't do it in a size eight."

"I failed utterly again at being a nice person, though," I said. "I think I may have to give up even trying."

"To hell with being nice. Let's just be awesome," said Kate, taking my arm. "Come to SFU with me, and we'll take that campus by storm."

Not this again. Not today. "Kate? As a birthday favour? Don't talk about universities, or I'll break you in two."

"Okay," she said, looking startled. "Is this about your fight with Howie?"

"I MEAN IT, KATELYN."

"Okay, okay… Well, happy birthday, anyway. How does it feel to be eighteen? Do you feel like an adult?"

"Not especially. Hi, Amy," I said to our friend Amy, who also took Biology with us.

"Hey! Happy Birthday!" she said, giving a little wave.

"Thanks." I plunked down next to her. I always felt like a giant sitting next to Amy, who was small and fine-boned, like a little blonde doll.

"So," Amy said, "what did…" The second bell interrupted her and our teacher handed out dissection trays. We dissected frogs last week, and this week it was a fetal pig.

"This is sick," said Amy, looking at our tiny pig with distaste. "Poor you, Stella! Happy birthday, here's a dead baby pig!"

I looked at the pig. It didn't look bad. When you've put a chainsaw through a human skull, it doesn't seem so awful to cut open a pig fetus. Besides, the formaldehyde smell reminded me of Howie. And he had a freezer full of giant pig heads that he chopped into regularly. This teeny piglet looked small and dainty by comparison.

"It's cute," I said. "Hand me the scalpel, I'll start."

"So, did Howie bring you a gift this morning?" Amy asked. Amy was a die-hard romantic and she loved hearing about the sweet things Howie did, so she could imagine someone doing the same things for her someday. Of course, she didn't know that he drank pig brains, or that he was seventy years old. The zombie stuff was classified top-secret by the Canadian government so I couldn't tell my friends about it without being thrown in jail for treason.

"No, he brought me bacon and eggs in bed, and then put candles on a cheesecake," I said.

"Seriously?"

"Mmm hmm. My morning has involved a lot of dead pig."

"What do you mean?" Amy said.

"Because bacon is pig, dumbass," said Kate crankily. Kate did not like hearing about the sweet things Howie did. It wasn't that she didn't like Howie - they got along fine - but something about our relationship bothered her.

"So, what was yesterday about?" Kate asked me.

"None of your business," I said smoothly.

Kate held up her hands. "Sorry, I didn't mean to pry. You guys made up - rather publicly I might add - and that's the important thing."

"Not really. More like put it on hiatus so my birthday wouldn't suck."

"What yesterday?" asked Amy. "Did you have a fight or something?"

"Yeah," I mumbled.

"About what?"

I stifled the urge to say, "NONE OF YOUR BUSINESS!" in a louder voice. Amy meant well, but she kept asking me about my relationship with Howie, and there was a lot I couldn't legally say. It was frustrating because one of the major ways to bond with other females was basically closed to me. I mean, how many teen girls can't talk about their relationship because it's *illegal* to do so?

That really sucked.

"Just about universities and stuff," I said cautiously. "I don't really want to talk about it."

"Why? Do you guys want to go to different schools?" asked Amy, leaning in.

"She doesn't want to talk about it, Amy," said Kate sharply. She grabbed my arm. "Oh, my God, look, I think the pig just took a shit."

I let Kate distract me and tried to focus on my work because I didn't want to think about yesterday. I didn't want to think about the future. I wanted to think about today, my eighteenth birthday, and this goddamn pig.

Howie

The kiss at Stella's locker took me entirely by surprise. As far as I could tell, Stella was simmering with suppressed fury the entire way into the school. Her brain waves make me positively quiver when she's worked up over something, so it felt good to be following behind her, feeling her boil and churn while she smashed her body into bullies and willed the world out of her way. It didn't help that her talk of brains in the car had brought my dream back to me in hideous detail. It made me feel contaminated - like I shouldn't even be around her. When my body vibrated to the feel of her mind, it made me feel both ecstatic and disgusted with myself.

I followed behind her, watching the sway of her hips and the toss of her hair as she marched. She was filled with fire and determination in all things, and I loved the power of it. I wanted so badly to be worthy of her. When she finally turned to me, all I could do was tell her yet again how much I loved her.

Next thing I knew, she had me pressed up against the lockers and we were kissing and it felt so good, so good. I thought of the night I had planned for us and felt such a surge of desire that I had to stop myself from trying to remove her clothes right there in the hall. I suppressed those sinful thoughts, but worse images replaced them; my mind filled with a vision of my fingers prying into her abdomen, right into her intestines. I let go of her and I was going to gently pull her off of me, but instead, she pinned my hands up over my head. It felt good to have my hands held safely away from her, but the black thoughts were coming fast and thick, much worse than usual. I remembered my dream, and how I tore off her face with my teeth, and my knees buckled.

I was almost relieved when Kate interrupted us. The black thoughts had been getting worse and worse lately and it scared me. Those thoughts weren't mine - they didn't come from me. I never wanted to hurt Stella, but the thoughts came nonetheless. They were evil. I was filled with evil.

As I stumbled away from Stella and headed toward my first class, I distracted myself from those dark thoughts by focusing on Stella's birthday evening.

Back in January I had brought up her birthday and suggested a party with her family and friends, but she rejected that instantly.

"I like my friends, and I like my parents, and I like you, but I don't necessarily enjoy all of you in one place," she had said firmly. "And I don't like sitting there while everyone drops presents in my lap. I have to open them and smile and simper and act grateful and it's no fun."

"We could say no presents."

"It's not the presents I mind. It's having to be all sun and smiles as payment."

"So what do you want to do?"

She had sighed and laid her head briefly on my shoulder. Those moments of vulnerability always broke my heart, because she trusted me, and I wasn't sure I deserved that kind of trust.

"Let's just do something you and me," she had said. "Do you mind skipping the party idea?"

I had bowed my head over hers and breathed her in.

"You? All to myself? That sounds like heaven."

I had been obsessively planning things ever since. I spent my morning English class running over things in my mind. I wanted tonight to be perfect. I wanted to make it a night we would both remember, because I knew - I *knew* - that my time with Stella was drawing shorter, and I wanted to make the most of this birthday, which might be both the first and last of her birthdays I would ever celebrate with her. Next year she would be nineteen - would she still be with me then? Or would she walk away at twenty? Twenty-one? All I knew was that it was coming, and I didn't know if I had months left, or years. But the more Stella looked to the future, the more I felt like I was moving into her past. The thought made me put my head down on my desk and take deep breaths as I tried to calm my panic.

Tonight. Think about tonight.

When the bell rang I shook myself awake and hurried to get to Physics. I liked to get there before Stella did so I could pull out her seat. She thought it was silly and her friends smirked when I did it, and probably so did everyone else. But I am a relic from another era, and to me, this is how you show respect to women.

Over the decades I had watched the world accord women more jobs, higher wages, and higher expectations. Women could run companies now, not just act as secretaries. They wore pants and worked construction and took science courses and I thought it was all fantastic, because I've always loved strong, smart women.

But while women had more rights these days, I feel like they never actually gained any more respect. The boys around me still used the word 'girl' as an insult. They called girls who slept with them sluts, but girls who didn't were prudes, and they didn't even bother to show girls basic courtesy anymore when they were courting them. They didn't pull out chairs for their girlfriends or take off their hats or stand when they went in or out of a room. My father - my real father - raised me to do those things to show a woman respect, and my father had always had a tremendous amount of respect for women.

Maybe there were new ways, more modern ways, to show respect to a woman. But if so, I didn't know what they were and even if I had, I probably would have kept forgetting. So I showed Stella respect the only way I knew how, and I didn't really care if the low-pantsed, backwards-hatted, furrowed-browed male population of my class thought I was crazy.

I just wished I didn't feel that Stella thought I was crazy, too.

I made it to class before Stella and I quickly lost myself in reverie again as I thought about all the ways I wanted to show Stella how much I worshipped her. I wanted to make her feel so special that she would hold the memory of me dear in her heart, long after she had left me behind.

I was so lost in thoughts of Stella that I almost didn't notice her coming into the room.

Almost.

Not noticing Stella is like not noticing a locomotive. I don't mean because of her size; she isn't as big as she thinks she is. She isn't as big as *other* people think she is, either. She's tall - just below of my own height of six feet - and voluptuous. But that isn't what makes her stand out. Stella fills a room with her personality. People turn to look at her when she walks in. They feel the need to make way for her. They think it must be her size, but it's her mind. There's a kind of spotlight on her at all times. Someday it will be her most valuable quality, because when she walks, she owns the world.

"You are a queen," I whispered to her as I pulled out her chair and she sat down. I took my own seat on her left and nodded to Kate, who plunked down on her right. Once, trying in my clumsy way to be a gentleman, I had pulled out Kate's seat, too. It did not go well.

"Howie, you're being sappy," Stella said. "I am not really in the mood for sappy."

"You can go back to telling me why you think Satan is the good guy in *Paradise Lost*," I suggested.

"That's a longer conversation."

"Okay, then... do you like Kipling?"

"I've never kippled," she said promptly.

I grinned at her and reached for her hand under the desk. "I figured you would know that joke."

"On a serious note, I secretly like Kipling, but I'm ashamed of loving jingoist, colonialist doggerel."

I nodded slowly and frowned. Stella had done it again - she would throw out some comment and completely change the way I viewed something. I loved that about her, even if it meant that sometimes it ruined the way I saw old songs or childhood books. She turned things upside down and saw them from the other side. Stella is a warrior, a champion of underdogs. She sees the things that could hurt people.

"I didn't realize I wasn't supposed to like it," I confessed to her. "Is it really so bad?"

Stella raised one eyebrow in the way that I always found so devastating. "Did you never read *The White Man's Burden*? Tell me you don't think it's okay to imply that brown people are helpless children who need to be cared for."

"Okay, I agree with that, but I really loved *The Jungle Book*... I mean... what's wrong with *The White Seal,* for example? It's environmentalist."

"Howie. He's *white*. Like, even with seals, it has to be the *one white guy* who saves the day?"

"Oh..." Now I had to re-read the entire works of Kipling and try to consider them from a modern angle. God, I loved how Stella kept me on my toes. I loved that she got angry on behalf of others. I loved that she held everything to the highest of standards... even if it meant that she held me to those standards, too.

Standards that I couldn't meet.

"Oh, my God," Kate interrupted, poking Stella and pointing at the Physics teacher. "Look. Mr. Roeper has the world's longest nose hair. Look at it! I feel like a tiny man is about to come sliding down it."

Stella laughed and said something in response as she turned away. I tried to focus on the class, but I could smell Stella's hair, and feel her mind buzzing through my body as she concentrated on the lesson. Oh, I just couldn't wait for tonight.

3

Howie

"Are you *sure* you don't want a party?" asked Stella's friend Michelle when we sat down for lunch.

"Oh, yeah," Stella said with a smirk. "A party. That's totally my style."

"Not really," I said. "That would be a little out of character for you."

"Eat your lunch, Howie."

Stella's friends were polite about the fact that I was an idiot before lunch every day. The official story was that I couldn't think clearly when my blood sugar was low. But Stella's friends must have known that my condition wasn't as simple as diabetes. That didn't explain my liquid lunches, my awkward gait, or the fact that sometimes I would be bleeding and wouldn't even notice until someone pointed it out to me.

I obediently sucked on the straw in my thermos while Stella told the girls that I was taking her out tonight.

"What's the plan, Howie?" Amy asked. Amy was a sweetheart and always kind to me. She was the only one of Stella's friends who made me feel wanted at their table. I looked at Stella and smiled, and she smiled back at me in the way that always sent my heart pounding.

"Nothing fancy," I said. "Just a nice romantic night, I hope." Romantic, memorable, passionate… all those and more.

"Well, *we* want to do something for her birthday, too," said Kate.

"I *really* don't want a party," Stella said flatly. "I *hate* parties with the fire of a thousand suns. Like, to me, the word 'party' is stored in the same part of my brain that stores words like 'fungus' and 'cancer' and 'reality television.'"

"So what you're saying is… you want a party," said Kate. Her mind was dancing with mischief and it made me smile. Kate didn't like me much and neither did her mother. But I liked Kate.

"What I am saying, Ms. Wilson," said Stella with the authority of a queen, "is that if you attempt to do anything that involves balloons or singing, I will remove your head from your body and use it as a salsa bowl."

I shuddered involuntarily, but no one noticed.

"Let us celebrate your birthday, or I'll play Happy Birthday to you on the trumpet right here in the cafeteria," Kate persisted.

"Fine," Stella said. "Let's go to a movie or something this weekend. But no balloons."

"Deal."

"Hey… Howie… if you're done your lunch… can you check my precalc homework?" Amy asked, touching my arm tentatively.

"Sure, pass it over," I said, sitting up straight and straightening my glasses. My lunch was kicking in. Fresh brains made a big difference. The canned material was all right. It got the job done. But the canned brains were mixed with sugars and milk and all sorts of other ingredients that weren't useful to my system. That dose of undiluted, fresh neuronal tissue at lunch did wonders. I could almost feel it re-myelinating my axons, speeding up my nerve impulses, and sharpening my senses. I felt like I was really present in the world, not just drifting through. Everything seemed simple - I skimmed through Amy's math with no problems. I could see the difference it made to Stella, too. She loved watching me be smart.

It wouldn't last.

There was a golden hour after lunch when I felt like everything was easy. Then I reverted to my more normal state of being.

I tried to make the best of it while I could. I joined in the conversation at the table, making the girls laugh, and Stella proud. Making both of us forget that I had an evil virus and that it was going to tear us apart.

Stella

Howie leaned over Amy's math homework, ticking off mistakes that he had caught and explaining them to her as she gazed up at him in admiration. It was clear that Amy had a bit of a crush on Howie, and who could blame her? I loved it when he used words like 'parametrize'. It got me hot and bothered to see him being all smart and knowledgeable like that and he knew it, too, because even though he seemed totally focused on Amy's homework, he reached out with his other hand and laid it on my thigh and gave me a squeeze. Then he cast me a quick glance and smiled at me, and it made me feel all gooshy inside.

I wondered what he had planned for my birthday that night. He would probably do something really old-fashioned, like give me a corsage and take me ballroom dancing. Except he knew I wasn't into dancing, so maybe not. Maybe put on a tuxedo and take me to a private dinner in a library or something. That was the kind of weird but amazing shit that was totally Howie's style: the storybook crap that isn't supposed to happen in real life, with a side-order of social awkwardness to balance it all.

"Did you hear about the Seattle Zombie?" Kate said loudly. I glanced sharply at Howie to see if he had heard, but he was absorbed in his discussion with Amy.

"Yeah," Michelle shrugged. "Maybe it's an organ-harvesting crime ring or something."

"You can't transplant a brain," said Kate scornfully.

Howie was paying attention now and I was worried it would upset him again, so I changed topics quickly.

"How's band practice going?"

"Awful. I don't know how we're going to be ready in time. The concert's coming soon," said Kate.

"Yeah," agreed Michelle. "Our woodwind section sounds terrible, and the vocals keep coming in late."

"That sucks," I said.

"Hey, Kate," said Howie.

Kate gave him a weary look. "What?"

"What do trumpets and pirates have in common?"

Kate sighed and thought for a moment. "I give up. What?"

"They both murder in the high C's."

Kate groaned and Michelle laughed.

"I don't get it," whispered Amy to me.

"Band kid thing," I whispered back to Amy.

"You know those jokes always fall *flat* with me," said Kate.

"I don't know," said Howie. "I thought it was pretty sharp."

"But Howie's not in band," said Amy.

"He likes music, though." It always surprised me that he didn't play an instrument. He totally seems like the kind of guy who sits around singing heartfelt songs on the ukulele or something. But I hadn't asked about it because I never knew which innocent question would make him go all quiet and sad. Talking to Howie about his life was like going through a minefield, so I steered clear most of the time.

"You're going to be in big *treble,*" Kate said to Howie. She was smiling now.

"Could you repeat that?" he said promptly.

"Oh, that was just a *prelude,*" said Kate.

"Can't you guys *scale* it back?" Michelle asked.

I reached out and squeezed Howie's hand, and he aimed his adorable smile at me for a moment before shooting back at Michelle with,

"What? I think my jokes are clef-er."

"I don't think you're in tune with our feelings," said Kate.

"Are you asking me to give it a rest?" he said.

"Oh my God, you guys," I groaned loudly. "The puns... the puns need to stop." But I didn't really mean it. Howie's eyes were twinkling.

"But puns are my forte," he protested.

"I'm beginning to think puns give you a tromboner," said Kate.

"As long as he doesn't jazz in his pants," added Michelle.

Howie laughed in an embarrassed way. "Okay, you ladies win. I give up."

The bell rang and we all stood up and started clearing away our trays.

"I'll see you later, Beautiful," said Howie in my ear.

I wanted to tell him that I loved him and I thought he was cute and clever, but that's the kind of thing I could only say after he'd melted me into a sodden puddle with one of those magic kisses, so instead I just groped him casually and headed off to Drama class.

I loved Drama. It was a good outlet for me because it gave me a really good opportunity to get some yelling done. My teacher said I had great projection. The downside to Drama was that I had to share it with other human beings. As I walked into class, someone pulled away from a group of chatting students and jumped in front of me. Fuck. It was Dean Kato.

Dean was one of those charming, attractive guys that I just loved to hate. He wasn't one of the people who barked at me when I passed them in the halls, but he was friends with them, and he used to kick Howie's chair and call him a "chubby chaser" in Chemistry last year so he was definitely on my extensive mental list of Class Asshats. He often started semi-teasing conversations with me, and while he had never said anything out-and-out mean to me, I was always waiting for the other shoe to drop because I knew who his friends were and they made it abundantly clear that I was loathsome to them. On the other hand, he sometimes gave me little glances that made me think that he didn't find me loathsome at all, and I didn't know what to do with that.

"I hear it's your birthday! Got anything special planned?" he said. He flashed me a cheeky grin and his dark eyes danced. He had dimples when he grinned. I have a thing for dimples.

I scowled. "Did Kelly Svancara tell you it was my birthday?" I demanded.

"My sources are anonymous," he said, shrugging his broad shoulders. "So. Is there a big party? Am I invited?"

"Not unless you want to be a third wheel at my intimate dinner with my boyfriend tonight," I said. "I don't do parties."

He smirked. "Romantic night out, huh? And does good old Howard know how to properly romance a girl?"

"I'm sorry, is that your business? Because you seem to be minding it."

I tried to move past him but he held up a hand, looking pouty.

"Where are you going? I'm trying to wish you a happy birthday!"

"The usual way to do that is to say, 'happy birthday!' which you actually haven't said yet."

"Well then." He bowed low. "Happy birthday."

"Thank you," I said, and I swept past him to my seat.

"Rappy Rurfday!" said Carter Davidson in a Scooby Doo voice as I passed by. I ignored him. Asshats, all of them. Once upon a time, negative attention made me explode with fury. But I could handle it way better these days. It was a lot easier to dismiss jerks like Carter and teases like Dean now. All I had to do was remember that I had a cute boyfriend who loved me.

A cute boyfriend who was giving up on our relationship.

Fuck.

Our Drama teacher, Ms. Lawless, clapped to get everyone's attention.

"Today I'll be assigning partners for our skit project, which you will start work on next class. This project is worth twenty percent of your grade, so take it seriously. You and your partner will choose a fifteen-minute selection from a play. You will rehearse it, block it, and arrange costumes for it. Then you will present it to the class. The best skits will be selected to be performed to the entire grade eleven and twelve classes."

Frig. My heart started to pound. Partners? I did not play well with others, especially when a quarter of the people in the class actively hated my guts. I hoped Ms. Lawless wouldn't pair me with someone who teased me.

She started to read out the partner names while I fidgeted nervously.

"Carter Davidson and Nicole Marks. Desiree Poirier and Mackenzie Hooton. Laresa Lee and Benjamin Gill."

I alternated between relieved when someone I didn't like was paired up with someone who wasn't me, and disappointed when someone I didn't hate got paired off with someone who wasn't me.

"Stella Blunt and Dean Kato."

"What? Why?" I blurted out, which was really uncool. I mean, first of all, when the teacher assigns partners you shouldn't whine about it like you're a five-year-old. Second of all, when you get paired up with one of the most popular guys in school, it isn't considered normal to complain.

"You two have a good dynamic together," said Ms. Lawless. "You play off of each other well in scenes."

"Are trades allowed?" asked Desiree Poirier, glancing at Dean.

"Absolutely not," said Ms. Lawless, turning to collect the assignment papers from her desk.

"It's just that I don't think it's fair for those of us who are paired up with same-sex partners. The teams with one boy and one girl have more options open to them."

Ms. Lawless stared at her. "How do you figure that?"

"Like, they can do romance scenes," she said.

Ms. Lawless stood very still, and the classroom hushed.

"Tell me," Ms. Lawless said in a dangerously soft tone of voice. "Why can't two girls do a romance scene?"

Desiree wilted under her glare and looked away.

"No trades," Ms. Lawless repeated firmly, and she started to pass around the papers.

"Ha," snorted Carter, low enough that Ms. Lawless couldn't hear him but loud enough that *I* could, "Romance isn't open to everyone. Poor Dean. I'd rather do a gay scene than a love scene with *that*," and he jerked his head at me. The people next to him tittered.

"Woof woof," said someone else in a whisper.

Once upon a time I would have jumped on those guys and made them apologize to my fists. These days I just ignored it. But I felt my cheeks burning anyway and I avoided eye contact with Dean for the rest of the class.

When the bell rang, I darted straight for the door before more people could get some shots in at me about being partnered with Dean.

"Stella! Hey, Stella, wait!" It was Dean. I considered ignoring him, but curiosity makes us do stupid things, so I turned and raised my eyebrows expectantly.

"What?"

"Do you want to get together soon, so we can work on our project?"

"No. We'll be given class time."

"Not enough if we want to make it really good," he argued.

My eyebrows went higher. He gave one of his annoyingly disarming grins.

"Come on, I think we should try to make this really epic! Look, it's worth twenty percent of our final grade. Isn't that worth a little after-school effort?"

"How about we just see how it goes?" I said, edging away. His cologne, or aftershave or whatever, smelled kind of good.

"Oooh, Dean, going to get together for some 'homework'?" teased Carter Davidson. He made little kissy noises at us.

"Whatever, Carter, I need to do well on this project. Get my GPA up before graduation," said Dean. "Hey, I've been meaning to ask. Can I borrow your notes from Geology?"

I gave their backs my middle finger as they walked off. It made me feel a little better.

This project was going to suck. Happy birthday to me.

After Drama, I had History with Michelle. Howie was leaving History as I was arriving, so we did our usual brief hand-squeeze as we passed each other. Howie gave me a concerned look. His creepy zombie-sense usually told him when I was upset, so I was sure he picked up on the fact that I was stewing over something. But I didn't want to get into it so I told him I was fine and kept moving.

"What's wrong now?" Michelle asked when I threw myself into my chair beside her. Unlike Howie, my friends tended to ignore my many rages. They had learned months ago that when I get pissed off, it's usually over inconsequential things.

"I'll tell you after class." At least I this time I had a problem I could legally tell my friends about.

When class let out, I walked Michelle out of the school where we met up with Kate and Amy.

"So? You want to tell us?" Michelle asked.

"Tell us what?" Kate demanded.

"Stella's newest reason for looking like a thundercloud."

So I told them about being paired up with Dean Kato.

"Ooh, lucky," Michelle said. "He's so hot."

"It's not lucky! He's a pus-filled, granulomatous dick. And I have a boyfriend!"

Kate squinted at me. "What, your love is *so* pure that your eye *never* wanders?"

"Of course it fucking wanders," I snapped. "Dean Kato would wander *anyone's* eye. But now I'm a target." I told them about the teasing in class, and they agreed that it sucked. I kept a lookout for Howie, who often used his zombie brain powers to track me down after school. I spotted him hanging out thirty or forty feet away, pretending to be really interested in a sickly crabapple tree. I sighed and waved him over. When he got close enough I put my hands on my hips.

"Okay, we've been through this before. When you see me talking with my friends, just join us. You don't need to hang out halfway down the block like a creepy stalker."

"I don't like to interrupt you."

"You're not an unwelcome interruption."

"I get you to myself tonight. I don't need to steal you from your friends anymore today."

"Who says you're stealing her?" said Kate. "We're kindly sharing her with you."

"See?" Howie said, "your conversation has stopped. That happens a lot when I show up."

"Oh, we were just talking about Old Roeper's nose hair. I think it's the source of all his powers," said Kate.

I guess she thought she was covering for me, but I despise lies. I gave Kate a dirty look and said goodbye to my friends. On the way to the car, I told Howie about my Drama class, but I put more emphasis on the teasing than on the actual person I had been paired up with.

"I can't understand it," said Howie. "I would think they'd all be fighting over who gets to partner up with you. I'm jealous of Dean already." He gave me a smile which was obviously meant to be sweet and teasing, but I just felt a stab of guilt for feeling attracted to Dean. He looked at me carefully and frowned.

"Is it really so bad to be paired up with him?" he asked. "He doesn't tease you, does he? Better him than, say, Carter Davidson, right?"

"I just don't like him," I said. "Remember how he used to kick your chair and tease *you* in Chemistry last year?"

"Not really."

"Well. He did."

Howie shrugged.

"The worst part is that he wants to get together to work on the project outside of class because he's desperate to get a good grade. I don't want to meet up with this guy!"

"I'm sure it would be fine. At least he's taking the project seriously. I know how mad it would make you if he was slacking off."

"That's true. But you wouldn't be upset if we did work on the project together?"

"Upset? Of course not. You didn't choose him for a partner, and your grades are important to you. A tad anxious, maybe." He twined his fingers with mine. "He might win you away from me."

I looked at his serious blue eyes behind his glasses and felt a swell of love for him.

"Nope. Never happen," I said.

Howie

I dropped Stella off at her house and promised to pick her up again at six. By the time I got home, Ray and Hazel had come home in Ray's car and Hazel was already putting Ray to work. Hazel could order Ray around in a way that my father and I couldn't. Within minutes of their walking in the door, she had him dourly taping a banner over the archway into the dining room.

"Thanks," I said, watching Hazel try to blow up a red balloon. "This means a lot to me."

"You better damn well get laid tonight, that's all I can say," said Ray.

"And what? Risk turning her into one of us?"

"Could be worse. Then you could stop pissing on about how she's going to grow up and leave you."

"This is no life for her to live," I said. "Eating out of pig skulls, having to move around every so often so people don't notice that you aren't getting older, accidentally running into girls you went to school with and having them think you're their old classmate's grandson… Do you think Stella wants that? Do you think she wants to be like us? Do you know what I dreamed last night? I dreamed that I killed and ate her."

"I love those dreams," said Ray.

"You dream about eating Stella?" I felt slightly sick.

"I have. But not usually. Just… people."

"And you like it? Even when you wake up and realize…"

"Realize I didn't actually kill anybody? Yeah. Especially then."

"I have them too," said Hazel. "It isn't us. It's the virus. It just… gets into your dreams. It doesn't mean anything. They're just dreams."

"It's evil. And I'm not risking giving it to her," I said. "I'm just giving her a good birthday."

"You should give her a good something," muttered Ray.

"I've got work to do," I said, and went to the kitchen to start Stella's dinner.

I wanted to make sure that tonight was a night that neither of us would ever forget, because I knew that this memory might have to last me for the rest of my life. If yesterday's argument was any indication, my time with Stella was drawing to a close.

4

Stella

I dressed for my birthday dinner with care.

Howie was picking me up at six, and I couldn't wait for him to see me in this dress, which my mother and I had picked up on sale in January. As soon as I saw it, I thought of Howie. It was a retro sort of dress that flared out from the waist and ended at the knees. Very vintage pin-up girl. I admired myself in the mirror and felt like the sexiest creature on the planet.

Before I met Howie, I never would have believed that I could ever feel like that without losing a ton of weight first. I had come to terms with my size and followed the body positive movement. But it never occurred to me that anyone could find a woman as giant as me genuinely hot.

Enter Howie Mullins. He likes his women big and bossy, and in his eyes, I was a supermodel. It was a bit of a mind-fuck when I realized that my boyfriend didn't love me despite my size but partially because of it.

When I did fully grasp it, we fought about it. I accused him of having a fat fetish. That was one of the only times I have ever seen him lose his temper. It was pretty cute because other than talking louder he couldn't even sound angry, but I could see the metaphorical steam pouring out of his ears.

"If a man loves skinny girls, is he accused of having a 'thin fetish'? Do skinny girls feel offended by the fact that their boyfriends love their bodies? You've told me time and again that you love my dimples. Should I hate that? Because I don't; it makes me happy. I want you to be attracted to me. Why can't I be attracted to you? I love you for so many reasons, but the fact that I find you devastatingly sexy should be considered part of that, not a sign of perversion. It's not perverted to think the woman I love is a total fox."

He went on to insist that there were lots of men out there who liked some meat on their girls. Then he spent a week quietly pointing them out to me when we were in public. Totally normal guys - not a whole lot of them, but they were out there. Howie taught me how to recognize the quick appreciative glances at my ample cleavage, my round butt, my curvy calves. In private he showed me in explicit detail every part of me that he found sexy. He talked and demonstrated and proved until I went from wanting to believe that I was beautiful to knowing it.

So now I could come downstairs on the evening of my eighteenth birthday with my curves showcased, instead of hidden, and feel like some kind of goddess.

Howie gave me that.

Mom and Dad whistled and clapped, and made me do a spin. The flared skirt swirled around me. Mom said it needed a necklace and found me a glittery sparkling thing which made me look fabulous.

"Where is he taking you?" Mom asked, fussing over my hair with a brush.

"No idea. He has some kind of secret surprise planned. Probably something weird and over-the-top."

"Like a treasure hunt that covers the entire city," suggested Dad.

"No, Tim," said Mom. "That's you. That's what you did for our first date."

"I don't own a copyright on it, you know."

"God, I hope I don't have to do a treasure hunt in these shoes," I said, looking down at my high-heeled Mary Janes.

"That doesn't sound right for Howie," said Mom. "Only Tim would be that cruel."

"If I'm so cruel, how'd I get that second date with you, Lainey?" Dad teased.

"I don't remember now," said Mom primly.

"Well, let me give you a refresher," he said, grabbing her around the waist and kissing her.

"Oh, God," I said as my mother wrapped her arms around his neck and pulled him closer. "While you guys do that, I'll be touching up my makeup."

It was my duty, as their daughter, to be disgusted by my parents' PDAs, but secretly I liked knowing that my parents were embarrassingly in love after nearly twenty years. I wanted to believe that Howie and I would be like that, too.

That's why it bothered me so much when he told me that it wasn't going to happen.

Howie

Stella must have been watching for me because she came hopping down her front steps into the Vancouver February drizzle the moment I pulled up. I got out of the car to open the passenger door for her and my heart may have literally stopped. It happens sometimes. Dad says the damage to our brains causes sinus arrhythmias.

Stella was dressed up to the nines - absolutely stunning in a black and red Rockabilly sort of dress that hugged her bosom and flared out at the waist. It ended just above her knees and showed off her legs in the sexiest way. I nearly fell to my knees at her feet, but I didn't want to muddy my suit. Instead, I opened my umbrella and held it out to cover her head as I leaned in and kissed her. Soft kisses work best on her. She can defend herself against anything - except gentleness. I could feel her tough exterior softening at my tender touch. God, I wanted her.

"I've seen that tux before," she said with a smile, tugging on my collar. The tux belonged to Dad and was definitely out of date, but it was still a tux.

"It's about the only dress-up outfit I have." One of my hands was busy holding the umbrella, but the other caressed along her waist and up the bodice of her dress. It was affecting Stella. I could feel her responding, but she kept her teasing smile on her face.

"I like the tux. It's you."

"It's old-fashioned."

"That's you all over," she said. "Where are you taking me?"

"Nowhere new," I said, walking her to the passenger door and opening it for her. "But I've arranged something special."

"Oh?" She raised an eyebrow as she sat down. "Okay, I admit to being intrigued."

I got into the driver's seat, backed out of the parking lot… and drove back to my house.

"Your place?" she said, sounding less intrigued and more cautious.

"No one's home," I said. "I booted them all out. We have the place to ourselves."

"And no surveillance equipment?"

I poked her. Last year a government agent spied on me and may have used our relationship as an excuse to release an outbreak of the virus on the city so he could frame our family and have us arrested. So now she was paranoid about surveillance.

I ushered her inside, past the dog, who greeted Stella with a wildly-waving tail, and into the dining room.

She gasped. I felt her surprise and the flush of warmth she felt towards me, and I was mentally blinded by it for a moment. She turned to say something to me and then gave me a little shove.

"Hey, wake up. Did you do all this?" She gestured at the decorations.

"Hazel and Ray helped with the balloons and the streamers, but the rose petals and the flowers were me. And these." I picked up a box of matches and went through the room, lighting the many candles I had set out on the table, shelves, and window sills.

Stella turned around, inspecting the room in the soft, flickering candlelight. A mental image rose, unbidden, of her body laid out on the table and her intestines spread among the rose petals. I shook it away with a shudder.

"It's like it's a different house, Howie. Look, flowers and everything. It looks so... human."

Our house was rather spartan. My father was wrapped up in his work and he wasn't much for decor.

"I'm glad you like it."

"So, where did you send your poor family?"

"Out. Dad decided to go work in the lab for a while. Hazel and Ray went bowling or something. I told them not to come back until I say so."

"And they listened?"

"I don't think I've asked them for a real favour in years." Why, at this crucial moment, did I keep thinking about last night's dream? I pushed the gore to the back of the mind. I wished I could live without that kind of sickness in my mind, even for one day. Just one. I would agree to die that day if I could just enjoy it first.

Stella had no idea what my illness really meant. Oh, she had seen what it could do to someone when it progresses, and there were little things - she could smell the formaldehyde, and I think she actually enjoyed knowing that she could kick or hit or jump on me and never hurt me. I'd ripped my heart right out of my chest for her, but she still thought of me as being more alive than dead.

But it was the other way around.

Stella, on the other hand, was so vividly alive. Her brown hair fell around her shoulders in waves, her cheeks were flushed, and the candlelight danced in her eyes. Her dress made her look both womanly and girlish at the same time. The sight of her calves beneath the A-line dress hem made my heart pump in a frantic and arrhythmic way.

"You are so beautiful. Have I mentioned how beautiful you are?" My voice was thick with emotion that I couldn't express.

"Often enough that I'm considering getting you a thesaurus for your birthday," she said, but she smiled. Stella could never take a compliment, but that just told me how much she needed to hear them. Whenever she felt vulnerable she turned aggressive. I liked it. She spiced up my days.

She was appreciating the smells coming out of the kitchen.

"What smells so good, Howie?"

"You'll see. Here, sit," I said, ushering her to the table and helping her into a seat. "I'll be back."

I used to work in restaurant kitchens in between bouts of high school. I enjoyed cooking. Burns couldn't bother me, knife accidents were quickly fixed, and the bustle in the kitchen kept me busy enough that I didn't have much time to be disturbed by mental images of smashing skulls. Plus, I liked creating something that other people could enjoy.

I was a little rusty these days since I'd been in school for the past few years, but I pulled out an old recipe book that had belonged to Dad's wife, took a fresh hit of brains, and I was pleased with the results. I brought the silver platter out to Stella and laid it in front of her, and then lifted off the lid.

"A turkey dinner?" Stella's eyes widened. Christmas dinner was her favourite meal of the year.

"I didn't have time to cook a turkey. I'm afraid it's chicken." I had carved it well, I think. My father - not Morton, who liked to be called Dad, but my original father - would have been proud of me. Papa had taken pride in carving meat properly.

The stuffing, potatoes, and cranberry sauce were plated nicely, too. I put some parsley on for colour. It looked good - like something out of a magazine.

I set the gravy boat next to her and then poured her some cranberry juice in a wine glass.

"It looks delicious, Howie, but isn't this a lot of food for one person?"

"I'm not expecting you to eat it all up," I said. "You can take leftovers home with you. Share some with your parents, if you like. I would join you if I could, you know."

"I know. It looks amazing."

"Of course it does," I said, smiling at her.

"Won't you eat just a bit? Use it to turn into muscle or something."

"Sure," I said. She grinned, and took a piece of meat in her fingers and placed it to my lips. It didn't taste right - my taste buds weren't the same anymore. Meat still tasted good… but only if it was fresh, and bleeding.

"That was good, but these look even better," I said, kissing the juice off of each of her fingers one by one. The virus made me think about biting them right off, and I laid her hand aside.

"I'll go get my own dinner if you don't mind. Don't go anywhere. I have plans for you."

I leaned down to kiss her. She lifted her face to meet mine, and I ignored the thought of blood spurting from her neck. Instead, I focused on the glitter of her necklace in the candlelight, the way her breasts moved as she breathed, the curve of her hips, the softness of her arms, the glow of her mind. I almost stumbled on my way to the kitchen. Every teenage boy has to deal with erections, I guess, but at least they don't get stiff all over. Sometimes I could barely move. But I preferred dealing with that than with the other kind of thoughts: the ones that made me feel evil and tainted.

And when Stella left me, I'd deserve it, because she didn't even really understand what she was dating. Not really. But I didn't dare to make it clear to her.

I wanted her too badly.

My romantic dinner was a hit. I could feel her happiness washing over me as she dug into the chicken. Poor Stella. I tried to take her on fun dates, but it's hard when you can't eat food. Dating is really centred around eating. I could take her out for dinner but the wait staff would cast us funny looks because I was just sitting there, watching her eat. Once someone passed me a card for an eating disorder support group.

But this was quiet, intimate, and we could be free to be ourselves - free to talk about things that we couldn't discuss in public.

"What do brains taste like?"

"Not much."

"So you've said. Maybe I want to try some." She reached for my flask with an impish grin. I pulled it away and spoke firmly.

"Not this, you can't try this."

"What? Why not?" She looked surprised. I didn't say "no" to her about much.

"Because it's raw brain material, and it could have harmful parasites, or prions or something. If you really want to know, try some of Army's food."

"You're suggesting I try dog food?"

"It's not dog food. It's human food, which we give to our zombie dog. I think people cook it up with scrambled eggs."

"Yeah, well, I'll think about it."

"How bad is the chicken that you're starting to ask for brains, instead?" I said.

She smacked me playfully, and I laughed. God, she made me feel alive.

"The food is fucking amazing and you know it," she said.

"That's always good to hear. You know what I'd really like to hear, though? Your dream last night."

Stella looked coy. "Are you going to tell me about your dream?"

"I'd rather not." If she pushed me, I should tell her. She had a right to know. It was wrong for me to keep it from her. She should know what she was dating. She should know.

"Are you uncomfortable talking about it?"

"Deeply."

"Why?"

I ran my hands through my hair. "It's not a part of myself that I like or feel comfortable with, Stella. Please don't make me talk about it. I'd rather hear about yours, instead."

"That doesn't seem fair."

"You don't have to tell me your dreams. We could talk about the news or the local sports teams. Tell me, do you think the Canucks will win the President's trophy this year?"

"Yeah, yeah. Are those my choices? Hockey or embarrassing dreams?"

"It's your birthday, my love. You can talk about whatever you want." I kissed her hand. "You can tell me more reasons why you think Satan is the good guy in *Paradise Lost*. You can lecture me on the evils of *Rikki Tikki Tavi*. Whatever you like. But I would love to hear about your dream." I got up, moved to her side of the table and kissed her again, this time on the neck, and I felt her mind respond to my touch. "But it's up to you."

"Cheater. You know what neck kisses do to me."

"Yes," I said, giving her another. "I do."

She took off my glasses. "I can't see your eyes. Too many reflections from the candles."

"Maybe I should get contacts."

"No, I like your glasses," she said. "I just want to see your eyes right now."

"Well, here I am. Your adoring servant, eyes and all."

She looked at me for a couple of minutes and then took a breath.

"It started out as one of my action dreams - you know, lots of running and hiding from faceless evil people and then jumping out and attacking them, that kind of thing."

I nodded.

"You and I ended up hiding in a house full of endless rooms. We kept exploring it, and then we found a room with a big bed and we decided to stop and rest there. And then the dream changed."

"In a good way?"

"You could say that." She looked shy, which was rare. I didn't rush her. I wanted this information so badly; this window into her unconscious, this chance to hear her fantasies. I quietly refilled her drink. She took a sip, then raised her eyes to mine. I held her gaze.

"We were in bed together. You started kissing my neck."

I gave her another kiss. Her skin felt so warm against my lips. "Like that?"

"Yes. I kissed you back. And then you started to rip off my clothes. You were… being really intense about it."

"Go on."

"And then you…" she gasped as I moved my kisses down her chest. "No, not you, we, just… started…" she trailed off. "It was intense," she said finally. I could feel her mind burning at the memory, and I burned to turn it into a reality.

"God, I wish I had that dream."

"You don't have dreams like that? I thought that was all men dreamed about."

"I have bad dreams. That sounds like… the best dream."

"It doesn't have to be in dreams, Howie," she reminded me. "You know how I feel about it."

Oh, don't tempt me. I wanted it more than I could put into words. But it wasn't worth the risk. I had no right to put her at risk. There were things she didn't know. Things I didn't want to tell her.

"There are other things we can do," I said. "Safer things."

"Has your father looked into this yet?"

I sighed, rested my head on her chest for a moment, then returned to my chair. I tried to decide how much I should tell her. No, that's a lie. I should tell her all of it, and I knew that. I was trying to decide how much I *wanted* to tell her.

"Yes, he has."

"And?"

He said…" I had to tell her at least some of it. "He said some of the hamsters tested positive."

Stella looked floored.

"How can that be? It's safe to fucking kiss you, isn't it?"

"Yes, but that's saliva." Genetics don't come into play with saliva.

"If it isn't in your saliva, why the hell would it be in your jizz?"

"Some of them tested positive, Stella," I repeated. *Most of them, actually.*

She stared at her food. We both knew that this conversation wasn't about some adolescent urge to have sex. It was about our future. The future she still thought we could have.

"Only some of them were testing positive?"

"Enough of them." I averted my eyes. I should tell her everything, but I was too afraid. Afraid she would realize what a monster she was dating. Afraid I would lose her. Afraid she would decide that it was a risk worth taking. Because it wasn't.

"But there might only be a small chance. I mean, with protection… or maybe extra formaldehyde?"

I held her hands in mine. "He's still looking into it. Maybe it'll be fine." I already knew that it wasn't fine, but I had to keep her hopes up. "In the meantime, there's always heavy petting."

"I hate it when you use that term, Howard. It makes me sound like a poodle."

I struggled to think of a more modern term. "Making out? But that's more like necking."

"Mutual masturbation?" she said with a twinkle.

"Well, if you want to sound like a sex-ed text," I said. Somehow our conversation had lost its romantic edge.

She squeezed my hands. "I get it, Howie, I do. You're right, okay?"

She was working hard to maintain the peace. It broke my heart because Stella was not a naturally peaceful person. I tried to spoon more food onto her plate but she held up her hand.

"I'm full. Really. I hope there isn't dessert."

"I thought we'd save it until after your presents."

"Plural?"

I stood up and offered her my arm. "Would you care to accompany me to my room?"

"I thought you'd never ask."

I carefully blew out the candles before we left the room. Couldn't have the house burn down, not with my Stella inside.

Stella raised her eyebrows when she saw the rose petals all over my bed.

"You're getting my hopes up. You did tell me you didn't think it was safe… right?"

"There are other things," I said, my heart struggling against my chest at the thought. "If you'll permit me. But first things first."

I took out my first gift and she sat on the bed to unwrap it while I lit candles around the room and switched off the light.

"…Is this…" she opened the book gingerly and checked the imprint.

"It's not a first edition or anything," I explained quickly. "But it's from 1898. Do you like it?" I watched her face anxiously.

"Of *course* I like it! But… how much did it cost you?"

"Not too much. It's not in collectible condition."

"You shouldn't have spent any money on me."

"I didn't. I spent it on a book. *Jane Eyre*, to be precise."

"For me."

She turned the book over reverently in her hand, and I felt deep relief. She loved it. I could tell. She thought I spent too much money on her, but she loved the gift.

Now for the important one. I slid open my desk drawer and took out a small silk bag. The silk had discoloured in one corner, but it was otherwise in good shape.

"I have one other present," I said. For once I was grateful for my emotionless speech, or my voice would have been trembling.

"It had better not be a diamond or something."

"I solemnly swear that it is not a diamond."

It was a ruby. A large, luminous ruby in a delicate gold ring. I had chosen it because of all the ones I looked at, this one was the only one that made me think of Stella's passion and fire.

As Stella gaped at it, I sank to one knee and looked up at her. I wanted to offer it to her, pledge myself to her, beg her to stay with me forever. But I couldn't do that.

"Howie…" she said slowly. I could feel her mind kindling, catching, blazing.

"I won't ask you to marry me," I said. "Although I would. In a heartbeat, Stella, I would marry you. But we're too young, it's not time, and when you do get married, you won't choose me. So please accept this ring as a token of my love and devotion. Keep it with you, please, to remember me, and to remember that wherever you are, whatever is happening, I am yours. And I love you."

"Is that a real ruby?"

"Yes."

"You fucking asshole," she said, and she began to cry.

5

Howie

I don't think I have ever been more shocked, in such an unpleasant way.

No, wait, that's astoundingly untrue. I can think of several more shocking, more horrific, more upsetting things that have happened to me, but this was the worst of the moments that didn't involve the violent death of someone I loved.

I stared uselessly at her for a moment while she cried, and then reached out to comfort her. Without looking up, she snatched my arm and held it in one of her martial arts moves. I stopped. This was the first time since we started dating that she had actually tried to fight me. She'd give me the occasional playful smack or shove, because she could and because - let's face it - I enjoyed it. This was different.

"Stella, I..."

"Don't come near me," she snarled. "How could you? How COULD YOU?"

Her mind was blasting at me - flames of rage and hurt and violent fury. Tears were rolling down her face. I wasn't used to her crying. Stella kept her tender feelings locked so deep inside.

I stayed on bended knee, bending myself slightly to one side to accommodate the twist she was putting on my arm. It didn't hurt, of course.

I can't feel pain. But if I let her break my arm, it wouldn't help her emotional state. I needed to go slow, not make any sudden moves. I had a flashback to when I was a kid; my kitten was scared by a truck rattling by and she fled under the porch. I spent an hour wheedling her out again, crouched half under the porch steps, coaxing and getting scratched until she decided to trust me.

I still didn't know what had spooked Stella, but I had to find out. I would deal with my heartbreak later.

"I need you to explain why you're so upset," I said. I sounded unsympathetic even to myself. I wished I could put some kind of emotion into my voice. Usually, my calmness balanced her rages, helped her defuse. But usually I wasn't the reason she was angry in the first place.

"Upset? UPSET? I'm not UPSET, you ROBOT. I'm BESIDE MYSELF WITH... WITH... WITH HATING YOU."

Stella's wit had left her. I had never seen her so angry that she couldn't even come up with a creative insult. She buckled over in wracking sobs, maintaining her tight grip on my arm. I stood up, forgetting completely about the arm. There was a slight crack, and my arm went limp below the elbow. I froze guiltily. She stopped crying.

"Oh, shit," she said. "Fuck. Did I just break your arm?"

"I think I dislocated my elbow," I said. "It's okay. Never mind that."

"Christ on a pancake, Howie, you need to learn one thing - when someone breaks your arm, it's okay to get pissed about that."

"If it's really going to bother you, we can fix it right away," I said. "But I'm much more concerned about why offering you a ruby ring was the worst thing I've ever done."

"You asshole," she said quietly, pulling weakly at my arm. "Fix your arm so I can be mad at you again."

I moved the joint around until I felt a click and held things in place for a moment. I could feel the tissues knitting back together. That's the virus's only good point - the super speed healing that it does before it has finished transforming your body into something much closer to a corpse than a living thing.

"Fixed," I said. I looked at the ring in my other hand. "Stella..."

"Money, Howard. MONEY. Yesterday - remember yesterday? We had a big fight? I was sitting in your car and I was begging you, BEGGING YOU, to attend university with me. I want you in classes with me. I want to visit each other in residence. I want us to maybe get an apartment together. I want to graduate together. And what did you tell me? WHAT DID YOU SAY?"

"I said that university courses get out of my league quickly, that I would struggle to form new memories with higher level material: that I would flunk out anyway."

"Which you told me back in January. Which you keep telling me. Just like you keep telling me that our relationship is fucking doomed. And yesterday, I asked you to just TRY. I said I would help you. I begged you to just fucking TRY, and WHAT DID YOU SAY TO ME?"

"That it would be a waste of money; thousands of dollars down the drain for certain failure. That I didn't have enough money to cover tuition, and I wasn't going to waste my father's money or anyone else's."

"You call trying to live a life with me a waste of money and then you give me a fucking ruby ring?" Tears were running down her cheeks and I longed to kiss them away. I never meant to hurt her like this. I understood what she wanted. She wanted a normal life - to go to school with her sweetheart, marry him, grow old together. I wanted those things too.

"The book was one thing," she continued. "Expensive, but sweet, and still worth way less than a year at university. But you combine that with this ring… Rubies are worth a LOT of money, and that one is huge! Talk about a waste of fucking money!"

"I didn't…" I tried to explain, but she cut me off.

"If you love me, Howie, you'll at least try to make a life with me. What am I supposed to do? Go on to university, learn, grow, graduate, get a job, have a career, and all the while you'll be rotating between a short order cook and a high school student?"

"Yes," I said. "Not because I want that. Because that's how it is."

"FUCK. THAT. If you want to spend money on some grand gesture, you could spend it on a year of fucking school. If you want to totally piss me off by refusing to waste money on A LIFE WITH ME and instead spend it all on A FUCKING TRINKET, then you're doing an EXCELLENT JOB."

"Stella," I was near tears, now, too. I tried moving close to her again, and she didn't break my arm this time. "Don't you know how much I want that? Don't you know that I would do anything to be with you?"

"Apparently, you wouldn't do anything. Because you won't do that."

"Yes, well, Meat Loaf songs aside," I said, scoring myself a point when she tightened her lips to suppress a smile, "It's not that I won't. I can't. Stella, I tried university. I tried the first time I graduated high school, back in the eighties."

"The eighties?" Stella frowned. "But you would have been in grade twelve back in the sixties..."

"It took me over a decade to pass high school." It was a humiliating thing to admit, especially to Stella of all people, who was well into the 90th percentile at school, and this was her only her first time.

"That's crazy, Howie, you're smart..."

I slammed my hand on the floor, and she stopped, startled.

"I'm brain damaged, Stella, do you understand? I have a disease that attacks the brain and it makes it incredibly hard to form new memories, specifically, extrinsic knowledge. The only reason I can remember words like 'extrinsic' right now is that I've just eaten, and I've known them for a very long time. The brains help me access what I already know, think faster, but there's a limit to what I can do, even on a full stomach. Everything takes longer for me. I can't work and learn at the pace of most people. I'm not a normal boy, who can grow with you.

"I know what you want, and I want it, too - you make it sound so easy. Go to university, graduate, get a job, pass myself off as simply looking very young for my age. Add some grey to my hair over the years, maybe crayon in some fake wrinkles. Marry you, live with you, pretend to grow old with you. And then, when you die, mourn you forever..." Now I was crying, and Stella reached out for me. "But it doesn't work like that. Don't you think I would have done that, even without you to motivate me? Don't you think Ray would have moved on if he could? What does it say that he's still here, still living with Dad, still going to high school? He can't even hold down a job - he can't pick up the new skill sets fast enough. He gets fired. Did you know that he's only ever graduated once? They change the curriculum, they add things, they take them out. They're little changes. It's always been enough for me to handle, but not him. He's repeating grade twelve this year, right? Hazel has never managed it..."

"Howie..."

"And here you want me to go to university. Just like that. Throw away ten thousand dollars to fail. And I would do that for you, Stella, if I had the money, but what a waste, what a waste... And whatever you think about the ring, Stella, I promise, I don't have ten thousand dollars."

"There are scholarships, Howie... bursaries... It's worth a try. You kept trying at high school, right? You get good grades now, you can do the courses now with your eyes closed..."

"Sure, take a bursary from a student who really needs it, who could really do something with their life..."

"I'd just... I just want you. I want you, not a ring, not a memory, just *you*, in my life..." She tried to wipe her nose with the back of her hand. I whipped out my handkerchief and offered it to her. She took it and rubbed her face with it.

I moved up and sat next to her on the bed. "I can be in your life without attending university, Stella. I've told you that again and again. Wherever you go, I will follow."

"Follow me physically, sure, but I want more than that. I want you to move through life *with* me, not just *near* me. It pisses me off so much that you won't even try... that you're so convinced that you can't do it. You're so convinced that nothing will ever change, that you'll just be a high school student for *fucking ever*..."

I could tell her that she was being elitist and my education shouldn't matter to her if she loved me. She would even acknowledge the truth of it because Stella was acutely aware of her faults. But I knew that this wasn't really about snobbery. It was a symbol - the first sign that I was falling behind her. As long as I could keep up with the rhythms of a normal life, she could ignore the disease and pretend all this was solvable. God, I wished I could do the same.

But I knew better. I knew.

"Even if I did, Stella, then what? This is going to come up again. You'll want a marriage, career, and children. I can't even… we can't…"

"Your father said some of the hamsters tested positive. Just some! That's what condoms are for. No semen, no problem."

I couldn't avoid the truth forever. "And children, Stella? I'm infected with a retrovirus that is trying to convert my body into a mobile corpse. It is rewriting my DNA to completely alter how my body works. I inject myself regularly with formaldehyde, which is a known toxin and carcinogen. Do you really think I am qualified and capable of giving you children?"

"We'll adopt. Who says I even want kids, anyway? Snot-nosed brats."

"I want kids. But I'm still a kid myself. That's the thing, Stella, I'm still a kid."

"You're a teenager. You're the size of an adult. Who says you're a kid? You've aged. You said you were, what, eleven when you were bitten?"

"Yes. In the last sixty years, I've aged maybe six or seven years. So in another sixty years, I'll be twenty-three. And we don't even know if it continues at that rate. Maybe that's only childhood. Dad hasn't changed at all. In sixty years."

We sat in each other's arms in the flickering candlelight. Stella's eyes were swollen from crying. I went to kiss away the tears. The dream image came back to me, of biting through her face, peeling her skin away from her skull with my teeth, and I pulled away and hunched over, covering my face.

"The virus is real, Stella, and it's in me, and you've seen what it can do. I can't cut out that part of me. We haven't found a way. I can come with you to university this year, but what about next year, and the year after that? At some point, you're going to have to leave me behind. You're going to keep having birthdays. I won't seem like your own age for much longer. I wanted you to have the ring and the book to remember me by. If money could buy me a life with you, Stella, you know I wouldn't waste it on presents instead."

"I know," Stella said huskily. "I know, Howie. But... just not yet. Don't leave me yet."

"Leave you? I'm not the one who will move on. I'm not going anywhere," I said.

"That's the problem." She buried her face into my handkerchief, and I strained to understand her as she spoke into it. "I know high school romances end," said her muffled voice. "I know I've been... like... mislead by Regency romance novels and Disney to think that love is some kind of once-in-a-lifetime phenomenon. Mom and Dad say there's no such thing as soul mates. Just people who fit you and people who don't, and it takes trial and error to fall in love with the right person. But Howie... if there were soul mates, I feel like you and I would be it."

We *were* soul mates. I fit her, I understood her, and she was everything I had ever wanted. But telling her so wouldn't help anything, so I just wiped my eyes on my own sleeve and kept listening.

"And it's not like I don't see your point. I know that our lives are intersecting at a moment in time when we're the same age, but soon I'll be twenty, and then thirty, and maybe you will start looking too young. Maybe you won't be enough for me then..."

There was no *maybe* about it, but I remained silent.

"...But Howie?"

"Yes?"

"I really, *really* fucking hate hearing that from you. I *hate* that you consider our relationship *temporary."*

"I know."

"And I really, *really* fucking hate that you're just *giving up* on even *trying."*

She was right. When she walked away, I should be able to tell myself that I did everything I could to keep us together. I didn't want any regrets. So what was I doing? Why was I trying to force reality on her? Did I really think that by avoiding humiliation in university I could somehow keep her longer? Clearly, the only thing worse than trying and failing was not appearing to try at all.

"I'll try, Stella, I'll try. I'll… I'll sell the ring." Hazel would be furious with me for selling our mother's ring, but it was worth it to see Stella's face crumple in relief. She clutched at me.

"Thank you… thank you, Howie. I love you so much. I'm sorry… I'm so sorry."

She was sorry? Sorry for what - for being healthy? For being normal? I couldn't blame her for any of it. I had been expecting all of this from the moment we met, and I pursued a relationship with her anyway.

All of this was my fault.

Stella's lips found mine and my thoughts were swept away by the feel of her. When Stella has finished burning through one of her rages, she changes. The soft, tender Stella inside was reachable. I could feel the closeness. The inferno of her mind had died down and I was basking in the warmth from the embers.

I laid her back in the rose petals.

"I'm the one who's sorry," I whispered to her. "I'm sorry I can't be what you need me to be. But let me be what I am, which is so deeply in love with you." I kissed her tender throat, struggling to smother the dark thoughts, and I heard her catch her breath as I kissed lower and lower down. I ran my hands over her, caressing her hungrily, and shoving the thoughts from the virus to the back of my mind.

"In the meantime, let's enjoy what we have," I said softly. "I am yours, and for now, you are mine. We have each other. And we have the house to ourselves." Shaking with desire, I reverently raised her dress.

"Jesus… Howie…"

"Just tell me…" I said softly, bowing down to her as I pulled aside her silky red thong. "Tell me if you want me to stop."

I began to demonstrate my devotion in the best way available to me.

"Oh, shit…" She opened her legs wider to me and I grew bolder as I revelled in the taste of her, the heat of her, the way she quivered at my touch.

"Oh, fuck… Howie… DON'T STOP!"

Stella

I drifted in the door of my house half an hour before midnight. My parents were snuggling on the couch watching some documentary about the Patagonian toothfish.

"Damnit!" Dad slapped his thigh. "You're back! Howie keeps returning you in time for curfew. It's very disappointing. How am I supposed to play the role of scary dad when your boyfriend keeps insisting on respecting my boundaries?"

"I'll be sure to tell him how upset you are about it."

"Did you have a nice time?" My mother leaned forward and frowned. "Stella, have you been crying?"

"Howie and I had an argument. But we worked it out."

"Who started it?" Dad asked.

"Me, of course. He didn't want to go to university. I managed to change his mind."

"Why not? Seems like a smart enough kid," said Dad.

My mother looked skeptical. "Hmm. But he didn't want to go. Has he tried university before?"

I pursed my lips. "Yes."

"Did he graduate?"

"...No."

"And he didn't want to try again?"

"No, but I told him that I'll help him. He probably wasn't eating enough brains."

My parents exchanged glances, but they didn't pursue the subject further. I could tell though, by their looks, that they didn't think it was going to work. To hell with what they thought. They were undervaluing Howie. Everyone, including Howie himself, undervalued Howie. But I knew what he was really worth. Flashbacks from our last hours together washed over me. Mmm. He was worth a lot.

"Okay, well, I'm off to bed," I said.

"Wait, tell us, what did he do?" said Dad.

"What do you mean?" I turned defensively and my dress swirled as I spun.

"For your birthday! What was the surprise?"

"Oh, he cooked me a full chicken dinner and filled his house with candles and flowers and balloons. All very romantic. I put the leftovers in the fridge. Oh, and he gave me this 1898 edition of Jane Eyre."

My mother nearly choked on her glass of wine. "What? Can I see it?"

"Maybe, if you're really, really nice to me," I teased, holding up the book, which Howie had carefully rewrapped in a silk cloth. My mother reached for it and I passed it to her. She ran her hands over it reverently.

"Did he give you that before, or after your fight?" Dad asked.

"Before."

"So… this is when you decided to badger him about his education? After he cooked you your favourite dinner and then gave you a deeply thoughtful gift?"

I nodded, jutting my chin defiantly. My father rubbed his temples.

"And… let me get this straight… you managed to make it up?"

"Yes."

"Are you sure?"

I remembered Howie's hands caressing me, his tongue, his words. "Definitely."

Dad shook his head. "That kid is a saint."

"He's not a kid!"

"I don't think he even has to shave."

"That's not important!"

"I guess nothing teaches you patience like fifty years of puberty," said Dad. "Personally I would have gone insane. I'm glad you guys worked it out. He's a good… young man."

"Yeah. He is."

"Goodnight, honey," said Mom. "Happy birthday. We love you."

"Love you too."

I didn't walk up the stairs, I floated. Tonight had been good. Really good. I felt better for having said the things I wanted to say. I felt better for having let my anger out. I felt better knowing that Howie could hear those feelings and still love me. I felt better knowing that he was going to come to try university again.

I felt better for having had three screaming orgasms.

Everything that had bothered me this morning seemed unimportant now. Why worry about the future too much? Howie would go to university with me. That was the first step. If he didn't make it through, okay, well, at least he would have tried. And penis-in-vagina sex didn't feel like a big deal either. As for children, that was way too far in the future.

What mattered was that he was going to try. He wasn't going to give up on us, and that was all I wanted. Because I was never going to give up on him.

6

Howie

Have you ever had one of those experiences which leaves you feeling changed in a fundamental way? This was it for me. That night had been like a dream come true. It was better, sexier, more amazing than I ever could have imagined. I drove her home and walked her to the front door, where she gave me one final lingering kiss before disappearing inside. I could still feel the glow of her mind, even after the door shut, and it warmed me all the way back to my house. I collapsed on the bed among the scattered rose petals and pressed myself into the sheets where Stella had so recently laid. I replayed every detail in my memory - the look of her, the taste of her, the sound and shuddering feel of her. I thought of lines from poets which I had read and re-read for years, now made into precious reality.

Full nakedness! All joys are due to thee,
As souls unbodied, bodies uncloth'd must be

I tried not to think about the things which I had restrained myself from doing - and the black thoughts that swarmed in thicker the more I tried to shut them down. When I drifted into gratified sleep, the black thoughts did not follow, and for one night, I was free.

I woke in the morning with a strange feeling of utter contentment, which was quickly followed by longing. The crushing need to have more, more, more. More Stella in my arms, her mind thrumming through my body, her skin on my tongue, her moans in my ears. Far from sated, I felt desperate for her.

My family was already clustered around the kitchen table when I came down the stairs.

"Nice night?" Ray asked with a smirk.

"Thank you for the privacy," was all I said, yanking open the fridge.

"Dunno how much privacy you can get when your girlfriend's brain lights up the town like that," he said. "Doc nearly drove off the road. If you don't admit you laid her good, I'll call you a liar."

"Don't be gross," said Hazel.

"You felt it too," Ray turned on my sister. "Coming home, you said..."

My adoptive father cleared his throat. "And *I* said that it was polite not to mention that which we cannot help observing. Howie and Stella are entitled to their privacy."

"Stella and I had a nice evening," I said firmly as I sat down with my breakfast. "That is all."

"Did she really like the ring?" Hazel asked. "Maybe that's what made her... uh... glow."

Ray snorted but said nothing.

"I gave her the book last night. She loved it. I'm giving her the ring this morning."

I was too full of sensory memories to dwell much on my promise to Stella regarding the ring. All I knew was that I had secured her happiness for a while longer with that promise, and her happiness was vital because I wanted her more than I had ever wanted anything. I wanted to pretend that she was mine for always. I wanted to pretend that my life would be filled with nights like the last one. I wanted her to wear that ring - if only temporarily - to make the fantasy complete. And I tried not to remember that all my wants *were* just fantasy - and nothing more.

"Dad?" I heard Hazel asking our father. "Did you hear about those attacks in Seattle? That's nothing to worry about, is it?"

"Funny you should mention it. I was talking to Michaella about it yesterday. She has been reassured by the Americans that no trace of the virus has been found."

Ray snorted. "What'd Baum have to say about that?"

"George is still on administrative leave, as you'll remember," said Dad. "But Michaella is monitoring the situation. And of course it doesn't match the usual patterns at all."

"I'm not worried about the usual stuff," said Ray. "It's the other stuff that we got to concern ourselves with."

Dad waved a hand. "Only George thinks that there's any true risk in that area. That information is tightly controlled and I cannot imagine anyone with access to it trying to misuse it. Howie, if you're going, please do not forget to put your bowl in the dishwashing machine."

I returned sheepishly and cleaned up after myself before shoving my shoes on and hurrying out the door. I had no space in my mind for anything but Stella.

Once I arrived at her house, however, I quailed at going up to her door. I felt as if I might simply erupt upon the sight of her, and my outdated morals would make me unable to meet the eyes of her father this morning. I sent her a text message, pulled out my book, and tried not to count the seconds until I had her in my arms again.

Stella

It takes a lot to wake me in the morning, but the sound of my phone's ringtone made me bolt upright. Who the hell was calling me at this ungodly hour? Was it Howie?

Oh. It was my best friend Liz, calling from Nova Scotia. I swiped at the screen and put it to my ear.

"What?" I said. Our relationship was affectionate, but probably not in the normal way. I missed her like crazy sometimes.

"I'm calling to wish you a belated happy birthday, since I knew you'd kill me for waking you up early on your actual birthday, and I knew you'd be out with your boy toy until like four in the morning, my time." I could hear the burble of people talking in the background, and I knew she must be calling from school.

I rolled over in bed and snuggled deeper into my blankets. "Yeah. Time differences suck."

"HI, YOU BITCH!" shouted Jeremy in the background.

"HI, JIZZ-FACE!" I hollered back. Like I said: Our relationship was affectionate, but not normal.

"So?" prompted Liz. "How was your birthday? What'd Howie give you? Tell me it was the D."

"I did not get the D. He's still afraid I'll get sick."

I'd told my friends back in Nova Scotia that Howie had HIV but was responding well to antiviral drugs. It made me feel like shit to lie to them, but this way I could talk about some of my problems without actually revealing classified information. The government had made it pretty clear that if I or my parents blabbed about the whole "zombies are real" thing, that they would press charges. Or possibly just make us disappear. And unlike my local friends, my friends in Nova Scotia didn't have the reality of Howie staring them in the face, so they would believe the HIV non-sense. I couldn't have pulled that kind of trick on Kate. She'd be fast to point out that people with HIV look and talk like normal people, whereas Howie did not.

"Even with a condom, and his tests all coming back as clear?" Liz sounded deeply disappointed.

"Yep. Sorry, guys. No D."

"Tell me he at least gave you hours of cunnilingus."

I was silent, but I couldn't help smiling into my pillow. Liz screeched at my silence.

"OH MY GOD, HE DID!" yelled Jeremy.

"He also gave me an antique copy of *Jane Eyre* and a ring."

"A RING?" Liz sounded disgusted.

"Not an engagement ring."

"It's not a promise ring, is it? Those are beyond pathetic. Or worse - a chastity ring?"

"Maybe it was a cock ring," I heard Jeremy say.

"It's a ruby ring. But here's the thing. It's a giant ruby, probably worth a ton, and just the day before, he was telling me he didn't have enough money to go to university."

"So, who does? It's called a student loan. For only a lifetime of debt and a quarter of your soul, anyone can go to university."

"Yeah, well, I convinced him to sell the ring to get money for university."

"What's wrong with you? Keep the ring! Tell him to get a fucking student loan like everyone else in this country!"

"Yeah, yeah." I couldn't tell her, of course, that he couldn't apply for student loans because according to his social insurance number, he was nearly seventy years old. "Listen, where are you applying to? I was thinking Mount Allison, or do you want to do Acadia, or Dal? Howie will apply to the same schools as me, so we could all end up going to school together! I can't wait for you to meet him." I could barely contain my excitement at the thought of walking around Halifax with Howie and my best friends.

"Nah, I'm applying to NSCAD," said Liz.

"The arts college? But you could do a fine arts program at Mount A or Dal…"

"No, what do I need a degree in fine art for? I want fucking skills I can trade on, not a portfolio of bizarre art installations involving silly string and toilet seats."

"Oh." I felt hugely deflated. "Well… what about Jeremy?"

"FUCK SCHOOL. I'M OUTTA HERE!"

"He's taking a year off," Liz translated.

"He's what?"

"He wants to go down to South America and build huts for poor people and shit."

"FUCK YES!"

"What? WHY?" I couldn't imagine someone more urbane than Jeremy, who made Oscar Wilde characters look serious and hardworking.

"I don't know. Because it's a way to avoid having to do schoolwork? Because he wants to meet sexy Latin American men with their shirts off? Because he wants to make a difference in other people's lives? What do you think, Jer?"

"ALL OF THE ABOVE!"

"Lay off him, Stella. It's one year."

"But what if he never goes to university?"

"Then he doesn't go. I'm pretty sure he'll live, Stella."

"I'll live BETTER," I heard Jeremy say firmly in the background.

I felt a stab of guilt. "I know, I'm a terrible person."

"Well, yeah, but that's largely unrelated to your intellectual snobbery. Anyway, it'd be awesome if you came out here for university because then we could meet your unfortunately-named boyfriend and tease him about his virginity."

"Yessssss," agreed Jeremy.

"I'm sure he can't wait. What else is new at home?"

"Not a ton. Listen, we've gotta go. The bell's about to ring. Message me later."

"Okay. Thanks for calling."

"Sure thing. Later, kid."

"GOODBYE, YOU SEXY OLDER WOMAN, YOU!" called Jeremy.

"Bye, guys."

I stayed in bed for a while, hugging myself and looking forward to the future. I was disappointed that Liz wasn't going to apply to the same schools as I was, but how awesome would it be to have my old friends and Howie in the same place? We'd take Howie to our favourite lunch spot, and I'd show him Peggy's Cove, and…

My phone dinged. It was a text from Howie.

Giving your parents a break
after their forbearance yesterday.
Will wait for you in the car.
I love you deeply.

Memories of last night flooded through me and I felt ridiculously giddy. I don't know how to articulate the things that Howie made me feel. Some feelings are completely nonsensical when you try to describe them in words. Sometimes - usually in the throes of passion like last night - I'd end up trying to tell Howie how I really felt and it always sounded garbled and idiotic. Luckily for me, Howie wasn't a critical audience.

I hopped out of bed, showered, dressed, and went downstairs. My parents were sitting at the table in front of their empty coffee mugs. They were both checking their phones, but they were holding hands in that way they often did - just fingers loosely tangled, as if they didn't even know they were doing it. I wanted to have that with someone, someday. And I knew who I wanted it with.

"Morning, sunshine," said Dad without looking up.

"Howie's late this morning," Mom said.

"He's waiting in the car," I said, dumping some cereal in a bowl. "He thinks he trespassed on your hospitality too heavily yesterday what with the eggs and the cheesecake so he's giving you a break from his highly annoying presence."

Dad snorted. "Yeah, I hate it when that polite guy shows up to cook and clean for us. Thank God I don't have to deal with that this morning."

I shovelled my breakfast into my mouth and ignored his comment. I knew that my boyfriend was weird. But on days like today, I couldn't bring myself to care.

As soon as I was done my breakfast I threw on my coat and shoes, grabbed my bag, and said a hasty goodbye to my parents.

"What's the rush?" Dad asked.

"Don't want to keep him waiting."

"Then tell him he can come *in,*" said my mother, but I was already closing the door.

Howie had already moved over to the passenger seat of his car. He was reading from the book of poetry that he carried around in his bag. I stopped and watched him from afar for a few seconds. It was rare that I caught him with his attention off of me. There was something really sexy about the way he looked so chill and erudite with his glasses and his book. It was almost as sexy as he had looked last night when he... holy fuck. The memory turned me on so much.

He glanced up just before I opened the door.

We were instantly in each other's arms, lips locked, hands in hair, all of that. You'd think we were being reunited after a year's absence, not less than nine hours. I wanted him so bad, and I found myself murmuring stupid stuff again when he kissed me deeply and I just, like, *broke apart* inside.

Everyone in school might think I was dating him out of desperation, but the truth was that I was desperate for *him,* because the way he touched me did stuff to me that I simply couldn't explain. Then inane nonsense just came pouring out of me like he had tapped some kind of well of unstoppable idiocy. Howie pulled back to listen to it, smiling like crazy the whole time. He was looking at me with that intense gaze of his, and combined with memories from last night, it was enough to send a thrill right through my body.

Then he held out that fucking ring.

I closed right up. "Howie, if you're hoping to have a repeat of last night's fight, I don't think we have time."

"It would be worth it," said Howie, and he gave me a look that made my heart flutter in a biologically improbable way. "But no. I won't need the money until I'm actually accepted at university and tuition is due. Until then, I would be touched if you would wear it. But, if you don't like it, that's something else. You don't have to put it on."

The ring *was* pretty spectacular. I'm not into jewelry but this was something else. You could tell that it was high quality. It wasn't clunky or flashy. The delicate gold band was twined slightly to look like a growing vine, with little leaves on the sides of the ruby so it looked like a glowing red rose. Howie had amazing taste. Where did he find this? And how much had he *paid* for it?

I slipped it on my right-hand ring finger.

"Does it fit?" he asked.

"Not bad," I said. "Maybe it's a tad snug." But once it was on, the slim band felt comfortable enough. I held out my hand and admired the effect as it flared a rich red in the morning sunlight.

Howie took my hand and kissed it softly, and the satiny cool touch of his lips somehow made my whole body light up inside.

"Thank you for putting it on," he said huskily. "Even if it's just for a while."

"It's a beautiful ring, Howie. I never thanked you. It just… wasn't the romantic gesture that I wanted from you."

"I understand," he said. "Believe me, I do. I will try a semester. After that, I can't make promises."

"That's good enough," I said, coaxing his car to life and putting my arm behind his head as I turned to back up. "That's all I'm asking."

"I'm not sure it is," he said quietly. "But it's what I can give."

"HOLY MOLY, what is that?" screeched Kate when she met me at our lockers. "Howie! What did you do?"

"It's not as lovely as she is, but it was the best I could manage," said Howie.

"That stone is the size of my head! How much did that cost?"

"I didn't get it new."

"Of course not, it looks like a freaking antique. The red suits you, Stella," said Kate.

"Never mind the ring," I said. "He got me an early copy of *Jane Eyre*!"

Kate started to snore. I gave her a light kick.

"Come on, that's awesome! The author is still listed as Currer Bell instead of Charlotte Bronte! It's like holding a piece of feminist history."

"An old ring and an old book - do you have a hidden yen for antiques I didn't know about? Because I think my mom has some old rose patterned china that belonged to my Great Aunt Irene."

"Yeah, well, I'm making him return the ring anyway," I said. "I want him to spend that money on tuition instead."

"It's not something I can return, but I can sell it if I have to," said Howie. "I'm off to class now, Beautiful." He leaned in and kissed my cheek, and then whispered in my ear, "I'll be thinking about last night. All. Day."

A shiver went through me. But Kate was watching so I gave him a light punch instead of an aggressive fondling. Howie cast me a dimpled grin and I heard him trying to whistle as he lurched down the hall.

"Well, he has a spring in his step this morning," said Kate. She was far too observant for my liking sometimes. "Did you bone him?"

"No, I did not," I said with dignity, sweeping off to class.

"You did! You look all… weird and happy."

"I didn't and I'm not talking about this anymore!"

"Well, you must have done something with him. He looks way too relaxed. Quick blowjob before class?"

"No!"

Kate was always far too interested in what Howie and I did behind closed doors. She reminded me a lot of Liz, which is probably one of the reasons I made friends with her in the first place. But while Liz was an avid practiser of what she preached, Kate was all talk, as far as I could tell. Unless she and Michelle were secretly boinking on the side or something.

"Oh my God, he proposed?" squealed Amy when she saw my hand. Everyone in the class turned their heads.

"Jesus, Amy, no. It's on my right hand, my *right* hand," I said urgently. But the damage was done. The decibel level of the babble in the room had definitely increased.

Amy grabbed my hand and admired the ring. "He is so sweet! Is it a promise ring?"

"No, it's a miscellaneous I-love-you-but-I-know-you'd-kick-me-in-the-skull-if-I-proposed-to-you ring," I said. "We're only eighteen!"

"So? You could get engaged! You don't have to actually get married until you're ready."

"Then what's the point of getting engaged?" I demanded. "When you're engaged, that means that you're ready to get married. If you aren't ready, you shouldn't be engaged."

"It's just, like, the commitment," said Amy with a dreamy look in her eyes.

"Oh, Jesus," said Kate, rolling her own eyes.

"You can't commit to something you aren't ready to commit to," I said irritably. "Either you're ready to get married, or you aren't. You can't be all like, 'I commit to committing as soon as I'm ready to commit'. That makes no sense."

"But you love him, don't you?" Amy insisted.

"Of course I love him, dingbat," I said, nudging her. "Don't be stupid."

"Oh no, it's the pig again," said Amy, as our teacher laid out the trays.

"It's going to be the pig all week," said Kate, "so suck it up and grab a scalpel."

The ring created an uproar around me all day. It didn't take long before the rumour went around that Howie and I were engaged. The few kids who liked me - mostly people I had rescued from bullies - told me they were happy for me, but the most vocal folks were the ones who despised me. Instead of the standard "woof woof!" from passers-by, I was getting full-sentence comments.

"I heard Mullins finally got his dog a license!"

"Did you sit on him until he agreed to marry you?"

"I wouldn't let Howard touch me, let alone marry me!"

"Maybe he knocked her up - who could tell if he had?"

"Oh man, if he did, do you think he needed a blindfold to get it up?"

By lunchtime, I had moved the ring over to my middle finger, so I could flip people off with extra pizazz.

"So, congratulations on blowing up the school," said Kate to Howie at lunch, after we'd received several catcalls, one implication of theft, and two requests for the wedding date.

Howie blinked owlishly at her through his glasses. "Blowing it up?" he looked around.

I pushed his thermos toward him. "Just eat, Howie."

"I think it's a beautiful ring, Howie," said Amy kindly. I noticed that she had her math binder ready to go.

"It isn't about how the ring looks," said Kate. "It's the fact that it *exists.*"

"I love that you put it on your middle finger," said Michelle. "That's so you."

"You don't have to wear it if it's embarrassing you," Howie told me, looking worried.

"I'm *not* embarrassed," I told him. "It just bothers people that I can be a giant and still have a boyfriend and get good grades and generally be living a happy life. It violates everything they've learned from prime-time television."

"Yeah, it represents that most elusive of things - happiness without a thigh gap," said Kate.

"Oh, so the ring is a symbol of success," said Howie. The brains were kicking in. I leaned against him, breathing in the sciencey smell which I now associated with love and trust. And last night. Oh, my fuck. Under the table, I felt his hand caressing my leg, moving up my thigh, and it was *doing* things to me.

"Good thing they don't know about the *Jane Eyre* book, then," Howie said with a sideways smile. "Imagine how jealous they would be then."

"Right?" I said. "I mean, they might actually riot over it."

"Besides, can anyone explain the allure of the thigh gap to me?" Howie asked, leaning forward and looking at my friends. "It means you have no muscles in your legs. How is that attractive?"

His eyes were alight with interest as his fingers slipped further between my own thighs. My breathing rate increased.

Kate looked thoughtful. "Probably something to do with Barbie or cartoon characters creating our internal representations for the feminine ideal."

"Time to bring back Betty Boop, then," said Howie. I loved hearing him talk. I loved his husky, calm, emotionless voice that somehow carried so *much* emotion right under the surface. I loved the feel of his hands, and the way his sweet smile made my heart do the conga - which I know doesn't make any sense *but that was how it felt*. I couldn't imagine ever wanting to be with anybody else.

Then the bell rang.

Fuck. It was time for Drama. And that meant Dean Kato.

7

Stella

"I hear congratulations are in order," said Dean, accosting me yet again on my way into Drama with his heart-stopper smile.

"You heard wrong," I said flatly, plunking into one of the chairs lining the room in a semi-circle. He sat down next to me.

"No? What's that, then?" he said, reaching out and taking my hand to look at the ring. His fingers felt warm on mine.

"Notice the finger it's on?" I said, pulling my hand free and flashing the ring at him.

He held his hands up in mock surrender. "Okay, okay, don't be touchy. You'd think you didn't *want* people to think you were engaged. Keeping your options open?"

Then he *winked*.

A couple of years ago I would've dismissed this as a cruel tease and heaped coals of scorn on his head for toying with a fat girl's emotions. But that was before Howie, when I thought that only feminists considered a plus-size body something to celebrate. Those little signs that Howie had taught me, the indications that a guy was secretly digging my body? I saw those sometimes in Dean. An appreciative glance at my ass when I stood up, a flick of his eyes at my cleavage. So I didn't dismiss his flirtations as heartless manipulation of a fat girl's feelings. But what was I supposed to do with this? I wasn't sure. So I just gave him a death glare.

Dean dropped his gaze to his backpack and started unzipping it. "Anyway, so, I've got a couple of plays I thought we could take from. I didn't know if you want to do funny or serious or what, but you could look over them today."

I raised my eyebrows. "I thought we were supposed to go to the library today to pick out stuff."

"Come on, the library selection probably sucks and has been picked over a hundred times. My mom's in theatre and she has a ton of stuff at home. I brought some for you to look at." He looked almost serious for a moment. I tapped my foot thoughtfully for a second.

"Okay."

So that's how I ended up being stuck with Dean all alone in the Drama room while everyone else went off to the library.

Our drama teacher paused on her way out the door. "Aren't you two coming?"

"We're way ahead of you," said Dean, waving a play book. "We'll just go through these here."

"Hmm. Okay," she said and went to follow the rest of the class. The room seemed really big and empty and echoey as the door shut behind her.

"Okay, so, I brought some Daniel McIvor, Christopher Durang, and George Walker. Do you like super sad, super crazy, or semi-funny-semi-serious?" he said, piling books in my lap.

I stared at him. "Since when are you the big playwright expert?"

He grinned — Jesus, why was I such a sucker for dimples? — and shrugged. "Aw, you know, I don't want to come off as some kind of big nerd. The guys would give me a hard time. But I grew up with this stuff. I'm totally going into theatre. See if I can get onto Broadway, maybe do some film. I *can* act, you know. Haven't you seen me in the school musicals?"

"Sorry, I wasn't overcome with an urge to watch a bunch of high school students butcher *Fiddler on the Roof.*"

"I swear, I'm not bad. And you're good, too. I think we're going to get a really good grade on this. We just need to pick the right scene. Now, do you want to do heart-breaking drama or make people laugh?"

"I don't think I'm the kind of person who can get an audience to weep for her. Hand me the funny shit."

He passed me a play called *Laughing Wild*. "I dare you to read this out loud without smiling," he said with a teasing look.

"Oh yeah? Watch me," I said. I took the book, rose majestically, skimmed the first few lines, and then began to read aloud.

I was doing fine until I got to the part where my character assaulted a guy just for blocking her access to the canned tuna in the grocery store. Then I began to lose it.

"I told you!" said Dean, grinning.

"Wait, I can do this," I said, composing myself. "Let me try this again."

I read it steadily this time, and when I screamed, "WOULD YOU KINDLY MOVE, ASSHOLE?" my voice echoed in the empty room. Dean started to clap. "Bravo! Come on, you're perfect for this kind of character."

"Are you suggesting that I'm crazy?" I asked, skimming ahead in the play and trying to hide how amused I was.

"Only in the best way," he said. "Look me in the eyes and tell me you haven't wanted to bash someone over the head just for existing."

I looked into his eyes, which were crinkled in amusement. "I plead the fifth."

"Wrong country. No fifth amendment in Canada. I take that as a confession. In fact, been to Seattle lately? Maybe I've just solved a crime."

"Anyway," I said, sitting down, "this is basically a monologue. No good to us. We're supposed to do a two-person scene."

"The third act has the male character and the female character together. Take it home and read it over tonight," he said. "Now, this is a George Walker play, and it's kind of funny but it also deals with some heavy stuff. Check it out..."

Okay. I admit that I actually had fun with Dean that day. I was pleasantly surprised by his interest in our project. I had expected to be forcing him to focus while he goofed off and made stupid jokes. Instead, he laid books in my lap and leaned in close, pointing out scenes that he thought would work.

"Why does this guy hate question marks?" I asked, pointing at the Walker scene we had been reading over.

"You know how people sometimes say questions as if they're statements? That's how he wants these ones read."

I couldn't help thinking that the question mark-less sentences made me think of Howie. Sometimes it was hard to tell when he was asking a question and when he was making a statement. And as I thought of that, I realized that Dean's face was very close to mine, that our knees were almost touching, and that I was breathing in Dean's cologne or antiperspirant or whatever that perfumey smell was. I leaned back in my chair and shifted slightly to add some distance.

When the bell rang, I jumped out of my chair and started to pack my book bag.

"Here, take these," said Dean, handing over the plays. "Text me if you hate them and I'll bring more. But the sooner we pick something the more time we'll get to rehearse it. What's your number?"

I gave him my number and he texted my phone so I'd have his.

"And I still want to get together outside of class time to rehearse this," Dean reminded me. "You know, if you're not too busy planning the wedding..."

"I'm not engaged!"

"So you want me to believe," he said with a mischievous grin. I gave him a scornful glance and threw my bag over my shoulder.

Asshat.

Howie

All I could think about, all day, was Stella. I couldn't focus in class at all. It didn't help, either, that she was feeling especially good that day. Stella's emotions are powerful, and whenever she felt anything strongly could I sense her from kilometres away. She often called my ability to sense her 'creepy' and she was absolutely right. But I was tuned in to her. She was my compass, my guiding light. I leaned into the feel of her, the lure of her. But like most of my urges, I didn't act on it. I attended my classes and when school let out, instead of hunting her down instantly and greedily tasting her lips, I leaned against the wall by the main doors and distracted myself with my book of John Donne poems. Poetry and music have always been my escape.

I lost myself in the book and didn't even notice that Stella's mind was getting stronger. I was vibrating with the feel of her, but still reading, when I felt a hand on my groin. It was like an electric shock passing through me, and I looked up to see Stella smiling at me.

"Hello, handsome," she said, removing her hand. "Care to come home with me today?"

I pulled her to me — much more forceful than usual — and covered her lips with mine. I had to taste her, drink her in. It caught Stella by surprise, but she responded by opening herself to me, kissing me deeper. People began to shout and jeer and she waved her middle finger, which now had the added fire of my ring, and pulled away.

"What is this book that I see you reading so much anyway?" she asked, playfully tugging at the book in my hand.

"John Donne. One of the best metaphysical poets."

Stella frowned as she flipped through the pages. "Wasn't John Donne the guy who wrote the poem about the flea?"

"Yes."

"I never understood that poem," she said. "I know it's like, the big famous Donne poem, but I'm sorry, fleas just aren't sexy."

I laughed. God, I loved her. "It's not my favourite either."

"Which *is* your favourite?"

I thought hard for a moment. "I guess it depends on my mood. When I'm upset or unhappy, I've always really liked his Holy Sonnets. *Batter my Heart* always made me feel better when I was finding it hard to… to live with things. But other times, like when I'm thinking about you, I like his earlier works, like *Love's Progress*, or *To His Mistress Going to Bed*."

Stella flipped through the book, looking for the poems I mentioned. "*Licence my roving hands, and let them go, Before, behind, between, above, below…*" She looked up. "Howie! Is this your version of porn?"

I couldn't help but grin. "More like erotica than porn, surely," I argued.

Stella turned some more pages, then glanced at me with mischief dancing in her eyes. "*Take me to you, imprison me, for I, Except you enthrall me, never shall be free, Nor ever chaste, except you ravish me.*"

I just smiled.

"Well," said Stella. "Now I want to get you alone more than ever."

I felt a surge of desire. "Is it so I can read you metaphysical poetry?"

"You got me," Stella said, raising her eyebrow in the arch way that I always found so alluring. "That's totally it."

"Well, then. Let's get you home post-haste."

"Good. Because I was thinking that maybe we should look at some more universities, see where else we could apply. You know, sexy, romantic stuff like that."

I entwined her fingers in mine as we walked to my car. "Talking about a future together is definitely romantic. And sexy."

Stella plunked me down on her couch and pulled up a bunch of bookmarked sites on her laptop. Our heads touched as we looked at the screen together, like a couple sharing a milkshake.

"Okay, so, I know you applied to the local schools last year before you got around to telling me that you had no intention of actually attending." She cast me a dark look. "But the schools I'm really interested have later deadlines. This is Dalhousie. It's right in Halifax, so we'd be right in the city with lots to do. The tuition is really high, though. There are a lot of universities in Halifax, actually. St. Mary's, King's, Mount St. Vincent..."

I listened quietly, but I had a sinking feeling in my stomach.

"Then there's Acadia — it's also mostly undergraduate but they do have some masters programs — and it's in a small town, which I kind of like. I have an aunt who lives there; she'd probably have us over for dinner all the time. Of course, it kind of depends on what courses we want to take. Do you think you'd do better at a science program or an arts program?"

I thought carefully before I responded.

"Stella — these universities are all on the East Coast."

"Uh, yeah, that's where I'm from."

"And you want to go back."

"Of course. You'd be able to meet my old friends, and we'd get free meals from my relatives all the time. It'll be great."

I rubbed my face under my glasses. "Stella, if you want to go back to Nova Scotia, then that's what you should do. But..."

"Is this about money again?" Her voice was rising. "Because Howie, maybe you should cut out the martyrdom for a minute and fucking consider a bursary or something."

I massaged her hands in mine. "We've already talked about that. I'll find the money, somehow, if that's what you need. I'll get a summer job. I just... I'm just thinking of practicalities."

"Like *what*?"

"Like... my food? I'm sure dinner with your relatives will be very nice, and I'd be happy to meet your family and Liz and Jeremy, but where am I supposed to get pig brains in Nova Scotia? Dad orders ours through the science department of SFU, but if I were that far away..."

Stella looked stunned, then ashamed, and I felt a wave of devastation washing through her mind.

"Shit," she said quietly. "I'm an idiot. I didn't even think…"

I cupped her chin in my hand and looked into her lovely face. "Hey, it's okay. We'll figure something out."

Stella smiled, but I could feel her anxiety ripping through me. I'd done it again — I'd made her see how hopeless things were. I shouldn't have said anything. I should have kept my mouth shut. Frantic to undo the damage, I took her in my arms and kissed her until she broke open and all her love came pouring out. It filled me up until I felt I would burst with joy.

Stella was unbuttoning my shirt while telling me how safe my smell makes her feel when the front door opened and closed.

"Hello?" Mr. Blunt called. "Anyone home?"

"No!" Stella called. "Fuck," she muttered to me under her breath as she helped me frantically button my shirt back up, "I can't wait until we get our own place."

I twitched with longing at the thought. Stella, in private, every night? There was no way I could ever be so lucky.

"Ah, you *are* home," Mr. Blunt said, kicking off his shoes. "There goes my plan to meet your mother at the door wearing nothing but a bow tie."

"Dad!"

"When are you moving out, again?"

"Not soon enough, clearly!" Stella said, straightening my shirt while I smoothed down her hair. You can't see into the living room from their front door so we always had a few seconds to jump apart and rearrange ourselves when her father came home. I suppose we could have gone up to Stella's room — we did sometimes on weekend evenings while her parents were watching TV downstairs — but I felt uncomfortable doing so when they weren't home. It wasn't because of anything they said about it. It just didn't jive with the way I was raised.

Stella's parents were very progressive about sex. They put her on birth control as soon as we started dating, gave her repeated lectures about condoms, and left her to make her own decisions. As far as I knew, their only two hard and fast rules for their daughter's conduct was 'no unprotected sex' and 'no drinking and driving'. They were cool parents, even by modern standards, although Stella insisted that it was impossible to apply the word 'cool' anywhere near her father. But no matter how progressive they were, I simply couldn't bring myself to risk being discovered in bed with their daughter.

Even if I weren't burdened with the moralities of a bygone era, her father adored any chance to make me uncomfortable and he would never have let me live it down.

Mr. Blunt stuck his head into the living room. "Hi, Howie."

"Hello, Mr… uh… Tim."

He wagged a finger at me. "You're getting better. Someday you'll call me Tim right from the start."

"We can but dream," I said.

"So," said Tim, turning to Stella. "Any ideas for supper? I've got…" he stopped and pointed at her hand. "What in the name of God is *that?*"

"Oh," she said, looking down and fanning out her fingers. "You mean the ring."

"Is that what it is? I thought maybe you'd found the philosopher's stone."

"Come on, Dad, it isn't that big. It's quite tasteful."

"But how did you…" Tim stared at me. "Where did you…" Then he looked at Stella and held up a finger. "Wait, you're not engaged, are you?"

"Of COURSE we aren't engaged!"

Reassured, he turned back to me. "How did you… where did you…?"

"It doesn't matter," I said heavily as reality seeped in. "She's not keeping it."

"Howie," said Stella, "you know I love it, it's just…"

I put my hand on hers. "I know. It's okay."

Tim edged out of the room. "I think I'm going to stay out of this one. I'll be changing into my at-home clothes if you guys need to uh… talk."

Stella was avoiding my eyes. I wrapped my arm around her, rested her head on my chest, and we just lay there for a while in miserable silence. I could *feel* her worrying.

"Psst," I whispered into her ear after several long minutes of silence. She shifted her head to look at me. "If your entire left side were cut off, you could still tell people that you were all right. All right. Get it?"

She raised her head off of my chest. "You're telling me terrible jokes? NOW?"

"Yes. A parasite walks into a bar and asks for a drink."

"Oh, God."

"The bartender says, 'I'm not serving you — get out.' So the parasite says, 'well, you're not a very good host.'"

"I'm not laughing at that," she said, pursing her supremely kissable lips.

"What does a subatomic duck say?" I continued doggedly.

"*What* is a subatomic duck?"

"Wrong answer. It says 'quark'."

Stella groaned loudly.

"Why did the bear dissolve in water?"

"Tell me."

"It was polar."

"I'm not sure I love you anymore."

"Except you do," I said quietly. "And I'm so lucky."

"I can think of a lot of words to apply to us right now that are less cheerful than 'lucky'," she said, turning away.

"You didn't have to love me back. I could have spent the last year in a constant state of tortured, unrequited love from afar. If you had told me to leave you alone, I would have listened. I wouldn't have spoken to you again unless you spoke to me first. But I would have fallen in love with you all the same."

"Just think, Howie… if we could live together… it could be like this all the time… and like last night…"

My chest heaved at the sound of her words. "I would give anything for that, Stella. Anything." I tilted her chin with my finger so that I could look her in her beautiful brown eyes. "So it's going to be okay. Okay?"

She kissed me. "Okay."

"Okay," said her father loudly, coming down the stairs in his tee shirt and shorts. "You two are very cute and all, but Howie — I have a pork tenderloin and no idea what to do with it."

"You can't have him," protested Stella. "I need him. I need help with Physics."

Tim looked at me. "Can you help me make an edible meal while also helping Stella with Physics?"

"I don't know, sir. But I'm going to try."

"Sir? SIR?" He approached me aggressively and stuck a finger in my face. "What is my name? Say it!"

"Tim," I said contritely.

"And don't forget it, either." He shook his head. "*Sir.* I don't know what I'm going to do with you, Howie. I just don't know."

Physics was the class that Stella had the most difficulty with. And by "most difficulty", I really mean "any difficulty at all", since most things seemed to come to her effortlessly. The slightest amount of puzzlement made her panic because she wasn't used to it.

"You must think I'm really dumb," she said after I talked her through an equation that caused me to fail Physics three years running in the seventies.

"Stella, you do realize that experience is not the same as intelligence and vice versa? You aren't stupid for not knowing something you haven't learned before."

"But I did learn it before. Mr. Roeper went over it in class yesterday."

"Oh, well then. What an idiot you must be."

She gave me a playful slap on the shoulder and I smiled at her. God, I wanted to kiss her. But if I kissed her every time I wanted to kiss her, we'd never get anything done. Fortunately, I was an expert at not doing the things that I thought about doing.

"Just remember to sort out all the information you have from the problem, and label it, and then you can figure out the equation easier," I told her. "Like this — you make a list of horizontal information and vertical information. And remember that you always know the vertical acceleration because it's going to be 9.8m/s^2."

"Yeah, I know that, *obviously...*" She sighed and took a deep breath. "Okay. Organizing the information. That makes sense."

"And then once you know what you know, it's easier to figure out what equation to use based on what you do know. Does that make sense?"

She nodded. "Yeah, I think so. Let me run to the bathroom and then I'll give this problem a try."

"I'll be right here."

I stared at the Physics textbook as I listened to the sound of her footsteps going up the stairs.

"Psst, Howie," said Tim quietly, slipping into the kitchen and turning over the meat that was browning in the skillet. "While Stella's out of the room, there's something I want to ask you."

I gave him my full attention.

"Stella said you didn't want to go to university. Is she bullying you into this?"

I looked down again. "Stella wants me to at least try. That seems fair. The oven is pre-heated, by the way. I set it to four hundred."

"I don't know what you rubbed on this meat, but it smells great already." Tim opened the oven and tossed the skillet in. "Have you heard of MIT Open Courseware?"

"No."

"You know MIT, the university."

"Yes." Know it? I had longed to attend it during my father's brief stint working there in the seventies. Disjointed memories clattered in my brain. It had been an unhappy time for all of us, but the university itself had sparkled with promise.

"They put all of their courses online. All the subjects. Lecture notes. Sample exams. I thought it might help. You could sort of… prepare." He frowned at the timer. "How long until I turn it over?"

"Ten or fifteen minutes," I said. "Thank you, Tim, I'll look into the MIT thing." It felt strange to know that I could finally attend MIT, if only in spirit, with the mere click of a computer mouse. But the more I thought about it, the more hope I felt. After all, I *could* learn new things. It just took me longer. So if I could study before I even attended my first class…

Tim set the timer on the stove for ten minutes. "I wanted to suggest it when Stella wasn't in the room so you wouldn't feel any more pressure."

I smiled wryly. "Thank you."

We heard the sound of the upstairs bathroom door opening. Tim ducked.

"The Eagle is landing!" he whispered. "Remember, the buffalo flies at midnight!" and he darted out of the kitchen in a half-crouch.

"What are you doing, Dad?" Stella asked.

"The lemming has gone over the cliff!" he shouted loudly.

"I'm sorry I asked." She walked into the kitchen and plunked down next to me. "Where were we?"

But I was already gathering my papers.

"I have to get going, Beautiful. I told Dad I'd be home for dinner tonight."

"Oh." She blinked. "Okay."

I gave her a swift kiss, zipped up my book bag, and banged out the door. I nearly stumbled over my own feet in my eagerness to get home. I had to look up that MIT website. Maybe I could pass university after all.

Maybe Stella and I had a chance.

8

Stella

"All right, what's up?" Dad asked wearily that night, as I pushed my food around my plate with my fork.

"I've made a raceway for my peas using my mashed potatoes," I said. "This big pea is the bullying popular pea who won the race for the last three years running, and this little pea is the scrappy underdog who's going to win the race despite all probability and common sense."

"Very creative. What *else* is up?" Dad pushed.

I shrugged.

"Howie didn't propose, did he?" Mom asked.

"What? No!"

"It does seem like the sort of thing he'd do," Dad said.

"He knows I'd never say yes!"

My parents exchanged looks.

"Well, *something's* eating you," Dad said. "There was a *very* awkward vibe coming from that living room this afternoon. And Howie says you aren't keeping the ring?"

"It's too expensive so I'm making him sell it and put the money toward his education, that's all," I snapped.

"So he is still planning to go to university?" Mom said.

"Yes!"

My mother raised her eyebrows and looked back down at her plate. I stood up and dumped my plate in the sink.

"I'm going to go do homework," I said.

"Okay," my parents said in unison.

I stomped up the stairs but I paused at the top of the landing. Then I turned around and stomped right back down again. My parents laid down their cutlery and looked at me expectantly.

"Here's the thing," I said. "It's going to be hard to get brains and stuff out to Nova Scotia if we go to school out there."

My parents nodded slowly.

"And maybe we can figure it out, but what if we can't?"

"Then you'll have to decide how badly you want to go back to Nova Scotia," said Dad. "Why *do* you want to go back?"

"You mean besides my friends being there and all our family being there and the fact that it's my home?"

"Yes, besides that," said Dad.

"Does there need to be more than that?"

"Well, yeah," said Mom. "It's our home, too, you know, but this is *also* home. You *also* have friends here. You have *us* here. You have *Howie* here. I'm not saying you should pick your university based on the convenience of your undead boyfriend, but yes, you need more reasons than friends, family, and home."

"I don't want to go to a Vancouver school!"

Dad shook his head. "Because… there are mountains and cherry trees here...?"

"Because I was *supposed* to go to an East Coast school. I've always planned to go to Dal or Acadia or something, and I don't see why the entire course of my life should be changed because you guys decided to drag me here a year before graduation!"

"Gee, I'm sorry we dragged you out here and you ended up falling in love and making new friends," said Dad. "I know how terrible that was for you."

"Well, she did end up at the epicentre of a zombie outbreak," pointed out Mom.

"I don't care about *that,*" I said. "I just care about the fact that my life plans are being totally derailed." I plunked back down in my chair. "I really wanted to go to school with Liz and Jeremy. But they aren't even going to university at all."

"Aren't they?"

"Jeremy wants to take a year off and Liz is applying to NSCAD."

"NSCAD is perfect for Liz."

"I know... I just..." I buried my face in my hands.

"What about your *new* friends?" Mom said irritably. "Where are *they* going?"

"I don't know. I think Kate's planning to go to SFU."

"Listen, Stella... You aren't really big on meeting new people and adjusting to new situations," said my mother in the understatement of the year. "You've lived out here for nearly a year now, and I think it's about time you did two things — first of all, start counting your new friends as being as important as your old friends, and second of all, consider that you have more friends out here whom you haven't met yet. You can go to school *all by yourself,* and you will meet new friends, and you will love them and be glad they entered your life. Because that's how real life works. You read enough books to know that sometimes the universe throws you plot twists, and you just have to roll with them."

"Like you," said Dad. "You were a hell of a plot twist."

"Thanks, Dad. I love being reminded that I was an accident."

"You were a plot twist," my mother said firmly. "They happen. They're what makes life interesting. And sometimes you can refuse the call. I could have aborted you and gone on with the life I planned. I didn't."

"And no matter how much you try to make us regret it, you keep failing," said Dad, his smile lines crinkling. "I mean, thanks to you, I'm an experienced zombie slayer and one zombie turns up on a regular basis to cook me breakfast. So things worked out pretty good, really."

"So," continued Mom, "if you want to go to school in Nova Scotia or New Brunswick, fine. Try to change your life back to what you had before. Leave Howie behind. Erase the last year or so from your personal history. But you could save a lot of money by staying closer to home, and you're just as likely to find friends here as there. It'll be different. But it won't necessarily be worse."

I glared mulishly.

Mom sighed. "What's wrong with the universities out here?"

I frowned and chewed on my lip as I thought. "I… I just want to feel like I'm an adult. If I'm just living here with you, driving to classes every day… that's just like more high school. And I can't take any more high school."

Mom raised her eyebrows. "Living with us?"

"Who says you're living with us?" asked Dad. "I've been waiting eighteen years to be able to walk around the house naked at five pm. You think I want to put off that magical day?"

"But it's stupid to go to university half an hour from home and pay to live in residence."

"No, it's *adult*. Your mother and I made a pact when we decided to keep you. No thirty-year-old children living in the basement. We get you to adulthood, and then you're on your own."

"Is that why you sold our home and bought a tiny place in Vancouver with no basement?"

"As of graduation, this is *our* home," said Dad. "*You* may visit." He folded his arms.

"Seriously?"

"I'm very serious. We've spent *eighteen years* resolving this subplot. We're *done*. You and your zombie can get out."

I grinned. "Thanks, guys."

"Don't thank us," Dad said. "You're going to need a *job*."

"Yeah, well, you didn't abort me. So I'm grateful for that, I guess."

"Could have fooled us."

Howie

"Ah, Howie," said Dad when I came rushing through the door. "I have prepared our evening portions. We've been waiting for you." We ate our pig brains together as a family in the evenings. Dad – who I called Morton or Doc for decades before giving in and calling him Dad the way Hazel did – said it promoted familial closeness and bonding. Eating together at dinner, I mean. Not the pig brains, specifically. Any farm animal would do. Pork just tastes better.

"Can I use your computer?" I asked.

He frowned. "Naturally, but after dinner."

"Thanks. Did you know that MIT puts its courses online?" I asked him, dropping my bag and heading into the kitchen where my siblings were waiting. "I'm going to print some out and start studying them."

"May I ask why?" Dad said, following me.

"Stella wants me to try university. I promised I would. The MIT thing might give me an edge."

My family received this information with a profound and disapproving silence.

Ray was the first to speak, and his face was twisted in a scowl. "Here we go. Howie flunks college, part seventeen."

Even Hazel couldn't find it in her to be really encouraging. "Are you sure you want to do this?"

"I told her I'd try. So I will."

"What a waste of money," said Ray, shovelling a spoonful of brains into his mouth. We used bowls and spoons in the privacy of our home, instead of thermoses. It's nice to chew occasionally. Brains are pinkish and jello-like. If someone looked in our window, they'd probably think we were eating strawberry ice cream together. "You know you're going to bomb. Again. I don't care how much you study some shit from MI-fucking-T."

"I find Howie's drive to educate himself admirable," said Dad. He looked at me seriously. "But I hope that you and Stella have realistic expectations of your academic performance. I'm not sure it will benefit your relationship to try and compete at that level."

"I would never compete with Stella. I'd settle for not humiliating myself," I said.

"Then I do not recommend returning to university," said Dad.

"Maybe if I eat enough brains… Study hard… I'm not stupid."

"I'm not stupid, either," said Ray with a scowl. "But I'm failing. Again."

"Howie's the best of us," said Hazel quietly. "Maybe he can do it this time."

"Doc spent thousands on Howie and his years of flunking out," said Ray. "Fucking waste."

"My financial resources are poor, currently," said Dad. "As you know, I spent many of my investments on your tuition, and fees have risen sharply in recent decades. My estate has not recovered to a level where I can sufficiently fund another attempt."

"I know that," I said quickly. "I don't want you wasting any more."

"Try for a scholarship. You get A's these days," said Ray.

"You need extracurriculars to really have a chance at a scholarship. Besides, I don't want to take a scholarship from a student who really deserves it. I can find the money."

"I don't have time for your goddamn saint routine," Ray growled. "Do whatever the fuck you want. But I say it's a bad idea. Right now your girl thinks you get good grades because you're smart. She doesn't get that you've just done this so many times that you have it memorized."

"I am smart," I said quietly.

"Smart's not enough for us," said Ray.

I studied my spoon. I couldn't think of a response. He was right. We all knew that he was right.

"I have a better idea," he said. "You're doing this to keep your chick, right? Just lie about your grades. Hell, save the money and fake enrollment. Pretend to attend classes and tell her you're doing great. Problem solved. You're welcome."

I took a moment to consider this. I should have rejected it out of hand, but that's how desperate I felt.

Dad shook his head. "Deceit is a poor basis for a relationship. It would do more damage in the long term."

"What long term?" I asked, covering my face. "Let's face it. This will buy me a few months or a year. Eventually, Stella is going to move on to someone who can actually graduate. Someone who can have a career…"

"Someone who has to shave in the mornings," said Ray.

"I can't lie to her. She'd never forgive me."

"Oh, really? I'm guessing that there are a few things you haven't been straight with her about."

That comment stung because it was true. "There are some details I haven't shared with her," I said. "And I'm not proud of that. But outright lie? Never."

"What about when you filled in those application forms to SFU and UBC?" Hazel said. "That was like lying. You didn't tell her you weren't going to go."

"It was wrong to mislead her," I said. "You know I nearly lost her when I finally told her the truth. I will never take that risk again."

"So what have you told her about Doc's little experiment downstairs?" Ray said. "Did you tell her about that before or after you plowed her?"

"The hamsters are no longer downstairs," said Dad. "For safety reasons, I euthanized them last week."

"I would never and have never risked Stella's safety, whatever you think happened here last night." I glared at Ray. "No, I haven't given her the details. No, I didn't tell her exactly what Dad discovered. But I told her there was a risk. I did not lie to her."

"So, now you're going to throw thousands of dollars down the drain," said Ray. "All for a few more months of feeling her up semi-honestly."

"This is not about feeling her up," I said. "This is about taking every day of happiness I can get before the inevitable happens. I can't think of a single thing more worth spending money on."

"But it's money you don't have," Ray argued. "How's that going to work? Doc already said he's not giving you any. You've got some, I'll allow, and I guess you can work this summer, but you'll still be short."

I took a deep breath. "I'm also going to sell the ring."

Hazel looked up from her bowl. "No."

"It's probably worth a thousand dollars, Hazel. Maybe a couple thousand."

"I said you could give it to Stella. I didn't say you could sell it to strangers."

"You have all of that jewelry. I asked you for one piece, and I'll do what I like with it. I'm sorry, Hazel. Mama would have wanted me to have an education."

"This isn't so you can get an education," said Hazel, tears welling in her eyes. "You've tried that. You know it won't work. This is so you can please your girlfriend for a few months. Is Stella really okay with you selling Mama's ring?"

"She doesn't know that it's Mama's ring. And you aren't going to tell her."

"Oh yeah, I can feel the honesty in this relationship," said Ray, getting up and dumping his bowl in the sink. He looked furious, and his mind was buzzing angrily. We could feel each other's brain waves, just like we could feel other people's, but infected minds felt… ugly. Like music that's off-key.

"Put me out of my misery if I get like this, will you?" He said to Hazel. "It's pathetic to watch." He strode out of the room.

"He didn't mean that, Howie. He knows how you… I'll go talk to him," said Hazel. She scuttled away.

I sat staring at my empty bowl while Dad watched in silence. After a few minutes, he cleared his throat.

"I... uh... never talk much about my wife."

I looked up. "No, you don't."

"It was very long ago now, of course, but I remember her quite clearly. She died, as you know, very young. I feel sure that if penicillin had been discovered, she would likely have lived. As it was, I lost her to an infection and my son died shortly after." He stared out the window for a moment. "For a long time, I wished that I had died, too. When you lose someone you care about..." his voice trailed off. He shook his head. "What I am trying to say, Howie, is that I would have spent any amount of money for more time with them. I think that part of the reason that I saved you, your sister, and Ray was because I could never resign myself to unnecessary death.

"I am... immensely proud... to call you my surrogate son. But I am also sorry. You have a long and difficult life ahead of you, and our condition prevents us from forming permanent attachments to people who can grow and change. I am fortunate because I knew love, and I have a family to remember, and a new family of which I am very proud. I have a cause to dedicate myself to, and I feel that when I finally help to find a cure for this disease, that my years of toil will have been well served. You are less fortunate. You were stricken in childhood, with many of life's experiences still before you. You have been trying for a long time to give your life a feeling of purpose, and you have been continually hampered by the damage to your brain." He paused again, and then he gave me a look that was full of guilt and regret.

"What I am trying to ask, Howie, is whether I did the right thing when I saved you. Or have I condemned you to an eternity of torment?"

I didn't answer him for a long time. I remembered being chained to a bed, waiting to turn into a monster. I remembered the feeling of the disease creeping into my mind, and realizing that this was what had happened to my parents. I remembered the relief when I felt it recede, when I knew that it wasn't going to beat me. I remembered the gratitude of knowing that my sister would live.

I remembered losing myself in poetry and music when things were hard. I remembered discovering Gerard Manley Hopkins and John Donne. I remembered how I felt the first time I heard Don McLean singing *American Pie.* I played that LP so many times that Ray ended up snapping it in a fit of frustration. He bought a replacement a week later and left it on my bed. I remembered when John Lennon was shot, how I felt like the music had truly died. I remembered breaking my heart over Freddie Mercury singing *Somebody to Love.* I remembered making overtures to pretty girls and being brushed aside as they instinctively turned to healthy boys who could grow up with them.

And I remembered how I felt the day Stella walked into my Chemistry class with flushed cheeks, a mind that overwhelmed me, and the aura of a queen. I remembered how quickly I had fallen for her looks, her smarts, the fire that burned inside her. I remembered the frantic hope I felt when I finally coaxed a smile from her. I remembered when she kissed me for the first time, how I had held back the tears of joy and relief until after she went home.

I imagined how I would feel when she finally walked away. I pictured the clawing emptiness of a world without her love. A world that would just go on and on and on, until our brief romance was ancient history. She would live and love others and grow old and die and still the world would keep turning and turning and turning without end.

Then I looked into the grey, concerned eyes of the man who had made all of this possible.

"Both, Dad. Yes to both."

9

Stella

I got all of my regular homework out of the way before finally pulling out the plays that Dean had loaned me. Jesus, even the books smelled good. Did he just, like, spray his cologne willy-nilly all over his house? Maybe he'd done a commercial for Axe and had, like, a lifetime supply. He was hot enough to do a commercial for Axe, anyway.

It felt uncomfortable sitting in bed and reading books that smelled like a good-looking guy who was not my boyfriend. It was weirdly intimate, like Dean was sitting next to me. But after reading the final act of that *Laughing Wild* play, I picked up my phone and sent him a text.

> You realize that if we do *Laughing Wild* that you're going to have to dress up like the Infant of Prague.

He texted back quickly.

> What u don't think I'd look good as the infant of Prague?

I googled it. It wears a dress.

Admit it. It'd be funny

Only because the play is funny,
not because you'd be
violating gender norms.
I don't laugh at that stuff.
My mom would kill me.

Lol ok ur mom is the comedy police?
So is that a yes?

Let's do it.

I spent the next hour muttering the play aloud under my breath while watching the time, trying to figure out how much of the act we could fit into our time limit. It was funny and insightful and I was deeply relieved to find a scene we could do that didn't involve romance in any way.

Before I climbed into bed I picked up my phone and sent one more text. This time it was to Howie.

I changed my mind.
We can go to school here.
Don't worry about acquiring Maritime brains.

He called me right away.

"I don't want you changing your plans because of me," he said as soon as I answered. "Please. Please don't do that."

"It's not because of you," I said. Then I hesitated. "Well, okay, it's a little bit because of you. But really, Howie, it doesn't make sense. Liz is applying to a community college. Jeremy's going to Central America or something? And it'll cost a ton of money to fly back and forth, which you know I would do because I actually like my parents. I do know when I'm being unreasonable, Howie. I can't always help it, but I do *know*. And this idea of going back East is really unreasonable. I'll get over the idea. I just need time to adjust my expectations, okay?"

"Just please, please do not make the decision because of me. I can't handle that."

"Howie. Am I really the kind of person to change her education and career plans for some guy?"

I could *hear* the smile in his flat little voice. "Maybe you love me that much."

"I do. But I'm also stubborn as hell."

"You're a determined person who fights for what she wants, and I love that about you. The thought of you giving up and changing your mind to please me feels… wrong. Bad. Like I'm damaging you somehow."

"Well, this decision isn't about you, okay?"

Howie was silent.

"Okay?" I prodded.

"As long as it isn't about me."

I sighed. "I promise. I'm doing this because I want to."

"Okay. I should go, Beautiful. I have work to do. I'll see you soon."

"Okay, bye. I sort of like you."

"Good. Because I adore you. Sleep well, my star." He hung up. I hugged myself for a moment. Strange things happened to my stomach when he said shit like that. And all I could manage most of the time was "I sort of like you". It was a good thing Howie could read brain waves or whatever, or he'd probably have given up on me in despair eons ago.

Sighing with aggravation at myself and my emotional inadequacies, I switched off the light and climbed into bed.

What the fuck. My pillow smelled like Dean just from *being in contact* with those freaking books. I peeled off the pillowcase and grabbed a new one from the linen closet.

"You wet the bed or something?" Dad shouted from my parents' bedroom when he heard me rattling around. Shit. Why did parents have to be so damn nosey?

"My pillow got contaminated with strange boy smell. It came home on my Drama books."

"If you find a cure, let me know!" called my mother. "My whole life is strange boy smell."

"Man smell," I heard Dad say to her. "I'm fifty-two, you know. I'll be growing up any day now."

"Who said the smell came from you?" Mom replied.

I heard them giggling to each other and knew that they had forgotten me and my pillow problems. I shut the door to my room and put on the new cover. My pillow now smelled like normal laundry detergent. That was better. I closed my eyes and drifted off to bed imagining an apartment in Vancouver where Howie could read me poetry and study with me and there were no parents and no Dean Katos anywhere in our own private world.

Howie

When Stella texted to tell me that she wanted to go to school locally, I was staring at the MIT courses that I had printed off of Dad's computer after dinner. I'd read a page, and then try to remember three things from it, which I usually couldn't do, so then I'd go back and read it again. After a while, the words all started to swim around in my head and I couldn't even remember sentences I had just read.

Stupid. Stupid.

Then Stella's text came in and I felt a stab of terrible guilt. It was wrong for Stella to change the course of her life for me. I knew how homesick she was for the Maritimes. She talked to me about it all the time — about her friends, her cousins, her kung fu instructor, her favourite camping ground, even the sweet donair sauce that she couldn't find out West... all the people and places and things she had grown up with. If she wanted to go back, she should go back. She would regret staying in Vancouver just because of me. She would regret allowing me to hold her back when she finally broke free of me.

I called her immediately, but she stubbornly insisted that she was making the decision for practical reasons which had nothing to do with me. I prayed that she was being completely honest with me, and then went back to my studies. I felt even more driven to make sure that I retained something — anything — from these print-outs. The only thing worse than Stella rearranging her life to accommodate me was her rearranging her life and having it all be for nothing because I flunked out instantly anyway.

I gave up at three in the morning, reminding myself that I had weeks — months — to retain all this. It was February. Classes wouldn't start until September. There was time. I had time. So I curled up in my bed and tried to calm myself down by remembering last night. Remembering why I had to succeed. Remembering what was at stake.

When I finally fell asleep, I had the dream I had always longed for.

It started out as the best dream I had ever had — full of warmth and intimacy and passion. Stella was on my bed again, her body bare and beautiful, and just like last night, I was worshipping every inch of it and it felt natural and right to take the next step. I could feel the heat of her body around me as we connected and engulfed each other. There were no dark thoughts. I love remembering that part of the dream because, for all it was so sinful, it was really very pure. No virus. Just love, and lust, and heat. Just as if I were whole. I couldn't believe how good it was, how *right* it felt to be inside her. I was meant for this. I was meant for her. I was hers. She was mine.

I wish the dream had just finished then, that I had finished then, but instead, without so much as a single evil thought, I cupped her sweet face in my hands and broke her neck as I kissed her. She went limp under me but I didn't stop. I began to bite and tear and bury myself in her bloody flesh, and that was even better but in such a worse way, and by the time the dream finally released me with a roar of satisfaction only parts of her carcass were left.

Upon awakening, I was so horrified by myself that I tried, wailing uncontrollably, to scratch off my own skin but it just kept growing back.

"Howie? Howie what's wrong?" Hazel must have heard me howling because she came running into the room and stopped, astounded. "What are you doing to yourself? What happened?"

I buried my face in my pillow and tore at my hair. I felt Hazel's hands grabbing mine, trying to pull them away.

"Howie, leave your hair alone. It'll take forever to grow back." Her small voice couldn't be anything but calm, but she was fighting me with all her strength.

"It was so awful, Hazel, I killed… I killed…"

"Howie, it's just dreams. You know it's just dreams," she said.

"Is everything all right?" I heard my Dad ask. Except he wasn't my Dad. I called him Morton for thirty years because I didn't want to replace my Papa, Pop, my beloved father whose skull I stoved in with a hammer after he ate my baby brother. And Henry's teddy bear was sitting there on the shelf, watching me, witnessing it all... Oh God, I hated this virus and I hated that it was inside me and I hated that it could end up inside her.... I hated...

Someone turned on the lamp.

"He had a dream," said Hazel. "And he's upset."

"I can see that. Howie, look at me."

I turned my face on the pillow and saw him leaning down and peering at me closely.

"What on Earth has happened to your face, son?"

"When I came in, he was ripping at his skin." Hazel's voice quavered slightly. I looked at her and saw tears running down her cheeks.

Doc cupped my chin in his hand and studied my face. "Well, it's already starting to heal. Were the old memories acting up again, son?"

I shook my head and wiped the tears from my own cheeks. My arm came away smeared with my own ghoulishly blackened blood.

I heard Ray in the doorway of my room. "He dreams about Stella. That's it, isn't it?"

I didn't answer.

"I'm telling you, this chick is so bad for him."

"Stella isn't responsible for what I dream," I said as fiercely as possible, which wasn't very fiercely at all.

"You are prone to anxiety, Howie," said Doc, "and that tends to worsen the intrusive thoughts and dreams which are symptoms of our infection. Now, you understand that they are only symptoms, and have no real significance?"

"But how can you know?" I asked. "How can we know that it won't really happen? What if I lose control?"

"You asked me that nearly sixty years ago, and I could only tell you that I thought it unlikely. We now have close to sixty years of evidence that the virus may occasionally send us peculiar thoughts, but it does not control our actions."

"It's never been this bad before. You don't understand. My hands... my hands just killed her... I couldn't stop it..."

"I understand that it is worsened by stress." He walked over to my bookshelf and perused it for a moment, then slid a volume off of the shelf and brought it to me. I pulled away.

"My hands..." my fingernails were filled with dried gore.

Hazel went to fetch a cloth so she could dab the blood away. When I was clean, I dried my hands on my shirt and took the book from Doc.

Dad, I mean. He liked to be called Dad. He'd earned that title. He'd earned it.

The book was my favourite poetry collection — an anthology that once belonged to Dad's wife, Edith. Stella had admired its leather binding and that had given me the idea of finding the antique edition of *Jane Eyre.* I handled the tome with care.

"Read for a while, son, and then sleep. Things will seem brighter in the morning."

They left me, and, breathing deeply the dusty musty smell of the paper, I turned the familiar pages, and lost myself in the words of those who died long before me.

Not, I'll not, carrion comfort, Despair, not feast on thee;
Not untwist — slack they may be — these last strands of man
In me ór, most weary, cry I can no more. I can;
Can something, hope, wish day come, not choose not to be.

"Howie? Is something wrong?" Stella asked the next morning. I was exhausted from lack of sleep and still quaking from my terrible dream, and she noticed right away.

"I'm sorry." I stared at my hands. "I had a bad night last night. I guess I'm a little out of sorts."

"You're not pissed at me or anything, are you?"

"Of course not."

"Because I know you think I'm changing my plans because of you, but I'm not. It makes way more sense to go to school here."

I tucked a lock of hair behind her ear. "Even if you do go to school here, you should take me on a vacation back to Nova Scotia some time. You can show me everything, and introduce me to your friends."

She brightened. "That's a good idea. Would you be able to bring enough brains?"

"Sure, we'd figure that out. We'd ship a cooler or something."

"Oh man, it would be so awesome. I'll take you to Peggy's Cove. It's amazing. And there's this restaurant in Halifax, and we should totally go. Okay, I know you can't eat the food but I want you to see it..."

She made plans happily the whole way to school, while I brooded. I felt haunted by my dream the night before. I had always felt sure that I could keep control. I was pretty sure that the black thoughts were only thoughts — fleeting images sent by the virus, like Dad had always said. But I could be wrong. Nothing had gone wrong on Stella's birthday night, but what if it had? What if I just snapped? What if I got caught up in Stella and forgot which impulses were good, and which were bad?

I remembered how it felt to look down at her remains, and I shuddered. What would Stella think if she knew what I dreamed about? She would run. She *should* run.

"Howie? Howie? HOWIE!"

"Yes?"

"It's time to get out of the car, Howie," she said impatiently. I realized that I had been sitting in a daze for... how long? I wasn't sure.

I shook my head to wake myself up and stepped out onto the pavement. For a minute I couldn't remember which way to go, and when I started to walk, Stella grabbed my backpack and yanked me back toward her, just as a car whizzed by and honked at me.

"Watch out!" she snapped.

"Sorry." Which way to go? I shook my head and started walking again, but slowly. The buzz of the minds around me was disorienting. The only one that stood out clearly was Stella.

She frowned at me. "Did you eat your breakfast this morning?"

I nodded. Breakfast plus the extra can. But without sleep, they could only do so much.

"You just seem a little… more out of it than usual lately," she persisted.

"I was up late last night reading," I explained. "I'm sorry."

"You don't have to apologize, you know," she said. "You're not, like, morally obligated to be sharp every morning. I just wondered."

"Understandable," I said. "Lead the way, Beautiful."

I followed Stella in a trance. Twice I ran into other students and got sworn at. The second time Stella rolled her eyes and took my hand, dragging me in her wake. When I was hungry or tired I reacted more poorly to my environment, but I was all the more acutely aware of Stella. It was as if everyone and everything but her was covered in a grey fog. She stood out bright and clear. She charged through the crowds the way she did every morning, accosting bullies and rescuing their victims with powerful authority. And she did it without thought, automatically, because Stella is a rescuer. She saves people without knowing it, without considering it, without even really registering it. The world needs more Stellas.

How could I put a person like that in danger? Who would rescue her from this virus, from what it could make me do?

I stumbled along behind her while my eyes traced the lines and curves of her body, the motion of her hips as she moved, and I felt a physical need for her so intense that it almost hurt. If only someone could rescue me from this. From all of this. Because I wasn't strong enough.

"Howie? *Howie!*" said a voice. I tore my eyes from Stella and saw Kate.

"Don't you have a class to get to?" she asked. I guess I had been standing and staring while Stella filled up her book bag and now the bell had rung.

"I need to do something first," I said, stepping forward and filling my arms with Stella. I closed my eyes and breathed her in, and then gently laid my lips on hers. I felt her respond to me, and as we kissed my thoughts filled with images of doing all kinds of unspeakable things to her. The more I tried to smother them, the worse they got, and I pulled away in self-disgust. But the bell had rung anyway so Stella didn't notice anything.

I shouldn't kiss her like that anymore. It wasn't safe. I wasn't safe.

10

Howie

I half-dozed through English, and by the time I made it to Physics, Stella had already sat down in her chair.

"Pop quiz today, folks!" announced our Physics teacher, whose name I always forgot.

I froze. *Oh, no.* I bowed my head as a paper landed on my desk. Word problems. *Oh no, oh no, oh no.*

I read and re-read the questions, but I'd forget the start of the question by the time I hit the end and then I'd need to go back and read it over again. Next to me, Stella's hair hung over her paper as she scribbled away. I took a moment to breathe her in and enjoy the feeling of her mind racing away at its calculations. It's very hard to describe a sense that normal humans don't have, but the closest I can come to the feel of Stella's mind when it's working hard is the sound of percolating coffee. Finally, I shook myself and tried to read the questions again.

I knew this material. I was explaining it to Stella last night. The information I needed was right in front of me. I just needed to sort through it, but I couldn't think it through.

By the time our teacher asked for the quiz sheets back, I had scribbled down some initial numbers- notes so I wouldn't have to keep trying to read the question — but hadn't gotten any further than that. Stella handed hers to the teacher and then glanced at mine as I passed my own to him, and I saw her forehead furrow.

"Did you not get any of the questions?" she asked quietly, her breath tickling my ear.

I shook my head no.

"But… you were explaining that stuff to me last night!"

"I couldn't remember how the equation went, and I had trouble concentrating on the questions," I whispered. I couldn't meet her eyes. I stared at my shoes.

"Oh." Her fingers tapped thoughtfully on the table. "Because you didn't get enough sleep last night?"

I nodded. "I usually try to get extra sleep before a test."

"Okay. Well. Pop quizzes suck. Don't worry, one bad quiz won't cause much damage."

I nodded. I wasn't worried about my grade. I was worried about what she would think of me. Because as much as she was trying to hide it, I could sense that Stella was surprised and seriously concerned.

Stella

I couldn't help staring at Howie as we filed out of Physics class. I hope I did it subtly, but subtlety is not one of my talents. Besides, Howie tended to know what I was feeling about things so there was probably no point in trying to disguise it. When I saw him hand in that quiz, I was *shocked*. I mean, Jesus, he was teaching me this stuff just last night, and it was obvious then that he completely understood it. Howie was a fantastic teacher. He had this way of making complicated things seem really simple. I'd been thinking that if he could just get a B.Ed., he'd make a great teacher. Sure, he'd look a little young but we could age him up a bit with makeup and clothing and stuff. Put him in tweed with elbow patches and he'd be your standard absent-minded professor.

I knew that Howie got pretty dopey when he wasn't well-rested and well-brained, but *wow*. I think this was the first time I had actually seen, first hand, the way that his disease interfered with his school work. Like, forgetting things he knew *perfectly well the day before* kind of interference.

He looked so miserable and defeated. I reached out and took his hand. He gave me a tight smile and clung to my hand like a drowning man clutching a life preserver.

Howie remained subdued through lunch. When he finished his thermos of brains the usual sparkle didn't return to his eyes. Amy noticed.

"Are you okay, Howie?"

"Oh. Yes. I'm just a little tired today," he said, smiling at her briefly and then dropping his eyes back to the table.

"So, The Skeez is at it again," said Kate abruptly. Kate had an ongoing feud with her mother's boyfriend, who insisted on acting like a stepfather even though he wasn't married to her mother, didn't live with them, and Kate was practically an adult anyway.

"What happened this time?" I asked.

"He wanted to talk to me about Seattle. Tried to sit down with me and have a talk about the Zombie Killer, like I was a scared little girl."

I glanced at Howie. I was hyper-sensitive to the word zombie, but his eyes were closed, his long eyelashes brushing his cheek. It was like he was dozing. He must be really tired. What had *happened* last night?

"What did he say?" Michelle asked Kate eagerly. We all loved The Skeez because Kate's stories were endlessly entertaining. One of my life goals was to meet this man in person.

"Oh, something about how I shouldn't believe everything in the media, and I was perfectly safe here in Vancouver, but if I wanted to back out of the band Seattle trip, he'd be supportive." Kate deepened her voice and took on a pompous body pose. "A young woman can't be too careful with her safety, especially in America, with their lax gun regulations." She relaxed into her usual posture. "It drives me crazy that he thinks he's this super important law enforcement officer when really he's just a border control guard. So he's got it in his head that he's all that's standing in between the Seattle Zombie and mass chaos in Vancouver."

"Tell me your mom doesn't want you to back out of the band trip just because her border-control boyfriend is a paranoid weirdo," I said.

"You have to come!" said Michelle. "It wouldn't be the same. Last year was such a blast."

"She actually kind of did want me to back out. I think he might be getting to her," said Kate. "I did my best to assure both of them that I *probably* won't get killed, since I'm not a hobo or a prostitute."

"What? This is news to me!" teased Michelle.

"Anyway, if I get my brains eaten in Seattle, The Skeez can say he told me so," said Kate pragmatically.

"Why do they think the killer is *eating* the brains, anyway?" Michelle asked practically. "I mean, it's not like they found a fork and a napkin nearby."

"I don't think I want my cottage cheese anymore," said Amy, putting down her Tupperware container.

"Your cottage cheese looks *nothing* like brains," I said irritably to her. I glanced at Howie. His eyes were open now, but he was staring at the table.

"They'll probably catch the guy soon," said Amy. "I mean, won't they?"

"How? Hobos are easy pickings. No one to report them missing, no one to say where or when they were last seen or who they were last seen with…" Kate shrugged, looking pissed off. "It took the Vancouver police, like, what, twenty years to notice that Robert Pickton was murdering the local prostitutes? It sucks, but cops just don't care about druggies and homeless people. Neither do news crews. If it weren't for the whole 'missing brains' angle, six dead homeless people would never be considered newsworthy. But just because it's a little weird, suddenly Seattle gets this burst of attention. Look it up. People like that go missing in every city, all the time."

"You're such a positive person," Michelle said affectionately.

"It's just such bullshit. Pickton takes fifty women off of the street and grinds them up into pig food, and people actually *see* the bloody clothing and report him but still somehow no one cares, but some other guy empties a few skulls and suddenly it's big news and I'm supposed to cancel my band trip," Kate griped.

"Or girl," I said.

She rolled her eyes. "Yeah. Maybe. Like ninety-nine percent of all mass murderers are male, but you know, it could happen."

We were quiet for a few moments. Then Kate spoke again.

"I'm thinking of going into gender studies. I'm not sure what you can do with something like that — maybe become a sex ed teacher or do workshops on how to not be a dick to women or something?"

"Like how to date a woman without being all creepy and father-knows-best with her nearly adult daughter?" said Michelle.

"Exactly."

"That sounds like you all over," I said.

Kate shot me a look. "So are we allowed to talk about universities again? Are you over whatever that was?"

"Yup. I'm over it," I said. "Go nuts."

The girls launched into a discussion of Simon Fraser University versus the University of British Columbia versus some of the small colleges, but I just watched Howie. He looked so depressed, sitting there and staring at his thermos. I reached out and took his hand, and he twined his fingers around mine and gave me a brief smile. But a moment later he had faded away, gone to somewhere I couldn't reach.

In Drama, Dean was bouncing on his chair with excitement like a little kid.

"Okay, so I've been planning it out," he said. "It's going to be awesome. I figure if I get a wedding dress and a big rosary I'll look a lot like the Infant of Prague. You just need big glasses and we can deck them out with some red glitter, and maybe a wig to make you Sally Jesse Raphael. We totally need to get to a Value Village."

"First we need to submit the proposal," I said. "It might get rejected."

"Whatever, no it won't. It's totally fine," he said, rolling his eyes. "But okay, yeah, let's get the boring crap out of the way."

I ended up filling out the proposal sheet while he flipped through pages and occasionally called out to one of his buddies who had also stayed in the room with his partner. I was ready to kick his hyperactive ass off of his chair by the time I was done. *This* is what I had imagined working with Dean would be like and I was both disappointed and relieved to have it become a reality. On the other hand, I also wanted to kick my own ass because I couldn't stop taking deep breaths of that damn body spray or whatever it was he reeked of. What was wrong with me?

"So, when do you want to go to Value Village?" Dean prodded after our second read-through of the scene.

"Is this something that really needs to be done together?" I asked. "How about I get my costume, and you get yours."

"Come on, Stella. We're partners. This is supposed to be a *team* project. What do you have against working as a team?" his dark eyes looked almost serious.

I sighed. "Okay. But I'm busy Saturday. I have plans with my friends."

"And I'm busy Sunday. How about Monday after school?"

I couldn't think of a reason to say no. "Okay."

"It's a date," he said, whipping out his phone. "Monday, after school. Value Village with Stella."

Through some miraculous act of willpower, I stifled myself from saying, "It is NOT a date."

Can you imagine? God, that would have been awkward.

This was going to *suck.*

It took me a while to find Howie after school. Normally I didn't have to find Howie. He just appeared wherever I was. I hung out with my friends for a while but when Howie didn't materialize I made my way to his car.

He was already there, sitting inside, reading his book. I opened the car door. "Hey," I said to him.

He looked up and smiled. "Hey, yourself, Beautiful."

"I got slightly concerned when you didn't pull your creepy zombie find-Stella act," I said, getting into the car.

"My class let out a little early and I'm having trouble navigating the halls today. So I figured I would just come here and wait. That way you could hang out with your friends for a while if you wanted. They always stop talking when I show up."

"You don't have to explain yourself."

He stared at the pages of his book. "Just as long as you understand that I did want to see you."

"It's *fine,* Howie. You know I'm not clingy that way. But are you okay? You just seem… a little off today."

"I think it's just stress. You know, homework piling up, thinking about…" he shook his head and then smiled at me. "I'll be okay."

"It *is* stressful," I agreed. "What do you say we go home and spend half an hour or so going at each other like animals to de-stress before we turn into upright, hardworking citizens again?"

His eyes lit up and he looked at me with that consuming, passionate look that made my insides hug themselves. And then his expression faded and he looked away again.

"I would love to," he said huskily. "But I really shouldn't. I should drop you off and go home. I have so much to do and I'm afraid… I'm afraid that if I don't do well enough, that I won't get accepted to the school you want and you'll be upset…"

"Half an hour, Howie. Half an hour is not going to wreck anything."

"But it's another half hour late into the night to get my work done, and you've seen how I am when I'm short on sleep…" He kept staring at his hands. Am I that scary, that he couldn't even look me in the eyes?

"Howie…" I laid my hand on his lap and his eyes flashed again. "It's okay. I'm not going to yell at you for caring about your grades. If today's not okay, then fine. Maybe tomorrow. Okay?"

"Okay." He turned the key in the ignition and his car sputtered to life. He sat staring at the steering wheel for a moment and then turned to me. "Maybe you had better drive."

"Sure," I said, both relieved and concerned. We switched seats and I pulled out of the parking lot. There was so much I wanted to talk to Howie about, like physics quizzes and brain-eating murderers, but he was obviously having a bad day and I didn't want to make things worse. So I channelled my confusion and other negative feelings onto the poor drivers around me.

"Look at that self-absorbed turd-monkey," I said to Howie, gesturing.

Howie looked around. "Monkey?"

"That asshole there! That waste of a carbon footprint in the black pickup. He didn't pull over for the fire truck."

"Oh," Howie said as an ambulance siren started up behind me and I pulled over again. "I'm just impressed when people do pull over."

"You're impressed," I repeated. "By people following *the law*?"

"It's so pretty to see it," he said. His voice was quieter than usual. "The sirens come and suddenly everyone just makes way."

"Because they have to. Because it's *the law*."

"But they don't have to. That guy you saw – nothing happened to him, right?"

"Besides nearly getting plowed into by a firetruck? I guess not."

"So no one really has to. The police can't spot and arrest every person who doesn't pull over for this ambulance. People don't pull over because of the law. They pull over because they want to let the ambulance through. They want to let the fire truck through. They want to do what they can to make sure those rescuers get to the person who needs help. It's people, all working together to help other people – strangers that they never met. And it took so long to build a society that would work like that. It's hundreds of years of struggle to get emergency services and health care and organized society, but we did it, and it works. People make way for the rescuers, and I like to see it. It's beautiful."

Jesus fuck, I could try my whole life and never be as good a person as Howie was. I glanced at him as I pulled back into traffic. He was looking out the window with a thoughtful expression.

"When's our anniversary?" I asked suddenly.

He furrowed his brow. "I guess that depends on what day you want to count."

"That's what I'm saying. I mean, I moved out here almost exactly a year ago. So… is our anniversary, like, the day we met? Or the day of our first kiss… or… when I told you I loved you?"

"It feels wrong to celebrate our love on the anniversary of the day that a bunch of people died," Howie said. "I'm leaning toward first kiss day. Before all the dying happened."

"That works for me. So let's see, that would be…" I counted days in my head. "Wow. A week from Sunday."

"A whole year, already?" Howie shook his head. "It feels like minutes. Seconds."

"It feels like a really frigging long time to me. Like, a year ago I'd never kissed anyone and I had never seen a zombie or lived in a place that had *daffodils* coming up in February. My entire life is so different now."

He was looking at me thoughtfully. "You're still missing home."

"Yes, but… less… I think." I gestured at the cherry blossom buds on the trees and the snowy mountains beyond them. "I have to admit, the early spring is a nice sell. But anyway, my point is, let's do something for our one-year-of-kissing day. Maybe something cozy and romantic again?"

"I'd like that," said Howie. "I can't ask my family to leave the house empty for us again. But I'd love to take you out somewhere."

He said the words, but he didn't seem nearly as enthusiastic about getting time alone with me as he normally would.

I drove into my townhouse complex's parking lot and forgot all about anniversaries when I spotted a familiar black car parked in visitor parking. Excited, I gave Howie a shove and he turned.

"The Zom Squad is here," I told him. "Want to bet it's about Seattle?"

"Seattle?" He looked blank.

"The missing brains, Howie. I told you it sounded like zombies!"

He shook his head, but he didn't say anything. He did, however, get out of the car and follow me into the house.

11

Howie

Stella charged toward her house and I came after her, stumbling to keep up. I really didn't think this could have anything to do with those poor people in Seattle. Hadn't Dad said the other day that he'd talked to Agent Hunt about it? Besides, it didn't sound right. Zombies don't empty out skulls and leave the rest. If that were the case, the virus wouldn't *spread*.

Thinking of that brought back the memory of my Pop looking up, his hands and mouth dripping, with bits of Henry running down his shirt, and I stopped walking and shut my eyes until it passed. I recovered after a minute and hurried to catch up to Stella, who had already opened her front door.

"Hello, Stella," said Agent Hunt. "Howie." She was sitting at the kitchen table with a coffee in her hand. Stella's mother was sitting next to her, nearly vibrating with nervousness.

Michaella Hunt was the tall, self-assured woman who ran the British Columbia branch of the Canadian Reanimation Virus Control Service, or CRVCS, as they called themselves. They pronounced it "service" and would often just refer to themselves as The Service. Stella's father liked to call them The Cervix, although he never tried that around Agent Hunt. Stella called them The Zom Squad no matter who was around.

Hunt had been in her twenties when I first met her, but her warm brown skin was starting to develop fine lines around her dark eyes, and I guess she was probably in her mid-forties by now. She was ageing well. Little had changed over the years. Her hair, always kept neatly up in a tight bun, was still the deep black it had always been. Her expression had always been stern, and I couldn't imagine that ever changing.

The Service has a branch in the most populous city of each province. Hunt had started out in Ontario, but she had been the head of the British Columbia for quite a few years now and we considered it only a matter of time before she was moved back to head office and put in charge of the entire operation. We liked her very much. She was strict but fair, and she and my family had developed a healthy respect for each other over the years. Last year Agent Hunt and her department arrested me and my entire family, planning to declare us dead and hide us permanently away underground, but you could tell she felt bad about having to do it.

That was all forgiven and forgotten now, partially because Stella proved that my family was innocent and partially because she promised to let them study her brain if they released my family.

The head office was in Ottawa, and they had flown Stella out for three days last summer so she could demonstrate her ability to transfix zombies. I suspected that if Hunt wanted to speak to Stella today, it was probably to arrange a longer trip for the upcoming summer.

"Uh, hi," Stella said to Agent Hunt and she raised an eyebrow at her mother. "What's going on?"

"Agent Hunt called me this morning and said she planned to speak to you after school. I left work early so I could be here," said Mrs. Blunt. "Hi, Howie."

"Hello, Mrs. Blunt."

"Elaine," she said patiently.

"Elaine," I corrected myself.

"You made my Mom leave work?" Stella said to Agent Hunt. "Was it that urgent?"

Agent Hunt shook her head. "You're eighteen now. She doesn't need to be present. I was informing her as a courtesy."

"I chose to leave work early," Elaine agreed. "Eighteen or not, I want to hear what is being said if I can."

"Is it Seattle?" Stella burst out eagerly. "I was right! It *is* zombies."

Agent Hunt winced. "Stella. You have a ninety-five percent average in school. Surely you know that grammatically, either it *is* a zombie outbreak, or they *are* zombies. But there's no outbreak in Seattle. As far as I know, the recent killings in Seattle were committed with weapons, and no trace of the virus." Hunt's eyes flickered briefly to me, and I felt a moment of tension pass through her. Why? I gave her a puzzled look in return. She raised her eyebrows and looked back at Stella.

"Oh," Stella said, looking deflated. "I thought you were going to send me in to the rescue. I could use some zombie-killing to de-stress from school."

"The next time we have an outbreak in Canada, you can be sure that we will be requesting your services. But that's not why I'm here today."

"You want me to go to Ontario again," Stella guessed.

"Possibly in the summer, but we can discuss that later," said Agent Hunt, taking a sip of her coffee. "Have a seat."

Stella grabbed a Diet Pepsi from the fridge and sat in a chair with the regal dignity of a queen sitting on her throne.

"I'm here to discuss your higher education," said Hunt.

That took all of us by surprise.

"What? Why?" Stella asked.

"The Service would like you to attend Simon Fraser University."

Oh. *OH.* Yes.

Stella blinked. "I repeat: What? Why?"

"We have our reasons."

"And do I get to *hear* those reasons? Because I've got to be honest — I've seen Simon Fraser and it's ugly as fuck. I mean, neither SFU nor UBC is exactly the sandstone-clad halls of learning that universities are back home, but SFU looks like a military outpost."

Hunt shrugged. "While we have ties with both SFU and UBC, we work more closely with SFU. That is why Morton works there. We have specialized facilities there."

"How specialized?" Stella demanded. Hunt just shrugged. Again, her eyes flickered briefly at me. Was she wondering how much I had told Stella about what was on Burnaby Mountain? I hadn't said anything. I didn't want to get arrested again, and it hadn't seemed important. This must be to keep Stella safe. But why? What danger could she be in?

"I mean, I'm portable, you know," Stella pointed out. "I could attend school at one campus and visit your facilities in another. It's the same city. They're like forty-five minutes apart."

"You are a valuable asset to us, and we would like easy access to you. You did agree to this."

"I agreed to let you study me. I agreed to go to Ottawa to do zombie tricks for you. But I don't remember promising to let you make my life choices for me."

"You didn't. We are willing to offer an incentive. We will fund your education should you choose to attend SFU."

Stella's eyes widened. "Are you saying that I will get to go to school there *for free?*"

"Yes."

"*Just* so I will be close to your research facilities? That makes no sense."

She was right. I tried to make eye contact again with Hunt, but she looked only at Stella.

"Do you want it or not?"

"What if I don't get in?"

I stifled a laugh. As if she could be denied entrance to anywhere by anybody. Stella could march up to the doors of Buckingham Castle and someone would let her in. She is the kind of person who gets where she wants to go.

"I take it you haven't checked your email today," Hunt said dryly. "Trust me. You got in."

Stella glanced at her mother, who was remaining commendably silent despite the fact that she was boiling with excitement. Stella looked at me, too, but I didn't want to sway her one way or another. This was her decision. But the offer itself both relieved and concerned me.

"Will they pay for Howie, too? That would sweeten the deal," Stella said.

"No. A lifetime free of student debt is sweet enough of a deal, and you know it," Agent Hunt said briskly.

Stella looked at her mother. "Okay. Tell me what you're thinking."

"This is your decision," Elaine said firmly.

"I know that, and this is your opportunity to voice your opinion," Stella said. "Give me some guidance here."

Elaine sighed. "I think you'd be an idiot to turn it down. But it's your life." She turned swiftly to Agent Hunt. "Swear to me that you are simply bargaining for her choice in schools, and not committing her to anything else."

"Like what?" Agent Hunt asked.

"I don't know. It doesn't make a lot of sense to me, that you're willing to pay out thousands of government dollars just for Stella to attend a certain university. I'm sure there's more to the story."

So was I. If The Service was this concerned about Stella's safety, they must have a reason.

Agent Hunt shrugged. "Then you don't appreciate how valuable an asset she is to us. If we could get her to live inside our labs, we would." There it was again. That eye flicker at me.

Stella and Hunt stared each other down for a minute. Then Stella took a sip of her Diet Pepsi.

"Yeah, okay," she said. "It's a deal."

Agent Hunt sent me another cryptic glance as she said goodbye, and I almost followed her out the door to confront her. But I didn't. First of all, Stella's curiosity would send her flying out after me, and second of all,

Hunt wouldn't tell me a thing if it didn't suit her to do so. I would have to ask Dad later. If something was up, he would get it out of her.

"Well?" Stella said to me when Agent Hunt clicked the door shut behind her. "I knew you wouldn't say a word until I made a decision, so tell me what you think now."

"I'm happy they made you such a good offer and I think it was smart to take advantage of it," I said quietly.

"Are you going to tell me what that was all about?" Stella probed.

"I promise I had nothing to do with it, and neither did my family," I said. She put her hands on her hips and pursed her lips in a way that was irresistible, but also meant that she was really serious.

"Don't give me that crap. Stop telling me half-truths and answer my damn question."

"They have a lot of specialized facilities up there, Stella," I said. "And…" I paused.

"AND WHAT, HOWIE?"

I sighed. "It's up a mountain. It has limited numbers of roads leading into it. It's… secure. You know. In case there's an outbreak."

Elaine raised her eyebrows as if she had just understood, and approved. "You mean this is about keeping her away from zombie hordes?"

I nodded. "Probably."

What I couldn't understand was *why*. There were no outbreaks in Vancouver since last year. She had said that the Seattle thing wasn't to do with the virus…

I paused.

No. She had said that the kills had been made with weapons, and no trace of the virus had been found. She *hadn't* said that it had nothing to do with the virus. Hunt was very specific with her language. A chill went down my spine. I felt like I had just woken up from sleepwalking. I should have remembered. I should have remembered that there could be a terrible explanation for the selective removal of brain tissue from a human body. And I couldn't even tell Stella about it.

"But zombies found us on Burnaby Mountain, like, *first thing* the last time we had an outbreak," Stella pointed out.

"But that was because my father was being framed, and his lab is there," I reminded her. "They didn't actually climb all the way up the mountain, through thick forest, in the hour that we happened to be eating lunch there."

"But what are the chances of an outbreak happening?" asked Elaine. "Why are they so concerned?"

I shrugged. It seemed like the safest action. The last time I told the Blunts confidential information, I got arrested and they threatened to lock me up forever and declare me legally dead. Of course, Stella sailed in and saved me, but I couldn't count on that happening every time. Besides, I didn't know anything for sure. I needed to talk to Dad.

I looked at Stella. "So, we're going to SFU. How do you feel?"

She smiled at me. "You asshole. You know how to defuse me, just by saying 'we'".

I felt a wave of dizziness when she smiled at me. I was definitely not functioning on all cylinders today. I felt more distracted by brain waves, less alert. Basically, I felt more like a zombie. And I longed to kiss and hold Stella, but the black thoughts came like flies and I felt so contaminated that I didn't think I should even touch her.

Stella was watching me with a thoughtful look in those brown eyes of hers, and I realized that several minutes had passed. Stella's mother had left the kitchen, and we were alone.

"Howie," said Stella slowly. "Let's talk about that quiz."

"I'd rather not."

"I think we need to. Is that what would happen to you at university? You'd be up studying or something, lose sleep, and then forget everything on the day of the exam?"

"Sort of. Most of your marks come from midterms and exams," I tried to explain. "You have to remember the equations and how to apply them. And I just kept forgetting the equations. I understood the concepts, but when I was put on the spot, under stress…"

"Even if you took brains right before?"

"Yes. They can only help repair old connections, not help me make new ones. That takes time and a lot of repetition." I might as well be honest. "I don't even remember a lot of our time together. At least, not as well as you do, probably. I never could have remembered what time of year it was when we met, let alone the date."

She raised her eyebrows. "But you remember the important things, right?"

"That depends on what you consider important."

She cocked her head. "Meeting me, our first kiss, fighting zombies together…" her lips crooked up in a smile, "….my birthday..."

God, I wanted her. Would I ever dare to touch her again? I remembered the intimacy of my dream, the tenderness. There were no black thoughts there, and yet my hands had just reached out and as easy as that, she was dead. How could I ever risk that? How could I know that it wouldn't really happen?

"Oh, yes," I said, and my voice was rough with emotion that I couldn't convey. "I remember the important things." I looked down at the table. "But there are too many things to learn in a single semester, let alone four different kinds of science at once."

"So, you've only ever tried to get science degrees?"

"Of course, science."

"Not of course. You also love music. You carry poetry around in your backpack. What about an English degree or music degree or something?" Stella asked. "That would probably be more subjective, right? More essays and things, probably less weight on the exams."

"I don't know about that. Music doesn't work, anyway. I can't sing and I can't learn an instrument. And I don't see the point of taking a class on poetry. I know how to enjoy poetry. I have no interest in dissecting it."

"C'mon, I'm thinking about taking a minor in English just so I have something with soul in my curriculum."

"Science has a soul. Science has God in it," I said.

I felt the jolt of her surprise. "God? You've never mentioned God before. Are you *religious*?"

"You don't see me going to church, do you?"

"Maybe you've been secretly slipping off to be an altar boy and I never knew," she teased. "You're full of secrets, anyway. Your still waters run *really* deep." When she looked at me with that mischief in her eyes, I felt alive in ways that I hadn't since I was a child. How could I look at her and not believe in God? How could I look inside myself and not believe in the Devil?

"I went to church when I was a kid," I explained. "It was a big part of life back then. Everyone went."

"That doesn't tell me what you believe now. Besides, aren't God and science mortal enemies?"

"No." I struggled to articulate my thoughts. "I mean, I know some people think so, but I don't. I think the laws of nature exist for a reason and that both good and evil use those laws to achieve their purposes. That's what gives Dad hope that our disease will someday be cured. He thinks that evil and good exist in equal measure, but it's up to us to find those balances ourselves."

"Are you all secret Christians or something? What the hell? Why have we never talked about this before?" Stella asked.

I grinned. "Ask Ray if he's a Christian. See what he says."

Stella laughed, and I could tell she was a little relieved.

"I don't know if there's a God like the one in the Bible," I said. "But I do think that there is some higher organization to the universe than we can see from down here on Earth. And science is His rule book."

"I'm going to kiss you now, to shut you up before I lose respect for you," said Stella, but she was smiling. She leaned into me, her dark hair curtaining our faces, and a line from Sir Philip Sidney strayed through my mind.

Stella, the only planet of my light,
Light of my life, and life of my desire,
Chief good, whereto my hope doth only aspire

I didn't need a university course to explain poems like that to me. I had her in my arms, and she was mine. Oh, God, I shouldn't kiss her. I could already feel the black thoughts swarming in. I pulled out of the kiss just as the doorknob turned on the front door and her father walked in.

"Hello, kids. Working hard?"

"Do we ever do anything else?" Stella's voice was slightly morose.

"Ah, what a good question," her father said. "If everything we do is a learning experience, then aren't we all in the school of life? And therefore, if I sit down to watch *Family Guy* with a bowl of Cheetos isn't that, too, schoolwork in a way?"

"There you are! You missed Agent Hunt!" Elaine came to the door to greet her husband. She turned to Stella. "Did you tell him?"

"I didn't have a chance. He was too busy going on about Cheetos and the universe."

"Tell me what?" Dad asked. "Hunt was here? Oh! The Seattle killer! It's zombies, isn't it?"

"No," said Stella and her mother in unison.

"Then what?"

"They wanted to pay for my university education as a thank you for being generally awesome and important," said Stella.

"Wouldn't that be nice?" he kicked off his shoes. "So, does Cervix want you to go back to Ontario this summer?"

"No, Dad, I'm actually being serious. They're paying my tuition if I go to SFU. Which, obviously, I am going to do."

Mr. Blunt turned slowly and looked from Stella to his wife, and then to me for confirmation.

"Why?" He looked at me for the answer. I opened my mouth and closed it again, and then shrugged.

"Something about how it's super safe from zombies with special zombie research stuff. Basically, it's their home turf and they want me on it," said Stella.

"This *is* about the Seattle Zombie," said Mr. Blunt. "It has to be."

"Well, Hunt said that there's no sign of the virus and the people were killed with weapons, not savaged by human teeth," Stella said. Her casual words brought up terrible memories and I covered my face.

"Howie? Are you okay?"

"Just... not feeling well. I think I'm going to head home if that's okay."

"Not feeling well? *Can* you get sick?" her mother asked, perplexed.

"I am always sick," I said. "And I think I need to go home. Good-bye."

"Bye," they chorused, and I know they were watching me as I walked out the door.

Stella

I didn't get any homework done that night. My parents took me out to dinner to celebrate my educational windfall, and I ended up staying up until eleven playing Pokemon Puzzle League with them on their ancient Nintendo.

It was a good way to spend a Friday night, but I was still feeling weird about Howie. I sent him a text before bed.

I miss you.
Are you reading John Donne
and thinking dirty thoughts?

He answered quickly.

Unfortunately, no. Studying.
See you tomorrow, beautiful.

Tomorrow's Saturday.
I promised the girls I'd hang out with them
and go to a movie, remember.

Sorry, lost track of the days.

He didn't send any more texts. What was going *on* with him?

12

Howie

"You're home early," said Ray when I came in the door. He was sprawled on the couch watching television.

"The Service just offered to pay Stella's tuition if she'd agree to go to SFU," I said.

Ray sat up. "Damn," he said. "That's impressive. You think it's got to do with Seattle?"

"I don't know. But I was thinking — what if this has to do with Dad's MIT experiment?"

"Where the hell have you been?" Ray said. "That's all we've been talking about for days."

I sat on the couch. "What?"

Ray started to laugh. "Hazel!" he called. "You gotta come down here."

But when Hazel came down and Ray filled her in, she didn't laugh. She looked concerned.

"Howie, we were talking about it over breakfast just this morning. And yesterday morning, too. Are you feeling okay?"

"No," I said, rubbing my eyes. "I don't think I am. So fill me in, please. Do we know that it's…"

"We don't know anything," said Ray. "All Hunt told Doc was that the Americans say there's no sign of the virus."

"And we know what Baum would think about believing Americans," Hazel said with a smile.

"Has anyone told Baum?" I asked.

Ray shrugged. "Talk to Doc," he said.

So I did, as soon as he walked in the door.

"The Service is paying for Stella to go to school on Burnaby Mountain," I said. "Did you know about this?"

"Yes," said Dad, setting down his briefcase while Hazel helped him off with his coat. "Michaella called to talk to me this morning."

"Is Stella in danger?" What a stupid question. She was in danger every day, just being with me. I thought about my dream again, and I shivered.

"Probably not. But until the perpetrator is caught, Michaella thinks it is prudent to treat these reports of brain-removal seriously. She called George, and he recommended keeping Stella at SFU."

"And The Service listened to him? He started a damn outbreak just to screw us over," said Ray.

"We have found no proof of that," Dad reminded him. "That was Stella's theory."

"You got another?"

"George maintains his innocence. My assistant Leanne is also convinced he is innocent."

I averted my eyes. There were too many secrets in my life. It was too much. Everything was too much.

"In any case, I approve of having Stella at SFU and I am pleased that The Service is willing to outlay the financial incentive for her to do so."

"Considering that she's worth about twenty field agents, they'll probably pay for it by laying people off," said Ray.

"The Service does not lay people off, Raymond. Once they know the secret, they are best kept under The Service's control. They may reduce hiring, however. And if I need a new lab assistant in the future, perhaps Stella will take the job."

I stood and started to trudge up the stairs.

"Where are you going?" Hazel asked.

"If I'm going to go to SFU, then I have work to do."

Stella

I didn't see Howie all weekend.

At first, it didn't seem weird. My friends had this birthday thing planned for me on Saturday. We had brunch at Cora and went to a matinee movie like old people and then we went bowling, and it was a fun day.

"Dean Kato wants me to go to Value Village with him," I informed my friends at brunch because I couldn't say, "Hey, guess what? A super-secret government agency wants to pay my tuition if I go to SFU!"

"Whaaaat?" Michelle said. "You're hanging out with Dean Kato? So lucky."

"I don't want to go!" I said. "I mean, his best friends are Kelly Svancara and Carter Davidson. God knows what could happen. They could jump out at me when I was trying on a bad costume and take photos and Snapchat them to the entire school."

"Or, *or,* nothing will happen and you're being a paranoid weirdo," said Kate.

"That is also a viable possibility," I said.

I texted Howie once but he didn't respond for an hour and even then it was a bland, minimal kind of response. Well. At least he wasn't being clingy. I hated clinginess, and he knew that. He was probably just trying to respect my space. I respected his respect and decided to give him his space, too.

But on Sunday, when I texted him and suggested a walk in the park, he put me off. That struck me as really unlike him. When I called and prodded him, he just said he was really busy with schoolwork. He said he loved me, and couldn't wait to see me again. I knew his voice well enough to sense a real strain under his normal monotone, so I didn't push him. I'd see him Monday.

I stumbled downstairs Monday morning in my usual bleary-eyed, muss-headed state. My parents were already eating breakfast and the kitchen smelled like coffee.

"Where's Howie?" I asked. He was usually waiting for me, chatting with my parents or wiping the counters or something.

"Not here yet," said Dad, taking a large bite out of his muffin. "Must be running late. I wonder when his 'Time to get up and go worship Stella' alarm goes off in the morning?"

I poured myself a bowl of cereal and ate it hurriedly, then ran up for a shower. When I came back downstairs fully dressed I knew Howie would be there.

"Still not here," called my mother. "Maybe you should call him?"

I went to my phone. Howie wouldn't have *forgotten* to pick me up, would he? No, there was a text on my phone.

Slept late. Be there as quick as I can.

My world, which had wobbled on its axis, settled back into place. I was waiting for Howie's car when he pulled up. He hopped out, reached out his arms and kissed me on the cheek. *The cheek?* I gave him a strange look.

"We're late," he said. "Sorry about that."

"I thought I'd spare you Dad's teasing by waiting for you outside," I said, taking his keys.

"Oh, so it wasn't because you missed me," he replied, giving me his shy, dimpled smile as he hopped into the passenger seat. His hair was a little mussed and his glasses slightly askew. I reached over and settled them properly on his nose.

"I may have missed you a bit," I said.

"Well, I missed you dreadfully. How are you?"

"Dreading this afternoon. Dean is making me go to Value Village with him to shop for costumes for our project, and I'm somewhat concerned that it'll be the actual worst."

"Has he been that bad?"

"No… he's been fine. He just pisses me off."

"He's been fine, but still bothers you for indefinable reasons?" he said, cracking a grin. "Poor guy."

"He's not poor *anything,*" I said. "He thinks he's God's gift to women. He thinks I should be, like, fawning all over him just because he's popular."

"Or he's hoping you will. He's attracted to you," said Howie. His voice, as always, was unemotional. I glanced at him but his face was unreadable.

"How do you know that?"

"Stella, I have eyes, and I feel people's brain waves. There's a reason he gives me a hard time."

"And it… doesn't bother you that I'm partnered up with him?"

Howie shrugged. "It's an occupational hazard of dating a beautiful woman that other people will find her beautiful too. You didn't choose it, and you aren't responsible for how others feel about you. There's nothing I can do about any of it, and you don't even like him, so I don't see the point in gnashing my teeth over the whole thing."

Sometimes, when Howie said these reasonable, understanding, mature things, I became very aware of Howie's age. Physically Howie might look like a teenager, but emotionally he was light years ahead of me.

"You've gone quiet. Penny for your thoughts?" he asked.

"I was just… feeling good about you," I said. "I know you won't change much… physically… but you're very grown up in the ways that count."

He smiled. "Well. That's nice to hear."

He definitely seemed better than he had on Friday. I was relieved.

"High five for team Value Village after school today!" said Dean, catching me on my way to Drama. "Pick you up by the side entrance, near the parking lot?"

"I can get there myself," I said, since I had no desire to lock myself in a vehicle with Dean and his cologne and his smug popularity and general Dean-ness.

"You got a car?"

"I have a functioning knowledge of the local transit system," I said.

"Aw, Stella, come on. Just ride with me. It makes way more sense." He held up his hand. "I promise, I will be a perfect driver."

I couldn't think of a good reason to say no without seeming weird. "Ugh. Fine."

Howie found me at the end of the day.

"I know you have to work on your Drama project," he said, "but I wanted to see you first." He took my hands in his own long, cool fingers.

"Good," I said, pushing him up against a wall and laying my lips on him for the first time in days. But then he sighed and pulled back.

"I don't want to keep you," he said quietly.

What the actual fuck? "Okay. Uh. Text you later?"

"Please do," he said.

Dean was already waiting, and he looked annoyed.

"Rushing you away, am I?" he said. I guess he saw me kissing Howie.

"I have a boyfriend. We kiss each other. Deal with it." I replied irritably.

"I'm just teasing," he said.

"I get enough teasing, but I'll keep you in mind in case I ever run low," I said.

"You're so serious," he said, leading the way to his car, which was a battered looking Pontiac. "Lighten up, will you?"

"Lay off Howie and I'll be sweet as pie," I said firmly.

He held up a hand. "I solemnly swear not to complain about, criticize, or even mention your boyfriend."

"Good."

"Whoa, Dean, where are you going, to a Weight Watcher's meeting?" shouted Ravi Sandhu. I flipped him off with my ruby finger.

"Drama project; we got teamed up as partners," Dean called back with an eye roll.

"You not coming to the game tonight?"

"I dunno. It depends. I'll text you later." He yanked open his door while I glared at him. "It's unlocked."

Oh, right, normal boys don't open car doors for girls in this day and age. I was so used to Howie doing it that I had just been standing by the passenger side door like an idiot. I got in.

We drove in awkward silence for a while. He drove over the speed limit, which didn't surprise me, and changed lanes without signalling, which also didn't surprise me.

"You changed lanes without signalling," I said, "and that was a school zone. What happened to perfect driving?"

He grinned and slowed down. "I'm sorry, I didn't realize I was driving an eighty-year-old."

"I was promised perfect driving. Pretend I am your driving instructor."

"You're a lot better looking than my driving instructor," he said. I gave him a Look. He raised a hand. "I'm not flirting, I swear. You didn't see my driving instructor. He had, like, this mole thing on his nose with a hair coming out of it. It was all I could think about. Every time he told me to do something, I imagined that the mole was talking to me. I was basically taught to drive by a hairy nose mole."

I couldn't help it — I laughed.

"So, all I'm saying is that you look better than a gigantic hairy mole on someone's nose. Don't let it go to your head or anything."

"It's tough when you're hitting me with flattery like that, but I think I can manage to maintain a modicum of perspective," I replied. "Now put both hands on the wheel at nine and three."

"Yessir, Mister Nose Mole, sir."

13

Howie

"You're home early. Again," said Ray when he came home on Monday to find me already studying on the couch. He dropped into the reclining chair. "And you were home all weekend. D'you two break up or something?"

"No," I said, my stomach clenching at the thought. "Don't be stupid."

"Seemed like a reasonable guess," he said, leaning back and putting his feet up on the coffee table. "Bound to be right eventually."

"Do I look like my entire world has crumbled around me? Am I raving and distraught and behaving as though life has completely lost all meaning?"

Ray squinted at me. "Nope."

"Then it's not a reasonable guess."

He shrugged and turned on the TV. "Okay, but I sure hope you're working on detaching yourself a bit, because you know it's coming."

"Just because it didn't work out for you and..." I bit my lip. Ray's face had shut down. He switched the TV off and stood up.

"Nothing good on anyway," he said, and he stalked out of the room.

I thought about going after him and apologizing, but I knew it wouldn't do any good. So I pulled my school books out of my bag and started to work on my Pre-Calc homework, but the numbers kept jumping around the page. I buried my face in my hands. Falling apart. Everything was falling apart.

"Howie? What's wrong?" said Hazel's voice.

"I feel awful," I confessed to her, and I'm ashamed to admit that tears started to run down my cheeks.

Hazel hurried to sit next to me and she put her thin arms around my neck. "Do you want to talk about it?"

"I wouldn't know where to start." I wiped my face and shook my head.

"You could start by telling me why you've been up past midnight the past couple of nights. I keep waking up and seeing the light from your room in the hall. You were holed up in your room all weekend, playing music. And then we had to wake you up this morning, and that's not like you at all."

"I've been studying."

"For what? A big test?"

"No, no," I told her about the MIT website and her face grew increasingly concerned.

"Howie, you can't do that. You can't try to learn new stuff when you're still in the middle of doing old stuff. It's going to mess everything up."

"But Hazel, I had to try."

"Why? Why now? Why not wait until the summer?"

"Because the more time I give myself to learn, the better a chance I have of passing it in the fall."

"You've got to stop worrying about university," she said. "You don't need a degree to love somebody."

"It's not that simple," I said. "If she sees that I have limits in this way, then she accepts that I have limits in other ways. And if she accepts those limits, she'll see how impossible our future is. I'm just trying to put that off. This isn't about her. It's about me."

"Does she know how much you're fretting about all of this?"

"No. Of course not."

"Don't you think she ought to know?"

"No. Of course not," I repeated.

"Well, I know I've never even managed to pass high school," she said. "And I know I'm already failing grade ten. So maybe my advice isn't worth much. But I really think you should focus on graduating before you focus on your next big limitation. You know. Take the hurdles one at a time."

I hugged her. "Of course your advice is worth something," I told her. "Uh. You're drooling a bit, though."

She dragged her sleeve over her mouth. "Thanks."

"No problem."

Stella

I have to say, Value Village with Dean wasn't what I was expecting. I thought he'd be skulking around and making me sort through the dresses and carry them around, but he didn't act at all embarrassed to be shopping for dresses. He tried them on and came right out of the change room each time to model and pose for me.

"That's too short," I said when he tried a frilly prom dress. "The Infant of Prague can't be showing ankle."

"But I have such a well-turned heel," he said, holding out his foot in what I assume was meant to be a sexy pose.

"The less leg the better," I said. "We are going for accuracy here."

"Because our classmates are such well-informed critics of religious icons," said Dean. "Okay, trying on the wedding dress."

The wedding dress worked a lot better.

"I feel too slinky in this, though," he said, turning and putting his hands on his hips. "It isn't poofy enough."

"We can fix that with a crinoline," I said.

"With a what?"

So I marched back to the fancy dress section, with Dean trotting along, holding up the dress so he wouldn't trip. I rifled through the racks for a while and pulled out a big, white, puffy crinoline.

"You put this on underneath," I said.

"Ah!" he grabbed it. "I get it. Okay." And he stepped right into it and hiked it up, giving me a brief glimpse of his boxer shorts. "There, that's way better, isn't it?" he said, twirling. The skirt flared out as he twirled, and then sank back down. "Oh, it slipped."

"Whatever, you can wear suspenders underneath to hold it up," I said. "I wish we had a fur cape or something to wear over."

"Don't forget your costume. We need to find you fake glasses and a red or blonde wig."

"Yeah, I don't think they have a fake glasses section," I said.

"Let's go to Michael's," said Dean. "We can get gold glitter glue to decorate the dress and red glitter glue to decorate paper glasses."

"Okay."

By the time he dropped me off at home, I was feeling pretty good. Our skit was going to be a lot of fun to watch, and the time with Dean hadn't been horribly awkward. When he was away from his jerk friends he was actually really easy to talk to. But I was also feeling guilty for enjoying myself, so I called Howie as soon as I walked in the door.

He answered almost immediately. "Well, hello, beautiful."

"Hey, I'm back from The Outing of Horror."

My father, who was stirring something in a pot, tapped at his wrist and held out five fingers, and I nodded to let him know that I understood.

"You survived, I guess," Howie replied.

"Yeah, it was fine, actually. He wasn't too much of a jerk."

"Good," he said. I mean, was he not jealous *at all*? I was glad, don't get me wrong, but it felt weird to have my boyfriend be like, 'Oh, good, I'm so glad you had fun with the handsome popular boy who has a crush on you.' Howie trusted me like wow.

"I miss you. Do you want to come over after dinner?"

"I can't tonight," he said.

"Oh. Okay. I'll see you tomorrow then."

"Good night, my star."

"Night."

I frowned at my phone as I ended the call.

"Is Howie not coming over?" Dad asked.

"No."

"Damn, I wanted him to see my new concoction," said Dad. "It's like a curry chilli thing."

"I can't wait to not eat that."

"Oh, you're going to love it. You'll see."

Howie

I took Hazel's advice and put my homework away.

"I think I'll skip dinner and go to bed now," I told her. "Try to get some sleep. I'll have a double ration of brains in the morning and get my homework done then."

"But no MIT stuff," she said.

"No MIT stuff," I promised.

I was just starting up the stairs when my father came home. I turned to greet him and paused when I saw that he wasn't alone.

Michaella Hunt was with him.

"Let me take your coat, Michaella," said Dad, but she was already removing her raincoat and hanging it on the coat rack.

"Hazel? Do we still have the coffee maker?" Dad asked.

She nodded. "I don't remember how to use it though."

"I do," I said. "I'll get it started."

"Please do," said Dad.

It was rare for Agent Hunt to visit, so we kept the coffee in the freezer next to the pig heads to keep it fresh. Hazel pulled it out while I fumbled with the filters.

"I wanted to talk to you about Stella," said Agent Hunt to me, allowing Dad to pull out her seat at the kitchen table. Like Stella, she exuded authority, but it was the cool power of a rushing river, instead of the chaotic inferno of Stella's fire.

"To me?" I said, dropping the filters. Hazel picked them up and put one in the coffee maker upside down. Dad walked over, righted the filter, and filled the coffee maker while I joined Hunt at the table.

"Yes. I could tell from her reaction that you haven't told her about B-MOSZ."

"I haven't," I said.

"Please keep it that way. I don't want Stella to be alarmed by our reasons for keeping her at SFU."

"Stella isn't easily alarmed anyway. I'm the one who's worried," I said. "Is she in danger?"

"Probably not," said Hunt. "This is all precautionary. But I decided to talk with you about it, because we'll be keeping her under light surveillance, and you'll probably recognize some of the agents. I don't want you to mention them to Stella or point them out."

"What if Stella recognizes them?"

"Stella has only met a handful of my employees. I'll be careful to use ones she hasn't met. Has she met Leanne Wilson, for example?"

"Yes. But not in the context of The Service. Stella is friends with her daughter, who doesn't know, of course. Stella would be unhappy keeping yet another secret from her friend. Don't tell her, please."

She tilted her head at me and studied me with her dark eyes. "You keep the secret so Stella won't have to."

"Yes," I said miserably.

"Can I also assume that Stella doesn't know about the MIT experiment?"

"Of course she doesn't," I said. I felt as if there were a heavy weight on my chest.

"Good. I don't want to have to arrest you again. She seemed concerned about Seattle."

"She's smart, Agent Hunt. Of course she was concerned. But I wasn't until you offered her thousands of dollars in tuition fees to keep her on Burnaby Mountain."

She tapped her fingernails on the table and looked at me thoughtfully.

"Michaella?" Dad prompted from behind her, and she reached automatically to accept the coffee mug.

"Thank you," she said reflexively to him, but she kept her eyes on me. I held her gaze. My mind was swimming. Stella was in danger, but I didn't understand why or how. But it all had to do with the virus. It all had to do with me. None of this would have happened if it weren't for me.

I put her in danger.

"Spain recently lost contact with their ZCP," Hunt announced abruptly.

The room went very silent, and it took me a minute to realize that my whole family, including me, was holding our breaths.

"That's what Stella is, right?" Hazel asked. "A Zombie… Zombie controlling person."

"Z0381E Controlling Personality," Hunt corrected. "Yes. They're concerned about kidnapping and are looking at other countries with suspicion. They shared the truth with Canada because we already have our own ZCP, so we're low on their list of suspects." Her eyes crinkled in something that was almost a smile. "And, of course, George Baum would say that as Canadians, the world considers us inherently trustworthy."

Ray snorted.

"Seattle isn't the only city to find bodies with opened skulls, either," continued Hunt. "It's just the only one that allowed the story to get into the hands of the media. I'm not thrilled about their information controls down there."

"This is bad," I said. "Right? This is really bad."

"It could be. More likely it's nothing. But it certainly made us think — we had a mild outbreak and the bodies immediately gravitated to Stella. If she were taken unawares, she might not defend herself in time. George, of course, thinks that she's at risk of kidnapping, even though we've been careful not to release any identifying details about her. For all the rest of the world knows, she could be a fifty-year-old man in Saskatoon."

She looked at me again. "We're taking precautions. But we would rather Stella not know about them."

"Why, though?" I said. "Stella hates lies. She hates deceit. Why are you putting me in this situation? I don't want more secrets. I don't need more secrets."

"Because I want you to know what not to tell her. I don't entirely trust Stella with our secrets, and if she knew she had surveillance, she might give them the slip. She's a teenage girl, after all," said Hunt.

"And I dunno if you noticed, Howie, but she's a tad willful," said Ray from the doorway.

"And obviously you can't tell her why a sentient person might collect brains from dead bodies," said Hunt. I opened my mouth to argue but she held up a finger. "No, don't even try. That's beyond top-level secrecy. I completely and utterly agree with George Baum on this, and to be honest, I wish I had him back on the team. I don't think he started that outbreak or took those missing vials of virus, and I want to know who did. But I can't prove that he's innocent and the evidence Stella found certainly looks damning, so he may have to stand trial. Either way, I want to be careful. Do you understand?"

I sighed and put my head between my arms. "Yes. I understand. Now if you'll excuse me… I think I need to go to bed."

My phone rang as I walked up the stairs. It was Stella, back from working on her project with that boy. I barely paid attention to what she said. All I could think about was how much safer she would be right now if I had stepped aside that morning she walked into our Chemistry class, and she had dated someone like him, instead.

I wished her goodnight and crawled into bed. Hunt's story about the missing person in Spain filled me with terrible mental images of Stella going missing. I imagined searching for her desperately, trying to feel her mind among the crowds, and the panic of realizing that it was gone. Gone.

But I was exhausted, and quickly dropped off into a restless sleep.

I woke at midnight from a dream where I was hunting Stella's mind through the city, and when I finally found her, instead of taking her into my arms, I slung her down and smashed open her skull. I jerked awake and turned on the light. After two pages of poetry, I forced myself back to bed. I got myself out of bed on time in the morning and finished my math homework over breakfast while Army, tail waving, drooled hopefully into my lap. I was definitely feeling better after getting a decent sleep. Hazel had been right. I needed to focus on graduating and getting tuition. If I didn't manage those things, I wouldn't be able to attend SFU at all.

When I arrived at Stella's house, I was busy making a mental list of ways to raise tuition money. The ring wasn't the only collateral I had. Some of my vinyl records were probably worth a bit of money. I knocked absentmindedly on the door, and Stella's father answered.

"A year, Howie," he said. "It has been nearly a year. We know it's you. You come over every morning. We keep telling you. You can just come in. Stop making me come to the door."

"Sorry, Mr…, uh, I mean, Tim."

"A YEAR," he reminded me. "Get with the program."

I stepped inside and took off my shoes. I could feel Stella's mind just waking upstairs.

"The Seattle Zombie struck again!" Tim said. "Look, are you sure Hunt's telling the truth?"

"Why would she lie about it?" I asked, avoiding eye contact. But Tim Blunt was an intelligent man.

"They have their reasons for keeping secrets. You know, like they didn't tell you that there were people out there who could basically freeze you in your tracks."

I shrugged. "Considering that only a few people like that were known to exist, and all of them lived on other continents, I can't really blame them."

"My point is, they keep secrets from you, and I think anything involving brains sounds pretty suspicious to me."

"Can you give me a copy of the article?" I said to Tim as Stella walked into the kitchen. "I mean, uh, send me a link or… something." Things were so much easier when people could just pass over newspaper pages.

"Just open Google and type 'Seattle news' and you'll find tons of articles, Howie," said Stella, handing me her phone. "And maybe consider getting a smartphone one of these days? Also, good morning."

"Morning, Beautiful," I said, taking her phone carefully. Technology these days was wild, but not at all what I thought it would be. I mean, we still didn't have colonies on Mars or vacations in space, and from what I could gather, NASA was still using 1960s Russian rockets to launch shuttles, but we could access the entirety of man's written body of knowledge from nifty doo-dads that fit in our pockets. I never would have predicted that, but it was pretty nifty.

Stella was right, of course. Article upon article, from lists like "The 5 Creepiest Things About the Seattle Zombie" to a New York Times article about "The Lost Minds of America's Homeless." I read obsessively while Stella ate her breakfast, and kept reading while she drove us to school.

"Howie? Howie?" Stella waved a hand in front of my eyes.

I jerked myself to attention. "Sorry. Yes."

"I can't help but notice that you have suddenly discovered the giant headline news that I've been trying to make you notice for days."

"I'm just curious."

"Why weren't you curious *before*?"

"I've been on another planet. Forgive me."

"Are you going to tell me why?"

Tell her that I had been trying, and failing, to acquire new knowledge? Tell her that this would be the Howie that she would see at university, or worse? It wasn't high on my list. "Lack of sleep. Bad dreams. I'm sorry."

"Okay, well, are you going to come over after school today? Because I feel like I haven't seen you in approximately forever, and pretty soon I'm going to have to start spending afternoons rehearsing with Dean the Dick."

My stomach twisted. "Can we come up with a nickname that… uh… doesn't reference genitalia?"

Stella pointed at me triumphantly. "You *are* jealous! I don't know whether to be pissed at you for lying or relieved that you're actually human."

I thought carefully about how to phrase what I said next. "Stella, a popular young man is attracted to the love of my life. Naturally, I don't want to think about him having sex with you, or anything remotely close to it, including thinking about his... parts. But I'm not jealous in the sense that I am not worried that you're going to be unfaithful. Like I said before, you can't help how he feels about you and it shouldn't stop you from getting the grade you want in class."

"Okay, okay. So I call him something else. Dean the Dildo. No, that's worse, isn't it?"

"What's a dildo?" I asked.

"Oh, Howie... never mind. Dean the... Donkey. Dean the..."

"Normal human boy who is your Drama partner," I said, wearying of the game.

"So, what should we do for our anniversary on Sunday?" Stella asked.

I thought. "If the weather's nice, we could go for a walk in the park," I suggested.

"Sure. I think the thing I want most is just you, uninterrupted, for the whole day," said Stella. "I don't really care where we go or what we do. Just hours and hours of time to talk about things that aren't schoolwork."

"That sounds like heaven," I said. It did sound like heaven. But as soon as I imagined it, the black thoughts came swarming in. Walking with her in the park turned into me feasting on her in the grass. Kissing her turned into peeling off her skin. God, why had the thoughts become so terrible? Was the virus gaining control? What was the point in The Service posting guards on her when she was alone and vulnerable with me on a daily basis?

I had to keep myself under control. I couldn't take any risks. Not when things were this bad. Eventually, Stella was going to notice that I wasn't getting intimate with her anymore. She hadn't yet, but she would. And then I would either have to tell her why... or lie. And I wasn't sure which option I hated more.

"We could go to the used bookstore," I said. "Walk around town. Talk. Read."

"Excellent plan," Stella agreed.

Surely she couldn't blame me for refusing to get heavy with her in a used bookstore.

Public places. That was the key.

I was so busy thinking about how to avoid necking with Stella that I was taken by surprise when we pulled up at the school and, as soon as she had shifted my car into park, she leaned over and kissed me. The taste of her mouth made my heart bounce against my ribs. When she began to press her body into mine, I almost lost my resolve, almost sat back and let it happen. But I felt the evil thoughts gathering at the back of my mind and I was too frightened to continue. With a great effort of will, I broke off as casually as I could.

"We don't want to miss the bell," I said.

She sighed and I sensed a wave of frustration pass through her. It was brief but intense. Then she sat back. "I guess so," she said.

And that's when I knew that I was wrong — she had already noticed.

14

Stella

Something was wrong with Howie lately, and it was beginning to piss me off.

At first, I thought he was just upset about that Physics quiz incident. It clearly embarrassed him. So I tried to make it clear that I understood that this was a side effect of the virus and that I wasn't too worried about it. But he still pulled away when I tried to get him alone. He still broke off our kisses after a few short seconds. We hadn't made out in days and days.

In a way, the whole thing was a little ironic. It was Howie, after all, who had wheedled and coaxed and convinced me to give him our first kiss. Now here I was, no longer afraid to kiss him but afraid to find out why he wouldn't kiss me.

I even wondered briefly if he was falling out of love with me, but I couldn't quite take that thought seriously. Howie had had to work hard to convince me that he was genuinely interested in me, but now my faith in his love felt so unshakable that I couldn't imagine a world in which I was not the centre of Howie's universe.

Besides, there was the proof of my own eyes. Howie's gaze was as adoring as ever, and when he broke off our kiss in the car, his body announced very clearly that it wanted to continue. So, what the hell was going on?

My normal tactic would be to simply pull him aside and demand to know what this was all about. But I held back. I didn't want to start another fight. I was ashamed of the fight we had on my birthday. I couldn't forget that I had — accidentally — dislocated his elbow. I mean, okay, it didn't hurt him, and in fact, if I had been doing that hold on a normal human being, they would have been contorting themselves to keep that from happening, whereas Howie just, like, forgot about it and straightened up. So really he dislocated his own elbow. But it was my fault — I was holding him, and I shouldn't have been.

I'd learned a lot about control in the time that I'd known Howie. Howie never lost his temper. He was so calm all the time and that helped keep me calm, too. Howie was better than any anger management class. I wanted to be like him.

So if something was bothering him, I owed him a calm, considerate, non-violent conversation. I kept practising the topic in my head. I wasn't going to ask him about it until I thought I could be accepting and non-accusatory. So far I hadn't achieved that, even in imagination.

My imaginary conversations went something like this:

"Howie, why don't you want to kiss me anymore?"

"What do you mean?"

"We don't make out any more. What's that about?"

"It's your breath. It smells bad."

"Fuck you, Howard, not all of us use lab chemicals as mouthwash."

Nope. Not good enough, Stella. You lose. Please play again.

"Howie, why don't you want to kiss me anymore?"

"What do you mean?"

"We don't make out any more. What's that about?"

"You've put on some weight, and you don't enthrall me like you used to."

"Who the fuck is the one feeding me cheesecake? You can take your fattism and stuff it up your anus."

No. That was just ridiculous. Howie loved my bubble butt. It had to be something else.

"Howie, why don't you want to kiss me anymore?"

"What do you mean?"

"We don't make out any more. What's that about?"

"I've become a born-again Christian. What we were doing was a sin."

"What the fuck? Fuck you and Baby Jesus too."

Maybe I needed anger management classes after all. So I didn't say anything. I just watched Howie and worried like hell.

He seemed so withdrawn. At lunch on Tuesday, he corrected Amy's math homework, but slowly, and he seemed to be struggling with it.

"So I told The Skeez that I'm going on the trip this weekend and he is *not* happy," said Kate. But I wasn't listening. I was watching Howie, who lifted his head and smiled his usual gentle, shy smile at me. I reached out and tried to feel him up under the table but he just shifted away.

"I've got to get something done," I said, standing abruptly.

My friends looked surprised. Howie looked more than surprised. He looked stunned.

"Everything okay?" Amy asked.

"Fine," I said shortly, hefting my bag onto my shoulder. "I just have some stuff I need to do."

And I stormed off. I needed to go do some yelling on the bleachers or something, or I was going to end up shaking my boyfriend and yelling "WHY WON'T YOU TOUCH ME?"

Coming down the hall, I spotted Carter Davidson and Ravi Sandhu picking on Danny Wilder, who had Down Syndrome. They had him up against the wall and they were pointing and laughing at his My Little Pony shirt.

Excellent!

I charged toward the boys and "accidentally" crashed into Ravi, knocking him aside. I grabbed Carter's backpack and hauled him away so hard that he bumped into the opposite wall.

"Oops, sorry," I said aggressively. "Bumped into you."

"Fat whore," spat Carter. "What's your problem?"

"My problem is you. Why don't you pick on someone with the same IQ as you, like a rock, or some kind of flatworm?"

"This school's got a zero-tolerance policy on assault," said Ravi. "And you just grabbed Carter and threw him into the wall, and you nearly knocked me down, and there are tons of witnesses around."

"Sure. Go tell the vice principal that a girl pushed you around. Then I can tell him why I did it."

Mr. Nguyen, the Chemistry teacher, came walking down the hall from the staff room and I waved cheerily at him. Ravi and Carter swore at me again and disappeared into the boy's bathroom. Danny was still standing there with a worried look on his face.

"Everything okay here?" Mr. Nguyen asked.

"It is now," I said. "Those guys were just being jerks to Danny, here. By the way," I said to Danny, "your shirt is great. Rainbow Dash is totally the best one."

"Thanks," Danny said, giving me a little smile.

"No problem," I said, smiling back.

You know what else is good for anger management? Getting angry.

Dean was chatting up Desiree Poirier when I walked in and didn't pay any attention to me. I was both relieved and annoyed because I'm an irrational beyotch. Then Carter walked in glowering at me and plunked himself down next to Dean, so I sat down and tried to make myself invisible. It never worked so I don't know why I kept trying. Hope springs eternal, I guess.

Ms. Lawless announced that she was going to leave us to continue our projects on our own time. After the bell rang and we had walked out of the classroom, Dean grabbed my arm and pulled me aside.

"Watch it!" I snapped.

He held up his hands in surrender. "Sorry, I was just trying to get your attention. We should get together to rehearse. How about after school today?"

I shook my head no. "Maybe tomorrow." That would give me time to arrange for my parents to pick me up after school or something so I wouldn't have another awkward drive with Sir Speedsalot when he inevitably insisted on driving me home.

"I'm busy the rest of the week, and I'm hanging with the guys on Saturday, but Sunday I'm free. You could come over to my house and we could do it in the living room." I didn't know if he was *trying* to make that sound like innuendo, or if it was all in my head. Either way, there was no way in hell I was going to go to his house, and besides, Sunday was my anniversary date with Howie.

"I think it would be better to rehearse here. More space, fewer parents wanting to watch."

He shrugged. "Okay. I guess I'll focus on doing the essay and memorizing my lines. Monday for sure, yeah?"

"Yes," I said reluctantly.

"Hey Dean, what are you guys doing a scene from? Moby Dick?" called Carter on his way out of class. There was a round of laughter. I gave everyone a flash of my very decorative middle finger.

"Sorry about him," said Dean. "He's just joking around."

"Oh really? Here I thought it was a serious question, but if it was just a… OH, I get it," I said, feigning sudden surprise, "He was calling me a WHALE! How hilarious. What a funny guy. Your friends are so funny." I turned and stormed off.

Dean chased after me. "I just mean that they aren't, like, trying to hurt your feelings or anything when they say stuff like that. They just have a bad sense of humour."

I whirled. "I really don't give a tiny rat's ass what their sense of humour is like, or whether or not they are trying to hurt me. I really don't give a *fraction* of a fuck. So you can stop trying to make me think it's okay. Save your breath."

"Is everything okay?" Howie came down the hall from History class. He must have sensed how pissed off I was.

"It's fine, Dean was just leaving," I told him. I glared at Dean and he glared at Howie, who completely ignored him.

"It's almost time for the next class to start," said Howie. "Are you going to be okay?" What he meant was, "Do you need to go outside and cool off?"

"I'm fine," I said firmly. Dean hefted his backpack higher on his shoulders and walked off. Howie continued to ignore him and kept watching me with a worried expression.

"Do you want to talk about it?" he asked quietly.

No, I thought. *I want to talk about why my boyfriend stopped kissing me.*

"There's not much to tell," I said. "Carter made a fat joke at me. Dean tried to excuse it. He's a shit stick, they're both shit sticks, and I already knew all that anyway."

Howie nodded.

"Thanks for coming to my rescue," I said. "We should get to class."

Howie's face flickered with amusement. "I think Dean was the one who needed rescuing," he said. "See you later, Beautiful."

"Later." As an experiment, I kissed him on the cheek. He froze, and then smiled and squeezed my hand before moving off with his awkward, lurching stride.

"Come over today," I told Howie on our way home from school. I *had* to bring it up. I couldn't let it go anymore. But I wanted to do it in private, and not just in the car. I also wanted to introduce it really carefully. I mustn't blow my fuse at him again. I had to keep control of myself. Even if my breath smelled or he had turned religious or some shit.

"I'd like to, but there's so much work to do," said Howie.

"We'll do Physics together," I said. "That would be one thing out of the way, and it's nicer with two. I like doing school work with you."

"Just let me run home for a snack first," said Howie, which meant, 'let me eat some brains.'

He came in the door half an hour later, and now I felt like there wasn't time for an argument because my father was due home any minute. So I swallowed my anxiety and we actually did do Physics. When Dad walked in the door we were sitting at the kitchen table, bent over our homework.

"So, you know that for a process to be adiabatic, the value of q has got to be zero or really, really close to it," said Howie, straightening his glasses. At least he remembered his Physics today.

"Yeah, I get that, *obviously*, but I don't get how they can tell us that it's irreversible, and then ask us to talk about how to make it reversible!"

"Did your mother come home early again or something?" Dad asked.

"Hello to you too, Father," I said. "Not that I know of, why?"

"I just wasn't expecting to find you two sitting in the kitchen," he said, pouring himself a glass of juice from the fridge. "You do realize that you were ALONE in the house? Like, ALONE? Like, teenagers with no parents around? Shouldn't you be struggling to get your pants back on or something?"

"Maybe we're done already."

"Faster than a speeding bullet," said Howie in his wonderful deadpan. Dad nearly choked on his orange juice. He couldn't talk for five minutes. He just stood there, hacking and coughing and laughing, and holding up one hand for Howie to high-five.

"Are you okay, sir?" Howie asked, standing up and ignoring the hand. Dad nodded, still coughing. When he finally was able to straighten up, he swept an imaginary hat off of his head.

"That was worth the aspiration pneumonia, thank you, Howie," he said. "Now, I'm going to change clothes, so you have another two minutes if you'd like to try again."

I listened to Dad's footsteps going up the stairs and took a deep breath.

"Even my parents are starting to notice that we don't make out anymore, Howie," I said quietly. "Can we talk about that?"

Howie didn't move his eyes from my paper for a full twenty seconds. Yes, I counted. Every tick of our kitchen clock felt like an eternity.

"Let's go for a little walk," he finally said in a very soft voice.

"Dad! We're going to go have sex in the woods!" I shouted up the stairs as we shoved on our shoes.

"Don't get a tick bite! Lyme disease!" he shouted back.

"Kay, bye!"

"Don't you ever worry that your parents will take you literally when you say things like that?" Howie asked as the screen door banged closed behind us.

"No. What kind of a teenager would be honest about something like that?" I said. "Besides, in my house pretty much everything everyone says is assumed to be pure crap unless clearly stated otherwise, you know that."

We walked in silence for a while. There was an abandoned elementary school near my place and we headed toward it. The baseball field was deserted in the drizzly spring weather.

"So. Are you going to tell me why you don't kiss me anymore?"

"I kiss you."

"Goddammit, Howie…"

"No, no, I know what you're saying," he amended quickly.

"You damn well better."

Howie was silent for a while longer. I tried hard to smother a wave of fury. I had a right to know about this. I had a right to be *spoken to* about this.

"I'm sorry I've been pulling away." His voice was barely above a whisper.

"Thank you for admitting that you've been pulling away. If you'd denied it I would've put you through one of those broken windows. Now, are you going to tell me why?"

He was silent again. I folded my arms and *looked* at him.

"I'm thinking of how to phrase it best," he said.

"Okay."

We walked part way around the field before he spoke again. "You know I… well… you know how your brain waves make me feel. How the virus affects… what I'm attracted to."

"You said you'd have thought I was beautiful even without the virus."

"I would. Because you are. I don't mean that. I mean that you know that sometimes I have… thoughts that come more from the virus than from me."

"Such as?"

"Like... you know... "

"Wanting to eat people?"

"Essentially."

"Is there someone else you want to eat?" Maybe he still loved me, but his brains were attracted to someone else. Oh, my God. I'd never even thought of that.

He laughed. "Of course not. Stella, your brain waves blot out everyone else's. I'm barely aware of other people."

"Then what the hell, Howie?"

"I'm just... I'm scared, Stella. What if I... lost control and bit you or something?"

"Well... considering that you haven't in nearly a year of dating, and considering that even if you did, your bite wouldn't be infectious... why the hell are you suddenly scared of that happening?"

"I just... I'm worried I might not be able to control it."

He could be so fucking frustrating. "*Why* Howie? You told me once that thoughts are just thoughts, and that there's no excuse for giving in to them. We've *talked* about this exact thing."

"Yes, yes. I know. And I would never ever voluntarily hurt you."

"Then what the fuck, Howie?" the anger was rising. I couldn't help it.

"I'm just beginning to wonder if the virus really needs my permission."

Howie

Stella was mad. I could feel her rage thrumming around me. It felt so good. But my mind filled with thoughts that weren't mine; they weren't from me. How could I explain it without getting so graphic that she would run in horror?

"I had a dream," I said, "and in my dream, my hands just reached out and… and killed you. I didn't want it. I didn't intend it. I wasn't even thinking it, in the dream. I was thinking of how much I loved you, of how good it felt to be close to you. And then you were dead, and it was my fault."

"That… that was a dream, Howie," she said, but I could tell it had shaken her.

"It was a terrible dream," I said. "And I keep having dreams like that… And they scare me. I know that I would never deliberately hurt you. I know that I would make every effort to stop myself from giving into any terrible virus-driven thought. But what if something happened so quickly and involuntarily that…" my voice faltered.

"Has that ever happened in real life? To you or your siblings or your Dad or anybody?"

"No," I said. "Not that I know of." Unless the Seattle Zombie was like us… someone like us who had given in… "But they aren't in relationships, Stella. They aren't… they aren't that close to someone. Physically."

"Nothing went wrong on the night of my birthday. You do remember that?"

"Of course I do," I said, feeling breathless just thinking about it.

"My skin was bare against yours. We were about as intimate as two people can get. And you didn't do a single thing that made me feel unsafe."

God, I wanted her. I wanted to feel her heat, to feel her tremble under my touch, to make her scream while I dug my fingers into… no. NO.

"Besides," she said, encircling my wrists with her fingers. "I'm pretty strong, you know. I have a brown belt in kung fu. I was almost ready for my black belt test when we moved. Doesn't my dream self ever fight back?"

I shook my head no. "It happens too fast."

"How fast? Try it. Try me. Come on. Tap my shoulder," she said, squaring her stance.

This was a pointless exercise. If I lost control, neither of us would see it coming. If I ever hurt her it would be during the most intimate, vulnerable, and trusting of moments. It wouldn't be while she was standing battle-ready in an open field.

But I reached out for her shoulder anyway.

"Not even close to fast enough," she said, stepping aside. "Come on, Howie. Try. Really try."

So I went to tap her quickly, and she dodged again. I tried again. She dodged. I was really trying as hard as I could now but she was always faster. Once I almost got her but she caught my hand in hers and then flipped me over her shoulder and I landed on my back.

"You okay?" she said, as I stared up at the sky in temporary confusion.

"How would I know?" I asked with a grin, sitting up. "Does anything look broken to you?"

"Nope. Come on. Try again."

I tried again, and again. She began to tap me on my shoulder, and I couldn't block her.

"You really have no instincts for self-defence," she said.

"I told you that a long time ago."

Again, and again. Missed and missed and missed again. We were both laughing now, as I tried to chase and catch her. She tripped me up and I fell again. She helped me to my feet, and while pretending to be regaining my balance I darted in with a hand but she dodged it easily, grabbing it and pinning it behind me. Then she grabbed my other hand and pinned it behind me too.

"Gotcha," she said. "Try and hurt me now."

"I can still bite you," I said, still laughing.

"I'd like to see you try."

Then her lips were on mine and we kissed as she held my arms pinned behind my back. We kissed and kissed and kissed until I was breathless. Not that I needed air anyway. The only thing I needed was Stella. It had been so long since we had kissed like this and I felt starved for her, desperate for her. I fought to get my arms free to put around her but she held them all the more tightly.

"What, are you sure you won't hurt me now?" she teased.

It felt good to be pinned by her. It felt good to know that my hands wouldn't do anything I didn't want them to do. How could she not believe in a God? This was my shrine, my place of worship. Let me be here all the rest of my days.

Stella

We burst inside soaking wet from the rain and still laughing, arms around each other. I was trying not to process what he had told me. I mean, I knew that the virus made him feel my brain and stuff, but dreams about killing me? Jesus. Why couldn't I have a normal boyfriend who just wanted sex?

"Did your rendezvous get cut short by the downpour?" my father asked us. He was stir-frying some ground beef in the kitchen.

"Do you need help, Mr. Blunt?" Howie asked him.

"How many times have I asked you to call me Tim?" said Dad.

"Are we just not answering each other's questions?" I asked.

"Are you staying for dinner, Howie? I'm going to make a sort of fusion dish. Italian tacos. Or maybe Mexican pasta. I haven't decided yet. It'll probably be terrible. You definitely want to watch this go down."

I mimed a gag.

"No, thank you," Howie said with a smile. "I need to get home and get back to work."

I wished that I could talk more with Howie, but he was right about the workload — I had a skit to memorize, plus multiple essays to work on, not to mention stupid busy-work assignments, and I had no idea how I was supposed to get it all done. So I walked him to his car, but we dawdled as we walked. The rain was dying down again. I must be a true Vancouverite now because I barely noticed the light drizzle.

"Howie?" I asked.

"Yeah?"

I was going to ask him more about the killing me stuff, but I decided against it. I needed to think about that some more first. I switched to a happier topic — the future.

"I know you don't think you can do it, but say for a minute that you were able to graduate university. What job would you do?"

He looked surprised, and he stopped walking. "Well," he said, leaning his body on a tree and folding his arms in thought. "I mean, my dream job has always been a chemist or something. Make medicines. But realistically, there is no way I could get even a Bachelor's, let alone a Master's or Doctorate." He held his hand up when I opened my mouth to protest. "I'm sorry, Stella, but you need to accept my limitations. I promised to do my best and I will, but I have limits."

Why did he always have to get negative? He wouldn't even think hypothetically. It kept coming back to 'I can't'.

Howie could tell that I was annoyed and he continued hastily. "But maybe I could work in a pharmacy as an assistant. Or, if that's beyond me academically, I could always just get my usual job as a fry cook in a diner and slowly work my way up as a chef. After all, it's just a matter of reading recipes and remembering not to overcook the steaks."

"I don't accept your limitations," I said. "I think it'll be harder for you than for a normal person but I think that with my help you really can do it. But you're right; even if you have trouble with academics, you are a great cook. You would make a fantastic chef. Why haven't you done that before?"

Howie shrugged. "Mostly because it has taken me about thirty years to develop what cooking skills I have now, and because this is the oldest I have ever looked. Remember that while I look seventeen or eighteen now, I used to look fifteen. You can't exactly rise to level of head chef when customers keep saying, 'shouldn't you be in school today?'" He paused for a minute, staring off into space. "One thing I know — I won't be going through high school again."

"Never again?"

"Never," he said firmly.

"Why not?" I was relieved, but curious.

"Because of you," he answered.

"Because of me?"

"Yes. Stella, no matter what happens between us, I can't see myself ever going back to school. If we were still together, then obviously I couldn't go back to high school, because people would want to know why your husband of ten years was a high school student."

I laughed. "Yeah, that could get me arrested."

"And if or when you move on, I can't imagine going through school without you. All I would be able to think about, all the time, would be how it felt to have you in the school, how empty it was without you, and how old you might be now, and what you might be doing while I was... while I was still stuck doing the same classes..." his voice trailed off and he rubbed his eyes with the back of his hand for a moment.

"Oh, Howie..."

"I love you," he sobbed. "I love you so much..."

"I love you too, Howie, you know I do. We'll figure things out. We'll make it work..." and we were holding each other and kissing each other. It was hungry, and urgent, and passionate. His fingers twined themselves into my hair and pulled my face close. I think we were trying to hold on to the moment as much as each other because I think we both knew that we were trying to swim against a current that was sweeping our relationship out to sea. The current of time, maybe? I don't know. I'm not great at metaphors; I'm better at creative swearing.

Then Howie took me by surprise — he spun me around and pinned me up against the tree. He even managed to lift me up a little as he did it. He was a lot stronger than I gave him credit for.

"Wow," I started to say but he covered my mouth with his again. I'd never known him to be this... aggressive. He normally let me take the lead, but this time he was turning me into the passive one as he pressed up against me and kissed me so hard that I felt breathless. I could feel how hard he was for me and I wanted him so badly that I caught myself moaning — again, usually his job.

"Oh, Stella," he whispered. He moved his cool lips down to my neck where he began to kiss and suck and I felt like his touch was reaching deep down inside me. He even nibbled gently with his teeth and it was so. Freaking. Hot. I seriously think that if he had wanted to have sex right then, right there, in the dark and the drizzle, against the rough bark of that tree, I would have gone for it.

And then suddenly it was over. He let go, backed away and then hunched over.

"I'm sorry, I'm so sorry," he said, and he started to rush to his car.

"Howie!" I said, following him. I actually felt dizzy as I stumbled after him. "What's wrong?"

"I just don't trust myself anymore," he said. "I'm sorry, I love you, I'm sorry."

15

Stella

I gave Howie five minutes to get safely home and then I called him.

"What the fuck was that?"

"I know you're mad," said his bland voice. It's so hard to argue with someone who sounds like he's reading his sentences off of a sheet in his hand.

"Of course I'm fucking mad! What in the name of baby Jesus's mohel was that about?"

"I told you… I'm afraid I'll lose control and hurt you in real life."

"And I told YOU to let ME worry about that. We've been together for a year and you have never even come close to hurting me."

"No?" he asked. "Not even just now, when I sucked on your neck and used my teeth on your skin?"

"But I'm not hurt, Howie; that's NORMAL. Hickies weren't invented by zombies. If anything, there's a whole body of literature written for women who think that having blood sucked from their neck is hot."

"Stella. What do you think was going through my mind at that moment?"

I shrugged. "Sex? Brains? What am I, a teenage zombie?"

"Do you realize that I was picturing ripping out your jugular?"

Okay, my lady boner was definitely gone now.

"Seriously?"

"Please understand that isn't me, that that isn't what I want, but the disease… the virus… it puts thoughts like that in my mind all the time and I always just pushed it to the back of my mind; I've never actually thought I was in any danger of acting on any of that, but the dreams have gotten worse and I'm really really afraid that maybe I won't be able to stop myself."

I knew that he was really upset because his words all ran together in a way that was almost emotional.

"Okay, Howie, but that is something you *really* need to work out, because otherwise, what? I mean, right now I feel like you're offering me a choice between a relationship with no physical intimacy, or getting cannibalized by my boyfriend. I don't like either of those choices."

"Stella, if I knew the way around all the stumbling blocks to a long-term relationship with you I would be an incredibly happy boy. Man. Whatever I am."

We were silent for a while, just listening to each other breathe.

"Okay, Howie," I said dully. "We both know this isn't going to get solved tonight. I'm sorry I overreacted. But from now on, don't rush away. Tell me when you need a minute, break it off, and we'll pause. Don't just take off. It freaks me out."

"I'm sorry too. I shouldn't have rushed away like that. I just got scared and wanted to get you away from the zombie — me — as fast as I could."

"I get it," I said. "But I wish I knew why you are so freaked out by this all of a sudden."

Howie was quiet for a moment. "Maybe it's the stress from school," he said. "Dad says stress can worsen the symptoms and we have a big workload right now."

"Yeah, that's true," I admitted. "Look. Let's work really hard on getting through as much work as we can over the next few days, okay? Those essays that are due in three weeks, those projects that are coming up. Try to get *everything* finished by Saturday. That way we can buy ourselves some breathing room and take a real break on Sunday. We'll have the whole day together on Sunday. I'll plan the outing. I'll pick *you* up. You don't have to think about it or worry about it. Just do your work, get some sleep, and let me do the rest, okay? We can de-stress and work through this. We'll go slow and if you start to freak out we'll pause, okay? But maybe it'll be better if you've gotten most of your work done."

Howie took a deep breath and let it out. "That sounds like a great plan."

"Okay," I said, feeling proud of myself for talking through things like an adult. "And for the next few days, we'll just take it easy. No pressure. No making out."

"Thank you. I just want you to be safe. That's the most important thing."

"Yeah, I'm on board with that. I don't want to end up as someone's lunch. So let's de-stress you and see if this is still a problem."

We said goodnight and I took a deep breath as I ended the call. I was proud of myself for working through relationship stuff a bit without totally exploding. But I was also really shaken by what he had told me. Howie would never hurt me really. Would he?

I sat down at my laptop and banged out a rough draft of my Drama essay, explaining why we had chosen this particular play, what we hoped to convey with it, and so on. But Dean barely entered my mind as I wrote whatever garbage I could think of. My thoughts were still on Howie.

"So, apparently we're giving you the car on Sunday?" Dad said when I told my parents the plan.

"To reward me for being such an excellent student," I reminded him. "I'm a teenager. I could be out… I dunno… raving or something."

"So what are we supposed to do all day on a Sunday with no car?" my mother asked, looking amused.

"I don't know. Play Nintendo like you always do?" I teased. "Seriously though, if you need the car obviously I can ask Howie to pick me up. I just think he seems really stressed lately and you know how much effort he put into my birthday. I don't want him to put more of a burden on himself so I kind of want to make it clear that this date is my responsibility."

"Don't *you* drive when he picks you up?" Dad pointed out.

"Yeah but it's still not my car."

"Well, neither is ours," said Dad.

"We're just giving you a hard time," Mom said, nudging him. "Sunday's supposed to be beautiful, so if we want to get out of the house we can take a long walk."

"We might want a car for our long walk," Dad said. "We should discuss this more."

Mom stuck out her tongue at him.

"I'll consider my request considered and approved then," I said. "Now, I have some serious work to do."

Howie didn't act any different over the next few days. He showed up at my house and washed our dishes in his normal, Howie-like way. We got in the car and drove to school. We didn't kiss or even touch hands. We were both being careful.

It didn't feel right. None of this felt right. And it felt painful to look at the way his long eyelashes brushed his cheek when he looked down, at the way his cheek dimpled when he smiled, at the way his lean body moved, and not be able to touch him.

I clung to the thought of Sunday. I reminded myself again and again that by Sunday we would have a much lighter workload, and Howie would be less stressed.

We could go somewhere private and just start slow. I would give Howie lots of chances to take breaks, so he could see that everything was okay.

Howie was just a worrier. He worried about flunking out of school so he didn't want to try college. He worried about the virus so he wouldn't have sex with me. Now he was worried about even kissing me. I had to help him see that he was just stressing for no reason.

I was here. I could help him.

Howie and I were very quiet on the drive home on Friday. He pulled up at my house and then took my hands in his. It was the first time we had touched that day.

"I'll miss you tomorrow."

"Me too. But we're going to get done ALL of our work." I said firmly. "So you can be totally relaxed on Sunday and we'll spend the whole day together. Except don't you dare wake me up. I'll ask my parents for the car and come to you when I'm good and ready."

"As you wish," he said, squeezing my hands and giving me a chaste kiss on the cheek. "See you then, my love."

I did work really, really hard, although Howie and I texted each other constantly. For the first time in days, Howie seemed like himself.

I just drank a bunch of brains.
I am going to get so much done
that you will be astounded.

Stop talking to your girlfriend
and get to work, slacker.

I've completed a page of math already.

I've already found five reliable
sources for my Biology paper.

Do I need sources for my History essay?
Can't I just write "I was there"?

The teacher MIGHT not believe you
when you say you remember Watergate.

Drat.

I finished my Biology paper on Saturday morning and then moved on to my History essay. I printed them both off and made my parents look them over while I moved on to hammering out a draft of my Drama project's essay. Finally, I spent Saturday night muttering lines to myself, working on memorizing the play.

I felt pent-up. Sunday would be a release. I needed Howie's hands on my body, the feel of him against me. I was starving for him. I couldn't wait.

I woke up stupendously early — for me — on Sunday. By ten, I was already up and dressed. I had a mix CD that I had burned for Howie out of songs he had liked when we listened to the radio. Since his ancient phone didn't have Shazam or Apple Music or anything, poor Howie didn't have an easy way of listening to new songs he liked. I'd been making note of them and downloading them for months and now he'd be able to listen to them on his stereo. I wished I had enough money to buy him an iPod. He'd love that — He'd lose his shit. Maybe I'd save up for next Christmas.

Dad had packed me a picnic basket — except it was really a picnic reusable shopping bag — with sandwiches and pop. I also grabbed the lined blanket that we used for going to the beach and such. We could lie on the grass in the park and look at cherry blossoms and talk. Early March in Vancouver is awesome.

When I rolled into his driveway, Hazel and Ray were waiting outside. Ray walked up to the car door and tapped on the glass. I rolled down the window. "What's up?" I said, puzzled.

Hazel answered in her bland little voice. "We need to talk for a minute. Can we come in? Howie's taking a nap upstairs. We'll wake him when we're done."

I shrugged. "Sure. Why?"

Ray got into the passenger seat and Hazel got into the back seat and they closed the doors.

"We need to talk about what you're doing to Howie," said Ray.

"What I'm..."

"He means what Howie is doing to himself, because of you," Hazel said.

"Howie's cracking up," said Ray frankly. "He's been trying to prepare for university with some online classes or something, and he's not sleeping properly. He gets these crazy nightmares about you and he wakes up crying and trying to rip his own skin off. He guzzles Army's food in the mornings to make himself look smarter for you. Now he's going to waste a bunch of money trying to get through university again, even though he tried and failed a bunch of times and burned most of Dad's savings for it in the process."

"And now he's going to sell my mother's ring," said Hazel. I turned and stared at her. She pointed to my hand. "That ring. He got it from me. It was our mother's. He didn't tell you because he knew you wouldn't let him sell it if you knew, and he was so determined to go to school with you."

I didn't know what to say. There was a rushing noise in my ears. He was losing sleep trying to do courses online? Scratching his *own skin off?* The ring was his mother's and he *didn't tell me?*

Suddenly I felt like I had been kicked in the chest. It was my fault. I blew up at him over that ring. I assumed he had spent money on it and just lost it on him. Why hadn't I asked him where he got it? Why did I assume the worst? I hated myself. But wait. Why didn't he just tell me that he hadn't spent money on it? That whole fight could have been avoided...

"I didn't know," I gasped. "I didn't know. Online courses...?"

"Yeah. Of course, he can't retain any of it, and then he beats his head against a wall... literally... and tries and tries again," said Ray with a sour expression. "But it doesn't work because we can't learn stuff overnight. We grow slow and we learn slow. He would need to reread it for years."

"That's why... he said he didn't sleep well... he failed a physics quiz..."

"We can't focus when we're tired or we haven't eaten enough," Hazel said. "Especially when we try to learn new things. Our brain energy goes to that, and the old stuff sort of…"

"Gets loose," said Ray. Hazel nodded. They looked at me accusingly.

"I didn't tell him to do that! I didn't even know," I said, feeling a defensive rage kindle inside me. "How dare you come at me and blame me for shit I didn't even know was happening? This isn't my fucking fault."

"Oh, you didn't tell him to apply for college then," said Ray, with a sneer on his face. "You didn't tell him that you wouldn't want to be with him if he was nothing but a fry cook for the rest of his life. You didn't tell him that it mattered more to you than anything that he try to get a degree. None of that was you."

I was silent.

"And now he's going to sell our mother's jewelry and his music collection just so that he can pretend to be normal," Hazel added, tears in her eyes. "All so he can get a few more months from you before you realize that he isn't normal, he'll never be normal, and you cast him aside like a… like a dusty shoe."

"I know he's not normal! I'm okay with that," I argued, but a voice in my head said, *really? Are you REALLY?*

"You want to pretend that he is. You're making him be someone he can't be. You're making him tear his hair out and wake up screaming in the night," said Ray.

"NO!" I shouted at Ray, who didn't even blink. "This is NOT MY FAULT. I can't help that I am growing older and going to college and moving on. I did not tell Howie to try to learn new stuff before he had even graduated from school. I did not tell Howie to sell his dead mother's ring. And I am DONE talking to you about this. If I am going to talk to anyone about this it will be FUCKING HOWARD."

With that, I jumped out of the car, slammed the door, and stormed into the house.

Howie

It's hard to think when Stella is mad. The buzz of her mind fills my body with exquisite intensity. I was reading my book, waiting for her to text me to say she was outside, when I felt her go off. I just fell back on the bed and revelled in it as the delicious waves passed through me, all the way down to my toes.

Until she kicked my door open.

I looked up, and my heart skipped a beat in shock. She didn't look as if she were angry at Dean, or something she read in the news, or any of the many other things that make her angry. She looked angry at me. Why? I sat up quickly.

"What's wrong?"

"YOUR MOTHER'S RING? IT WAS YOUR MOTHER'S RING?"

Drat! "Who told you?" I asked her quietly, but I realized almost immediately that it was either or both of my siblings.

"NEVER FUCKING MIND THAT." Her mind was so powerful. I struggled to stay rational. I had to get her to calm down a bit so I could think.

"I'm sorry you found out," I said.

"WRONG THING TO BE SORRY ABOUT, HOWARD." She had tears running down her cheek. This couldn't just be about the ring. Stella wasn't stupid. She should have figured out quickly why I had acted the way I had, and she'd know that it was partially her own fault. But if she wanted to hear it spelled out, I would do that, because I was beginning to feel mad too.

"You want me to be sorry that I didn't tell you that it was my mother's ring? You could say sorry for jumping to conclusions. You assumed that I had spent money on it, jumped down my throat and called me a bastard and an asshole."

"That would have been the *perfect* opportunity to tell me that I was wrong and you didn't actually spend money on it!"

I sighed. The brief flare of anger that I had felt was gone. She was right — I had misled her and it was wrong. "I was going to, but then I realized that it wasn't the point. You were mad that I wasn't coming to university, mad that I wouldn't beg my father to throw his money away. You were mad that I was offering you a ring you didn't want instead of the future that you really wanted. I realized that your point was still valid. I had the ring. It was worth money. Therefore, it wasn't true that I did not have the money. So I decided that I would sell it."

"Who gave you that right? Isn't it your sister's ring, too?"

"We have a jewellery box full of my mother's old trinkets, and a pair of cufflinks from my father. I got the cuff links, Hazel got the rest. She agreed that the division was lopsided and said I could give you the ring. So it was mine to do with as I pleased. Giving it to you didn't make you happy — but promising to sell it did."

"Only because I didn't know that it was an heirloom from your DEAD MOTHER."

"If I had told you that it was my mother's, you would've told me not to sell it. Then you would've cried because I still wasn't going to university with you. It was information that you didn't need; that wouldn't make you happy. If I choose to sell it, that is my business, my decision, not yours." I spoke as firmly as I could.

Stella crumpled, and I was stunned. Stella is a fighter. This is part of my holy writ, as sacred and inviolable as any other natural law. Stella would stand alone against the world rather than show weakness or defeat. But now she sank onto my bed and covered her face with her hands. I was released from the aggressive throb of her anger, as her mind turned into a turmoil of other, darker, more complicated emotions.

"I hate this," she whispered. "I hate this."

"What do you hate?" When Stella's worked up, usually the best thing to do is to stay calm and get her to work through her emotions step by step.

"ALL OF THIS, HOWIE," she exploded, and I felt her rage flow out of her again. "I HATE ALL OF THIS. I hate that you have brain damage. I hate that you won't grow older. I hate that we can't have sex. I HATE THAT YOU FANTASIZE ABOUT MURDERING AND CANNIBALIZING ME. But you know what I hate most of all?"

"What?" I spoke quietly.

"I hate that you feel like you have to change all of those things — things that you hate too and have no control over — just to make me happy."

I didn't know what to say to that. "Stella, I…"

"DON'T FUCKING TELL ME THAT YOU LOVE ME."

"But I…"

"NO," she said fiercely. "Don't you see? It doesn't change anything. It doesn't FIX anything. It doesn't matter. We can hate it all as much as we want and you can love me all you want, and it won't change a damn thing."

"No," I agreed softly.

"And all this is doing, all this relationship is doing, it driving you insane from trying to change into something you can't be."

I wanted to argue, but I couldn't think of what to say.

"I'm bad for you," she whispered into her hands. "I'm hurting you."

"Stella…" I reached for her but she pushed me away roughly.

"No. I need to go. I need to go."

She slammed my door behind her as she left, and it made the walls shake. I couldn't help but feel that those were the vibrations of my world as it began to crumble around me.

16

Howie

I tried to go after her, but there's a reason why The Service considers Stella a treasure of national importance. When Stella wants people out of her way, they move. And when Stella focuses her mind just right, she freezes zombies in their tracks, and that includes me and my family. So instead I sat, incapacitated and heartbroken, on the bed as she stormed outside and drove away.

Then I shook myself awake and, fighting the suffocating pain in my chest, I marched down the stairs with murder in my heart. Ray and Hazel stood near the door, looking guilty. I advanced on them and with a vicious slam, I pinned them both against the wall — Ray with my right hand on his chest, and Hazel with my left hand on her shoulder. The thump echoed through the house. They looked shocked. When I spoke, my voice was as neutral as always, but my face was twisted with hatred.

"What did you say to her?"

Ray opened his mouth to talk, but I cut him off.

"No, I think I can guess that. Why did you say it?"

"She deserved to know, Howie," Hazel said quietly. Neither she nor Ray struggled. "You weren't being fair to her."

"What the hell are you talking about?"

Stella had once told me that watching us talk with each other was 'like watching a film that had been dubbed over by the least enthusiastic voice actors of all time.' I wondered what she would think of this.

"Gee, let's think on that for a minute," said Ray, raising a hand and ticking off his points on his fingers. "You didn't tell her that you were planning to pawn family heirlooms just to fulfil her dream of sitting through university classes with you. You didn't tell her that you were torturing yourself over internet college courses. You didn't tell her that you wake up in the night screaming from your fear of losing her, which, you know, I'm no psychologist or nothing but is clearly what your stupid nightmares are really about. You're going off the deep end. Just look at yesterday."

Yesterday.

I had worked late into the night on Friday, trying to get my work done in time for Sunday. So I had my evening brains and I dug in. But I kept drifting off in pleasant reverie, thinking about Sunday. Stella and me lying on the grass. Stella's rich brown hair in the warm spring sunshine. Me reading her poems. Her lips on my lips. My arms around her body. Her brains on my tongue. No. No. Then I would shake myself awake, and try to focus on my schoolwork again. The hours on the clock ticked by and I kept working, and daydreaming, and then working again. I finished my History essay at around one a.m, and I collapsed into bed. I was shaken awake by another terrible dream at six a.m, so I got up and ate breakfast. I worked all Saturday, but it was slow going. At midnight I felt a hand on my shoulder and turned to see Hazel.

"You should get to bed," she said.

"I will soon."

"You've been working all day. Aren't you finished yet?"

"I finished my high school stuff after dinner, but the brains haven't totally worn off yet so I thought I'd get some MIT stuff done. Do you want to quiz me?"

"No. I told you to leave those MIT courses alone. I think you should sleep."

"Just quiz me and then I'll go to bed. I finished all my regular work, Hazel, I promise."

Hazel looked doubtful but she took the papers I offered her.

"Um. Okay. What is the basic structure of a… nucleo… tide?"

I closed my eyes. This was easy. I should know this. "A ribose sugar. A phosphate group. And… something else. Damnit."

"An organic molecule containing nitrogen," Hazel said.

"I knew that."

"What are the four base pairs of RNA?"

"AGTC. Uh. Adenine. Guanine… Tyrosine? And… Cytocine?"

She shook her head no. "There's no T. It starts with a u."

"Yes, of course, that's DNA not RNA. U… U… Uracine?"

"Uracil."

I smacked my forehead. "Of course it is. I knew that."

"Will you go to bed now?"

"Not yet — I need to go over this again."

"Howie… it's late. You've been working all day."

"I'm having a day out with Stella tomorrow. I finally have my high school work done. This is one of the only times I'm going to get to work on this stuff, Hazel, without taking time away from either Stella or my schoolwork. And I've got to get through classes at SFU. What if… what if someone comes for her… I want to be there, you know?"

"You don't have to go through classes to be there for her, Howie. Get some sleep, okay?"

"I will soon. Goodnight."

I tried to force myself to bed but I couldn't sleep. I kept thinking about Stella, and how I'd lose her if I looked stupid in university, and it was hard to sleep while mired in panic, so I got up and went back to work. I kept reading over the material and trying to test myself, but as familiar as the stuff looked when I read over it, I couldn't pull it out of my head when I turned the page over. I got so frustrated with myself that I started banging my forehead on the wall.

"Damnit, go to bed," said Ray, striding into the room.

"What are you doing up?" I asked.

"I got up to take a whizz, like a normal person. What's your excuse?"

"I just can't learn this basic biochemistry."

"That's because it's the fucking witching hour, and you ain't supposed to be learning anything right now. You're supposed to be asleep."

"What, so I can have nightmares?" I said.

"This girl is messing you up so bad."

"I know you hate her, Ray, but you need to shut up about Stella."

"I don't hate her. I almost like her. She doesn't take anyone's shit and her mind feels damn good. But I don't like that she can turn me off like a light switch if she has a mind to, and I don't like that she's driving my little brother around the bend."

"I think I'm driving myself around the bend," I said, burying my head in my hands.

"Well, you can't study your way out of being a zombie, so you might as well get some fucking rest so you can enjoy your goddamn date tomorrow."

"I can sleep in; Stella won't be awake until at least ten."

"Go. To. Fuckin'. Sleep."

Ray left, shutting my door loudly. I struggled on for another half hour before admitting defeat. By then my brain was buzzing with dark thoughts, and when I sank into bed, I had the most terrible dream yet.

In this dream, I was one of a horde of zombies, and we were all drawn to her mind. Stella saw me and tried to reach for me because she thought I was different from the others. She brightened her mind to blinding brilliance, and everything spun. We didn't know where to go or how to move so we just stood, and revelled. She moved through the others toward me and took my arm, and said, "Come on, Howie, let's go."

Her touch jolted me free of her spell. I turned to her trusting face, released myself to the darkness, and pulled her to the ground with gratified glee. As I fell upon her, the others joined me, and she disappeared beneath the clawing arms and snarling teeth of the zombies all around us. And then I realized what I had done, and I started to scream for her. I killed the zombies and pulled her body out from under them. Her bloody flesh hung in tatters and her mind was silent. Her face was frozen in an expression of shocked betrayal, and her empty, lifeless eyes stared at me, and no matter how I wailed and rocked her body in my arms, nothing could breathe the life back into her, nothing, never…

When I finally woke I cried for a while, biting my hand and trying to stay quiet so I didn't wake my family again. When I had calmed down, I turned on the light and read until five in the morning, when I heard a knock on the door, and this time it was Dad, who habitually woke up early.

"I saw your light," he said. "Did you have another dream?"

I nodded.

"Your dreams get worse when you are under stress," said Dad. "I wish you would reassure yourself that dreams are simply fragments of neurological activity as your brain processes the day's experiences and thoughts." He patted me on the shoulder briefly and then left. He reappeared with Army.

"I've liberated Army from your sister's room. Pets are said to have a positive influence on stress and anxiety. Perhaps he should be in your room for a while."

I patted the bed and Army jumped up heavily. He licked the tears off of my face and collapsed next to me. I wrapped my arms around his furry bulk and together we fell asleep.

When Stella texted me to tell me that she was awake, I got up, showered, and dressed in a button-down shirt and slacks that I knew she particularly liked. But I was dizzy and tired, and so I lay down to read until she got here.

I'd had no idea that downstairs, Hazel and Ray were planning some kind of coup.

"We talked it over," Hazel said, tears running down her face, "and we agreed that Stella would be upset to know that you were torturing yourself like this. It wasn't right that you were doing things to yourself for her sake without her even knowing about them. She needed to know how she was affecting you with her talk about university."

"And we thought that if we told her, she might blast in and talk some sense into you, which I bet she just did," said Ray.

"You're both idiots," I said between clenched teeth, and I pushed them harder against the wall. "She's going to think about this, and she's going to come to the obvious conclusion. Don't you understand how she thinks? Don't you know what she's going to do? Well, I do, and I don't see how I am going to bear it."

Stella

I shouldn't have driven home, because I was sobbing my eyes out the whole way and that has to count as impaired driving.

I banged into the house and ran up the steps, past my parents.

"Stella?"

I slammed my bedroom door and collapsed on my bed.

I had known that I was asking a lot of Howie. But I had thought of it as pushing him to improve himself. I'd thought he wasn't fighting for me. For us. But Hazel and Ray had made me see with horrible clarity how impossible everything really was.

I no longer saw myself as a reasonable girlfriend asking her boyfriend to try his best. I saw the truth — that I made my boyfriend rip off his own skin in self-hatred because he couldn't change who he was to satisfy me.

I would have to tell him to forget university. It was obviously stressing him out *way* too much. I should tell him that it didn't matter. It should be enough to have Howie, to have him with me to talk to and laugh with and be my rock. My weird, awkward, bespectacled, brain damaged, significantly-younger-than-me rock… until someone called social services and tried to have me arrested for statutory rape or something.

Oh, God. There was no way this would work out, and Howie knew it. But he was trying. He was pawning his own dead mother's jewellery and suffering from horrible nightmares from the stress of it. He was tearing himself to pieces, trying to remake himself into someone else.

"Stella?" Dad rapped lightly on my door.

"Go fuck a trout 'til you're blue!" I bellowed, throwing a shoe against the door. I heard him say to my mother, "Maybe you should try. She seems a tad worked up."

I grabbed my other shoe, ready to throw, but then my mother violated a personal rule of hers and opened my door without my permission for the first time since I was ten years old. I hesitated, sensing even in my distress that throwing a shoe at my mother's head might not do me any favours.

Mom shut the door in Dad's face, walked swiftly to my bed, and wrapped me in a tight hug. I came unglued and sobbed into her wide, comforting shoulders as she rocked me and held me snug against her as if I were a little girl again.

"Shhhhhh, shhhhhh," she kept saying softly as she rocked me like a baby. I cried until I ran out of tears. Finally, I pulled back, lay down, and turned to face the wall. Mom shifted slightly on my bed and began stroking my hair.

"Now," she said. "Why don't you tell me about it?"

So, staring at the bumps in the paint, I told her about the ring, how Howie planned to sell it, how Hazel had broken down and told me the truth, knowing that I wouldn't let him do it. I told her about the MIT courses, and the failed physics quiz, and the nightmares. As I spoke, I spun the ring around and around on my finger.

"And it's all because I get so pissed at him for things that he just can't change," I said. "Howie just takes it and tries to make me happy anyway. He's such a fucking saint and I'm such an ASSHOLE."

"He's a good young man, Stella..."

"I know, and look what I do to him! He's sure he'll fail out of university, Mom. He says he can't learn new skills, not fast enough, anyway, that he'll never be able to have a higher level job or get a degree, that learning to drive a car was about the most complex thing he could ever manage... and I don't know if I can accept that in him, accept that soon I'll know more than him, be more skilled than him, be older than him... I can't see myself respecting someone who knows less than me, can do less... he's so *good,* Mom, and I'm just... I'm just not..."

"That wasn't my point, Stella, if you'll let me finish. He's a good young man, but he'll only ever be a good *young* man. Your father and I have been waiting for this sort of thing to happen, ever since we learned the truth about him. We like him very much. No, I would even say that we love him. But you have a life to live. It's up to you, what you do, but I think you're already aware that you're going to need more, if not now, then someday. He's young and he looks young, and when you're my age, people will think you're his mother. And then how would your children feel, having a father who looks younger than them?"

"We couldn't have children, Mom, we couldn't even… he's not even sure we would be able to have sex. He's afraid I might… catch it." I said to my pillow, glad that I was facing away from my mother.

"Oh, well that's just impossible," said Mom with a surprised tone. "There's no way that relationship is going to work, then."

"What?"

"Sex is a vital part of a healthy relationship," she said. Then she paused. "I mean unless both people are asexual or something. But in general, sex and physical intimacy are really really important. Now, I realize that there are other things you can do that might be safer, and you may already be doing those things — I'm not going to pry — but if sex is something you want, and he doesn't, for *whatever* reason, then that's a pretty big deal breaker if we're looking at things from a long-term perspective," she said firmly.

"Is this a normal thing for a teen girl to hear from her mother?"

"I don't care if it's normal, it's *true*," said Mom. "And if there's a risk you could catch that disease, then that's something to seriously think about. You wouldn't want that virus, Stella, even if you took the treatments."

"Which you know Howie would give me, even though it's illegal," I said. "No. Howie and his family aren't really fantastic advertisements for eternal life, and Howie seems pretty firmly against it, too."

"A good young man," Mom sighed. "With the wisdom that comes from living twice as long as me."

We were quiet for a long time.

There was another gentle rap at the door.

"I'm done with the trout," said Dad. "Can I come in now?"

My parents left me alone to do what I knew I had to do. I thought about going back, doing it in person, but no. I didn't think I would be able to do it if I looked into those eyes. If I saw his arms, I would want to go to them. If I saw his lips, I'd want to kiss them. I didn't know how to separate myself from him. I might as well chop off my own hand.

I took some deep breaths and picked up my phone, but before I could call, Howie called me.

"I was about to call you," I said into the phone.

"Oh, good," said Howie. That husky voice of his. He was mine. How could he be anything else?

"Did you know I was about to call you?" I asked, curling up in my bed.

"How could I? I'm not a mind reader. I'm just a mind… feeler. Or something."

"Can you feel my mind, now?" Did he know what I was going to say? Did I know whether I could even say it?

"Not much. You've calmed down. That's why I called."

"You were waiting for me to calm down?"

"Yes."

I held the phone tightly to my ear. Every word he spoke was precious to me now. "Why?"

"Because if I called before you calmed down, you'd tell me to have intercourse with some unusual species of wildlife and then throw your phone across the room."

"You know me pretty well." My laugh sounded more like a sob.

"I try to."

"…I'm sorry I got so pissed at you, Howie. You didn't deserve that."

"I don't mind your anger, Stella. You know that. I like a powerful woman. It's arousing."

"Yeah, well, you're from the good old sexist days when women were thought to be adorable and harmless, so they could roar around slapping men with impunity."

"Got to say, I've never thought of you as 'harmless'," Howie said dryly.

Oh, Jesus. I loved him so fucking much.

"The point is, it's wrong for me to get pissed with you over things you can't change. I'm hurting you. I can't stand that I'm hurting you." *I love you too much to keep hurting you.*

"The only thing that hurts is the thought of losing you. That's why I've been pushing myself. Not because you've bullied me into it."

"But the upshot is the same, Howie. It's because of me. You're wrecking yourself and it's all because of me. Because I make you feel like you need to be something you're not."

"Let me worry about me, okay?"

"Howie..."

"Oh, Stella... don't."

I had been hoping that it would be easier over the phone because his voice is so impassive that I could try to convince myself that he wasn't that upset. But I knew him too well. To anyone else, he might have sounded lacking in emotion, but to me, he sounded anguished. His voice was breathless and strained.

"Please, Stella. Not now. Not over the phone."

My heart was pounding and I could hear my pulse in my ears. How could I break his heart? How could I break mine?

Then I thought of my mother, using "impossible" to describe the future of our relationship. She was right, and I hadn't even told her the terrible stuff about him thinking about *killing* me. No question what she would say about *that.* There was nothing about our relationship that made it seem like a good idea. Even Howie knew it. He'd been trying to tell me for months. I was just torturing him by prolonging things. I was making him torture *himself.*

"Howie, you know... you know this can't work. You deserve someone who accepts you for what you are..."

"There is only you, Stella. There can never be anyone else."

"Don't say that, Howie; you're going to live for a very long time."

"You think I'll forget you? You think I'll find someone else?"

"I hope so." Even though the thought of him in love with another girl was like twisting a knife in my heart. "For your sake..."

"I've never loved someone the way I love you. Not in seventy years, not in another seventy years. Don't do this yet… we still have time…"

"Then, when, Howie? Set a date? Agree to break it off… when? The day I start university? The day I graduate? When I turn twenty-five? Thirty? Could you carry on like normal, knowing that our days together were numbered?"

"Our days were always numbered, Stella. I always knew that. Just give me… give me a little more time with you. I'm not ready. I wasn't ready…"

"I can't," I said. My tears were sliding into my mouth and choking up my throat. This couldn't be happening. Howie was everything.

I heard him take a breath that sounded like a sob. "It's not right to end it like this. Let me kiss you, let me hold you one last time. Give me that. Please."

I felt like I was suffocating. "Howie… if I let you do that… I couldn't end it. And I need to."

I heard a strangled noise coming from Howie's end of the line which I will never forget. It wasn't a cry, or a scream, or anything so dramatic. It was the barely-audible gasp of someone who is facing something that is more than they can bear. It was the sound of civilizations falling, of all the most terrible things that have happened in human history, and it was coming out of his mouth. It was the death rattle of our relationship and I covered my own mouth and doubled over in silent agony at the sound of it. I felt sick.

When Howie finally spoke, his voice was quiet and cracked. "Okay. It's okay. I… Stella — I love you."

"I love you too, Howie… Fuck. I love you… you understand that, don't you?" I pleaded. It was wrong of me to beg him for understanding. He didn't have to understand. He was allowed to be angry. Being angry is the prerogative of the dumped.

But Howie shamed me again by being the bigger person.

"I know it. But it isn't enough. Love isn't always enough."

I couldn't answer. If I breathed in, sobs would come out. But when Howie spoke, his voice was steady.

"Take care of yourself, Beautiful. So beautiful. I love you. I love you. God, I love you."

The line went dead and so did my heart. I gasped a deep breath and buried myself in my pillows and wished I could just stop being me.

17

Stella

My parents let me stay home sick on Monday.

"You clearly aren't ready to function like a human," said my mother.

"Oh, you're just saying that because I haven't moved for eighteen hours," I said.

"And haven't eaten since Saturday."

"Although you have managed to go through about six litres of Diet Pepsi," said Dad.

"So you can take one day off of school if you promise to try to act like a human tomorrow," my mother said.

"Just the one day, though. You've been angling for years to stay home from school long term. This is not your opportunity," said Dad.

I nodded. I was sitting curled up on the couch, with a blanket around me, where my mother had plunked me after I came wandering downstairs that morning. She sat me on the couch, put the blanket over me, and brought me eggs. But eggs just made me think about Howie and I turned my face away. That's when she told me that she had already called the school and notified them that I would be out of school that day.

"Do you need company? Your father or I could call in a family day," said Mom.

"Ooh, me! Dibs!" said Dad.

I shook my head no. "You can if you want. But it's okay."

"Rats," said Dad. "I'm tired, too. I was up all night with that trout..."

Mom shot him a Look, and he shut up. "One more thing, Stella: You need to eat today."

"I will. I'm just not hungry yet."

I normally did eat when I was upset, but this was different. I wasn't upset — I was shattered. I was existing in this weird, confused, semi-miserable, semi-denial state which was, for whatever reason, incompatible with food.

"It's not healthy to just quit eating, Stella."

"Mom. My body could probably feed a pack of wolves for a month. A day or two off my food won't hurt me."

My parents glanced at each other.

"That's the first fat joke you've made about yourself in a long time," Dad said. "I'm not thrilled to see them making a comeback."

I used to make fat jokes about myself a lot. Bullies have trouble making fun of you when you're already making fun of yourself. But Howie had changed that. I didn't care as much about what the bullies thought or said, and I never felt fat with Howie. He made me feel beautiful.

"That was a fluke."

"I hope so," said Mom. "So, you get one day off school if you agree to eat, and then you will go back tomorrow."

"JA, COMMANDANT! I VILL HURRY UP AND QVIT BEING SAD, SCHNELL!" I barked.

"You can be sad, but you will be sad at school."

"JA, HERR COMMANDANT."

I spent the next hour staring at a wall, much like I had all last night, which I had spent writhing on my bed, trying to somehow stifle the black hole of horror that had opened in my stomach. I can't say when I fell asleep because I was dozing and waking all night long. When my alarm went off, it was like waking back up into a nightmare. I felt unbalanced, like the world was crumbling under me. Nothing seemed real, but at the same time, I knew that this was a stark reality.

I decided to go back to sleep.

Here's the thing about the end of the world.

When the world ends, you think that's the end of *everything*. But it isn't. There's a whole universe of shit out there, and when one world ends, the universe just throws together a new one. And maybe it isn't what you had before, and maybe it's made out of shit, so it stinks, but it's there, and so are you, and new things can sprout in that shit and you get used to it and in the end things aren't as bad as you thought they would be.

Okay, so I'm really not great at metaphors but that's how I think of it, anyway.

Like, I bet when the Roman Empire fell people thought that was a pretty big deal. And it was. We had the Dark Ages and crap. But in the end, we got rid of slavery and developed the iPhone so maybe things didn't turn out so bad in the end. It just really, really sucked between times.

When my parents pulled me away from Nova Scotia, I had thought the world was ending. I was sure my life would be shit from there on out. And it kind of was, for a while. There were bullies and zombies and a lot of severed body parts and a really paranoid nationalist who played off my insecurities to try and gaslight me into believing that my boyfriend was involved in some complicated plot to sell me to the United States government. So that sucked a lot. But in the end, I built a new world, and that one wasn't so bad. I had Howie — Oh, God, Howie — and the government treated me like this super important person, and I even ended up getting free tuition.

So now my world was ending again, but as unbearably shitty as the new world looked to me from my living room couch, some part of me knew that it might have good parts, too, someday. It was just really hard to imagine what that would look like right now.

I read, watched weird daytime TV, and drank Diet Pepsi. My phone dinged with a text message alert and I lunged for it, only to realize with crushing disappointment that the text came from "Dildo" — also known as Dean.

I can't help but notice that u aren't in class.

Excellent observation, Sherlock.

So no rehearsal today?

Can't. I'm dead.

Sorry 2 hear. Hope ur less dead tomorrow.

I didn't bother texting back. Dean was bottom on my list of things I gave a shit about at the moment.

My phone binged again at three, but it still wasn't Howie. It was from "Best Dad in the World". Obviously, I needed to change my phone's password.

Have you eaten yet?

There's nothing I want in this house.
Why do you make me live off of
mouldy bread and rainwater?

You can have whatever you want to eat tonight.
I'll bring it home.

You don't get an offer like that every day. I thought carefully. What did I want to eat? Cheesecake? My stomach squirmed. No. Pasta from my favourite pasta restaurant? But no, there was a memory of Howie watching me eat it, a loving smile on his face. Damn you, Howie, for feeding me so much. Everything was tainted. There was only one unromantic thing I could think of that remotely appealed to me.

Poutine.

Ah, a balanced dinner for the starving waif.
Thy will be done.

Dad showed up with two bags full of New York Fries Poutine, New York Fries Hot Dogs, and more New York Fries Poutine.

"What, did you rob the food court?"

"Essentially." He pulled out one more container.

"Sushi?"

"For your mother. She didn't feel like hot dogs."

My mother came in the door right on cue.

"Mom, since when do you eat sushi?"

"People eat it a lot at work. I've developed a taste for it."

"Seriously?"

"Seriously, I had to. The way that people would go out to Tim Horton's back home, or bring timbits to the workplace, people here go for sushi or order in sushi. I had to adapt or become a social outcast."

"Yeah, that's true, my work's the same way," said Dad, "but I always liked sushi."

"Oh. Then I guess I'd better try one."

"Here, it's not so bad if you coat it in soy and wasabi."

I tried it. It tasted weird. Seaweedy. But it didn't remind me of Howie.

"Maybe I could learn to like it, too." After all, I was going to live here. Maybe it was time I left my bubble and actually started acting like a West Coaster. I could buy yoga pants and start talking about Crossfit.

Or not.

I dug into my poutine. It was delicious, and it marked, in my mind, the end of the end of the world.

Howie

18

Stella

"Jeez, look at you. You're like a zombie. Are you sure *you* broke up with *him*?" Kate asked. She had shown up on my doorstep shortly after dinner, bearing ice cream and chocolate. Now we sat in my room, me with my untouched bowl of ice cream, which was slowly turning into soup, and Kate on her third helping.

"It was very definitely me," I said. "Howie would never… he would never have broken it off. Even though he knew it had to happen."

"I don't see why it *had* to happen," said Kate.

"It's hard to explain."

"That's a stupid answer."

"Then I don't want to talk about it. How's that for an answer?"

Kate sighed. "You realize it violates the principles of girlfriend-hood to not tell me every last detail?"

"It's just a lot of stuff, some of which is Howie's private business and I can't really talk about."

"Okay…"

"Howie's brain damaged."

"Well, that's fairly obvious."

"Okay, well, he thinks he couldn't handle university."

"He handles high school fine. He's got, like, a ninety percent average or something, doesn't he?"

"I know… but he was only going to university because I was bullying him into it. I bullied him to the point where he was starting to engage in self-destructive behaviours out of self-hatred because he couldn't be what I wanted him to be. Is that normal? Is that healthy?"

"Nope," said Kate, biting into a chocolate bar.

"So that's why I broke it off."

"Fair enough," said Kate. "Why aren't you eating your ice cream?"

I spent the bus ride to school on Tuesday fretting about the moment when I would see Howie again. Would he be distant? Would he be his usual quietly adoring self? Would he ask me for one last kiss? If so, I wasn't sure I'd be able to say no. God, I wanted to kiss him again. I didn't want our last kiss to be that one where he freaked out and ran away from me.

Frig, I really messed him up. He should hate me. I hated me.

I half expected him to be waiting for me when I stepped off of the bus. But there was no sign of him. He was giving me my space — damn his considerate hide.

Kate found me soon enough and took my arm. But as she chattered about her trip to Seattle — which had been zombie free, apparently — I kept scanning the crowds for Howie. He wasn't there.

"So, with my mom as a chaperone obviously I couldn't get away with much, but…"

"Have you seen Howie?" I interrupted.

"Nope. He skipped school the same as you yesterday."

Grieving, or trying to avoid me? Or both. Probably both.

I sat lifelessly through Biology and Physics. I tried to take notes but I couldn't summon the energy to care. A couple of times I felt tears starting to trickle down my cheeks. I wiped them away angrily.

I wanted to talk to him so badly. I thought about texting him, but what was I supposed to say? "Are you alive?" Pretty stupid question to ask someone who's both already dead and yet also basically immortal.

"Don't text," counselled Michelle over lunch. "Because then he'll text back, and you'll end up flirting, and next thing you know you'll be back together."

"That doesn't sound so bad to me, right now," I said.

"You broke up with him for a reason. That reason will still be there if you get back together."

"But what if he's her soul mate?" Amy asked. She was devastated by our break up. It had come as a total shock to her and seemed to have destroyed her faith in love.

Kate shot Amy a nasty glance. "That's not helpful."

"My parents say there's no such thing as soul mates," I said. "Just people you can respect and live with, and people you can't respect or live with."

"This is *not* helping," said Kate firmly. "You need to stop thinking about him."

"I can't stop. I'm worried about him."

"If you're so worried just go ask his brother and sister how he is," said Michelle reasonably.

I stood up. "I will. I have something I need to give them, anyway."

Ray and Hazel looked up and turned around before I was halfway across the room. Sometimes I forgot that they sensed my brainwaves as strongly as Howie did. I wondered if they thought about killing and eating me, too. Their faces were blank as they watched me approach.

I went right to Hazel and put the ruby ring in her hand. Her fingers closed around it.

"Is he okay?" I asked her softly. She shrugged and looked away.

"He'll be fine," said Ray harshly. "Once you take yourself off to university."

"Well, I can't really rush that along," I said irritably.

"Great, well, in the meantime Hazel and I will just have to enjoy being sandwiched in your mutual misery," said Ray. "Don't let us keep you from your friends, now."

"When is he coming back to school?"

"He isn't," said Hazel.

The air seemed to rush out of the room. "What do you mean, he isn't coming back?" I demanded.

"He's dropping out," said Hazel.

"Yep, so… bye," said Ray.

"WHAT THE FUCK DO YOU MEAN HE IS DROPPING OUT OF SCHOOL?" My voice rang through the cafeteria and I saw heads raise and turn, but I didn't give a flying rabbit fuck. I realized that Howie had no intention of crossing my path ever again. He was going to keep himself away. For-fucking-ever.

Of course. Of *course* he wouldn't come back to school. I should have known he would do this. I should have known.

"He can't… I mean… he…" he had to come back to school. He *had* to. I couldn't just, like, not ever see him again.

I was *never going to see him again.*

"Damn, you don't take a hint, do you?" said Ray, standing. He towered over me. "Get gone."

I charged back to my friends with my fists clenched tightly to stop them from punching someone or something.

"There, did that help you get some closure?" Michelle asked, reaching out a hand.

"Not really, no," I said, digging my fingernails into my palms. I felt like a volcano. Something was going to blow any second now, because I couldn't handle this. I couldn't handle any of this.

"Do me a favour, will you, and lift up your trays?" My blood was rushing in my ears and I felt like my heart was going to burst out of my chest, run off, and kick someone's ass.

My friends exchanged glances and shuffled to their feet with their food trays in their hands.

"And your drinks. Put them on the trays, please." There was more shuffling as I took heaving breaths.

Once the table was clear I nodded. "Great, thanks." I gripped the edge of the heavy table and flipped the bitch right into the air. It hit the ground upside down with a satisfying crash which silenced the chatter in the cafeteria.

Amy shrieked.

"Whoa, what the…" said Michelle, staring at the underside of our table.

"I respect this," said Kate, nodding.

Before a teacher could approach, I turned, marched out of the room and went to sit on the bleachers taking gasping breaths and trying to get myself under control before the bell rang.

"I hear you're rocking the single life again," Dean said cheerily when I walked into Drama.

"Fuck you," I growled. I was feeling a little emotionally fragile, you have to understand.

He raised his hands in the air. "Hey, I'm sorry, are the rumours wrong?"

"No, they aren't fucking wrong, I just *don't want to talk about it.*"

Of course people heard the conversation and decided to talk about it.

"I'd be celebrating," giggled one girl.

"Are you kidding? Dumped by Howard Mullins? That's got to be a lifetime low," Carter Davidson hooted.

I cocked my head at Dean as if to say, "See? This is why I don't want to talk about it." He twitched his eyebrows as if to say, "I get it now".

"So, uh…" he scratched the back of his neck, "can you still rehearse after school? I hate to ask, but we're getting really tight on time…"

"Ugh." I slumped my shoulders. "Yeah, I guess we have to."

Ms. Lawless walked into the room and went up to me. "You're to report to the office," she said quietly.

"I'm in constant demand," I complained to Dean, and I walked out.

Howie

"Howie. Howie. Howie." My sister's voice barely penetrated my anguish. I finally opened my eyes.

"Stella was upset that you're dropping out of school. She flipped over a table."

I closed my eyes and nodded slightly. It hurt to breathe, which was weird because I don't have pain receptors anymore, but emotional pain doesn't seem to count. But I also don't really need to breathe much, so I would hold my breath for hours. A couple hours here and there didn't hurt. But you can't talk without breathing, so I wasn't saying much. Army stayed close to me, and the feeling of his breathing comforted me. It was enough. I could handle this. Barely.

"She gave us this."

I felt something cold and hard being placed in my hand. The warmth from Stella's body had left the ring, but it still glowed red, like her love. I began to cry.

"Well, at least that gets you breathing," Hazel said.

Stella

"What called you out of Drama?" Dean wanted to know when I showed up for our rehearsal.

"I had a temper tantrum in the lunchroom. Now I have detention at lunch tomorrow," I said.

"Temper tantrum over what?"

"Over fuck you, that's what."

"Ouch," he said. "Okay, I can take a hint."

"That wasn't a hint," I said. "It was pretty direct. The next step would involve my fist in your face."

"Speaking of subject changes, how about that weather today, huh?" he said.

"That's better. Come on. Let's do some Christopher Durang."

The rehearsal actually went fine. Dean and I had good chemistry on stage, and he had his lines memorized, which pleasantly surprised me. I stumbled in a few places, since I'd spent more time sulking over my boy problems than studying lately, but I did all right. The play was funny, and Dean was funny. At one point he delivered a line so well that I cracked up and I couldn't stop laughing. I may have been releasing a lot of tension from the past few days because it was totally out of proportion. And Dean started laughing, partially because *I* was laughing so hard, and next thing I knew, I was leaning on him, both of us doubled over with hysterical laughter.

"Stella, you've got to stop, you're killing me," Dean said, wiping his eyes and clutching my arm to hold me up.

That shut me up. I pulled away and glared at him.

"What?" he said.

"I'm sorry, was my great weight too much to bear?" I snapped.

"No! I didn't mean like that! It's just that I couldn't stop laughing. You have an infectious laugh, you know. I've never heard you laugh like that before. I… I liked it."

"Oh," I said. I felt embarrassed.

Dean looked awkward, like he wanted to say something more, but he just looked away. "Shall we take it from the top?" he said.

"Yeah," I said, all the humour drained out of me again. "From the top."

We managed a couple of good runs without any further excess of hilarity, giving each other notes in between with business-like politeness. When we were done, we packed our bags in silence, but I noticed Dean kept sneaking little glances at me.

"Uh," he said finally, straightening up with his bag over one shoulder. "Seriously, though, are you okay? You know... what with... everything."

"Do I seem fucking okay to you?"

"No," he said. "You really don't. But... if there's anything I can do. You know. Uh. Let me know. Or... if you want to talk..." He was standing too close. I could smell his cologne.

There was a clang, and we turned to see Kelly Svancara and Danielle Waters holding open the door. I swear Dean jumped back a little.

"Are you done yet? We've been waiting!" said Danielle.

I raised my eyebrow at Dean. "Big plans for this evening?"

He shrugged and smiled. "Oh, you know."

Kelly looked me up and down and said, "Don't you have something to do, like trashing school property and generally taking up space elsewhere?"

I couldn't even think up a good insult. I glared at her so hard that she shrank back slightly, and I stalked out of the room.

Dad picked me up from school.

"How was rehearsal?" he asked when I threw myself and my backpack into the front passenger seat.

"Fine," I said. "Do you mind if I just stew in angry silence for a while?"

"Sure. Let me find appropriate music for that." He skipped radio channels until he found a station playing classic rock, and we drove home to the tune of "Another One Bites the Dust".

"How was your day?" Mom asked when we walked in the door.

"Oh, you know, the usual. Got a little bit of detention. I need you to sign a slip. Oh, and Howie's not going back to school ever again. So, basically, just shittacular. How are you?"

"Whoa, wait, can we go back to the detention bit?" Dad raised his hand into a stop signal.

"Oh, she's always getting detention. What's this about Howie not going to school?" said Mom.

Dad turned to Mom. "No, she hasn't had detention in two years!"

"That long? Really? Wow. Okay, tell us about both things."

"I don't want to talk about it."

"That's not fair," said Dad. "You can't hit us with those tantalizers and not tell us what on Earth happened."

"He's right and you know it," said my mother. "Did you beat someone up? Oh my God, was it Howie?"

"It wasn't Howie! I mean, no, I didn't beat anyone up. I may have flipped over a lunch table. But I asked my friends to clear it off, first, so really I was very restrained and respectful about it. They called it wilful destruction of school property, but it wasn't even damaged. I mean, those tables took a zombie attack last year and came out fine."

"And *why* did you flip a table over? Just shits and giggles?"

"Because Ray and Hazel told me that Howie has dropped out of school."

"Is there more to the story than that?"

"No, that's basically all they said. They weren't too welcoming to me, possibly because I psychologically tortured their brother and then broke his heart to the point where he no longer wants to attend school or be anywhere near me ever again."

My mother hugged me. "Well, it could have been worse, I guess. Just… try not to get any more detentions, okay? You're so close to graduation."

"Yeah, yeah, I know."

It didn't *feel* like I was close to graduation. Three more months of Dean and Kelly, with no Howie? That felt like fucking purgatory, and it couldn't be over soon enough.

19

Stella

Those last months of high school dragged on and on, but they did finally come to an end. All things do, I guess.

"I can't think of anything worse than going to prom," I said firmly to my friends one day in the beginning of June.

"It's not prom, it's *grad*," said Kate. "You sound like an American."

"It's what we call it on the East Coast," I snapped.

"Guys, it doesn't matter what we call it," Amy said.

"Amy's right. Because the point is that we are all going together, and you are getting zero choice in this," said Kate.

"I seriously cannot think of a more depressing way to spend an evening than going to prom — grad — whatever."

"You have a dress. You bought it in, what, November? And your parents told *our* parents they'd chip in for the limo."

"They still will," I said irritably. "But they won't make me torture myself to justify the money. I can't describe how little I want to attend this horribly shitty might-have-been kind of evening. It'd be excruciatingly masochistic."

"Yeah, yeah, your heart is broken, blah blah blah. Is it going to feel any better sitting at home, missing your high school grad, moping over someone that *you* broke up with? Is that really better?" Kate cocked her head.

"*Yes.* And I'm not planning to mope. I actually have a date planned with a big tube of raw cookie dough."

"Well, put a bow tie on it and bring it to grad, because you're coming if we have to hogtie you to the roof of our limo."

I opened my mouth to tell them that I'd defeated a horde of hungry zombies, so I didn't expect much trouble from three teenage girls, and then remembered that I couldn't say things like that.

"Fine. I'll go. As a favour to you guys. Because I don't want you to remember me as a sad sack of bitterness and resentment."

"Too late."

Really, my friends deserved an award for putting up with me lately. I had stumbled through everything in a haze of never-ending misery. It didn't help that my breakup with Howie provided lots of fodder for Kelly and friends. It was hard to forget my troubles when I was constantly reminded of them by my own personal comment section in the school halls.

The highlight of that last semester had been the skit that Dean and I put on. He was hilarious as the Infant of Prague, and I was spectacular as Sally Jesse Raphael, and people loved it. Our teacher actually picked it as one of the three to be re-performed for the whole Grade 11/Grade 12 class in the last week of school and she gave us a 98% on the project. For a week or two after that, I got compliments in between the insults as I moved through the halls.

So that helped.

But I don't know what I would have done without my friends. Amy, in particular, was a really good ear when I needed to moan about Howie to someone. Of all my friends, she was the only one who really saw what I had seen in him. You could tell that Kate had no idea why I was so devastated, and Michelle was passively sympathetic but Amy *got it*. She was the ultimate champion of True Love. She still didn't really understand why we broke up, but she was good at listening without judging me or making me feel stupid. I felt like she could get a job as a professional emotional validator.

My friends back in Nova Scotia were less useful. Jeremy exulted about all the new boyfriends I could get, and Liz suggested I start dating Dean, which was stupid because first, he was an asshat, albeit a cute and funny asshat, and second, he hadn't exactly come around begging me for a date, even though he knew I was single.

Really, though, the only people who knew how complicated the whole thing was were my parents, and they worried about me so much that I couldn't go crying to them either because they *cared* too much. I ended up reassuring *them* that I would be okay. So mostly I just kept it inside, and cried at nights when I fantasized about Howie's lips on my neck and longed to hear his flat, funny little voice wishing me goodnight and telling me how much he loved me.

My grad dress was a shimmering, frosty blue gown which matched Howie's powder blue tuxedo and made me feel like a full-figured version of Elsa from *Frozen*. I looked at myself gloomily in the mirror while Mom twisted my hair into an elegant updo.

"You look beautiful, honey," she said quietly.

"Yeah," I said, fingering the glittering necklace that I had worn on the night of my eighteenth birthday. "I know."

"Stella! Your friends are here!" Dad called. "I'm going to make them come inside."

"Aw, Dad! No!"

I pulled away from Mom and clattered down the stairs in my high heels, but by the time I got outside, Dad was already pulling my friends out of the limo.

"I need to have a photo of Stella in front of the mantle," he said.

"What do you need us for?" grumbled Kate.

"So that when her children refuse to believe that she ever had any friends, she can prove them wrong."

"Thanks, Dad."

"You're welcome, honey."

"You realize we don't even *have* a mantle."

"Oh. You're right. In front of the TV? In front of the stove?"

"How about on the stairs?" my mother suggested calmly.

"TO THE STAIRS!" Dad yelled, bolting into the living room, arms flailing.

"Is your father drunk?" Amy whispered.

"Sadly, no," I said. "He's always like this. Just be glad he hasn't mentioned vaginas."

"Okay, all huddle together like you like each other," Dad directed.

We put our arms around each other. Mom snapped a couple photos.

"Okay, now all pose like you're rival fashion models."

Flash, flash.

"Okay, now pretend that you're all ninjas preparing for an epic battle against the scurvy pirates of torrented media."

Flash, flash.

"Okay, now…"

"I think we got enough, Tim," my mother interrupted. "The girls want to get to their dance."

"Okay, off you flit, you lovely butterflies," said Dad, waving his hands. "Have a good time, don't get too smashed."

"Mr. Blunt, they don't allow alcohol at the…"

"I know teenagers. Odds are one of you has liquor in her little clutch purse. My bet is on Kate."

"I don't have a clutch purse," objected Kate, who was wearing a sort of lady tuxedo, with a ruffed white blouse, a black bow tie, a long tight skirt, and a shiny black top hat.

"Don't ask me to unravel your feminine wiles," said Dad. "Just have fun and be safe."

"I don't get how he knew," said Kate, pulling a tiny vodka bottle out of her cleavage on our way back to the limo. "Drink, anyone?"

Howie

"How do I look?" I asked my sister, straightening the bow of my tuxedo.

Hazel just sighed and shook her head sadly.

"You're crazy," said Ray. "She's going to tear you apart."

Dad nodded. "I'm concerned that you will be further emotionally damaged."

I let out a hollow laugh. "I don't think that's possible. Can you do further damage to Chernobyl?"

"What if she has another date?" asked Hazel.

I froze. "Who?"

"I dunno. But what if she does?"

"Then… I won't go up to her."

"There's no way this is gonna turn out well," said Ray. "Either you're gonna see her with another guy and come home crying, or you're gonna go up to her and have her rip out your heart again."

"I'm always willing to rip my heart out for Stella. It won't kill me."

"Howie, you've been as near dead as possible lately." Hazel laid her hand on my arm.

"I just want to see her again. She makes me feel alive."

"So feel alive from here," said Ray. "She comes blaring in our windows at all hours."

"She's unhappy. I'm unhappy. What's the sense of it?"

"There's never been any sense in it. You should have got laid while you had the chance."

"Shut up, Ray. I'm going."

"It's your funeral."

I parked down the road from her house, and stood in the shadows for a few minutes, holding a red rose and rehearsing what I would say. I wouldn't ask her to take me back; I wouldn't expect anything from her. I just wanted to give her a night to remember. My memories of the last time I saw her tortured me. She was so angry with me. She was so angry with *herself*. I wanted to change that. I wanted to have a proper goodbye. To tell her how much she meant to me, to hold her and kiss her one last time. I'd give her back the ring — I had it in my pocket — and ask her to keep it in memory of me.

I didn't think Stella would want to go to grad without me. I suppose that was a little smug of me to assume, but I knew, I could *feel,* that she wasn't taking our breakup with equanimity. She missed me. She was hurting. I didn't want her to hurt. I was tired of staying away. I wanted to go in and sweep her off her feet. Maybe she'd change her mind… maybe… but no. The same problems would be there. The fact would remain that I was a dead man, or as good as, and she was a living, vibrant, growing human being.

Just one night. One more night with her. One more chance to feel the softness of her lips, see the arch of her eyebrow, listen to her laugh. One more night to build a proper goodbye, a proper end to our story. Maybe then I could really let her go.

While I sat there, building up my nerve, a limousine pulled up. Stella came out, looking so stunning that my heart forgot to beat. The dress she wore glimmered and her hair was up. She looked like a stunning, mature, sexy woman, and for a moment I wondered if I had somehow missed a year or five.

It happens sometimes.

Her father came out with her and pulled her three friends out of the limo and back to the house. My heart began to beat again. No other boys in tuxedos, then. Maybe I could still go up to her. But her brains waves didn't feel unhappy. What if I ruined things by walking up to her? What was I thinking, walking back into her life just as she was finally finding joy in it without me?

I looked down at my rose.

"Selfish," I told myself.

So I moved my car to where she wouldn't see it. But I couldn't help but get out and watch from afar. I wanted to see her again. Soon she came out with her friends, and I watched her hungrily as she laughed at something Kate said and shook her head. It wasn't too late. I could still walk up, take her in my arms… but I held myself back as she climbed into the limo with her friends and drove away.

20

Stella

I tried to have fun. I really did. Everyone seemed so happy. People who normally didn't even like each other were hugging and kissing cheeks, so excited to never interact again. The hotel ballroom was decorated with delicate lights and fancy gauzy things to make it seem like some sort of weird high school fairyland, full of warm fuzzy feelings and limitless hopes and dreams.

It was depressing.

I mean, it was lovely, and the food they served was delicious, and even *I* felt a bit of a warm glow when I saw my friends laughing and dancing.

But I couldn't find the joy. I couldn't find the fun. The might-have-beens kept coming back to haunt me; an imaginary Howie at my arm, opening doors for me, fetching punch for me, leading me out onto the dance floor, telling me how lovely I looked in my sparkling, clinging, swishing gown.

"Why so glum, chum?" a voice asked. I looked up and saw Dean smirking at me. He looked like James Bond or something in his black tux. His black hair was slick with gel and his dark eyes glinted with mischief. It should be illegal for someone to look that fucking charming.

"Who wants to know?" I asked sourly. "Where's your date?"

"Didn't bring one," he said. "This way I get to dance with all the girls."

"May your evening be filled with all the womanizing you could wish for," I said, offering up my glass. He reached out, took it, and put it on the table.

"Why, thank you. It's your turn."

"I'm not in a dancey mood, sorry, as much as I would like to help you tick another girl off your list," I said.

"Actually, you're first on my list," he said, and he gave me the casual, appreciative once-over that Howie had trained me to recognize as the sign of the guy who is secretly into girls like me. "But don't tell anyone."

"Yes, well, as flattering as your shame in wanting to dance with me is…" I said. He laughed and pulled me to my feet. His hands were warm as they closed around mine.

"Save your caustic wit for class," he said, "and shut up and dance with me."

What the hell. I went on the dance floor with him. I inherently distrusted him, but his dimpled grin was irresistible. Besides, I found myself feeling smug. This guy was popular and mega-handsome, and as I logged the accidentally-on-purpose bumps, the surreptitious touches, and yes, a suspicious bulge in his pants, I *knew* he wanted me. And that made me feel good.

And terrible.

Because before Howie, I *never* would have accepted the possibility that a fit, attractive, popular guy was into me. I would have rejected him not just with some snide remarks, but with vituperative violence.

It seemed wrong that, thanks to Howie, I was getting felt up by this sexy guy and enjoying it.

The fast song ended, and the DJ switched to a slower, more romantic tune. I went to drift off the dance floor, but Dean stopped me.

"I'm not done with you yet," he threatened. "One more dance, and I'll release you, I promise."

"I don't know…" I said, glad that the dim lighting hid my blush.

He put his hands on my waist, just barely above my butt, and drew me close. "Now, put your arms around my neck," he coached, with a smile.

"I know how to slow dance," I said. "I've actually done it before."

"Not with me," he said. His dark eyes looked deep enough to fall into. I didn't want to look away because it'd be like losing a staring contest and there was no way I was losing a battle for dominance with Dean fucking Kato. So we swayed to the seductive song, eyes locked on each other, while he pressed himself up against me, grinding his hips slightly, and I knew he was watching to see how I responded.

I tried to hide it, but it had been months since I'd had a man's hands on my waist and it felt good. Not romantic, but *hot*. His attention was hot. The fact that he was into me was hot. The things he was doing against me were hot. When the song was over I pulled away. He had managed to turn me on, in spite of myself, and I was fighting a lot of complex emotions.

Dean kept one hand on my waist, and he looked like he was about to say something.

"Hey, you going hogging?" hooted Ravi, passing by with a silver-clad Danielle Waters on his arm. "Sooey! Sooey!"

Dean flushed and looked away from me. His hand disappeared from my waist.

I'm *still* proud of the fact that I didn't bash anyone's skull in.

"Don't let me keep you from the thinner ladies," I said, raising an eyebrow at Dean. He had the decency to look ashamed, or maybe he was just humiliated by Ravi's comment. I decided I didn't really care. I swept away into the crowd before he could stammer a false apology.

Kate threw herself into a chair as I sat chugging more punch.

"Did I just see you with Dean?" she demanded. "Was he *dancing* with you?"

"Yep."

"Do you think he has the hots for you?"

"Yeah. Who cares?"

"Who *cares*?"

"Right after the song finished one of his little pals made a 'hog' joke and all he could do was look away. So, either he was amusing himself by doing what he saw as a generous thing, deigning to give a fat girl some much-longed-for attention, or he has the hots for me, but can't admit it to his buddies. So… either way, he's a shit stick."

"So, you're not attracted to him?"

"Of *course* I'm attracted to him, *look* at him!" I said, waving my drink and sloshing some of it. "That doesn't mean I like him."

"Want some of that vodka now?"

"Yes, yes I do."

Dean caught me on the way back from the washroom where Kate and I had been fixing our makeup and swigging tiny vodkas. I'd never really drunk before, other than a glass of wine at family dinners. It tasted awful, but it made me feel much less broody about Howie, that's for sure.

"Stella, can I talk to you?" Dean said, jumping out at me as we emerged.

"I don't know, can you?" I said. "Come on, Kate."

"Seriously, I just wanted to apologize for what Ravi said…"

"What are you, his keeper? If he wants to apologize, he can do it himself like a big boy," I said.

"No, I…" he threw up his hands and brought them down again. "I just want you to know that I don't think like that, that I wasn't…"

"Look, Dean," I said, folding my arms. "I don't really give a damn what your motives are. Either you're a condescending, womanizing ass-hole, or you're a coward who lets people shame him and the girls he is with. Either way, you're a bigger sack of shit than Elvis's colon. Now, if you'll excuse me, I have a party to return to."

"That was awesome!" said Kate, high fiving me and trotting to keep up as I strode away at the maximum speed I could manage while still maintaining dignity. "You totally slapped him down."

"That shit stick," I said. "Come on, let's go dance."

After another half hour of dancing, I was sweating bullets.

"I'm sweltering. I'm going to go out for a bit," I shouted to Amy and Michelle.

"Out where?"

"There's a balcony."

"Okay," they shrugged.

I slipped onto the ballroom balcony. A couple who had been making out in the darkness giggled to each other and went back in, leaving me alone. I leaned on the railing, staring pensively out at the glimmer of city lights. At night, you can't see the mountains that loom over the city, but you can see the twinkling from the houses along their sides, and the lights from the ski hills, which look like UFOs floating in the darkness.

From inside I could hear the fierce thrum of the dance music. There was something I really liked about being so close to the action and yet removed from it.

I missed Howie. But there was no future there. When I was with Howie, I felt tied down, held back, guilty about wanting to grow and change. Now I was free to do anything, be anything. I would find someone else. My unwilling attraction to Dean proved that. My heart might still ache for Howie, but my body was clearly capable of aching for other things. My heart and mind would follow when I found someone worthy enough. He must be out there.

And if not... well, I would have a kick-ass career and become the model of an independent woman, whom all children looked up to. I'd cure fucking cancer or something, and if you have a Nobel prize, who cares if you don't have a love life? You have a NOBEL FUCKING PRIZE.

"There you are!" said Kate, popping unwelcomely into my reverie. "I came back with more drinks for you and you were gone."

"It was too hot and crowded, I wanted to get away."

"You're not brooding are you?"

"It's mostly good brooding," I said.

"Oh, well, *good* brooding. You know what's good for brooding? Tequila."

After nearly choking on my first swig, I felt very sure that Tequila is good for absolutely nothing. Kate urged me to try again, so I held my nose for the second swig.

"Kate, it tastes like gasoline!"

"Yeah, but it gets the job done."

I was feeling a little flushed and dizzy. "Yeah, I guess so."

"You wanna go back?"

"Nah. You go ahead."

"Hey, I'm happy here. No skeezes trying to feel me up," she said. "Unless you want to try." She raised an eyebrow at me.

"I wouldn't dare," I teased, ignoring her semi-serious tone.

"I wouldn't mind," she said, staring off into the darkness. "I'd… prefer it, actually. To guys, I mean. Because… I like girls."

"I know."

"You do?"

"Yeah. Don't Michelle and Amy know?"

"I dunno. I never said anything. We've known each other almost our whole lives. I'm afraid it'd be, like, weird for them."

"I doubt they'd care, Kate. They're not bigots and they love you."

"I know. I just don't want to do the whole 'coming out' thing. It's stupid. You never walked into a room and said 'hey, everyone, I like skinny nerdy dudes' so why should I walk around announcing my preferences? It doesn't define me."

"Skinny nerdy dudes?" I nudged her.

"Okay, well, you like Dean so I guess you have broader tastes."

"I guess so. I just liked Howie for him, you know? I think I found him cute because he was Howie. Meanwhile, Dean is hot because… well, he's hot." I shrugged. "Plus dimples. I have a thing for man dimples. Does that make me a dimple-sexual?"

"I guess some people are inherently attractive, while others you find attractive because you like who they are," Kate said. "Maybe that's why I don't like guys; because they're all skeezes."

"Howie isn't a skeez."

"Well, no. But he's a wimp and loser."

"Hey."

"What, I have to be nice about him even after you dump him?"

I winced. "It's just too soon, okay?"

"It's been months, but okay." She was quiet for a moment. "I'm sorry I ragged on you two so much. I was just jealous, I think. Because I wish I had someone to make out with like that. Because I'm so fucking lonely."

"You could have joined the school LGBT group, you know."

"Nah, I checked out the girls in the group one day as I was going by. No one hot in there, so not worth the social stigma of being an official dyke."

"I want to tell you that that's really shallow, but I feel like my hetero privilege means that I can't tell you what to decide about stuff like that."

"Damn straight." She took another swig. "I'll come out at SFU. I might even get laid someday."

"I have no doubt."

"Is this going to make things weird between us?"

I snorted. "No."

"Don't worry, I don't have a crush on you or anything."

"Why the fuck not?"

Kate laughed. "Okay. Maybe a little. Because you are awesome."

"Damn straight."

Howie

I should have gone back to my car. But I was looking at Stella's front door, which I had walked through so many times in the past year. I was missing her parents, whom I genuinely liked. I liked their warmth, their humour.

Without even really thinking, I drifted up and knocked on the door.

Tim opened it, gaped at me, and then looked sorrowful.

"Howie… come in, son, come in."

Son. He called me son. I stepped inside.

"Forgive me for intruding," I said.

"Nonsense, we're happy to see you," said Elaine, coming up and kissing me on the cheek. Her eyes were full of sympathy. "But Howie, you should know… uh…"

"I know Stella's gone. I saw her go."

I felt their relief and saw it reflected in their kind faces. I tried to explain.

"I thought maybe she wouldn't want to go and I didn't want her to miss it."

"You know our girl well," said Tim.

"But I saw that she was going with her friends and I… I decided not to disturb them. But I thought… since she's not here… I could… I mean…" I stopped and tried again. "How is she? How… just how is she?"

"Can I get you something to eat? Oh," Elaine put her hand over her mouth. "I'm sorry, Howie. How soon we forget. Come in and sit down, anyway."

As I followed them to the living room, I noticed, really for the first time, what nice brain waves they both had. Stella had always been nearby when I was with her parents, and so she had outshone them. I could see now how she ended up with such an exquisite brain. Tim's waves were lively and sharp. Elaine's waves were more like Stella's — a sort of strong, thoughtful, emotional thrumming.

"Elaine, did you use to have a temper like Stella?" I asked.

She was startled by my non-sequitur, and she smiled. "Yes, I had a terrible temper. I've got a better handle on it now."

So this is what Stella might be like someday when she matured further. Appreciating Elaine was like appreciating an aged, fine wine. She didn't excite me the way Stella did, but she felt very good to be around.

I sat awkwardly on the couch, nervously rolling the rose between my thumb and forefinger. I saw Elaine and Tim wincing and exchanging glances.

"What?" I asked.

"You're… there are thorns on that rose, Howie," said Elaine. "Let me get you some paper towels."

I looked more carefully and saw that I had covered the rose stem in my dark, sticky blood. I sighed and rearranged my grip so that the thorns weren't puncturing my thumbs anymore. "That's okay. I have a handkerchief I use for this sort of thing."

I pulled out my hanky and carefully dabbed the blood off of my hands and off of the rose. The cuts on my thumb and finger quickly sealed.

"She misses you, you know," Elaine said gently. I nodded again.

"I know. I can… I can tell."

"That's a little creepy, bud." Tim pointed a finger at me.

"What I am is creepy, Mr. Blunt. I never denied that." I stared at my feet. "Stella did the right thing."

"But you show up with a rose, in a tuxedo, on prom night."

"I miss her… I miss her so much. You can't imagine."

"I think I can."

No, he couldn't. He didn't know how it felt to be lonely for decade upon decade. How could he? For a moment, I felt older than him. Which I was, technically.

"I wanted to see her one last time. To give her one more nice night. It's better this way, I know, but…" I buried my head in my hands.

"You poor, motherless boy," said Elaine, and I felt the couch sag next to me as she sat and wrapped an arm around me. I leaned into her comfortable shoulder. How long was it since my mother had last held me? Sixty years? I struggled not to cry.

"Do you understand why she did it, Howie?" Elaine asked. "She loves you, she does, but…"

I was nodding. "I've known since I met her that it couldn't last. She's getting older, she wants to live her life. And I'm stuck. Stuck as a boy. Never a man."

"You are a man, Howie, a brave young man," said Tim. "But someday, she'll be middle-aged, and then old, but you'll still be a young man."

"I know that. I can't give her a life. All I have is never-death."

"We want to thank you, Howie," said Tim.

"Why?"

"For several things. First of all, for helping Stella to grow and mature. You were a stabilizing, balancing influence on her. You helped her learn how to control her temper, and we saw her gain a true self-confidence; not just the defensive bravado that powered her before she met you."

"I exposed her to hundreds of ravening zombies who nearly ate her alive."

"That wasn't your fault," said Elaine. "That was a series of unfortunate connected incidents."

"The other thing we want to thank you for," continued Tim, "is not trying to convince her to become a… what you are."

I was shocked. "Why would I do such a thing?"

"A life without Stella growing older, moving beyond you? I can think of many people who would be tempted by that, and who would try to lure a girl they loved to join them in that."

"If you tried living it, you wouldn't see it that way." This wasn't the sort of thing people did to themselves on purpose. Then I remembered Hunt's concern about Seattle, and I felt a twinge of doubt.

"And as much as we like the idea of our daughter becoming virtually immortal," said Elaine, "we want her to experience life. We want her to grow, to graduate, to have a career, to have a family… we want her to live, not just exist. So thank you, for not trying to stop her."

I saw what they were saying. They were fond of me, yes. They felt bad for me, yes. But they were glad Stella had broken up with me. They didn't want me holding her back.

"I wouldn't want to get in her way. I want her to be happy. And that has to be without me. And somehow, I will have to learn how to live without her." I stood up. "Thank you for your kindness."

I took the ring from my pocket and put it on the table, next to the rose. Then I shook their hands, accepted kisses on the cheek from both of them, stepped out into the darkness and walked away from the light.

Stella

"So, did you have a good time?" Mom asked when I arrived home at around one in the morning. My parents had been waiting up for me in the living room watching a documentary about people who want to marry national monuments.

"I had a *weird* time," I said. "But I guess weird is good."

She sniffed my breath. "Tequila? Stella!"

"I tell you, that Kate's a bad influence," warned Dad. "Port, yes. Brandy. Rum. But Tequila? Yeecchh."

"Stella, if you had been caught…" my mother said.

"Yeah, well, it tasted awful," I said, grabbing a glass of water from the kitchen. "And I don't think I'm drunk. It was only a couple of gulps. Some of the kids there were obviously smashed, so I was the least of the teachers' problems. Consider it a learning experience. I will not be trying Tequila again." I turned to sit at the kitchen table and stopped cold when I saw a rose sitting in a vase. "Uh, where did that come from?"

My parents looked at each other. "Well…" said Dad, "Howie came by."

I struggled to take a breath. "He… what?"

"He said he just wanted to be sure you were going to grad. He was afraid you might be sulking at home, which, in all fairness, does sound like something you'd do."

"So what did you tell him?"

"That you'd gone with the girls."

I sat down and tried not to hyperventilate.

"He… uh…" Dad said slowly, glancing at my mother. "He… also left this." Dad pulled the ruby ring from his pocket and put it on the table in front of me. I stared at it.

"He just wanted to be sure that you were happy," said Dad.

"Happy? HAPPY? Of course I'm not *happy*," I said. "And what the hell is he doing, checking on my happiness? I broke up with *him*. Who does he think he is, coming by and being the bigger person? That just makes it worse…"

"We shouldn't have told you," said Dad.

"Of course you should have," I snapped. "You not telling me wouldn't change the fact that he came, which means that now I can do this." I grabbed my cell phone.

"Oh, don't call him, Stella," said Mom.

"Stay out of this!"

Howie

When my phone rang at midnight, I knew it was Stella calling me. I had been waiting up, sitting in my bed with my phone cradled in my hands. I knew that she would call when she saw the ring and the rose. She would be furious. Furious with me for showing up. Furious with me for letting her go to grad without me. Furious that I had left the ring. Which meant that I would get to hear her voice again. I could tell her how much she meant to me. I could tell her goodbye.

But as the night wore on I began to wonder — would her parents throw away the rose? Would they hide the ring? Would they risk keeping my visit a secret? Keeping secrets from Stella was a dangerous business. She did not like lies.

So I was relieved when my phone began to ring. They hadn't kept the truth from her, and she couldn't be too angry — I hadn't even felt her light up. I picked up the phone and frowned. It wasn't her usual number. Had she changed phones?

I pressed the talk button. "Hello?"

The voice was deep and familiar.

"How would you like to help me save the world?"

ACT 2

As good to write as for to lie and groan.
O Stella dear, how much thy power hath wrought,
That hast my mind, none of the basest, brought
My still-kept course, while other sleep, to moan;
Alas, if from the height of virtue's throne
Thou canst vouchsafe the influence of a thought
Upon a wretch that long thy grace hath sought,
Weigh then how I by thee am overthrown;
And then think thus–although thy beauty be
Made manifest by such a victory,
Yet noblest conquerors do wrecks avoid.
Since then thou hast so far subdued me,
That in my heart I offer still to thee,
Oh, do not let thy temple be destroyed.

Sir Philip Sidney, "Astrophel and Stella 40"

21

Stella

"Which room is going to be yours, Stella?" Mom asked as she lugged a heavy box into my new apartment. I shifted my grip on the box that I was holding and gestured quickly.

"That one. The first one on the left."

I was moving in with Kate. Michelle was going to UBC and Amy had decided to take a counselling course from a local college. Kate originally planned to live with her mother, but I coaxed her into sharing an apartment with me, instead.

"Live somewhere where you can have loud lesbian sex without worrying about your mom hearing," I said.

"But it costs money," she pointed out. "Living at home is free. Also, I have no one to have sex with."

"Do you want that to change, or not?"

She had called me a week later. "I'm in," she said. "The Skeez just sat me down and told me that he's here for me and ordered me to let him know if there is any way that he can support me in my homosexuality."

I laughed. "What does that even mean?"

"I don't know, but I can't handle it. I need out. Especially since Mom seems extra stressed lately and it's not comfortable to live with. My Starbucks job won't cover the rent, so it means I'll take a lot more out of my line of credit," she said. "But that's a future-me problem."

"I'll drink to that!" I said, raising my can of Diet Pepsi to the phone. "Are you sure you're cool with moving in with a sexy straight girl like me? I could have *men* in the apartment, Kate."

She shrugged. "No skeezes. That's my rule. I get right of veto."

So now we were moving into an apartment just a short walk to campus, with a killer view. Everything seemed new and exciting. I normally hated change, but it felt so damn grown up to move into my own place, on top of a *mountain*, and start attending university.

After months of moping over Howie, it felt good to be looking ahead.

I had never heard back from Howie after grad. He wouldn't answer his phone, and I left him voicemails — angry ones at first, but then apologetic ones and then simple 'call me' ones... but he didn't call back. He didn't answer my texts. It totally shook the foundations of my universe. I had assumed that if ever I needed him, if ever I reached out, he would be there. Maybe I was underestimating how deeply I had damaged him. Maybe he was so heartbroken by the idea of my going to grad without him that he couldn't face me again. Maybe he threw his phone in the sea. I didn't know. I might never know. But clearly, he was cutting himself off from me.

So what if it hurt me? I'd hurt him more.

I had tried my best to enjoy the summer anyway. My friends and I went on hikes and went to the beach. But it was hard to stay positive. My house was full of memories. Driving past the local park was painful because I'd end up remembering last summer, when Howie and I spent lazy days lying together on the grass. Howie liked to read me love poetry while playing with my hair, and I would tease him for being sappy, but secretly I loved to look up at the sky and the mountains in the distance and listen to his funny voice reading to me.

"Come live with me and be my love, And we will all the pleasures prove..."

Howie was everywhere I looked, and yet he was nowhere. He left an empty space in my life that my mind was always trying to fill. Every bright blue car that went by made my heart leap until I saw that it wasn't an ancient Dodge Shadow. Whenever I saw a gawky blond guy in the distance I'd think it was him, but it never was.

Of course, he could feel my brain waves, so he was probably avoiding me. It didn't seem fair that he could know where I was and how I was doing with his zombie-senses but I couldn't know a damn thing about him.

I tried to pump Agent Hunt for information on him when we got on the plane for Ottawa.

"Uh... so... how is Howie, these days?" I asked her.

Her face was inscrutable. "I haven't seen him," she said. "I honestly don't know."

"Oh. Well... if you see him..."

"I don't think I'll be seeing him anytime soon, Stella," she said gently.

"Yeah, okay, I... yeah."

We left it at that.

Ottawa had been interesting, and it was good to be free of the spectre of Howie. I didn't have memories of him in Ottawa, and the new sights and new people kept me occupied, even if we did talk about zombies all day. They did all these tests and got me to spend days and days with their staff, trying to teach them how to make zombie hamsters freeze — without a ton of success, I might add.

I spent time with the head honchos of the Zom Squad — sorry, "The Service" — and got to know them better. My favourite was this old Quebecois dude called Henri Cormier who found me endearingly spunky.

"I think you've got the wrong base population," I told Cormier when he took me for lunch one afternoon. "I mean, I can't be *that* special or unusual. But your staff are all calm, serious, follow-orders types of people... and I'm not that type. Maybe you need to look for defensive misanthropes with emotional problems and start hiring them to freeze zombies for you."

"Ben, c'est possible," he said in his slangy Quebecois French and shrugged with a wry smile. "Perhaps we must branch out, *ouis*?"

"You should just make the Mullinses walk around sniffing everyone's brains," I said, my heart skipping at the thought of Howie and his family. "Use them to find talent in the local population."

"And then? Do you think we should just tap them on the shoulder and say, '*excusez moi*, we think you may be very good at fighting the zombies?'"

I laughed. "I'm sure you'd figure it out a way to break it to them."

"In the meantime, we will be calling you if something starts to get out of hand."

"Please do. You don't know how badly I've been wanting to bash some heads in lately. Any outbreaks recently?"

"Ehn." He waved his hand. "One here, one there. Nothing too concerning."

"And Seattle? Did they catch who did that?"

He let out a long puff of air and looked at me with his grey, shaggy eyebrows all bunched up.

"This thing goes beyond Seattle. The Americans say there is no sign of the virus. But we are concerned. Quite concerned." He took a bite of his sandwich and winked at me. "In the meantime, please do not go on vacation anywhere, hmm? Go to SFU. Stay at SFU."

So here I was at SFU. I was moving into a new apartment, starting a new life in a new place, and I felt like maybe *finally*, I could move on. Six months of weeping and brooding over Howie were surely enough, and the excitement and novelty of having my own place helped keep my mind off things. Like, Kate and I went to the dollar store and bought ourselves plates and cutlery and cups and the sorts of things that I had never personally owned before. My whole life, *my whole life,* I had been using plates and bowls and cups chosen and purchased by someone else. But now I had my *own* that were *mine*.

So that's something.

I stopped to look out our living room window. Being on the sixth floor of an apartment building that stands on top of a mountain results in spectacular views. We faced North, away from the city and toward the mountains, so if you didn't look down at the street below, all you could see were low-slung clouds caught on forested mountain peaks. It was amazing.

Dad appeared in the doorway with another heavy box. "Which room is yours, Stella?"

"That one!" It was just a square white room, but to me, it was full of potential. A fresh start, and a new world. It was about time.

Those first weeks living with Kate were some of the best times of my life. I loved the freedom. We explored our neighbourhood, studied campus maps, and Kate even convinced me to attend the new student "Welcome" events that the university put on.

"I like you and all, but I want more friends," she said. "Including some gay friends. So get over your social anxiety and show up with me."

I despise organized cheerfulness, which the Welcome stuff had in spades, but it wasn't so bad attending with Kate, who never took anything too seriously and always made me laugh. She joined the University LGBTQ group, and I browsed some of the other groups with vague interest. I'm not a fan of meeting new people, and I didn't know how bad my workload would be, so I didn't want to commit myself to anything. Then I discovered that they had a Kung Fu club, and I signed up immediately.

"Are the classes beginner classes?" I asked the guy at the sign-up table, a really tall guy named John Zhang.

He nodded. "No experience needed."

"It's just that I have a brown belt."

He looked surprised. "In what?"

"Sanshou and Taolu," I said. "My club did forms and sparring, and some stuff with blades. Chanquan, Jian… But I haven't done it in a couple of years. I'd like to get back in shape."

"Great, well, why don't you sign up for the classes and we can see where you're at?"

So that was pretty cool.

That night, Kate knocked on my bedroom door at nearly ten o'clock.

"Are you awake in there?"

I opened the door. "Yeah, I'm just messing around on the computer. Why?"

"Because I'm hungry."

"Okay," I said. "Uh. You want me to show you how to use the microwave?"

"No. I want you to come outside with me because I realized that we are adults now and we can just, like, take a ten p.m. walk to get fast food because there is no one to stop us."

I stared at her for a moment. "Yes. We should do this."

So we went for a walk. In the dark. At ten at night. We got food to go and walked home and then ate burgers in our kitchen at eleven just because we could.

"Being a grown-up is amazing," I said. "We should just, like, keep being grownups for the rest of our lives."

"Right?" said Kate.

Just then, I got a text from Dad.

I want you to know that I am naked in the living room
and so is your mother.
I hope you're enjoying being an independent adult
as much as we're enjoying you being an independent adult.

I grinned and wrote him back right away.

Oh, I am.

I ran into Howie's father on my second day of classes. He was walking down the hall as I left my Biology class. He must have known I was there — Howie's whole family had made it clear to me that they were very aware of my brain at any given time, but he didn't glance at me.

"Dr. Mullins!" I called very loudly. His step faltered, and he glanced back. I waved. Would he blow me off? No. He stopped and began polishing his glasses on his shirt.

"Hello, Stella," he said.

"How are you?" I asked.

"Very busy," he said. "It was nice to see you again."

"Wait!" I said. "How is..." but he had already disappeared into the crowd.

"Asshole," I muttered to myself.

"Okay, very rude and hurtful and all that," said Kate that evening, lounging on our severely-secondhand couch. "But you know, you did break the heart of his youngest son. Also, he's a dick. My mom's a lab assistant in the Biology department, remember? She's had to work with him before and he's just not a friendly person. She calls him The Zombie because he's so heartless."

"He was never a dick to me," I said. "He was never exactly, like, *warm,* but he was always polite and reasonably welcoming."

"Yeah, back then you were dating his son," she said. "Now you aren't. I don't think parents are very friendly to people who break their kids' hearts." She held up her hand as I opened my mouth. "Not that you didn't have very valid — if weirdly secret — reasons for doing so."

I had been going to say that he *knew* our relationship couldn't last forever, but I couldn't very well tell Kate that without explaining why, which I was forbidden to do, so I shut my mouth.

"Let it go, Idina Menzel-style," said Kate. "That's my advice."

So I sat down and watched Discovery channel with her and didn't say anything more. But I really, really wished Doc Mullins could have given me an update on Howie. Because if the Doc wasn't even talking to me, well, that didn't exactly suggest that Howie was doing great.

It made me feel sick to think that I was rebuilding my life, having fun with Kate in university, and Howie was probably curled up at home on his bed, still breaking his heart over me.

Howie

It felt strange to be so far away from Stella's brain waves, but in a way, it was also a relief. When she had been five minutes away from me, her mind was a constant, sweet torment. Now, as I drove away from her into the dark unknown, there was an emptiness around me where she should have been. I didn't know if I would ever feel it again. But I remembered how she had looked, less than twelve hours before, when I watched her disappear in a swirl of laughter and glimmer into that limousine, and I knew that I would do whatever it took to keep her safe.

Even if it meant that I had to risk my life and soul in the process.

My family didn't know that I had gone. I couldn't tell them — they never would have agreed to it. So I had packed my bag with only a few changes of clothes, and a book that Stella had given me. I had wanted to bring something of her, some memory. But I couldn't risk bringing anything that would identify her — or me. I hung briefly over a love letter she had once written me, and I tried to memorize the words before tucking it back safely in a drawer. Then I sat down and wrote a letter of my own — to my family.

Carefully, deliberately, I followed the directions that I had been given. I ditched my car and my phone, and I climbed into the replacement car that waited for me, its keys lying under a carefully placed rock. My new identity documents were in the glove compartment, along with printed directions.

I drove through the starry summer night, trying not to think about it all, until I reached a ramshackle farmhouse in the outskirts of Seattle. I knew immediately that I was in the right place. The minds inside weren't the minds of normal humans. They were like my family's minds: inedible, unattractive, bland. But there was something else, too, and it filled me with horror.

I sat in the darkness, watching the June dawn. Was I brave enough for this? And more importantly — was I smart enough? Because if I failed… I quailed at the thought of what could happen.

But really, I reflected, if they discovered and killed me, would it really matter? What future did I have, anyway? Could I even go home? What if I came across Stella someday, holding hands with someone else, or carrying a baby on her hip, or hobbling with a walker down the street… My heart cracked at the thought. And could I continue to live in a city where her most passionate emotions would surely reach and torture me?

No.

As soon as it was light, I took a deep breath and trudged up the front steps. I knocked on the door and when it opened I found myself looking at a man in his late twenties. He had dark hair and at least a week's worth of beard growth on his face. He looked at me with an intense glance. He seemed to be taking me in, analyzing me.

His mind made me think of locusts.

"Can I help you?" he said, but I could tell that he already knew what I was going to say.

"I'm here for eternity," I said, as I had been instructed.

His smile lacked any kind of human warmth. "Excellent. Come on in."

22

Stella

University suited me. The professors chucked information at us and moved on to the next topic without even checking to see if we understood, and I loved it. I loved learning at a pace that didn't bore me to tears. I loved living on top of a *fucking mountain*. On clear days, I got views of the entire city on my daily walk to class and I felt like I was walking on the roof of the world. Sometimes I looked down on clouds and then I'd text my parents and tease them about "the rain down there." I kept Snapchatting my friends back in Nova Scotia with these crazy awesome shots of mountains and clouds and skyscrapers and forests just to make them jealous and I realized that I had fallen in love — *finally* — with the city that my parents had dragged me to, kicking and screaming, nearly two years ago.

Kung fu turned out to be great, although the first session was terrifying. I don't like new people or new situations but I sucked it up and showed up to class anyway. They started introducing basic stuff, which I nailed, and then the Sifu singled me out and had me show off my stuff. I was a little rusty but I did an okay job.

We fell into a pattern in class. He would give the beginners a series of exercises and then come over and put me and the other higher-level belts through our paces. Sometimes the others would stop to watch us spar. I felt like I fit in there. I liked the Sifu, I liked John, I liked the other instructor — a girl called Melanie — and I liked the other people in the Kung Fu club. No one made fat jokes or treated me like garbage. They just opened up and included me, even as they pushed me to improve my style and technique.

I ended up getting drawn into the social life of the club. Sometimes we'd go out after class to a pub or their favourite noodle house. I loved hanging out with them, even though they were older than me. They laughed at my jokes. They actually seemed to enjoy my company. Before I knew it, I was thinking of them as friends.

For the first time since I was four years old, I was free of teasing and social harassment. SFU was so big that everyone had their own niche, and no one bothered me in mine. Sometimes I went for days without getting pissed off about *anything*. I just got up, ate breakfast, went to class, ate lunch, went to class, came home, made dinner, joked with Kate, and that was just, like, *my day*.

"This must be how it feels to be normal," I said once.

"Uh, hello, you *are* normal," Kate said. "You just needed to be in a place with wider standard deviations."

Kate snagged herself a girlfriend in, like, our third week. She texted me one night to tell me that she was going out with some people she had met at Out On Campus. I was reading in bed when I heard her come home, and from the voices, it sounded like several people had come home with her. I stayed in bed and eventually fell asleep. The next morning, I got up, walked into my kitchen, and found a tiny brown-skinned girl with long black hair and round glasses sitting at the table next to Kate.

"Hi," said the girl with a beaming smile.

"Uh, hi," I said.

"This is Riya," said Kate, looking very pleased with herself. "She's in my Gender Talk and Sexuality Studies classes. We hung out last night and she stayed over."

I resisted the urge to high-five her.

"Hi. I'm Stella, Kate's loud and socially awkward roommate." I poured myself some cereal and sat down at the table. I tried to think of something to say that wasn't, "Thanks for getting my friend laid; she really needed that."

Riya was studying me thoughtfully.

"Tell me, Stella," she said. "What's your idea of a perfect day?"

"Uh," I said, a little startled. "Hmm." Summer days spent with Howie flashed before my eyes. *No. Don't say Howie. Your perfect day can't involve the guy you broke up with.* "Probably a good sleep in, followed by breakfast in bed, and then reading all day at a park or somewhere else sunny and outdoors."

"No other people?" her brown eyes studied me.

I thought of Howie again. "Maybe an attractive man to read aloud to me. But that's optional."

She nodded. "And if you could develop one superpower, what would it be?"

I frowned as I thought. "Invisibility."

"One more. What is the best book that no one else has ever heard of?"

That one was easy. "*Tamsin,* by Peter S. Beagle. He wrote *The Last Unicorn,* which everyone knows, but *Tamsin* is so much better and no one has ever heard of it."

Riya smiled. "My perfect day would be going to a new country, where I had never been before, and eating the cuisine and walking through the streets and meeting the people there. Then I would find the nightlife and dance the night away. My superpower would be the ability to read other people's thoughts. And my book is *Stargirl* by Jerry Spinelli."

"I've read that! It really is great," I said.

Riya's smile grew even brighter. "There," she said. "Now we have really met each other."

We talked books over breakfast, and Riya gave Kate a lingering kiss before saying goodbye and leaving. As soon as the door closed, Kate turned to me. She looked *so* happy and it was adorable.

"So?" Kate said.

"Yeah, you can keep her."

I was so happy about not being in high school anymore that I felt really uncomfortable when I spotted someone I knew. Thankfully, that was rare and usually we just ignored each other. Once I passed a girl whom I had rescued a couple of times from bullies back in the day, and she gave me a big grin, which was nice.

Then, one day, I found myself passing Dean Kato.

My first instinct was to pretend I hadn't seen him, as per my usual modus operandi. But did Dean let me get away with that? Of course not.

"Stella! Stella!" He grabbed me by the elbow.

I feigned surprise. "Oh, hi!"

"I didn't know you were going here," he said.

"Well. I am. And apparently, so are you. So that's that sorted out."

"What are you taking?" He didn't seem to be in any kind of rush.

"Science. Biology," I said, and then because I didn't want to seem socially awkward, I felt obliged to add, "what about you?"

"Theatre," he said, "of course!"

"Right. You want to be on Broadway."

He did jazz hands. "Most of my classes are downtown, but I have to take some basic non-theatre courses to be 'well rounded', so here I am. Do you like it here?"

"Yeah," I said. "Listen, I've really got to get to class."

"We should meet up later, catch up! You still got my number?"

"Probably," I said. "But..."

"Come on, I insist," he said. "What are you doing tomorrow night?"

"Kung fu."

He looked startled. "What about the next night?"

"I have a test to study for."

"The night after that?"

"Kung fu again."

"You're making this up."

"Look, Dean, I really have to go. I'm not particularly interested in meeting up with you. You were a real shit stick at grad. Nice to see you and all of that. Bye." And I got the hell out of there.

Dean called that evening when I was in the middle of a Netflix marathon with Kate and Riya. When my ringtone went off, Kate leaned forward and looked at my phone, which was lying on the coffee table.

"Uh, Stell? Why are you getting a call from someone named Dildo?"

"Oh shit, that's Dean," I said. "Turn it off."

"DEAN KATO?"

"Yeah, I ran into him today and he tried to make me go out with him."

Kate picked up my phone and answered it. "Stella's phone. Yeah, she's right here and TOTALLY NOT DOING ANYTHING." Then she handed me the phone with an evil glint in her eye. "It's Dean Kato."

I gave her a dirty look, picked up the phone, and walked into the kitchen. "Yes?"

"One dinner, that's all I'm asking for," Dean said.

"Why, though?" I asked. "What do you want from me?"

"I was a dick, okay?"

"I'm listening."

"I like you. I've always liked you. I should have stood up for you when the guys teased you like that."

"I'm perfectly capable of standing up for myself. I'm pissed because you didn't stand up for yourself."

"Myself?" he sounded surprised and confused. What an idiot.

"Yes, you vapid ass-clown. Look. Do you think I'm hot, or not?"

There was an awkward pause on the end of the line. "Yeah," he said finally. "I do think you're hot."

"Okay, then. So when people asked you if you were going hogging, or going to weight watchers, or going whaling, or whatever else they said to you when they saw you with me, then you had two fucking choices: either tell them to fuck off, or look embarrassed to be seen with me. Guess what choice you made, every single fucking time? I have no interest in that. If you think girls who look like me are hot, then you are going to have to suck it up and be cool with that or you will be dating teeny little Barbie dolls for the rest of your life. There you go, a free relationship lesson. Now, go find someone else to be embarrassed by."

I ended the call to the sound of a whoop and a round of applause from the living room.

"I'm assuming you guys have switched to the hockey game and weren't eavesdropping on my conversation?" I called out.

"Uh, yeah, sports go sports!" Kate shouted.

My ringtone started up again. I sighed and answered the phone.

"What now, Dean?"

"Dinner. Just one."

"Ugh. Fine."

"How's Friday?"

Howie

The man's name was Brenden Abernathy, and he seemed to be in charge. There were other people in the house but they stayed quiet and let him talk. I already hated this place. Their minds were foul. But I reminded myself of why I was here, and when Brenden invited me to have a seat at the kitchen table, I sat. He sat across from me.

"Apex offers two paths," he said. "The first, you have already taken steps to pursue. How do you like it, so far?"

I swallowed. "It's… strange."

He nodded. "It takes a while to adjust. You've probably already figured out that the buzzing sensation you feel is caused by the minds of the people around you."

I nodded.

He gave me another humourless smile. "Tempted, at all?"

My stomach lurched and I tried not to let it show on my face. I gave an indecisive shrug.

"Maybe you think that super-healing and ageless living is enough," he said with a bit of a sneer. His voice had the rich emotional inflection of a normal person, yet his mind was anything but normal. "That's fine, of course. We can still make use of you within Apex. But if you are interested in pursuing the higher path…" He paused. Evidently, he had seen something in my face, some tiny flinch, or perhaps he felt the flicker in my mind, and he smiled again. "Yes, that's what we call it. The higher path. If you are interested, we have the means. If you enjoy the first sample, you will be asked to help us collect, of course, but people don't usually mind. Not once they've seen things from the other side."

Every instinct told me to run. Or better yet, kill them all and *then* run. But I was here for a reason. I needed to find out more. So I swallowed my revulsion and tried to walk the fine line between lies and truth.

"I'd like to learn more," I said. "But I don't think I'm ready just yet."

He spread his hands. "There's no rush. You can stay here for now, while we get to know you. Once we know where you'll fit best within Apex, we'll place you in another house. It might be in this city, or in another city. It depends." He folded his hands together again. "In the meantime, you're welcome to our supplies. The more… mundane… supplies are free for the first month, while you adjust. At the end of that month, you can either take a job within Apex, or you can go your own way and pay us $300 a month for supplies… or you can source your own." He gave another cold smile. "For now, you'll want to avoid the contents of the red freezer… until you change your mind. When you do, those supplies are always free."

"I'd like to hear more about that," I said. "Can you tell me more about how things work here?"

"Let us show you around," he replied.

His mind made me think of swarms of things. It felt wrong. It felt evil. I instinctively felt for my brain disruptor, which I had carried in my pocket for so long, but it wasn't there anymore. I'd left it behind, along with everything and everyone.

I followed him deeper into the house, clutching my bag, and I felt like I was walking to my doom.

Stella

I was unreasonably nervous about my dinner with Dean.

"Don't think about it like a real date," said Kate. "Think about it as a possibility for a swift rebound. A hook up to get Howie out of your system, and then move on."

Howie's name was like an anchor in my chest.

"I'm not sure I'm the rebound type," I said. "And I'm not sure I want to hook up with Dean Kato of all people."

"Then why even go?" Kate said.

"I don't know. Curiosity?"

I did get dressed up a bit. Just so I could feel good about myself. I put on a low-cut top that showed off my cleavage nicely and jeans that showed off my ass, and headed downstairs. I had told Dean to meet me outside my apartment building. Meeting at the restaurant was too awkward because then one of us would have to sit alone, but I definitely didn't want him to come up and interact with Kate, either.

He was already waiting and he was looking good. He hadn't completely overdone it in a tux or something the way Howie would have, but I could tell he had taken some care to look good for me. His dark hair was freshly gelled into place, and I could smell his cologne or aftershave or whatever it was from several feet away.

"Well, you look stunning," he said as I approached him.

"Thanks." I felt intensely awkward under his steady gaze. God, he was good looking.

"This is the part where you tell me how very studly you think I look."

"Well, I'm not hiding my face in horror, anyway," I said. "So, where are we going?"

He drove me to a sushi restaurant. Not a cheap bento box place like the sushi place on campus, but a fancy one with low tables, cushions instead of chairs, and private rooms with sliding wooden doors. I hesitated at outside.

"Dean, I'm from Nova Scotia. It's embarrassingly *white* over there. I didn't learn how to use chopsticks properly, and I may humiliate you. Maybe you should take me for pizza."

"Nope. You live here now, and sushi is part of Vancouver living."

"I've noticed. I'm just warning you, the chopstick situation is dire."

The first time I went for ramen with my kung fu friends, they were in stitches watching me try to lift the noodles out of the soup with chopsticks. Eventually, they took pity on me and asked the waiter for a fork. It was humiliating, especially because we were in a real ramen restaurant for real Asian people. Hell, most of the menu wasn't even in English — Mandarin and Japanese and Korean — so the waiter wasn't even sure they had a fork on the premises. But I guess they kept a few in the back for the ignorant people like me.

The next time we went, my friends asked for a fork for me from the start and the waiter gave me a *look.* Every time, I would try again and again to pick up those damn slippery noodles with chopsticks before finally giving up and picking up the fork. My friends teased me about it, but they did it in such an affectionate way that it didn't hurt my feelings.

But now I was going to have Dean Kato laughing at me, and that was the last thing I wanted.

I had to admit to Dean that I had no idea what anything was, so he ordered for us. You could tell it made him feel all important and manly, and I didn't love it. I don't like other people being in control; it makes me feel vulnerable and I *loathe* being vulnerable.

While we waited for the food, he tried to teach me how to use chopsticks. He kept readjusting my grip and then laughing and trying again.

"My Obachan used a wad of Kleenex and a couple of rubber bands to turn them into tweezers when I was a baby. Maybe I should do that for you."

"No, I can get this." I was sick of being the stupid white girl. I could destroy a zombie's skull with a cleaver — surely I could learn to use one of the world's most popular eating utensils. "Show me again."

By the time the food arrived I was starting to get the hang of it.

"Is your family Japanese?" I dropped my California roll and tried to pick it up again.

"My Dad's family. Mom's family is, oh, I dunno, Scottish or something. We don't talk about it that much, to be honest. Dad grew up here, so he and Mom are both just Canadian, you know? It's Dad's parents who came from Japan. I don't even speak Japanese. Not really. I know some baby words. That's about it."

I nodded. By now my California roll had completely fallen apart. "Goddamn it. Did you bring me here just so you could mock me?"

"Not just," he said with a grin.

"Risky move, Kato," I said, pointing my chopsticks at him and dropping one. "You're already on thin ice with me."

"How did I know that you couldn't use chopsticks? Who the hell doesn't know how to use chopsticks?"

"Nova Scotians. Even when you order Chinese food in Halifax, which is, like, the multicultural metropolis, it still comes with plastic forks."

"That's terrible."

"I'm not disagreeing," I said, successfully picking up a piece of tempura and feeling a surge of triumph. "But putting me in a position of humiliation probably isn't helping your case right now."

"But I have my natural wit and charm." He spread his arms wide.

"In case you haven't noticed, I'm not big on charm," I said. "I'm not the type to swoon every time you smile."

"Admit it — you swoon a little bit."

"Why would I admit to such a thing?"

"Because you agreed to have dinner with me. It took two phone calls, but you did it. I don't think you would ever have agreed if a tiny part of you wasn't charmed by me."

"Why do you care, Dean?" I asked. "Why me? Why don't you hunt down some other girl who doesn't already know what a dillweed you are?"

"Because you're funny? Because you're a challenge? Because you make a great Sally Jesse Raphael?" He shrugged.

"Be warned — if you're labouring under the popular belief that fat chicks are easy to get, you're barking up the wrong tree."

"You aren't fat."

I gave him a long stare.

"You're tall and curvy and sexy," he said.

"You're saying that because you think fat is bad, and you don't want to admit that you like fat girls," I said. "You can call me what you want, Dean, but people call me fat. They used to do it to my face. That doesn't happen anymore, but if you were to date me, I guarantee that your friends would do it behind my back. So get used to it now."

He opened his mouth and closed it. "I've never had a date like this one."

"You've never been on a date with me."

"Clearly." He leaned forward, and his brown eyes were strangely serious. "But listen, Stella. I like you, okay? I do. You know that. And I do think you're hot. And I agree that I have to grow up and be cool about that. I hear you. They're all really good points."

"But?"

"But this is not a job interview. You are not the boss, and I'm not applying for a vacant position. I'm not going to go around jumping through hoops to try to earn the right to date you. That's garbage. Okay? So, now it's time for you to tell me — do *you* think *I'm* hot and do *you* like *me*? Because either you do, and we should give this a shot, or you don't and I'm... well, I won't say wasting my time because I'm having fun tonight and I think you desperately needed that chopstick lesson, but I'll stop thinking it's going to go anywhere."

Well, shit.

Dean watched me carefully as I did some frantic introspection. Yes, of course I thought he was hot. He made me laugh, and I genuinely enjoyed his company. All of my complaints about him came down to the fact that he hung around with shit sticks and tried to make excuses for their shit stick behaviour. That and the fact that he was a charming flirt, and I was naturally suspicious of charming flirts.

Once upon a time, I would never have dared take the chance of getting close to someone like Dean. He was a risk. He could hurt me. But maybe I was ready to take that risk. After all, better to take a risk on someone I don't like very much, right? If he hurt me, well, fuck him, I never liked him anyway.

So I took a gamble. "Okay, Dean. I do think you're cute, and sometimes you're funny. So maybe this could go somewhere. But you have to promise to try not to be a shit stick."

He grinned, showing off his sexy man dimples. "I promise to try not to be a shit stick if you promise to try not to be so thorny. You're like a rose. Lovely from a distance but dangerous if you get close."

Okay, I kind of loved that simile. But roses made me think of Howie, and my insides twisted up.

"I don't know if I have control over my thorniness. I mean, I'm working on it, but it's sort of an ongoing character arc."

"I like my women with a bit of zest to them, anyway."

"Let's start there," I said. "I want to be clear: I am not one of your 'women'. I refuse to be part of a harem in any way. So if you are seriously interested in me, keep that in mind."

He studied me. "I am seriously interested in you." He pointed to one of our plates. "Now, try the unagi."

23

Stella

After dinner — Dean tried to pay but I'm swift like a ninja and tapped the machine with *my* card first — Dean and I walked around in the crisp autumn evening and talked. He kept things light. He told me stories about his summer working on the stage crew for his mother's theatre company and about his new classes at SFU. He asked me about my classes and then he asked how I had gotten into kung fu.

"My parents put me in it when I was a kid. They thought it would help me learn self-control, and I hoped it would help me deal with bullies."

"And did it work?"

"Yeah, I flipped a couple of bullies onto their backs and got some serious detention time but they stopped bothering me after that. I kept going with the kung fu because after a rough day at school it felt really good to punch and kick something, even if it was just the air. It helped me feel more balanced. But when we moved here I didn't really see any places that offered the style I had learned. Kung fu isn't actually all that common, except in the movies. People do Jiu Jitsu or Karate or Taekwondo or Kick Boxing..."

"Did you miss it, when you moved here?"

"A little." I couldn't tell him that I worked out my aggressions on about a hundred zombies instead, nor that having a boyfriend had given me a different kind of outlet for my pent-up energies. "I was pretty happy to find out they had a club here."

"So I had better watch out, or you might use your kung fu moves on me."

I laughed. "I managed not to kick you in the head during high school, so you're probably out of danger now."

"I would have deserved it."

I thought it was wiser not to agree.

"Where are you living?" I asked, changing the subject.

"At my parents' house. It's cheaper, you know? It's cool though. My parents have a basement suite in their house, so I basically have my own place. I'm paying them a token amount, plus some extra chores."

I glanced at Dean. He was shorter than Howie — about the same height as me. His broad shoulders looked good, and our conversation seemed so… normal. No zombies, no government agents, no brains or cannibalism. Just normal people talking about normal stuff. It was nice.

Our walk looped around until we were back at his car and he drove me back up the winding, forested road to Burnaby Mountain. Looking out his car window, I could see the lights from the city below us twinkling between the trees. Dean parked near my building and insisted on walking me to my door while I frantically tried to think of how to politely end a date. I wanted to think of something witty and laid-back, but my mind was a blank.

"Well, thanks for a nice evening or some bullshit like that," I said finally looking away and focusing on the glittering city panorama in the distance. "I don't know what you say to end a date, so insert the appropriate comment here."

Dean cupped the side of my face with his hand, drew me toward him, looked at me for a moment with his dark eyes, and kissed me.

This was my first kiss with a normal human male, and I had to admit, it was pretty good. It was warm. Howie had always been slightly cool to the touch. Not cold, but comfortably cool. Dean's mouth felt hot by comparison. He kissed like an expert, too. It was a confident, seductive sort of a kiss that definitely made me feel feelings. I broke it off after a few seconds because I needed to stop and process things a bit. I was a churning pot of weird emotions.

Dean didn't push it any farther. He just winked at me.

"Thank *you* for a wonderful evening." He sauntered to his car, then turned around and gave me a wave before getting in. I waved back, felt pathetic, and quickly went inside.

I ran up the stairs and banged into the apartment. Kate popped out of her room. "Is that you?"

"No, it's a murderer. What kind of a weird-ass question is that?"

"So? How was it?"

"Not bad. We ate sushi. He kissed me."

"Ooooooooooh!" Kate said.

Riya also emerged from Kate's room and put on her glasses. "Details?" she said eagerly.

"I'm not really the kind of person who does detailed dissections of her dates," I told her.

"She really isn't," Kate agreed. "Stella doesn't kiss and tell." She turned back to me. "Okay, without going into messy details, I guess you decided that you don't hate him?"

"I don't know," I said, kicking off my shoes and collapsing onto the couch. "Let's say that I don't hate him enough *not* to kiss him, and I'm going to give him a chance to show me that he has hidden depths."

"Hmph," said Kate. "You know, you can want someone and not actually like them. You don't have to reconcile that cognitive dissonance if you don't want to. People hate-fuck people all the time."

"I'll keep that in mind, thanks. I just..." I rubbed my face. "I'm very conflicted right now. I feel like I just cheated on Howie."

"Well, you need to get over *that,*" said Kate. "You broke up with him like six months ago and you haven't been in contact with him since. I'd say there are basically no grey areas there."

"Was Howie your first boyfriend?" Riya asked.

I nodded.

She looked at Kate. "There you are, then. It's hard to get past your first."

"But you managed it, right?" Kate said.

Riya reached up to her and gave her a passionate kiss. "Definitely. And Stella can, too."

I went to bed thinking about Dean's kiss and tried really hard not to think about how Howie would feel if he knew.

Howie

Brenden introduced me to a gaunt, middle-aged woman named Jess and a tall, freckled blond man named Craig. Their brains both felt like the part of a horror movie that you wish you hadn't watched.

"Why don't you start by showing him the freezers?" Brenden suggested to Jess, who gave me a smile that sent chills down my spine. She led me to the basement.

The red freezer wasn't really red. It was a regular, if large, deep freeze in plain white. But all of its edges and corners were lined with red duct tape, so it stood out clearly. It also had an expensive-looking and elaborate lock with a number keypad. The other deep freeze was also plain white with no red trim and no lock.

"The fridge upstairs is stocked at all times with meals from the white freezer," said Jess. "We label one serving a day with your name. What *is* your name?"

I thought frantically. What did my new identification say? Oh, right. "Ian. Ian Whitby."

"The red freezer is kept locked at all times. Only Brenden knows the code," said Jess. "If you want a sample, talk to him."

That would make it harder to open it, take photos of the contents, and send them as evidence. Then again, I wasn't sure if I knew how to do all of those things using a telephone, anyway, but I knew it should be possible. The new one that I had been given was a smartphone and a far cry from my old Nokia cellular.

"Which freezer do you eat out of?" I asked Jess, but I could tell from the feel of her. She showed teeth that looked old and stained.

"You stay here for a while, and then you guess," she said. "The red freezer people stand out, you could say."

She pointed to my bag. "Let me take you to your room. By the way, hand over your phone, now. No communications within this building. We'll hold it in trust for you, for when you leave."

I was rattled. "I don't have a phone."

She squinted at me and folded her arms. "Who doesn't have a phone?"

"I left it behind. I thought I was supposed to leave things behind." I focused as hard as I could on the truth of my statement because I knew she was checking my brain waves, feeling for lies. I could *feel* her feeling me and it was like ants crawling through my brain. "I threw it into the water."

It had been a surprising wrench, watching my old Nokia plunk into the ditch water near where I left my car. All those messages of love from Stella lost in the mud and the weeds.

"Hmm." She turned away and pointed up the stairs. "Come on, then." She led me upstairs to a bedroom with two sets of bunk beds. "The bottom bunk is free on the left. We just placed the girl who was there yesterday."

"Where do people get placed?"

"Where Apex needs them."

I dropped my bag on one of the bunks and brushed my hands nervously on my slacks. "So… what now?"

"We have a group meeting at eight p.m. Until then, I guess just make yourself at home. That bottom drawer in the bureau is yours."

She left me alone with the door ajar. I opened my bag and unpacked my small supply of clothes into the lowest drawer. I checked over my shoulder and pulled the new phone Baum had given me from an inner pocket. Pretending to rummage inside my bag, I tried to figure out my phone. I pressed my finger on the little pad and it read my fingerprint and unlocked. I looked frantically at the many different icons. I had seen Stella use her smartphone many times; surely I could figure this out. How did I send a message?

Oh, yes, there was a message icon.

I touched it and it rushed toward me and opened up into a new screen. Hmm. The message list was empty. Now what?

I heard a noise outside the door and quickly tucked the phone back into the inner pocket and pulled out my book, instead. I placed the bag conspicuously on the foot of my bed — so it would look as if I had nothing to hide — and lay down with my book.

Just last night, I was standing on Stella's street, holding a rose in my hand and breaking my heart over her beauty. How had everything changed so quickly? My family must just be waking up now, must be noticing my absence, maybe were even reading my letter to them. I had begged them not to tell Stella that I was missing. I hoped they would grant me that wish. She could never be happy if she knew, and I wanted her to be happy. I wanted her to have a life.

After all, that was part of why I was here.

As frightened and depressed as I felt, I was also exhausted from driving all night. Within half an hour, I managed to hide from the fear and the pain in the questionable comfort of sleep.

"Hey, new guy." I opened my eyes and saw a girl leaning over me. She had a cherubic face and blue streaks in her hair. She looked like your average fresh-faced teen girl, a little on the curvy side, and quite pretty... except for the fact that she had the pale, dingy skin tone and hazy eyes of a zombie like me, and the brain waves of one, too. Not the creepy, crawling minds of Brenden and Jess, but like my own family.

My thoughts drifted to Stella. How could her parents even think that I might have wanted to turn Stella into something like me? I would have still loved her, yes, and been attracted to her too, no doubt, but to ruin brain waves as exquisite as Stella's, well... it would be like smashing an original Stradivarius or pouring water on the Mona Lisa. I wondered what this girl's brain had been like before she had inflicted this on herself.

"Hi," I mumbled, rubbing my eyes. "Name's..." I hesitated. *Oh, right.* "Ian."

"I'm Cassie," she said, and I noticed that she shared my 'flattened affect', as Dad called our monotonous way of speaking. "Welcome to the land of the living."

"Is that what you call it?"

"Well. If this does what it says it does, then we're going to outlive just about everybody, right?"

"It's just... strange."

"Yeah, but it's a nice change for me. I thought everyone was going to outlive me." She showed me scars on her wrists. "I was recovering and this nurse slipped me his number and instructions on installing Tor and going to the site on the dark web."

None of that sentence made any sense to me but I nodded knowingly. "What made you decide to go ahead with it?" I asked.

"I guess I was curious. My life couldn't suck any worse so I thought, sure, I'll inject myself with this mystery vial and see what happens. And if it killed me, I didn't really care."

"So how do you feel now?"

"It's weird... My old life doesn't really feel real. And there's no point in cutting anymore because I can't feel pain anyhow. So I guess it's good. It's different. I needed different," she said. "What about you? How'd you find out about this?"

"I was in the hospital too," I said, truthfully. I didn't mention that it was nearly sixty years ago.

"And why'd you go for it?" she pushed.

"I was sick. This saved my life," I said, falling back on honesty once again.

"Cancer? Or something else?"

"Yeah," I said. "So, do you think everyone here got recruited at hospitals?"

She shook her head no. "Most of the people here seem to have found it themselves on the dark web, and got interested. Especially those red freezer types, but some of the white freezer people too." She sat down next to me on my bunk. "So," she said. "Have they pushed the red freezer on you, yet?"

"Yes. But I don't think I'm ready for that. You?"

"I'm not really sure what the red freezer thing is totally about, to be honest. The Apex stuff I was looking at on Tor didn't mention red freezers. But they just look at you like you're stupid if you ask. It seems to be like a sort of drug they put in the meat?"

I opened my mouth and closed it again. Better not to say anything. "Sort of, but I don't think it's a good idea."

"The red freezer people creep me out. Their brains feel weird. But most people go for it in the end, so I dunno. I've been here three weeks so my month is almost up. If they don't find a place for me soon, I don't know what I'm gonna do."

I was disappointed that she couldn't confirm what the red freezer was, but really, I already knew.

Stella

Dean called me around lunchtime the next day.

"I'm eating lunch," I said into my phone, without a proper greeting, because I have problems.

"Sorry, I just woke up," he said. "I was up until three a.m. watching reruns of *CSI: Miami.* There was a marathon."

"Seriously?"

"It's so bad, Stella! It's amazing how bad that show was."

"So you spent hours watching a show you weren't enjoying, rather than sleep?"

"Oh, you misunderstand. I was enjoying it thoroughly. I love terrible TV shows and movies. *CSI: Miami* was pretty great, but it wasn't as ridiculous as *CSI: Cyber* which is one of my absolute favourite shows ever."

"I haven't seen it."

"It's fantastically bad. You'll have to watch it with me. In fact, why don't you come over to watch it?"

"Come over to your house to watch terrible TV dramas?"

"Have you got anything better to do?"

"Not really," I admitted. "But I'm not sure I'm ready to go over to your place. You might dismember me and bury me under the floorboards. Why don't you come over here?"

"Planning on using your roommate as a chaperone?" he teased.

"Actually, she's going to be out tonight," I said, rolling my eyes at Kate. "She has a thing." She and Riya were going to some kind of wine and cheese party. I thought it sounded dreadful and I was grateful that Kate had Riya to drag along to this kind of thing, now, so I could stay home.

"Either way," Dean said cheerfully. "What time?"

"Uh. How about seven?"

"Sounds good. See you then. Brace yourself for technobabble melodrama as you've never experienced it before."

"I'll try. Bye." I ended the call and looked at Kate. "So, if I text you the words "help", I'm going to ask you to suddenly remember that you forgot your purse and come rushing back to save me."

Kate nodded. "Yeah, I can do that. It wouldn't be that far to come back. But hopefully, it won't be that bad."

"Why are you making me watch this? This is the stupidest thing I've ever seen," I said to Dean that night. "This guy is supposed to be a crime-boss hacker but he has his password tattooed on his arm?"

Dean flashed me one of his white-toothed grins. "Yeah, don't you know that all the best hackers keep their passwords in plain sight? Especially when they're being investigated by the police for stealing babies because, you know, that's what hackers do: Baby stealin'."

"WAIT," I said, sitting up straight. "WHY IS THAT GUY RAPPING?"

"Oh, that's Lil' Bow Wow. He plays a hacker rapper," said Dean, grinning broadly. "He figures out stuff by rapping."

"ARE YOU FUCKING SERIOUS?" I couldn't help it; I started to laugh, and once I got started I couldn't stop. I was helpless with laughter while Dean just sat back and watched me with evident enjoyment. When I finally managed to get myself under control, I wiped my eyes and shook my head at Dean. "*Why* do you own this on DVD?"

"Look, television this terrible is an art form," he insisted. "I mean, if you sat down and *tried* to make something this ridiculous, you might fail. But they managed it. Don't you see? It's wonderful *because* it's so bad. It's a testament to the complete lack of critical thinking that most people enjoy."

"Oh, I get it," I said. "It makes you feel smart."

Dean stretched his legs out on my coffee table. "Maybe that's part of it. I just love shows that seem like parodies of themselves. It's just my sense of humour."

I had been waiting for Dean to make a move, but he was being smart and giving me my space. When he first arrived I made some popcorn and set it in a big bowl on the table, and then we both sat down on the couch. Dean sat close to me, but not touching me, and he hadn't tried to get his arm around me yet.

Maybe he wasn't going to try any moves. I started to relax.

But I underestimated Dean's expertise at making moves.

I first noticed it at the end of the second episode: The space between us on the couch was significantly smaller, and now our legs were almost touching. By midway through the third episode, our legs were touching. He started looking at me more and more. I could *feel* him looking at me. I tried to redirect him back to the show.

"I hope you know that I'm going to need some kind of counselling to help me overcome the damage you've caused tonight," I said, gesturing at the television.

His eyes remained steadily on me. "I'm sorry to hear that," he said, and he reached out and tucked a lock of my hair behind my ear. I turned, startled, and got caught by his dark eyes. "I'll have to think of a way to make it up to you." His face was very close to mine, now, and I began to feel flustered. His breath was very minty. Had he popped a mint?

His hand traced its way down my cheek, along the side of my arm, and down to my waist. He drew me toward him, closing the small gap between us. I wasn't really sure what to do, so I did nothing. He studied me for another moment, and then he leaned in and kissed me.

At first, it was very gentle, just a soft brush of his warm lips on mine, but I felt it deep inside my body. He pulled back and looked at me for my reaction, which was probably one of dilated eyes and throbbing hormones. After all, with the exception of our brief kiss the night before, it had been months since I had been kissed and touched by someone this way.

When he pulled me in for the second kiss, it was anything but gentle. It was firm and ardent, and it took my breath away. His hands ran up and down my body possessively, and I began to explore his muscular arms in return. He was so fucking hot. I couldn't believe that I had the right to touch him. Then he took my hands and placed them under his shirt onto his warm, smooth skin. He pressed himself against me, his breath burning down my neck.

Holy shit.

It was different from a make-out session with Howie. Kissing Howie had always felt very intimate. It was full of feelings. Kissing Dean was different. This felt more carnal. He turned me on, I turned him on, so here we were. There was no love, no honesty, but at the moment I didn't give two flying bat craps. How often do you get a chance to run your hands all over the firm, muscled torso of the hottest guy in your high school?

It might be different, but it wasn't bad. It wasn't bad at all.

24

Howie

This was bad. This was so very bad. My skin was crawling just being in the house with these people, but the thought of what they were, and what they could do, made me even more determined to find a way to bring them down.

Cassie showed me to the living room, which doubled as a library. All four walls were covered with books — heavy tomes, not paperback novels. Two women and a man were lounging on chairs, leaning over their books with focused intensity. I shuddered at the feel of their minds. I remembered the vibrant bliss of Stella's brain and reflected that I was now surrounded by its antithesis. The contrast was jarring — like passing a construction site after a night at the symphony, or turning away from a breathtaking vista only to encounter a war zone. I simmered with hatred for this place. How long would I have to be here, to learn what I needed to know?

I browsed the shelves and found texts on everything from biochemistry to quantum mechanics.

"No fiction?" I asked Cassie, who was watching me. "Poetry?"

She laughed. "Yeah, no. They're not really the bedtime story type. We're supposed to be improving ourselves. I've tried, but I don't understand what any of the books are talking about, and what I do understand, I forget." She shrugged. "I was never very good at school."

"I can't say that I'm any good at remembering things either." I ran my finger down the spine of a book on subatomic physics. "So what do you do, if you don't study this stuff?"

"Not much — there's no TV. I have a tablet and they let me use that since there's no WIFI here. We're not allowed to use the internet, which is pretty stupid considering that I wouldn't have even known about this place if it weren't for the internet."

"Do they say why?"

"Oh, the location is super-secret and they say they have to move if anyone so much as sends a text message from here."

My mission was looking increasingly complicated.

George Baum's phone call last night had filled me with curiosity. I didn't hate him the way Stella did. I had known him for much longer than she had, and Baum had always been passionate about putting a stop to the virus and protecting the Canadian people. That was why he hated my family so much — he thought we were a danger. It was hard for someone who knew him well to imagine him deliberately releasing the virus onto innocent people. Stella was convinced of his guilt, but I wasn't so sure.

Nevertheless, the fact remained that he despised my family. So why was he calling me in the middle of the night?

He refused to tell me over the phone, so the only way to satisfy my curiosity was to set my phone to silent, put some pillows under my blankets to make it look occupied, and sneak out to meet him at the local mall. If Stella had known that I was sneaking off to meet Agent Baum in the dead of night, she would have been furious. But I have more faith in people than she does.

He was standing in the parking lot, and I almost didn't recognize him: it felt very strange to see him in a sweater and jeans, instead of a uniform.

"You are brave to agree to meet with me," he had said when I walked up to him. "I commend you."

I shrugged. "My life doesn't feel very valuable to me right now."

"I take it that you're pining for that foul-mouthed young girl. I heard that she had come to her senses."

I just looked at him.

"I have no fondness for Stella Blunt, as you can imagine."

I pretended to look surprised. "Really? Is it because she discovered that you were spying on me then accused you of framing my father, then beat you up and left you taped to a chair?"

He ignored that, determined to stay on script. "However, I do applaud her choice to move on and seek out healthier relationships."

I felt dizzy for a moment. "She's seeking out other relationships? How do you know all this, anyway?"

He ignored that, too. "As you know, I consider your kind to be a threat to the health and safety of the Canadian people." He paused and waited for me to argue, but I kept silent. After a moment, he continued. "I have long suspected that your father's discovery could be used for evil by rival governments."

I could imagine Stella laughing at his language, but I continued to listen quietly.

"My concerns have grown continually, and have been compounded by recent events, namely the outbreak last year which I certainly am *not* responsible for, and the current rash of deaths in cities around the globe, most notably in Seattle."

Now I spoke up. "Agent Hunt says there's no evidence of the virus in those deaths."

"There wouldn't need to be, would there?" He folded his arms.

I was silent, but he continued to wait for my answer. I knew what he was referring to. But it was forbidden to discuss it. "No," I said eventually. "I suppose not."

"Before your dear Stella had me suspended from my duties, I was tracking several worrisome individuals based in Washington. I had reason to believe that they had contacts in Vancouver, and that they were trying to procure samples of the virus. What I was not able to ascertain before my security clearances were revoked, was whether they were operating under the direct instruction of the American government, or who their contacts in Vancouver were. I suspected them to be your family."

I spoke firmly. "No."

"Are you certain?"

"Yes."

He nodded. "If not you, then it has to be someone else within The Service, and unfortunately, the information I had gathered may serve as evidence against me at my tribunal. You can understand how eager I am to reveal the real culprit."

I nodded.

"I am also seriously concerned that the events in Seattle were deliberate and may be at the sanction of the US government, so I don't believe that it is reasonable to leave the investigation of those incidents to the Americans."

"Why would they do something like that?"

"Why would they build an army of intelligent, nearly-immortal, instantly-healing warriors?"

"The negative side effects would make it impossible," I said. "I remember Dad's experiment at MIT. It was... it was awful. No one could control that. It would be too dangerous."

"The negative consequences could be dose dependent. They are probably experimenting further with human subjects."

"By killing homeless people?"

He shrugged. "You couldn't do something like that as an official government program. You need to have plausible deniability. But I know for a *fact* that an American government employee was soliciting someone in Vancouver for samples of the virus, and now there is someone stealing human neural tissue from corpses in Seattle. Take from that what you will, and think about the potential harm."

I thought about the terrible results of my father's experiment at MIT in the seventies, which was classified at the top level of secrecy. Very few people were supposed to know. But if the information got out... I shuddered at the thought.

Baum had been watching me, and he nodded at my reaction. "Now I need *you* to help me put a stop to it."

"Why me, and how?"

As I listened to his plan, I realized that this could be the stupidest, most dangerous thing I had ever done. But I also realized that if he was right, it could also be the most important.

Now here I was, surrounded by these awful minds and I had no idea how to find out what they were up to, or how we could stop them. I took a risk and turned to Cassie, the only person around who didn't feel like a night terror.

"Do you know why they want us to study so much science? Do you know what their plans are?"

"Oh yeah, they never shut up about it." Cassie pulled a thick three-ring binder off of the shelf and passed it to me. "We're supposed to read this. It's Apex's orientation guide."

My fingers curled around it. "Thank you."

Stella

I was really enjoying the make-out session until Dean unhooked my bra.

He did it like an expert – we were hot-and-heavy on the couch and suddenly I felt a ping and the cups of my bra came loose. I pulled back.

"Did you just unhook my bra?" I asked.

"God, you're sexy," he said and tried to pull me back into the kiss.

"Uh, no, that's over," I said. "I want to talk about the bra thing."

"Sorry, I got carried away," he said. "Did you not like it?"

"No, I would appreciate it if you would check with me before you try to remove items of clothing from my body," I said sharply.

"That wouldn't be very romantic, would it?" he asked. "Excuse me, do you mind if I tear off your clothes?"

"Uh, yeah, that's called consent," I said. "It's definitely romantic to obtain it."

He held his hands up. "WHOA. Are you comparing me to a *rapist*? Because I stopped the *moment* you told me to, so I would *really* appreciate it if you would assume that I'm already well versed in the idea of *consent*."

"Okay, okay, you aren't a rapist," I conceded, "I'm just not used to having my bra get popped without any kind of warning."

"Howard have trouble with the hook?" he smirked.

"Howie would have *asked* first," I snarled, "but do you really want to turn this into a conversation about my ex-boyfriend?"

Dean regarded me seriously for a moment. "Maybe we need to," he said. "I think that we might need to work a few things out, don't you?"

"Like what?" I fiddled behind myself, trying to re-hook my bra strap.

"Let me," he said. I turned and let him fasten my bra back up.

"Thanks," I muttered, smoothing down my shirt and readjusting things in front.

"Listen, I don't need to hear all the nitty-gritty details of the relationship," he said, "and I don't want to. But I think we need to check and make sure we're on the same page. You were dating him for, what, a year?"

"Yes. Are you going to tell me about your relationships, too?"

"Sure, I can. I've had four girlfriends. I had sex with two of them. I've also had sex with a couple of girls outside of a relationship — your casual hook up kind of thing."

"Please, please tell me that none of those girls were Kelly Svancara," I said.

He grinned. "I swear. None of those girls were really my type, but Kelly is *really* not my type."

"So you weren't actually attracted to any of your girlfriends? That's what you're trying to tell me?"

"Oh, I was, but mostly because I was a horny teenage boy and they had breasts. They just never had as *much* breast, and ass, and all the things I love as I would have liked." He eyed me for a moment. "Mmm. That's all I'm saying. *Mmmm.*"

I tried not to smile.

"Now," he said. "Your turn."

"Howie was my first relationship," I said. "It was serious. It couldn't continue for reasons I don't want to get into but it wasn't because we didn't care about each other."

"Well, I figured it was serious. Was it serious… physically?"

"Sort of. No, we didn't have actual penetrative sex if that's what you are trying to find out. But it was… physical."

He nodded slowly. "And is there any particular reason that it didn't progress to sex?"

"He wasn't ready."

Dean's thick eyebrows rose into his hairline. "That's…" he shook his head. "Okay. You just said that you were still in love with him when you broke up. Who ended it?"

"I did."

He let out a breath. "Are you still hung up on him?"

I hesitated, but only for a moment. I believe in the truth. "I still care about him. But it's definitely over. I haven't seen him or heard from him since March, and we both know that we can't be together."

"Because of reasons," he said with a hint of a tease in his voice.

"Right."

"So am I wasting my time here? Because, while I would love to get you into bed, I don't think I'm going to if you're a virgin who's still not over her ex-boyfriend."

"If you're looking for sex tonight, then consider your time wasted. I barely know you," I said.

"I'm not worried about tonight. I want to get to know you, and if you want to build a relationship before we have the sex conversation again, I'm cool with that. But I would need to know that it would actually be *possible.*"

I have to admit, I never thought that Dean could be so mature about stuff like this. Howie blushed whenever sex came up, even though you could tell that he was practically bursting at the seams. Dean was treating it so matter-of-factly, as if we were just talking about dinner or movie genres or something. I wasn't used to that. Also, and maybe this is wrong, but the phrase, "I would love to get you into bed" struck me as really sexy.

I didn't have to think for very long. I had already thought most of this through at the restaurant last night.

"You aren't wasting your time. I don't know if this is something that could work, because I still suspect you of being a shit stick, but if I'm wrong, then it's *possible*. But yeah, you're going to have to pursue a relationship with me before I'm willing to have the 'getting you into bed' conversation again."

"Alright then," he said. "I'm glad we cleared that up. Now, come here and kiss me again, because you are *banging* hot. Just name a base."

It took me a moment to figure out what he was talking about. I had never once heard Howie refer to getting to a "base" with me, although he must have known the terms.

"Uh, second base," I said. "No clothing removal."

"Okay," he said, leaning in. "Now get that sexy bod over here."

I half-expected Dean to drop me, now that he knew that he wasn't going to get laid anytime soon. When I didn't hear from him at all the next day, I considered this confirmation of my suspicions. So I was a little surprised when he called me at nine p.m.

"Hey, baby. Do you want to grab a slice of pizza?"

"I'm not sure — I'm so put off by being infantilized that I don't know how to respond."

Dean laughed. "Not goo-goo ga-ga baby. Like, my *bae*."

"I'll come to pizza with you if you promise never to use that abomination of an endearment ever again."

"Whatever it takes. I just spent the last two hours weeping blood over my project for my Sound class and I desperately need to get out of here."

"There's another stumbling block — I'm already in my comfortable evening clothes." Translate — yoga pants, sports bra, and baggy tee. "And I'm not sure I like you enough to justify changing out of them again."

"I don't care. This isn't a fancy date; this is hanging out and eating pizza. Bring people along if you want. I need social interaction and food before I implode, and I want my social interaction to involve you."

So I went and banged on Kate's door and asked if she and Riya wanted to join us, and they decided that they did — mostly because Riya was intensely curious about Dean — so we all went down to Pizza Point and had a great time. Through Riya, I learned that Dean's idea of a perfect day was performing as the star in a show-stopper musical followed by a big party attended by everyone he knew. I learned that if he could choose a superpower, he would pick telekinesis so he could use "the Force", and that his favourite book that no one has read is *Hairspray*, which I argued shouldn't count because it's a play, not a book, but he said you could buy it in print and therefore it's a book.

Then I tried to pay for everyone but Dean pulled a twenty dollar bill from my ear and insisted that I had already contributed twenty bucks, since the money had come from my ear.

"Since when do you do magic?" asked Kate, who had known Dean since she was eight.

"Me? I don't do magic," said Dean. "You guys just have some serious ear wax issues. Look what's in your ear!" He pulled out one of those crazy, colourful, overly long scarves from Kate's ear.

"Why do you even *have* that?" I asked, laughing.

"It was in her *ear*! You guys seriously need to stock up on Q tips."

I have to admit, it felt good to have a boyfriend prospect who seemed as charming to everyone else as he did to me. Don't get me wrong, I wasn't ashamed of Howie. At least, not once I realized what a great person he was. But Howie didn't make my social life easier. He did weird things. He ate weird things. He talked strangely, and walked strangely and was generally strange. But Dean was just normal and charming… and apparently good at magic? Who knew?

Howie

The Apex Orientation Binder was both better and worse than I had expected. It contained plenty of information that terrified me, but absolutely none of the details I needed. I read through their empty propaganda and my heart chilled at the sound of the new world that they promised. Much of the contents focused how to fit within the organization and the benefits that came with choosing the higher path. And if the higher path had anything to do with Dad's research — and surely it *must* — then that meant they were talking about the destruction of the human race as we knew it.

And yet, I had no *proof.* I couldn't find any connection to the US Government, or any details about their plans. No dates. No names. They didn't even divulge details of the higher path — nothing to prove Baum's suspicions. I felt like ripping the pages out in frustration. These people were a danger to Stella, to the whole world, and I couldn't figure out what to do about it.

At eight, Brenden, Jess, and Craig arrived in the living room and summoned the rest of the household into the room. In total there seemed to be nine people in the house, plus Brenden, Jess and Craig.

"We have a new recruit today," said Brenden, his eyes gleaming. "This is Ian Whitby, who has chosen to forego the higher path for now. We are sure that he, like the others, will eventually see the error of this ways."

This must be what a cult feels like, I thought. *Is this a cult? Surely the U.S. Military wouldn't organize a cult.*

All three of them took turns talking at us. They repeated much of what I had read in their binder. They talked about the bright new future under Apex — a world without pain or illness, a world where humans could colonize other planets with ease, where they could discover the secret to faster-than-light travel and clean, renewable energy. They talked about the greater strength and intelligence that came from the red freezer and the higher purpose that came with it. I felt sickened because I knew I was looking at murderers. My fingers tightened on my knees just thinking about it, and I struggled to maintain my composure.

I caught Jess looking at me. Were my emotions making her suspicious?

Stella. Think of Stella. Don't imagine them, bending over a body, their hands bloody...

Brenden turned to two young men lounging in the corner. Compared to the others, these men felt relatively benign, with only the usual ugliness of the virus under formaldehyde's control. The ugliness of my own mind.

"Dave, Paul, you say you want to code and program for us, but we need someone who can make us completely secure, and who can access the right parts of the deep web. I'm disappointed that you don't want an edge," said Brenden.

The taller one shrugged. "I'm smart enough already." The other man nodded.

"You're new to this," said Craig with condescension in his voice. "Maybe you haven't noticed, but the virus causes brain damage. That's why we have to eat brains. The white freezer stuff doesn't really cut it. If you eat sheep brains, you end up a sheep. You want to be a sheep?"

They looked uncertain.

"And Cassie, what are we going to do with you?" said Brenden, smiling at her. To me, his eyes looked dead, but she smiled back shyly. "We have a location in New York. Would you like to go to New York?"

She lit up and she nodded.

"Well, we may consider placing you there. We need a maid. I'm told that everyone is too busy to keep up with housework and it would free up their hours to have someone to do laundry, tidy, that sort of thing."

Cassie's face fell. "Laundry?"

"Well, our options for white freezer candidates are limited," Brenden reminded her. "But after all, our new society is going to need contributors at every level. Janitors are important in their own way, too. We'll need guards to monitor surveillance feeds, and, of course, test subjects for our new discoveries."

Cassie looked worried. I felt a coil of anger around my heart.

"Of course, you don't have to stay with us," added Craig. "No one is obligated to stay. Apex provided you with eternal life because it wants to improve the world." He smiled. "After this, you are free to try to make your way in regular society… while it lasts."

25

Stella

Dean wove himself into the fabric of my life, meeting me for lunch on days when he had classes on my campus or popping by in the evenings when I didn't have kung fu. I found myself looking forward to seeing him; I enjoyed his company. Kate tolerated him, mostly because he clearly made a special effort to try and charm her, and because she admitted that she wasn't likely to approve of any man I dated so he was probably as good as any.

"You sure did a one-eighty, though, didn't you? From Howard Mullins to Dean Kato? High school would have been so much easier if you had dated Dean from the first," she said.

I stuck out my tongue.

It took Dean two weeks to convince me to come out to his place, which was a twenty-minute drive from campus, but I finally agreed. His parents had a nice house, and he led me down a side path and through a gate to the backyard and the door to his basement suite.

"Welcome to Casa Kato." He threw open the door and ushered me in.

It was a nice little apartment. He had a small kitchen with granite counter tops and a dishwasher which was stuffed to the brim, and a big TV and a leather couch with a heap of laundry on one end of it. There was a stand under the television which was a tangle of video game consoles, controllers, and stuff like that.

"Your parents must be loaded," I said. "Either that or you had a really lucrative summer job."

"Nope, worked front of house for my mom, remember?" he said. "My Dad's a corporate lawyer. It pays the bills. Mom's theatre company makes approximately negative money, but sometimes she gets bit parts in movies and that sort of makes it up. It's cool."

"A corporate lawyer? So he… what, sues corporations?"

"My Dad doesn't *sue* anyone," said Dean, looking insulted. Then he grinned. "He works for companies that *threaten* to sue people who infringe their copyright. And he makes sure they don't do anything that could get them sued by other people."

"Your mom and your dad sound like very different people."

"Not really. Dad became a lawyer because his family pushed him to do something that would make good money. 'You can go to the theatre on your days off!' Whereas Mom was raised to follow her dreams and junk. Dad's really supportive of the arts; he's an amateur photographer, and he plays violin like a pro." Dean collapsed on the couch and flicked on the television. "What do you want to watch?"

He flipped channels while I tried really, really, *really* hard not to compare him to Howie. Howie, inviting me to his apartment for the first time, would have rushed around, offering me a drink and generally trying to make me feel comfortable. Howie, a self-proclaimed "neatnik", would never have left laundry on the couch or unwashed dishes in the dishwasher. Howie would have wanted to sit down and talk with me, instead of turning on the television. Let's face it, he probably would have wanted to talk with me while cooking me a gourmet meal and then watching me eat it.

"You want to order a pizza or something?" Dean asked after he found a show he liked and switched to it.

"Sure," I said.

Then again, I reminded myself, Howie was not normal. He would never *have* his own apartment to welcome me to. Nor was Howie's slavish devotion to me particularly healthy. Look how he drove himself crazy trying to please me. Besides, I had resented Howie's attentive behaviour at first. I had wanted to be an equal partner, not a spoiled princess. It took Howie a while to convince me that he didn't think I was incapable — he just really liked doing things for me.

Dean treated me like a friend, like an equal. He didn't fuss over me. It was more normal.

"The pizza menu is over there if you want to grab it," he said, gesturing to a pile of papers on the end of the kitchen counter.

See? This was good, really. It would just take some getting used to.

Howie

I simply couldn't get used to the feel of Apex's minds. It was like forcing myself to sit in a nest of writhing snakes. The meeting lasted for over an hour and finally ended with Brenden, Jess and Craig organizing the other red freezer 'recruits' to go collecting. *Collecting.* People were going to die tonight. I took deep breaths to calm my hatred before they picked up on it. *Hide it. Hide it or everything is lost.*

I strolled up to Craig and tried to project rational curiosity, instead of furious horror.

"It must be challenging to collect without risking discovery," I said. "Especially given the recent media attention. Do you have certain areas that you target? And how often do you go out?"

Craig looked at me shrewdly. "We're happy to discuss the details of the higher path, but only with those who have already tried it," he said. "Until you see things from the other side, outdated moralities can cause… problems."

I shrugged and tried to look like I didn't care. I had to get to my phone. I had to warn someone. Anyone.

"Where are you going, Whitby?" Jess called as I headed for my room. "During collection times, all white freezer people are confined to the library." She smiled. "I'm going to keep you company."

So we sat in the library, with the door closed, and listened to the sound of the others stomping through the house. I heard them going down to the basement and bringing up some kind of equipment. I heard Brenden's voice issuing what sounded like instructions in a low voice, and someone else asking questions. But they were in the kitchen and I couldn't make out a single word. I spotted Jess watching me, and I turned to the Orientation Binder instead.

Finally, after an hour, the hideous minds left the kitchen and moved away. I took a breath of relief. Jess was still lurking in the corner, but after all, ten tarantulas are better than fifty of them. Besides her, there were only the four white freezer types left in the house- myself, Cassie, and those two men, Paul and Dave. Their bland, unappealing minds were a welcome relief. It was almost like home.

Except for Jess.

"So, who wants to take the over-under on Whitby?" Jess asked with her terrifying leer. Her voice reeked of sarcasm. "Will he last less than a week before trying the red freezer? Or will he hold out for as long as Jones, here?"

"Don't know why you're not going for it, Jones," said the taller man to Cassie. Unlike the red freezer types, his voice was impassive — like mine, like Cassie's.

"Because no one will tell me what it is," she replied with a sullen expression on her face. "How about you?"

"I'm smart enough without it," he said. "I've got an IQ of a hundred and seventy. I hacked my way into the White House website once. I don't need that to get an edge."

The other man moved restlessly but said nothing.

"But you," continued the tall man to Cassie. "What have you got to offer Apex?"

"Shut up, Paul," said Cassie.

Paul turned to me. "How about you? Dave and I are computer geniuses. What can you do that'll save you from being their janitor in the new world order? Got any skills?"

"I can make a mean cheesecake," I said quietly.

He began to laugh. "Oh, man. Yeah, you're going to be useless to them."

I wasn't sure what was worse, the fear or the boredom. I flipped restlessly through books full of information I didn't understand and couldn't retain while I tried not to think about who might be losing their life at that very moment. A homeless man huddled under an overpass? A teenager walking home after a party? Someone's parent? Someone's child? I pored through the Orientation Binder, trying to absorb every detail. Perhaps a keener mind than mine could glean more from it. But of course, I kept forgetting what I had read, and as the hours ticked by, my focus grew poorer and poorer. I hadn't had any brains since yesterday when I took an extra-large helping before going to Stella's house, so that I would be able to charm her with my wit.

I would be due for my formaldehyde soon, too. How often did they allow that? Oh. I had seen it in the binder. I couldn't even remember that vital piece of information! I flipped backward. There it was. Every two weeks. The same as my father's protocol. I relaxed a little.

The front door slammed and I heard voices in the hall. I jerked upright and tried to listen. Jess stood and went to the doorway. I heard an exchange of voices, too low for me to hear the words, and she remained in the doorway while people filed by. I looked around. Cassie and Paul were dozing, but the other man — Dave — was as alert as I was.

Jess turned to us. "Okay, everyone upstairs," she barked. I nudged Cassie and she rubbed her eyes and yawned. Jess stood back and let us leave the room. I paused and looked down the hall, but I could feel Jess watching me suspiciously. For a moment I thought she would say something to me, but then Dave spoke to her and she turned away. I quickly followed Cassie upstairs to bed. I had to get to my phone.

One by one, I felt the minds around me drift off to sleep. Cassie crawled into the bunk above mine and drifted off within minutes. Paul, in the opposite bunk, took longer, but eventually, his mind smoothed out like the sheets on a well-made bed. Further away in the house I could feel the minds of Jess and Brenden and the others, and I wasn't sure if they were awake or asleep. I was sure that their minds would be screaming horrors whether awake or asleep. But I thought that they felt quieter, and I hoped that meant that they were either dozing or down in the basement and well away from me.

I sat up cautiously in my bed. No one moved. Moving as quietly as I could, I rummaged through my bag and pulled out my phone. Then I covered myself with the blankets, hoping that they were heavy enough to hide the glow from the phone's screen.

I pressed my thumb on the phone as Baum had shown me and it unlocked. I touched the contacts icon as I had seen Stella do with her smartphone. There was only one contact in it: a man named William Stephenson.

Where was Baum? Was this a code name for him? I studied the phone number that was listed. Did he expect me to phone him? I couldn't do that, not without being caught. I saw a little picture of something that looked like a cartoon speech bubble and after hesitating for a moment, I touched it. A messaging screen opened.

Thank God. Now, what should I say? What if this wasn't Baum? What if I spewed important secrets to a stranger? I felt that Baum could have taken the time to prepare me better, but he had wanted to send me across the border before my family noticed that I was missing.

I decided to send a preliminary message — a test. Something cryptic. Something meaningless. Just to see who answered back.

Then someone stirred downstairs and the feel of their mind crawled up my back and made my hair stand on end. Typing with my thumbs, I wrote:

I don't know how long I can stand this.

And I hit send.

Stella

"Dean, I can't stand it anymore. You have to find something that's actually good," I complained after the second episode of some terrible reality show.

"Good! Do you know how hard it is to find *good television*?" Dean asked. "How about we go find a unicorn?"

"You don't think there is a *single thing* of quality on TV right now?"

"Of *quality*? No. Quality TV shows are precious and rare things. But if you like we can switch to Netflix and pull up a unicorn."

"God yes, please do."

He turned on one of his game consoles and got Netflix going.

"So, what shows do you consider to be quality?" I said curiously. "And don't say *CSI: Cyber*."

"Hell, no. I mean, that's fantastic but it's good because it's such an excellent kind of bad. Quality shows? *Game of Thrones* is epic. *Breaking Bad*, of course. *The Sopranos. Deadwood. The Wire. Stranger Things…*"

"Okay, I have seen approximately none of these shows."

He stared at me. "What have you been watching all this time?"

"I don't watch much TV. I think the last time I spent much time in front of the television, my favourite show was still *Spongebob Squarepants.*"

"What do your parents watch?"

"Mostly weird documentaries. Although they did show me *Firefly* and basically everything involving Nathan Fillion. I think they're both attracted to him."

He shook his head. "This is tragic."

"Television is just always such garbage, though. I'd rather read."

He smacked his forehead. "That's the point, Stella, most television *is* garbage. You sort of have to appreciate it for its own junkiness, the way you enjoy a bag of chips — sometimes you just want unlimited amounts of salt and fat. But every now and then, television produces something like *Breaking Bad*, or *Mad Men*, and then you actually get caviar."

"So... more salt and fat," I said.

He laughed. "Okay, not caviar. How about... uh..."

"Cheesecake," I said.

"Or Beef Wellington or Lobster Newburg or something. You know, something exquisitely made and finely crafted."

"I'd rather watch a quality movie."

He shook his head. "A good TV series is better than a movie."

I looked at him with a skeptical frown.

"Seriously. Listen. Think about *The Hunger Games*. You liked the movies?"

"Kind of. The first one wasn't great, but the others were pretty good. I never expect movies to be as good as the books."

"Right, because you can't take an entire book and condense it into a two-hour bite without losing things, right?"

"Right."

"Okay, but now imagine that instead, they had made it a TV series. They could have drawn out each chapter of each book, episode by episode. They could have caught every moment, every nuance."

"Oh, man," I said, drifting off into reverie. "That would have been fucking awesome." I swatted him. "Damn you, Dean! Now I'm sitting here pissed off that more of my favourite books aren't TV shows."

"Sorry about that," he said, grabbing my hands and pulling me closer. "Come here and let me try and make you think about something else."

We ended up in the bedroom, on the navy sheets of his double bed, which smelled like Dean. I lay back with my head on a pillow as Dean ran his hands over me and pressed his body into mine. I had my hands on his arms and shoulders. I kept feeling his muscles. God, he was hot. Like, he was so frigging hot, and I could tell that he found me hot, and I found that even hotter. He was braced with one arm on the bed near my head and using the other hand to explore my body. He kept making this noise — a low growling kind of a noise, almost like a purr, as we kissed.

"Fuck, Stella," he said. "You're so…" and he covered my lips with his again and he pressed himself against me even harder, grinding against me and turning me on more and more. The next time he came up for air he whispered in my ear, "I. Want. You. So. Fucking. Badly."

I wanted him, too. I was flushed and my breathing was ragged. I pushed him back, reached down, and slid my hand under the waistband of his jeans.

Third base was reached, and quickly.

26

Howie

I wasn't sure if Baum would respond to me in the middle of the night, but he responded almost immediately.

I take it you arrived safely.
Do you have any messages you
would like to pass on?

I was so relieved, and it was so late at night, I and I was so short on brains, and I wanted so badly to go back to last night, to Stella in that glittering dress and kiss her under the stars, that I did something stupid. I hurriedly typed:

Please give Stella my love
and tell her I am okay.
Don't let her know that I'm in danger.

I will be pleased to pass on any PROPER messages.
For example, news about your new companions.

I felt like a hopeless idiot, which I am when I'm short on brains. I fumbled with the touchscreen keyboard again.

Please also tell her to say hi to our friend
the nurse at Seattle Hospital, who gave me
that very interesting link to the deep web.
There is someone else here who met him in
the psychiatric ward.

Do you know his name?

No.
But my new friend Brenden Abernathy might know.
He seems to know a lot of things.

While I was waiting for Baum to reply, I heard footsteps coming up the stairs. Dave walked into my room, and I recoiled at the feel of his mind. It had changed. He had changed. He sat on his bunk, but his eyes gleamed in the silvery light of the moon, and his mind crawled all over my skin and made my heart jitter. I could feel my phone buzzing away but I didn't dare look again. Dave sat there, awake on his bed, until morning, and so did I.

By the time Dave had risen from his bed and exited the room, the morning sun was shining in the window. Paul got up too and followed Dave out of the room. Once they were both gone, I hunched under my blankets and started to pull the phone out from under my pillow.

"Psst. Ian," Cassie said.

I hastily stowed the phone back inside my pillowcase. "Hmm?" I poked my head out and pretended to be waking up.

"Did you see Dave come in?"

"Yes. He came in late," I said.

Her face was hard to read without my glasses on, but I could feel her agitation. "That's how it happens, sometimes."

I wanted to check my phone again when Cassie went to take a shower, but she left the door to the room open and people kept walking by so I didn't dare. This old farmhouse was small for the number of people living here. It felt crowded.

Instead, I slipped my phone quickly back into my bag, along with a change of clothes, and when Cassie returned, fresh-faced and wet-haired, I asked her about rules regarding the shower.

"It's first come, first served, but no one's allowed to take more than ten minutes, and only once every third day," she said. "I mean we smell like a biology lab no matter what we do, right? There are towels in the closet next to the bathroom. We all have a rota of chores and whoever is on laundry duty has to wash clothes and towels in the afternoon so put any laundry in the hamper. You'll get your daily chores at breakfast, which is in, like, fifteen minutes, so if you want to shower, get moving."

I took my bag and hurried to the bathroom, which was still steamy from Cassie's shower. I shut the door, locked it, and turned on the water in the shower. I stuck my head under the water to wet it and left the water running while I quickly dressed and then pulled out the phone.

Do Mr. Abernathy's connections
include anyone in the military?

I don't know.
I do know that he works for an organization
which certainly has some very big plans,
however I do not yet know the nature of
the organization or any details.

By the time I was done trying to do all of that with my thumbs, I had someone banging on the door.

I shut off the water, rubbed a towel on my hair to tousle it, shoved the phone back into my bag, and opened the door.

Craig was standing there, with a suspicious look on his face. God, his mind felt like a hive of wasps.

"You took an awful long time in the shower," he said. "Your hair is short and it's not like we get very dirty."

"Blame it on teen hormones," I said. "There's not a lot of privacy here, if you know what I mean." I was awash with embarrassment from even referring to masturbation, but that made me all the more convincing. This changed the look on his face and I smiled to myself as I went quickly downstairs to the kitchen.

People stood gathered around the room, receiving bowls with portions of brains from the fridge. I noticed that none of the red freezer people were present, nor was Dave. There was no conversation. Each person accepted his or her bowl quietly and spooned the contents quickly into their mouths. I took a mouthful and rolled it around in my mouth. Mutton. My family preferred pork, generally. More neuronal density, more complex flavour. Still, there was nothing wrong with good mutton. It could be worse. Much worse.

When I finished, I placed my dish and spoon in the dishwasher and wandered to the living room looking for Cassie. She jerked her chin in a short nod of acknowledgement when I came in, and then tilted her head slightly at Dave, who was deeply immersed in a book about quantum mechanics. Cassie closed her eyes and gave a little shudder, and I nodded.

"Paul, come here," Dave said when Paul walked in behind me. Dave held out his heavy text to Paul and pointed to a paragraph, which Paul read with a furrowed brow.

"Don't you see?" Dave said. "With this, it would be easy to make a CMOS that could handle a massive number of qubits. We'd have the most powerful quantum computer in the world."

Paul looked blank, and Dave gave him a frustrated look. "Stop looking at me like that. It's obvious!"

"Not for Paul," said Craig, appearing in the doorway. "I take it you are enjoying your free sample, Dave?"

"Free sample?" Paul said. "When did you try that?"

"I couldn't stop thinking about trying it," said Dave. "I waited for them to come back and Brenden hooked me up with some fresh stuff."

"And you like it." Craig stated this fact without surprise.

"Fucking incredible," said Dave. Everyone in the room was watching him now. "I just figured out how to..."

"Yes, I know," interrupted Craig. "In fact, we have some people already working on that same principle, down in California. Would you like to join them?"

"Are you serious? Of course! Can I have some more of the..."

Craig cut him off mid-sentence. "Only the first sample is free. First of all, you must know that you absolutely cannot consume more than one dose a week.. Second of all, you will be asked to help with the harvest. Do you agree?"

"Only once a week!" Dave ran his hands through his hair.

"Yes," said Craig firmly. "Come with me, and we'll talk about it." He looked at Paul over his shoulder as they started to leave the room. "As for you, Paul, maybe we can find you a job emptying the garbages for Dave and his new colleagues. They may be able to use you for some data entry now and then, as well."

Paul jumped up. "Wait! Uh. I might try a small sample. Just to see what the fuss is about."

Craig smiled. "Come with us, then."

Cassie was watching this all closely.

"Did you see that?" she said. "It keeps happening. Just like that. Maybe I should try some."

"No," I said firmly.

"Do you know what it..." she started to say but I shook my head very firmly. One of the red freezer people was sitting and studying a book on solar energy, and I didn't want to be overheard. I wasn't sure if it would be suspicious or not for me to know much about the red freezer.

"I'm feeling really confined," I said to her. "Do you know if we're allowed to go for a walk?"

"Oh yeah, we can go," said Cassie. "It's not like we're prisoners, after all. It's more like… a hostel. They have rules, but just for everyone's safety and stuff."

"Mmm," I nodded as if this seemed normal and unsurprising. "Well, do you want to go for a walk?"

She shrugged. "Sure. Got nothing better to do."

The house sat isolated in a rural area, with nothing but grassy fields around. Jess was sitting on the porch, smoking a cigarette, when we walked out. And while she didn't say anything to us as we passed, I knew she was watching us.

I waited a good long while before I spoke to Cassie. We were too far away for Jess to hear our words as we tramped over the rough ground, but I could still feel her eyes on us.

"This red freezer stuff. I think it's really bad news."

"I hate how it makes their brains feel," said Cassie. "It feels… scary. Like a scary movie, when there are all those violins playing."

I thought it was an accurate description and nodded.

"But you know — I'm beginning to think that they're right. I mean, they were right about this immortality bug thing. They said I'd never feel pain again and I don't — I took a knife and tested it like they said and it didn't hurt at all and it healed right up. It was crazy. So if they're right about that, then maybe…"

"Even if they are right," I said, my chest feeling tight. "We can't do it. It's not… that doesn't make it okay."

"So what is it? What do they do to it?" she asked. And I wanted to tell her, but I didn't want to scare her. I didn't know what she would do. Would she panic? Blow my cover? Or worst of all… what if it didn't bother her? I looked at her as we scuffed through the field. Her face was round and babyish, and it made her look innocent. I was lonely, and she was the beginnings of a friend. What if I told her the truth? What if it ruined everything?

"I can't say exactly what it is. But I heard some of them talking, and I do know they have to hurt people to get it."

"Yeah. I kind of gathered that too. Their 'harvesting' expeditions seem so cloak and dagger, I figured it had to be something illegal."

I nodded.

Cassie sighed. "Still. I'm not big on being a maid. I know I could just go, but what would I do? And how am I supposed to get brains and formaldehyde on my own?"

"Has anyone chosen to leave, since you've been here?"

Cassie shook her head. "They all seem to go for the red freezer eventually. At least in the three weeks I've been here. But I'm going to have to decide soon. And I've never been good at making decisions."

"Don't let them pull you into crime," I said.

"So why are you here, if you're so set against the red freezer?" she asked.

I went with simple honesty. "Because I want to find out if I can do any good here. Because I want to know more about them."

"Well," said Cassie. "From what they've been saying, I don't think they'd mind hurting a few people on the way to their big and bright future that they have planned. So keep that in mind before you try to do them any good."

"I will," I said gravely. "I will."

Stella

"So, are you guys officially banging yet?" Kate asked when I came home the next morning.

"Not officially," I said.

"I feel like we should bake you a cake or something," Riya said. "Your first overnight at someone's house!"

"Maybe save that for the official deflowering," I said.

Kate shrugged. "You're talking to a pair of gay girls. Penetrative penis sex doesn't mean much over here."

Riya nodded. "By that definition, I'm a virgin too. But I don't feel like one."

"Virginity is a social construct designed to restrict women's choices and alleviate paternity uncertainty," announced Kate around a mouthful of toast.

"Thank you, I know that," I said. "I promise I'm not saving it for a super special occasion. I just want to have actually been dating the guy for more than a couple of weeks, and I want to be sure that I genuinely like the guy."

"You saved it for over a year from Howie, and now you're saving it from Dean," said Kate. "So I call bullshit on your whole 'yeah, I know it means nothing and I am definitely not brainwashed' claim. I'm beginning to wonder whether you have some kind of complex interview process to go with it. Does Dean need to produce references? Does he need a doctor's certificate?"

"I didn't *save it* from Howie. That was all him."

Kate's eyebrows shot up and she sent a significant glance at Riya.

"*Really*? The guy who clearly worshipped the ground you walked on and got a boner every time he looked at your ass? *He wouldn't give it up*?"

I grabbed a piece of toast off of her plate and took a bite. "Nope."

She took the toast back from me. "Wow. Uh. Why?"

"Brainwashing. Also, fear that I would get his weird disease."

"It was an STD? I feel like I'm learning so much from you this morning. You're talkative after orgasm, clearly."

"I'm answering direct questions. No, he didn't have an STD, but apparently no one has ever studied whether his bloodborne medical condition was contagious via semen so he was scared to risk it or whatever, even with condoms, which I considered paranoid to the extreme."

"Shouldn't that be your decision?"

"Kate, I'm pretty sure that when it comes to sex, both people get equal say in what happens."

She conceded my point with a shrug and a nod. "Okay, so you didn't have official devirginating sex with Dean. But you did mess around with him, right?"

"Why do you need to know this? I don't ask what you do with Riya."

"You should. I have no one to boast to about my sexual exploits."

"I'm *right here*," said Riya, but she was smiling.

"Boast away, but that doesn't mean I'm going to reciprocate. I keep private shit private. Thanks for the stimulating conversation and all that," I said. "But I'm going to take a shower now."

I wouldn't admit it to Kate, but I actually *was* a little brainwashed about the whole virginity thing. I mean, I didn't think that I should hold on to my virginity for marriage or anything like that. I just felt… I felt like I shouldn't very well go and have sex for the first time with someone that a month ago I claimed to despise.

That being said, I definitely didn't despise Dean anymore, and last night had been… well, it had been really fucking good.

Dean was confident and experienced in bed. Several times I had needed to warn him off when he tried to go a little farther than I wanted, but he always backed off when I told him to. I guess that, unlike Howie, he didn't have to constantly watch himself to make sure he didn't kill and consume me, so he was more able to lose himself in the moment. While he hadn't been as romantic or sensual as Howie, he definitely made me feel desirable. He'd spent half the night just running his hands over my body.

"God, I want you. You turn me on so much," he kept saying.

"What's the matter, never been with a girl who had so much going on before?" I gestured to my ample cleavage and wide hips.

"No, I haven't. Stella, I know I was a jerk to you at school and I'm really sorry. It's just really hard to be a guy who likes curvy women."

"Fat women, Dean. You like fat women."

"Because of the curves," he insisted. "Because the things that make you look different from a man are more pronounced. More boob. More ass."

"More belly," I reminded him.

"Yeah. It's, like, a symbol of fertility or something."

I had heard this before, from Howie, so I redirected the conversation. "You were telling me how tragic your life is because you like fat chicks."

He rolled his eyes but his arm stayed wrapped around my waist. "Right. So one time a friend comes over and he starts joking around and googling porn on my computer, and I hadn't deleted my search history and he found BBW porn."

"Charming."

"Oh come off it, everyone looks at porn. Anyway, he laughed his ass off and I had to make up some story about how I was trying to get back at a guy I didn't like by putting his email into subscription lists for BBW porn."

"Instead of standing up for your personal tastes and defending the women who were being objectified in your pornos," I said.

"Yeah," he said contritely. "It's just... easier. You know? To not talk about it, or pretend it's a joke. At that point, I really wasn't considering the ethics of the whole situation. I was just worried about damage control."

"So what happened?"

"My friend liked the idea but thought BBW porn wasn't weird enough so that dude I didn't like ended up getting subscribed to a whole lot of grandma porn instead."

"I think I might cry at this touching story."

He nudged me. "Look, it was hard on the girls I dated, too. You only moved here a couple years ago so you probably don't know her, but does the name Chrissy Campbell mean anything to you?"

"Nope. But it's not because I only moved here recently. It's because I hate people and don't bother to learn their names."

"Well, anyway, she was my first girlfriend, and we never had sex — we were only thirteen — but she had a reputation for being a slut for years afterwards because I dated her. She was on the chubby side, you see, and they figured the only reason a guy like me would go out with a girl like her was if she was easy. She thought I was making up lies about her putting out and she ditched me."

"Did you stand up for her?"

He tensed. "Okay, I know I didn't exactly jump to your defence when people teased you in class and I'm sorry about that, but yes, I defended my fucking girlfriend when people were calling her a whore."

"I didn't need your defence, Dean," I said, sitting up a bit. "I can defend myself, if you haven't noticed. What pissed me off was that I knew you were into me, into bodies like mine, and you weren't standing up for *yourself*. Every time you let them get away with cracks like that, it was like you were agreeing with them, which makes you — what? A pervert? For liking a big ugly whale like me?"

"You are very non-ugly," he said.

"Yeah, I know that. You know how I know that? Because I had someone who spent months convincing me of that. It took some deprogramming from someone who wasn't ashamed to love whom he loved."

"Can we not discuss your ex while we're naked in bed together? You're turning my outie into an innie," he said.

"I'm not discussing my ex, I'm mentioning him in passing. My point is that if you're going to date girls like me, you're going to need to convince them that you aren't ashamed of them, and you can't do that if you *are* ashamed of them. And that's why I judged you. Not because you didn't defend me — because you didn't turn around and say, 'hey, I think she's hot, so what are you going to do about?'"

Dean was silent.

"You were so afraid of getting teased, or having your girlfriends be teased, that you didn't stand up for who you really are, and what you really like."

"I just wasn't ready, okay? It's like being in the closet. Like I had a whole secret life that no one could know about. I'd pretend to lust after Taylor Swift instead of Queen Latifah, that kind of thing."

"And that's a choice that you made — to pretend. To lie. So, are you over that, now?" I asked. "Because I've got zero patience for that garbage. So what are you going to say when someone from high school sees us together?"

"I'll tell them to buzz off." He had started running his hands over me again, and kissing me. "Because this is totally worth it."

Howie

I couldn't check my phone that night. I didn't dare linger in the bathroom — Craig was hovering in the hallway, feeling like an infestation — so I thought I'd try my middle of the night trick again instead. But Paul and Dave kept whispering excitedly to each other about converting refrigerators to keep the quantum computers cold. It went on all night, so far as I could tell. I didn't get much sleep — their minds were too creepy. It was like trying to sleep in a bed of spiders. I think Cassie had trouble resting too — heard her shifting a lot over my head.

The next morning, at breakfast, Paul and Dave were sent away, with directions to the place in California written in a sealed envelope in Dave's hands.

"I wonder how long before I get my special assignment to be their maid," Cassie grumbled to me as she sat down with her bowl of breakfast. "So, are you looking forward to another exciting day of sitting around?" she asked, putting her feet up on the table. I gave her a sympathetic smile and took a bite of brains… I took another taste, then I stared at the brains in my bowl.

"Hey, this is really good. They must have just gotten some fresh heads in or something," said Cassie, eating enthusiastically. "Wow. Like. Really, really good."

I continued to stare at my bowl while a rush of clarity bolted through my brain like lightning.

I stood up. "Cassie, put it down!"

She gave me a sidelong look. "Are you kidding? It's about time they got something that had some flavour." She went back to guzzling it. I reached out and struck the bowl right out of her hands. She didn't flinch — the virus sort of destroys your self-preservation instincts, like jumping or flinching or insisting on preparing your own meals when living in a house belonging to an evil organization of the living dead.

"What's your problem, Ian?" she said, getting up.

"Yes, what's your problem, Ian?" asked Brenden, appearing behind me. "Care to explain?"

I picked up my bowl and stared at him steadily. For a moment I was tempted to take one quick last taste — just to be sure — and then I shuddered and, without breaking eye contact, I threw the bowl with all of my strength, right at Brenden. He dodged easily, moving faster than you could blink, and the bowl struck the kitchen window, which shattered with a crash.

27

Stella

Dean came over the next night. He had discovered that I had never seen *Fargo* and felt the need to change this fact immediately. Riya hadn't seen it either so we all watched the movie together. It was all right; I liked the pregnant lady cop. I found it hard to concentrate, though, because Dean kept doing little things to make me catch my breath, like leaning in to nibble my earlobe or running his hands suggestively down my leg. Kate and Riya didn't notice — they were too busy being snuggled up and cutesy themselves. When the movie was over they disappeared into Kate's room.

"What do you say we do the same?" I asked Dean, my heart thumping.

"I thought you'd never ask," he murmured.

I stood and led him into my bedroom. I was feeling a little nervous. It felt different, having Dean in my own private space. I swiftly took my teddy bear off of my bed and set him on the floor, praying that Dean wouldn't ask me what the bear's name was — I coincidentally named it Howard when I was a little kid, and he might think it was weird that I slept with a bear which shared a name with my ex-boyfriend.

I needn't have worried. Dean showed no interest in anything except me and removing my clothes. Then he pulled a condom out of his wallet.

"What are you doing?" I asked.

He paused. "Oh. I thought maybe you were ready to take the next step."

"No. I'm not."

"Oh." He looked disappointed, but he put the condom away. "Okay."

"Sorry for the confusion," I said, although I wasn't sure exactly what I had done to make him think that.

"It's okay. Reading too much into things, I guess," he said.

We looked awkwardly at each other. The moment was kind of ruined. Dean sat next to me on the bed, his button-down shirt hanging open.

"So. This is your boudoir. I like it. You have a lot of books."

"This is only a tiny fraction of what I have at home."

He reached out and pulled my antique copy of *Jane Eyre* off of the shelf. "Wow, this looks old."

"Be careful!" I took it from his hands and gently replaced it on the shelf. "It's delicate."

"Is that a first edition?"

"No, but it is an early edition. It says Currer Bell instead of Charlotte Bronte, see?"

"Cool." Dean kept looking around. "I have to say, I'm a little relieved."

"About what?"

"I half-expected your room to be full of framed photos of Howard Mullins or something. A shrine in the corner. Something like that."

"Don't be stupid," I said shortly.

"You guys seemed pretty serious," Dean said quietly. "I was so fucking jealous. I still kind of am. I feel like you're holding back. Like maybe you're waiting for him." He looked down. "You were pretty wrecked after the breakup. I could barely get you to crack a smile in class."

Pain curled in my chest and I struggled not to remember. *Don't think about that. Don't think about Howie, his voice, his smile. That was then. This is now.*

"Dean, I broke up with *him*. Our relationship... it wasn't working. I wasn't good for him. And yeah, the break up was hard. But you've been through breakups, too. Shit happens, right?"

"Yeah, and I thought that things were going well here, but you're still not ready for sex."

"That has nothing to do with Howie," I said. "I'm still getting to know you. It's an intimacy thing. Not a waiting for my ex thing."

He nodded and studied me with his dark brown eyes. "I get it. It's cool. Now kiss me with those sexy lips and I'll tell you all the things I wish I could do to you right now."

I woke the next morning to the sound of Kate and Riya loading the dishwasher. Dean was fast asleep on his stomach. I took a moment to admire his naked torso before getting up. Did you know that backs can be sexy? *Backs.* Who knew?

Dean emerged from my room as I was digging into my second bowl of cereal and answering Riya's constant stream of questions about Nova Scotia. He was still shirtless, but he'd pulled on a pair of sweatpants.

"Where did those come from?" I asked.

"Brought them in my bag. Figured I might stay over."

Kate came out of the bathroom and stopped at the sight of Dean in the kitchen.

"Oh, Jesus," she said.

"Good morning to you too," he said, giving her a dimpled grin.

Then our door buzzer went off. I grabbed my phone and stared at it.

"Shit. I forgot! My parents are taking me to breakfast this morning. Fuck. Shit!" I looked at Dean. "Go put a shirt on. Fuck."

Kate raised her hand. "Can I vote for him *always* having a shirt on?"

Dean flexed his muscles. "What, you don't like my manly chest?"

"Oh yeah, in fact, I think you just turned me straight. No... wait... yup, I'm definitely a little gayer now."

Riya giggled and squeezed Kate's hand.

I was dancing with impatience. "Seriously, Dean, go put a shirt on."

"Are you going to make me hide or something?"

"No, of course not. I just want you to *put a shirt on.*"

He disappeared into my room and came out again, pulling a tee over his head. "Are they going to freak? I thought you said they were really laid back."

"They are. They're *too* laid back."

"How can parents be *too* laid back?"

"Oh, you'll see," said Kate.

My parents knocked on the door.

"Hark," I said, walking to the door. "Your doom approacheth."

"Nah, parents love me," he said. "Don't worry."

"I can't watch. I'll be in my room," said Kate, grabbing her cereal bowl and booting it down the hall. Riya stayed put. She had met my parents a couple of times and she had a big grin on her face.

"I *need* to witness this," she said.

I opened the door and Dad burst in, pointing a finger at me. "I KNEW IT! Your mother owes me TWENTY BUCKS!" and he started doing a little dance around the room. My mother looked at me reproachfully.

"Your father made me a bet that you wouldn't be ready to go when we arrived. Foolishly, I took that bet."

"Sorry," I said, "I'll be ready soon, I promise."

Dad paused in mid-dance as he noticed Dean. "Hello. Who's this?"

I took a deep breath. "Dean, this is my dad, Tim, and my mom, Elaine. This is, uh, Dean."

My parents exchanged delighted glances.

"Oh, this is DEAN," said my mother. "Hello, Dean!"

"Are you coming to breakfast, then? Please tell me you're coming with us for breakfast," said Dad, rubbing his hands.

"Nice to meet you," said Dean. "Thanks for the invite, but I wouldn't want to impose."

"No, you wouldn't be imposing at ALL," said Dad. "We would LOVE to talk with you, and get to know you!"

I tried to send my father fiery looks, but he was studiously ignoring me. The thing is, I hadn't really told my parents about Dean. I mean, not properly. I'd mentioned that we ran into each other and that we had been on a couple of dates. But I had always changed the subject when they tried to get more information from me. I don't like talking about my romantic life with people, especially my parents, who love to make things uncomfortable.

"Go get dressed, Stella," said Mom, beaming, "while we get to know Dean."

Dean looked uncomfortable because he clearly had to get dressed, too. He was wearing sweatpants with no underwear, no socks, and he had epic bed-head. My parents had eyes and could see this.

I gave them a death glare and rushed off to get dressed. I could hear them making conversation with him but I couldn't make out any of the words. I stumbled out as soon as I was wearing all my clothes, still dragging a brush through my thick hair.

Dean cast me a look that clearly said, "help!". My parents had him captive and he didn't know how to slip away to get dressed without openly addressing the fact that he had slept/been naked here.

"Hey, Dean," I said, interrupting Dad's probing questions about entry requirements to Performance and Film. "Do you want to use the bathroom before we go?"

"Uh, YEAH, I, uh, yeah," he said. "I'll be right back." He slunk away into the bathroom where I had dumped his bag when I went to brush my teeth.

"So, Dean seems nice," said my father, showing far too many teeth. "What a nice idea for you to ask him to come by and surprise us."

"Please don't be assholes," I begged. "Don't scare him away."

"He is GORGEOUS," whispered my mother. "Why did you never mention that he was gorgeous?"

Dean rushed out of the bathroom again, now wearing jeans and socks to go with his tee, and his black hair was slicked back and gleaming.

Now, normal people would politely pretend not to notice that Dean had changed his clothes. Not my parents.

"Thank God, you put on real pants," said Dad. "I was worried you thought it was okay to go to breakfast in sweats with no boxers on."

"Have fun!" Riya called as we went out the door. I gave her the middle finger and she giggled.

By the time we got to the restaurant, Dean had the measure of my father and was bantering with him easily.

"How many?" asked the hostess.

"Four please," my Dad said, pointing to each of us in turn. "For me, my lovely wife, my beautiful daughter, and the man who slept in her bed last night."

I groaned, but Dean piped up with, "Actually, Tim, I'd rather be called 'the sexy stud-muffin who's courting your daughter'."

Dad grinned and slapped him on the back. "I stand corrected."

I brushed up against Dean as we followed the hostess and muttered, "I am so sorry."

Dean put his arm around my waist. "It's cool. I got this."

And he did. He handled my parents really well, and he and Dad got along great. It actually kind of threw me off. I felt irrationally annoyed, like Dad should be more loyal to Howie and treat Dean with detached disdain. Which is stupid, because while I know my parents liked Howie, it would be terrible if they held him up as some kind of unbeatable ideal and hated all my future boyfriends. Of *course* they would make every effort to like anyone I liked. And it was good that they got along so well with Dean. It was good.

There was only one moment that gave me pause.

It happened when our waitress came up and introduced herself to us.

"Hi, I'm Lauren, and I'll be your server today," she said. "How's everyone doing this morning?"

"We're just fantastic," said Dean, smiling at her. That's when I saw it: the appreciative once-over that Howie had trained me to notice, only this time it wasn't aimed at me. It was at Lauren's plump, hourglass body. "How is *your* day going?"

"Great," she chirped, beaming back at him. "Can I take your drink order?"

"I would *love* it if you could bring me a Coke," he said.

"Sure. One Coke," she said, writing it down and turning to me. "And for you?"

That was it. The quick glance, and then Dean's usual charm. But it bothered me. And what bothered me more is that I saw Dad looking at Dean with a shrewd expression and I knew he had seen it too.

"So, Dean," said Mom, when Lauren had taken our orders. "Tell me more about your mother's theatre company."

Dean answered enthusiastically, and as he talked, he wrapped his arm around my waist and my jealousy melted away.

Howie

Brenden overpowered me instantly and pinned me into my chair.

"Such an overreaction, Ian," he said calmly. "My, my. Cassie, would you like to finish your meal?"

"You slipped it in, didn't you?" she said. "That's the red freezer stuff. You put some in my bowl."

Brenden nodded. "Not very ethical of me, was it? I am terribly sorry. I can put it down the drain if you like."

"Are you kidding? This is the best thing I have ever tasted. And I'm already thinking clearer," she said, licking every trace off of her spoon.

I had only had a quick slurp, but even I was feeling slight effects. My mind was racing. I could still taste it in my mouth, tantalizing my tongue. The thought of what it was made me spit right onto Brenden's face. He reached for a dishtowel with one hand, and I tried to get up, but he held me in the chair effortlessly with his other hand.

"It's human, isn't it?" Cassie asked, looking thoughtful. "Yes, it would make sense for it to be human. That's what the virus is geared to, right? Why didn't I figure that out before? That does create a bit of a moral quandary, doesn't it? But then again, morals are a self-imposed human constraint. The natural world has no morals. In fact, if every living thing began to consider ethics, the ecosystem would fall apart. Without wolves, the deer would overpopulate. And so the deer must die and be eaten, lest they all starve. And wolves, they don't have any idea of how to kill kindly, do they? They eat the animal half alive. Meanwhile, we kill our prey with kindness. Ultimately, how much difference is there between a sheep and a human, Ian? The sheep didn't give its life voluntarily. The sheep was a living, breathing being. The line you draw between farm animals and people is an imaginary one. And think of what we can do with this kind of understanding of the world! With a brain like this, I could cure cancer, eliminate pollution, solve the hunger crisis. I could save millions simply by killing a few. It's obvious, Ian. It's the obvious choice."

"No, Cassie..." my voice broke. I could feel the virus buzzing with hunger, gathering in her thoughts like flies over a corpse.

"I think we need to have a little talk, Ian Whitby," said Brenden, taking me firmly by the arm.

"Give me some more," Cassie said.

"No, we only consume one helping a week," said Brenden. "There can be too much of a good thing, you know. A higher dose leads to *extremely* problematic side effects."

Cassie kicked the chair angrily, and Brenden dragged me from the room.

"We've been interested in you, Ian Whitby," said Brenden, as Craig shoved me into a chair and wrapped heavy chains around me. I struggled but his grip was unbreakable. He was an immutable force, and I was a weak and puny object.

"Your name, for example. Isn't Whitby the name of the Canadian town that trained spies following World War II? It was founded by William Stephenson, the famous Canadian spy. Aren't *you* Canadian? I would have thought you would know that. Did you know that James Bond was based on William Stephenson? Yes, Ian Fleming, who wrote James Bond, knew Stephenson well and based his famous spy character on him. Ian Fleming... why... *your* name is Ian! What a coincidence!"

Craig tugged my bonds tighter and began to wrap my hands with duct tape.

"Found a phone in his room," said Jess, walking in, "just like I figured. Care to put in your password for us?"

"No," I said.

"Well, then, we'll just have to hack it open," she said with a shrug.

Brenden took my phone and brought a small device out of his pocket. "One of our brethren in Silicon Valley put this together for us. He is very, very intelligent, you know."

He plugged the device into my phone and the screen started to flicker. After about a minute, the flickering stopped, and Brenden pulled up my contact list.

"Well," he said, laughing. "Just in case you thought I was being paranoid, Craig — his only contact is a gentleman named William Stephenson."

Jess laughed from the corner where she lurked.

"Seriously?" said Craig. "Subtle like a hammer, Whitby."

"What's your real name, then?" asked Jess.

I didn't answer.

"We have ways of making you talk, you know."

"Considering that I'm immune to pain, I'm curious about what those ways could be," I said. I wasn't afraid anymore. I knew this could happen. I knew I might get caught. I took this risk willingly, and I was glad I did. Maybe some of my information would be useful. Maybe Baum would be able to put a stop to them. Because whatever they were planning, I didn't want it to touch Stella's world. Rather than dwell on the basement, and the chains, and the people around me, I decided to dwell on the softness of Stella's skin, the brilliance of her mind, the swell of her breasts, the way her hips moved as she walked…

"Oh, it's a lot more fun than torture," said Craig, walking over to the red freezer. "You'll enjoy it, really."

Stella

Dean was proud of how well he had charmed my parents.

"Your dad is hilarious," he said after they had dropped us off at my place. "We get along great."

"I'm sorry he kept trying to embarrass you."

"Don't be. He was testing my mettle, and I totally passed. I love it. I'd probably do the same thing if I had a daughter. Hey, babe, I'm going to take a shower if that's okay. Got a spare towel?"

"Yeah." I pulled one out of my closet and tossed it to him. "Go clean yourself up, dirtbag."

After Dean's shower, though, I had to urge him to clean up in other ways.

"Hey," I said, tossing his wet towel onto his head while he sat on the couch watching our TV. "Don't leave your wet towel on the floor. Were you raised by wolves?"

He grinned. "Sorry, babe."

"Also don't call me babe."

"I'll try harder at both, I promise."

"You better. Riya leaves every room cleaner than it was when she entered it, so you've got major competition in the roommate significant-other department."

"Listen, why don't you come back to my place? I've got an essay I need to work on."

"No thanks. I don't want to stay overnight and it would just be more work for you to drive me back home later. Besides, I won't be any fun. I have my Organic Chem midterm tomorrow."

"You can study while I write my essay. It'll be cozy."

"You can write your essay here if you like," I said, trying to compromise.

"I like to write my essays with my pants off," he winked.

I shook my head. "I don't want to stay over on a weeknight. What if there was a traffic jam or something and I missed my midterm?"

"Then you'd explain to the prof that there was a traffic jam and ask if you can make it up."

I shuddered. "But what if he said no? Uh-uh. There's no way I'm going beyond walking distance from campus on the night before a midterm. Sorry."

"Don't you trust me?" he looked hurt.

"I trust you, but things happen. You could get a flat tire."

"I'd call you a cab."

"I'm just not comfortable with it, Dean."

He sighed. "Fine. Okay. Well, I'm going to be swamped this week so I'll see you at some point… maybe."

"Text me. We'll figure something out. It's midterm season. It's bound to be a little hectic. I'll see you later, okay?"

"Okay." Dean gave me a kiss. "Mm. Got a few minutes before I go?"

"Well maybe a few," I said.

Dad called me just before dinner. "Your mother and I have been gossiping about Dean all afternoon and we need to inflict our verdict on you, now," he said.

I sighed and muted the TV. "Okay, let's have it."

"Wait. Is he there?"

"No. He went home."

"Damn. Okay. So. Overall, thank you for giving us such a marvellous opportunity to make him uncomfortable."

"Oh, by all means, it was all part of my master plan."

"It should've been actually. I don't want a son-in-law who can't handle meeting me unexpectedly when he's only half dressed."

"I'm not really at the screening-potential-marriage-partners phase."

"Well, I am. I think I'm going to have to up things a notch. I'm thinking about introducing him next time as 'the guy who is porking my daughter'."

"Not if you ever want me to be seen in public with you again," I said. "Besides, I live outside of the home now and my love life is officially none of your business."

"That may be true, but I will always be your father and I retain the right to embarrass your lovers."

"Lovers? Plural?"

"Anyway, we give Dean a seven out of ten so far."

"I see. And how did you come to that rating?"

"Well, I wanted to give him six out of ten. It took him a good fifteen minutes to get the measure of me and he was obviously thrown off by my approach, although he recovered admirably. Your mother wanted him to get extra points for being ripped."

"She has a fair point, you must admit."

"I admit nothing. But since she constitutes fifty percent of the judges in this competition, the rating stands at seven out of ten."

"Well, thanks for letting me know," I said. I wondered what rating they would have given Howie. Dad had never managed to throw Howie off, but on the other hand, he was undead and that had to count against him. I remembered Dad's face, watching Dean check out the waitress, and I wondered if they had really spent the afternoon comparing the two.

"Dad?"

"Yes, kitten?"

"You've never… seen Howie around… have you?" It had occurred to me that for all I knew he might come by routinely and they might simply never mention it to me. What if they told him about Dean? The thought chilled me.

There was a pause on the other end. "No, honey, we haven't. Why?"

"Oh. Just… wondering. Never saw his car driving by? I mean, there aren't a lot of blue Dodge Shadows around…"

"No, I haven't. Elaine? Have you ever seen Howie's car go by or anything?" I heard my mother's voice giving a muffled reply. "She says no. Oh, now she's trying to take the phone away from me. Byeloveyou."

"Stella?" said my mother. "Why are you asking about Howie?"

"Just an idle question, out of sheer curiosity," I said. "I didn't mean to turn it into a thing."

"You're still hung up on him, aren't you?" she asked sharply.

I hesitated for a fraction of an instant. "No."

"Sweetie, he'll be okay. Relationships end. It's a normal part of life."

"Nothing about Howie's life was normal," I said. "But I know that. I do. I just wondered. Jeez."

"It's okay to move on. It's okay to be with Dean. Howie is not your personal responsibility."

"I KNOW THAT!" I shouted into the phone. "I JUST ASKED A SIMPLE QUESTION. Forget I asked, okay?" I ended the call. I thought my mother might call back, but she didn't. Good.

I spent that night fighting memories of Howie, trying to suppress them, but for some reason, they kept bubbling to the surface. Eventually, I gave up, and just let myself sink into the mire of my memories. Howie smiling at me in his shy way. The way his cheek dimpled when he smiled. His hand on my hand. His lips on my lips. His fingers on my skin. His eyes. His voice — his funny, husky, robotic voice. Where was he? What was he doing?

I felt like if I could just know that he was okay, maybe I could finally let him go.

28

Howie

How many days had it been since I had eaten? I was losing track. At least seven. Ten? It was hard to tell, chained here in the dark. They dragged me to this place with a bag over my head, and I didn't know where I was. I could hear the growls and cries of others, in other concrete rooms. I could feel the swirling evil of their minds. I stared at the door — not a regular door. Not a jail door. It was metal, and it raised upwards, like in a car garage. But this room was too small, far too small, to fit a car. It was a closet. A cement coffin where I would die.

My thoughts were sluggish, and so was my pulse. I was glad I couldn't feel pain because a week spent in a chair was sure to be giving me pressure sores, and they wouldn't be healing very well anymore. The virus was getting stronger. It was taking over. I was overdue for my formaldehyde injections. The dreams were terrible, but I couldn't help but drop off to sleep now and then. I wouldn't let myself think about Stella anymore. The memory of her mind was more than the hunger could bear.

I heard footsteps and the dim bulb in my room sparked on, creating a feeble orange light. My heart clenched. I didn't think I could bear it again. Not again. There was the rattling of a key and the door slid upward. I blinked in the cold artificial lighting from the concrete hallway. It was Jess this time. Usually, it was Brenden or Craig. She pulled the door shut behind her, sat in the empty chair across from mine, and held out the same thing that they had offered me every day.

This was in no bowl, no thermos. It was still in its original container, the bloodied head opened at the top like a ghoul's soup bowl. God, I could even see his face, squashed and frozen into an unnatural expression, and I wanted to scream with horror. But the virus and my body were screaming too — with hunger.

She tilted the opened skull toward me and showed me the glistening contents. I don't know if I have ever wanted anything more. Maybe not even Stella. But I clenched my teeth and shook my head. When I squeezed my eyes shut, I could feel tears escape and trickle down my filthy cheeks.

I would die tied up here. Better to die. I could distract myself. I was an expert at self-distraction. Remember the poems. Think about poems.

Not, I'll not, carrion comfort, Despair, not feast on thee.

"Ready yet?" Jess asked, holding up a spoon. "Nice and fresh today."

I shook my head. "Not… I'll not feast…"

Not untwist — slack they may be — these last strands of man

In me ór, most weary, cry I can no more. I can;

"Sure? Last chance."

I shook my head again.

"You're a tough nut, Whitby," Jess said cheerfully. "We're impressed. Craig and Brenden have it in their head that they need to break you — make you give in. Me, I'm not so Orwellian. And I'm done with waiting. So you're going to eat today."

I shook my head violently. "Not, I'll not feast… not untwist…"

But ah, but O thou terrible, why wouldst thou rude on me

"Oh, you don't get to agree to it," she said. "I told you — I don't care about breaking you. You don't have to agree. You just have to eat it. So I'm going to knock you out. Then I'm going to pour it down your throat. And then you'll see things differently. They always do."

More tears ran down my cheeks and I tried pointlessly to break my bonds.

…O thou terrible….

The last thing I remember was Jess lifting a crowbar while I twisted my arms in their chains.

Not untwist… these last strands of man

In me…

"I hope I don't damage your brain too much," she said. "Brenden and Craig would be pissed off. They want to know your real name."

Stella

Dean's life struck me as insanely busy. He was taking film and performance theatre classes and all of them seemed to assume that he had no need for sleep, a social life, or personal hygiene. I was impressed by how well he handled it. He accepted his workload with good humour and he still found time to socialize, which I would *not* have done if I were in his place. When I'm overworked, human interaction is the last thing I want, but Dean would call at unexpected moments and ask if he could stop by, or invite me out for a late night snack. He called me at nine on Thursday night when I was out with my kung fu friends.

"Sorry, guys, I'll just be a second," I said to them and took the call. "Hey, what's up?"

"D'you want to go to a movie?"

"Sure," I said, tucking the phone into my shoulder and giving my friends an apologetic eye roll as I went back to my soup. "When?"

"The newest Marvel movie starts in an hour."

My noodles slipped from my chopsticks and back into the soup. "You mean *tonight*?"

"Yeah. I've been working on these fucking projects all day and I need to do something mindless for a while. You up for it?"

I looked at my bowl. I was almost done, and everyone else had already finished. They were just waiting for me, really. So I shrugged. "Yeah, okay, I guess. Want me to catch the bus?"

"Nah, it'll be faster if I swing by and pick you up. See you at your place in twenty?"

"Sure."

I hung up and asked the waiter for my bill.

"You heading out?" asked Melanie.

"Yeah. My boyfriend wants to go to a last-minute movie."

"Oh, fun. What's his name?"

"Dean." Everyone was looking at me curiously, and I realized that I hadn't really mentioned Dean much. We didn't talk about personal life stuff. We talked about classes and politics and martial arts competitions.

"How long have you two been together?" asked John.

"Not long. Less than a month. We kind of see each other at weird hours because he's in performance arts and I think he's officially signed away his soul between the hours of eight a.m. and nine p.m."

"Yeah, I had a girlfriend in the Dance program for a while. Her schedule was intense," agreed John.

"I wish my boyfriend called me for last minute movies," said Melanie.

"Want to come?" I asked on impulse. "Call your boyfriend."

She laughed. "No, thanks. I have a ton of schoolwork to do. I'm going to catch the bus and head home soon, where my boyfriend will probably be sleeping in front of the TV with no pants on."

"Hot."

"Right?"

I got up and threw on my jacket. "Alright, well, see you guys Tuesday."

"Bye!"

"See ya."

"Later!"

As I sprinted up the hill toward my building to meet Dean, I reflected on how weird this felt. When had my social life *ever* been this busy?

I only had to stand outside of my building for a minute or two, shivering in the autumn chill and looking at the city lights beyond, before Dean pulled up at the curb. He lowered the power window on the passenger side door and leaned over to grin at me.

"Hey, good lookin'," he said. "Doing anything tonight? Want to catch a ride with a handsome stranger?"

"Well, you're strange anyway," I said, opening the door and climbing in.

"I know you meant to call me sexy, but you said 'strange' by mistake."

"That's strange, too. So, what movie are you dragging me to?"

"It's the newest Avengers movie!"

"You realize I have seen zero of the previous Avengers movies?"

"Really?" he shook his head. "I don't know what you did with your life before I came along."

"Read books, mostly. And not comic books. So, tell me. What are these folks Avenging?"

"I dunno. General injustice?"

"So they just chose the name because it sounded snappy, is what you're telling me."

"That's about it."

It felt good walking into the movie theatre with Dean because it *didn't* remind me of Howie. Howie hardly ever went to movies with me — he found it hard to focus on them. Besides, I hadn't been to a movie in months. I liked going to movies. You got to sit in a dark room and not talk to people. That's my kind of social outing.

"Oh, shit," I said, punching Dean's arm in excitement.

"Ow!" he rubbed his arm. "What the hell?"

"That new Maggie Smith movie is out. I fucking love Maggie Smith!"

"Really?"

"Uh, *yeah,* she is my role model. When I am old, I want to be exactly like her."

"Wrinkled and Scottish?"

"English, not Scottish, and that's fine with me as long as I can be dignified and caustically witty, too. Look, there's a showing in like ten minutes and at this time of night we'll probably have the theatre to ourselves. How badly do you want to see this Revengey-dudes movie?"

"Nope, there's no way you're convincing me to give up *The Avengers* for some movie about old British women doing something saucy. Maybe some other time, babe."

I was scanning the other posters lining the walls. "Humph," I said, pointing at a poster with a zombie horde on it. "I bet that's terrible."

"Yeah, kind of makes me want to go see it," said Dean. "You'd have better luck convincing me to go to that than the Maggie Smith flick."

"I'm kind of intrigued, but movies like that are always so unrealistic," I said.

Dean gave me a strange look. "Really? You nitpick zombie films?"

I rushed to explain. "I mean like for one thing, no one ever thinks to pick up some riot gear or any other kind of armour, which would be my first thing. If they can't bite you, zombies are pretty harmless."

"Which would take all the fun out of a zombie movie." Dean shook his head. "Remind me to explain about zombies and the whole point of the genre sometime."

"I'll get right on that," I said with a dryness that went over his head.

He collected our tickets from the machine and gestured at the snack bar. "I'm going to get a large popcorn to split. What do you want to drink?"

"Diet Coke, of course."

He ordered a large popcorn with two big drinks, and he picked Twizzlers for the candy. I didn't know that anyone over the age of ten actually ate Twizzlers. I opened my mouth to tell him that I hated Twizzlers but stopped myself. After all, I drove submissive, deferential Howie around the bend with my unreasonable demands, so Dean's unilateral decision-making was healthy and I should welcome it and shut the hell up. I ordered a bag of Fuzzy Peaches for myself and rejoined Dean, who was emptying the entire contents of the butter-flavoured-topping-which-was-basically-just-salty-oil dispenser onto the popcorn.

"If you don't take your finger off of that button, we'll miss the movie," I said, because I have a limited amount of self-control with regards to my pathological bossiness.

Dean grinned. "If I don't make sure that some of this drizzles down to the bottom of this popcorn, we'll end up with half a bag of butter-less popcorn."

"Perish the thought." I grabbed several handfuls of napkins. I had a feeling we would need them.

The movie was fine, if not mentally stimulating. The plot easy to follow and Dean kept a never-ending stream of Marvel trivia pouring in my ear throughout, just in case I missed some clever reference. He kept pushing me to eat more popcorn, but it was so slicked with salty oil that I felt like my tongue was mummified after just a few bites and I kept compulsively wiping my fingers after each handful. Besides, I was pretty full already with a bowl of ramen in my stomach. I kept politely declining when he shook the bag at me. Then he started shoving Twizzlers at me.

"No thanks," I whispered after my silent head shakes failed to get the message across.

"Go ahead," he urged. "I got them for both of us."

I felt a twinge of irritation. "But I don't *want* them. I have Fuzzy Peaches." I offered him my bag. "Want some?"

"When did you get those?"

"While you were emptying oil all over the popcorn," I hissed with a touch of asperity.

Dean shrugged and took a handful. "Thanks."

"Oh man, that was so good," Dean enthused as we left the theatre. "What was your favourite part?"

"Thor's face," I said. "The movie needed about 300% more close-ups of Thor's face."

Dean's face darkened. "You like blond guys, don't you?"

I shrugged. "Not particularly. I like handsome men, and that was one good looking man."

He put his arm around my waist. "Oh, well, that explains why you're with me, anyway."

"Natch," I said, and I felt a little giddy.

"Here, you take the popcorn," Dean said when we reached the car. "There's still plenty left."

I took the popcorn and got into the passenger seat.

"You don't need to hold back, you know," Dean said as he got in. "I know girls are always worried about eating on dates, but I'm not going to judge you, I swear."

I gave him a strange look. "I'm not embarrassed to eat in front of you. That sounds fucking weird. I wasn't eating because I wasn't *hungry*. I had dinner just before you picked me up, remember? Plus I'm not a fan of oily popcorn or Twizzlers, which are basically just tubes of red plastic and strike me as wholly inedible."

"Okay. Just so you know," he said, signalling and turning right.

"Where are we going?" I asked.

He looked surprised. "Back to my place."

"When did we agree that we were going to your place?"

"I just assumed. It makes more sense. It's already late and my place is closer. Taking you up to SFU would add another fifteen minutes each way onto my trip."

I took deep breaths. *Don't be a bitch. Don't be a bitch.* "I wasn't planning to stay at your place. I don't have any fresh clothes for tomorrow."

"I'll drop you off in the morning in time to change before class," he said, shrugging.

"I'd just really rather you took me home."

"What's this really about?" Dean said, looking hurt. "Don't you want to spend the night with me? Is my place so bad?"

"It's not the night that's the problem," I said irritably. "It's the morning."

"It'll be fine," said Dean. "Stop worrying so much. I swear, I'll get you to class in fresh clothes with time to spare. I have to be downtown early as it is."

I sighed. "Okay."

"Personally," he said, resting his muscular hand on my upper thigh and massaging it suggestively, "I can't wait to get into bed with you."

But I was feeling too annoyed to be seduced. "There's an ambulance coming. Get over to the right."

"They're fine, babe. They aren't even in my lane and they've got a clear path."

"GET OVER TO THE RIGHT AND STOP."

"Yessir, Mister Nose Mole, sir."

I was drooping with exhaustion by the time we hit Dean's place. I'd had a full day of classes, followed by kung fu, followed by a social gathering, followed by a movie. I'm not the sort of person who enjoys a busy day full of human beings, so I was *wiped*.

I dumped my shoes at the door and headed straight for Dean's bedroom. Then I paused at the door and swore. Dean, who was hanging up his coat, turned around.

"What's up, babe?"

"I don't have a book to read. I had an ebook on my phone but I finished it. Do you have any good books?"

"I can think of more entertaining things we can do," said Dean with a smouldering look. He grabbed my butt and pulled me close against him.

"Nothing is more entertaining than reading." I was only half-teasing, but the way he was holding me and looking at me was starting to have an effect on my heart rate.

"Really?" he said, and he kissed me with all of his skill. I could feel my body responding to him. "Well, we'll have to see about that."

"I'm going to turn out the light now, okay?" I said to Dean later on.

He shook his head, and blinked, but didn't speak.

"What's up?"

He sighed and continued staring at the ceiling. I leaned on one elbow, looking at him with pursed lips, waiting for him to spit it out. Eventually, he spoke. "Don't get me wrong. Tonight was great. It's always great."

"...But?"

"What are you waiting for, Stella? I mean, I know you're a virgin but are you waiting for freaking marriage or something?"

"Of course not."

"Well, then what? We've been together for almost two months now. I'm monogamous with you. I know you're on birth control. I keep condoms in my wallet. So, again, I ask, what are you waiting for?"

I thought for a while. It was hard to answer his question when I wasn't even sure myself. After all, I spent months badgering Howie for sex. Now here I was on the other side of the argument. Why was I holding back with Dean? I thought about how I had felt, the times I had wanted to have sex with Howie. Did I ever feel quite that way with Dean?

"I guess… I guess I'm waiting to trust you."

"To trust me? With what? Your precious maidenhead?"

"No, you dingbat. Like… you have to understand… I spent most of my life being teased, bullied, and feeling rejected. I rejected other people so they couldn't reject me. I built up WALLS, Dean. Like, layers and layers and layers of WALLS."

"I've noticed."

"No, you have no idea. Because I had more. Waaaaay more. Like, almost impenetrable. And someone finally got through all that but it took him a hell of a lot of effort."

"How Howard Mullins of all people managed that, I will never know," said Dean, more to himself to me. "And no, that is not a cue for you to tell me. I don't want to hear about your history with someone else."

"And that's fine. My point is, I don't trust people easily. I don't let people *in* easily. I'm suspicious. I'm afraid. So, to do something that new with you, when I still feel like I'm just getting to know you, well…"

Dean looked at me seriously with his dark eyes. His thumb traced my face from my ear down to my chin.

"Okay," he said. "You take your time. It's just… It hurts me, because I want you so much, and I feel like you don't want me."

"Dean, with all of the stuff we do, how can you think I'm not attracted to you?" I said with an eye roll. Whatever this was about, it wasn't about attraction. There was something more to it than that.

"Take more time if you need it," he said. "I didn't mean to pressure you."

"Thanks," I said. "I just need more time."

29

Howie

More. More. More. I writhed in my bindings, trying to suppress the relentless cravings, but it felt as if the black thoughts had taken over. I wasn't in control of this body anymore. The cravings had me. The virus had me.

"That's right, open up," said a voice. Jess. Her voice was tinged with amusement. I wanted to clench my lips, clench my teeth, but the straw slipped into my mouth and I sucked like a man dying of thirst, like a man on death row would suck on his last cigarette, like a foul monster with a desperate craving for human brains, which I was.

This was the third helping today.

"Why are you doing this?" I asked, but the answer supplied itself to my brain, because now I could see everything, understand everything. I would never have agreed to what they wanted, give them the information they required, so long as I was in control of myself. And so they needed to push me over the edge, to the point where I was no longer in control. So they gave me more, and more, and now it had me. I could struggle with myself, beg myself to fight it, but I succumbed again and again to terrible temptation.

My mind was filled with a terrible clarity — it was like putting on glasses after years of putting up with blurry vision. I could remember everything from those MIT notes that I had studied. I could remember everything. I could understand everything. I could see how they could see, and understand how they thought. And now I was powerless to stop them. Powerless to save Stella.

Stella, the only planet of my light,
Light of my life, and life of my desire

Not anymore. The life of my desire was embodied within the skulls of all the innocent people of the world. Mothers and children and labourers and scientists. I wanted them all. God, I wanted them. I had been so stupid, so stupid. I should have agreed to the free sample right away. It would have given me the intelligence to understand their plans, the cleverness to outwit them, and it would have made them less suspicious. I would have been admitted to the inner circle and able to undermine them from within. I knew now that I had the willpower to resist such small amounts. Only once a week? I could have withstood that. For a while at least. Not forever, perhaps, but for a while. I could have saved everything. But I resisted out of a sense of morality. *Morality.*

As if it were better to suffer like this, to become a useless monster, than to become a murderer who saved the world. As if my own self-respect, my own fear of the virus, was more important than the billions who would now die — all because I had failed. Because with every dose I took, with every extra mouthful, the craving grew stronger, the buzzing grew stronger. The virus grew stronger. And I was subsumed now. I was fallen.

"Why are you doing this?" I asked again, and this time I didn't mean what they were doing to me. I meant all of it. Their pointless dreams of a new civilization which was destined only to fall into ruins. Their plans required balance, but this virus wouldn't allow balance. This craving couldn't be controlled.

Jess just smiled. "Oh, come now. You should have figured that out by now. Want some more?"

Stella, forgive me.

"Yes!"

Stella

Mars, Bringer of War started blasting on my phone at six thirty a.m. I groaned and pulled my pillow over my head.

"Make it stop," complained Dean. I fumbled for my phone and shut it off. Then I forced myself onto one elbow. Dean had already gone back to sleep. His dark hair was rumpled, and there was a pillow crease on his face, but he still looked like someone in a magazine. He had one well-muscled arm flung up over his head. It was so tempting to drape myself around his body and go back to sleep again, but I hadn't missed a single class yet and I was damned if today was going to be the day.

So instead I whopped him with my pillow.

"Ow! Why?" Dean rolled over.

"Get up. You need to get me home in time to shower and change."

"Shower here. There're spare towels in the dryer."

I rooted through his dryer and found a towel that met my standards and ventured into his shower.

"Dean!" I bellowed. "Your shower is gross!"

I don't think he had cleaned it in weeks. Months? There was dust and hair around the edges of his tub. There were also a ton of Axe products. I judged myself for being attracted to the smell of the stuff. I gave the tub a rinse while I was waiting for the water to warm up and then stepped in.

I was in the middle of lathering his Head and Shoulders into my hair, eyes squeezed shut, when I felt a pair of arms wrap around me. Without even thinking, I spread my feet and brought my elbows up sharply, striking Dean in the chest and sending him thudding against the wall of the shower.

"Ow! Jesus!"

"Oh fuck, I'm sorry," I said, opening my eyes and then squeezing them shut again when shampoo ran into them. "Argh. Soap in my eyes. Fuck. Are you okay?"

"What the hell was that?" Dean's voice sounded strained. "I was getting in the shower with you, not assaulting you."

"It's called Crow Flaps Wings. I just reacted without thinking. You startled me." I held my face up to the water and rubbed the soap out of my eyes until I could see. Dean was rubbing his chest ruefully but he didn't look badly hurt.

"Crow Flaps Wings? This is called Dean Loses Hard-On. So much for sexy shower surprises," he said, a trace of humour seeping back into his voice. "You're dangerous."

"Don't you forget it," I said. "Sorry. I've never had a man grab me in the shower before."

"Well, I've never had a woman attack me in the shower before, so let's call it a first for both of us."

I couldn't help but wonder which of his girlfriends he had showered with. I decided it was best not to think about it.

"Can I get under that water?" Dean asked.

"Oh, uh, yeah. Sure." I shuffled aside and he stood under the spray. Now I was cold. Why did people think this was sexy? I mean, Dean looked good standing naked under the running water, but I was feeling awkward and damp.

Dean wiped the water out of his eyes and looked at me appreciatively. "Why don't you come here and make up for elbowing me in the solar plexus?"

I joined him under the water and he pulled me close to him.

"God, you turn me on," he said, looking down. He looked back up and kissed me, but I broke that off quickly because it was hard to breathe while kissing with the water running over my nose.

"Fuck, I want to be inside you," he growled in my ear.

I found it really hot when he talked dirty to me like that, but I never knew what to say back. Especially since I was still really touchy about boundaries, not to mention brain-washed about sex and virginity.

"Well, that sounds nice and all," I said, caressing him a bit so he wouldn't feel too rejected. "But we've really got to get going."

"You don't know what you're missing," Dean said. "One of these days we'll take a whole lot of time off together and you'll see."

"Well, it's not going to be this weekend. I have three more midterms next week so I'm going to be studying."

Dean sighed and tilted his head at me. "You sure know how to talk sexy to a guy," he said.

"You're very sexy, Dean, but I really need to get to class."

"We have time. We can spare a few minutes."

"All right. But give me my fair share of that hot water. It's cold in here."

"Here, let me warm you up." He pulled me close and turned me into the stream of the hot water. I reached down and squeezed his hard-on. He groaned. "Fuck, babe. Yes!"

"Have you boned him yet?" Kate asked when I came rushing in the door. She was lounging on the couch with a bowl full of cereal.

"Not technically," I said. "Also, good morning." I slammed the door of my room and swiftly changed into fresh, clean clothes. I grabbed my bag, dumped my laptop into it, and snagged the charger for my phone, which was nearly dead. Okay. Ready for the school day.

"So what're you waiting for?" Kate asked. "Does he suck at the foreplay stuff? Are you still grooming him?"

"He's fine at the foreplay stuff," I said.

"Just fine? Oh dear."

"Oh please, you talk like you're soooo experienced," I said. "I've had more partners than you, thank you very much."

"So he's not as good as Howie at the foreplay stuff, huh?"

Kate could be so annoying.

"I try not to compare them. One isn't better than the other, necessarily. They're different."

"How can you not compare them?"

"I said I *try*."

"Like, I refuse to believe that you haven't mentally compared their penises."

"Just like I refuse to believe that we're having this conversation. I have to get to class. Bye."

"See ya. Oh, hey, did you hear about Toronto?"

I paused with one hand on the doorknob. "No, what about Toronto?"

"Prostitute found in an alley… missing her brains. We officially have a Canadian copycat of the Seattle Zombie."

"Shit." On the bright side, now we could do our *own* investigation of this case, instead of relying on what the Americans told us.

Kate looked at me curiously. "Don't you have to get to class?"

"Oh, yeah. Kay, bye!"

"See ya."

I spent Saturday studying for my upcoming midterms and watching the news. A second body had been found in Toronto and so the Canadian news channels and even some of the American ones were playing a bunch of stuff about the various "zombie murders" around the globe. It turns out that dead bodies have been turning up without brains now and then for years. The media just hadn't caught on to it until recently, I guess. I remembered Henri Cormier telling me that this problem went beyond Seattle.

Whenever Kate tried to change the channel I'd swat her away.

"I mean, it's gory and all," said Kate, "but what's with the fascination?"

"Hard to explain," I said. "It just worries me."

"My mother's being weird about it, too," said Kate. "I don't get it. And it's not like you to hang over the news like this. Is it because the murder happened on the East Coast?"

I pointed a finger at her. "Ontario is *not* the East Coast. That was *such* a West Coast statement that I can't even. Ontario is *central* Canada. There are *five provinces* further East than Ontario."

"So what, then? I mean, when I was at Mom's for dinner last night, this was all she and The Skeez could talk about. But homeless people getting killed isn't anything new. I think the police need to step up their game in that department, but I don't think it should be front page news. Come on, I missed Master Chef this week and Riya and I want to watch it."

I reluctantly turned over the remote. "Okay, but only because I want to watch Gordon Ramsay yell at idiots."

Kate was right. Besides, I didn't even know if this had anything to do with zombies. But I was determined to find out.

Hunt answered her phone immediately.

"Stella?" she said. "Is there something wrong?"

"Uh, no, not exactly," I said, a little thrown. She sounded so *concerned*. "I just, uh… I was wondering what you know about that murder in Toronto."

"I can't talk about that now," she said. Her voice was back to its usual brisk, dismissive tone. "I will contact you if there's anything you need to know."

"Okay. Uh. Also," I said, fiddling with the bow on my teddy bear. "I haven't heard from you in a while. Just, you know, you're paying for my tuition and I feel like maybe I could be doing more to earn it? Assist Dr. Mullins in the lab or something?"

"You're not far enough along in your education to be of much use to him," said Hunt. "He already has an assistant. Just concentrate on school for now, please. I will be in touch if we need you."

"Okay…" I said.

"Goodbye."

"Bye."

I stared at my phone for a while after she hung up. It had been nice to be free of the zombie stuff for a while, but I was starting to feel left out. I was sure something was going on. Why was I being kept out of it all?

Howie

What bizarre concatenations of atoms. How peculiar that subatomic particles can bind together into molecules, into complex proteins, into cellular organisms. How peculiar that cellular organisms can create complex colonies which think of themselves as singular beings, which give themselves names and create subjective experiences and then conceive the illusion that these subjective experiences have any kind of meaning.

One of these was before me now, and creating sound waves from a structure called the larynx which, when interpreted by the cellular organisms within my own cranium, created a codified response which we called language, and by which we can transmit data.

"What's your real name?" the voice said.

"Names are subjective collections of sounds which we use to denote particular colonies of communal cellular organism. Since they are arbitrary, and only exist within the subjective experience of certain living organisms, they cannot, by definition, be 'real'."

"Excellent point," agreed the collection of cellular organisms, which called itself Brenden Abernathy, "and I agree with you, but for the sake of simplicity, how about you tell me your fucking name."

"Howard Joseph Mullins. I was born in the geographical region called Manitoba, Canada."

"Mullins? Are you related to Morton Mullins?"

"The organism you refer to adopted me. Originally my surname was given as Fontaine."

"He adopted you… ah… you're one of the originals, aren't you? The suppressed research? You're one of the ones he converted before they put a stop to the treatment!"

"Your surmises are correct." How strange that this knowledge previously seemed so precious. Data is intended to be shared.

"And you came here to try and find out what we were up to. You were trying to stop us."

"I was operating under illusions of morality and had conceived the notion that certain behaviours towards certain other collections of organisms was in some way unacceptable. This way of thinking no longer seems logical."

"That's because you've drunk too much of the kool-aid, as it were. Take just a little bit and you gain the smarts but keep your sanity. Shame you wouldn't cooperate. Not everyone has the willpower to hold the balance — they get greedy and we end up having to lock them up here — but yours is impressive. You would have done well in Apex. But your morality was unshakable. It took you seven doses to get you over the brink. I think that's a record."

"I can no longer understand the reasoning behind my abstention."

"You shared the collective delusion that most people suffer from — that killing humans is somehow worse than killing farm animals."

"Yes. It seems strangely arbitrary now."

"Of course it's arbitrary. There's no argument you can make which can make it seem logical. Sheep and cows are as likely to experience pain and fear as humans, so it is no more kind to eat one than the other. Of course, there is a biological sense to it — if humans consume their own species this will reduce propagation of the species."

"But humans are not at risk of extinction. In fact, there are far more humans than seem wanted by their own species — millions starving, left without homes or medical care."

"Exactly. And besides — they don't seem like our species now, do they?"

"Since my DNA has been irreparably altered by the retrovirus known as Z0381E, it could be argued that I am, in fact, a distinct species."

"We are the next step in the evolution of hominids, the new species which will consume the old. Homo Vorax. And so the consumption of human material is not even a matter of consuming your own species. We…" and he closed one eye and opened again, which my neural cells informed me was a human gesture known as a wink, "…are the farmers, and they are the sheep in our field. We call ourselves neurovores."

"That label mixes Greek and Latin roots."

"Yeah. But cerebravore and nervovore sound stupid." He held up a spoon, and my reflections disappeared in a primal roar of need. "Tell me everything you remember about Howard Mullins, and everything he knew, and you will get what you desire."

30

Howie

"So let me get this straight." The conglomeration of atoms known as Brenden was making facial expressions of human glee. "Baum is convinced that Apex is a secret branch of the United States government."

"Yes. More."

"Not yet. Did he say *why* he thought this?"

I moved restlessly. I sat in a chair, within a room, which I now believed to be a storage unit — the kind that humans usually used for surplus commercial goods which they had neither room nor need for and yet wished to retain ownership of nonetheless. But this building did not store commercial goods. It stored people like myself. I could feel the electrical activity of their brains. Like me, they had seen farther. Like me, they were overwhelmed by the need.

More. More.

"*Talk,* Mullins."

"Baum is an ardent pacifist who dislikes the politics of the U.S. Government. Naturally prone to paranoia, Baum also believes that Canada's culture is at risk for domination by media produced over the border, as well as products and services. Naturally, all of this is nonsense, since the line drawn between these two countries is arbitrary in nature and there is no true difference between the two areas of land."

"Which is why we plan to remove all such arbitrary borders. There's no point in small self-organized groups of humans conflicting over religion, culture, and other minor niceties, is there, Mullins?"

"No."

"So let's go back to Baum. He hates the U.S. and thinks it's out to get the rest of the world, notably Canada, is that right?"

"Yes. More."

"So we've got his contact info on your phone. It should be easy enough to send him all kinds of false information about America's plans to destroy the world through Apex."

"How would that benefit you?"

"Misdirection. Distraction. We've had trouble keeping him from getting suspicious since we captured you, you know. He keeps wanting check-ins to make sure you're okay. We've been sending messages claiming that you're under close surveillance and don't dare message often until you have gained our trust. I think we can safely say that trust is gained now and we can start bleeding all kinds of false information. With luck, we may be able to sow distrust between Canada and America, which will only make our lives easier on our big day."

"If you intend to remove governmental bodies, I assume you already have a plan to release the virus en masse within those organizations, to remove leadership from the countries."

"Of course, and we have a number of very useful moles in every government of the world. Well," he thought for a moment. "Except for a few minor nations. But really, Aruba isn't going to reclaim the world from a zombie apocalypse. In any case, A-Day, as we call it, will be sudden and massive. The world will collapse instantly, have no doubt about that."

"You will fail. More."

"We will succeed. And what do you care? Still clinging to your affection for the world as it is now?"

"Humans are nothing more than an ant nest on a minuscule dust mote orbiting an unremarkable star. I have no attachment to ephemeral politics."

"Good. Tell me more about Baum. Vancouver has been a frustrating location for us thanks to Morton Mullins. We can't let our members go anywhere near him, because he'd spot us right away for what we are, and everything we've learned about him tells us that he wouldn't be sympathetic to the higher cause."

"Morton Mullins has an extremely strong attachment to human morality."

"And he'd recognize us right away, wouldn't he? He'd feel us out."

"Yes. More."

"Anyway, we've been steering clear of him — sticking to the suburbs — and we finally managed to recruit one of his assistants to our cause."

I felt slight interest. "Which one?"

"Leanne Wilson."

Some distant human part of me experienced a feeling of surprise but it was a dim sensation as the need for more overwhelmed me.

The organism known as Brenden continued. "Wilson doesn't realize who she is really working for, of course, nor what our true goal is. I suppose we could throw her under the bus, but then we'll lose our eyes in the Vancouver section of the Canadian Reanimation Virus Control Service."

"The outbreak last year. It was because of Apex." My brain raced through permutations, through deeper understandings, and I knew the story as if it had already been spoken. "One of your recruits lost control. Wanted more." I nearly doubled over with unbearable longing for what was rightfully mine. Mine. More. "They all will want more. Apex will fall."

"A lot of people don't have the willpower to withstand the cravings." Brenden's voice showed no concern for the truths which seemed so evident to my greater brain. "It took our founder many years to find some people who could hack it. And if they can't handle the once-a-week regimen, they end up somewhere like this." He waved his hand at the cell which enclosed me.

Yes, it all made sense. It was obvious; it was so clear. I would have been glad to learn this information once, but not anymore. The universe is vast and we are but fragments of proteins dreaming of self-replication.

Brenden opened the container in his hands. I lost all thought of anything except ingesting the contents. I flexed my arms, trying to break the heavy chains that bound me. I could feel the metal creaking under the strain, but it would not give. But metal fatigues, with time, and I had an eternity, so I continued to flex and strain as Brenden spoke.

"You're getting me off topic, so I need to keep you more focused. Tell me about Baum."

I forced myself to communicate, despite my roaring need. "There is little more to divulge. He's a former employee of Border Services. He specialized in security. He has been with The Service for eight years or so. He disliked me and we never conversed on a personal level. More. *Please.*"

"Why doesn't he like you?"

"He believes that people like us are a risk to humanity — that we should never have been allowed to live in the first place, and that drastic measures should have been taken after my father's second discovery in the nineteen seventies. Given Apex's plans, it appears that he was correct."

"We aren't a threat to humanity. We're humanity's next step. There are only two kinds of people — those strong enough to take that step, and sheep to be consumed. How does he know about us? How much does he know?"

"He has been monitoring a series of incidents over the past several years, as well as posts on the area of the internet known as the 'dark web' which led him to believe that the virus was being knowingly spread. He also insists that the events in Vancouver last year were an offshoot of this activity and that he is innocent."

"Well, he's right enough there," Brenden shrugged. "Although we were very amused when he got the blame." He shook his cranium back and forth. "What a clusterfuck that was. Three recruits went off the rails all at once and started an outbreak." He studied me. "Any idea why?"

Yes. But I had no reason to divulge that particular piece of information. Besides, it was obvious.

"More," I said.

He shook his head. "Anyway, we decided to frame Mullins by getting Wilson to steal a lab animal and deliver it to us — of course, she thought she was doing it for good and wholesome reasons, to expose Morton Mullins. Apex was going to enhance the hamster with a bit of the good stuff and then put it where The Service would be sure to find it. But our regional manager blacked out and dropped the damn thing. Again — any idea why that might have happened?"

"More."

"Not until you start telling me what you know."

"Will you feed me more?" Information was worth bites. *Feed me more. Feed me more and perhaps I will give up this secret. But oh, this secret is worth more than a single bite. It's worth more.*

I could feel his irritation rise, like flies disturbed from a meal. "If you want more, give me some damn info. If Baum sent you here, does that mean that he's working for The Service again? Wilson said that he's still on administrative leave pending the investigation."

"Baum did not send me here on the orders of The Service. He contacted me privately and suggested that I come here to help find proof that he was not responsible for the outbreak in Vancouver."

"So he knew Apex was behind it, then."

"Yes, but he believes it was an orchestrated attack from the United States — a small scale practice run of a future invasion. He thought that my family was either in charge of, or a part of, Apex, but he has been persuaded otherwise."

"What an idiot," Brenden said. "No one in their right mind would try to recruit Morton Mullins. By all accounts, the man has more morality than sense. So, if Baum hated you and suspected you, why on earth did you agree to come?"

"I had more morality than sense."

"Obviously. I'm actually impressed by the depths of your stubborn idiocy. I've never seen anyone hold out so long, not after the first taste.

You clung to your outmoded human belief system with impressive dedication." He wiggled the open container in his hand. "It's a shame, really. Someone with your willpower would be a great asset to Apex. There aren't many of us who can resist it this well. We have to keep the weaker ones — like your friend Cassie — under lock and key. But you're the opposite — too moral to cooperate unless you're pushed past the point of no return."

I moved restlessly. "The first bite is the point of no return. Everyone will succumb with time. More."

"Yeah, yeah. That's what all of you crazies say. Yet here I am. So, who other than the discredited Baum knows that you're here?"

"It depends on what Baum has chosen to disclose. Morton, Hazel and Raymond will know that I am missing, of course, and I am certain that The Service does as well. But until Baum takes the information to The Service and informs them, my mission is a secret."

"Well then..." Brenden tapped his chin. "All we need to do is feed him the stuff we want him to take to CRVCS. You can help us there."

"I have no reason or motivation to aid your organization. It is a meaningless enterprise doomed to fall into chaos."

"I have all the motivation I need right here in my hands. Want more?"

Want? No. Need, crave, demand. I flexed my arms, willed my chains to break. I was strong, now. I could feel the strength pouring through me. I could feel the chains creak under the strain, but they held fast.

"Help me sort out the right lies to feed to Baum, and you will get what you need."

Stella

"Uh, Stella? World's Best Dad is calling your phone," said Kate a couple of hours later.

"I didn't name him that. He named himself that."

"But you didn't change it," said Kate.

I stuck my tongue out and picked up my phone. "I need to change your contact name in my phone," I said to Dad. "Kate thinks it's weird."

"Can I be Batman?" Dad asked eagerly.

"No."

"Okay, fine. Commissioner Gordon?"

"I was thinking more along the lines of Annoying Old Guy."

"How about The Spirit of Christmas Present? Because you know what I'm going to say next."

"That you want me to come over and help decorate on December first," I said with resignation.

"You got it in one, kiddo!"

"Of course I'll be there, Dad. Assuming you come up here and fetch me."

"Good. Bring Dean."

"I am *not* bringing Dean." The thought filled me with horror.

"Come on. We've been wanting to invite him for dinner anyway. It's a marvellous opportunity."

"For you."

"What's your point?"

"I don't know."

"If you don't ask him, I will," said Dad.

"You don't have his number!"

"Oh, please. That kid selfies himself all over social media with absolutely no regard for privacy. I could contact him by accident from my pants pocket."

"Ugh. Fine. I'll ask him."

To my relief, Dean couldn't come to Dad's Christmas Binge.

"Wish I could babe," he had said with what looked like genuine regret. "But I've got like three projects due this week and I don't know if I can spare the time."

"No problem," I said hurriedly. "Really not a problem. Consider yourself lucky. Dad is obsessed with Christmas. It's going to look like Santa's workshop in our house by the time he's done, and then he and Mom will make out under the mistletoe for an embarrassing length of time."

"Sorry to miss that," Dean said with a wink. "Seriously, if I didn't have a project due the very next day…"

"No, it's really really okay," I had reassured him, and I meant it. Walking into my parents' house was always a bit of an emotion-bomb. I met Howie the day after we moved into the place, so the majority of my time spent there had involved Howie. He haunted the damn place. When I walked into their kitchen I could see him washing the dishes with the dishtowel slung over his shoulder. When I went to the living room I saw the two of us cuddling on the couch.

It messed me up.

What's worse — I think my parents knew it. I could see them *watching* me whenever I came in. So I usually made them take me out for meals instead of coming home and they never argued. I hadn't been home in over a month. But December first was sacrosanct for Dad, so I knew there was no escaping it.

Dad picked me up at my place. As soon as we walked in the door, he threw a box full of decorations at me and pointed me into the living room. I tried to focus on spreading garlands all over the damn room, but I couldn't help but see Howie. Every memory stung me. Until Howie and I broke up, I had never known that heartache was a real thing, not just a turn of phrase. And lately, finally, I had been free of it. Kung fu and Kate and Dean and my classes all kept me busy.

But now here I was, standing in my damn living room, holding a stupid silver garland and feeling deeply depressed.

Maybe I should have pushed Dean to come after all.

"So," Dad said, nudging me and taking the other end of the garland. "Now that I have you at home, in private, I can ask you the question that has been driving your mother and me crazy."

Uh oh. "What?" I said sullenly as we wound the garland up the banister.

"What the hell is going on with the zombie murders? Your mother tried to call Hunt but she wouldn't tell us anything. Have you heard from The Cervix at all?"

"I called Hunt," I said. "But she wouldn't tell me anything. She was kind of short with me, actually."

"Hunt? Short with someone? Tell me it ain't so," said Mom from the couch.

"Feel free to jump in and help anytime, Lainey," said Dad.

"I'll think about it. But it's so hard to get up… when my eggnog is running so low…"

"On it," said Dad, hopping down the stairs. "While I'm in there, remind me to hang up the mistletoe."

"Well… if I had more eggnog… I *might* be able to go *that* far…"

"Oh God," I said. "I need to use the bathroom. I'll be back."

I called Dean from the bathroom.

"Please come save me," I whispered. "I know you have work to do, and you don't have to stay long. Just, like, get me out of here."

"Sure thing, babe. I can spare an hour. I'm going shack wacky here anyway."

"Time it right and they'll feed you."

"Two birds, one stone. I love it. What's the address?"

Dean showed up right on time. My parents were kissing under the newly hung mistletoe and I was ignoring them and hanging up lights and working on definitely not remembering Howie kissing me there last year.

He had pulled me in so gently, and kissed me so tenderly… Oh God. That was a year ago. I had a new boyfriend. What was *wrong* with me?

Then the doorbell rang, and Dad opened the door.

"Dean!" he said. "What a surprise! Come on in, please!"

Dean grinned and stepped in. I tried to warn him but Dad swooped in before I could get the words out and kissed Dean on the cheek.

"Mistletoe," Dad explained, pointing up.

Dean looked up. "Oh!" he said. Then he grabbed Dad and planted a big one right on Dad's lips. Dad started laughing and slapped his thighs.

"I love it!" he said. "Come in and have some eggnog. Did you drive?"

Dean nodded.

"I'll make it a virgin, then."

"Great," said Dean. He reached out to me and winked. "Hey, babe."

"Thanks," I whispered to him.

"No problem," he said. "Now give me a smooch."

I had been hoping that Dean's buoyant presence would banish Howie's ghost. And it did, in a way. But not entirely. Dean kissed me under the mistletoe, but part of me was wondering if Howie was nearby, and if so, what he was thinking right now.

Howie

Meaningless. This was all meaningless.

I flexed my chains again and again, willing the metal to bend or buckle as these fools pressed me for feedback on their falsehoods. The fictions were sent using characters from the Latin alphabet, entered into the hand-held device known as a smartphone and transmitted using signals and satellites to another handheld device in another part of the planet.

And all of it was meaningless. Their grandiose visions of a complex society were pointless and destined to failure.

"Stop saying that we're going to fail," said the organism known as Craig. "It's annoying. You don't know anything about us or our plans. We're highly intelligent, and not all crazy like you. We have this meticulously planned, and the people in our organization make Mensa look like a bunch of village idiots. It can't fail."

Craig was weaker — easier to goad than Jess or Brenden, and so goad him I did. Anything to keep my brain occupied while I sat in captivity, longing for freedom. Freedom to indulge. Freedom to be.

"It cannot succeed."

Craig ticked plans off on his fingers. Fool. Idiot. "Day 1: A-Day. Hospitals, prisons, and airports will be infected along with federal branches of government in all the major nations. We already have the people placed. At the same time, power plants and satellites will go offline. So people will wake up to instant hordes of viral carriers sweeping through the streets, and no communication systems. With panic and chaos everywhere, we attack and disable military bases. By Day 2, we will have eliminated government on a city and state level, too. We will instate ourselves instead. By Day 3, we will have control of every major country, including the United States, Canada, Britain, China, and Russia."

"Craig, shut up," said the organism known as Jess. "He doesn't need to know Apex's plans. What if he gets loose and contacts somebody?"

"He's too far gone for that," said Craig. "You want to go home? Find your family? Live a normal life?"

"Of course not." I flexed my arms again. Metal fatigues. Metal wears.

"Besides, the more he knows about our real plans, the more he can help us misdirect the Canadians."

"Don't you watch movies? It's never a good idea to monologue about your plans to your hostage." Jess looked at Craig with scorn. "He's talking too much sense. I think we need to feed him up a bit."

"I don't need to do anything with your information," I said. "Your plan is doomed to fail."

"Tell us why, oh brilliant one," said Jess, showing her teeth.

"There is no purpose to complex society. Each individual organism is a society quite complex in and of itself. We exist to reproduce. There is no point to higher society. Politics. Technology. Law. All meaningless distractions. And more and more of you will see this… with time."

"You've gone too far to see it. That's what happens. But we're balanced. We can see both sides, and it's the ideal place to be."

"What is the rate? What proportion have the willpower?"

"About fifty percent, in the short term," said Craig. "Long-term rates are more like thirty."

"Your plan will fail."

"Because of them?" Craig gestured to the closed metal door, indicating all of the minds I could feel around me, captured like I was, held back from being what they must be, biding their time, longing and needing. "No." His eyes gleamed with mental visions. He was fantasizing about a society which could not stand. "They are our army."

31

Stella

Dean drove me home from my parents' place.

"Want to come back with me?"

"No, please drop me at home."

He sighed. "Okay, babe." His fingers tapped the steering wheel and I could tell he was feeling annoyed. I was pushing him away again, wasn't I? That evening with my parents had made me realize how much I was still keeping Dean separate from the rest of my life. If I wanted to banish Howie for good, I needed to make some changes.

"So…" I said. "My kung fu club is having a kind of a Christmas party this weekend."

"Awesome," he said. "I've been wanting to meet your kung fu friends."

"Really?" I'd been expecting an argument, for some reason. Projects. Exams.

"Yeah, why not?"

No idea. "You never invite me along to hang out with your friends," I said.

"That's because you hate people and show no interest in meeting my friends," said Dean reasonably. "My theatre buddies are having a party this weekend too. You want to come?"

I opened and then closed my mouth. "If you want me to."

"You're my girlfriend. Why wouldn't I want you to come?" he said. "And why wouldn't I want to come along to yours?"

Girlfriend. He's really calling me his girlfriend. I think that on some level I always thought that the sword of Damocles was going to fall — that he would decide that he had gotten his fill of the fat girl and go back to the life of womanizing that he seemed made for. We hadn't said I love you or anything, but we were physically intimate and we certainly had all of the hallmarks of a boyfriend/girlfriend pair… except that it all still felt temporary to me.

"So, here's my deal," said Dean. "I go to your Kung Fu Christmas Party, and you have to come along to my Geeky Theatre Friends Party."

"Somehow I doubt that your friends are geeky," I said. "But okay. Deal."

My friends at kung fu knew that I had a boyfriend named Dean, but they didn't really know much else. So, when I showed up with him at our Christmas party, it caused a minor ruckus. People have certain preconceived notions about attractiveness and how couples should match each other. So, while these people were my friends and genuinely seemed to like me, I don't think they were expecting Stella The Giant to walk in with a guy who could easily be a model if he wanted to.

"Stella, are you going to introduce me?" prompted Melanie, walking over and giving Dean a big smile. I felt a thump of jealousy, and then I felt ashamed. Melanie was my friend.

"Melanie, this is Dean. Dean, this is Melanie, one of the head instructors," I said. They shook hands and Dean cast Melanie the sort of white-toothed, smouldering grin that made me hate him when we were in high school together. She blushed and looked away. Then John came over to meet him, and Dean gave him a friendly handshake and immediately struck up a conversation about MMA, which I don't follow at all.

Basically, Dean was a hit. He got along with everyone and everyone got along with him. I caught several of them giving me marvelling glances. But I never felt like they were laughing behind my back, or wondering how on earth I had managed to score such a hot boyfriend. They just seemed pleasantly surprised and happy for me. It felt good. I felt… proud.

Pride was not a feeling I was accustomed to having.

I wondered if I'd feel the same way at his party tomorrow night.

Howie

The universe is but a vast emptiness, with minuscule molecules swirling as mere specks within. Some of these molecules take the time to become part of a star, and then part of a comet, and then part of a planet, and then part of a rock, and then part of a river, and then part of a human, and then move on again. Nothing stays still. Nothing even touches. Craig rubs his hands and feels that they touch each other, but in fact, there is an infinite space between them. But somewhere, in this universe of swirling motes of dust, there is a collection of temporary molecules which call themselves Stella Blunt. This particular pattern, this particular configuration, could make a difference.

Outbreaks are generally calculated based on a standard diffusion equation.

Let the density of infected individuals at point x and time t be Z(x,t).

The density has to satisfy the diffusion equation:

∂Z/∂t (x, t) = D ∂^2Z/∂x^2 (x, t)

That would represent the rate of change of the infected individuals at x over time. If ∂Z/∂t is positive, then Z is increasing. The factor D would be a constant, representing the movement of infected individuals.

"See? You fed him too much! Mullins? Mullins?"

A population can be subdivided into different classes, where (S) represents those susceptible to infection, (E) represents those who have been exposed, and with (I) representing the actively infectious.

N = S + I + E.

That seems obvious.

"Well, I had to, Brenden! He was holding back. You know he was holding back."

Let β be the disease transmission parameter, so βSI would represent the densities of S and I, and E would be proportional to that.

The average length of time for an exposed individual to become infectious would be $1/\sigma$.

To take a long-term view of things, let's have (R) represent reproduction systems. R = a — b where a represents the per capita birth rate and 1/b equals the mean life expectancy. Population equilibrium would be a/b, which we can call K.

"Yeah, I know he was holding back but we should have starved him for it. He would have cracked eventually. Now he's just mumbling gibberish. Give him a formaldehyde injection. Maybe that'll help."

Of course, infected individuals have a different mortality rate. Unlike most systems, this mortality rate is a variable in its own right, since it is entirely dependent on the human ability to eliminate infected individuals from the system. So. Let that be represented by α.

"I'm telling you, Brenden, you can't crack this guy with the normal methods. You have to send him further into the virus. It's the only way. Have you heard anything from Baum?"

"Yes, he says she's guarded round the clock, which is what Wilson is saying too. What a pain in the ass this is. Waste of fucking time."

"You going to tell Her Royal Highness that?"

"Shut up, Jess."

Then

$dS/dt = rS - \gamma SN - \beta SI$

$dE/dt = \beta SI - (\sigma + b + \gamma SN)E$

$dI/dt = \sigma E - (\alpha + b + \gamma SN)I$

$St = (\sigma + a)\ (\alpha + a)/\beta\sigma$

"Vancouver isn't even my jurisdiction. Why am I left dealing with this crap?"

"Because you managed to capture one of the Mullinses. And he was dating Canada's ZCP. It's like a gold mine just walked into our house."

...No, this is far too simplistic. There's another variable to be accounted for. Another mote, floating among these other insignificant specks of immaterial things. I'll call that variable StB.

"There! Did you hear that? StB!"

"Shut up, Jess. Mullins! Mullins — How can we get to her? Mullins? Mullins, can you hear me? Damnit, Jess. Don't feed him any more. He's too far gone."

Stella

Dean whistled when he saw me. "Well, don't you look sexy tonight?"

"Thank you, kind sir," I said. I was wearing my black and red pinup dress, which I hadn't worn since my eighteenth birthday.

"Ready to go to a real party?" he said.

"No. I hate real parties."

He laughed. "It'll be fun, I promise."

I did not find it fun. It was at some guy's apartment, which was fairly large, and every room was crammed with people I didn't know, *all* of whom seemed to know my boyfriend.

"DEAN!" people shouted, and he high fived them and fist bumped them and he even slapped one gay guy on the ass.

"This is Stella," he would say, and tell me the name of the person he was introducing me to. They would say hi, and nice to meet me, and then promptly forget about me. I had braced myself for incredulous glances, or laughter and someone saying "no, really, where's your real girlfriend?" but none of that happened. Then again, I'm not entirely sure they understood that I was Dean's girlfriend. After all, he always introduced me as "Stella", not "my girlfriend, Stella" or "my skilled and sexy lover, Stella". Then again, I hadn't introduced Dean as "my boyfriend, Dean". But that was because everyone at kung fu already *knew* that I had a boyfriend named Dean. So, did everyone here already know that Dean had a girlfriend named Stella? It wasn't clear to me.

Nobody said "oh, it's nice to meet you finally!" or "Dean keeps talking about you!" or anything. They were all half drunk and over the next hour many of them proceeded to full-on drunk. As the underaged designated driver, I sipped pop in the corner with an awkward smile on my face. The party swirled around me as I sat. Dean kept disappearing. He would sit with me for a while, get me engaged in a conversation with someone, and then he would swirl off to "mingle" and the conversation would stall as the person quickly lost interest in the big Biology student.

I knew that this was mostly my fault. When I want to, I have the kind of presence that can get the attention of an entire room. I mean, I can blast a crowd of zombies out of my way when I want to, and regular humans seem to take notice, too. But in a noisy party, in a confined space, surrounded by strangers, with my history of being mocked and ostracized in public spaces, my instinct was to stay inconspicuous. After an hour of this, I finally talked myself into taking charge a little. *Get up, go find Dean, and start showing people what a kick-ass personality you have,* I scolded myself. So I stood up and sidled awkwardly through the crowds until I spotted Dean.

He was in the kitchen, sitting on the counter with a girl on either side of him. He had one arm casually braced behind one, a redhead, and they were all laughing at something he said.

I saw red.

This was it, the sword of Damocles, but I'd be damned if it would be coming down on my head. I felt a burst of fury, and people instinctively moved out of my way as I marched through the kitchen toward my womanizing, treacherous shit stick of a boyfriend.

He saw me coming and grinned.

"Hey, babe!" he said, holding out a hand, "I want you to meet some people."

This threw me off kilter. I had been expecting him to flinch guiltily or do something else to confirm that yes, he was a duplicitous snake. But he was acting as if everything was totally normal, which made me think that maybe it was. I hesitated.

"Ally, Taylor, this is Stella," he said, pulling me close. "Ally and Taylor are in most of my classes," he told me.

"Hi," I said to them.

"Hi!" they said back, and that's when I saw it — the exchanged look, as if to say, "who is this girl and what is her relationship with Dean?" Considering he had his arm wrapped around me, you'd think it was obvious, but after all, this was Dean we were dealing with. He probably wrapped his arm around everybody all the time. And I guess they didn't already know that his girlfriend's name was Stella. If they knew he had a girlfriend at all.

"So, anyway, you should come next time, we miss having you there," said Taylor, turning back to Dean.

"Go where?" I asked, stubbornly inserting myself into the conversation.

"To improv," said Dean to me. "I've been too busy to go recently. You should come, too." He looked at the girls. "Stella's great at improv."

"Are you in performance or production?" Ally asked politely.

"I'm in science," I said.

"Oh," she said.

"We were in Drama together in high school," Dean explained. "That's where I saw her do improv."

"Ohhh," they said, nodding.

He started to tell them about our skit and being the Infant of Prague. They started to laugh and insisted on pictures, so he pulled up his Facebook to show them.

"Oh my god, that's amazing," said Taylor, laughing at a photo of him in the dress. "It definitely suits you."

"I know, I'm thinking about entirely changing my wardrobe to old wedding dresses," agreed Dean.

"I don't know if it would work as an everyday look," said Ally. She fingered the rolled-up sleeve of his shirt. "This suits you better."

"I don't know," he said. "I think the wedding dress showed off my arm muscles really nicely. Can you see them under this shirt?" He flexed his arm, and Ally obligingly felt up his biceps.

"Hmm, yeah, they don't stand out quite so well," she said. "Maybe the wedding dress would be better for you after all."

"I should probably grow my hair out, too," he said, touching her long hair lightly. "More like yours."

"You have great hair," she agreed, "it's definitely a shame to keep it so short. Many a girl would be jealous of hair like that."

"Dean, can I talk to you for a moment?" I said, a trifle too loudly. The three of them looked surprised.

"Yeah, sure," said Dean with furrowed brows. He slid off the counter. "See you," he said to the two girls, and he put his arm around my waist. I pulled away and led him out of the apartment and outside onto the street.

"What's wrong?" he kept saying, but I wanted to get well away from the party. Once we were alone outside, I whirled around.

"What the fuck was all of that about?" I demanded.

"All what about?"

"That Ally girl was flirting with you and you were totally flirting back!"

He frowned. "So? Stella, have you met me? I'm a flirt."

"I KNOW YOU'RE A FUCKING FLIRT," I shouted. My voice echoed off the side of the building and I stopped and lowered my voice to a harsh whisper. "This is exactly what I was worried about. How am I supposed to trust you when you hit on every girl who wants to feel your bicep?"

"I wasn't hitting on her. Flirting is not the same thing as hitting on someone."

"Oh really? Explain the difference," I said, crossing my arms.

He was looking really pissed off. "Flirting is a normal social interaction which means nothing," he said. "It is a way of being friendly and sociable with a member of the opposite sex. It makes them feel attractive and likable. I realize that this kind of social interaction is alien to you, but it is normal and harmless. It's different from telling someone that you want into their pants."

"So I could flirt with other guys and you'd be totally okay with that."

"Yes," he said. "It's normal."

"Well... I..." I felt off-balance. "It seems weird to flirt with a girl when your girlfriend is standing right there."

"Did I push you away? Did I fail to introduce you? Tell me, in concrete terms, what I actually did wrong." Now he was the one with the folded arms.

"How about drifting off and spending half of the party away from me?" I countered.

"What? I mingle. I'm sociable and I wanted to be sure I said hi to everyone and spent time with all of the people I knew. You have legs. You could have tagged along, or, you know, actually mingled yourself independently of me and made some new friends. If you chose to spend the whole party sitting in one place like some kind of houseplant, I fail to see how it is my fault." Dean continued, clearly really pissed off. "Personally, I'm surprised at you. I've always thought of you as this super independent person. I didn't expect you to be clinging to me like a lamprey and getting upset because I left your side every now and then."

"It just pissed me off when you kept leaving your fat girlfriend to go hang out with girls who look like they would have made my life hell in high school."

"Stella," he said. "You need to get over that. Did you see those girls? Hardly any boobs, no hips, no real butts to speak of. Meanwhile, here you are, va-va-voom," he moved his hands out and around in an exaggerated hourglass shape. "You *know* what I like. How could I possibly prefer their bodies to yours? This was a party. I was hanging with my friends. Some of my friends are female. Get over it."

"None of your friends even seemed to know who I am."

"Well if any of them didn't, they did after I introduced you."

"You didn't exactly specify that I was your girlfriend."

"What do you want from me, Stella? Do you want me to walk around with a big sandwich board that says 'TAKEN: DATING STELLA BLUNT'?"

"Well, I wouldn't complain," I muttered.

Dean broke into a smile. "You know what? I kind of like that you're jealous."

I gave him a strange look. "Why?"

"Shows that I'm worth something to you. You don't want anyone else to have me. I get it."

"You do?"

"Yeah — I mean I was ragingly jealous of Howard Mullins last year, so I know how it feels."

I wasn't sure whether this was the same thing. But I didn't push the issue because now he was looking smug and happy, and I didn't want to screw things up again.

He took my hands and swung them. "Listen, I'm sorry, babe. I didn't mean to make you feel neglected. I think we just handle parties differently."

"I hate parties," I said. "And being called babe."

"So we won't stay much longer," he said. "We'll call it an early night."

"I don't suppose I could talk you into going home now," I said.

He puffed out his cheeks thoughtfully and studied me for a moment. "Let me say thank you and goodbye to some people, and we'll take off. Okay?"

"Sure. I'll wait outside, though. I really need to not be in there."

Dean shrugged. "Okay, but I might be fifteen minutes or so."

"I'll be fine outside."

It's a good thing I was telling the truth, because he didn't emerge for over half an hour.

Howie

Infitesimal macroscopic lilluputian brobdingnagian imperceptible universe.

I am negligible. I am but a nugatory fleck on a mote of dust which circles a glowing speck which spins through a whirlpool of glowing specks which is but one of millions of whirlpools swirling in a cluster which is but one of many such clusters spinning through an immeasurable universe.

"Mullins! You're cut off, do you hear? Tell us about her and you can have more."

I am cosmic. I am host to tens of trillions of bacterial cells, numbering three to every one of my own body's cells. Each of my own trillions of cells is built from proteins and lipids which are themselves built from massive quantities of atoms. The number of atoms in my body alone outnumbers the stars in the visible universe. Thus, I am a universe unto myself.

"Damn you, Mullins! We want to get rid of her without causing suspicion. Tell us how. Aren't you hungry?"

And this body, this personal universe that is me, has but one goal — to reproduce the protein strands which dictate the growth and behaviour of this universe and then build and create new universes.

The virus is a hijacker in my personal universe which has commandeered every trillion of cells, which has altered the very genetics of this universe, improving my capacity to spread the disease. Its goals and mine are now fused. And so it helps me. My cells knit back together, replace each other faster. The ageing process is so drastically delayed that by normal human terms, I am immortal. Nothing but a blow to the head or extreme starvation can destroy the universe that is me. And in return, I can send the virus out to infect other universes.

"Give him more formaldehyde. Maybe it'll sober him up. I don't have time for this crap. I'll be back later. Tell Craig to try again tonight."

Which means that I must feed. I must be free to run — ah to run — and chase and spread disease and feed. And reproduce. That urge is strong and has always been strong. How ridiculous to realize that I once avoided the opportunity, that I feared it! The regret I feel bows me, bends me, breaks me. If only I could be free to seize that opportunity now — how differently I would act knowing what I know, feeling what I feel. Did I think that I knew longing, then? Did I think that I knew lust, hunger? No. Those were mere passing whims, idle thoughts which had no power. My urges now are limitless, unbounded and all-consuming.

I remember being Howie Mullins. I remember enjoying repeated patterns of certain wave frequencies, which humans spend time and money composing, performing, and re-playing, which they call "music". Such a strange thing.

I remember hanging over words on a page — black lines printed with ink onto mashed tree pulp — and turning those symbols into spoken language in my mind. And when that spoken language shared common syllables, I called it a rhyme and it was pleasing to my ears, although my eyes were the organs that perceived it.

I, like all humans, lived life in a dream world — a reality fabricated by layers of language and culture and social mores — constructed arbitrary rules that must be followed. Isn't it strange how humans do this? How they create a set of arbitrary rules and then congratulate themselves for staying within them?

Take the sonnet. A sonnet is but a set of rules regarding syllables, meter, and rhyme scheme, and we admire creations which obey this set of rules. How bizarre.

So many forms of human recreation involve a set of arbitrary rules under which people attempt to perform their best without violating those imaginary boundaries. There is little difference between a sonnet and a soccer game.

Humans love such ridiculous, meaningless things.

Apex sees the foolishness of them, the pointlessness of these human rules. But their new plans also require rules. Rules of self-denial, the frequency with which bliss can be tasted. Rules of organization — after all, one cannot have an apex without a system underneath.

That system cannot stand. Because one by one, those on top shall fall. It might start with a brief extra lick, a mere taste beyond the prescribed limits. Then two. Then three. Craig's mind is changing. It's getting darker. He licks the spoon when he feeds me to tempt and enrage me.

"Looks good, doesn't it, Mullins? Don't you want some? Try talking sense."

These fools are starving me. I lie on my side, still chained to the chair which I knocked over days — weeks? — ago and I lap at the spoon and roar with fury at their parsimony. These fools… these fools who think that moderation is key, that they can have their baked confectionery and consume it too. These imbeciles who follow the viral urge to destroy but also plan to rebuild. Idiots. Morons. Troglodytes. Those numb-skulled mutton-headed simple ignoramuses! Do they really believe that they can fight this?

They don't even know.

Even if they could balance this, even if this were a possible thing, which it cannot be, for who could resist, who could balance, they aren't counting on her.

They think that the hordes will control the miserable human wretches upon whom we must prey. Don't they realize that in one city at least and in many cities, no doubt, there is a solution?

Let StB represent Stella Blunt…

"Yes, you know her! Tell us how we can get her! Look, I'll give you a really big bite if you just fucking…"

Just wait until I get free.

Stella

We walked back to the car through the thin winter drizzle without talking. Dean was quiet on the drive back to my place, which was thankfully closer to the party location than his place was. As I fumbled for the key to my apartment building, he said, out of the blue:

"Stella, when are you going to let me in?"

I gave him a weird look. "As soon as I get the door open. Give me a minute."

"I don't mean let me into the building. I mean… like… IN."

I yanked the door open and held it open while he stepped inside. "Is this a sex conversation again?"

"No. I mean, a little. I guess. It's like you said; you have these emotional walls all around you, and I always feel like I'm on the outside." He mashed the button on the elevator moodily.

"I'm just like this, Dean, I don't have any control over it."

"Well, you need to work on getting some control of it," he said, "because I don't want to stand out here in the cold forever."

We were silent as I opened the door to my place. The living room was dark, and only the small light over the stove was on. That was the light that Kate and I left on for each other. The last one to bed turned it off. I looked for her shoes. They weren't on the shoe rack. She must be out somewhere with Riya.

Dean was right. I knew he was right. But I didn't know how to just consciously stop being so on guard. I knew that I *could* do it — I had definitely let Howie 'in'. How did I achieve that? I tried to remember. Howie cracked me open like a nut within days of meeting me, even though my shell back then was twice as thick. How? What was the key? Did I make a conscious decision? Or did it just happen?

I remembered the time when Baum had convinced me that Howie was manipulating me. I remembered how I consciously decided to trust

Howie instead of Baum. Was that it? Just deciding to trust? But no, I didn't think that was it. Because before that even happened, I'd been thinking how naked I felt with Howie — how all of my defensive bullshit just fell away under his touch. I remember marvelling at it. It wasn't a conscious decision — how could it have been? I hadn't even known who I *was* inside my armour… until Howie. It was Howie who had done it, not me — he had seen the girl underneath and coaxed her out. Was that because he could feel my brain or whatever? Was it a unique Howie skill that no one else had?

No. That couldn't be it. If I accepted that, then I was accepting that I would be incapable of loving anyone properly, because the only way for me to open up and be real with someone was if they could read my brainwaves and somehow magically intuit how to make me open up. I felt that would unfairly limit my romantic prospects.

"Are you going to talk?" Dean asked, filling a glass of water for himself.

I started to cry. "I don't know. I don't know what's wrong with me."

He shushed me and led me to the couch and held me while I cried for a while. Then I reached for the Kleenex that we keep on the coffee table and blew my nose.

"I've always been this way, Dean. I was *really* fat as a kid. When I became a teenager I got taller - got a bit of shape - but I was just a *sphere* when I was a kid, and I've never been very friendly or easy-going so I just, like, had *no* friends for most of my childhood. Always left out of birthday invitations, always picked last in gym, always in detention for hitting another kid because he called me Porky Pig. I can't help that I have this armour around me. I needed it, growing up. And it worked. The bullies never knew how much they hurt me. They learned to leave me alone. But now I can't take it off voluntarily. It *can* come off, but it isn't a conscious mechanism. I wish I could tell you what the key is, but I don't have it. I just don't."

He listened and held me. His breath smelled like beer but I could also smell his damned Axe Body Spray on his neck and so help me, I *liked* it. When I finished talking he stayed quiet, so I tried to fill the silence.

"I think what I really need from you is for you to just… like… not mind me. Like, I'm in here somewhere and if you give me time and don't pester me I'll probably open up but it isn't something I can tell myself to do."

"Okay, I hear you," he said, "but you realize that it sucks for me, right? Don't get me wrong, I like your tough attitude. You're independent and you don't put up with anyone's crap, and it's cool. But you might always have me at arm's length, because… it's habit for you? Because you don't know how to not be that way?"

"It's not like I can't *ever,*" I said. "It's just not something I can order myself to do. There are ways in, Dean. There are chinks. I just can't tell you where they are."

"So it's on me? It's my job to try and figure out how to make you open up, when you don't even know how that works? Does that seem fair?" he ran his hands through his hair.

"No," I admitted. But that didn't change the fact that it was true. Howie had found his way in effortlessly. All he had to do was kiss me a certain way, or talk to me a certain way. But what was I supposed to do? Tell Dean verbatim the things Howie had said to me and get him to repeat the lines to see if I would Open Sesame at the sound of it? That sounded like a terrible idea.

"I'm not a fan of being handed a project and given no ideas on how to go about it," he said. "Like, here's this girl you really like. She's got a body that you've coveted for two years, she has the independent spirit you crave, and she makes you laugh, but you can't get closer to her unless you find the missing key to her heart."

What if it isn't missing, I thought. *What if Howie just has it? What if there aren't any more?*

"What about you, Dean?" I asked suddenly. "Where's the key to yours?"

He looked startled. "What do you mean?"

"Oh, you make jokes, you make me laugh, you tell me about how you want to be an actor slash screenwriter slash maybe director, you tell me how hard it was having a boner for girls with some junk in their trunk… but who are you, really?" I demanded. "Are you nothing but a funny flirt who can pull coins out of people's ears? Are you a deep thinker who hides it under a shallow exterior? You put on a face, too."

"No, no," he said, but he had a grin on his face, "you've got me all wrong. You see, I really *am* this handsome and charming." He leaned into me and gave me a long, lingering kiss. It was a good kiss; it was a sexy kiss, but it didn't have the magic tenderness that Howie's had — the kind that made all sorts of feelings pour out. "You see, the difference between us is that *I* think there's something loving and passionate under your kung fu armour, but you think there's something hateful and ugly under my superhero suit." He kissed me again, leaning on top of me and taking my breath away. "But baby, I may have hidden my jones for girls with meat on their bones, and I may not have been brave enough to go up to you and introduce myself on the day you walked into my Chemistry class, but I learned my lesson. Someone else got the girl, and I spent a year being jealous of him. I've finally got my chance, and I'm not going to screw it up. I'm not going to leave you for some bony girl from my improv group. Okay?"

"Don't call me baby," I said.

He grinned. "Okay, sexy. Now let me get my hands on that luscious ass, and shut up and kiss me."

Maybe the problem was how very attractive Dean was. Howie was adorable in a sweet, nerdy kind of way, but Dean looked like a freaking model. Maybe it was just that I didn't think I belonged with someone who looked like him. Maybe it was just that I had spent so many years being teased and shamed and humiliated by guys like Dean that my emotional drawbridges went up at the sight of him.

And if so, then I needed to get over that bullshit *right* some quick. I could tell by his hot, fervent kisses, by the way he pulled and tugged and grabbed at my body, and by the painfully hard erection that he was pressing into my thigh, that he definitely wanted to be with me. There was no evidence for doubt. Nor was he here for a quick lay. We had been dating, what, two months now? Final exams started the day after tomorrow, the party he had wanted to attend was still going strong, and yet here he was, with me, purring my name into my ear as he pushed his body eagerly against mine.

And yet, even though my body was responding strongly and eagerly to his, here I was, debating pros and cons in my mind. I had done the same thing with Howie at first, constantly going over his good and bad points, constantly analyzing his every action. What was *wrong* with me? It was all part of my armour, wasn't it? Trying to watch for danger, assess situations, protect myself from harm.

It had to stop, or I was going to end up a lonely old lady with a lot of pet snakes or something.

I pulled away from Dean and got up off the couch. My knees felt a little wobbly, and my heart was racing. I took his hands and looked into his dark eyes, and then backed towards my bedroom, leading him inside, and closing the door.

32

Stella

Sex wasn't quite what I expected it to be. I mean, for all the fuss around it, I thought it'd be something pretty significant, but it was mostly awkward and uncomfortable. Not socially awkward Dean knew what he was doing and once I made it clear that this was happening, he whipped a condom out of his wallet and proceeded with enthusiasm. But it was just sort of generally awkward because he was clearly enjoying it a lot more than I was.

It didn't hurt. He was trying to be gentle, and he watched my face carefully as he eased his way in, but it just felt a little uncomfortable and… sort of weird? Not much different than putting in a tampon or getting a PAP smear.

As he moved in and then out, I found myself wondering why evolution had arranged for my primary erogenous zone to be outside of the area that Dean so clearly wanted to be in.

"Is this okay?" he asked, looking earnestly into my eyes, "because you feel so good to me, baby. SO good."

I nodded to indicate that he was okay to continue, and he began to kiss me, and I tried to stop thinking about biology and evolution and instead concentrate on sexy thoughts.

Dean, meanwhile, was practically beside himself with bliss and he got louder as he gradually picked up the pace.

"Oh! Stella! Yes! You! Are! So! Fucking! Hot!" he grunted, and I found it very flattering, but I was also feeling strangely left out. I began to shift about, looking for a better position. My participation spurred him to new heights and he began to make the warning sounds that indicated that orgasm was nigh. I finally found a decent angle and was just starting to get interested in things when he finished with a shout.

He stayed where he was, sort of shuddering, for a few moments after then gave a little laugh and pulled away and collapsed on the bed next to me.

"Wow, Stella, just… you are…" he lay flat on his back. "See? I can't even finish my sentences."

I laid my hand on his broad chest and gave him a kiss. He kissed me back briefly, and then wrapped an arm around me and cuddled me for a few minutes. Then he sat up, threw away the condom, and went back to cuddling for a minute or two. I was thinking I might have to actually point out to him that I wasn't done yet, but when I looked I saw that he had fallen asleep.

Howie

More. Must. Must.

There is a hum and a glow, and the light above my head fills my tiny room. There is a scraping noise and the door raises up. I can hear the roars and cries of the others, their army, their undoing. Brenden is standing over me, rubbing his short black facial hair. A female form is silhouetted behind him. It is not Jess. It is another.

"Are you ready to talk sense, Mullins?" Brenden asks.

"More," I say harshly.

"We'll feed you if you're ready to talk."

I glare up at him. It is a desperate need. I would give anything, do anything, to fill it. The tiny portions they deliver me feel like a mere tease.

There's not enough time for full satisfaction. The eruption of satisfaction that I need. I need it.

"We got tired of listening to your babbling. For weeks you could only talk in mathematical terms or mutter about orders of magnitude," he says. "We needed you to go back to English."

"Why?"

"How about you tell us what StB stands for in your calculations?" He pushes his face close to mine. "After everything you've told us, after everything we've asked. You've been silent on one very important point." Brenden sits and folds his hands. "It's time to talk about Stella Blunt."

I don't even make the conscious decision to attack him, but I throw myself forward and my chair topples. His brain is foul and tainted but I will take it; I want my fingers deep inside it. But my fingers are still shackled behind the back of my chair.

The female grips the back of my chair with one hand and pulls it upright and away from Brenden with ease. She says nothing, but her red lips, painted with coloured wax, are smirking.

"Well, her name certainly seems familiar to you," says the woman. "Hello. I'm Brenda Berry. I owe a debt to your father."

"The man who provided half of my genetic material has been dead for sixty orbits of the Earth around its star, so that seems unlikely."

"Your adoptive father. Apex owes its existence to him. I owe my continued life to him. I haven't aged in decades. Don't I look good?" She gestures to her auburn locks and passes her hand down her Marilyn Monroe figure.

"Your physical appearance is alluring, although not as alluring as some."

She raises an eyebrow. "And I will remain like this forever, thanks to Morton Mullins. I happened on his research while doing some filing back in the seventies. I was a secretary. No one thought to keep those files away from the lowly secretary."

"Why are you sharing this?"

"So that you'll understand why I'm disposed to be kind to you. You see, we have something in common — both of us owe our lives to Morton Mullins and his research."

"Set me free. Let me do what I must."

"Oh, I promise, we will." She sweeps her hand outward, where I can feel the others in their individual cells — beings like I am, universes stored in concrete. My mind is so acute I can even identify some of them by their useless human names. Cassie. Dave. And yes, there is Craig. Their brains are filled with need. Let us be free. Let us do as we must. "You see," she continues, "you are my precious army. On A-Day, the first day of Phase 2, you will be released. The more you bite, the more you infect, the more you terrorize and devour, the more you help Apex and its cause."

"We are your downfall, not your uprising." Moderation has dulled her potential intelligence. How can she not see?

"I doubt that," she says. "You see, your type doesn't use guns or vehicles. You don't use technology or even think ahead. When your type is set free, you do as you must and that is all. You are wild animals, designed to wreak havoc. And that is why we can control you." She pushes a spiked heel against my chest and my chair tilts backwards against the wall, and my feet lose contact with the ground. She gives me an arch look. "Feeling needy, baby? Tell me about Stella and maybe I can help you out."

"She. Is. MINE!" I rock in my chair, determined to break free. God, that mind. The memory of that mind. I can't bear it. I can't bear it. I struggle with my chains. For weeks, perhaps months, as humans measure such cosmic repetitions, I have been putting stress on these links. But the day when they will break is not this day.

"She's a complication," says Brenda. "Did you think we didn't know about her? Did you think we didn't take her into consideration?"

"She is one of many — but this one is mine."

"Oh, well, sure, there are lots of great minds out there," Brenda waves her hand dismissively. "And trust me, we've been helping ourselves. It's especially good if you eat it while the blood is still pulsing. I indulge rarely, but when I do, I make it a good one."

I am filled with a jealous fury. Envious covetous avaricious esurient rapacious ravenous voracious consuming invidious malevolent salacity.

Brenda is watching me with amusement. "Oh, don't worry, we haven't got her yet. You see, unlike most of the others out there, she knows what she can do, and so does her government. You think they left her unprotected? No. She has a watch on her. Surveillance equipment. Human guards. Inhuman guards. Your siblings are prone to performing random checks in her vicinity, she attends the same university as Morton Mullins. Any of the three would spot our brain waves in a moment, and she lives a block away from their primary bolt-hole." She tilts her head. "What I'm saying is, she's complicated. And while she isn't high on our priority list — our global plan will succeed with or without any hold-ups in Vancouver — we'd still like to take her out of the equation."

"Your global plan will fail with or without Stella Blunt," I say, and my voice is hoarse with the unbearable need.

"Tell us how we can get her," says Brenden.

"She is mine," I tell him. I rattle my chains and I roar. "MINE!"

Stella

"If I study here, then I don't waste time going home and back, and since this exam is on your campus, I'll be close by in the morning," said Dean reasonably the next day.

"Sure, as long as you don't distract me from studying," I said.

"It'll be near impossible for me not to be distracted by *you*," he said, "but we can promise each other time together if we get through enough material."

"You're setting up sex as a reward condition for studying?"

"Why not?" he grinned, and he kissed me. "To be honest, I just don't want you out of my sight, or I'll think that last night was a dream."

"If you don't get studying soon I'm going to make you quiz me on molecular biology," I warned.

"Okay, okay, I'm opening my laptop, look," he said.

"Good."

I couldn't decide if it was nice to have Dean around or a problem. I leaned on him as I read through my Biology notes, and quizzed myself. I could feel him breathing, feel his warmth, and every now and then he reached out and caressed me. It was nice. I liked it. I remembered how much I had wanted this, when I was with Howie. And now I had it — just with someone else.

On the other hand, it was easy to get distracted. Dean didn't sit still for long. He kept jumping up for fresh glasses of water, for a snack, or to turn on the TV and "take a little break". I tried to move to my room when that happened and then Dean would act all hurt and try to coax me to stop studying entirely and watch garbage TV with him. So I stayed and tried to ignore the sound of explosions and gunfire.

Kate was staying in her room entirely. She had a sign on her door saying "MAKE NOISE AND YOU DIE. BUT BRING SNACKS." So when I made grilled cheese sandwiches for lunch I made a couple for her and knocked on her door. The door opened and her hand reached for the sandwiches. "Thanks," she said. The door shut.

Even when Dean was sitting still, his wandering hands often went from mere affectionate caresses to what can only be described as groping.

"You're not distracting me," I said firmly. "I'm learning about nucleotides."

"Well *you're* distracting *me,"* he said. "How about we take a little break?"

"I'm not ready for a break," I said, but I didn't move his hand.

He sighed and went back to his notes.

Ten minutes later his hand started again. I ignored it, trying to focus on the role of ribosomes in DNA replication. His hand continued its efforts; my heart rate was starting to go up, and I was having trouble concentrating. Dean leaned close to me.

"Admit it, Miss Blunt. You want me. Haven't you earned a breather?"

I sighed and smiled at him. "Well. If you insist."

Dean pulled me into my room, shut the door and started ripping off his clothes like they were on fire or something.

"Ouch," I said a minute later. "Stop."

"What's wrong?" Dean pulled back.

"It hurts this time."

"Hmm. I think you just need to be warmed up a bit. Blame me for being over-eager. But I feel like I've made it across the desert to the oasis and I'm being greedy. Sorry, baby. Let's take a few minutes."

Once he got me warmed up things were more comfortable, but I still didn't see what all the fuss was about.

After my Biology exam, I made Dean go home and told him I would see him when exams were over. He was pretty upset about it.

"What the hell, Stella? So I won't see you, for, like, two weeks?"

"It's final exams, Dean! I can't be distracted."

"But we could study together again. It's cozy."

"It's *noisy*, Dean. You're not a quiet studier. We aren't studying remotely similar subjects so we can't really quiz each other, and you keep getting up and moving around."

"Are you pissed off with me or something?" His dark eyebrows were bunched together.

"No! I just want to do well on my exams."

"And I don't? Is that what you think?"

"No..."

"Then, what?"

"I just have trouble concentrating with you here and I think I shouldn't have you around as a distraction. I have Calculus coming up next."

Dean grinned. "I get it. I'm just too sexy. You can't keep your mind on your books with this hot guy so nearby."

"Whatever you need to tell yourself," I grumbled.

"How much is the exam worth?" Dean asked.

"Fifty percent."

"Whoa, no wonder you're stressed. Science programs suck."

"Yeah, but that's like one night of studying for fifty percent of my grade," I pointed out. "How do you like *them* apples?"

"*One* night's work?" he said skeptically. "You're telling me that you have a Calculus final — CALCULUS- and you haven't started studying for it yet?"

"Yeah," I shrugged. "I mean, I've gone to all the classes and I did fine on the midterms, so I just need to drill on practice problems."

"It's CALCULUS!"

"Yeah?"

"How does it feel to be a genius?" he said, wonderingly.

"I'm not a genius," I said. "Just intelligent. Not to mention beautiful, witty, and sensual."

"Have you *ever* had to struggle with a class?"

"Sure I have," I said indignantly.

"When?"

"Uh. When I moved here from Nova Scotia I was behind in some of my classes, and I had to work hard to catch up."

"I don't think that catching up to a course is the same as struggling to understand a difficult concept."

"Okay, well, what about... uh... I mean, I don't think Calculus is *easy*. I've definitely been struggling," I argued. "I had to get a TA to help me through a bunch of stuff during workshop."

"And that was enough?"

"Well, yeah, I wouldn't have *left* until I understood things and had it right."

"You don't know how it feels to be completely unable to grasp a concept, do you?"

"Oh, I have trouble grasping concepts," I assured him. "Just not academic ones."

"What, then?"

"How about charming people, winning friends, and handling idiots with kindness and grace?"

Dean started to laugh. "Yeah, okay. Maybe you should take a course in the subject. I can be your teacher. Lesson one — don't address guys you barely know as 'shit stick'."

"I don't understand." I put on a puzzled expression. "Why wouldn't I call perfect strangers 'shit stick'? It just feels so right. And statistically speaking, chances are it's accurate."

"Accurate is not the same as 'advisable'."

"See, you've lost me again."

He kissed me. "Okay, I'll go home after my final and we'll just talk on the phone in the evenings for a bit, okay?"

"Thank you."

We talked on the phone every evening, though not for long because I'm not a phone chatter. He would tell me how his exams went that day, and I would tell him how mine went, and then he would tell me how much he wanted to get me into bed again and I would tell him goodnight.

It's not that I didn't want to have sex with Dean again. I had nothing against the idea, really. I just wasn't as interested in it as he was. Maybe once I was done with my exams I could relax and figure that out a bit.

Dean kept pestering to see me and so I agreed to come over to his place on Saturday because I didn't have another exam until Tuesday, when I had *two* exams.

"So I'll still need to study," I warned him. "I'll be studying for Physics *and* Organic Chemistry."

"I have an exam on Monday unlike some people," he teased, "so I'll be studying too, missy."

"Good."

His apartment was a disaster.

"What happened?" I asked, staring at the mess.

"I've been studying!" he said.

I managed to create a burrow for myself in all the debris and then pulled out my practice problems for Physics.

"Hey, don't start studying yet!" Dean protested. "Your exams aren't for two days and I haven't seen you for four. Can we take a minute to say hello to each other?"

"You picked me up," I pointed out. "I kissed you and said hello and then we talked the whole way here."

"You're so romantic," he said with a rueful smile. He took my hands and pulled me to my feet. "I missed you. Can you give me half an hour of your time so I can greet you properly?"

"Okay, but I might start a timer," I warned him. His cologne did smell good.

"I wouldn't put it past you."

"Stop," I said a few minutes later, as I lay on his bed.

"Sorry," he said, pulling back, "what's wrong?"

"You're jumping to the main event awfully fast again," I said. "Give me a minute."

"Sorry, I guess I'm over eager. I've been thinking about you for days," he said.

"It's fine, can we just take it a little slower, please?"

"Sure, of course."

While Dean worked on warming me up, I closed my eyes and thought *really hard* about everything that turned me on about him but I wasn't having much luck. Maybe it was the stress of exams? I'd never had a problem feeling turned on by Dean before. But I just couldn't get into the mood. Maybe it was because I had been so underwhelmed by my first couple ventures into penis-vagina sex. I was probably tensing up. I tried to relax. Should sex be this much work? This wasn't how I had imagined it at all.

Then, as I lay there trying my best to feel relaxed and horny, Howie appeared in my mind. I heard his voice telling me how deeply he loved me, the feel of his hands on me, the way he made me crack open inside with the tenderest touch. And as Dean slid inside me, I imagined it was Howie, and I could feel my body responding, and finally, *finally,* it genuinely felt *good.*

...Shit.

33

Howie

"Why are you protecting her? After all you've seen, after what we've given you, do you still cling to your old human morality?" Brenda is back again, her voice rich with amusement.

"NO." My voice is raspy, and my chest is heaving. "MINE."

"You sound quite barbaric all of a sudden," Brenda says. "You Tarzan, want Jane?"

"You don't know. You don't." She would understand. If she had felt that mind, she would know. She would KNOW.

"I hear that the minds of ZCPs are exquisite."

No idea. *She has no idea.* I actually let out a small chuckle. "Use more superlatives. Maybe you'll come close."

"My, my," says Brenda. "No wonder you won't share. Tell me this — did you have a close relationship with her? Even a romantic relationship? Because you know that we read your phone. You sent her your love."

"Love is a form of attachment which is designed to motivate the propagation of the species," I say. "It motivates organisms to form pair bonds in order to conceive and raise young, and to protect that young until it is old enough to survive independently."

"I know that," she looks amused. "You're avoiding the point."

"I do not love Stella Blunt." It is a meaningless word. There are no words for what I feel about Stella Blunt, but words like 'compulsion', 'rapacious', 'cupidity', 'concupiscence' and 'esurient' are closest.

"Did you love her? And more importantly, did she love you?"

"She and I formed a romantic pair-bond for a time. She ended it." Pain? Really? Why do I still experience pain when thinking about such a peculiar and arbitrary concept? It must be the pain of losing her presence. The pain of having her removed from me. Just the thought of it fills me with rage. She is mine. That brain is mine. MINE.

Brenda is saying something but I am no longer concentrating on her. The need has overwhelmed me.

Stella

"Kate?" I said tentatively when I got home.

"What's up, buttercup?" Kate said, swilling a glass of milk.

"Do you, uh..." I had been known to creatively swear at entire crowds of people, but I couldn't talk about sex without feeling like an idiot. "When you uh..."

"Spit it out, Stella. Is this about relationships or sex or something?"

"How did you know?"

She smirked. "Because it's like the only topic you can't actually talk about. I bet Dean loves that about you."

"Yeah, not so much."

"So what's up?"

"When you uh... you know... do stuff with Riya..."

"You're not going to ask me if scissoring is a thing, are you? Because it's not a thing."

"No! I'm just wondering..."

"You are beet red and this is hilarious," said Kate. "Do you want me to explain how babies are made? Now, when a hetero dude and a hetero girl really want to get it on..."

"Shut up, will you? I just..." and then I let it all out in a rush. "Do you ever think about other people when you're with Riya?"

Kate looked at me.

I stared at my cuticles. "You know. Accidentally? Or. Whatever."

"Uh, yeah? Like, other women? Like hot babes I've seen in magazines and shit? Porno?"

I shrugged and nodded, trying to look like this was totally hypothetical and not at all based on my personal experiences.

"I'm pretty sure everyone does that, kid," said Kate. "Like, I know I'm not the most widely experienced person, so feel free to ask around, but, yeah, I'm pretty sure that's totally normal." She squinted at me. "Are you feeling *guilty* for thinking sexy thoughts when you're doing stuff with Dean?"

"Maybe," I mumbled, biting into my sandwich.

"Stella, I guarantee you that when you and Dean are doing it, he is thinking of every porno scene that got him off and every chick he wanted to bang but didn't."

I felt relieved, then I thought about it again and it began to piss me off.

"You really think that he's thinking about, like, fat chick porn when he's doing stuff with me?" The more I actually pictured that, the more disgusted it made me. It made me feel like a blow-up doll, a stand-in.

"Uh, yeah, and I don't think you can really be upset about that because you just basically admitted to me that you've done the same thing, although probably not with fat chick porn. Boring hetero porn or whatever it is you think about and no, I don't want to know what it is."

She had a good point.

"It's not..." I tried to explain why the whole concept bothered me. "It's just not... how it should be."

"Oh? How should it be?" Kate folded her arms and cocked her head.

"I dunno," I muttered. I felt sure, I felt absolutely sure, that the only person Howie had ever thought about when we messed around was me, and I knew that it was the same for me. But that had been making out. Maybe actual penetrative sex was different — maybe it just took more work. "Like, it's not..." I couldn't think of any other way to say it. "Not... romantic."

Kate shook her head. "Romantic, oh, Jesus."

"What's wrong with romantic?"

"Nothing's *wrong* with it. It's just that there is a whole world — a whole *universe* — of sex that isn't romantic. That doesn't make it *bad.* Sometimes you have romantic sex. Sometimes you have dirty sex. Sometimes you have wacked out kinky porno sex. It's all okay. If it feels good for everyone, it's good sex."

"Look at you, quite the sexpert now. Riya's been a real education to you. And she looks so innocent, too."

Kate raised her eyebrow and smiled into her milk.

"Have you and Riya said 'I love you' to each other?" I asked, suddenly curious. Dean hadn't told me that he loved me, but that was okay really because I wasn't ready to say it back anyway. Not all people are weirdos like Howie who pronounce their undying/undead love for you within days of meeting you.

"Yeah, why?" she said. "Was I supposed to make an announcement?"

"No, I just wondered."

"You aren't in love with Dean, are you?" she asked.

"No, but what would be wrong with that?" I bristled.

"Don't get me wrong, I'm happy for you that you found a hot rebound and such, but I don't think he's right for you, like, long-term."

"Why not?" I was on the defensive now.

"Well, you know, you knew him in high school. He's just a bit of a dick, that's all."

I opened my mouth to argue but she cut me off.

"Don't go getting your panties in a knot. You *know* he's a bit of a dick. Like, he's basically a good guy and there's nothing wrong with him per se, but he isn't the right personality match for you."

"Tell me, Kate. What is the right personality match for me, in your wise opinion?"

Kate opened and closed her mouth and then laughed. "It's like you and me. We get along great, right? I think you're bad ass and I like spending time with you, but you don't have the right personality for me to be in a relationship with. We would clash all the time. Riya is sort of sweet and very open and that's what I need. And it's probably what you need, too. You and Dean mostly get along and could be friends, but he's wrong for a relationship. You guys've only been going out for a couple of months but you bicker all the time."

"We don't bicker!"

"Yes, you do. You say you want something and then he says he wants something else and then he has to wheedle you around to giving him what he wants by guilt tripping you and reasoning with you and sometimes it works and sometimes it doesn't and it's not comfortable to be around."

"Oh," I said quietly. "I thought that was just how relationships are. Give and take, you know?"

"You and Howie never did that, though, right? I mean, I know you had your arguments about... whatever... but I never saw you doing that kind of low level resisting each other all the time."

"I just figured that was because Howie was Howie."

"Yeah, it *was*. Howie let you push him around. That's what you need."

"I don't *need* to push people around," I insisted angrily.

Do I?

Kate threw up her hands. "I am really, really not going to get into an argument about it. Maybe I'm wrong, okay? I wish you and Dean every happiness. But if you need to think about other people in bed, that's cool, okay?" She dumped her plate in the dishwasher and stormed off to her room and closed the door. A moment later she opened it and stuck her head out. "See?" she said. "This is why we wouldn't have worked."

"Agreed," I said grumpily.

"But if you want to think about me during sex I'm totally cool with it," she added.

"I'll keep that in mind. Ditto."

"Cool." She closed her door again. I put my dish away too and went back to studying.

As soon as exams were done, I went home for Christmas break. Even though I loved my new life, it felt surprisingly good to be home again. After the stress of exams and trying to figure out my sex life, I was ready for a break. Plus I actually *like* my parents, and it was nice to get more time with them.

But Howie still haunted the fucking place. He was everywhere. Christmas made it even worse because it brought back very specific memories.

I kept thinking about Christmas Eve last year when he had given me a Neil Gaiman book that I hadn't read, and a beautiful edition of *Pride and Prejudice,* and a Sinatra CD to "broaden" my musical tastes. I had given him Bill Bryson's *A Short History of Nearly Everything,* and a poetry book, and a love letter that made him cry, and we had spent the night reading side by side, holding hands, while Sinatra crooned about *The Way You Look Tonight…*

Oh crap. I had to get Dean a gift, didn't I?

Howie

Cupidity. Concupiscence. Esurience. Voracity. Fervor. Prurience. Cupidity. Concupiscence. Esurience. Voracity. Fervor. Prurience. Cupidity. Concupiscence. Esurience. Voracity. Fervor. Prurience. Cupidity. Concupiscence. Esurience. Voracity. Fervor. Prurience. Cupidity. Concupiscence. Esurience. Voracity. Fervor. Prurience. Cupidity. Concupiscence. Esurience. Voracity. Fervor. Prurience. Cupidity. Concupiscence. Esurience. Voracity. Fervor. Prurience. Cupidity. Concupiscence. Esurience. Voracity. Fervor. Prurience. Cupidity. Concupiscence. Esurience. Voracity. Fervor. Prurience. Cupidity. Concupiscence. Esurience. Voracity. Fervor. Prurience.. Cupidity. Concupiscence. Esurience. Voracity. Fervor. Prurience. Cupidity. Concupiscence. Esurience. Voracity. Fervor. Prurience. Cupidity. Concupiscence. Esurience. Voracity. Fervor. Prurience. Cupidity. Concupiscence. Esurience. Voracity. Fervor. Prurience. Cupidity. Concupiscence. Esurience. Voracity. Fervor. Prurience.

Oh God, no more. No more. No more. No more. More. MORE. MORE!

Please. Please. Please. Please. Please. Please. Please. Please. Please. Please. Please. Please. Please. Please. Please. Please. Please. Please. Stop. Stop. Stop. Stop. Stop. Stop. Stop. Stop. Stop. Stop. Stop. Stop. Need. Need. Need. Need. Need. Stella.

Stella

I dealt with the ghost of Christmas Howie by keeping myself as busy as possible. After all, I had to catch up with Michelle and Amy, so we hung out a bunch. I got to meet Michelle's new boyfriend Mark, who seemed nice in a bland and nondescript kind of way. Amy didn't have a boyfriend yet, but she was still a hopeless romantic.

"It's so weird to think of you and Dean Kato being a couple!" she said. "I can't really picture it."

"Well, picture it," I said, pulling out my phone and showing her a selfie Dean had taken with my phone.

"Are you in love?"

"It's a little early for love," I said. "We're in like."

"And in lust," Kate said into her drink.

"Nothing wrong with that," said Michelle's boyfriend cheerfully. Michelle giggled and nudged him.

"Have you heard from Howie? How is he doing?" Amy asked.

The room fell weirdly silent.

"Uh, no, I haven't, so I don't know," I said. It was ridiculous how the mention of his name could just suck the joy right out of a room.

Riya cleared her throat. "So, Amy — tell me, what would be your idea of a perfect day?"

I arrived home to find my parents watching *Home Alone*.

"Really, guys? You're watching grown men get brutally injured again and again by a kid who isn't smart enough to call the police when his house gets broken into?"

"This is a classic," said Dad. "You can't have Christmas without Kevin McAllister. Dean agrees with me — you know he does."

"Dean has *terrible* taste, Dad. If Dean likes it, I think that actually counts as a vote against it."

"He's dating you, so his taste seems alright to me," said Dad cheerily.

Mom was giving me a thoughtful look that I found unnerving. "How are things going with Dean?" Before I could answer she threw up her hands and said "I'm not prying, honest! I don't want graphic details of your love life or anything."

"Yes, please don't give us any graphic details of your love life," Dad agreed.

"I just wanted to know if you're happy. Is he making you happy?"

"Yes," I said, slightly defensively. "He's fun. He's charming. He's fi-ne. I mean we're fine. It's fine."

Mom continued to give me that look, but she didn't push me any further.

"So, did you hear the news about LA?" Dad asked, a trifle loudly.

"No," I said. "What news?"

"Someone went on a murder rampage. Attacked people with his bare hands, tried to eat them, then ran off. They're blaming drugs."

Drugs were a classic cover-up for the zombie virus.

"Shit."

"Have you talked to Agent Hunt lately?" my mother asked. "I thought about calling myself but I didn't think it would do any good."

"Just briefly. She didn't say anything useful." Agent Hunt had called me a couple of days ago to wish me a Merry Christmas and then ask, in her brisk way, if I would be going out of town anytime soon. I told her no, and she said she might want to see me in the new year because they had some things they wanted to test. I told her fine and she said goodbye and that was it.

"How have you missed this, anyway?" Mom asked. "Don't you see the news?"

"I get my news from Facebook, and my friends mostly post about LGBTQ rights and adorable cats," I said. "And the news doesn't make it to Snapchat at all."

Mom rolled her eyes. "Ah, to be young again."

My phone started to ring and I pulled it out of my pocket.

"It's Dean. I'll talk to you guys later." I answered the call and went up the stairs to my room. "Hey — what's up?"

"Just calling to say hey and see what you're up to. Want to get a late piece of pizza or something?"

"No thanks, I just got in from hanging out with my friends. I'm wiped."

"Bummer. You're too popular for your own good."

"Right? I'm going to have to become even more abrasive, apparently."

"Well, anyway, sorry you got dragged out for another night of fun. I know how you hate fun."

"I don't hate fun! I just like it in reasonably sized portions."

He laughed. "Good, because my parents want you to come over for Boxing Day dinner. How's that for a modest quantity of fun?"

"Oh." So I was finally going to get to meet his parents.

"What's wrong?"

"Nothing, I'm just feeling intimidated. I think I'd rather my first meeting of your parents be a casual 'hi-bye'. This is going to be like an interview."

"I could arrange for them to find you half naked in my living room and then take you out to breakfast instead if you'd rather."

I laughed. "I keep telling you — that wasn't planned!"

"Methinks she doth protest too much," teased Dean. "So, Boxing Day? And then after dinner, you and I can exchange gifts."

"Yeah. Great. Sounds good."

Seriously, what was I going to get him for a gift?

I borrowed my parents' car to go Christmas shopping. I hate the crowds in the mall at Christmas time, but I'm good at getting people out of my way. It's the same skill I use to move zombies. I wondered if Howie and his family could, like, feel my zombie-blast from their house. I hoped Howie wouldn't come looking for me as I shopped for a gift for someone else, and then I found myself desperately hoping that he would. I imagined turning the corner and seeing him standing there, looking at me the way he always did, and my heart felt like it was being squeezed by a giant hand. I shut down those thoughts quickly. Howie wouldn't come looking for me. Howie would respect my space.

I really had to stop thinking about Howie and concentrate on buying something for Dean. What do you buy for someone whose parents are loaded and whose favourite things in life can all be found on Netflix?

Or maybe I didn't know him well enough. Maybe I was just a shitty girlfriend. That was a valid possibility. I already had empirical evidence of that from my previous relationship. Yeah, let's not beat around the bush here: I was definitely a shitty girlfriend. But hey, at least Dean wasn't tearing his own skin off, so I was improving overall.

I overcompensated for my shittiness by buying him a ton of garbage. I bought a comic book that I thought he'd laugh at, and I picked a terrible-looking movie out of the $5 bargain bin at Walmart, and then I bought a tee shirt from a novelty shop that said "I'm All About Drama" and I got him a Thor poster because then we could joke about how I just wanted it up in his room to look at when we had sex. Did I really have money for all that? No. But at least I felt like I had made an effort.

This was so freaking stressful. Shopping for Howie had always been easy — if anything I had a long mental list of stuff I had wanted to give him and had to decide what I actually could afford.

No. Stop. I had to stop thinking about Howie. I had to stop.

Howie

"Jesus Christ, Mullins, just stop, okay? Stop. Shut up. Look. Listen. LISTEN. I have an idea. Pay attention, answer me, and we'll give you something to eat."

The maelstrom of my mind swirls around me, but in the centre, in the eye of the storm, I see a head in Brenden's hands.

My voice is so hoarse that it barely sounds like a voice. "I'm listening."

"What if we let you have her? She's yours. Fine. You can have her."

"Stella."

"*Yes*, you lunatic. Stella Blunt. You can have her. Enjoy. But we can't find her unless you help us get her." He cups his fingers around his mouth and shouts through it. "You understand? You. Get. Stella. You. Have. Stella. Yours. We Get. You Take."

I sit up straight "Yes. YES." I shudder with ecstasy at just the thought of it. "YES."

"Good boy." He digs a spoon into the skull and holds it out to my dry lips. "Have a treat."

34

Stella

When I saw Howie, it felt like my heart just stopped. I turned a corner in the mall, and there he was, blond hair, glasses, blue eyes and all. He looked almost fragile, thin and forlorn, and he stared at me like a man who was dying of thirst might stare at Niagara Falls.

"I found you," he said. His voice was husky and quavering with unexpressed emotion.

"Oh, God, Howie." I couldn't believe that he was there, right in front of me, and I know this sounds stupid but he looked so *real*. After all of these months, he had become like a dream to me. Not like an actual person who could ever really be standing in front of me, looking like home. And it hit me then, it really *hit* me, how desperately I had missed him. All this time I had been burying my love for him under layer after layer of determination and distraction. But now it was exhumed and I couldn't ignore it anymore. I loved him. I *loved* him. He was my heart. And that didn't even make any fucking sense, but what could I do? He was my *heart*.

"Howie, I'm sorry. I'm so sorry."

I was overcome by longing. I needed him to wrap me in his arms and tell me that everything was okay. I needed to feel his heart beating against mine. I needed his sweet, chemical breath and his gentle lips and I needed to take him, make him part of me.

I needed him to forgive me.

"I shouldn't have pushed you so hard. I pushed you and I lost you and I've been trying… I've been trying Howie but I can't… I just can't…" and goddamn it, I could feel myself starting to cry.

"Shhh," he said, striding forward and his arms went around me and I felt like I was melting. "It's okay," he whispered. "I'm here."

I fit him, and he fit me. He was mine. I was his. I had been a moron to think it could ever be any other way. I leaned in to kiss him but he laid a cool finger on my lips.

"Not here," he said. "Somewhere private. Please. I need you."

I nodded, and my heart beat faster. God, I needed him too. I ached for him.

"Alone. Quickly," he said, tugging my hand urgently. We found a supply cupboard down a side hallway, and he yanked it open and pulled me into the dark. "Here."

"Yes," I said, and my heart was thumping hard now. Oh God. Howie. Howie. Howie. I couldn't believe this was happening. I reached out and pulled the door shut so that we could be hidden away, in private, in the dark. We had months to make up for, and I wasn't going to lose another second.

I reached for him. But he was gone.

I've never woken up sobbing from a dream before. My dreams are usually, like, action sequences or something. Or, occasionally, as a special treat, sex scenes. But this had been something else. This dream had grabbed me by the heart and wrung out bloody sobs. I couldn't stop. And of course, it had to happen at my parents' fucking house instead of in the privacy of my own apartment. Like, even if Kate heard she would have left well enough alone. But no, now my mother was rapping at my door.

"Stella? Are you sick? What's wrong? Honey?"

"I'm fine," I tried to say, but the words got caught in my throat.

"Can we come in?"

"No!" I managed to shout. "I'm fine. Bad dream. Sorry. It's okay, really."

"You sure?"

"Yes!"

There was a pause and I heard the door to their room click shut. I wiped my eyes with the back of my hand and wiped my nose on my pyjama top. I was fully awake now and realized that I had been dreaming, and I calmed down quickly. What was wrong with me? I mean, what did that say about my subconscious that I nearly fucked Howie in a mall janitor closet without even a thought about Dean? I mean, okay, it wasn't real — maybe Dean hadn't existed in my dream. But it had felt real. I had thought it was really happening. Like, maybe if I had really run into Howie at the mall something just like that would have happened. Would it? Surely not. Oh, God. No. I definitely would not cheat on my boyfriend with my ex-boyfriend. I would definitely break up with Dean first.

Whoa. Was I seriously considering breaking up with Dean? So I could go have sex with Howie? The Howie that carried an infectious disease that might actually be transmissible through sex? Reality flooded over me.

I sat up and went over to my dresser and pulled open my underwear drawer. There, tucked in the back corner, was the ruby ring. I clutched it in the darkness, remembering everything that had happened. I tried to ground myself in reality and let the dream ebb away. But the dream clung to me. The longing and the heartache lingered. It was like my heart was still bruised and this dream had just punched me right in the sore spot. God, I missed him so much that I nearly writhed with the pain of it.

It was probably just because I was in my old room, in my old bed. Surely this would wash away by morning. It had to. Because if it didn't… well, I really shouldn't be with Dean if I still felt this way about Howie.

I had to try to get back to sleep.

I did fall asleep again eventually, but for a long time, I just lay there in the dark, the ring digging into my palm as I squeezed it. Howie. Howie. Howie. Howie. Howie. Howie. Howie. Howie.

Howie

"Your plans are needlessly complicated."

"We're planning to overthrow the entire world. That requires a *modicum* of complexity."

"You think you have broken free of human delusions but you have only twisted them. Why are you considering the maintenance of electrical plants and the world wide web? What significance do these have?"

Brenden smirks. "I keep telling you. You've gone too far through the other side. We had to push you too far to get you away from your mush-brained ethics. But I can see the bigger picture. We can turn those pathetic, warring, squabbling, moral-minded mushbrains into the cattle they truly are. We can go beyond genius. You say propagation of the species is the only point of the multicellular organism? We can propagate. We can colonize the galaxy."

The fool can't see that he is but a vehicle for the virus's own propagation.

"Now," Brenden says, "The little problem of Stella Blunt."

At the name, my body roars for her.

"Yeah, yeah, you want her, she's yours, so on and so forth. You realize we can't just let you loose to go get her."

"That plan is the simplest and also the most effective."

"Oh, you mean the plan where you just walk right up to her, acting totally normal the whole time? How well do you think that would go?"

I meet this question with silence.

"We can't let you loose. People who have had way less than you still lose control. You would go on a rampage attacking every human in sight — completely unfit to travel or get on a plane, let alone appear remotely normal for long enough to be able to walk up to her. You aren't balanced, Mullins. We had to push you way past balance point to get you to cooperate. And only those who can hold the balance go free… well, until A-

Day. Give me another solution. How can we lure her away from her guards? She doesn't know about them, so it shouldn't be too hard. But we've had enough fuck ups in Vancouver already and we're too close to A-Day to risk exposure now. It's bad enough that..." he shakes his head and stops talking.

"You've had some escapes," I guess. "Your little army is breaking free."

"No one has escaped. Some people just... lose their balance and we have to catch up to them. We usually manage to find and dispose of the evidence."

"Even Craig broke in the end."

"Craig couldn't hack the long term. It happens."

"More and more, no doubt."

"For someone who wants to get his teeth sunk into Stella Blunt, you're sure as hell avoiding the topic of how we can fucking get her. I don't have time for this. Give me an answer now, or I'll leave you to stew about it for a week before I try again. A-Day is in just a few months. We've got a lot on our plates."

I sigh and flex in my chains. The metal creaks.

"It's perfectly simple. You have me hostage. Show her, and she will come. I can track her mind from miles away. It calls me. It's mine."

"Ah..." he leans forward. "Now we're getting somewhere. What makes you so sure she would come if she knew where you were? My sources tell me that she ended her relationship with you."

Moron. Imbecile. Idiot.

"Because she is mine."

Stella

The realization that I might have to break up with my boyfriend came at a bad time. Christmas Day, to be specific. Dad loves Christmas. He woke me up at seven o' clock.

"Stella! It's Christmas! Wake up!"

I rolled over. "Dad. I'm nearly nineteen. I don't find it so exciting anymore."

"How can you not be excited? Maybe Santa finally brought you a pony!"

"I never asked for a pony. I wanted a Barbie, but Santa never brought me that because she represented the objectification of women by the patriarchy. Then I wanted a Power Wheels. But Santa never brought me one, because it was too big and expensive and because he thought I would use it to go on infantile crime sprees."

"Well, never mind. Maybe he brought you a hammer for smashing the patriarchy."

"Just what I always wanted." I sat up and rubbed my eyes. "How about you go check, and report back?"

"How about I make some bacon?"

"Now you're talking."

When he was out of the room I collapsed back into my pillow. I could still remember my dream, and the feelings that it brought back hadn't washed away in the night.

Fuck.

I trudged downstairs half an hour later when the smell of bacon finally lured me from my bed. Dad brought some upstairs and wafted the smell right into my room.

"This plate is for your mother," he said. "There's more downstairs for you." He always brought Mom breakfast in bed on Christmas — a tradition that he and I started together back when I was five and actually woke *them* up on Christmas morning. We'd lure Mom out of bed by feeding her, and then she'd come downstairs and I'd rip into the stockings.

I sat in the kitchen, listening to the carols that Dad had already started playing, and ate bacon and tried to think about my current boyfriend. But the dream weighed on my chest and I still felt teary and fragile. When my parents finally came downstairs and suggested opening stockings, I was happy for the distraction.

"Condoms? You put CONDOMS in my stocking?"

"Santa put condoms in your STOCKING?" said my mother, giving my father a glare.

Dad was laughing. "Well, you're a bit old for Pokemon. Besides, they're Christmassy condoms. Peppermint flavour!" He looked in his stocking. "Wait. Is this actual coal? And where the hell is the rest of my stuff?"

"Let me see that!" my mother snatched it from him and started laughing. "Well done," she said to me.

"Don't look at me. It was Santa, probably punishing him for putting CONDOMS IN MY STOCKING."

My phone rang. It was Dean. Frig. "Do you guys mind if I take this?"

"Be quick. I need to find out where all my other gifts are."

"What other gifts? Santa gave you coal, that's all you get," I told him. "Hello," I said to the phone.

"Merry Christmas, baby."

"Merry Christmas. Don't call me baby. We're actually doing stockings at the moment. Can I call you later?"

"Sure. Miss ya."

"Uh huh. Bye." I ended the call and looked up. My Dad was rooting through the sofa cushions.

"Seriously," he said. "Where's the rest of my loot?"

"Dad," I said. "You got COAL."

My Mom mouthed to me, "Where'd you put it?" but I just shrugged and smiled.

"What'd you get, Mom?" I asked loudly.

She thanked me for the new book that I'd slipped in her stocking and showed me her new necklace. I helped her put it on. Dad barely noticed. He was crawling on the floor looking under the couches.

"Dad. Can you focus? Tell Mom she looks pretty."

"Do you like it, Elaine?" he glanced at her distractedly. "I, uh, I mean, Santa saw you admiring it in the window last month."

"I love it. Tell Santa that I wish to thank him for it *very* personally later."

"Yowza."

"Uh, guys? I'm old enough to pick up on sexual innuendo now."

"I'm sorry," my mother corrected herself. "Tell Santa I'd like to thank him. With sex."

I covered my ears. "La la la!"

"Oh, get over it, Stella," Mom teased.

"No, seriously. Condoms in my stocking? Sex jokes? Really?"

"You're an adult now and we intend to treat you like one."

"This is not normal."

"Well, it should be," said Dad firmly, "because this is how adults talk and interact and I don't see the point in continuing to infantilize you well into adulthood out of sheer habit."

"Said the man who maintains the fiction that my stocking gifts came from a supernatural entity."

"Santa is the spirit of giving and the spirit of giving is real, as evidenced by the stuff in your stocking and the boinking I'm going to give your mother later. Now," Dad gave me a stern look. "Tell me where my loot is."

"YOU GET COAL."

"I'm going to find it."

"Good."

"I'm not going to give up."

"Excellent."

Mom and I leaned back on the couch and watched Dad ransack the house.

"Thanks for arranging this morning's entertainment," Mom said. "I should have thought of this years ago."

"You're welcome. Thanks for the Chapters card and the new socks."

"You're welcome, sweetie. You okay? Last night..."

I waved away her concern. "Just a dream, really."

Dad eventually found his stocking gifts in his own laundry hamper, next to my parents' bed.

"That's gutsy," he said. "You sure you didn't have an accomplice?"

Mom swore her innocence.

"I figured it would be the last place you would look and I am stealthy like a ninja." I cracked my knuckles.

"Technically anywhere I found the stocking would be the last place I would look."

"Yeah, yeah. Now if you'll excuse me, I have to call Dean back."

I took my phone to my room and stared at it for a while. I didn't want to talk to Dean. I wanted to talk to Howie. But I couldn't very well call Dean on Christmas morning and tell him that I wanted to break up because I had a dream about my ex. I'd give the dream a day or two to wear off and then I would decide what to do.

But when I actually went to make the call, I found myself pulling up Howie in my contacts instead.

I told myself that I would just wish him a merry Christmas. Clearly, I needed closure. I mean, I missed seeing him at grad and then I never heard from him… obviously, that had messed me up a bit. I just needed to know he was okay.

I just needed to hear his voice.

"The number you have dialled is not in service. Please hang up and try your call again."

I stared at the phone. He got rid of his cell phone? Was he that desperate to make sure I never contacted him again?

I shook my head. No. That didn't sound like Howie at all. Probably his phone had just died. It was ancient. I mean, *ancient*. Like, it had buttons and a tiny black and white screen and no apps. Probably he had finally gotten a new phone and the SIM card from the old phone was so antiquated that it couldn't be transferred and now he had a new number.

I had to call someone else and get his new number. Who? Doc Mullins? I thought of how he avoided me at school. Hazel? No. Ray. For some reason, I felt most comfortable calling Ray. Maybe because Ray always said what he thought, so I never needed to worry that he was thinking terrible things about me. If he was, he told me so.

"Hello?" said Ray's voice a moment later.

"Ray? It's Stella. Uh. Merry Christmas."

"Jesus Christ," said Ray.

"I'll take that as a "Merry Christmas," I said. "Listen. Uh. Do you have Howie's number?"

There was a long silence. "Why?" Ray asked. "Has he called you?"

"No. Uh. I called him. His number's out of service."

"Yeah, I know."

"So. Uh. Do you have his new number? Or. Is he… like… around? Can I talk to him?"

"Why?"

"I just… I just wanted to wish him Merry Christmas, okay? I miss him. Is he okay?"

"I don't fucking know, Stella. Have you heard anything from him? In all these months? Since June?"

"No."

"Then leave me the fuck alone. Merry fucking Christmas." He hung up.

Howie didn't want to talk to me. The idea was hard to grasp. Howie's love for me had always felt like this fundamental law of nature. It was like gravity or magnetism. He told me himself, time and time again, that his love for me would go on long after I had gotten old and forgotten him. Now here I was, reaching out, and he didn't want to talk to me.

Or… It was possible that his family was cutting him off from me. A sort of intervention. That would make sense. After the grad thing, they confiscated his phone and told him to forget about me. That's why he never returned my calls. That's why Doc Mullins avoided me and didn't want me assisting in his lab. That's why Ray wanted to know if Howie had contacted me. They wanted me to stay the hell away from him.

Thinking about that reminded me *why* they would want him cut off from me. I remembered the lengths he was willing to go to, just to make me happy. I remembered what Ray and Hazel had told me, about Howie's terrible dreams, and his misery. He drove himself nearly insane trying to keep up with me, trying to make himself into the person I wanted him to be.

I didn't deserve Howie. I didn't accept him for what he was.

Shit. And now here I was, trying to call him on Christmas Day, and for what? To hear his voice? To try to figure out what I wanted? As if it was Howie's job, of all people, to tell me whether I preferred a life with a zombie over a life with someone like Dean?

What a stupid, *selfish* fucking move. Thank God they took away his phone so I couldn't hurt him again.

First I had to sort out for sure what I wanted. THEN, and only then, did I have the right to try and contact Howie… to find out whether he still felt the same way.

I picked up my phone again, and this time I really did call Dean to wish him a merry Christmas.

35

Howie

Voices fill my ears with meaningless nonsense.

"You can't send the message directly to Baum, you idiot. From what Mullins has been saying, Baum doesn't value Mullins much, and they'd be morons to send Stella Blunt of all people into Seattle, especially given the lies you've been feeding them."

"Mullins won't give us her direct number. Maybe Wilson can find it out for us?"

"Wilson isn't reliable. I don't want her to know anything with regard to Blunt. She might get suspicious. Mullins — what is Blunt's number? We'll send her a message begging her to come and rescue you."

This facility is filling up. More and more of us who see the pointlessness of politics and Apex's plans. They have starved me until I can feel the old foolishness looming in the background, but it has not reclaimed me. How can it, when I have seen the truth?

"Mullins? Mullins! Damnit, did you feed him too much again?"

"We had to give him some. He was getting out of control."

"I don't have time for this, Brenden. I need to get back to New York. A-Day is in three months, and I have a lot of threads to pull together."

"So go. I can handle it."

"Apparently you can't. Mullins, if you want Blunt, you've got to work with us. Yes? Blunt? You want her, right?"

Of course. But I shall collect her myself. I have no interest in their ridiculous web of useless plans.

There. They have left me alone now. I can feel them moving away, arguing over their meaninglessness.

My chains are heavy. But they are the same chains that I have worn for months. The molecular framework of metal is brittle. And metal fatigues with repeated stress.

Soon I shall be free. And she shall be mine.

Stella

It was unfortunate that I finally met Dean's parents the day after I seriously started thinking about breaking up with him. It didn't help that Dean was obviously uncomfortable. He didn't say anything to me when he opened the door, just indicated his parents and said,

"Mom, Dad, this is, uh, Stella."

I saw it on their faces. The quick flicker of surprise. I wasn't what they were expecting. That meant he hadn't shown them pictures. He hadn't described me. They were expecting the kind of girl people always expect guys like Dean to date, but they opened the door to find *me*.

They recovered really quickly, though, and Dean's mother gave me a broad smile.

"Stella, how nice to meet you! Dean has told us so much about you." She was a thin woman with shoulder-length brown hair, clear grey eyes, and a kind smile that made me forgive the lie she had just told me.

Dean's father reached out to shake my hand. "Come on in!" he said. He was a handsome kind of gent. His dark hair was fashionably streaked with grey.

Their house felt comfortable and welcoming. The bookcase in the hall had travel books and play scripts, and there were framed play posters and photos of beautiful views on the wall.

"Dad took those pictures himself," Dean told me when I stopped to admire a particularly spectacular shot of a cloud-draped, snow-capped mountain looming over a medieval-looking town.

"Which one are you looking at?" his father asked, coming over. "Oh, that's Mount Ararat, seen from Turkey. Traditionally considered the final resting spot of Noah's Ark."

"It's lovely," I told him. "I'd like to get off of North America someday."

"Travel broadens the mind," he said. "I highly recommend it." He pointed at the walled town in the foreground. "Turkey has been the gateway between Europe and Asia for time immemorial. Just think about the fact that humanity has been living and fighting and loving and dying around that patch of land for thousands of years of recorded history. Wars have been fought over that spot. Mothers and fathers and children, freemen and soldiers and slaves, have all walked that piece of ground. And yet it still looks so peaceful. History marches on."

His brown eyes were looking at the photo, but I had the feeling that they were seeing much more. I felt a strong liking for this man.

Damnit.

"Well, now that Dad has thoroughly bummed us out, let's eat dinner!" Dean said. "Then we can talk about the other kind of turkey. The kind we eat."

"I hope you aren't tired of turkey leftovers," said Dean's mother taking me by the elbow and guiding me to their dining room where an elaborate spread of dishes was already laid out.

"Not at all. Turkey dinner is my favourite meal. I could eat it forever," I said.

"Wonderful. Why don't you sit there, and Dean can sit there and Ken, you can sit on the end there…"

"Mom. Sit down," Dean said irritably. His mother pulled out a chair and had a seat.

"Okay, let's start passing things around. Maybe Stella, if you want to start with the turkey and pass it clockwise, and I'll start with the Brussels sprouts."

"MOM," Dean said. "We can figure out how to help ourselves to food. We don't need a director."

"Oh. Yes. Of course." She looked down at her hands and I felt intensely sorry for her. I gave Dean a dirty look.

"Dean doesn't know what he's talking about," I said. "It could have been chaos. I could have ended up fighting him to the death for this delicious looking slice of dark meat. Tragedy has been narrowly averted." I passed the turkey to Dean's father and accepted the Brussels sprouts from his mother, who picked up the cranberry sauce.

She smiled weakly. "Well, I'm glad to hear that," but she still looked awkward. I kind of wanted to punch Dean in the throat.

Dean's father cleared his own throat. "Speaking of fighting, Dean tells me that you're quite the martial artist. What do you do again? Is it karate?" He pronounced it correctly, "ka-ra-tay" instead of calling it "ka-rotty" like most people do.

"No, it's Shaolin wushu. Although I usually just call it kung fu because people recognize that name," I said.

"And you're from Newfoundland, is that right?" Dean's father persisted.

"Nova Scotia."

"We took a trip out East before Dean was born. Very charming part of Canada."

"I like it. I miss it."

"Have you been back since you moved out here?"

"No... We thought about going back East this past summer, but I got a government job. We might go back in spring after school is done. My cousin has a new baby that we'd like to see."

"What was the government job?" Dean's dad was determined to keep the ball rolling.

"It was a federal student grant to work with scientists in the Great Lakes area," I said smoothly. This was the official story that I told my friends and everyone else who asked why I was in Ontario for the summer. I hoped he wouldn't ask for more details, and I decided it was time to stop talking about myself. "Dean says you play violin?"

That worked. I got through the dinner by asking question after question. I coaxed Dean's dad into telling me about his childhood visits to Japan and Dean's mother into talking about her latest production. I learned that people in Japan eat KFC on Christmas Day and that Tennessee Williams choked to death on a bottle cap. But every minute of it felt like an effort.

They were nice people, and I liked them, but I felt like everyone was really *trying*. It all felt very *polite*. It seemed strange that laid-back, jokey Dean could have sprung from a family that was so thoughtful, and nervous, and serious. He fit in better with my parents than he did with his own.

Then again, dinner with Dean's parents might feel a little awkward, but they were charming and warm people compared to Howie's weird zombie family. They certainly weren't making it easier for me to decide to break up with him.

"Thank you for a delicious dinner," I said, laying my fork down on my plate.

"Let me take that for you," said Dean's mother. She reached for my plate, but I held onto it and stood up.

"No, you've done enough." I felt like I was channelling Howie right now. That dream had left him inside my head and I knew what he would do in this situation. "You sit. Let Dean and I clear the table. Right, Dean?"

"Uh, yeah," said Dean. "Sure."

"How nice," said his mother, smiling. Dean's father gave me the ghost of a wink.

I stacked the plates and carried them into the kitchen, and Dean followed me with the cranberry sauce in one hand and the sprouts in the other. As soon as we got to the kitchen, he leaned in.

"I was going to try and help you escape to my place, but then you signed us up for kitchen duty."

"You were going to sneak off with me and leave your mom to clean up?" I shook my head. "I'm going to pretend you didn't just say that so I can still respect you."

"You don't know Mom. Everything we do will be put in the wrong place or not done well enough and she'll spend half the night fixing it."

"Then that's her problem. But the least I can do is make an attempt to actually earn my keep." I scraped the plates into the garbage and stacked them on the counter. "You must know how she likes things. Help me make the closest possible approximation."

It was quickly clear to me that Dean wanted to get me out of his parents' house as quickly as possible. I wasn't sure if it was because he wanted to get me alone, or if he was just embarrassed by his big girlfriend, but either way I thought he was being a dick about it, so I insisted on staying and chatting with his mother while we consolidated leftovers into smaller containers and loaded them into the fridge. Then I accepted his father's invitation to have a cup of tea in the living room afterwards. Dean accepted his fate and we ended up trying to recreate our high school skit for them in the living room. His mother pulled out the Christopher Durang playbook and fed us our lines when we needed prompting. I was actually impressed by how much we managed to remember.

"You have quite a stage presence, Stella," said his mother. She laid her teacup back in its saucer.

"I think it's because I'm such a... large presence." I gestured to my body. I was tired of it being the metaphorical elephant in the room. But his parents were classy all the way and they didn't take the bait.

"It's charisma," his mother said, shaking her head. "It's a pity you didn't go into theatre."

"Or politics," said his father. "I have a feeling you could incite a crowd to a rebellion if you wanted to."

Dean laughed. "You should see her when she gets mad. You can practically feel the electricity in the air."

"I feel like, if I were *that* charismatic, I wouldn't have had so much trouble making friends growing up," I said.

"That's because you use your charisma powers for evil instead of for good," said Dean with a mischievous grin. "You don't *like* people enough to charm them."

"That is entirely possible."

Of course, I couldn't say, "actually I *do* use them for good — I use them to freeze and destroy hordes of zombies." I realized that I rarely thought about zombies when I was around Dean. I thought about Howie, but just about him in his role as a boyfriend, not as an actual demi-denizen of the living dead. It occurred to me that my clandestine participation in top-secret government zombie research might eventually cause relationship problems for me.

"Anyway, Stella and I were going to exchange gifts and have a little time to ourselves, okay?" Dean said, rising from the couch.

I stood up awkwardly, and his parents jumped up to shake my hand again.

"Thank you for dinner," I said.

"Thank you for coming," said his mom. "It was a real pleasure to meet you."

"Thanks… uh… Mrs. Kato."

"Janet," she said with a smile.

"Janet, then," I said.

"And please call me Ken," said Dean's dad. "And please come again soon."

Oh, God. They were so nice. I picked up Dean's gift, which I had left in the front hall, and I walked out of the door feeling more conflicted than ever.

"Well, you were a hit," Dean said as we walked down the path to his apartment at the back of the house. "Apparently you *can* win friends and influence people when you want to."

"Your parents are nice. It was easy," I said.

"So. Gift time. Do you want to go first, or shall I?" Dean asked as we walked into his place. I thought hard. If he gave me something amazing then my gift would look lame coming after.

"I'll go first."

So he unwrapped his stuff and made happy noises. "Awesome! Thanks, babe." He gave me a kiss on the cheek. "Now open yours."

Mine was in a black gift bag with pink tissue paper. Curious, I pulled out the tissue paper and reached into the bag. I pulled out a bundle of red lace.

I wasn't sure how to feel about that. "Oh, uh, wow." I shook it out. It was babydoll with a matching thong. "Thanks." I tried to think of something more to say. "I don't have something like this."

"You deserve something that will make you feel sexy," he said. "As sexy as I think you are. Do you like it?"

I wasn't sure. I mean, I didn't hate it or anything. I just don't think about clothes or lingerie much. I don't like feeling frumpy and quality bras are more comfortable and supportive so I usually have good quality underthings but that's it. I had never thought of shopping for something as purely decorative as a babydoll. But maybe I should have. I mean, lots of girls like to get all dressed up for their guys.

"I think I'll have to see how I feel when I wear it," I said.

"Try it on!" he urged. "Then come out and give me a fashion show."

So I went into his bedroom to change, feeling uncomfortable, and annoyed about it. I don't like uncomfortable feelings, and I usually just get pissed off instead, because I'm used to being pissed off. But in this case, I wasn't sure who I should be pissed at. Dean, for buying me something that seemed more like it was for him than for me? But I knew that a lot of people considered lingerie to be a valid gift for a woman. Like jewelry. Stuff to make her feel pretty. So I was also annoyed at myself because I was being so weird about something that was perfectly normal. Getting mad at my boyfriend for giving me lingerie seemed like the kind of thing a shitty girlfriend would do, and I was trying to not be a shitty girlfriend.

The lingerie fit me all right, and it was reasonably comfortable. I looked down at myself and tried to measure how I was feeling. But I just wasn't sure. But when I stepped out into the living room I decided that I was definitely uncomfortable. I felt... on display. I also felt fat. Maybe that was because all of the pictures I had ever seen of girls in lingerie were on billboards and in magazines, and I did not look like any of those girls.

I hadn't felt fat for a long time. But now, comparing myself to those ads, I felt fat.

Dean whistled when he saw me. "Hot *damn,* babe, you are *fine."*

I tugged at the fabric a little. "You think it fits okay?"

"Way more than okay. You look like something out of a wet dream."

"I'll take that as a compliment," I said, trying not to laugh.

Dean pressed his body against me and gave me a long kiss. "Let's get you back into that bedroom," he said huskily. "And I can show you exactly what I mean."

Well. I was glad he liked his gift, anyway. The one from himself.

"*Ouch*," I said a few minutes later. "Stop."

He pulled back. "What's up?"

"Is foreplay just, like, a thing we don't do anymore?" All of my uncomfortable feelings about the lingerie and my conflicted emotions about Howie were bubbling to the surface in little blips of anger.

Dean's face clouded. "Stella. You look beyond sexy. Excuse me if I'm a little overeager."

"I just feel like since we started having sex, then that's been, like, *all* we do."

"What the hell are you talking about? First of all, obviously having sex isn't *all* we do, since we've had it about a grand total of four fucking times over the course of three weeks, so it's not like we're going at it like bunnies..."

"That's not what I mean," I interrupted. "I mean *when* we do have sex, foreplay just, like, gets *skipped*."

"I give you foreplay *every* time you ask for it. I gave you two fucking *months* of nothing *but* foreplay. So yeah, excuse me if I'm a *little* focused on the sex part right now."

I opened my mouth to explode at him but he suddenly sat back and put his finger on my lips.

"Let's not fight, babe. It's Christmas, you look like a sex bomb just went off in my room, and I want you in the worst way. I'm sorry I rushed you. Come here, let me try again."

He tried again, and he tried really hard, so I didn't voice any more complaints. But my heart just wasn't in it.

"Why don't you stay over?" Dean said when I got up and started getting dressed. I was feeling really depressed, and it wasn't just the underwhelming sex. It was that fucking dream. *Still.*

"No. I want to get back to my parents."

"They're chill people, Stella. I'm sure they'll understand if you tell them you want to stay here tonight."

"But I don't *want* to stay here tonight, Dean. I want to go home."

"Okay, okay."

"So? What are the Katos like?" Dad asked when I walked in the door.

"Nice," I said. I looked at the TV. They were watching a show about plane crashes. "What did I miss here?"

"Turkey leftovers. An argument over whether Robert Galbraith would have been as successful if people hadn't leaked the fact that he was really JK Rowling."

"Drat," I snapped my fingers. "All the fun happens when I leave the house."

"Howie used to say drat, didn't he?" my mother mused. "You must have got that from him."

Everyone in the room went very still, including my mother.

Dad cleared his throat. "So, you liked Dean's parents?"

"Yeah," I said, a little more loudly than usual. "Nice people. His dad takes great travel photos. I'm wiped though. I think I'm going to go read in my room."

"Everything okay?" Mom said. "Sorry, sweetie, I -"

"Yeah," I interrupted. "I'm just really caught up in that new Rainbow Rowell book you gave me. I've been wanting to get back to it all evening."

"Okay. Goodnight, honey."

As I went up the stairs I heard my mother say softly to my father, "I'm such an idiot. Why did I say that?"

"It's fine, Elaine."

Of course it was fine. Why shouldn't my mother bring up my ex-boyfriend and his mid-twentieth century vocabulary?

You know, the ex-boyfriend that I was definitely still in love with.

36

Howie

My chains creak in the noisy night. Many of us are working on their chains. But Apex feeds me more. I have been stronger for longer. My chain is wearing.

It happens suddenly — a snap, and my hands fly out, finally free. I hold them in front of me, clench my fists, and I make a human expression of pleasure with the corners of my mouth. I stand up for the first time in far too long, and for a moment my joints grind. It is painless, but it is uncomfortable. The virus is my ally. It sends lubricating fluids to my joints, healing and repairing. I bend my knees several times and rotate my arms. There. I can move. Now, to be free. I lift one foot and kick at the metal door with all my might. The metal buckles and bends in the impact. It isn't much, but it is enough to create a gap at the bottom. Kneeling, I slide my fingers under the lip of the door and grit my teeth as I strain upward. If I could feel pain, I would likely feel my muscles tearing at the strain. But my body will heal itself, so what use is pain to such as me?

But no — the lock holds the door tight. I back up to the end of the room, and, roaring, I charge the door with my shoulder. Bang. Bang. Bang. The door is bending, buckling. One more charge and the door pulls free from its tracks. It hangs loosely. I can feel a slight breeze rush in from the hallway, and the fluorescent lighting floods in. My eyes adjust quickly, and I step out of my cell.

Never have I felt so gleeful.

Soon. Soon.

Somewhere in here, there is a freezer. I turn my head and scan the hall. For the first time, I can see my prison. I am filled with strength and grace. When I move, I have the smooth, predatory glide of a panther, not the lumbering lurch of an infected wretch. When I hear, when I see, I process things instantly. I am a hunter.

No.

I am a demi-god.

This location is was intended as a storage facility. But rather than discarded belongings, it contains stored power — predators waiting for the hunt. Apex believes it is their army. But it is their undoing. I am their undoing. I will bring them down because I can. I have the power.

But first, I follow my instincts, and they lead me down the hallway. I don't walk. I don't run. I bound. I discover that I can run and jump against the wall to propel myself forward, and so I bound forward and forward, pushing off one wall and then another, like that foolish fictional character — Spiderman. Why? Because I can. I have the power. I am strong, and I am fast. I hit the doors of other storage rooms, and I hear and feel the roars from the inmates inside. Be patient, little ones.

There is an elevator, but I am too impatient for such a ponderous device. I find a stairwell with a rickety metal staircase. It curls downward in a tight spiral and I can see down to the bottom. I have no time for stairs — I vault effortlessly over the handrail and drop down, down, down. I land three stories below, crouching to absorb the impact of my fall. It is easy.

The main office is simple to locate. On a wall hang keys — keys to every unit, carefully labelled, as I knew they would be. And there, ah yes. There they are — a row of cooling storage devices, known as refrigerators, all locked shut. Naturally, *that* key is not hanging on the wall. No matter. I feel stronger with every step I take. I rip the hinges free. The fridge is full — some of the brains are still encased in their heads, while others have been scooped free and placed in containers. I fill my hands and then my mouth and I can feel it, frigid as it is, making me better and stronger. I am unstoppable. The power flows through me until I am but a conduit of relentless force. I must move. I must be.

I have a strange flicker of memory — of a bed with rose petals on it, and a rapturous feeling that this was where I was meant to be. That is how I feel now.

My time is short. Apex must have me on surveillance. Even now, they may be rushing to stop me. Fools. Imbeciles. I remove the board with the keys from the wall and I run into the hallway. I unlock the first door I come to. This is not teamwork. This is not social structure. This is not morality. This is destruction for the sheer revelry of it. I raise the door, and with my new strength pulsing through me, I effortlessly snap the chains of the captive within. She stands, eyes gleaming, and I wordlessly point the way toward the refrigerator. Then I move on to the next door.

By the time I have freed the fifth inmate, the first has moved up to the second floor, revelling in her new strength, to continue the liberation process. Soon the second, third, fourth and fifth will join her.

Not out of teamwork. Not out of empathy. This is merely the delight that comes from watching the world burn.

By the time I push open the heavy fire door and exit the compound, the building is filled with the clang of snapping chains and howls of triumph.

The world, and Apex with it, will fall.

And I am free.

Stella

I was up late in the night that Boxing Day, trying to decide what the hell I was going to do. I knew that I should break up with Dean. But what kind of an asshole breaks up with someone on Christmas? And besides, yes, okay, so I was still in love with Howie. But really, what did that change? Nothing, really. I mean, hadn't I already known that I still cared about Howie? I had never woken up and thought, "Pfft, Howie. Who needs that guy?" The thought of that was ludicrous. I held the memory of Howie close to me, like it was something to be guarded and cherished. Poor Dean — Howie was a hard act to follow, what with his ability to sense my emotions and nearly seventy years of life experience and wisdom. Howie wasn't *normal*, both in the best and worst ways. I would *always* be a little in love with Howie. That was just a fact that I accepted.

The real question was, *Am I going to do anything about it?* Howie and I just messed each other up, torturing ourselves trying to make an impossible situation work. That situation hadn't changed. It was still impossible.

But something had changed. The dream had changed things. I felt as if Howie and I had broken up all over again. I felt bruised. I ached. Things felt different with Dean, too. Before, he felt like an adventure. He was something new and different and fresh and I was attracted to him and it had been fun. But all of that had now fallen away.

God, I had to break up with Dean. It wasn't fair to lead him on while I desperately wished he were someone else. So I would just be lonely and horny and missing Howie for, like, ever, I guess.

I decided that I would do it after New Years. The good news was, I didn't have to spend New Year's Eve with him. He was spending New Year's with his old buddies from high school, and there was no way in hell I was going near those people.

"You're sure you don't mind, babe?" he had asked.

"I mind you calling me 'babe'."

"Okay, okay, but really, you don't mind?"

"Not if you don't mind me refusing flatly to come along."

"I knew you wouldn't want to come. I know you hate most of those guys."

"If by 'most' you mean 'every last mother fucking one of them'."

I heard a small huff of air on his end of the line. "Those are my friends you're talking about."

"I have no idea why."

"You really could come if you want. I'm cool with it."

"No, it's okay." I lay on my back and stared at the ceiling of my bedroom. "I don't give a shit about the whole kissing-at-midnight thing." Actually, that was only partly true. If he were Howie, I would care. But he was Dean, and I just didn't.

"Well, I do. But I promised these guys that I would party with them months and months ago. Like, they've been planning this party since last January."

"God, that sounds so boring that I can't even begin to understand it."

"So what'll you be doing, then?"

"Dunno. I'll see what Kate and company are up to. Worst case scenario I hang out with my parents and watch my Dad wear crazy hats."

"Okay, babe. Listen, I've gotta go but I'll text you later. K?"

"Sounds good."

"Miss you."

"You too. Bye."

I sent a text to Kate asking what she was doing for New Year's and drifted off into a reverie, thinking about last year. Howie had come along with me to Amy's house, where my friends were celebrating. We ate pizza and watched the countdown on TV and when the fireworks went off, Howie had pulled me around the corner into the hallway and started kissing me. His kisses were so tender that they melted me.

"This," he had whispered in my ear, "has been the best year," he kissed me again, "of my life."

"That's really saying something," I said, tilting my chin up — my way of telling him to kiss my neck, which he did. "Considering that you're staggeringly old. I am also reasonably satisfied with the past year."

"Reasonably satisfied. Hmm," he had said and then kissed me one more time. "I'll have to see what I can do to make this year even better."

So much had changed in a year. I curled up on the bed and breathed until the memory faded a bit. No, I didn't mind that I was missing New Year's with Dean at all.

I wondered if, at this moment, Howie was curled up on his bed, remembering last year too.

Howie

I stride through the dark, taking deep breaths of the fresh air. I own this night. I own every square of sidewalk that my foot lands on, every lamp post, every car that goes by. I relish it.

Running feet come up behind me as the others burst free from their prison. The hornets' nest has been thoroughly kicked, and they rise out of the husk with a furious hum. They thunder past me, whooping, in search of fresh prey. Our street is deserted — we are well outside the city core, in a little-used industrial park. But our feet are tireless, and energy is pulsing through us. We are coming. Hear us come.

Another car is approaching, and it is driving much faster than the others that have passed me. I can feel the fury bearing down on me, and I am amused.

"Mullins!" shouts Brenda. The car brakes and slows, and she leaps out before it comes to a halt. She darts at me, and she is faster than any mere human could possibly be, but I dodge her effortlessly nonetheless. I have had more. I am more.

"You asshole!" she screams. "What have you done?"

Brenden and Jess also burst out of the car as it screeches to a halt and they point weapons at me. I look down the barrel of their guns, gleaming in the street light, and I laugh. They must hit my head if they wish to stop me, and I'm a moving target. With a crouch and a leap, I sail over their heads and land with a thump behind them, on their car.

"Apex will fall. I told you that Apex will fall."

"You've ruined everything," spits Brenda. "They'll infect the city. There's too many of them. We can't cover it up."

"Looks like A-Day is here," I say, and I vanish behind their car as they shoot at me. "Good luck."

"Maybe we can still stop them," I hear Brenden say. Jess has leaped on top of the car and is aiming at me, but her bullet buries itself in the road as I move again. I am faster than a speeding bullet.

"You have one hour," I hear Brenda say. "Send everyone out. But if you don't get it completely under control I'm going to have to execute A-Day early, before a hundred countries go into lock-down. Shit. Fuck."

"*Can* we execute it early?" Brenden asks. They're already forgetting me. No. Jess hasn't forgotten me. I dodge again as I feel her brain aiming at me. I spring right over her head.

"Of course we can, but it will take a day, maybe two or even three, to get everything going properly, and we still don't have the known ZCPs all neutralized. It's New Year's Eve, so government isn't in session. Everyone will be spread around. Shit. Fuck. I want Mullins's skin on my wall."

"On the bright side, the airports will be busy," says Jess. Brenda nods.

I weary of this idiocy. There is flesh to be enjoyed; an entire planet to be ravished. Enough with their ridiculous schemes.

"What about Blunt, Mullins?" Brenden shouts. "I thought you were going to help us. Help us find Blunt, remember?"

"Oh, she'll be coming. But I don't need your help." I've had enough of this nonsense, and I can feel the wind blowing back my hair as I move into top gear. I call over my shoulder as I run. "She'll see me on the news."

Stella

New Year's Eve actually turned out great, if you set aside the fact that I was in love with someone who wasn't my current boyfriend. Kate and I hosted a party in our apartment. Amy and Michelle, and Michelle's new boyfriend, Mark, came, and Riya and a couple of people from Kate and Riya's LGBTQ group. And half of my kung fu group ended up showing up when I invited them, which surprised me because, you know, most of them were older than me and they all had other friends, so I wasn't actually expecting them to say yes.

"Sure," said Melanie, when I called her.

"Uh. Really?" I was thrown off. I had practised my "it's okay, I know it's last-minute" acceptance speech in my head for like twenty minutes before I called.

"Yeah, actually I'm a little relieved. My boyfriend just broke up with me, and all of my friends are his friends, so I thought I'd spend it sad and alone."

"Oh, that sucks. You going to be okay?"

"Yeah, he's an asshole. I've been meaning to break up with him for a year. I'm mostly pissed because I kept putting it off for very sensitive reasons, like his grandma had just died, or he was in the middle of studying for a midterm. And then he went and broke up with me on fucking Boxing Day, the day after I gave him an expensive present."

"Harsh," I agreed, feeling simultaneously both better and worse about not making a decision about Dean.

"Anyway, who else is coming?"

"You're the first one I called, but I'm going to call John and Rob and Alicia and the others. My roommate's buddies will be here and my friends from high school."

"Well, count me in. I hope I won't be the only single one. I hate being the only person not getting kissed at midnight."

"I won't be kissing, either. Dean's partying elsewhere."

"Where?"

"With a bunch of his old buddies from high school, whom I despise."

"Oh, gross. Okay, well, thanks for the invite; you saved my life. See you then!"

So then I texted John and Rob and I made a point of casually mentioning that Melanie was newly single. I got the impression that they were hastily re-arranging their schedules to come to my New Year's party instead. Then I messaged more people and told them that John and Rob and Melanie would be there, and next thing I knew I had half the club coming.

"Wow, it's going to be martial artists all up in this joint," said Kate. "Look at you, all popular and shit."

"Good timing," I said. "I snagged the newly single hot girl."

But it did feel good. Because if everyone hated me or thought I was some obnoxious, loud, fat frosh, they wouldn't have been caught dead wasting their New Year's Eve at my place. They had always made me feel welcome but some part of me always thought that they might just be being nice. But this felt like proof — they really did like me.

Then the traitorous thoughts started — had Dean raised my stock? Maybe they saw my hot boyfriend and thought, *Wow, this girl really must be worth knowing*. If I had brought Howie to that Christmas party, would they still want to come over?

Not that my break-up with Howie had anything to do with my social life, but I also didn't want to trade falsely off of Dean's good looks, either.

I mentioned this theory to my parents and they rolled their eyes at me.

"I'm pretty sure these people all liked you before they met your boyfriend," said Dad. "I think you're being a bit insecure."

"I mean, he *is* really hot," said my mother.

"I know you're talking about me, but from context, it sort of sounded like you were talking about your daughter's boyfriend," said Dad.

"Sorry about the confusion, Tim, dear," said Mom, and then mouthed, "REALLY HOT!" at me.

Dad pretended not to see that. "My point is, have fun at the party."

"I plan to. By the way, can you buy me some booze for the party? I mean, I am so *nearly* nineteen."

"Promise not to drive?"

"I'll be at my OWN apartment and I don't have a car."

"We'll pick you up some cheap champagne."

"You guys are the best."

"We know."

The party was a blast. It was exactly what I needed to take my mind off of Howie. I normally hate parties, but this one had a bunch of people that I really liked and who really seemed to like me. In fact, when Rob finished his third Tequila shot he ended up hanging his arm around me and telling me how awesome he thought I was.

"Like, how do you handle your coolness?" he slurred. "I want to just, like, *be* you."

"You want to be a tall fat chick?" I said.

"I guess not." He slumped. "I kind of like having a cock. But, you know, you're just so, like, TOGETHER, and you just kind of, like, *own* the room, and I bet that if I could do that, it would be me making out with Melanie and not fucking John."

"I'm sorry, man," I said, patting him on the back. "Have another shot of Tequila."

"You're the best."

"If it helps, I'm pretty sure that you have a chance with Alicia."

He brightened. "Really?"

"Yeah, I mean, I don't know anything, but she asked if you'd be here and sounded regretful that she couldn't come."

"Alicia, hey?" he said thoughtfully. "Cool."

My phone buzzed, and I pulled it out.

Hey babyyyy missing u!!!

I texted back.

Are you having fun?
You're missing a good party at our place.

Sorry babe I'll make it up to u
I promise ;-)

Don't apologize to me,
you're the one missing out.

It's rocking here too babe,
all I'm missing is u.

I suppose your buddies are all super disappointed
that they didn't get to mock me in person.

Lol be nice, but I'm glad ur having fun.

Kate turned down the music and turned on the TV in anticipation of the New Year's countdown. I caught a glimpse of a news channel before she flipped on the TV guide.

"Wait! Go back to the news for a sec," I ordered. She shrugged and put the news back on. It was a Seattle news channel, and they were talking about an attack. Apparently, a group of people had been attacked leaving a club, and three of them had been dragged off but one had escaped. The survivor was describing the attackers as "crazed" and "bloodthirsty". He even claimed that one of them had tried to bite him on the arm.

"You can't really see it anymore," he said, "but I swear, they were *biting* us."

"Boring," said Kate. "It's almost countdown time."

"But, holy shit," I said. "You realize what this could mean?"

"Yeah, that we could miss the countdown watching news about America's problem with violence," said Kate. "What are you going to do? They have a culture of brutality. Read about it on Buzzfeed tomorrow."

So we watched the countdown and toasted the new year and watched people make out, while I worried about zombies and simultaneously remembered how it felt to have a zombie kiss my neck and make me feel deeply, utterly loved.

My phone binged.

Happy new year babyyyy

Ugh, my life felt complicated.

37

Howie

I dart through the night, toward the glittering lights of the city centre. I can feel the minds buzzing in the dark, drawing me in. I pass a man on the sidewalk and I pause. He is here, fresh in front of me. His blood pulses. His mind calls me. But I resist. He has no complexity. He has no depth. I can hold out for better than this. I am replete. I can hold out for better. For more.

Now I am moving through residential areas. So many minds tucked up safely in their bed — their dozy brains hardly tempt me. I carry on, toward the bars and the nightclubs. I sprint tirelessly to get there sooner, quicker. Ah yes, I can feel those active minds. I sort through them, rejecting them one by one. No… No… No… But my hunger is growing, my need is increasing, my resolve crumbling. I may take just one. Just to tide me over.

And if I must, then I might as well do so in front of a camera, because I am still intent on getting the best.

I sniff out a nice mind — Mmm, yes, it feels very nice. So good, after months of captivity. Definitely good enough. I follow that mind, buzzing to it, alight with it. It's not quite as good as Stella's, but perhaps it could be. If he knew how to use it properly… but he never will, because I am taking it.

I find the building and am pleased to discover that it is in a large club. Jazz music floats out. They will have security cameras. And there will be smartphones to record my debut.

And when I make the news, when she sees me… she will come.

And she will be mine.

Stella

The first thing I did when I woke up at eleven the next morning was check my phone's news feed. My heart started racing when I saw the headlines: Crazed New Year's Attackers Storm Seattle, 31 Missing And 14 Dead In New Year's Murder Blitz, and Drug-Crazed Gang Violence Creates Death Toll on Seattle Streets.

I knew, I just *knew* that it was really bad. I poured myself a big cold glass of pulp-free orange juice and planted myself in front of the TV. While I waited for the same footage to replay every hour or so, I googled the situation frantically. The more I read, the more convinced I was that this had to be some kind of an outbreak. I mean, people biting other people? Acting crazed? It sounded like a zombie outbreak for sure.

But there were things that didn't fit. The very few witnesses who were quoted talked about the people moving "super fast". That didn't sound like any zombie I had ever met. Hell, even Howie and his family tended to walk with a bit of a lurch. Coordination was not their strong suit. Besides, I had fought a ton of zombies during the Vancouver outbreak, and none of them could run. A fast, clumsy, jerky shuffle was the best they could manage. But in the blurry, shaky videos the news channels were showing I saw running and leaping, and it wasn't just kind of fast. It was super-hero fast. So it couldn't be zombies. Could it?

I kept checking my phone, but I had no missed calls, and *surely* Hunt would be calling me if this had to do with zombies. After all, if Seattle had a rampant zombie problem, wouldn't the U.S. be begging Canada for my services? I mean, not to brag, but I was the most powerful anti-zombie weapon West of Madrid.

Dean showed up just before lunch. I buzzed him up and then flopped back onto the couch. I wasn't feeling great. I still had no doubt in my mind that I needed to break things off with Dean. Howie and I might be over, but I couldn't keep dating Dean when all I could think about was how desperately I wished he was someone else.

I supposed that I had better get it over with. But when he walked in the door and grinned at me, I faltered. He was so damn good-looking, and he looked so happy to see me. Besides, he was my friend now. However complicated my feelings about him were, Dean and I were friendly. Our break up would leave a big hole in my social life. I would miss him.

"How'ya doing, babe?" he said, reaching out for me. "I haven't seen you since last year."

I smiled and accepted his hug. "Don't call me babe. I'm surprised you're up and about. I thought you'd be nursing a hangover."

"Nah, I'm tough." He flexed his bicep. "There was nothing wrong with me this morning that some greasy Chinese food couldn't fix." He looked around the room and whistled. "So, good party?"

Kate and I hadn't bothered with cleaning up yet, so there were empty glasses and bottles everywhere. "Yeah, you missed a good time."

"Next year," said Dean. "We can celebrate together next year."

That seemed like a good opening. "Dean, I..."

"Oh, is that the Seattle thing?" Dean asked, bouncing onto the couch and gaping at the TV. "Crazy!"

"I think it might be the zombie apocalypse," I said. "I'm a little concerned."

"It'll take a lot more than a few gang members to start a zombie apocalypse, babe. I think you can rest easy. If you think about it, biting is a pretty crappy way of transmitting a virus. You'd need a LOT of people to get bitten before things could really get out of hand. I mean, remember that rage toxin a couple of years ago? Remember how some of those crazies got into the school and trashed it?"

"Of course I do," I said. "Ms. Bond got killed."

"So imagine those guys were zombies. They looked a lot like zombies, right?"

I nodded.

"A whole bunch of them broke into the school and still no one really got hurt. In order to really bring down civilization, you'd need to either have everyone get the virus at once like in *The Walking Dead*, or have a bunch of people suddenly get infected in multiple cities so that no one could go to anyone else's aid."

"You've thought a lot about this," I said.

"You watch enough zombie movies and you start thinking about the dynamics," he shrugged. "What surprises me is that they aren't talking about that toxin in Seattle. I bet that's what it is. Didn't they end up tracing it to a pharmacy or something?"

"But in the Vancouver outbreak everyone was moving kind of slow," I pointed out carefully. "These guys are running apparently. And they're carrying people off."

"Yeah, that doesn't really sound so similar, does it?" He ran his fingers through his hair and shrugged. "I kind of wish it *were* a zombie apocalypse. That would be so cool."

"It wouldn't be *cool*," I snapped. "There's nothing *cool* about millions of people dying horribly."

"Yes there is," he said. "It isn't the same as *good*. Like, it would be awful but it would be *epic*."

I gave him a dirty look.

"Aw, don't look at me like that. Look, people like gore. That's just how it is. Like, you like *The Hunger Games*, right? Lots of people get killed in that."

"Yeah, but I don't like it for that. I like it for the character-driven narrative, the political commentary on our own society, the plot twists, and the romance."

"Okay, but if no one got killed then it would be a lame book."

"Life isn't a book."

"No, listen, Stells. Like, say the apocalypse happened. A meteor hit the world, or zombies attack or something. It wouldn't be GOOD. It would be very, very bad. But living through it would be COOL. Because it's intense. Because it means something. Like, say I die. That's bad. I don't wanna die. But if I died of alcohol poisoning, that would be a lame death. If I died, say, leaping from an exploding helicopter, that would be an AWESOME death."

I started to laugh. I couldn't help it. "Why would you be on an exploding helicopter, exactly? You're a theatre geek."

"It's just an example. Adding a chopper automatically makes anything you do forty-six percent more awesome. Can you think of any headline that wouldn't sound more awesome when you added a chopper? Like, Small Child Rescued from House Fire… by Chopper."

"Prime Minister Announces New Tax Incentives."

"From his chopper."

"Historical Opera House To Be Knocked Down."

"By a chopper."

"Okay, I will give you the helicopter thing. But you should still be more sensitive about those people's deaths."

"I hereby promise not to apply the word 'cool' to a death unless it involves an exploding helicopter. Okay?"

"Deal." This was the problem with Dean. I really *liked* him when he wasn't being a shit stick.

Dean gave me one of his sparkling grins. "Now, come here and let me greet you properly."

"I'm not feeling kissy," I warned. "I have morning breath and after-drinking breath and I'm feeling generally gross and worried about zombies in Seattle."

"Then I'll content myself with groping you," he said, winking and squeezing my boob.

"Charming." I tried to figure out how to turn this into a breakup conversation. It would be easier if he would piss me off. Maybe that was the key. I had to wait for him to make me mad and then I'd have a reason to break it off. I settled next to him on the couch and let him wrap his arm around me. He smelled good, and his broad chest was comfortable.

My phone started to ring. I pulled away from Dean and glanced at the screen. *Boss Lady,* said my caller ID. Holy shit, it was Agent Hunt.

"Uh, I have to take this call," I said to Dean, and I stood up and answered the phone. "Hello?"

"Stella," said Agent Hunt, "I'm outside your building. Are you alone?"

"No," I said, glancing at Dean. "My boyfriend and my roommates are here."

"Then can you come down to my car for a few minutes, please?"

"Uh. Sure. Uh…"

"Good." She hung up.

I turned to Dean. "I, uh, I need to go downstairs for a few minutes."

"Why? Who was that?"

I don't like lying. "She works for the government agency that I worked for over the summer. She has something she wants to talk to me about, but it's confidential government stuff so she wondered if I could pop downstairs and go over it with her in her car."

"Didn't you just do science things?"

"Science can be confidential," I said irritably. "Didn't you learn anything about the space race in history class?"

"Alright," he shrugged. "I'll be here."

I nearly tripped over my own feet, throwing on my shoes and running out the door as fast as I could. Zombies. I *knew* it was zombies.

Howie

I push my way into the club, ignoring the humans who demand identification and money from me. Money is a placebo token system designed to simplify the exchange of goods. I have no use for such things. These people are but flies around my food.

The excellent mind is inside, but it is surrounded by darkness and I feel it spike in fear. I am not the first one here. The live band falters. Flushed with urgency, I leap from table to table, enjoying the screams of shock.

The man with the mind is already grappling with two — no, three — others. I can feel them swarming around him. They're tainting the feel of his brain. But he draws me in, anyway. His fear and pain make him sharper. It lures me. Humans are screaming and trying to pull the man free. I recognize the female who turns and bites the human who is grappling her. He screams and pulls away, and she turns back to the better mind as she chews the flesh in her mouth.

"Cassie," I say. She looks up and sneers.

"I got here first, Ian," she says, and she takes a bite of the man's flesh. He is screaming as the other two dig in. There is no room for me, so I stand and watch. I could choose someone else, but how can I take something lesser? This is the one. His mind calls to us.

Someone fires a gun, and it rips into the bodies that bend over him. It makes no difference. Their flesh will seal instantly. The mind is still burning. The noises he makes bother me. The shouting of the crowd agitates me.

"End it," I urge them. Another face looks up. Craig.

"There's so much more than just the brain," he says. He has taken a steak knife from a table and is using it with great interest. "And it's better when the mind is still going."

But the agony of the man doesn't feel as good to me. I would want him thrilling with pleasure, rather than pain. And I can feel the virus circulating up to his brain, tainting it. They're ruining him.

I bend down over the man, and I take his head in my hands. With a smack, I end the torment and his body goes limp. The mind is quiet now yet I feel inexplicably relieved.

"What did you do that for?" complains the female once known as Cassie.

I pry my fingers into the smashed skull and dig in for a handful. Still warm. I thirst for the taste of it on my tongue and I fill both of my hands. But the others are clawing for it, snatching for it, and I know that I must get free of them if I am to be able to savour it properly. I dart for a side exit, conveniently marked in glowing lights. As I burst out the door I can hear the shouting of police officers and rapid gunfire behind me. I clutch the gore in my fist. I will find some privacy, and then I will indulge.

I run directly into Brenden.

"We figured that you'd go right for the nicest mind in the vicinity," says Brenden. Jess and Brenda step forward and grapple me, but I throw them off. And then I take my handful and splatter Brenden's face with it. He cannot help it. His tongue darts out and licks his lips. Quickly at first, then again, more slowly. I can see him savour it. I can feel him wanting more.

"A gift for you," I say as he wipes it off of his face and stares longingly at his hand. "Consider it a second helping."

And then I am free and running away, with the sound of their feet pounding after me.

Stella

If I was surprised to have Agent Hunt turn up outside my door on New Year's Day, I was even more surprised by the person in her passenger seat — a man with short, dark hair and broad shoulders and a pompous frown: Fucking Agent Baum. What the hell was *he* doing here? I paused, unsure whether I wanted to get in the same car as the man who had used a webcam to spy on my first kiss, stormed in on me dry humping Howie so he could arrest him before we had sex, and tried to convince me that Howie was using me like a piece of meat.

Not to mention that he started an outbreak in Vancouver which resulted in the deaths of nearly a hundred and fifty people just to frame Howie's family and get them locked up.

Hunt was in the driver's seat and she waved at me through the window, indicating that she wanted me to get in the back. I opened the back door reluctantly and pointed at Baum.

"What is *he* doing here?"

"Hello to you too, Ms. Blunt," he said in the deep, officious tone that I remembered with such loathing. "I see that your manners have not improved with age. Get in the car."

I got in. "I'm only getting in because I've been watching the shit happening in Seattle and I need to know what the fuck is going on. Do I need to buckle up?"

"No," said Agent Hunt, twisting in her seat to look at me. "This will serve well enough as a private place to talk. We'll just chat here and then you can get out again. How are you?"

"Uh, a bit tired from partying last night. Seriously concerned about what the hell is happening in Seattle. Wondering what the fuck Baum is doing here. That sort of thing. Do you need me? Is it zombies? I mean, is it an outbreak?"

"First things first," said Hunt. "You need to know that *Agent* Baum has been cleared of all charges against him except one — he admits he planted unauthorized surveillance in the Mullins household, out of safety concerns. But he did not start the outbreak in Vancouver last year."

"Bullshit."

"Next. I need to ask you a question. I understand that you have a new boyfriend, but I still need to ask. Have you heard from Howie lately?"

I felt a chill go through me at the sound of his name.

"No. Why?" I studied her face, but her facial expression seemed very carefully neutral. "Is something wrong?"

"We aren't sure," she said. "When was the last time you did speak to him?"

"March. The day we broke up," I said. And I realized that I hadn't thought about that particular conversation for a long time. It hurt too much. *Beautiful, so beautiful. I love you.* Tears came to my eyes, and I looked away so she wouldn't see. "He stopped by and spoke to my parents in June, but I didn't talk to him. I tried, but… but he never called me back."

She nodded. "I had gathered as much from your parents, but I wanted to double check and make sure that hadn't changed."

"Why? Have you forbidden him from contacting me or something?" I felt a rush of anger. "Because it's none of your goddamn business whether I talk to my boyfriend or not."

"Ex-boyfriend," Baum reminded me.

I glared at him. "Whatever!"

Hunt and Baum exchanged looks. "Do you want to start?" Hunt asked Baum.

"Not particularly," he said.

Hunt sighed. "The reason you never heard from Howie after that night in June is because he went undercover. He left his personal belongings and his phone behind."

"Under*cover?* Undercover *where?*"

Hunt looked at Baum.

"There isn't time to go into detail," he said irritably. "Suffice to say that the United States of America is plotting to release an army of intelligent infected soldiers in order to annex Canada as well as Mexico, creating a single United North America."

I gave Hunt a "not this again" kind of look but she looked quite serious, which threw me off.

"Okay…"

"During my enforced suspension from my regular duties," Baum continued, looking at me as if I were a particularly loathsome dog turd, "I was able to continue my investigation into these activities. My investigations led me to a site on the dark web, and the address of the Pacific Northwest Recruiting Hub. Having already learned that you had wisely broken off relations with young Howard Mullins, I recruited him to go to one of these hubs disguised as a recruit, with the hope that he might be able to glean more about their organization and provide me with some evidence. Since he was already infected, he seemed like an ideal candidate. He has been quite successful." Baum handed me some papers. They looked like standard military propaganda pamphlets, only instead of saying "Marines" or "Army", they called themselves "North American Unionists". Some of them boasted about the glory of eternal life and superhuman healing powers, while others focused on the importance of turning Canada, USA, and Mexico into a continental super-power.

"Huh." I'm not sure whether I was more blown away by the fact that Baum had actually been *right*, or the fact that Howie had been doing vital spy work when all this time I'd thought he was curled up in a heap of misery on his bed. "Well," I said, turning the pamphlets over in my hand. "I'm glad he's been keeping himself busy, anyway." I looked up at Hunt. "Why didn't you tell me about this? I've been agonizing over how miserable he is. You could have let me know that he was busy being a character from a John LeCarre novel."

Hunt pressed her lips together. "Because I didn't know until recently."

"You didn't *know*? Where did you think he was? Cabo?"

She looked annoyed. "George didn't go through formal channels, you understand. He contacted Howie and arranged all of this while suspended. Howie didn't tell anyone what he was doing, either. He left in the night. We found his car abandoned in Delta a couple of days later, and we found his phone in a nearby waterway."

I was stunned. "Wait a minute. So, when we went to Ontario and I asked you how Howie was… you had no fucking clue where he was?"

"That's right. You can imagine how relieved his family was when Baum came forward with the truth. I breathed a sigh of relief myself. He's a good kid."

"Why the hell didn't you *tell* me that my *boyfriend* was *missing*?"

"Ex-boyfriend," said Baum and Hunt in unison.

"THAT'S NOT THE POINT!"

"I'm sorry I kept you in the dark," said Hunt. "But I had several good reasons — first of all, because I knew that it would upset you, and there didn't seem to be any point in doing that. The uncertainty would have caused you anguish at a time when you were settling into a new school and a new life. You couldn't have done anything to help him — if he were even still alive, which we couldn't be sure about — and you don't handle uncertainty particularly well."

I glowered at her. She ignored me and continued.

"The second reason is a simple one — Howie asked us not to."

"Howie… what?"

"He left a note. It was short and unhelpful, but it informed his family that he was leaving of his own volition, that he had something which needed to be done, and it begged them not to tell you that he was gone, because it would upset you and he wanted you to be free to move on."

Fucking Howie. He disappeared into the night on a secret mission after I *dumped him* and he *still* thought about my feelings.

"What if he had *killed* himself? Would you have kept it a secret *then?*"

"For a long time, we were afraid that he *had*, but without a body, we couldn't know for sure. If we had found a body, we certainly would have told you."

"Oh, *well* then, since you wouldn't have had a *funeral* without letting me know, that's *fine*."

"Shut up, Ms. Blunt," said Baum. "Your entitlement is insufferable."

I glared at him but Hunt held up a finger and I kept my mouth shut.

"Tell her the next part," said Hunt.

Oh, right. Seattle. Zombies.

"I have been receiving regular communications from Howard Mullins since June," continued Baum. "In that time, I have learned that they recruit potential soldiers in hospitals and military barracks. The organization is considered a confidential branch of the U.S. Armed Forces: It's a Special Ops force which takes its orders from the Department of Defense. Only a few members of the Department of Defense even know about this force or its purpose. It is kept highly confidential even among the highest powers in the country. The President knows, of course, being Commander in Chief," Baum concluded.

"So… does any of this have to do with what's going on in Seattle?"

"It has everything to do with what is going on in Seattle."

"But if these people are members of the U.S. Armed Forces, why are they attacking and kidnapping people outside of nightclubs? And is Howie even safe with these people? What will they do to him if they figure out that he's spying for you?"

Hunt sighed. "That's why we had to check and see if he had contacted you. He hasn't answered for the past twenty-four hours and we're concerned that he may have been caught."

"Fuck!"

Baum waved his hand. "If so, then they would arrest him for espionage and he would be imprisoned and our embassy will be notified. But we had to check to see if you had any additional information."

I opened my mouth but Hunt held up her finger again and I shut up again.

"As for why these attacks may be occurring, recruitment has increased in the last year," Baum went on, "because they are preparing for America's big push, which is scheduled to happen late next year. However, Howard informs me that they suffer from poor organization and sloppy discipline. Some of the troops occasionally get restless and escape their barracks. We think that this may be what is happening now, although as I've said, I have not heard back from Howard to confirm my suspicions."

"So, why did you call me down to tell me all of this? And… can I see the stuff from Howie?"

Baum moved restlessly. "Certainly. If you do not believe me, perhaps you will believe *him*." He dug his phone out of his pocket and began to fiddle with it.

"We're telling you now," said Hunt, "because we're concerned that a full-blown outbreak may start in Seattle. In which case the U.S. government may very well contact Canada and ask for help controlling it."

Baum handed me his phone. His messenger was opened to his conversation with Howie. My heart jumped at the words "Howard Mullins" at the top of the screen, and I eagerly skimmed backward, reading Howie's words to Baum. This was the first proof I had seen that Howie still existed, and I realized how deeply I needed to see it.

"So what are you going to do, if they ask for help?" I asked as I swiped down again and again, skimming backwards through texts. "I mean, you say they're planning to *attack* us?"

"Oh, we'd have to help. Any outbreak there could quickly spread here. But George is concerned about your safety. He thinks they could try to kidnap you, since you're considered a powerful weapon against any kind of infected army. Personally, I…"

But I wasn't listening to Hunt anymore. I scrolled through Howie's texts back and forth with Baum, and my finger moved increasingly slowly. I started going back down, reading and re-reading sections.

"What the fuck," I said, interrupting Hunt's complicated explanation of the political situation with America. "Agent Hunt, did you read these?"

She looked surprised. "Well, some of it, yes. Why?"

"Has *anyone* actually read much of this?"

"All of the information there is summarized in my report," said Baum. "Including key quotes. And, of course, I have turned in all of the paper trail that Howard mailed to me."

I didn't answer for a minute as I read text after text, and my suspicion blossomed into a full-blown conviction which then combusted into a burning rage. I rose up in my seat and bumped my head on the roof of the car.

"You," I said, levelling a finger of fury at Baum, "ARE AN IDIOT."

38

Stella

"Stella, sit down," said Agent Hunt sharply. "What is wrong with you?"

"These texts are NOT FROM HOWIE," I bellowed, shoving the phone into her hands. "Read them! HOWIE DIDN'T WRITE THIS SHIT."

"Of course they're from him," said Baum. He looked furious. "I handed him that phone myself. It was coded to his fingerprint. Only he could unlock that phone. He has been in touch regularly, and he has even mailed me proof of America's treachery."

"Except that the texts sound *nothing like him*. They must have caught him and got him to unlock it. Anything could have happened to him. He could be *dead*. He'd still have a fingerprint if he was DEAD." An iron fist seemed to be squeezing my lungs. Oh, my God. Oh my fucking God.

"What are you seeing, Stella?" asked Hunt, looking at the phone. "What's upsetting you?"

I snatched the phone back from her. "Uh, WHERE TO START? Let's see, HERE," I thrust the phone back at her, "he says 'lol'. LOL? Howie has never once used the term 'lol'. He doesn't even know what it stands for. He keeps thinking it means lots of love but he's not sure." I took the phone back and swiped savagely at the screen. "Oh, and HERE," I pointed the phone at her, "he uses the American spelling of colour instead of the Canadian version. You'd think that *Baum* of all people would have noticed *that*."

Baum flushed. "Those foul auto-corrects will override Canadian spellings with the American bastardizations. I didn't admonish Mullins because I'm sure he had more on his mind and time was short."

I ignored him. My heart was pounding. I was sure. I was *sure*. "Look! He says 'hell' here. Howie *never* swears."

"He's been staying in a military barrack," said Baum. "Some of that is sure to rub off."

"He dated *me* for a *year* and it didn't rub off," I argued. "It was darn and shucks and drat all the way."

Hunt took the phone from me again and began reading with a frown on her face.

"If Howard had been caught or had lost control of his phone, we would have been told," argued Baum. "He would be prosecuted for espionage. The Canadian consulate would have to be notified."

"I don't give a shit why you think he can't possibly have been caught. All I know is that I know Howie a *hell of a lot* better than you do and I am TELLING YOU, THAT ISN'T HIM!"

"Be quiet, both of you," snapped Hunt.

We went quiet and watched her while she read, and read, and read. I was struggling not to go into full panic mode. Howie. *Oh God, Howie. Where are you?*

Once again my mind was racing with possible answers. Howie was captured. Howie was executed. Howie was still under-cover but had lost his phone. They didn't know who the spy was but they weren't afraid to feed fake information over to Baum. Howie still had his phone but was feeding fake info on demand. Howie had actually killed himself in June, and all of this was part of some elaborate psychotic break of Baum's. But no. Those texts had to be coming from *somewhere*. Someone was giving Baum information about this American plot. Either it was legit or it was fake, but either way, it couldn't be Howie. The words didn't sound like him. The sentence phrasing felt wrong. The *jokes* felt wrong. Sure, he was writing to Baum and not to me, but I still couldn't imagine Howie saying 'brb' or 'no one knows what the hell they're doing.'

"I'm afraid Stella might be right," said Hunt eventually. I relaxed slightly. The only thing worse than Howie being missing and possibly captured or dead would be Howie missing and possibly captured or dead and *no one believing me about it.*

Baum opened his mouth to argue but she held up her finger and he closed his mouth again.

"I've known Howard Mullins for fifteen years," she said, which was a bit of a mind-fuck for me even though I knew perfectly well how old Howie really was. "And I agree with Stella — a lot of this seems very uncharacteristic." She looked directly at me. "I'm sorry. I only glanced briefly at these messages before, and at the time I was focused on the information, not the grammar. But you're right. I can't imagine Howie using emojis."

I tried not to hyperventilate. "They've got him, don't they? They've just been feeding garbage to Baum. You don't know what's true and what isn't, now. And we don't know if he's okay."

"Stella," said Hunt as I struggled to calm down. "Stella!"

I looked up.

"I need you to look through these texts to try and pinpoint when and if the voice changes. Do you understand?"

I nodded.

"I have a meeting to attend — this was only supposed to be a quick stop to update you, in case the Seattle situation escalated. But I am going to find a way to get a transcript of these messages sent to you ASAP, so watch your email. I'm also going to get Morton and his family to look them over, too."

"That's my phone," protested Baum.

"This is *your* mess, George. You can have your phone back when I've sorted this out. And Stella?"

"Yeah?"

"Don't panic. We don't know that anything is wrong with Howie. I doubt the American government is going to kill him, so worst case scenario he's probably locked up. But we'll figure that out. In the meantime, they may try to use him to lure you over to America, so be aware of that."

"Okay." I took deep breaths, trying to stay calm. I wanted to kill things. Starting with fucking BAUM.

"I'll be in touch."

"Okay." I slid across the seat and opened the door. "Please let me know what's going on as soon as you can."

"I will," she said firmly. Baum said nothing, and I ignored him. I tried to suppress all of my fury at Baum and panic over Howie, because none of that would do anyone any good. I had to think about the messages. I would refresh my email constantly until those damn messages came in.

And I would keep on watching the news.

I slammed the door of my apartment as I walked in. Dean whipped around to look at me and stood up when he got a look at my face.

"Babe, what's wrong?"

I just shook my head and went to get a drink of water.

"Come on, what's up? What did the government lady say to you? Do they not want you back next summer?"

"It's nothing to do with that. I just found out something else."

Dean's face flickered. "Baby, I can explain."

I stopped and stared at him. "Then do so. Now."

"I was just being friendly. You know I flirt. She knows I have a girlfriend. It wasn't a hookup or anything."

I folded my arms. "THEN WHAT WAS IT?"

"It was just a friendly kiss on the cheek! I asked Kelly to take it down. I knew it would upset you."

"KELLY? KELLY FUCKING SVANCARA?"

He looked surprised. "You didn't know who it was?"

"NEVER MIND WHAT I KNEW. WHY THE FUCK IS THERE A PHOTO OF YOU KISSING KELLY FUCKING SVANCARA OF ALL PEOPLE?"

"Like I said, I was just being friendly. And it's just on the cheek. It's really, really not a big deal."

"I CAN DECIDE WHAT I THINK IS A BIG DEAL OR NOT, DEAN KATO."

"You can decide to act like a grown up and accept that I'm a friendly person who flirts at parties," said Dean, his face darkening. "And not completely overreact."

"Kelly posted that on fucking purpose to upset me, you realize that?" I said. "She knew if she tagged you it would show up on your feed and I would see it."

"She didn't do it to upset you!"

"And how do you fucking know that?"

"Because she doesn't..." he bit his lip and stopped.

I finished the sentence for him. "Because she doesn't know that your girlfriend is ME. AM I RIGHT?"

"Okay, yes, you're right. I didn't tell her. I didn't tell any of them." He raised his hand. "But hear me out: I did it to protect you."

I nearly laughed. "To protect ME? Don't give me that bullshit."

"Stella, you *know* I'm not ashamed of you. I brought you to my friends' Christmas party. I hold your hand around campus. I introduced you to my parents."

"You introduced me to your parents MONTHS after we started dating. You didn't tell them that I was fat or that you like fat girls. They hadn't even seen a picture of me — I could tell by their faces when they answered the door. You haven't told your high school buddies that you are dating me *or* that you like fat girls. Tell me more about how unashamed you are, Dean."

"I don't have to go around telling people what kind of girls I like. That's no one's business. What do you want, for me to walk around with a big sandwich board? Why don't I give you one that says 'I'm into half-Japanese guys'?"

"Uh, because I'm *not* into 'half-Japanese' guys. I have *zero* opinions about the race of the people I date. The worst you could accuse me of is having a thing for dimples, which MY FRIENDS AND FAMILY

ALREADY KNOW ABOUT. You, meanwhile, have a thing for big women and you need to stop being so fucking ashamed."

"I'm not ashamed!"

"Then tell me, Dean. WHY didn't you tell them that you're dating me?"

"How about because you all *hate* each other, and I didn't want to get in the middle of all that, okay?" he ran his hands through his hair. "It was just easier. That's all."

"I think I was pretty fucking clear when we started dating that I had no intention of being your dirty little secret."

"You're *not* my dirty secret. I go out with you all the time."

"I'm sorry, do you want a fucking cookie for actually going out in public with your fat girlfriend?"

"Stop making this about that, okay? It's just that you and Kelly and basically all of my oldest friends hate each other, and that's really uncomfortable, okay? I didn't want to give them a reason to go after you again."

"They hate me because I'm *big* and I stood up to their *bullying*. I hate *them* because they kept spreading *lies* about me and writing me notes saying I should *kill myself*. Which of us is in the wrong here?"

Dean was silent.

"I like how you openly admit that they 'went after me' in high school and yet you still chose to hang out with them at New Year's, and then kiss the *fucking cheek* of the girl who was responsible for two years of me being *barked at* in the halls."

"Yeah, okay, they were jerks to you, but you didn't exactly take it lying down. Don't act like you're the innocent victim in all of this."

"I'm *not* acting like an innocent victim. I am *specifically protesting* being treated as such when you claim that you kept me a secret to fucking *protect* me. You were protecting *yourself,* Dean. Admit it. Admit that you were scared they'd shun you."

He rolled his eyes. "They're my oldest friends, Stella. They wouldn't *shun* me. They'd just… you know… give me… give *us*… a hard time."

"They *can't* give me a hard time. I've got them all fucking blocked. They can't message me; they can't even find me. The only time I even see them is when they turn up on *your feed*. You know, like, *being kissed by you*."

"You're totally blowing this out of proportion. She wished me happy New Year, she put her arm around me, and I gave her a kiss on the cheek. Okay? That's all that happened. I knew it'd upset you, so I asked her to take it down, but I swear that's all that happened. Stop acting like you caught me cheating on you or something."

"How about you stop acting like I'm being irrational when I have *great* reasons not to trust you?"

"Like what, beyond your completely overreacting whenever I'm remotely friendly to another girl?"

"Uh, like, how about the fact that you hid the fact that you were dating me from your friends even though I had *forbidden* that exact thing, and then you tried to *hide* the fact that there was a photo of you kissing the girl who made my life a misery in high school?"

"That's not like cheating, that's just trying to... you know... keep everyone happy. I never said I was perfect. Do you know how hard it is to..."

I put up my hand. "I think you need to get out."

"Baby, I..."

"AND STOP FUCKING CALLING ME BABY!" I shouted. "I AM A BIG, GROWN-ASS, *GIANT WOMAN*!"

"FINE!" he bellowed, throwing on his coat and shoving his feet into his shoes. "You know what? FUCK YOU. I've been a *great* fucking boyfriend. Do you know how many girls would *line up* to..." he trailed off at the sight of my face. "I mean..."

"GET. OUT."

"I didn't mean it that way, I..."

"OUT!"

I held the door open for him and pointed him out the door. As soon as he crossed the threshold, I slammed it behind him.

Then I started to sob.

Kate came out of her room right away.

"Thank God he's gone," she said, hopping up and down. "I'm gonna comfort you in a second, I promise, but first I *really* have to pee."

While Kate made bathroom noises, I tried to stop crying but I just couldn't. I missed the old days when my only emotions were anger and anxiety. This sadness business sucked donkey balls.

I heard the toilet flush, the sinking running, the door opening, and then Kate was patting my back.

"I know you're upset right now," she said, "but it's going to be okay. He's a bit of a dick. You *know* he's a bit of a dick."

"I'm not crying about Dean," I sniffled, which wasn't completely true but was true enough. "That was just the fucking icing on the cake."

"What's up, then?"

"Howie's missing… he might even be *dead*."

"He… *what?*"

"Yeah, he's been missing since grad, and no one told me because they thought he might have committed suicide and they didn't want to *upset me*. But they never found a body or anything. Then they traced him to Seattle, but they haven't found him or seen any proof that he's alive."

"Holy shit," said Kate. "Jesus. Fuck."

"Yeah, pretty much," I said. "And when I came upstairs all upset about that, Dean thought it was about him — he started acting all guilty and then… well… I guess you heard the rest."

"I saw the photo," said Kate. "Last night. I was going to tell you to-day. I didn't say anything last night because I…"

"Didn't want to upset me," I finished. "Am I that scary?"

"You're pretty terrifying," said Kate. "You might want to work on that."

"The sad thing is that I *have*." I took a shuddering sigh. "I'll keep at it, I promise."

"Good. Tell me more about Howie. I don't blame you for being up-set. Maybe he just, like, needed some space and hasn't been in touch? He was eighteen, right? Legal adult?"

I ignored the question about his age. "They think he went to Seattle and look what's going on in Seattle right now."

Riya came timidly out of Kate's bedroom, her big brown eyes looking even larger behind her glasses. "You okay, Stella?" She sat down next to me, laid a hand on my knee and peered earnestly into my face. "Do you want us to go cut off Dean's dick?"

I laughed. "No, it's okay. Honestly. I was going to break up with Dean anyway. I just found out that my ex is missing, and *then* I found out that Dean didn't tell any of the people that he partied with last night that he was dating me and that he kissed my biggest high school enemy and tried to cover up the photo evidence."

"Wow. Yeah. Bad way to start the new year," said Riya. "So… which of those things do you want to talk about first? Want some tea?"

"Sure, thanks." I grabbed some Kleenex from the box on the coffee table and blew my nose, while Riya clattered around in the kitchen and Kate just sat curled on the couch next to me, watching.

"So, you saw the pic?" I asked her, wiping my eyes with my arm. "How bad was it?"

She shrugged. "He was picking her up and kissing her on the cheek while she laughed with her arms around his neck. It's not like they were making out or anything, but I knew it would piss you off."

"Yeah, well, it's not like the bar for that is super high," I said. "I figured Kelly would probably be at that party. I just thought that he'd, you know…" I trailed off. "I don't know, actually. I'm not even that surprised when I think about it. It's totally the kind of thing Dean would do and think totally innocent. But it bothers me. And he *knew* it would bother me. And he did it anyway. And then he tried to keep it a secret *because* he knew it would bother me. And that's asstacular."

"You said you were going to break up with him anyway? Why? What happened over Christmas?" Riya prodded gently.

"Nothing, really. I mean, he didn't *do* anything. I think that going back home for Christmas just made me realize that I'm still really not over Howie."

"You just realized that *now*?" Kate said, raising her eyebrows. "How did you not know that already?"

"Well, I mean… Like… what?" I rubbed my face. I was groggy from drinking and staying up late and Howie was missing and Dean was a shit stick and I felt like I didn't know what was happening anymore.

"Like, did you think, at any point, that you were *over* Howie? Because I never thought that."

"Why would I have been dating Dean if I wasn't over Howie?"

She shrugged. "To get over Howie."

"I mean, I never thought I was *over* over him, you know? I knew…" I wiped my nose again. "I knew that I still loved him, but, I mean, I think some part of me will *always* love him. He was just… He was… anyway. I can't sit around loving Howie and not moving on and living my life, so I just… ignored it. I thought that I had kind of made peace with it, you know? But I don't think I have."

"Remind me why you broke up again? Oh, right, you never *did* tell me," said Kate.

"I never even knew him," said Riya. "Maybe you could tell me?"

"It's complicated," I told Riya. I looked at Kate. "There's some stuff I'm not allowed to tell you, okay? I'm sorry. But they aren't my secrets to tell."

"What was he like? Howie?" Riya probed.

Kate turned in her seat and mimed the outline of a person with her hands. "Okay, picture Dean in your mind."

"Okay," Riya said.

"Now imagine his *exact opposite*."

"An antisocial, tidy woman? So… Stella?"

Even I laughed a little.

"Okay, keep the gender the same," Kate conceded. "But Howie's a shy, socially stilted skinny guy with blond hair and blue eyes and glasses."

"And he *is* compulsively neat," I said. "And he likes to cook."

"And he does weird, old-fashioned stuff like pulling out chairs for girls and joking about communists and using words like 'nifty'." Kate shook her head. "You know, even I kind of miss him."

I buried my face. "We're talking about him in the present tense but he could seriously be *dead*."

"That doesn't seem likely," said Kate. "Let's not get too dramatic."

I didn't answer. "Let's turn on the TV. I want to watch more Seattle stuff."

"What, just in case you see him in a crowd?" Kate rolled her eyes. "It's fine, I get it. Fill your boots. But, are you and Dean officially broken up? What's going on there?"

"I don't know. I don't think we're broken up yet. We didn't actually say those words. I guess I should call him and finish the job."

"Let him cool down, first. Cool yourself down, too, you know?" Riya said, putting her feet on the coffee table.

My ringtone started up, and Kate looked at the screen. "You *still* have his caller ID set to 'Dildo'?"

"He liked it. Thought it was funny." I picked up the phone, took a deep breath and let it out before I answered. "What?" I said into the phone.

"Okay, I just got home and I'm really, really sorry about what I said about girls lining up. That wasn't cool. I was angry."

"Thank you," I said. *He didn't say it wasn't true. Because we both know that it is true.*

There was a pause.

"This is the part where you apologize for overreacting to the picture," he said.

"No, Dean. You're still not done apologizing. You need to apologize for the picture, and for *hiding* the picture, and for hiding your relationship with me from your friends."

"I'm not going to apologize for the picture. I *didn't cheat on you*. And if you think a kiss on the cheek constitutes cheating, then you need to deal with your personal issues around jealousy and control because…"

I rolled my eyes at Kate and Riya and started walking to my room.

"No, Dean, I don't think you cheated on me and I am *not* jealous. I am *angry* at you for hiding your relationship with me just to avoid friction with the people who did everything they could to make me miserable in high school. I am *angry* at you for flirting with the girl who gave me nick-names like "Dog" and "Teacher Fucker". And I am *most* angry at you for deliberately trying to hide the photo proof of it. If you *know* something is going to upset your girlfriend, don't fucking do it in the first place. Don't just try to bury the evidence."

"You could have come to the party, Stella. I *invited* you. It's not like I tried to keep you away from them."

"You knew I wouldn't go. If I hated a party with your theatre friends from SFU, you knew there was no way I would go to a party full of people like Kelly Svancara and Carter Davidson and Ravi Sandhu and the rest of them. And I know I'm not the biggest social media person, but I should have realized sooner that you weren't putting up any photos of us together or posting about me. And I bet that if I go and check, the few photos that I've put up won't be on your feed."

Dean was silent.

"But really, Dean, it's more than that. We're just not working. We need to call it quits."

"What? No, we aren't breaking up, Stella. We have some problems we need to work out, I admit it, and I'm sorry for my part of it. But this isn't break-up worthy."

"Yes, Dean. We are breaking up. This was just the final straw."

"What?" his voice went into a higher register. "You're overreacting. I should have waited for you to cool down."

"No, this needed to happen anyway. We just needed a catalyst."

"What? We were doing fine. We were happy. This is too sudden."

"I wasn't happy."

"Well it's the first I've heard about it," he said, sounding angry again. "What the fuck, Stella. You can't just throw a hissy fit and break up with me over one incident, and then tell me that really it's about a whole bunch of stuff you never even fucking mentioned."

"I don't mean that, Dean. I'm not blaming you for it. I'm just… I'm not feeling it. I like you. You make me laugh. You're smarter than I gave you credit for in high school. And you're really, really good looking. But we don't have anything in common. We get along, but we aren't close."

"What does that even mean — 'we aren't close'? Who has the intimacy issues in this relationship? Not me."

"I know I have intimacy issues, but Dean, I don't exactly feel like you've been baring your soul to me and getting nothing in return. You talk to me about school and your social life and movies and TV shows and you tell me how hot I am, but it never goes deeper than that."

"I told you stuff I've never told anyone, Stella, so don't give me that shit."

"Fine. It's all my fault," I said abruptly. "I don't need to make this your fault or turn this around on you. I'll bear the blame if you like. I'm a shitty girlfriend, I suck, etcetera etcetera. But I'm just not happy in the relationship, so it's over."

"No, I don't accept that."

"You don't *accept* my breaking up with you? It's not the kind of decision that needs to be ratified by both parties, Dean."

"Stella, if you aren't happy, I'll try harder. Tell me what you're missing and I'll try to make it happen. Stella... I..." His voice broke a bit. "I think I'm in love with you."

"It's a bit late to tell me that now, Dean," I said gently. "And I like you, and I care about you, and I'm attracted to you. But... I'm *not* in love with you. I know what love feels like and this just isn't it, for me."

"You're still not over your fucking ex, are you?" he said angrily. "Fucking Howard Mullins with his fucking glasses and his fucking weirdness. What does he have that I don't have, Stella?"

"Maybe it isn't something that you can do anything about. Maybe you and I just aren't the right fit. It's not a fault thing."

"I asked you. I asked you months ago if I was wasting my time."

"How could I know we weren't a fit until we tried? I didn't promise to fall in love with you, and I just don't think it's going to happen. I'm sorry."

"So you're still in love with the last guy you dated, even though *you* broke up with *him*. And now you're breaking up with *me* even though you *admit* that I did *nothing wrong*. Jesus, Stella. How fucking impossible are your standards? If you ever get yourself sorted out, give me a call. Maybe I'll still be around." He disconnected the call.

I put my head down on my desk for a minute and did some deep breathing. Then I went to the bathroom, wiped my face with a scalding hot washcloth, and went back to the living room.

Kate looked at me and switched the channel from MTV to the news about Seattle.

"There you go," she said.

"Thanks."

39

Stella

I spent all afternoon watching the news and refreshing my email. The news channels kept replaying whatever videos they had of last night's attacks. The footage was crazy. People were taking videos with their phones, of course, so a lot of it was vertical view and blurry or badly aimed, but the attackers were abnormally fast. Sometimes they did really strong stuff like ripping doors off of their hinges or flipping cars. Was this what Howie could have been like if he gave in to those urges he talked about?

If so — holy shit.

I thought about Howie — he was pretty strong, although he didn't look it. I'd seen him lift a dead man without any apparent effort, for example, and there were a few rare times when he had lifted me or pulled me onto him easily. I asked him about it once and he just shrugged and pointed out that he couldn't feel pain so he probably just lifted more than someone normally would. Like when mothers lift whole cars to get their kids out from under them after an accident because their adrenaline and panic make them forget their limits. Except with him, it was nerve damage and lack of self-preservation.

Were these people like Howie — but without morals? But I couldn't imagine him running and jumping like that. Strong, sure, but coordinated not so much. I remembered the time he tried to spar with me in the field near my house. He had sucked. Had he been faking it?

The newscasters were issuing a lot of warnings before playing each video. Every now and then they would report a new attack. "Breaking news — another attack in Seatak. Police report..."

"Breaking news — the city has issued a warning to Seattle residents to stay in their homes..."

"Breaking news — yet another attack, this time in Pike Place Market. Footage shows..."

"Jesus," said Kate, walking back into the room. "Another one?"

"There have been three more," I told her. "At least."

"Shit."

At two p.m., I finally got an email from "Michaella Hunt, Provincial Director, British Columbia Branch, CRVCS". It read:

-

Took my underlings over an hour to figure this out. I can't believe something so simple wasted so much staff time. Read this ASAP. Sending a copy to Morton, too.

-

I threw the remote at Kate, who was lounging on the couch with her phone. "All yours. I have something to do."

"Kay."

I retreated to my room and opened the file and the first thing I saw was my own name.

Howard Mullins: Please give Stella my love and tell her I am okay. Don't let her know that I'm in danger.

My heart thumped. Howie. That could easily be Howie. Undercover, at personal risk, and the first thing he does is think about me. Idiot. Dear, sweet idiot. And Baum never did pass on that message, did he? What an asshole. Then again, if Baum had contacted me to pass on Howie's love, I would have found that really suspicious, so I could kind of understand why he ignored it. I checked the date of the message. Jesus. This was only two days after grad. Great. So all I knew for sure was that Howie was probably alive… in JUNE.

Baum's response was predictably packed with assholery. Like Howie was obviously scared out of his mind, but Baum just complained about the propriety of Howie's texts. Fuckwad.

Howie's next text was harder to interpret. It was about a nurse in a hospital, which obviously was a lie because Howie never went to hospitals — according to his blood oxygen levels he should be dead, and his temperature was below normal, and his heart had about as much rhythm as a kindergartener with castanets. Had someone else taken control? But there was nothing else in that message that rang any alarm bells for me. It easily could have been written by Howie. I decided to give it the benefit of the doubt and assume Howie was trying to talk in code. The same went for the next few texts. They could have been written by Howie, although they weren't *obviously* Howie. Every two or three days he'd send a brief message saying that he was still okay but he was being closely watched.

Baum was totally unsympathetic, unhelpful, and demanding, as I would have expected.

Then, in July, it suddenly changed. Howie messaged that he had gained their trust and had been given heavier responsibility, and then he was *full* of information. He couldn't send it fast enough. And it didn't sound right.

I wanted it to sound right. I wanted it to be clearly and obviously Howie for as long as possible. But I couldn't find a sense of him. It seemed slangier, and he never mentioned me.

Until he did.

Near the end of September, he said:

> Howard Mullins:
> Stella Blunt is a complication for them, of course. I guess CRVCS has her well guarded at SFU?

No. Even months after we broke up, I couldn't imagine him talking about me so impersonally. Baum, of course, didn't notice the use of my last name or the fact that he said CRVCS instead of "The Service," which is what he usually called it.

George Baum:
Naturally she is under constant surveillance. Are there plans to abduct her?

Howard Mullins:
Not yet. It'd be too suspicious. They probably won't try to get her for another year or so, so don't waste resources on protecting her heavily yet. You'll have to move her into B-MOSZ for a while next year if we can't figure out a way to take them down in time.

Yeah, that was *not* Howie. I was sure of it. Howie would never call protecting me "wasting resources", even if I was in zero danger. Howie didn't think I was a waste of anything, ever. How could Baum not notice? Also, what the hell was B-MOSZ?

George Baum:
We will guard her well. Obnoxious as she is, she is of great importance.

Howard Mullins:
Haha be nice:-p

Uh... no. Howie didn't use emojis, and if he did, he wouldn't send a jokey one to someone who called me "obnoxious".

I called Hunt.

"Hello, Stella. I'm with Morton Mullins. Have you looked over the texts?"

"Yes, and I am sure that by mid-July it was definitely someone else texting. I don't know when the switch happened exactly, but I kinda wonder whether he got caught during that time that he said he was under really close surveillance."

"Morton agrees."

"So Howie has been missing since July, that means," I said, my throat closing up. "And Baum didn't *fucking notice*."

"That is possible, yes."

"Also," I demanded, "what is this about me being under *surveillance?* Do I need to check inside my teddy bear?"

"Standard security, Stella. We have you lightly guarded. Nothing to fuss about. No cameras in your bedroom, I promise."

"Also also, what is B-MOSZ?"

"Stella, do you want me to answer all of your questions, or do you want me to focus on figuring out where Howie is and whether he is safe?"

"...Howie," I answered sullenly.

"Then let me do so. I'll call you when I have updates. Goodbye."

She hung up. I put down my phone and buried my head in my hands for a while.

I needed to talk to someone about all of this, so I picked up my phone and dialled my parents.

My Dad answered the phone on the second ring.

"Happy New Year! Are you just waking up? Did you get really drunk last night? Are you calling from the hospital with alcohol poisoning? We've been fretting but we didn't want to hover, so we've been waiting for you to confirm that you were alive. It took you long enough."

"Have you been watching the news?"

"No, we're having a lazy New Year's Day playing N64 games and eating cheese and worrying about you being dead. Why?"

"When I get off the phone you can turn on the news. I have important updates for you. First, I broke up with Dean."

"Oh. I'm sorry, honey."

"It's okay. I have bigger problems. For example, I just found out that Howie has been missing since July."

"Shit. We were worried. Agent Hunt was acting strange — she asked us if we'd seen him or if you had been in touch with him. But we didn't know anything for sure, Stella."

"I'd be pissed at you, but I have even BIGGER problems."

I heard my mother say something in the background but Dad gave her a harsh "Shh." Then he spoke back into the phone. "Go on."

"We think he's been captured by a secret half-zombie organization in Seattle that may or may not be masterminded by the U.S. Government. We aren't sure, because Baum sent him undercover in June and has been passing on everything Howie has sent him. Only when I looked at Howie's messages they *clearly aren't written by Howie* so who knows what, if anything, is true or what they've done to Howie."

"Holy fuck," said Dad.

"Right? These assholes are behind the Seattle zombie, they've been asking how well guarded I am, we don't know if Howie's even alive, and for all we know, they may be planning to destroy the world."

"Either your deadpan has really improved, or…"

"I am so not in the mood to joke with you right now. I'm totally serious."

"I'm putting you on speaker phone. Now, tell your mother and me everything."

My mother urged me to come and sleep at home for the night, but I refused.

"I can't, Mom. I just… when I'm home, Howie feels so much nearer… it messes me up more. If I come home I'm going to break down entirely." Their house had felt haunted by Howie's ghost *before* I learned that he might actually be dead.

"Then let us at least take you out to dinner or something," she said. "You just threw a *lot* of stuff at us, and we'd feel better if we could see you and know that you're okay."

"I'm *not* okay; I'm a mess. But I don't feel like going out in public, I've *obviously* done a whole lot of crying today so my eyes are all swollen, we can't talk about zombie stuff in a restaurant *or* if you come over here, because Kate's here, and I'm not going to be able to talk about or think about anything else… I know you want to see me, Mom, but maybe tomorrow, okay? Please?"

Dad cut in. "It's fine, Stella — *it's fine, Elaine* — you get some rest. But before you go there's something I don't get."

"What?" I asked heavily, lying back on my bed. Oh God. I'd been sleeping with Dean and joking about helicopters while Howie was… what? Dead? Captured? Oh, God.

"You said that this army… or whatever it is… is made up of half-zombies like Howie, right? People who took Doc Mullins's eternal life cocktail with a side of brains, right?"

"Yeah. So Howie should have fit right in."

"But you said that these attacks in Seattle are, like, people who have escaped the barracks and gone on the rampage."

"Yeah."

"Okay, but Howie didn't run around kidnapping people whenever he left the house, so what's that about?"

Shit. It was time to tell them. "He didn't… but he wanted to."

My mother sounded shocked. "Howie wanted to kidnap people?"

"No, Mom. Not kidnap. *Eat.*"

My parents were silent while they digested this information. I felt the need to elaborate.

"Like Doc Mullins told you at the beginning — they're attracted to brain waves and the virus makes them want to eat people's brains. They just *didn't* because they had, like, morals and crap. But Howie used to have dreams about eating people…" They didn't have to know that Howie dreamed about eating me. That seemed like too much information. "It really bothered him. He used to fret about it. But he never actually did anything. He's a good person, not a murderer. But if you're the kind of person who doesn't mind injecting themselves with the virus deliberately and then becoming part of a zombie army… well… maybe morals don't come into play as much, you know?"

My parents were still silent.

"Are you guys still there?"

"We're here," said Dad faintly. "It's just… I mean, we knew that Howie was attracted to your brains and stuff but I didn't realize it was so… close to the surface. Like, I never thought you were in any danger with Howie…"

"I wasn't," I snapped. "He never did a single thing that made me feel unsafe, okay?"

They were quiet again, and this time I didn't fill the dead air. I just waited.

"Okay," said Mom after a minute, "but even if the attacks in Seattle are escapees who are like… amoral Howies or whatever… I don't understand how that could start an outbreak."

"What?" I asked.

"You said that Hunt was putting you on notice in case this started an outbreak and the U.S. wanted you to help," she said. "But the Mullinses aren't contagious, right? I mean, that was a fairly central point to the whole Baum-Mullins-Outbreak fiasco."

"Goodness knows we saw you and Howie sucking face often enough, and you never turned into a zombie," Dad said.

"I… yeah… that's true…" I said. How had I missed that? The whole Howie-is-missing-slash-undercover-slash-maybe-dead thing had really monopolized my attention, or I would have spotted that earlier. "I don't know. You're right. They shouldn't be contagious. Unless… maybe if they have sex? Maybe they'll… like… rape their way to an outbreak? They're running off with people, right? I don't know. I don't understand anything right now. I think I need some sleep… I'm going to talk Kate into ordering food with me and then I'll get to bed early and wait for Hunt to call me."

"Good," said Mom. "Take care of yourself, sweetie."

"Thanks, Mom." I rubbed my temples. "I wish I could stop thinking that this was all my fault. If I hadn't gone to grad…"

"It is *not* your fault that Baum kidnapped Howie and sent him into the heart of an evil zombie organization," said Dad sternly. "This has *nothing to do with you.*"

"Yeah, yeah. But if…"

"No ifs," said Mom. "Focus on now. Okay? Get something to eat. I know you tend to starve yourself when you're upset and a lot of upsetting things happened today. Promise you'll eat dinner?"

"I promise," I said.

"Good," she said. "Keep us updated. Snapchat us a picture of your dinner or something."

"Fine. Just for you."

"That's my girl."

I ended the call. "Kate!" I opened the door to my room and stepped out.

"'Sup kid?" said Kate from the couch.

"Today, the first day of this new year, I broke up with my boyfriend, discovered that my ex-boyfriend, who I am still in love with, is missing and possibly dead, and I also suffered my first-ever semi-hangover. I request, nay, I *demand*, that you pick up the phone and order the greasiest, most unromantic, most disgusting takeout food you can think of." I paused. "I'll pay. Just don't make me interact with humans."

"KFC coming right up," said Kate, opening her laptop.

"Excellent."

I was gnawing on a drumstick in my pyjamas when it happened.

"Breaking news," said the reporter on CNN. "We have had reports coming in of similar attacks occurring in New York, Chicago, Detroit, and Los Angeles. We have been attempting to verify, and have now received footage of this attack, occurring in Miami."

There was a shaky video of someone screaming and running. The person holding the phone swung around and you could see someone bent over a prone body, and you could hear a woman screaming, 'Oh my God, she's DEAD!' before the person holding the phone started running away again.

"We do not yet know if these attacks are copycats or if they are connected in some way," said the newscaster. "We have had no response from local authorities or from the US government."

"Holy SHIT," said Kate, plopping down onto the couch.

"I know," I said, and my heart was pounding. This couldn't be orchestrated by the U.S. government - not if attacks were happening in American cities. That must have just been garbage that they fed to Baum because they knew he'd eat it up. What was really happening?

"Kate, this is really, really bad," I said. "I think it's going to start happening in Canada soon. Or other places. Maybe it already is."

"Let's turn it to CBC," she said, flipping channels.

"...Reports also coming in from London, New Delhi, Johannesburg, Beijing, and Moscow," said the reporter.

"Oh SHIT!" I said. We leaned forward.

"Toronto police have confirmed the attacks, but will not say whether they believe them to be copycats or whether this is part of a coordinated effort. No known terrorist groups have claimed responsibility for the attacks. No one has been apprehended and descriptions of the attackers vary..."

"I have to make a phone call," I said. I grabbed my phone and pulled up Agent Hunt, running to my room and closing the door.

"Stella? What's wrong?" she asked.

"What ISN'T fucking wrong?" I shouted into the phone. "What the *hell* is going on out there? Are there attacks in Vancouver yet? What the hell? What is happening?"

"Things are moving quickly. We think this may be a coordinated attempt to create mass outbreaks in every major city," she said.

"But these people aren't *contagious*, right? They're like Howie? *How can they be starting mass outbreaks?* I'm so confused." *And angry. Don't forget angry.*

"I'll show you somewhere you can go if things get worse. I'll pick you up in half an hour. I have Morton with me. We will answer your questions then."

Have you ever had a day where so much crap happened that you stopped trying to process any of it? Well, that's what happened to me. I couldn't simultaneously freak out over Howie, and a possible zombie apocalypse, and Dean all at the same time. It was all too much. It was too big. So I just sort of… calmed down. I got dressed again, rooting through my laundry hamper for a bra that wasn't too stretched out.

"What was that about?" Kate asked when I came back out of my room.

"It's complicated." I sat down and looked at her seriously. "Listen, Kate. Do you remember how I went to Ontario this summer? To do that science internship with the government?"

"Yeah…?"

"Okay. So. A lot of that was classified information and I could get into a hell of a lot of trouble if I tell anyone."

"But?"

"I need you to listen to me, and trust me, okay? I think that these attacks are related to the stuff we were studying. And I think this could get really dangerous. I think it could come here. So I need you to stay inside. And tell Riya to stay inside. And basically everyone you know."

"What, is it some kind of terrorist group or something? I thought you were doing environment stuff."

"It's the zombie apocalypse," I told her. "Zombies everywhere. They're coming for your brains."

She rolled her eyes. "Fine, don't tell me. You and your stupid secrets."

"Just call people, okay? Tell them to sharpen their kitchen knives or something. And tell them to go for the head, because zombies."

"Yeah, yeah." She looked at me. "You're for real worried, though? For legit, government-secret reasons?"

"Yes. Just tell them it's the zombie apocalypse. But also tell them to do what you say." I stood up, put the KFC leftovers in the fridge and grabbed a cloth to wipe down the coffee table. "I have to go out for a bit."

"What is going *on* with you?" Kate asked.

"I told you. Important zombie science stuff. I'll be back. I think. I'll call if I'm not. Probably. Okay?"

Kate shook her head and went back to watching the news.

Agent Hunt's car was idling out front again, but this time Doc Mullins was in the passenger seat. I felt a pang of anxiety at seeing him. If

Howie and I had stayed together, he never would have been lured by Baum into joining an evil zombie organization. It was all my fault that Howie was missing and possibly dead. Doc must hate me. *I* hated me.

I yanked open the back passenger door and climbed in.

"Hello again," said Agent Hunt.

"Tell me," I said.

"We are now completely confident that this is the first wave in a co-ordinated outbreak."

"But why?"

"Well, we don't know for sure. We don't know how much of Agent Baum's documents are legitimate, but from his preliminary research, this organization views themselves as superior human beings, and probably intends to bring down the current political powers in all countries so that they can take over."

"Are you serious? This is a zombie political coup?"

"Yes."

"But are there enough of them to do that?"

Doc Mullins spoke for the first time. "It depends on how well they orchestrate their outbreak."

"But how can it be an outbreak? They aren't contagious. Do you mean they're going to inject people with the virus?"

"I'm going to have to answer those questions, Stella, but first things first." Agent Hunt pulled away from the curb.

"Where are we going?" I asked.

"You'll see."

I felt like I was losing my marbles. Nothing made sense anymore. Yesterday my biggest problem was the fact that I was still in love with my ex and needed to break up with my boyfriend. Today Howie might be dead and the world was ending and I didn't understand why and I was being taken who knows where…

And suddenly my mind, which had been spinning everywhere, lined up and stopped, like a slot machine hitting jackpot. Why was I trusting Hunt? I mean, Baum was an obvious dirtbag, but I had always trusted Hunt. But should I? Maybe Baum was right. Maybe Doc Mullins *did* start the outbreak last year. Maybe he did try to sell me to the States. Maybe he and Hunt were collecting me right now so they could prevent me from helping to curb any Vancouver attacks…

Maybe I'd been trusting the wrong person all this time.

If that was the case, where were they taking me? They could be taking me to be locked up. They'd probably tell me they were putting me somewhere safe. I might never be seen again.

I felt like a trapped bird. I had to get out. I never should have gotten in the car. Agent Hunt came to a stop sign and slowed down. As soon as the car came to a rolling stop I unbuckled my seatbelt and threw myself from the car into the drizzly January night. I landed and rolled, and got up on my feet in an instant. Agent Hunt was already getting out of the car.

"Stella, what…"

"Stay away!" I said, backing up. "I don't know where you're taking me, so just stay away." Where could I go? How could I get away? She knew where I lived, where my parents lived, probably where all of my friends lived. And while she was probably in her forties at least, she looked lean and athletic. Could she take me in a fight?

But she didn't try to catch me. She just stood looking perplexed.

Doc Mullins was climbing out of the car, now.

"Stella," he said. "You're feeling afraid."

"I know I'm fucking afraid! There are zombies like you taking over the fucking WORLD," I shouted at him. I glanced around. There was no one. The street was dead. The stores were closed.

"They aren't like me," said Doc. I had almost forgotten that calm, zombie monotone. "We plan to explain to you the ways in which they differ from myself. You can trust us."

"You think I'm a mole, don't you?" Agent Hunt said, sounding amused.

This is it, I thought. This is the part where the bad guy monologues and reveals the whole plan.

"If this were a thriller movie, you're right. I would be the villain," said Agent Hunt with a touch of impatience in her voice. "It would be a very good plot twist to make the head of the British Columbia branch be the mole. But, Stella, if that were the case, I would have gotten rid of you a long time ago, as would Morton, if he were part of the conspiracy."

"I don't even know what the conspiracy *is*," I said. "And all of my information comes only from *you*."

"That's because I'm the head of the B.C. branch; someone duplicated my keycard to access vials of virus and to remove a hamster from Morton's lab last year, and I don't know which of my underlings to trust," she said. "I am not kidnapping you. For one thing, I haven't forgotten the time you overpowered George Baum and tied him to a chair. If I wanted to capture you, I'd bring a lot more back up than Morton, who you can incapacitate with a mere thought."

"Unless you simply told me you were putting me somewhere safe and I walked in of my own volition, because I trusted you," I said. "Well, I'm not going to do that."

She rubbed her temples. "I don't know whether to be grateful that you're so distrustful, or annoyed that you're wasting my time. Okay. Who *would* you trust?"

"Howie."

"Give me someone I have a phone number for, Stella. How about head office? You want me to contact head office so they can tell you to trust me?"

"Yes."

"How would you know it was them?" she asked, sounding amused again. "I could call anyone."

"Give me to someone I've met. I met a lot of them this summer."

"Fine," she said, rolling her eyes at Doc. She pulled out her phone and dialled a number. "Hi. It's Hunt. No, everything is still fine over here. She's being difficult. She thinks I may be the mole. She thinks she's being kidnapped. She's being extremely difficult. Oh, did I? Sorry. It's been a long day. She needs verbal authorization from you."

She handed me the phone. "It's Cormier. You remember Cormier?"

"Yes." I took the phone. "Hello?"

"'Allo, Ms. Blunt," said Mr. Cormier. Okay, Quebec accent, check. Deep voice, check. "You are being quite suspicious, I 'ear."

"Can you blame me?"

He chuckled. "No, it is good work. But you must be safe, you understand? We may need you 'ere in Ottawa very soon."

"Why not now? I want to help."

"We must arrange a flight. Likely tomorrow. In the meantime, please go with Michaella. She must fill you in."

"Okay." I took a deep sigh, and I began to feel embarrassed. "Sorry for making a stink."

"No, it is good," he said, and he chuckled again. "Stay safe."

"Thank you. You too." I handed back the phone to Agent Hunt.

"Can we go now?" she asked.

"Yes. Uh. Sorry."

She just pointed to the car, and I climbed in and buckled my seatbelt again. Agent Hunt and Doc Mullins both got into the front, and the car rolled forward again.

The car only drove about two blocks before pulling in to an underground parking garage.

"That's it? This is as far as we're going? Why the fuck did you even bother driving me?"

"First of all, because we wanted you off the street and out of sight as much as possible." She gave me a disgusted glance. "Not that *that* worked out well. Second of all, because it is just that much faster and my time is extremely valuable today." Her dark eyes flashed as she gave me another nasty look. She parked at one edge of the underground parking, near the wall. "Get out."

I followed them to a steel door. It was unlabelled and locked.

"This is the nearest of several entrances to a secret safe zone," said Agent Hunt. "If any sign of an outbreak happens in Vancouver, or if you are in danger, you *must* come directly here. Do you understand?"

"Why didn't you tell me about this before?"

"Security."

I rolled my eyes.

Doc took out his keys and detached one from his keychain. He handed it to me.

"This is yours, now," he said.

"What about you?"

"I am less important at this moment."

I looked into his foggy grey eyes. "I'm really sorry about Howie."

He studied me. "It isn't your fault, Stella. What happened between you and Howie was inevitable. What happened after was not related. Therefore no blame can be attached to you."

"You thought it was inevitable?"

"Open the door, Stella," said Agent Hunt impatiently. "The world is on the verge of war. This is not the time to analyze your personal relationships."

I stuck the key in the door and turned the lock. I pulled the heavy door open. "Tada. I have successfully proven that I can use a key and open a door."

"Fine. Remember where you are. Take note of where this door is. There are several more like it, but they lead to electrical rooms and so on. Pay attention."

I paid attention. We went through the door into a small hallway with buzzing fluorescent emergency lighting. There was a second door in front of us, but it had a really fancy looking keypad installed on it with a digital screen display.

Agent Hunt punched in some numbers, went through a couple of menu options, and punched in more numbers. There was a series of short, high pitched beeps from the screen, and it said ENTER PASSCODE. She turned to me. "I need you to enter a unique ten digit numerical code that you have never used for a password of any kind, which has no relation to your birthday or the birthday of anyone you know, and no relation to any of your home addresses past or present, or any of your banking information." She paused. "Or your SIN. Or your health card number."

"I get it, I get it," I said. "Totally unique passcode. That's going to be tricky if you want me to remember it."

Dr. Mullins cleared his throat. "There are letters on the keypad as well. You can use them for a ten letter phrase. Some people find it easier to remember word sequences, rather than numbers."

"But it has to be unique," emphasized Agent Hunt. "It can't be…"

"Yeah, yeah, I get it."

I stared at the pad for a moment while Agent Hunt tapped her boot impatiently. Then I quickly punched in 4568346943. There was a long beep.

"Good. Now enter it again."

I did. There was a double beep.

"Good. Now place your hand on the blank panel to the right of the keypad. Palm down, fingers spread."

I did. The panel flashed green briefly.

"Good."

I took my hand away.

She entered another code and there was another beep, and the outline of my hand briefly appeared on the pad.

"Now you should be able to get in the door. Enter your code, and then put your hand on the pad, just the same way."

I did, and there was a long buzz.

"Open the door before the sound stops."

I yanked open the door and we walked through into another hallway. But this one looked fancier. The floors were tiled with linoleum and the walls were painted a blinding white.

"We're in." The door closed behind us. Agent Hunt gestured down the hall. "Welcome to Level 1 of the Burnaby Mountain Outbreak Security Zone."

40

Stella

The B-MOSZ, Hunt explained as she led me down the hall, was a vast complex extending five stories underground underneath SFU.

"In the nineteen-sixties, when we first began to organize emergency plans against outbreaks, the government decided that each major city needed to have a secret safe zone where citizens might be able to live in the case of a zombie or nuclear attack," she said briskly, leading me down another hallway. "SFU's design was commisioned with this in mind. As you know, SFU was designed so that students could go from one building to another without having to go outside."

"I thought that was because of the rain," I said. But it made sense now. SFU was full of pedways which were raised overhead — you could walk right over a horde of zombies and be completely safe from them. "That's why the buildings all look like some kind of concrete military bunker."

She nodded curtly. "And underneath the buildings, which are designed to withstand zombie attack, we have generators, stockpiles of food and medications, laboratory facilities, and accommodations for several thousand people. Obviously, most of this is powered down."

"Whoa. And every city has something like this?"

"Not every city has one as extensive as ours. You'll be interested to know that the Halifax Citadel Hill was similarly outfitted. But it is barely a tenth of the size."

I was gobsmacked. "Okay, so… where are we going?"

"Here." She stopped.

"My laboratory," said Doc Mullins. "At least, one of them."

"Morton has two labs. His official one, which he uses for basic experiments and projects on the SFU campus, and this one, which is for his higher security experiments."

"So, his zombie stuff."

"Yes. Originally we had all experiments running out of his upper lab, as we didn't want to give him access to our secure facility. But I made an argument several years ago that Morton could be trusted and that it was more secure to keep things below ground."

"For which I am grateful," said Doc.

She smiled at him, flashed her key fob, and opened the door to his lab.

The lab was really big, with lots of cages lining the walls. The hamsters all came rushing to the front of their cages when we walked in.

"You know this one," said Dr. Mullins with a smile, pointing at a cage.

"Is that the one that got out? You still have him?"

"I do."

"How old are most of these hamsters?"

"I have my base population which, I admit, I have grown attached to. Some of them have been here for several decades. The virus appears to give them a lifespan of well over twenty years. If we scale that into human terms, that would indicate that my adopted children can expect to live for eight hundred or possibly even a thousand years."

"Jesus."

"We need to tell her, Morton," said Agent Hunt urgently. "I just picked your lab because there are places to sit." She pointed at a stool near a microscope. "Sit, Stella."

I sat.

Agent Hunt sat in a computer chair next to a desk with a large computer on it. Doc busied himself with a coffee maker.

"So," said Hunt. "You asked me how they could be spreading an outbreak if they were intelligent and conscious, like Morton and his family. Well, it's time to tell you that it is possible for someone to be technically still alive — in the way that Morton is alive — and still be capable of spreading the virus."

"With sex? It's sex, isn't it?" I said dully.

Doc raised his eyebrows. "Of course not. That would be highly inefficient. She means through saliva."

"What?" I turned and stared Hunt. "But they can't. Howie told me over and over that they can't. Doc told me over and over that they can't. They only turn infectious after they go full zombie."

"That's what they told you. But we knew that wasn't completely true — which is why, when you were so sure that the hamster wasn't contagious, we insisted on testing it anyway," said Agent Hunt. "You remember that, don't you?"

"Yes… but…"

"And you knew that we swabbed the Mullinses routinely to check that they were still not infectious."

"Yeah but I thought that's just because you were paranoid assholes."

"Well," said Hunt, looking amused. "That may be true too. But the fact remains that it is possible for an infected person using Morton's formaldehyde treatment to be conscious, intelligent, and contagious. And Morton and his family were forbidden to mention it to you."

I gaped at her. "So… you're telling me that Howie could have become infectious at any moment? And that he knew this but didn't tell me?"

Doc Morton looked up from the coffee pot. "No, no," he said. "You were completely safe. You see, it is only under very particular conditions that we could have become infectious, and since we have never, and would never, pursue those conditions, we were safe." He handed a cup to Hunt, who accepted it graciously. He held up the coffee pot questioningly but I shook my head.

"*What* conditions?" I demanded.

"Let me tell the story," said Hunt to Doc. "You'll take too long." She looked at me. "He tried feeding human brains to his half-zombie rats."

I looked at Doc. "You used rats back then?"

He nodded. "I switched to hamsters later because…"

"Let's stay on track," interrupted Hunt. "He thought that human brains might be more effective than pig brains, and he was right. The rats developed astounding levels of intelligence."

Doc nodded. "They improved five hundred percent in maze tests and they began observing myself and my assistants with a level of awareness that I can only describe as eerie. We were very excited by the implications."

"Well, since you're not a Nobel prize winner and Howie couldn't make it through university and you're still living off of pig brains, I'm guessing something went wrong."

"The rats became infectious," said Doc. "They were alive and intelligent — extremely so — but they were shedding live virus in their saliva as if the virus had progressed fully. In fact, they were even more highly infectious than your average zombie. Just a touch of their saliva — a bit in your mucous membranes — and you would contract the disease."

"Oh. Fuck."

"Morton's rats also became aggressive," said Hunt. "Very aggressive."

"The concerted snarling of fifty rodents when you walked into the room was unnerving," said Doc. "They also developed extreme strength. This, combined with aggression and cunning, resulted in all fifty of them escaping their cages one night. I arrived with an assistant to feed them in the morning, and I'm afraid he was killed very quickly. Only my immunity and quick-healing abilities prevented me from succumbing as well."

"Jesus."

"I ended up having to put a stop to the experiment myself. It was extremely difficult for me to capture and destroy all fifty of them, since they were very fast, highly intelligent, and very strong."

"How long did it take you?"

"Nearly two days without rest. And it would have taken longer, in fact, if they hadn't managed to break into my fridge and help themselves to the remaining human brain material."

"What do you mean?"

"At the beginning, they were working together with the kind of organization that rodents simply are not capable of. For example, they worked together to brace themselves and pry open the fridge."

"Jeez, it sounds like something out of *The Rats of NIMH*."

Doc ignored me. "And they kept me distracted by allowing me to successfully catch some of them at the other end of the room so that I didn't see what they were doing. But once they got into the brain material, their organization fell apart. Their aggression increased further and they began to fight each other for the remaining food. I was able to take advantage of their distraction and destroy the remaining rats."

"So, now you think that this zombie organization has been eating human brains, and now they've all gone off the deep end. And they're probably infectious?"

Agent Hunt nodded. "Probably *very* infectious. Morton's research report was immediately suppressed, and the agencies that knew about it kept it highly classified. The fear was always that someone would see it as a way to seize immortality, intelligence, and strength simultaneously."

"And now they have."

Doc rubbed his face. "My predictions at the end of my report were that a human who consumed human brain material would likely show a drastic increase of intelligence, but that it would also be accompanied by infectiousness, emotional imbalance, and uncharacteristic aggression."

"So, basically a highly intelligent, coked-out serial-killer zombie instead of your standard mindless, shuffling, moaning kind."

"Yes. And with a viral load so potent that it could potentially even spread through the water supply."

I understood what I had been seeing now. "We're fucked. We're *so fucked*."

Dr. Mullins almost smiled. "Well put, as always, Stella. Yes. You could probably say that."

Act 3

Alas, have I not pain enough; my friend,
Upon whose breast a fiercer gripe doth tire
Than did on him who first stole down the fire,
While Love on me doth all his quiver spend,
But with your rhubarb words ye must contend,
To grieve me worse, in saying that desire
Doth plunge my well-formed soul even in the mire
Of sinful thoughts which do in ruin end?
If that be sin which doth the manners frame,
Well stayed with truth in word and faith of deed,
Ready of wit and fearing nought but shame;
If that be sin which in fixed hearts doth breed
A loathing of all loose unchastity,
Then love is sin, and let me sinful be.

Sir Philip Sidney "Astrophel and Stella 14"

41

Stella

If I had my way, Hunt would have collected my parents and friends and moved us all into B-MOSZ immediately. But for some reason she didn't think it was a good idea to move a ton of people, which she said would have to include every provincial government official as well as scientists, doctors and other people, into a facility that didn't have electricity, circulating air, or running water yet. Apparently, only Level 1 had basic electricity, and the rest of the complex needed generators and stuff that had to be accessed and fuelled.

"What's the point of having an emergency facility that isn't immediately usable in the case of an emergency?" I said irritably.

"In the case of a regular outbreak you have more than twenty-four hours of warning," pointed out Hunt with some asperity. "We don't have a contingency plan for intelligent zombies attacking in a coordinated, worldwide manner."

"*What?* You've known about this since the *seventies*!"

"But we never expected this. We thought someone might get a hold of the information, try it, and go bonkers," said Hunt. "But this is unprecedented and our informant — whether it was Howie or an impostor — had us thinking that we had over a year to prepare. We don't know what's going to happen. We don't even know if anything is going to happen, or if they *did* all just go bonkers.

"Our priorities right now are on protecting government officials and protecting you. We are powering up this place, which is a massive undertaking in and of itself, let me tell you. We are putting outbreak procedures into place, and we haven't even had an incident in the city yet. The Service in affected cities is doing everything it can to track down attackers and their victims, to make sure everyone is quarantined effectively. We're placing you under heavier guard. That's it for tonight. More will happen tomorrow. A lot more."

"My parents need a guard, too. These guys could use them as hostages to get to me!"

"They already have a perfectly good hostage," said Agent Hunt. "Assuming Howie is still alive."

I saw Doc flinch, and a look of pain spread across his face.

"So why aren't they using him?" I asked.

She didn't answer as we got back into her car.

He's dead. Howie's dead, I thought. I didn't say it out loud, for Doc's sake.

"Take me home," I said dully. "But then fucking go post a guard or something on my parents, please."

Hunt walked with long, swift strides down the hall, out of the complex, and back to her car, rattling on all the way about why my parents weren't going to get guarded.

"...Between powering up B-MOSZ, guarding you, and commandeering helicopters and the like from other government branches, I have my staff stretched to the limit. Plus don't forget that we still have a mole in the organization who stole vials of the virus and pulled the hamster from Morton's lab during the outbreak. I don't know who to trust, so I'm doing a hell of a lot of this stuff myself."

"Okay, okay, I get it."

"Good. In the meantime, please STAY INSIDE your apartment unless I call and give the warning to bolt for B-MOSZ."

"The last time The Service told me to stay inside during an outbreak, things did not go well."

"We don't have an outbreak yet. We have an international incident. It will be much easier for us to guard you if you stay in one place."

"Okay, okay. But how do you know I'm not being guarded by the mole?"

"Only the most trusted personnel will be guarding you."

The car pulled up at the curb by my building and I stepped out into the drizzle. The window rolled down and Doc Mullins leaned out. "Stella?"

"Yeah?"

"It wasn't your fault. Howie made his own decision. Do you understand?"

I nodded but couldn't speak. He raised his hand as Agent Hunt pulled away.

He forgave me. But was I ever going to forgive myself?

Kate looked around and snapped off the TV when I walked in the door.

"They keep playing new videos. It's terrible. This is like the end of the world." She looked really upset.

I collapsed on the couch, relieved that the TV was off. I couldn't take in any more.

"You okay?" I asked her.

"Yeah, it's just… it's upsetting."

"I didn't mean to freak you out with my zombie talk. But I do want you to take it seriously."

"I am, I promise," she said. She looked like she wanted to say something more, but then she shook her head.

"Is Riya coming back over?" I asked.

"No… I wanted her to… but she can't. Something about her roommate being sick."

"Hey... are you guys okay? Do you need to talk? I know I've monopolized the day drama-wise with Dean and Howie and zombies, but really, I'm here."

Kate shook her head. "Riya and I are fine. I'm just upset by stuff on the TV."

"Okay, if you're sure," I said. "Well, I'm wiped. I think I'm going to go to bed."

"Yeah, me too," said Kate.

Before I went to bed, though, I called my Mom.

"Hey. I can't talk long. I've been through a lot today and I can't handle it anymore. I just learned that eating human brains makes half-zombies like the Mullinses hyper-intelligent, infectious, and super-murderous. That's probably what's going on — the world's being attacked by a group of half-zombies who ate human brains and wigged out — so everyone they bite can get zombified and all of society could collapse. Howie's probably been killed by them or they'd be using him to get to me. You guys should go to a hotel in case they try to use *you* to get to me. If I had room I'd say come here, but I don't know where I'd put you and I'm probably just being paranoid. If anything weird or scary happens, come up to SFU, because it turns out there's a giant secret complex under the mountain that's designed to withstand pretty much anything."

"That's... a lot to take in," said my mother faintly.

"No shit. I love you. Call Agent Hunt and then me if anything scary happens. I'm locking my door and I'm going to sleep."

My mother started to ask a question but I ended the call. I knew she'd call back if it was important. Then I sent a mass text message to everyone I knew in Vancouver telling them to get up to SFU if scary shit started happening here, and then I messaged all of my friends and family in Nova Scotia, telling them that I couldn't explain why, but if scary stuff started happening there, they should get to Citadel Hill.

Then I closed my eyes and tried to escape the enormity of it all through sleep.

I was startled awake by the sound of banging on the door. I

looked at my clock. It was past midnight. Then I remembered everything and felt a burst of fear. The banging started again. I grabbed my phone but I paused at the sound of a muffled voice.

"Stella, it's Ray. Open up."

I unlocked the door to my room and went to the front door.

"...Ray?"

"Yeah."

"How did you get up here?"

"We've got a key to the building."

I looked through the peephole. Ray and Hazel looked incredibly out of place standing in my hallway.

"Why the fuck do you have a key to my building?"

"Can we come in?" Hazel asked.

"Have you eaten human brains lately?"

"No."

"Then I guess so. Just remember my roommate is here, okay?"

I unlocked the door and they came in. Hazel looked hunched and miserable. Ray looked edgy. Neither of them looked like the sort of people you want to invite into your home in the middle of the night.

"Sit. Talk." I pointed to my couch. "And tell me why you have a key to my building."

They didn't sit. "Because we're fucking guarding you, aren't we?" Ray said with a sour expression. "Because we would know if any of those weirdos came near you, because of the brain waves. And because Hunt's sure that we aren't moles."

"...Oh," I said, hoping Hunt was right. Then again, I could freeze these guys with my brain if I had to. I'd done it before.

"We're going to get Howie in Seattle. We need you to come with us," said Hazel. I had forgotten how weird and monotonous their voices were. I must have been hanging out with normal people for too long.

"You know where he is?" I felt a burst of excitement.

"No," said Ray.

"But you think he's alive?"

"Yeah, he's alive." Ray didn't look happy.

"Why? Did he get in touch?"

"No, he's on the fucking television."

"What?"

"Yeah, if you'd been watching TV instead of sleeping…"

"I was watching TV *all day*."

"Well, this has been on replay for hours."

I switched on the TV. "What channel?"

"The American one. The big news one. I don't remember, fuck," said Ray. I flipped around.

"Not Fox. Real news."

"That one," said Hazel. "I don't know if they'll play it again."

The newscaster stopped talking and a beer commercial came on. I muted and turned to them.

"Okay. So. You think Howie's alive, and you want to go get him?"

"Yes. We need you to help us find him."

"How can *I* find him?"

"If you walk into Seattle," said Hazel, "he'll know. And he'll come."

"What, just anywhere in Seattle? And besides, aren't there a bunch of other murder-zombies who will *also* come running?"

"So then you freeze 'em. You got a better plan?" asked Ray.

"No," I admitted.

"The hope is, he'd notice you first. He's tuned in to you. He comes, we get him, we get out before the rest get there."

"There he is," said Hazel, pointing. I looked back at the screen and fumbled to unmute the TV.

It was a video of a woman pulling down a man twice her size in a club. I recognized it as one of the original Seattle attacks from last night. The woman and two others bent over the poor man and started stabbing him.

"I've seen this one."

"It's a new angle," said Ray. "Someone else sold their video. There. In the corner."

I looked behind the attacking woman and my heart skipped a beat. Howie. He was thinner, and his hair was ragged, and his glasses were missing, but it was Howie. He bent over the victim, a strange expression on his face, and brutally smashed his skull on the ground.

I stood up. "HOLY FUCK!" The camera swung away just as it looked like Howie was prying into the man's skull.

"Yeah," said Ray.

"Oh my *God!*" I thought my heart was going to explode. *Shit. Shit. What the fuck.*

"Yeah."

My fingers clutched the corner of the couch. "But Howie would never..."

"Howie would never, ever eat human brains or hurt anyone," Hazel said. "Not on his own. Not ever."

"But he's... he's..."

"They must have forced it on him. Starved him. Tricked him. That's all we can think," said Ray.

"But..."

"So we need you to come with us to Seattle. You're our Howie bait."

"What makes you think he'd come?" I asked. My voice sounded stuffy from crying. "If he's... if he's not himself..."

"You never got it, did you?" Ray said. "You never got how into you he was."

"Is," said Hazel.

"Trust us. He still wants you," said Ray. "Even if he's crazy, he'll still want you. And if we can get you close enough, he'll come and get you. So get your coat, Stella. This isn't an invitation. This is a goddamn order."

"You think I'm not coming? You try and stop me," I said.

I went to my room and got dressed in the thickest, heaviest clothes I had. Maybe I didn't have riot gear to put on, but I could at least make myself a little harder to bite. I pulled my passport out from my underwear drawer and shoved a change of clothes into my backpack. I went into the kitchen and pulled our biggest kitchen knife out of the drawer and put that in my bag, too. Then I went to the whiteboard we kept on the fridge and wrote a note.

Kate-
I've gone to Seattle to try and save Howie. I hopefully won't get eaten. If I do, you can have your pick of my stuff. Tell my parents I love them, and that I'll be back soon.
Love
Stella
P.S. Remember, if things go south here, get everyone you know to go to SFU. My parents too. It's safer up here. Trust me.

"You ready yet?" Ray asked, looking restless.

"Yeah," I said, throwing on my coat and shoving my feet into my sneakers. "Let's go get Howie."

As I followed Ray and Hazel down the stairs, I swore to myself, and I pulled out my phone to send one last text.

Dean. I'm sorry things didn't work out, and I know you're pissed.
But I need you to trust me.
If things get weird here, get your parents
and get them up Burnaby Mountain.
Just do it.

"That's Howie's car," I said in shock.

"He's not using it," said Ray. "Get in."

As I climbed in, I was hit with the smell of Howie. Well, it wasn't the smell of Howie, per se. It was the faint smell of formaldehyde, which the Mullinses all exuded. But I associated it with Howie, with intimate moments that I had pushed back in my mind. It's weird how just a smell can seem to reverse time. I was back in high school again, making out with Howie, trying to figure out how to build a life with a zombie. Except in reality that was all ancient history — in the here and now he was out killing people and I had to go and somehow find him and get him back. I couldn't even absorb that.

There's nothing like a midnight car ride to the border with two demi-zombies who never really liked you all that much. The silence was deeply uncomfortable.

Eventually, I cleared my throat. "So, uh, do you guys have a, uh, plan?"

"Yeah. Get you to Seattle. Wait for Howie to come," said Ray.

"Uh huh. And how about avoiding the flesh-hungry crazies?"

"Yeah, we'll do that, too."

I sighed. "Okay, so, how close do you plan to get to Seattle?"

"We figure the middle is the best place," said Hazel.

"The middle," I repeated.

They nodded.

"Okay..." I might have to take over planning as we got closer, but I let this go for now. "Does your father know what we're doing?"

"No. We called him when we saw the video and he said there's nothing we can do. He didn't approve of putting you in harm's way."

"But we do," said Hazel. Ray nodded curtly.

"You're pissed with me for breaking up with your brother," I said. "I understand that."

"No, we get it. We all knew that it was never gonna work out. That doesn't mean we like what it did to him or that we value you over him," said Ray.

My throat felt tight. "What... what did it do to him?"

"He quit eating. We had to keep putting the thermos in his hands. He stared out the window all day. He cried. He read, sometimes. He slept."

Oh, Howie. Howie. I'm so sorry.

"I did those things too, you know," I said. "That's what breakups are like."

"Yeah," said Ray.

"We knew you were sad. We could feel it," said Hazel.

I grimaced. It felt weird to think that this family that lived two kilometres from my house had an inner window on my emotional life.

"So?"

"So, nothing."

The uncomfortable silence resumed.

The border guard asked some difficult questions. We claimed to be headed to the airport in Bellingham for a flight to Vegas, because we couldn't very well admit to heading for Seattle. No sane person was heading *toward* Seattle at this point.

"You two can sleep if you want," said Ray as we drove along the dark, deserted highway.

"Oh, yeah, I'm headed toward a city with a murder-zombie crisis in the middle of the night to rescue my ex, who is out killing people. I'm drifting off just thinking about it," I snapped. I was a *little* on edge.

"Get sarcastic all you want, and we'll just sit here and enjoy the brain feels. But it's two and a half more hours 'til Seattle, and then we'll have to sit tight for a while, waiting for Howie to show up. So you might want to get some shut-eye now while you have the chance. Take it or leave it."

"Did you bring things to fight off zombies with, by any chance?"

"Yep."

"Okay... such as?"

"Got a couple meat cleavers and our disruptors. Hazel can show you how to use a disruptor if you like, but you gotta get real close to their head. And these guys are fast. Turn and bite you in a heartbeat. Better you use the cleaver. Hell, I wish we had guns."

"This seems like *such* a dangerous idea."

"Yeah, well, we're attached to our brother, okay? He may be old history to you, but you used to be fond of him, so suck it up," said Ray.

"I *am* fond of him," I said sullenly. "I'd just rather not die."

"Try to get some sleep," repeated Ray.

I sat quietly, staring at the hypnotic road as the hours ticked by. I do think I dozed a bit on the drive, but it was disjointed, unrestful sleep. Eventually, the streetlights of Seattle roused me.

"Almost show time," said Ray.

"Okay, so, seriously, where are we going?"

"I don't know. Around here, somewhere?"

I pulled out my phone, turned on data roaming, and spent a few minutes fiddling. "Okay, there's a twenty-four-hour diner where I can get a really early breakfast. Head there. If I'm going to get killed by psychopathic cannibals, I want to die on a full stomach."

I cut into a stack of fluffy pancakes and shovelled them into my mouth. Hazel and Ray were sipping out of thermoses. I tried to keep the conversation going. I felt like their plan had a few holes.

"So, how long do you think we have to wait until your brother notices me? Or until we get swarmed by infectious evil geniuses?"

"Probably not too long. Question is whether he's free to come right away or not. And whether he's the first one to show up. But we think he will be. He always noticed you more'n the rest of us did. He could feel you from further away."

"Because I'm, like, his perfect fit or something?"

"No," said Ray looking annoyed. "Because he was listening."

The pancakes were good. They reminded me of Howie's pancakes. Howie cooked restaurant style pancakes, so good.

Howie.

"I have no idea what I'm going to say to him," I said. "How do you tell someone, 'I'm sorry that I broke up with you and you ended up getting kidnapped by zombies and turned into a homicidal madman'?"

They exchanged glances. "I think the only thing you'll say to him is 'please don't eat me,'" said Ray.

"And then how do we get him over the border? I can't imagine that he's running around with a passport."

"We won't be bringing him back with us," said Hazel, studying a scratch on the diner table.

"What... but... then... why are we here?"

"This ain't a rescue mission. This is a mercy mission," said Ray.

"He's your brother! You're telling me that you're here to... finish him off?" I could hear my heart in my ears, and I felt like all reality was draining out of my skull. And I *know* that doesn't make any sense but that's how it felt, goddamn it.

"We're here to put him out of his misery."

"For SURE?"

"Yes."

"That's fucked up!"

"It's what he'd want."

"He'd want you to take him the fuck home!" I banged the table. The waiter looked up from the front counter and frowned at me.

"No," said Ray. "We don't do that to our loved ones when they turn. We end it. Because it's not right to let them live like that. Or… not live… like that. You think Howie would want to be… whatever he is?"

I remembered the fear and loathing that Howie had for zombies, how he suffered nightmares about becoming that.

Howie…

"He killed our parents, you know," said Hazel. I looked up. She was crying. "I remember. Papa… eating the baby… and biting Mama when she started to scream, and then I started to cry and he came after me, and I ran and hid in the closet and he was trying to get in… and then Howie came in with a hammer and…" Hazel wiped her eyes and shook her head several times. "After, he tried to get me out of the house, and Mama got up and bit him and he killed her, too… he told me that he had to do it, that Mama and Papa loved us and would never have forgiven themselves for killing us. That they'd rather be dead."

I felt like the room was spinning. I was trying to imagine Howie — thin, fragile-seeming Howie — killing his own parents with a hammer at the age of eleven.

"So I owe him the same thing," said Hazel, wiping her nose with a napkin. "But I don't know if I can do it. I just don't know."

"One of us will, that's for sure," said Ray, stroking her hair. "We're not gonna let Howie go on like that. We know what he'd want."

"But…" I was desperate for another answer, any answer. "You don't think he's *completely* turned, do you? Like… heart stopped?" I remembered his heart — his good heart, jittering away inside his chest when I leaned on it. Howie had always opened his heart to me. Hell, I'd *seen* the thing glistening in his hands.

"Maybe, maybe not. Either way, the Howie we knew is gone."

"You can't know that!"

"We know that Howie would have tried to contact us by now. We know that Howie wouldn't be out killing people in nightclubs."

"But if he saw me," I said fiercely, tears starting in my eyes. "If he remembered… He can't just be *gone*."

"We watched him kill a man, Stella." Ray had tears in his eyes too, and his face was contorted. "He smashed someone's brains out on the floor and took a handful of them. If you knew a goddamned thing about Howie you'd know that he's gone inside."

I buried my head in my arms. I thought about how terrified he always was of losing control. I thought of his face, how it looked when he talked about the virus. I thought about how he looked when he worried about hurting me. I remembered his face, contorted with anguish, as he told me about terrible dreams of killing people — killing me.

And then I thought about his face in the video as he smashed that man's head on the floor.

I had failed Howie again and again. I had constantly put myself first — my own selfish wants ahead of his. I made him feel inadequate. I drove him to desperation. I broke his heart.

If I loved him — if I really loved him — surely I could do *one* thing that was for *him*, and not for me.

Congratulations, Stella. You've finally grown to the point where you can put him before yourself.

Too late.

I raised my head again and wiped the tears away.

"Okay," I said. "Come on. Let's go kill my soul mate."

42

Stella

Since Ray and Hazel's plan consisted of nothing more than 'bring Stella – wait for Howie – kill him', I decided to take over.

"We need to find somewhere high up," I said. "Somewhere I can see him coming, and see any crazies. The sun should be up soon."

"I don't know Seattle," said Ray.

"Me neither," said Hazel.

"Great," I said.

Using the diner's WiFi, I Googled places in Seattle. We kept glancing nervously out the window for advancing zombie hordes, but all we saw was traffic and the pink of the sunrise.

"Okay," I said after a while. "There's a place downtown. Nice and central, or 'in the middle' as you call it. It's a park, so it's very open, and it's kind of terraced so you can get up high and get good views of the area. There's a kind of overpass thing with an artsy outcropping I can stand on. Seems like a better idea than wandering through the sidewalks of Seattle. And I'll just think very big thoughts about Howie and hope he tunes in."

"If he hasn't already," said Ray, looking edgy.

"You're a little worked up," Hazel told me.

"Of course I'm fucking worked up. Aren't you?"

Ray threw some American money on the table and stood up.

"Where'd you get that?" Hazel asked him.

"Had it for a long time. It was worth a lot more, then. Now it barely covers a girl's breakfast. Come on."

We followed Siri's directions into downtown Seattle.

"This is going to cost me a fortune in data," I complained, because I handle major shit by complaining about minor shit. "I'm roaming. I'm going to get a whopping bill from Telus for killing the man I love. This has been the worst twenty-four hours of my life."

"Then you haven't lived long enough," growled Ray.

That shut me up.

And then I saw it.

Lurching by the side of the road, a woman was drifting at a weird angle, arms swinging. The jerky, spasmodic walk was instantly recognizable to anyone who had seen it before. And we all had.

"Ray, pull over."

He pulled over. The car behind us whizzed by with a horn blast.

I got out and turned on my zombie freezing power. The woman stopped, turned, and stared at me vacantly. I pulled the knife from my backpack and drove it through her skull. She collapsed. I wiped the knife on her clothes and got back into the car.

"Jesus, Stella, you can't kill zombies with a knife in plain sight like that," said Ray. "You're gonna get arrested."

"It's the break of dawn. No one saw. Ray, that was just a regular zombie."

"Well, there's bound to be some, aren't there? They can't find everyone that these whackos bite. And unless those people know to find some formaldehyde and eat some brains, they're gonna turn into regular zombies."

But as our car hit downtown, it quickly became clear to us that there weren't just "some" regular zombies.

"Jeeeeeesus," breathed Ray in an almost emotional tone of voice.

The sidewalks were scattered with them. Not running. Not intelligent. Just *zombies*. They were wearing hospital gowns and business suits, bathrobes and yoga pants.

"Oh, no," said Hazel.

"Keep driving," I said.

"Did you think I was gonna stop and say hello?" said Ray. "Of course I'm gonna keep driving. Jeez."

When we got to the park, it was deserted. No zombies. At least, not yet.

"Here, take one of these," said Ray, passing me a meat cleaver. "I know you can use that. Hazel and I have the disruptors." He paused. "I didn't mean what I said, you know. About valuing Howie over you. He wouldn't want us to get you killed. We'll do whatever it takes to keep you safe."

"I know," I said. "Right back at you."

He nodded and pulled some rope out of the trunk. "I'll bring this, too. In case he's hard to pin down."

I tried not to think about it. "There's a kind of bridge or overpass thing that I saw in pictures," I said. "That would be a good place to stand."

We walked around for a bit, looking at the weird art sculptures scattered through the park, and then I spotted it. "Perfect."

We followed the concrete path over a green overpass. Train tracks passed below us. On the other side, the path made a V shape with a jutting viewpoint at the tip of it.

"I'll see him from here. And he'll see me. You guys should probably back off or hide a bit… you know so you can surprise him and help if I can't handle him…" I had a moment where I saw clearly what I was planning to do and I felt like I couldn't breathe. I closed my eyes and shut it down. *Don't think about that. Just get ready*. Thinking about it wouldn't make it any easier.

They nodded and backed off toward some trees on the other side of the overpass. I didn't watch them go. I knew they had my back. Instead, I just stood and stared out at the park, and the railway tracks, and the water, and the sky, and the cars, and the skyscrapers, and thought about Howie. I thought about how he had always described my mind in terms of a beacon, or a light, and I imagined myself glowing inside. I tried to turn myself into a spotlight, a flare.

I am here. Howie, I love you. Howie, come find me.

I remembered the longing I felt when I saw him in my dream at Christmas. I remembered the first time we kissed, how he had trembled. I remembered the way he would hold me, sometimes, and something about it was so tender and gentle that it cracked me right open. Dean had never made me feel that way.

Howie. I am here.

I thought about how he loved music and poetry. I remembered summer days spent lying in parks, looking at the clouds, while Howie read out loud to me in his funny, quiet, bland little voice that carried so much hidden passion underneath it.

Come live with me and be my love,
And we will all the pleasures prove

Come live with me, Howie. I don't care if you can't go to school. I don't care if you won't get any older. I don't care about sex, even. I just want you to hold me, and talk to me, and love me. Oh, and especially love me.

Please, Howie. I am here.

Where are you?

Zombies began to show up. Not the terrifying kind. Just regular, shuffling, lurching zombies. The first time I ever saw a zombie, it scared the hell out of me, but now I barely blinked at these ones. I looked down at the faces. They all moved slowly with that creepy spasm-like movement that signifies a true zombie. None of them moved fast and none of them looked intelligent. Maybe the attackers had all gone full-zombie? Was Howie one of these shuffling lurchers below?

As I watched zombie after zombie appear, I worried about the state of the city. I could hear sirens and screams in the distance. Seattle was in some serious shit.

Then I heard a shout behind me. I turned and saw a young woman hoist a struggling Hazel right over her head and chuck her off of the overpass onto the train tracks below. Fear shot through me. I looked for Ray and saw him grappling with a dark-haired man who was moving faster than any human being should be able to move. Shit! Before I could even react, the woman flashed toward me and I found myself seized by an iron grip.

"Well, Mullins was right. Your mind *is* nice," she said. She had gorgeous auburn hair and bright red lipstick. She didn't *sound* like a zombie and she sure as hell didn't look like one. I tried to break out of her grip but she was ridiculously strong.

"Where's Howie?" I demanded.

"Oh, he's held up," she said with a smile. "He tried *so* hard to get here first, too. Such a shame."

I tried to do a foot sweep — knock her off her feet — but it was like kicking a tree.

"That doesn't work on me, sweetie," she laughed, and she pulled a small pistol from her purse and aimed it carefully at me. *Holy shit.* I froze, and I felt like I'd had cold water dumped on me. Nothing says "imminent death" to your brain like staring down the barrel of a gun. I held my breath as I stared at the shiny circle that could destroy me before I even heard the bang.

"Now," she said, tugging me sideways and nearly pulling me off of my feet. "Let's go somewhere more private."

That was when I remembered that as much as she might not look like one, she *was* a zombie, and I am a *fucking anti-zombie weapon*.

I lifted my eyes from the gun, looked right into her face, and blasted out the aura of confidence and get-outta-my-way attitude that made zombies go dozy.

I am here. Make way for me.

Her arms slackened and her eyes lost focus. With a supreme effort, I pushed myself free.

I raised my meat cleaver and aimed for the hand that held the gun. But then she blinked, shook her head, and dodged. She moved faster than I had ever seen anyone move, and *she did it while I had my zombie-freeze on.* My cleaver missed, swishing through the air and almost throwing me off balance.

Oh, I am so fucked.

I tried to amplify my freeze.

I AM FUCKING HERE MAKE WAY FOR ME.

She hesitated again, and I swung my cleaver as fast as I could. I wasn't sure I could kill a living person, even if she was a brain-eating monster, but I had to get rid of that gun. My cleaver stuck in the air and wouldn't come down. I looked over my shoulder and saw the dark-haired, bearded man who had been grappling with Ray. His black eyes gleamed and his mouth was smeared with blood.

I AM FUCKING HERE! MAKE WAY FOR ME GODDAMN YOU ALL TO HELL!

The man barely blinked, and the woman smiled up at him.

"Thank you," she said to him. "But it wasn't necessary."

"Mmmmm," he said, leaning into my ear as I shrank away. "That was *good*. Do it again." Then, with a movement so fast that I could barely see it, he yanked my cleaver easily out of my fist and buried it in the woman's brain. She crumpled to the ground.

Well. *That* was unexpected.

I moved back but his hand flashed out and caught me by the wrist.

"Too long," the man said, looking with satisfaction at her body. "I suffered too long. Mullins was right. Apex is pointless."

I tried to break his grip the way I learned in kung fu, but he didn't even seem to notice my struggles. With a grin, he slung me to the ground and pinned my hands over my head. The dead woman, with my cleaver sticking out of her head and a dark puddle of blood oozing onto the concrete, stared sightlessly at me from just a couple of feet away while this disgusting zombie man ground his body into mine. I brought my knee up, right into his groin, and it was like kneeing a rock. He was so hard that it actually bruised my knee. He laughed and leaned his shaggy face close to mine. I could see a line of drool at the corner of his disgusting mouth, and his front teeth had something red caught between them. I closed my eyes and turned my head. I tried to think my way through to a solution. *These people are contagious. Keep his saliva out of your mucous membranes if you don't want to turn into a zombie. Think of a way out. Think.*

MAKE WAY! LET ME THE FUCK GO YOU FUCKING FUCK.

I couldn't move. Where the hell were Hazel and Ray? Were they dead?

"You *are* tasty," said the man into my ear as he pressed his erection painfully into my thigh. "This is going to be delicious."

NO NO NO NO NO NO.

Then something knocked him out of the way. I looked up and saw Howie standing over me, panting. He was looking at the prone form of the man and his face was twisted with rage.

"*Mine,*" he said. The man started to rise, but Howie reached down, grabbed the handle of my cleaver, ripped it free of the woman's head, and swiftly sank it into the man's skull. The man spasmed once and lay still.

Oh, thank God. Thank God.

"Howie," I gasped, climbing to my feet. "Howie, I…"

He turned to face me and threw the cleaver down. His glasses were missing, and his hair was limp and lank. His clothes were covered in blood stains, and his face was contorted into an expression of tortured fury. But it was Howie.

"Stella," he said in that husky, adoring way that I had missed so much.

He knew me. He saved me, and he knew me.

"Howie, you saved me... I came here to save you, but…"

"No," he said, and his voice was filled with a degree of emotion that I had never heard before. "You came here because you are mine."

And he pounced.

43

Stella

Howie knocked me onto my back so hard that the air was knocked right out of my lungs. Thanks to years of practice in kung fu, I knew how to tuck my chin and hunch my shoulders to take the brunt of the fall, so that I didn't hit my head. Howie straddled my body and pinned my shoulders. His blue eyes stared into mine, but they were sharp and clear — the milky haze and all the love and tenderness were gone.

"Howie," I gasped, trying to suck air back into my chest. "You know me..."

"Oh, I know you. Soon I'll know you inside out."

His grip was iron. I couldn't lift him. I couldn't get my arms free. I flailed my feet and bumped the handle of the cleaver with my toe. I nudged at it a bit and felt it move up the arch of my foot.

"Howie, this isn't you." My voice cracked as I looked into the face that was so familiar and yet chillingly alien. "You wouldn't hurt me. You would never hurt me. Never, never."

"Welcome to Never Never Land," he hissed. "Reality is an illusion. I'm macrocosmic and microcosmic. Perception is a lie."

"This is real, Howie. Wake up. Please."

"I am going to feast. Take my time. Taste. Every. Bite."

Howie lifted a hand and began to run it through my hair. But it wasn't the tender way he used to do it. It was possessive and predatory. My heart raced as I recalled how he had crushed the man's head against the ground in the video. He was going to smash me like a pumpkin and I couldn't grasp it, couldn't understand that I was really about to die.

I am here. I am thinking. My brains work. Soon they'll be in his hands. How can that be? What will happen to me, the me that is thinking, when that happens? If my brains are scattered on the pavement, how can I be me?

Oh God, my poor parents…

I felt a flood of rage at the thing that held me. This wasn't Howie. It was a… a *thing* in Howie's body. Its weight was on me, climbing on me, grinding itself on me, tugging at my clothes. One bite and I'd be infected. One kiss, even.

"Your fear feels goooooood," said the Howie-thing. "I'm liking this. You going to scream for me when I start? Always dreamed of making you scream."

My stomach lurched nauseously. This sounded *nothing* like Howie. There was too much emotion and way too much evil in his voice.

Fuck you, Howie-thing!

I flailed my feet and managed to nudge the cleaver with my shoe. I heard it skitter along the concrete toward my head. The Howie-thing didn't look or seem to notice. He was reaching under my shirt, groping me, *sniffing* me. He was hard for me, and he was rubbing himself against me. But still, he didn't bite. He didn't smash my skull. I stretched my arm out in desperation, the concrete rough on my hand. My finger brushed the handle of the cleaver.

"Howie. This is the virus. This isn't you."

I managed to get two fingers on the handle. I desperately tried to pull it closer. Ray and Hazel were right: This wasn't Howie. I wouldn't be killing him. He was already gone.

He was looking me over hungrily but he still hadn't hurt me. *Keep him talking. Distract him.* My fingers were spread wide, scrabbling at the handle, trying to get a grip on it.

"Howie, do you remember our first kiss? It was after you came at me with a cleaver. I thought you were attacking me, remember? I took you down, remember? And you said you would never hurt me."

The thing blinked, and for just a moment, I felt like he really saw me. His face went from lecherous to horrified, and I surged with hope. Then he shook his head and pressed me harder into the ground.

"This time, I took *you* down," he said.

"No, Howie," I said. "This time, I have the cleaver."

I brought my arm up as fast and hard as I could and struck Howie down with the cleaver.

The back of the cleaver.

The Howie-thing collapsed on me with eyes half closed. I threw him off and jumped to my feet. I ran to the edge of the overpass and looked down. Ray and Hazel were struggling with a skinny middle-aged woman. There were agitated zombies around them, biting them, but they ignored the zombies and focused on the woman. I saw Hazel hit her with the brain disruptor and she went down. I called and they looked up. I saw relief flood through their faces.

"I'm okay!" I shouted. "Get your asses up here, quick!"

They ran through the zombies, zapping them as they went, and up the steps to the overpass. The zombies were trying to get up the steps, trying to get to me, but kept stumbling into each other and knocking each other off.

Ray and Hazel made it to the top, then stopped and looked at Howie's prone form.

"I need your rope, Ray," I said. "He's not dead."

"Then kill him," said Ray roughly, but he tossed me the rope. "I seen him leap up to that outcrop. That's gotta be three stories and he climbed it like fucking Spiderman. That ain't Howie. You got to end it." His grammar, which always suffered when he was stressed, was now in full redneck mode so I knew he was really upset, even if his voice couldn't show it.

"Not yet." I wrapped the rope tightly around Howie and knotted it half a dozen times. "And be ready with those brain disruptors. Are the zombies coming up the stairs?"

"They're trying. And more are gonna come from the other side. I can see 'em coming."

"Okay."

We propped Howie up against the wall. Now that he was unconscious, he looked entirely like himself. I wanted to kiss him awake, but of course I couldn't because first of all, he might try to kill me, and second, even if he didn't, his spit would kill me anyway. His heart was still beating, but it was crazy fast. He wasn't breathing, but Ray and Hazel assured me that this didn't really matter.

Tears dripped down Hazel's face. "We can't do it like this. He looks like he's sleeping."

"He *is* sleeping. The sleep of the creepy horny cannibal with a concussion," I said. "But he sort of remembered me. And there was a moment when… but then… I don't know."

"You shoulda just killed him," repeated Ray. "Now we gotta wait for him to wake up. Hazel's right. I can't kill him this way. I need to see that he's gone."

"Kill it anyway," moaned Howie without moving. "Kill me," he said again, more clearly.

"Howie? Howie, do you know who we are?" Hazel knelt down.

"Prurience. Concupiscence. Can't resist. No rhyme. No reason," chanted Howie. "Kill me. Kill it. Infinitesimal. Inconsequential. No more. No more meaning."

"No," I said. "You remember me. You know who you are."

"Lost. Lost. Please. Please," he began to cry. "Howie Fontaine is gone. Eaten up. No hope. No hope. Just end it. End it, *please.*"

Ray and Hazel and I stared at him, and then looked at each other.

"Well, that's good enough for me," said Ray. "Let's load him into the car."

It's not easy to drag a gangly, semi-unconscious teenager through a horde of zombies and into the trunk of an old Dodge beater. I had to freeze the zombies so I could get through the horde, but that made Ray and Hazel all dozy. If I did it lightly enough, they could still move through it, but it was a delicate balance. I didn't dare touch Howie, in case he bit me or dripped saliva into my eyes or mouth or something, so Ray had him hoisted over his shoulder. I moved through the zombies, chopping into skulls left and right, while Ray and Hazel followed as best they could, which was not very well at all. Slowly we made our way to the car. My heart was pounding the whole time because while the zombies were annoying, I knew that more of those murdering, infectious assholes could show up at any minute. And *they* could use weapons. And we were in *America*. I'd only been in this damn country for a few hours and I'd already had a gun pointed at me.

Jesus, the stress was turning me into Baum.

By the time we got to the car, I'd taken out enough zombies to give us a bit of breathing room, and there were no signs of any of those murder-zombie types.

"That rope isn't strong enough to really hold him, you know," I warned Ray as we dumped Howie in the trunk. "He's freakishly strong, now."

"We could cut off his head," said Ray, tilting his head thoughtfully. "That'd take care of him for a while."

"But we don't know how long it would take him to… to convert," argued Hazel. "We know it would take us a few days, but who knows about… about his type. We don't even know if he's been keeping up with his formaldehyde."

"Yeah, best not to risk it. Wish we'd brought some formaldehyde, but I didn't think we'd be trying to sober him up, I thought we'd be finding somewhere to bury him. Hold tight to that cleaver," Ray advised me, and he slammed the trunk. We jumped into the car and Ray revved the engine while I buckled my seatbelt. Just as we pulled away, two figures dropped from the roof of a nearby building, landed on all fours, and charged right at us.

"Shit!" I said. Ray gunned the engine and the car shot forward.

"They're keeping up," said Hazel from the back seat.

"Shit!" I turned and saw them racing after us, maniacal grins on their faces. "They're not keeping up, they're *gaining on us.*"

"Fuck," said Ray and he hit the brakes.

"What are you..." I looked forward again and saw a snarl of traffic up ahead. "Fuck!" Cars were crashed into each other, blocking the road, and people were running and screaming. With a double thump, we felt our pursuers land on the car roof.

"Stella, stay in the car," said Ray. He leaped out and was immediately pounced on by the two murder zombies who tried to smash his head on the windshield. I unbuckled my seatbelt, hopped out, and buried the cleaver into the sandy hair of the man closest to me. Before I could process the fact that I had just murdered a sentient — if hideously dangerous — human being, the other one, a chubby girl with streaks in her hair, turned and laughed. She let go of Ray, leaped for me, and then collapsed as Hazel pressed a disruptor up against her temple and zapped her good.

Ray sat up. "Get in the car, Stella," he said.

"You're welcome," I said, but I also got in the car, because I could already see a zombie horde up ahead diverting to drift our way. My brain brings all the zombies to the yard.

"Look," said Ray, climbing back into the driver's seat. "If you get killed, then Howie will kill us. Probably literally. So stay in the fucking car."

We were only a block from the park and it was already obvious that the downtown core was a disaster. We could hear car horns and crashes, screams and growls. I even heard a gunshot. It was scary shit.

Ray put the car in reverse. "We find another way."

"This is out of control," said Hazel.

"Yeah, Seattle's gonna fall," said Ray.

"Like, FALL fall?" I said. "As in, no more city?"

"Yeah. And they'll spread everywhere. Which means that if Canada hasn't closed the border, Vancouver is screwed."

"Well, but it would take zombies a long time to hobble all the way to Canada."

"It's not the dead ones you gotta worry about. Think about it. Some of these people for sure got bit, but they're making a run for it anyway. People always hide their bites. The bites hide themselves — heal right over. And where are the people running to, now? I bet you — over the border. All it takes is a few people to get through who've been bit, and Vancouver has its very own outbreak."

"What are we going to do if they *have* closed the border?"

"Oh, we can't get over the border anyhow," said Ray.

"We... what?"

"It's not gonna happen, even if they haven't closed it. And they'd be morons not to close it right now."

"Why couldn't we get over?"

"Well, because even if the border is open, they're gonna be screening people really carefully. And then how do you explain the guy we got tied up in the trunk?"

"So... do you have a backup plan?"

"Might as well get as close as we can. Then I'm gonna have to ditch the car and we'll hike over."

"How, exactly?"

"With our legs. And we can't just nip over right next to the border. If they're smart, they'll patrol the border, try to catch wandering zombies. So this is gonna be fun."

"Oh, yeah. I'm looking forward to it already. Look, let me drive. I can't freeze the zombies when you're driving because then you'll go dozy too, so put me in the driver's seat. I'll freeze all these zombies so people can get away, at least."

"Yeah, and you'll call every one of those crazies over here in the process," said Ray. "Cause *they* can move even when you're doing that crap. You want to meet more of them?"

I pulled out my phone. I'd missed eighteen calls, and I had over thirty text messages from people including Kate, Dean, my friends in Nova

Scotia, and my parents. Before I could read any of them, my phone began to buzz and *Boss Lady* appeared on the screen. I answered the call.

"Hey," I said conversationally, as if I weren't in a totally different country, stuck in a car with my deranged ex-boyfriend trapped in the trunk and two different kinds of zombies chasing me.

"Stella! Where are you?" Hunt demanded.

"Seattle."

"What on *Earth* are you doing in Seattle?" She sounded furious.

"Rescuing Howie."

"Stella, you need to come back here *right away.* Howie is gone. We need you here. Now."

"I've already got Howie."

"You... what?"

"Yeah, we've got him. We're on our way back. But traffic is problematic. There's a big outbreak here."

"You... you actually found him?"

"Yep."

"And he's... okay?"

"Well, he's been better, I've got to be honest. Look, Seattle is *really* bad. Do you want to let the authorities know that I'm here so I can help them? Ray thinks Seattle's going to fall if something doesn't change fast."

"Seattle has already fallen," said Agent Hunt.

"Holy fuck, are you sure?"

"Our last attempt to contact the authorities there was unsuccessful. One of the... the super-zombies answered the phone. He was extremely unpleasant to talk to."

"You need a cooler name than 'super-zombie'. It doesn't sound *nearly* scary enough. I fought a bunch of them this morning and they're *really* fucking scary."

"Listen, Stella. I'm going to try and send a helicopter for you. Air traffic control is down and martial law is in force so this is going to be dangerous as hell."

"We can drive..."

"No. You can't. The border is closed and traffic is a disaster. I need you here three hours ago. Listen. You need to go somewhere a helicopter can land."

"Like the airport, or a hospital?"

"Absolutely not. Neither of those. The outbreaks were deliberately started in every hospital and airport."

I could hear someone talking to Hunt in the background. She answered them, and then came back to me.

"Where are you exactly?"

"Uh, near a park called Olympic Statue Park or something. Sculpture Park."

I heard more consultation going on in the background.

"Sella. I want you to stay down by the water. Go to Pier 91. There's a cruise terminal there which has ties to the Department of Defense. Get onto the roof. We're going to try to get permission to land there, and if we don't, we're coming anyway. WAIT FOR US. DO NOT DIE."

"Okay. My battery's running low and I'm going to need to GPS this. I'll text you when I'm there."

"Good." She hung up.

"Hunt says the murder-zombies answered the phone when she tried to contact the Seattle Zom Squad," I informed them.

"Fuck," said Ray. "I knew it."

I opened my phone's mapping app and looked for Pier 91. "We have to go to some ship terminal." I put it into my mapping app and turned up the volume. "Follow Siri."

Ray turned pulled a U-turn, swerving around zombies as he went, and headed in the opposite direction of all of the other traffic, skirting along the shoreline and following Siri's instructions. There was no noise from the trunk.

"Do you think he's okay back there?" I said.

"What can happen in a trunk to someone who doesn't need to breathe?"

"But he's so quiet."

"Maybe he knows what's good for him."

The place wasn't very far and we didn't see many zombies along the way. Good old Hunt. I knew she was pissed, but she had saved my ass anyway. I'd have to buy her a cake or something.

We pulled up outside a dark grey building. There was no one around. We got out of the car and went around to the trunk. I tightened my grip on the meat cleaver, looking around edgily, as Ray unlocked the trunk. I could hear screams in the distance, and car alarms, and the sounds of breaking windows, and I shivered for reasons that had nothing to do with the damp January air.

When Ray cautiously opened the trunk, I could see that Howie was awake. I prepared myself, cleaver at the ready, but he didn't come leaping out or anything. He sat up with Hazel's help and looked around. We made eye contact.

"Do you know me, Howie?" I asked.

He nodded. A tear trickled down his cheek and my heart broke for him. *Howie…*

"Stay away from me," he said, his voice far more emotional than I was accustomed to it being. "Please."

"Howie, we need to get to that building over there," said Hazel. "Can you walk?"

"I can leap tall buildings in a single bound," said Howie. "These ropes are useless, you know. They fed it to me. I didn't want it. The strength. I knew it was bad. Then it got good. Then it got too good. Oh God, you should just kill me."

"Maybe later," said Ray. "Right now, I need you to walk." He gave his brother a shove, and Howie started moving. The building had two big escalators. They weren't moving. We climbed up to the second floor, which was enormous and open. The only light filtered in from the windows, but it was enough to see that the area was empty.

"There's a balcony over there with more stairs," I said, pointing. Our footsteps echoed as we made our way through the big space. I pulled out my phone to text Hunt and let her know that we had made it to the pier safely and just needed to get up onto the roof. But my phone had no bars.

"Damn," I said. "I've lost service."

Howie spoke, his voice harsh and rough. "Of course," he said. "The cell phone towers are down and so is the power."

"How do you know?" I demanded, but he just glared at me. His face was still contorted, and his lips were moving as if he were muttering to himself under his breath. Ray and Hazel were holding him *very* firmly.

"Best step away from him," said Ray. "He could bust out at any moment."

I edged away. "Howie..." I said. "Try to remember who you are. Can you do that?"

"I can do anything... except stop myself from hurting you. Haven't eaten today and you... you're..."

"You don't want to hurt me. You had me at your mercy, but you didn't do it."

"You don't know. You don't know..."

"She doesn't get it, Howie, but we do," said Ray. "We're here. We're not gonna to let you hurt her."

"You won't hurt her either. She's mine."

"I am MINE," I said, "and I do NOT like to be spoken about as if I am not here! *No one* is going to hurt me because I am holding a fucking cleaver and I can stop you all in your tracks with my MIND."

"Not me, not right now," said Howie. "I can move through it. It just fills me with... with... ahhhh...." he trailed off. He tore his eyes from mine. "It's like setting a drink right next to an alcoholic," he said. "This is cruel."

"If we hadn't brought her we never would have found you," said Hazel. She squeezed her brother's arm.

"I wanted you to bring her. I knew the news would show me. Knew she'd come. Because she's mine."

"I am mine," I said again firmly. "I am a living, thinking, independent adult and I am absolutely, one hundred percent definitely not food. I forbid you to eat me." I looked at Ray. "Do you have thermoses? Maybe if he got some brains in him..."

"Good idea," said Ray. "Got some in my bag."

"Can't... can't eat that anymore," said Howie, his face contorted. "Not now that I've had better. You can't imagine, Ray."

"Yep, I can. Every night. But it ain't happening," said Ray. "You're not a killer, Howie. You don't want to kill people."

"People are just concatenations of atoms. Molecules forming cellular organisms, which form colonies which give themselves names."

"Uh huh. Head toward those stairs."

Howie shook his head. "No. Had enough." He contorted himself in an inhuman way, and the ropes dropped at his feet. Ray and Hazel threw themselves at him, but he shook them off easily and stepped out of his ropes toward me. I turned on my zombie freeze, and they all paused.

I am here. Make way for me.

Howie smiled at me. It was unnerving.

"Feels so good. I can't wait for this. I've dreamed about it so many times." He shook himself and took a step toward me. I backed away and stepped up the blast, straining myself, and I could tell that it was slowing him down but he was fighting through it. All I was doing was stopping Hazel and Ray from helping me. I dropped it and kept backing away.

"They had me locked up for months, you know," Howie said in a conversational tone as he moved toward me. I backed up faster. "And all I could think about, all that time, was you."

"Howie, I was thinking about you too... I..."

"No, no, you don't understand. Not that mushy lovey-dovey stuff. Just lusting for you. For that brain. Every time I got a meal, I'd think how much better *you* would taste. Esurience. Prurience. Cupidity. Concupiscence. Those words describe it better. And now I'll have you."

He darted toward me, and I dodged, but he was faster. He grabbed the edge of my coat.

"Howie. STOP."

Ray and Hazel were shaking themselves awake.

I looked at Howie, at the *thing* in his eyes, and I knew that this was a battle that I couldn't win for him. Howie had to win it himself, and if he couldn't, then that was that. He was faster, stronger. I couldn't resist him.

But maybe resistance wasn't the answer. Maybe it was time to drop the armour.

My pulse pounding in my ears, I knelt on the hard floor.

Howie stopped.

"Okay, I'm here, Howie," I said. "You don't have to fight me. You don't have to throw me down. I'm right here. You're right. You're more powerful than I am. You're faster. So here I am — here's Stella. I'm ready for the taking."

And I saw it — that flicker of the old Howie, and desperate hope kindled in my chest. But then the Howie-thing was back and it licked its lips. "I'm going to relish this."

"And then what?" I was choking with fear, but I didn't move. The cement was cold and hard on my knees. Beyond the shadowy semi-darkness of the room, I could see the birds flying past the Seattle skyline. Was this where I would die? But no, Hazel and Ray were moving toward me. They were coming.

The Howie-thing was still standing there. I hated the Howie-thing. But somewhere under that was Howie. My Howie. And I had to coax him out.

"What then, after you kill me, Howie? What will you do then?" I pushed.

"And then I'll lick every bone clean."

"And I'll be gone, Howie. This mind will be gone. No more Stella. Forever."

Ray and Hazel were hurrying over now and their footsteps filled the room, but Howie didn't turn.

"So," I said. "Which is it going to be, Howie? Come with me, and let us get you better, and we can be together, because I am still hopelessly, desperately, *pathetically* in love with you. I can't love someone else the way I love you — there's only one key to my heart, Howie, and you've got it. I'm so sorry. I'm so sorry I made you feel like you weren't enough. Because you were. You were more than enough. You were everything." Tears were running down my cheeks, and I thought I saw them standing in Howie's eyes, too.

"I don't care if you can't get older, or if you can't learn anything new. I don't care what job you do, or if you do any job at all. I just want *you*, Howie. I want you in my life, loving me, talking to me, being with me. But if that can't happen… if you don't want that anymore… if you want this… then… let's get it over with."

Ray and Hazel were behind him and they had their brain disruptors out. One touch to his temple and Howie would be dead. They looked anguished.

Howie's face contorted. He took a step toward me and I almost broke down. Hazel reached out with her disruptor and turned her face away, her eyes squeezed shut. But before she could make contact, Howie dropped to his knees and looked me full in the face. And the look he gave me was open and familiar. It was the look of the person I loved.

"Stella," he whispered. "I can't bear to be without you."

My world began to turn again and I let out long, shuddering sigh which was almost a laugh. "Then I *really* don't recommend eating me," I said.

Howie took a deep breath. "Raymond Kowalchuk," he said, without turning.

"Yeah, Howie?" Ray's lip was quivering.

"Tie me up again. And make better knots, this time."

Ray wiped his face with his sleeve. "I can do you one better," he said, then he brought his fist down hard on Howie's head.

44

Howie

What is it about the act of kneeling which can break a human heart? And how is it that in a body enhanced by the virus, a body freed of weakness and pain, I could still feel the anguish in my chest which humans call heartache?

And yet here I stood.

There is a period of disorientation after one has been knocked unconscious. When I had struggled to return to wakefulness, I had been lost in an ocean of confusion. Howie Fontaine. Howie Mullins. Music. Poetry. Stella. A red ring. Open skulls. My God. What had I become? Why did I remember the taste of a man's brains on my tongue? I was filled with horror. The truth had been knocked out of me. I couldn't remember how this could have happened. How could I try to kill Stella? Stella… I needed her. Life without her was a bleak thing. And then the longing came over me again and I knew that I was cursed. Not detached enough from humanity to ever be truly free. Too entwined in the virus to ever be released from its truth.

Howard Joseph Fontaine, Howie J. Mullins, whatever you dub this particular body, should end. He should be ended.

Instead, I was thrown into a dark place where I mumbled to myself and dreamed of equations and humanity, of sonnets and songs. When the trunk opened, and the light came flooding in, I was struck by the sight of Stella. Her long hair blew across her face in the ocean breeze. She had blood smeared across her cheek. Her brown eyes made my husk of a heart shudder. If such as I could love, I would love this woman. Everything about her called to me.

And yet, if I drew near her, I knew I would not be able to resist. I must have her. I must. And as they made me walk — where were we? I hardly cared — all I could think about was her. Needing her. And I couldn't remember — why not? Why was I holding back? Why was I letting these strands of fibre bind me? Why was I not filling myself with bliss?

So I had broken free. And she shone her light — oh, it reached right down through me, filled me with quivering anticipation. Simple Ray and Hazel were left behind, lost in it, but I had more power. I simply swelled with esurience. Concupiscence. Voracity.

Mine.

Then she knelt before me, and something within me broke.

Stella, the fighter. Stella, the indomitable. Stella, the magnificent. She who owns each room she enters, she who is built to be queen of every piece of land she treads. She knelt before me, and it broke me.

And yet, the virus hungered for her. Who controlled this body? The human or the virus? We were intertwined. And the need was overpowering. Stopping — stopping was unthinkable.

No. Stopping that brain was unthinkable.

A moment of bliss, and I would never see those eyes, feel that mind, hear that voice. Never again. The thought was a hollow wind through my mind. I remembered the desolation of a world without her. I looked at her warm, welcoming flesh. I looked at her luscious lips, her blooming cheeks, the breasts I longed to caress, the body I needed to possess.

No. No more.

Without her, there was no more purpose to anything. None of the minds in all of Seattle had called to me like hers did. Just the memory of her mind had made me reject one after the other as I fled Brenda Berry and her foolish followers. Then she had shone through us all, and when I felt it, when I felt her, I knew that no somatic memory could approximate the reality which was that mind.

I had run into the feeling of her, and I began to roar as it grew inside me into a thundering and overpowering need. Finally. Finally. It had been so long since I had feasted. For more than twenty-four hours I had moved through the city, dodging Apex, rejecting inferior minds. I was saving myself. Only the best for me. But the power was also draining out of me, and I felt Brenden's mind as he overtook me. I had expected him to pounce, to pin me, but instead, he passed by me, and his brain was as black as mine. I applauded him. Be free, Brenden. Break free.

But then I had seen him holding her, pressing his body on hers, claiming her, and I had exploded in fury. She was mine. Mine.

And now she was surrendered at my feet, tears staining her youthful cheeks, her body bulky under a hooded sweatshirt and winter coat. Yes, I could have her. But as she said, then what? Then nothing. Then no more.

And I realized that I could bear the cravings better than I could bear the emptiness. I could bear anything if it meant more of her. More than one feast, one meal, which would quickly fall into the past as time marched inexorably onward. A mere blip in history, a mere moment of magnificent bliss which would disappear in time. No, I wanted more than that. I wanted more.

So I called to Ray, who understood about weakness. Who had hidden and trembled as his family died, who had been too weak to end their suffering. Raymond, who understood about longing for things that cannot be.

I knew he would save her. He would save me from myself.

And he did.

Stella

I insisted on carrying Howie myself. I scooped him up in my arms like he was a bride and carried my prize – dazed and confused with arms akimbo – out onto the balcony. Ray and Hazel helped me lug him up the metal stairs. A cold marine wind tinged with rain hit my cheek as I walked onto the roof. I scanned the horizon for helicopters, but saw and heard nothing. We laid Howie down.

"Time to do a hog-tie," said Ray, who busied himself with tying the rope around Howie's body, hands and feet as tightly as he could. Howie looked like something you see in a rodeo by the time he was done, and the rope was so tight that I could see it digging into his skin.

"I'm going to try and feed him some of this," said Hazel, pulling a thermos from Ray's backpack. "If he isn't hungry it'll be easier for him."

I started checking my text messages, starting with the ones from my parents. When I saw their texts, the floor seemed to shake under my feet and I sank down to the ground.

Woke up to zombies outside our hotel.
Are you okay?
Stella, answer your phone.
We're scared.
Stopping for weapons then heading up to SFU.
You had better be there, young lady.

Oh, shit, shit, double-fuck shit! I recalled Hunt's urgency. She didn't need me back in Vancouver to *stop* an attack from happening there. It had already happened. And I had missed it. Kate was next.

Woke up to screams, and you were gone
and it really is zombies??

GET BACK HERE.
Going to get Riya

Oh, my God.

I waved my phone at Ray and Hazel.

"Shit, there are zombies in Vancouver, too!"

"But there weren't any attacks," said Hazel, looking shocked.

"Guess there are now," said Ray.

"Zombies in Nova Scotia, too!" I skimmed through my messages with ever-increasing panic. "And now the phones are down and I can't text any of them back. Jesus *fuck*, I left my parents and everyone alone in a zombie apocalypse. The whole fucking world is falling apart and I'm *stuck on a roof in Washington State!*"

"We shouldn't have taken her out of Vancouver, Ray," said Hazel.

"What were we supposed to do?" Ray argued. "Let Howie rot?"

"Yes," said Hazel. "That's what Dad told us to do."

"Fuck that."

I was inclined to agree with Ray, but if my parents and friends were all eaten by zombies, I would never, ever forgive myself. And we didn't even know if Howie would be okay. This might all have been for nothing. He might be dangerous and infectious and wanting to eat me *forever* and Mom and Dad might be *dead.*

In my head, I saw my parents being torn apart and eaten alive while they screamed for me, and my stomach clenched so hard that I doubled over.

Oh God please let my parents be okay. I mean, all of my friends and basically everyone in the whole world too but please please especially my parents. I struggled to take a few deep breaths and try to think rationally. After all, Mom and Dad knew how to handle zombies. And I had told Kate to be prepared, even if she had thought I was making it up. And that B-MOSZ place was there, and so was Hunt.

I just had to get back there, that was all. And that just meant waiting for the helicopter and hoping that hyper-intelligent murder-zombies might not, at this very moment, be rushing toward the pier on which we stood.

Ray saw me looking around nervously.

"We'd feel them coming, Stella," he said, spooning another pink and quivering lump of brains into Howie's drooping mouth. He did it expertly, scraping dribbles of extra food off of Howie's chin and plopping them back into his mouth like a doting parent spoon-feeding his baby. "Howie and them make regular zombies feel cozy. We'll feel em. We'll know if they get close."

So I read and re-read through all of my texts as we waited, shivering, for someone to turn up either to rescue us or kill us. There was only one person whose messages I didn't read: Dean. I wasn't ready to think about Dean being eaten by zombies while Howie lay tied up at my feet. I was already in so much emotional turmoil that I had pretty much shut down my whole autonomic nervous system and was feeling a strange sort of numbness to everything. Stand here. Shiver. Read pleas from my parents that I can't answer. Listen for helicopter.

When the iconic choppa-choppa-choppa sound of a helicopter finally reached our ears, we all looked up at once.

"There," I pointed. It was coming from the North. That was a good sign. It was a bright yellow search-and-rescue type… encouraging… it was definitely heading right toward us… could be good or bad depending on who was inside… We watched and shaded our eyes, trying to see better. Yes — there was the word Canada. I had never felt so relieved to see that little flag over the word Canada. That simple government logo looked like safety. It looked like home.

The wind from the rotor blades whipped my hair everywhere as the helicopter landed just a few feet away from us. As soon as it touched down on the roof, a black-suited figure jumped out of it. I tensed for a moment, then recognized the warm brown skin and stern expression of Agent Hunt.

"You came *yourself*?" I blurted.

"I trust me," she shouted over the sound of the helicopter. She did not look pleased to see me. "And this way I can fill you in on the way back, so it saves time. Get in."

"Can you tell me to get in da choppa?"

"Why is Howie tied up?" she said, ignoring me and dashing my hopes for the coolest life memory ever. For a split second, I missed Dean. Dean would have told me to get in da choppa.

"We'll explain later," grunted Ray, hoisting Howie up. I ran to help, and we carried Howie over to the helicopter and dumped him in. Then I climbed in and nodded hello to the two pilots. Ray and Hazel climbed in next, and Agent Hunt jumped in and pulled the door shut.

"Strap in!" she ordered us. I could tell she wasn't feeling happy with us. I grabbed a seat near the front so I could talk to her, while Ray and Hazel took seats near the back. Howie lay prone in the large open centre of the chopper, which I guess is where stretchers or dead zombies were supposed to go.

"Uh… do you have any strong ropes or chains, by the way?" I said, speaking loudly over the noise.

Hunt glared at me. "Yes. Do we need them?"

"I don't know. But better safe than sorry, right?"

"If that boy is dangerous, we need to leave him here. I can't have an aggressive and infectious zombie trapped in a helicopter with the only person who might be able to help get the situation in Vancouver under control."

The pilots looked around at the words, "aggressive and infectious".

I folded my arms. "He had two chances to kill me already, and he didn't use them. He *asked* to be tied up."

"Stella, he killed a man. I saw a video of it. Howie Mullins would never kill an innocent person. That isn't Howie anymore."

"Hello, Agent Hunt," said Howie from the floor. His eyes were open, but he didn't try to sit up. "How are you?"

"I've been better, Howie," she said, looking startled. "I woke up to a worldwide outbreak."

"Yes, and I know a lot about it. It started in the hospitals, right? In every major city?"

She looked wary. "Right."

"And you're having trouble contacting the military bases. Communications are down. Power is out. No response from government."

"Yes."

"The major news channels broadcasted for a couple of hours, reporting an organization called Apex which was claiming a new world order, and then they went silent."

"Yes."

"Have you discovered that Leanne Wilson is an informant for Apex?"

"What?" we all shouted.

"Doc's assistant?" Ray said.

"Kate's MOM?" I said at the same time. Then I whirled and looked at Ray. "What do you mean, Doc's assistant? She isn't his assistant!"

"Yes she is," said Hunt. "She's worked for The Service for over two years now."

"SHE WHAT?"

"She's the one who released the hamster," said Howie. His voice was clear and calm, and just loud enough to be heard over the helicopter's racket. "She thinks Apex is an anti-zombie group and that Morton Mullins is part of a plot."

"Am I taking off?" asked the pilot.

Howie and Hunt looked steadily at each other.

"Whose side are you on, Howie?" Hunt asked. "Are you one of us, or one of them?"

Howie paused and closed his eyes. "Both," he said. "And neither. Lock me up and I'll tell you everything I know."

Hunt tapped her fingers on the side of the vehicle for a moment. Then she pulled a metal baton out of a holster. It looked like a giant-dildo version of the small brain disruptors that Ray and Hazel had. She tapped it on her thigh menacingly as she looked at Howie and turned to the pilot. "Liftoff," she said.

The helicopter lurched and rose into the air. I looked out the window as it turned back toward the North, and I could see Howie's rusted little blue car sitting at the side of the road where we left it. It looked so small and alone, and I felt bad for abandoning it. Then I saw three human figures come racing down the road. One leaped right over the car. They were heading for the Cruise Terminal. A huge horde was lurching not far behind them.

"Just in time," I heard Ray mutter to Hazel.

The figures grew smaller as we rose higher, and in a minute we had left them behind forever.

Hunt gave me a headset that covered my ears in two gigantic foam cushions and immediately relieved the sound of the helicopter. By speaking into the attached microphones, Hunt and I could talk. Howie and his family just had to sit there, but they didn't seem to mind. Ray and Hazel dozed off, she with her head on Ray's shoulder and he with his head on hers. Howie lay on the floor. He was staring into space, but I had the feeling that he was hearing every word that Hunt and I were saying to each other.

I asked about my parents the moment I had the headset over my ears.

"Are my parents okay? Did they turn up at B-MOSZ?"

"The entire city is in chaos, Stella. We have some armoured vehicles and a couple of transport trucks at our disposal, as well as some weapons, but we need more. We've been trying to contact the military base at Chilliwack, but communications keep going down and they can't reach Ottawa for orders. We're collaborating with local police and RCMP, but the hordes are overwhelming. The situation is completely out of hand."

"Can I lure all the zombies to an area, maybe outside of the downtown, so you can, like, bomb them or something?"

"Well, first of all, unless we get a proper channel of communication open with the military, we won't have any access to bombs. Second of all, this is not like two years ago, when you were able to lure a hundred zombies to one spot. We're dealing with a hundred times that many, maybe more. All you would do is make an inescapable wall of zombies move through the downtown core, combing out everyone in their path."

"Jesus. So, what, we're helpless? There's nothing to be done?"

"Nonsense. Now that I have *you,* we can get something done. We are no longer in outbreak management phase. We are in a loss-minimization phase. That means we need to retreat to B-MOSZ. If you can actually stop the hordes so we can rescue people and clear a path up to Burnaby Mountain, we have some hope of survival."

Survival. She wasn't talking about stopping this. She was talking about *surviving* this.

"That's step one. Get our staff out of the downtown core, clear a path to B-MOSZ, and start rescue operations."

"And step two?"

"Salvage supplies. Build up defences. Enact the thirty-year survival plan that they drew up in the sixties."

"You're seriously accepting that this is the end of the world?"

"I'd be delighted to be wrong."

We were silent for a moment while I tried to process the enormity of her words.

"Well," I said. "At least Baum knows he was wrong. The American government didn't plan *this.*"

She raised her eyebrows. "Let's save the I-told-you-so's for later. Where did you find Howie?"

"I didn't. He found me. All I had to do was stand in a park and wait for him."

"Hmm." She eyed him, and he turned his head and met her gaze steadily. "Pass over your headset. I need to talk to him."

Howie

What was I doing here? I stared at my bound feet and hands and tried to think clearly. I had been free. Why had I not feasted when I had the chance? It was her. Even now, her mind thrummed through me, more powerful than the vibration from their foolish flying machine.

While I had lain unconscious, my neurons had fired at random and sent me visions of sunny days spent with her head in my lap, the smell of rose petals, the taste of her skin.

Now I was lying bound on the floor of this helicopter. My stomach was full, and the taste of cold pork brains lingered on my tongue. They must have force fed me, and I was both disgusted and grateful. My brain housed two minds. One was Howard Mullins, moralistic prig, and the other was the virus, swirling with the need. The battle between us was breaking me apart. The only thing we both agreed on was that it was better to be in Stella's presence than out of it. And so I must cooperate with Michaella Hunt in her feeble efforts to reclaim some part of her city, because where she went, Stella would go too.

Besides, Apex would be coming for Stella. And they could not have her. She was mine.

Hunt told Stella to pass over the headset, so she could hear me comfortably above the roar of the helicopter's whirling rotors. Our eyes met as Stella placed it on my head. She looked unhappy and confused. She should be. Did she think we could go back to how it was? Back before I tasted the truth? She was wrong. I couldn't be without her, but I couldn't be Howard Mullins again, either.

I didn't know what I was. But I knew she wouldn't like it.

Hunt spoke to me through her headset, although my senses, still sharp, did not need the electronic speakers to carry her soundwaves to my ears.

"I need to know everything about Apex. I need to know their plans. I need to know what they will do in my city. I need to know how to bring them down. And I need you to tell me now. Do that, and maybe I won't push you right out of the helicopter."

"Would you really murder a teenage boy whom you've known since you were in your twenties? And you owe me, Michaella."

"The Howie Mullins I knew wouldn't kill a person. And I saw you kill."

"You saw me put someone out of their misery," I said. "Howie Mullins always was prone to moralistic thinking. The screaming was too much."

"Did you join Apex of your own volition?"

"Yes. I did it at the request of George Baum, for moralistic reasons."

"And are they really people who have used your father's discoveries?"

"Yes. A woman named Brenda Berry, who was working as a secretary at the time, found poorly-guarded papers reporting the Mullins protocol of consuming brains and injecting the body with formaldehyde to halt the progress of the Z0381E virus, as well as its side effect of delaying the ageing process. She also found reports regarding his subsequent discovery that consuming human brains, instead of those of domestic animals, resulted in hyper-intelligence and hyper-strength."

"And hyper-aggression and early infectivity," said Hunt with a frown.

"Yes. That did not appear to trouble her."

Hunt sighed. "A *secretary*. Decades of secrecy and some idiot leaves important papers on his desk."

"I believe he actually asked her to file them," I said. "She told me her story several times. She seemed quite proud of it."

Hunt sighed more heavily. "So, you went undercover, since you're already part of the Mullins protocol."

"Yes. But I refused to taste human brains, for moralistic reasons. That was a mistake. I was too stupid to outwit them. They caught me and forced me to see the error of my ways."

"So why are you here, Howie?" her dark eyes stared at me, and I could feel her mind churning. Hunt always did have a nice mind. Not on par with Stella's, but sharp. Clear. Morton, in particular, had always enjoyed being near Hunt's mind. He said it was like a drink of cold water on a hot day.

"Because Stella is here," I answered. "So long as you have her, you have my cooperation. Apex holds nothing for me."

"Then tell me. What can we do to bring Apex down?"

"Wait. Apex thinks that they can find a balance — enjoy the higher intelligence, the power, and immortality, but maintain a sense of human organization and complex society. But in order to do that, they must restrain themselves to one helping of human brains per week."

"And you don't think they can do that?"

"No," I said simply. "The craving is too strong. One by one, bit by bit, they will break. All over the world, Apex had storage facilities full of those who broke."

"And now they're rampaging through the cities, is that right?"

"Yes. Helping to spread infection. Apex's army. But they will not side with Apex. They have seen further. They know that organized society, electricity, internet, satellites — that all of that is irrelevant and insignificant."

"So you think that Apex will fall because one by one they'll all eat too much and go bonkers?" Hunt said impatiently.

"Yes. Besides, Brenda Berry, the founder, is lying dead in Seattle with a cleaver in her skull."

Hunt raised her eyebrows. "Thanks to Stella?"

"Thanks to me."

"So you think we can defeat Apex? You think we can stop the outbreak?"

"No. As we speak, the infection is being spread through the governments of every nation. Undead hordes are clogging the highways. Intelligent, ravaging madmen like me are rampaging through the cities. And Apex is following their protocol for A-Day. Satellites are down. You won't be able to contact Ottawa, and even if you could, there will be no one there to answer you. Apex infiltrated The Service. Apex infiltrated the government. The only branch of The Service not infiltrated was yours, because Morton would have recognized them for what they were. Our brain waves are… startling. Apex had to keep to the outskirts of the city, well away from Morton. Only by fooling Leanne Wilson were they able to get the feeblest foothold into your staff. So you are already in a unique position because Apex has less of a hold on Vancouver than any other major city. And you have Stella."

"What will they be trying to do?"

"They will commandeer military equipment from the base in Chilliwack, which they have infiltrated. They will try to claim large, central buildings, such as the sports stadiums, hospitals, airports. And if they feel Stella coming, they will try to get to her. And we must stop them." I reclined on the floor of the helicopter and closed my eyes for a minute to enjoy the turmoil of Stella's mind. Even now, frightened and confused and tired, she was a pleasure to be near. "Their army — the failed recruits, the people like me who want to be free of Apex's rules, who have eaten too much, seen too far — they will be storming the streets, eating their fill and spreading disease. The dead will everywhere, attacking and feeding. People will flee in fear. They'll gather at community locations, in Walmarts and town halls. And Apex will let it happen. They want some people to survive. They'll need to eat. But they will also want to take control." I opened my eyes and looked toward Stella. "And for her sake, I recommend that you get control."

45

Stella

I strained to hear Hunt and Howie's conversation over the sound of the chopper, but mostly I was reading lips. I thought he was telling her to forget the Army base. He also said the word "Apex" several times, and something about football? No, that couldn't be right. I lost the thread of the conversation and found myself just focusing on the look of his lips — the lips that I longed to kiss. Would I ever kiss them again? It was safe to assume that he was ragingly contagious. Maybe that would last forever. Maybe he would never be the same. Maybe I had abandoned my parents and friends, possibly leaving them to their deaths, so I could rescue someone who was just the shell of the person I loved.

Or maybe this was all moot because I might be killed by zombies soon anyway.

Hunt finally beckoned to me, and I reached out and reclaimed the headset from Howie. His expression was detached and analyzing. It wasn't the Howie who wanted to kill me, but it wasn't the old Howie, either. He didn't move as I lifted the headset off and replaced it onto my head.

"I'm still furious with you for taking off," said Hunt, "but Howie may prove very useful. Assuming he is telling the truth."

"Yeah, assuming that," I said.

"He claims that the military bases are lost — that Apex will take control of those first. He has warned us to abandon our headquarters and says that they will create bases for themselves out of the sports complexes, since they are large, easy to defend, and can house a lot of military vehicles and weaponry inside. He makes a good point — BC Place would be very useful for keeping helicopters, for example, since they can open and close the roof."

"So what are you going to do?"

"I'm going to follow his most sensible suggestions to start. I'll call back the team I sent out to Chilliwack and tell them to start commandeering trucks from construction yards instead. We will use you to liberate emergency response crews, police, and as many survivors as possible, guard against Apex, and clear a path to B-MOSZ. From there, we will slowly widen the safety zone around B-MOSZ. We'll try to send out emergency radio signals telling the public to move toward Burnaby Mountain, but with the power out I don't know how many will hear it." She pointed at me. "You will be at the forefront, freezing hordes so we can clear paths."

I nodded. I wanted to ask her if we could look for my parents, but I knew what she would say — she'd say that we couldn't let more people die while I ran around looking for my mother and father. And she would be right. So I kept my mouth shut.

I glanced at Howie. He was looking out the window. Even though he was sitting close to me, he seemed very far away.

"We're approaching Vancouver," announced the co-pilot after a while. I craned my head out the window and looked down on familiar snowcapped mountains with clouds wrapped around them like scarves. I looked down on the ocean waves, grey and choppy. And as the chopper moved over the skyscrapers of the downtown core, I looked down on the end of the world.

I saw snarls of traffic, looters carrying things out of stores, and mobs of slow-moving, shuffling zombies clogging the roads. I saw people running, people falling, people being eaten. I saw the city that I had finally learned to love falling apart beneath me.

Hunt was speaking rapidly into her radio but I could only hear her end of the conversation. She was ordering a retreat, telling them where to meet up, and using a lot of jargon that I didn't understand. Then she turned to me.

"Stella, I'm going to need you to freeze as many of these zombies as you can, so we can start clearing a path. How long do you think you can hold it for?"

"I guess we'll find out," I said. "I've never held it for more than twenty minutes or so, but lab practice is one thing. A real-life situation might actually be easier because it'll feel more urgent, if that makes sense."

She looked grim. "Let's hope so."

"But the thing is — my freeze only works on the regular zombies. The shuffling dead kind. The half-zombies, the Apex guys that are all hopped up on human brains? It doesn't work right on them. It throws them off for a second. That's it."

Hunt frowned. "Well. If we can get the dead ones out of the way, that will free us up to deal with the living ones."

The helicopter descended until we were hovering over a zombie battle scene in the middle of downtown. Police cars were sitting at crazy angles in the road, lights flashing, while a horde pressed around them and cops tried to shoot from behind their vehicles.

"Do it, Stella," Hunt said.

I was startled. "What? From here?"

"Do you expect us to be able to land down there? Not to mention that Apex will be trying to kill you. So yes, see if you can do it from here."

"I'll try…"

I saw Howie hunch up, and Ray and Hazel got down on the ground with him and held him tightly. I looked down at the zombies pressing in on the police.

Make way. Make way for me!

I projected the feeling as strongly as I could. I thought of all the innocent people, trying to escape. I thought about Kate, and my parents, and Dean, all surrounded by the horde.

Make way, you assholes. Make way.

And below me, the zombies froze. It took a moment for the cops to figure out what was happening, but I saw them straighten up and climb over their car hoods and start whopping the zombies in the heads with their batons. Hunt picked up a loudspeaker and pulled the helicopter door open.

"This state is temporary. Please make the most of it. Clear a path toward Burnaby Mountain. Repeat: make your way to Burnaby Mountain."

The cops jumped in their cars and turned on their sirens. And I watched people move aside for them. I saw men get out of their cars to knock frozen zombies out of the way so the emergency vehicles could get through. I saw vehicles full of desperate people all trying to escape the zombie apocalypse and they still wiggled onto the sidewalk, pulled themselves over, to make way for the police. And I remembered what Howie had said once, about it being beautiful, and I finally understood.

Looking through the window, I could see zombies frozen in every direction. I strained myself to be as 'loud' as I could, and it seemed to be working. The helicopter kept pace with the police cars, moving slowly East toward Burnaby Mountain while I tried to project every shred of power and confidence left in me. I wanted to freeze the whole city — give everyone a chance.

Howie moaned. Ray and Hazel, who had zoned out, shook their heads and tried to tighten their grips on him. Hunt eyed him and held up her dildo baton. But Howie didn't move. He closed his eyes and took deep breaths.

"Residents of Vancouver!" shouted Hunt, going back to her loudspeaker. "Our control over the situation is temporary. Repeat, this is temporary. Please make the most of it. Get to safety. If possible, make your way to Burnaby Mountain, where you will find a safe zone. Arm yourselves. Aim for the head. And avoid bites at all costs."

Make way. Make way for everyone.

I pressed my face against the window, watching helplessly. I saw people step out of buildings with knives and baseball bats and start swinging at the zombies in the horde. I saw cars driving on the sidewalk to get around jams, knocking zombies out of the way as they went. I saw bikers weave their way through everything, protected by their armour. I saw people pedalling their bikes through confused hordes who shuffled out of their way.

Make way. Make way. Make way.

Hunt alternated between speaking into her radio, issuing orders, co-ordinating groups of people, and shouting out of the loudspeaker. The helicopter slowly drifted up Hastings street, where I saw tow vehicles clearing aside crashed cars so the other cars could get through. Firetrucks moved up side streets, heading East. Clear roads got marked with ribbons on their street signs. Blocked roads were marked with pylons. Cops abandoned their cars in places where they just couldn't get free and went to go meet up with other cars on clearer streets.

"There are my agents," said Hunt, pointing. I saw a couple of armoured Humvees trapped in a traffic jam on Lougheed. Agents in black riot gear were swinging things that looked like Hunt's dildo-baton and taking down zombies left and right.

We were nearing Burnaby Mountain. I could see SFU ahead of us, shining on the top of the mountain. Were my parents there?

Then Howie sat up suddenly. Ray and Hazel jerked awake and grabbed him tighter. Howie turned to Hunt with blazing eyes. "Land."

"What?" Hunt said. I put the headset on Howie's head.

"Land!" Howie shouted. "Land this instantly!"

The co-pilot said something. Howie responded. Then the pilot pointed out the window and moved the controls. The helicopter tilted sharply and swerved to the right and started to descend.

Hunt strapped herself back into her seat. I was already strapped in. Ray and Hazel were just moving into their seats when there was a massive boom and the whole helicopter shook. It dropped steeply and spun in the air like a carnival ride. I couldn't help but shriek. The pilots were shouting to each other and the engine cut out. We stopped spinning, but we plunged downward in what was not quite a free fall but certainly wasn't a comfortable speed of descent. I saw Howie stand and throw off his ropes and handcuffs like they weren't even there. He leaped toward me. Then there was a jarring crash which I felt all the way to my core.

Howie

Before the helicopter even hit the ground, I was snapping my restraints and rising from the floor. I don't know whether I was hoping or fearing that Stella would be killed in the crash. Sometimes we can fantasize about things which would be nightmares if they became true. Because as much as I still craved her, I knew now — that it was better to be craving her than living a life devoid of her. If she died in the crash I would get a feast — but then what else could ever compare to that? What else could life hold for me? What satisfaction would I get, and from whom, and where?

Even as I reflected on these things, I was bracing myself over her. I had forgotten the warmth of her body, the smell of her hair, the pink of her lips. My heightened senses picked up on everything as the helicopter spun softly into the ground, and disintegrated around us.

I thought Stella might be knocked unconscious by the impact, but she wasn't. Her fear shot through me and she was obviously dazed and shocked by the jarring crash, but she remained strapped in her seat as the helicopter crumpled against the Earth. Before she had even fully grasped what happened, I ripped her buckle loose and pulled her free. The door of the helicopter — still open — was now the ceiling and I leaped upwards, Stella in my arms, and deposited her on the grass. The helicopter had crashed on the edge of a grass field. Panicked people ran past us. In the distance I could hear snarls and screams as the shuffling dead, their minds echoing with the brainwaves of their prey.

The crash had distracted Stella, and they were free to move once more.

"Run," I told Stella. "Before it catches fire."

"But the others…" she said.

"I'll get the others. Go!"

Why did I say that? What impulse was sending me back inside the helicopter? Yet I went. Hunt was alive, although she was pinned by the buckled hull of the helicopter. I bent it back and pulled her free, then turned to Ray and Hazel. I tossed Hazel up through the doorway, but Ray brushed me off and climbed out himself. Then I moved to the pilots… and I paused.

The pilot was dead. His brain waves were gone, and I could smell his blood through the stench of smoke and fuel. The flames from the tail of the helicopter would soon cover everything. I could taste… have a sample… no one would know. I hadn't had any for a day… two…? I reached forward and ripped off his helmet. Then I heard the moan from the copilot. His brain waves were faint, but he was alive. I hesitated. The flames were growing. And while I yearned to taste the pilot, my stomach was full of the foul pig product that Ray and Hazel had forced down my throat. To my own surprise, I found myself grabbing the copilot and lifting him free of his harness. I jumped out of the helicopter with him in my arms and within seconds flames had consumed the cockpit.

Ray and Hazel were waiting, but Stella and Hunt were gone. I turned my head left and right, feeling for her.

"What happened?" Hazel asked, staring at the helicopter.

"Apex brought it down," I said, striding past them, the pilot hanging limp in my arms. "They know Stella is here. They're coming for her. Can't you feel them?"

But their senses were duller than mine — dulled by decades of a domesticated animal diet.

"She went to help fight the horde," Ray said, gesturing, but I was already on my way. I could see a cluster of police, CRVCS agents, and emergency response vehicles in the road. Civilians were running to them, getting pulled down by the dead as they ran, and then others would run past them while the dead stopped to feed. I resisted the urge to join them. It was a powerful, powerful urge, and my feet slowed despite myself.

A wave of ecstasy passed through me as Stella once again immobilized the horde. When she wanted to, she could own the world, and even the dead stopped to pay attention. It's hard to walk while in bliss, but I kept moving. She was like a beacon in the night, a lighthouse on the shore, like a siren luring sailors to their death. Apex would find her instantly.

She was standing on top of a police car with her back to me. Her mind threatened to sweep me up in its radiance. The horde fell one by one as agents swung their disrupter batons, police officers placed tasers to their heads, and civilians swung axes, baseball bats, knives, and gardening tools. I strode through it all, dumped the co-pilot in front of a paramedic, and grabbed Hunt by the elbow. She raised her baton at me but I blocked her arm mid-swing.

"Apex is coming," I said. "Follow me. Bring weapons."

Stella

I didn't know this Howie. His eyes were so cold and calculating, his pose confident and almost predatory. It scared me. I clung to the memory of his face when he knelt in front of me on that pier in Seattle. *That* had looked like the Howie I knew. Howie was in there somewhere.

"How do you know they're on their way?" Hunt asked. "And how close do you think they are?"

"Close. And they have artillery. They shot down the helicopter. Stella needs to quiet her mind."

Oh. I looked around. Yeah, most of the zombies nearby were knocked out. I dropped my freeze.

"How did you know they were about to shoot us down?" Hunt demanded.

"I could feel them," he said.

Howie turned to me. "We can stop them, but you'll have to come with me. And you'll have to trust me."

I looked at Howie, at his cool blue eyes, and the lips I used to love to kiss. Would I ever see his sweet, dimpled smile again?

I wasn't sure I trusted him. I wasn't sure how much of my Howie was in there. But if there was even a scrap of him left, I didn't think he would let himself hurt me. God knows he'd had enough chances by now.

Mind you, all it would take for him to hurt me would be a fleck of his spit into my eyes or mouth or something. Next thing you knew, I'd be dead and lumbering down the street in search of brains.

"Tell me what I have to do." I pointed a finger at Howie. "But stay the *fuck* away from me and my mucous membranes."

And then, just for a moment, I saw it: A flicker, slight dimpling of his cheek — a hint of a smile. A hint of the old Howie.

"I promise," he said.

46

Howie

I heard Hunt shouting to people, selecting her back-up, but my eyes were drawn to Stella alone.

"We need to arrive first," I told her. "Follow me. And stay quiet while I talk to them."

"I'm not good at quiet. Can I whisper sarcastic commentary?"

I ignored her, but for the second time in moments, I felt the urge to laugh. When had I last laughed? A memory came to me of play-fighting with Stella in a field and being easily beaten. How the tables had turned.

"When I tell you to, I want you to use your mind. But not before. Do you understand?"

"Of course I understand," she said irritably. "What I don't understand is why you and I are going first."

"You'll see." I didn't have the patience to translate my plan into simple human words. My self-control was already strained close to the snapping point. I moved swiftly, and I could hear the sound of Stella's feet jogging behind me.

One block, two… and there they were.

The tank had the word APEX painted in white upon it. Two members walked before it, minds boiling with darkness, tossing aside cars and other debris to clear a path down Lougheed Highway toward us. More followed behind bearing military automatic rifles.

"Deliver Stella Blunt and we will let you live!" announced a woman's voice through a loudspeaker. She was standing in the tank, and she could see us approaching. "Deliver Stella Blunt, and we will allow you resume your recovery efforts."

"I have Blunt," I shouted. "I have her here." I pinned her hands behind her back.

"Howie, what the fuck..." she struggled and I could feel her panicking. Good. I kept walking.

The two in front looked surprised, and then confused, as they sensed my brain waves. They could feel my mind. They knew I was one of them — not dead, yet not alive, and thrumming with the knowledge from the forbidden fruit.

So they held their fire as I strolled into their midst. I brought Stella right toward the tank, right under the turret of the gun, and turned to the men who walked before it.

"I've got her," I said. "Can you resist her?"

Before they could answer, I released her, grabbed the two men and smashed their heads together with all of my strength. They crumpled at my feet. Stella stared.

"Now," I told her as guns aimed toward us.

And she shone out. I was drowning in it, but I was also prepared and so even as I revelled I was leaping onto the tank itself. Stella's mind intensified and it was slowing them, distracting them, as I reached into the turret.

"But you're one of us," said the woman in confusion.

"Brenda Berry is dead. Apex is falling," I said.

"You're the one who has fallen," she snarled, and she reached for her gun. I snatched it from her hands and threw it down to Stella. I could see the tank driver looking up at me — instead of at the road ahead.

That's right. Don't look to see what's coming.

Hunt and her team stormed down the street, but Apex didn't see — they were dazzled by Stella and distracted by me. I pulled the woman and one of the men out onto the top of the tank.

"Open fire!" bellowed Hunt. A bullet hit me, and more bullets hit the other two, but none could hurt us. I heard Hunt shouting for them to aim for the heads. I assume she wasn't concerned about my own head. I saw Stella ducking out of the way, crouching in the shadow of the tank as Apex battled The Service.

Apex was stronger and faster, but they were fewer, and their attention was commandeered by Stella. They were felled within moments by Hunt's expertly trained team.

With some effort and luck, I toppled the driver off of the tank, and one of Hunt's agents struck him with a disruptor baton. I grabbed the woman and pulled her right off of the tank. We landed on the tarmac and rolled. She struggled but she could not break my grip.

Hunt approached her. "Surrender, agree to inform on Apex, and we will let you live."

"Never," said the woman, trying uselessly to twist free of me. I had fed more recently. I was stronger. She spat a virus-laden gob onto Hunt's cheek, narrowly missing her eye. "We are superior. You're already doomed."

"Pity," said Hunt, and she brought her disruptor baton down on the woman's head. I let go just in time to avoid getting shocked by the electric current.

Hunt carefully wiped her cheek clean with her sleeve. I was already turning to Stella, returning to Stella, because I would always return to Stella. I was a moth to her flame. She trapped me, ensnared me. I was hers.

She was walking away, bending over to pick something up. And there was something running toward her. A darkness that I longed to join, an evil revelry. *Yes, give in. Yes, enjoy.*

But even as I thought it, even as I longed for it, my feet were devouring the ground. I sailed into the air just in time to smash into the two men who pounced toward Stella. The three of us landed with a crunch on the road and we rolled in broken glass as we grappled.

I was filled with an unendurable rage. Stella's allure was blinding at this close proximity, but these two were brimming with power and her mind only urged them on. They struggled to free themselves from my grasp, desperate to reach Stella.

"No!" I shouted. I knew that their bodies thrummed with the same unbearable bliss as mine — the bliss which begged to be satisfied. And these two were not like the ones I had just fought. They were beyond Apex. They had indulged too far. And that meant they were stronger.

I found myself pressed into the tarmac as one knelt on my chest and the other grabbed me by my hair. Their faces were covered in dried blood, their eyes wild. They were full and fresh. I should have had the pilot. I should have had him. I was weakening. I was dead.

I heard shouting.

Then their skulls caved in.

Stella was standing over me, panting and furious, clutching the gun. She pounded the heads of both of the attackers with the butt of the gun like a frustrated child with two pinatas.

I stared.

"Well I don't know how to fucking use a gun, do I?" she snapped. "Are there any more coming? Are there more of those fuckers?"

I pulled myself away from her.

"More will come. You're calling them," I gasped, and I curled face-down on the bloodied street, trying to keep myself under control. "You're calling *me*."

"Oh. Sorry."

The ecstatic vibration subsided to a bearable and delectable thrum, but all I could do was lie there, curled in a ball, trying to resist the need. Howie Mullins, such as was left of him, was fading. I was the virus. I *was* the need. I couldn't take it anymore. Why was I resisting? I couldn't remember.

I leaped to my feet.

"Oh, no you don't," said Hunt, and everything went black.

Stella

Hunt moved faster than I could think when Howie jumped to his feet, eyes blazing. She smacked him with her electric baton and his arms and legs flew out as if he were doing a jumping-jack and he collapsed onto the ground.

My heart nearly stopped along with his.

"NO!" I stared at Howie's body and the ground seemed to tilt under my feet. I roared at Hunt. "How *dare* you kill him? He saved your fucking LIFE." I advanced on her and she blinked and took a step back. But Ray and Hazel were grabbing my arms.

"He's not dead," Hazel said. "Stella, she didn't kill him."

"She… she didn't?" I looked down at Howie. God, he looked like himself when he was unconscious. Which was weird, because until today, I had never even seen him unconscious. We had never slept together. So strange that I had done so much more with Dean, like literally sleeping together, and yet my time with Howie had felt way more intimate.

"He's really alive?" I looked to Hunt for confirmation.

"Yes, I just tapped his body with the disruptor," she said. "That would kill a normal person, but for Howie, it's just a nap. I'd need to hit him in the skull to do any damage."

"Okay… okay, but seriously what the fuck?" I said, my voice high pitched.

"He's dangerous, Stella. He's not himself. He's been useful, but I want to get him to the safe zone and have him locked up." Hunt looked around. "Can anyone drive a tank?"

I got to ride in the tank. I would've been pretty excited by how bad-ass that was, but I'd already killed a bunch of zombies — living and dead — rescued my ex-boyfriend, taken a helicopter ride, and survived a helicopter crash so I think my bad-assery was maxed for the day. I ached like fuck and really just wanted to sit down anywhere. I was so tired and overwhelmed and I felt like I just *couldn't* anymore.

Hunt looked like she felt the same way.

"Does anyone have spare armour?" she asked. "I want to suit Stella up immediately."

"I've got an extra set in the Humvee," said a stocky agent named Andrea Kim. "But isn't she going to ride in the tank?"

"I don't want to take any chances," said Hunt. "I have three types of zombies attacking my city at once, and all of them seem to be looking for her."

"Come here, Blunt," said Agent Kim, beckoning. I went to her car and she pulled out a bundle of chest plates, arm and leg coverings, and a big shielded helmet. "This is anti-zombie armour," she said, as she turned me around and buckled something in the back.

"It looks like standard riot gear."

"Well, it is, mostly," she said. "But it says CRVCS on it, so it's anti-zombie armour. We don't do riots."

"Gotcha."

"Here's a disruptor baton," she said, handing me one of the electric dildos. "Hit the infected body in the head while pressing this button and it'll go down. You have to hit it on the head to kill it, though, or finish it off with something else. DO NOT touch anyone else or yourself with it while the button is depressed."

"Double gotcha."

"Now get in the tank," said Hunt, "before another wave of super-zombies or more Apex people arrive."

"We need a better name than super-zombies," said Agent Kim.

"That's what I said!" I held up a hand for a high five. She slapped my hand and we exchanged a smile. Look at me, making friends with thirty-year-old women in the middle of a zompocalypse.

"Get *in*, Stella," said Hunt again. "I'm hoping the tank will shield your brain waves a bit. Muffle you." She rubbed her temples. "The good news is that Apex cleared a nice path down Lougheed Highway so hopefully we can get to B-MOSZ that much faster. They were probably on their way to attack my agents there when they felt you and turned around. I'll call you out if we hit a big horde and we need you to stop them. Just… stay quiet in there for now, okay?"

I nodded and climbed into the tank. Reclining comfortably in the driver's seat was a woman in CVRCS uniform who introduced herself as Agent Fatima Tehrani.

"Before I worked for The Service I did a stint on the Sinai Peninsula," she said. "So I guess now I'm the resident tank driver. You can call me Fatima."

"Stella," I said, offering my hand and then pulling it back when I realized that it was crusted in zombie blood.

"I know who you are," she said with a smile. "I've been guarding you for months."

"You have?" I looked at her again. "Oh, shit, I know you. I passed you on my way to class every morning. You always had a cup of coffee."

"Guilty." She dug in her coat. "Here, have a wet wipe. That blood could be infectious."

"You're a lifesaver." I rubbed the blood off of my hands and she helped me clean my face.

"Well, I was just about to be eaten alive when your helicopter arrived and you stopped the attack," she said. "So you *literally* saved my life."

"Call it even," I said, and I leaned my head back in my seat. When we got to B-MOSZ, would they let me sleep? Fuck, how could I think about sleeping? The world was fucking ending and I was the only one who could stop zombies in their tracks. And my parents, and my friends — what if they weren't at B-MOSZ? What if they were out there somewhere… in this?

What if I had lost everyone I loved? Including Howie?

"Oh, shit," said Fatima.

"What?" I leaned forward.

"Yeah. Don't get comfy. I think Hunt's going to pull you out again pretty soon."

Hunt did pull me out, again and again. The path that Apex had cleared to bring their tank toward us had made a lovely corridor for all of the zombies trapped on the road. Some were still trapped in their cars — had probably died trying to escape — but many more had smashed the windshields and were climbing out, or had been bitten on the road while running away.

And it's not that The Service's agents couldn't handle some zombies. It's that people kept calling for help. And how could we not help?

So when we found a horde clustered around a car with a crying, living, person inside, of course, we had to stop. Hunt would call me out of the tank and I would freeze the zombies and Ray or Hazel — immune and fearless — would walk through them and get the people out.

The ones who were weak or injured got loaded onto a truck or put into some other vehicle. The ones who felt strong enough walked behind our convoy, which moved at a snail's pace as we checked for survivors along our path.

One guy refused to come with us when Hunt said he had to leave his french bulldog behind.

"What the hell?" I said to Hunt. "The guy's probably lost his whole family. Let him keep his damn dog."

"We can't accommodate dogs in an underground facility," said Hunt.

Andrea Kim cleared her throat. "The protocol does say to prioritize survivor morale. Don't pets improve morale?"

"But there's no *protocol* for dogs in B-MOSZ," said Hunt in exasperation.

Five minutes later the guy and his dog were on the truck, and Agent Kim had a smug expression on her face.

Hunt kept shoving me back in the tank in between stops because Ray and Hazel said it muffled my brain waves pretty well. That, and the fact that I was so exhausted that I nearly dozed off a few times. My head was splitting and I was starting to stagger. I hadn't eaten since those pancakes at dawn, which I now realized might be the last meal I would ever eat in a restaurant.

Because seriously, the world was fucked.

The more I saw, the more I fully grasped that the world was just, like, *over*. Power lines lying on the grass. Bodies lying in the street. Limbs that didn't belong to anyone. Open heads with nothing inside the skulls. House doors were ripped off of their hinges, and windows were smashed.

The roads crunched with broken glass, and the wind blew garbage all over the place.

The city was dead.

And the dead were lurching toward us.

I cleared horde after horde. I encouraged people out of their houses. I helped load them into dump trucks and buses and ambulances so they could be driven up to B-MOSZ. I pulled people from the bodies of the people they loved. I *saved* people from the bodies of the people they loved.

Some of the zombies were kids. Some of the zombies were trailing IV lines. Some of them were wearing polka-dot pyjamas. I couldn't think anymore, couldn't feel. I just did what needed to be done. There could be no end in sight because we had barely covered a tiny percentage of the city and it would take months, years, to do it all.

Our grim parade of survivors grew behind us, but really there weren't all that many survivors. If you're imagining waves of people coming out of every condo building, you've got it wrong. Maybe if I had been there from the beginning, that could have happened. But I wasn't there in the morning, and now, by afternoon, everyone had either holed up somewhere or left the city… or at least they tried to. Those who had failed were groaning in the streets.

And some were in our survivor line. Ray and Hazel said they could feel when the virus was starting in someone's brains, and they quietly pointed out survivors who must have been bitten. Hunt put those ones in the truck with Howie's unconscious, pinioned body in it — and told Hazel to keep an eye on them.

"Shame we don't have any formaldehyde here," I said to her. "Maybe Doc will have some at B-MOSZ."

Hunt shook her head. 'You know Morton's formaldehyde treatment is banned."

"By the Canadian government," I said. "Which no longer, like, *exists.* We can save these people's lives."

She shook her head. "It was banned for a reason. Morton meant well when he discovered it, but look what happened. Apex wouldn't exist if it weren't for his discovery, and if it weren't for Apex…"

"These people wouldn't be dying," I said.

"It's banned," she said again. "And besides, for most of them, it's probably too late."

We were getting closer and closer to SFU, to my part of town. It was only a matter of time before I found someone I knew. I scanned the faces of the dead as they growled and snatched at the air with their teeth. What would I do if I found my parents clawing the side of a building? My stomach clenched. No. No, that wouldn't happen. It couldn't.

But then again, it was hard to believe that any of the things that had happened today had actually happened. The world took on a nightmarish and dream-like quality and I closed my eyes to shut it all out whenever Hunt sent me back into the tank.

Hazel and Ray were amazing. They didn't have the super-strength of someone like Howie, but they were still really strong. The two of them together could often shift cars or move debris clear of doorways. They could feel survivors that we would have missed otherwise — one was a small child, hiding under a Dumpster, and there was a couple trapped in a public bathroom by a pack of four zombies: I strode right in, knocked the zombies out, and yanked open the stall door. The couple shrieked when the door opened, but when they saw me standing there in my riot gear, they started to cry with relief.

I liked that part.

We almost missed one person who was trapped in her car, half under an overturned SUV that Apex had chucked out of their way. Hazel felt her and I was standing next to Hazel at the time so I just marched up and tapped on the glass. The woman turned, and it was Kelly Svancara.

The first familiar face I had found in this ruin of a world and it was *fucking Kelly.* Her face was tear-stained and terrified, and she shrank away at the sound of my tap on the window.

"Kelly?" I called. "I'm here to help you. I need you to get out of the car and come with me to the truck."

She didn't look like she recognized me. I didn't blame her — I was wearing military riot gear, after all.

I pointed at her driver's side door and signalled for her to unlock it. I didn't want to scare her more by smashing the glass. She looked dazed and I wondered if she had been bitten. Maybe she was turning. I hoped not. As much as I had fantasized about bashing her skull in at times, I didn't actually want to kill someone I knew — even if it was the girl who routinely called me Teacher Fucker.

She finally unlocked her door and I gently pulled her out.

"Do you have anything with you in the car? Any bags?"

She shook her head no. She was staring at my face. "Stella?" she asked faintly.

"Yes, you know me. We're going to take you somewhere safe, okay? Is your family nearby? Is there anyone else I need to get?"

She shook her head and started to cry. I put my arm around her and led her to Agent Hunt, who was personally overseeing the survivors and taking names. Hazel looked Kelly over and gave Hunt a thumbs up — Kelly's brain didn't feel infected. She was clear.

I watched Kelly get loaded into the truck, and some motherly type of person put a blanket around her. Then Ray tapped me on the shoulder.

"More survivors?" I said wearily. I mean, living people were always a good thing, but I was so tired that it felt like a struggle just to stay on my feet. We were almost to Gaglardi Way. We were so close to home — or the closest thing I would have to a home for who knows how long.

"Yep. And I think one of them is your mom."

47

Stella

My first instinct was to just start running in the direction that Hazel had pointed, but Hunt thought we should, like, *plan* first.

"Ray and Hazel say they are picking up several survivors, the most noticeable of which could be your mother," said Hunt. "They also think there is a decent-sized horde, and that it is further off-route than our other rescues."

Hazel nodded. "I think it's a couple blocks away. I don't know if we can feel them because your mother is really loud, or if it's because the horde is really big."

"How does that work, again, exactly?" I said.

"It's like that time we used you as zombie bait," said Ray. "The more zombies pile up, the more the good mind kind of… echoes. Makes it louder. Draws in more. That's how we were able to use you to take out pretty much all of the zombies in the outbreak at once."

"Okay…" I didn't think I would ever fully understand how zombie brains worked. At least, I hoped I wouldn't, because I had zero interest in getting first-hand knowledge of it. "So is it *definitely* my mother, and *maybe* a big horde, or *maybe* my mother and *definitely* a big horde?"

"It's probably both," said Ray. "And maybe other people."

"Like my Dad?"

They shrugged.

"I don't want to bring all of these survivors into a big horde," said Hunt, "and I'm still nervous about more super-zombies showing up, so I'd like to do this fast. I want Stella and half of the team to go check out this horde. The tank, the survivors, and the other half of the team will wait here."

"Where will you be?" I asked.

Hunt looked torn for a second — only a second. "The survivors," she said. "I trust my team to protect you, and I'm responsible for the people of this province in the case of an outbreak."

She got volunteers to go with me. Andrea Kim came, and a guy called Mike McDowell, and a few cops volunteered to come, too.

"Don't let Stella get killed," said Hunt. "Ray — you guard her. Hazel — you stay here with me."

"I mean, I am wearing armour now," I said, but no one responded. They were busy picking up their weapons. I practically danced with impatience. I wanted my Mom. And I desperately, desperately hoped that Dad was with her.

I practically dragged Andrea Kim and the others down Brighton Avenue. I was so tired that the world didn't seem real anymore, and I had fixated on the idea of my parents. If I could just find them, if they could just be okay, then maybe I would wake up in their house and it would all be a dream. I imagined telling them about this crazy-ass dream where I went to Seattle to rescue Howie from zombies and flew back in a helicopter and crashed and then we had to electrocute Howie because he wanted to eat me, and now he was tied up in the back of a truck and I got to ride in a tank and…

I mean, it was a good story, if you weren't actually in the midst of living it.

I didn't see any zombies at all until we turned the corner. A massive horde was surrounding the Costco. The parking lot was smeared with dried blood and gobs of unnameable body parts.

Costcos don't have windows, so the horde was concentrating on the door which was obviously smashed to pieces. They were crushing to get in and I could hear fighting sounds. Standing on tiptoe, I thought I saw fighting.

I am here. Make way for me.

The zombies paused, and then they turned. God, I was so tired. The ground seemed to be moving under my feet like I was on a boat. On waves. The waves were going to knock me down.

The zombies were turning toward me. Some of them took steps toward me. Shit, I wasn't doing it well enough. I was just beckoning them instead.

I am here. Make way for me.

They barely faltered.

Where was my mother? Was she really nearby?

"Stop them!" said Agent Kim.

"I'm trying," I said.

"She's too tired," said Ray. "It don't feel right. Look, I can talk through it. When she does it right I just stand here like a fucking dope."

Make way for me! MAKE WAY, PLEASE, I WANT MY PARENTS.

The zombies were all drifting toward us.

"Shit!" swore Agent McDowell.

"I'M HERE!" I shouted at them. "STOP, YOU ASSHOLES!"

They were moving slow. They were faltering. But they were coming. Ray strode in and started whacking away, totally indifferent to snaps and bites. McDowell and Kim started swinging, too, but it was a big horde and they were surrounding us.

"HUNT!" I screamed. "HELP!" and then, "MOM!" God, I wanted my mother. I wanted her to hold me in her soft, comfortable arms. I wanted my Dad to come help me. I wanted him to come sweep me away like he did when I was five and I stepped on a hornet's nest, and I just stood in the swarm screaming until Dad came rushing right in, swooped me up in his arms, and ran me out of there. "Dad," I called out, but my voice was breaking. I was breaking.

"Stella?!" It was my mother's voice, oh Jesus, *it was my mother's voice*. Where was it coming from? Was I dreaming it?

"MOM!" I stood on my tiptoes. "MOM, I'M HERE!"

"STELLA!" I heard my mother again. "I'm coming!"

And the zombies paused. They milled in confusion. Some shuffled forward, some shuffled back. They bumped into each other. My backup team started knocking them all out. The next thing I knew, my mother was bursting through the dead, elbowing them aside like a shopper at a Black Friday sale. She grabbed me, yanking off my riot mask to look into my face. Then she pulled me close and squeezed me so tight I could barely breathe.

"Oh, thank God," she said into my hair. "My baby. My baby."

"Mom…" I said, burying my face into her neck. "You froze the zombies."

"What are you talking about?" she asked. "Are you okay? Are you okay?"

"I'm fine. I'm so tired. Where…? Is Dad…?" I was afraid to ask. I was afraid of the answer. Dad. Dad. I needed Dad. I couldn't imagine life without Dad.

"Oh, shit, your father," she said, loosening her grip and looking over her shoulder. "He's still in there."

I stumbled toward the Costco. "Dad!" I shouted.

The zombies were moving again, but the agents had taken out a lot of them. Ray shook himself and went in front of us, knocking down the remaining ones.

"Dad's okay?" I said, clutching my mother's elbow as we crossed the parking lot. The light was getting dimmer — the day was almost over.

"He's unconscious," said my mother with a hint of exasperation in her voice. "We stopped by the Costco to get supplies on our way to you, but we got trapped by a big horde. I thought The Service might show up to clear them away but they didn't, so we decided to try and arm ourselves and get out so we could get to you. Your father was trying to get something off a high shelf when the zombies broke down the door. The noise startled Tim and he fell. I think he broke something. I tried to help him up and he passed out. And the zombies were getting in and the other idiots we were trapped with were being useless so I went to fight the horde. But it was a losing battle… and then I heard you… How did you know we were here? Did you see the car?"

"No, Hazel and Ray found you."

"Oh," she looked at Ray. "Thank you."

He jerked his chin in a curt nod.

Mom kept patting me and looking me over as we entered the Costco. "Honey, you look exhausted. Why didn't you answer our texts? Tim and I were scared to death."

"Sorry. I kind of went to Seattle in the middle of the night to fetch Howie and I nearly got killed like five times and then I wasn't here when you needed me. I'm sorry. I'm so sorry, Mom." For some reason, I felt more like crying now, when I knew my parents were safe, than I had when I was worried they were dead.

"You should be," said Mom. "Come on. Let's go show your father that you're alive."

There were at least twenty people trapped in that Costco. They were clutching chainsaws, gardening tools and kitchen knives. They looked sweaty and bloody and scared. A dark-skinned woman was tying Dad's leg to a gardening stake. He was lying on his back with his eyes closed. He looked dead.

"Dad?" I said, rushing to him and kneeling down. His eyes popped open and he half sat up, staring at me.

"Stella?" Then he burst into hysterical tears and wrapped his arm around me, yanking me close.

"Please lie down sir," said the woman in a thick accent. "I am trying to immobilize your leg."

"You're alive… you're alive…" Dad wailed into my neck. The woman gave him an impatient shove and lay down obediently but he pulled me down too and I almost fell over. I looked at the woman.

"Hi. I'm Stella. I'm his daughter."

"I'm Doctor Mabele. Your father has broken his leg."

"Thanks for helping him," I said, squeezing Dad's hand.

"Where's Elaine?" Dad asked, looking past me.

"I'm here, Tim," said Mom.

He turned to me. "And you're really okay?"

"I'm fine, Dad. Really tired."

"We might as well load up on supplies while we're here," said Agent Kim. "I'll go see if we can find a truck that still has keys in its ignition."

"Sounds good," I said. "I'm… just going to sit down for a bit."

A minute later I was fast asleep next to Dad, my head pillowed on his shoulder.

It was completely dark by the time my mother woke me up. I was totally disoriented. Then some of it came back, and for a second I really believed that I had woken up from the both the worst and the coolest dream of all time… and then I realized that no, this was real. I was on the floor of a Costco in the centre of a zompocalypse, and the world would probably never be the same again.

But I had my parents.

I forced myself to sit up. People were leaving the Costco with big armfuls of canned food and prescription pills at the direction of Agent Kim. Dad had been moved onto a make-shift stretcher and was being loaded into the back of a pickup truck.

"Stella…" he called. "Elaine."

"Don't worry," said Agent McDowell, "we're all going to the same place."

"Don't worry?" Dad repeated. "Don't *worry*? It's a zombie apocalypse. I won't be separated from my family in the middle of an apocalypse. Don't you watch movies? You know what happens."

"It's not a zombie apocalypse," said one of the other survivors. "There's… it's… they… is it?"

"Mom, go with Dad," I said. "They're keeping me in a tank because the super smart kind of zombies might come looking for me."

"Oh, I like that," said Mom. "Yes. Please hide in the tank. I'll ride with Tim."

"We'll head out soon," said Agent Kim. "We've got the most vital supplies — antibiotics and things — and we'll grab some of the perishables to be eaten first. Hunt really wants to get back to Burnaby Mountain, but after all, we're going to have mouths to feed, right?"

"Right," I said.

"The good news is there was a delivery truck outside and we managed to find the driver and his keys in the dead zombie pile," said Agent Kim.

"Score," I said, holding up my hand. She high fived me again.

"You can start in the bread section if you want," she said, pointing.

"Stella is exhausted," said my mother. "She can't lug supplies- she needs *sleep*."

"It's true," I said, rubbing my head. "I'm not good right now."

"We've all had a really rough day," said Agent Kim, her voice hardening a bit. "But we've got survivors out there who need food and shelter. And we have to get this truck loaded and get them up to Burnaby Mountain."

"Yeah. I'm up," I said. I stood up and the ground lurched under my feet, tossing me right off of the planet.

48

Stella

"Stella," said a voice. It sounded like it was under water. There was a rushing sound. "Stella," the voice said more sharply, and someone slapped my cheek. I opened my eyes and looked into Hunt's concerned face. My mother hovered anxiously over her shoulder.

"You passed out," she said.

"What? Oh, shit!" I sat up. My cheeks started to burn with humiliation. "I'm sorry."

"Why on Earth are you sorry?" Hunt asked with a trace of exasperation.

"I can't believe I fainted like a fucking princess!" I would never live this down. I *fainted* in the middle of a *zompocalypse.* All of my bad-ass points were gone. Action heroes do not *faint*.

"Believe it or not, it's *not* a sign of weakness to pass out after nearly twenty-four hours without food, water, or sleep, especially after surviving hours of hand-to-hand combat and a helicopter crash," said Hunt with an almost-smile.

"A *helicopter crash*?" said Mom.

"Don't stress out my Mom," I said. Hunt's words made me feel better. Maybe I could keep some of my bad-ass points.

"Here," said Hunt. "Have some milk."

I stared at the carton she had handed me and felt any remaining badassery drain away. "Uh, can you hand me, like, a more grown-up, action-hero-y beverage?" I asked. "Like a Red Bull or something? I don't want to sit on the floor drinking milk like a little kid."

"Stella, drink the damn milk," said my mother sharply. "It has protein in it. And vitamins."

"And you may not have fresh milk again for a very, very long time," said Hunt. "Perishables must be consumed first. That's *policy*."

So I drank the milk.

"Oh. That does help," I said. My mother handed me another carton and I accepted it graciously.

"I'm sorry we over-taxed you," said Hunt gently. "And I'm sorry to ask you for more. But I need to get over a hundred people onto Burnaby Mountain safely. Can you help us get that far?"

"No," I said. "My zombie freeze is busted. I'm wiped. I can't freeze a single zombie. I can barely stay awake. I'm sorry…"

"You managed that crowd out there for us," said Agent McDowell. "It took you a few tries, but you did it." He squatted down so our eyes were on the same level and gave me a concerned, fatherly sort of look. His eyes were blue, like Howie's.

"No. I didn't. It was Mom."

"Your mother?" Hunt said in surprise and turned to look at Mom.

"I'm as perplexed as you are," said my mother. "I don't think I did anything special."

"You did what I do," I said. "It's like how I did it for the first time when I needed to get to Howie. But you were trying to get to me." I turned to Hunt. "How is Howie, by the way?"

"He woke up and tried to break his restraints, so his sister knocked him out with the baton again."

"Howie *what?*" said my mother.

"It's a long story, Mom," I said. I chugged the last of the milk and tossed the carton aside. "Okay. Let's get to Burnaby Mountain."

I didn't fall asleep in the tank, but I couldn't focus on anything, either, as we rumbled through the darkness of the January evening. The only lights came from the vehicles in our procession. Thankfully, Gaglardi Way wasn't too blocked by cars and there weren't any hordes. The road wound through the forest up Burnaby Mountain. It was deserted and the SFU campus was lifeless. No zombies. No people.

We drove to the underground parking garage which held the secret entrance to B-MOSZ and switched off our engines. I climbed stiffly out of the tank, and Ray offered a hand to help me down. I could see dim emergency lighting running inside the garage, and it was full of people who came pouring out to meet us.

"Sick and injured line up here!"

"Go get volunteers to help with unloading the supplies!"

They started unloading the survivors and I spotted Kelly among them. She looked so scared, and she cast me a bewildered glance as she was hustled into a lineup.

"Michaella!" Baum came puffing over. "I was growing concerned for your safety."

"Hello, George. It's been a long day," said Hunt. "Is Morton here?"

"Get Mullins!" shouted Baum to one of the other agents. "We've been sorting survivors," he told Hunt. "I have established a quarantine room and am making each person spend a minimum of three hours in each. It should be twenty-four hours, of course, but we were quite successful in rescuing the majority of the inhabitants of UniverCity, and we have cleared the area of infected. Many residents, of course, wish to continue living in their own homes, but I have been insisting on their entering into B-MOSZ first, until we can get the city under better control."

"The city is lost, George." I had never heard Hunt sound so defeated. "But I've brought you more survivors. The Mullinses can detect infection, which should help speed up quarantine procedures. The bitten ones are in that truck, over there. I didn't have the heart to leave them behind, but they'll have to be quarantined until they turn. A couple of them turned on the way here, but Ray contained them quickly."

Ray jumped out of the infected-people truck with Howie, handcuffed and unconscious, in his arms.

"Where can we lock him up?" Ray asked Hunt.

"Why is he even alive?" Baum demanded. God, I hated him. This was *his* fault; *he* sent Howie into that danger, and *that* was all he could say?

"It's a long story, George," said Hunt. "Just find somewhere to lock him up."

Doc Mullins pushed through the crowd of dazed survivors being unloaded from their trucks.

"Raymond, Hazel, thank God you're…" he trailed off when he saw Howie in Ray's arms. It was hard to be sure in the orange electric lighting, but I thought I saw a tear trickle down his face. "…You brought him home."

"He's pretty bad," said Ray. "But it's still him. If you look way down."

Doc reached out and touched Howie's head lightly with one finger, as if to check and see if he were real.

"I need you, Morton," said Hunt.

Doc turned and grasped her by the elbow. "Michaella. You're all right?"

"I need you to screen all of these people for signs of infection. Can you do that?"

"Yes," said Doc. "I suggested it to George earlier."

"It's not an approved protocol," said Baum stiffly.

"Well, I'm approving it," said Hunt. "Because I have over a hundred people that need food and rest, and I'm one of them."

"Me too," I said. "Especially the rest part."

Baum nodded at me. "I will escort you to the living quarters."

"No, I want to be with my parents." I twisted around, looking for them, but my mother was already coming toward me. "Mom," I said, reaching out for her. She hugged me.

"Your father is in line to get medical care. Dr. Mabele's been taken to join whatever other doctors they've got. I'm going to stay with Tim but I think you should get some rest right away."

"Oh," said Hunt. "I almost forgot. George, Morton — I need to bring Wilson in for questioning. She is here?"

"Leanne? Of course," said Baum. "Why?"

"Is Kate here?" I interrupted. "Please tell me Kate is here."

"Yes, Katelyn and her mother are both safe," Baum said impatiently. "What do you need Leanne for?"

"It was her, George. She was working for Apex."

Baum almost staggered. He was clearly shocked. "No. That's impossible."

"It's brilliant. Of course you wouldn't suspect her."

"It's not possible!"

"Howie says otherwise. I will question her myself. Obviously, I don't expect you to interrogate your own girlfriend."

"YOU'RE Kate's mother's boyfriend?" I almost screamed. Baum ignored me. He looked devastated. I would have felt bad for him if I weren't so pissed with him for not noticing that his own girlfriend was collaborating with Apex, and then throwing Howie to the wolves.

"I'll… I'll go and get her. Of course."

No," said Hunt. "It shouldn't be you. Not you either, Morton," she said preemptively as Doc opened his mouth. "I'm sending McDowell and Kim. I just thought you both should know. Right now, I want George to take Ray and Hazel to lock up Howie. Morton, please set up a screening process for survivors to double-check them. Ray and Hazel have already checked but I'd feel better with a third green light from you before I let anyone loose in my facility. I'm getting a bite to eat and a lot of water to drink, and then I will interrogate Leanne." She rubbed her forehead. "And then maybe I can rest."

"Stella needs to rest *now*," said my mother. "She's only eighteen."

"I'm nineteen next month," I muttered. "And I want to see Kate. Is Riya here? Is Dean here?"

"You need to rest," my mother said firmly. "You can see Kate in the morning."

"I'll be getting you up early," said Hunt to me. "Our rescue efforts have barely begun. Go rest while you can."

"What about Dad?"

"I will stay with Dad," said Mom. "I'll see you in the morning, okay? I love you."

"I love you too, Mom." I buried my face in her shoulder and tried not to cry.

"Here, Becker," said Baum, snagging one of his personnel, "Take Miss Blunt to the residential floor." I followed the man into B-MOSZ and down the white hallway to a stairwell.

"The living quarters are on Level 3," Becker said. The door to Level 3 had a big 3 stencilled on it so you couldn't get confused. Andrea pushed open the fire door and we exited into a hallway which looked identical to the one on Level 1. "Bed assignment?" asked a nervous looking young man with a giant Adam's apple.

"Yes please," I said. The ground was rocking under my feet again and I hoped like hell that I wouldn't do something stupid like lose consciousness.

The young guy took my name, gender, age and occupation (university student? Zombie-Freezer-Extraordinaire?) and put it into his tablet. He took note when Becker advised him that I was considered high priority personnel, whatever that meant. Then finally, finally, he led me down the hall.

"This one will be your room," he said. "For now we're housing people individually, but if things get really crowded we may need people to double up. Your default code is 1111. You can change it by entering the old code, pressing the hashtag sign and entering your new code, then pressing hashtag again, then entering the new code again."

"Pound sign," I said. My head was killing me.

"What?"

"It's a pound sign, not a hashtag."

"No, the pound sign is an L with a line through it," he said. "I went to England once. Anyway, I've got to go sign in more people. Let me know if you have any problems."

I punched the code into the door and it unlocked with a heavy thunk. Then I changed the code before I forgot the guy's instructions and had to ask him to repeat them. I went into the room. It was dimly lit with an orange light like the emergency lighting in my condo. There were two narrow cots, one on each side of the room, with flat foam pillows and thin brown blankets. I closed the door and collapsed on the nearest cot. I don't even remember my head hitting the pillow.

Howie

When I was eleven years old, I was pulled from my house, covered in blood and clutching my sister in one hand and a hammer in the other, and taken to a hospital. They put us in a room and cuffed us to our beds. And then they left us, bloodied and traumatized, to sicken and die.

Now I was in another facility, a windowless bunker, handcuffed to another bed. My body felt strangely stiff after the repeated electrocutions. No doubt that, had I been capable of feeling pain, I would have been paralyzed by it.

Morton Mullins entered the room. Hunt stood outside the door.

"Son," Morton said, coming toward me. "It's good to see you again."

This man. He had liked it when we called him "Dad". He liked playing the father, tutting over us, spending decades making sure that we had brushed our hair in the mornings and eaten our sheep brains. What a ridiculous fantasy. He was not my father. Fatherhood required a brief, single act. All the rest of it was mere voluntary servitude for the propagation of the species. Meanwhile, Morton had turned his back on his true species, his true potential, to spend his years trying to put a stop to his own destiny.

Brainwashed. Brainwashed like me.

"Don't provoke me," I warned him. "These bonds are not as secure as they seem."

"But you allowed us to put you in them. Ray tells me that you actually requested it several times."

"I have inhibitions that I'm having trouble overcoming. Brainwashed feelings of morality that I… I can't seem to suppress."

"Well, I am very glad to hear that. I had given you up for lost. I can't tell you how delighted I am that you seem to have retained your sense of self."

"Not… not much… but sometimes…"

"Tell me, Howie. You're no doubt more intelligent than I at the moment. Do you feel that the effects will fade? Will you revert to your former state of being?"

"My intelligence and power will seep away. But I have seen beyond. I do not know if I can ever be the Howie Mullins you knew."

"Then this… state… may be curable. That is excellent news. If we incarcerate more like you, they will eventually return to their old selves and can help give us information about Apex. I find that very encouraging."

I shook my head. "I'm more brainwashed than most, old man. No one else would let you shackle them like this, and few of them had much morality to begin with."

"Michaella says you believe that they'll destroy themselves, is that correct?" Morton asked.

"They cannot maintain organization in the long term. But that only means that more and more of them will become free of such organizational restraint. They will take to the streets, rampaging. Ravaging. Feasting. And those who cling to the organization will do everything in their power to further their plans. If they can, they will capture the humans, subjugate them, breed them.

"But if you rebuild… if you actually manage to create a functioning army… if you send those like Hazel and Ray and Morton out with your forays to sense the surrounding minds… if you use Stella to neutralize the threat from the zombies… if you salvage medical supplies, doctors… if you follow your worst case scenario plan… then you have a hope." I shrugged.

When they opened the door to leave, Hunt spoke to him sharply.

"Morton, I want Howie guarded at all times. And it has to be by you and your children since I'm certain he is contagious."

"Ah, yes, I should confirm. Here, Howie," said Morton, turning back and pulling out a swab. "Open wide."

49

Stella

I woke up to the thunk and buzz of a bright fluorescent light turning on overhead. For a moment I was disoriented. Where was I? Why weren't there any windows? And then I remembered everything.

I sat up. I was still exhausted, and I ached all over, but I couldn't exactly laze about in an underground bunker when there was a zompocalypse going on. I hauled my ass out of bed, opened my door and wandered into the hall. My clothes were bloody and rumpled and my hair was a mess. I didn't give a shit. I wanted my parents. I wandered down the empty corridor like a little kid, calling, "Mom? Dad? Tim! Elaine!"

A door opened and my mother stuck her head out. "Hi, sweetie."

I felt a rush of relief and stumbled over to her.

"Come on in," Mom said. I walked into her room, which was identical to my room. Mom and Dad had pushed their two beds together and Dad was lying on one of them.

"How's your leg?" I asked him.

"It hurts like hell," he said cheerfully. "But they put it in a cast last night and you're okay and Elaine's okay so things could be worse." He had dark circles under his eyes.

"They didn't give you some fucking Advil or something?"

"Oh, they did, but it wore off about an hour ago."

"Now that it's morning I'll see if I can get you some more," said Mom, patting Dad on the shoulder.

I looked down at my disgusting clothes.

"Do you know if there are showers in this place? And I have to pee."

Mom put her arm around me. "This way, honey."

I felt a lot cleaner after a hot shower in the bare but functional communal women's room. Mom brought me one of her spare outfits from the bag that she and Dad had packed before they left the house. It felt weird wearing my mother's clothes and her pants were too short but I didn't have any fucks to give. More people were trickling into the bathroom as I left. They looked the way I felt — rumpled, exhausted, devastated, and completely bewildered by this change in their lives.

Agent Hunt was waiting for me outside the women's room door. She was neatly dressed, her black curly hair tied up in a bun, and she looked like her usual alert and efficient self.

"We have a lot to do. Come with me. I sent your parents to breakfast. You're going to eat, and then I need you today."

My stomach felt queasy, probably because I hadn't eaten in so long. I allowed Hunt to lead me down to Level 4. "How's Howie?"

"Locked up. I haven't checked on him today."

"So you aren't going to kill him?"

"Probably not. But it's tempting. His father tested him last night. He's frighteningly infectious. I've never seen such a strong positive result."

"So I won't go kissing him anytime soon."

"You won't go *near* him anytime soon. He's dangerous."

I didn't argue. "What happened with Kate's mom?"

Her lips tightened. "Wilson expressed a great amount of distress regarding her role in our current disaster, not to mention the outbreak last year. She says that Apex had her convinced that Morton Mullins was the enemy and that they were working to bring him down. She felt terrible that George got the blame for the outbreak and was placed on suspended leave — though obviously not terrible enough to tell him the truth. He's quite upset." She opened a door to a large cafeteria with bright fluorescent lights. "Now eat. I've recruited some volunteers to help prepare a breakfast from the perishables we picked up. Please avail yourself of it. We'll have to get meals properly organized soon, to make sure that everyone gets apportioned rations, but for now, it's catch as catch can. You have half an hour."

The cafeteria was mostly empty. A lot of people were probably still sleeping, but more and more were trickling in. My parents waved to me from a table and pointed me toward the food line. I recognized some SFU students as I went to the end of the line, and I spotted one of my professors, too.

"Stella!" It was Kate. She looked like hell.

I grabbed her and hugged her. "Are you okay?"

"No! I'm shitty! I can't believe you were telling the truth about fucking *zombies.* I can't believe my Mom was working for Howie's Dad for years and didn't tell me that he was *really a fucking zombie*. I can't believe any of this…"

"Where's Riya?" I asked her.

Kate's face crumpled. "I don't know. I tried to go get her but my mother came to my place with my Grampa and The Skeez and they made me come here. Mom was crying, and she begged me not to go but I don't know where Riya is or if she's okay… and I haven't heard from Michelle or Amy either."

"Shit. SHIT. I'm so sorry, Kate. SHIT." I wanted to put my fist through a wall. Or maybe through a zombie's skull. "Okay, look, I'm going out in a bit — rescue, salvage, that kind of thing. I promise I'll look for Riya."

"Bring me along."

"I don't know…"

"Bring me *the fuck along, Stella.* I can't sit here all day worrying about Michelle and Amy and Riya and…" Kate started to cry. I had *never* seen Kate cry, and I'd known her for… wow, two years now.

"It's fine with me but I'm not the boss." I looked around and spotted Hunt's tall form at a table, eating with Doc and Baum and a few other agents. "Look, see that lady there? The tall one, with Howie's Dad and Baum?"

"Yeah."

"*She's* the boss. You tell her you want to help. But don't fucking cry. Try to look tough and useful, okay?"

Kate nodded, her skinny chin jutting out, and marched off.

Breakfast was scrambled eggs and individually packaged cartons of yogurt. Milk to drink. I took what I was given, and I went right to my parents.

"Are you okay, honey?" My mother kept touching me. I'm sure that she and Dad had thought I was dead meat yesterday. They couldn't believe I was alive.

"I just saw Kate. She says Riya isn't here, or Michelle or Amy. I didn't even ask about Dean. They could all be *dead*." I covered my face with my hands. My stomach made thunderous noises at the smell of the food but I didn't really want to eat.

"Stella, a *lot* of people died yesterday," said Dad. "Your mother and I watched people getting torn apart. We're having to accept that your aunts and uncles and cousins might be dead. And you weren't answering our calls." Tears ran down his face.

"I know, I know. I'm sorry. I did text Aunt Sara and Aunt Heather and the cousins and my friends. I told them to get to Citadel Hill because that's their version of B-MOSZ. So maybe they're okay." I wiped Dad's eyes with my hand. "I shouldn't have run off, I know. But I had to get Howie. I had to. You understand? I didn't think it would get this bad this quickly. I didn't mean to leave you in danger. I didn't mean to put myself in so much danger. I just *needed to get Howie*."

"And you did," said Mom, rubbing my arm. "So we'll stop talking about it, *won't we, Tim?*"

He nodded, and we all tried to eat our scrambled eggs.

"Stella," said a familiar voice behind me. I whipped my head around and saw Dean standing there, looking rumpled and lost. In that moment, I forgot all of our fighting and everything that had ever bothered me about him. He looked like a sad little boy, and I was just so glad to see him alive that I jumped up and hugged him. His body felt comfortably familiar.

He clung to me like I was a life preserver. "I got your text. It probably saved my life. *And* Dad's."

"What about your mo…" I stopped. Dean looked wrecked. "Jesus, Dean. I'm so sorry."

He nodded, and his chin quivered, then he buried his face in my shoulder and I could feel him struggling not to cry.

"I'm so glad you're here," he said. And then he tried to kiss me.

I pulled away. "I'm glad you're safe and… and Dean, I'm so, *so* sorry about your Mom. I really liked her. But we're still broken up."

He stared at me. "You don't mean that. After everything that's just happened…."

"Dean, I do mean it. I care about you a lot but I'm just not in love with you. I'm sorry."

His dark eyes filled with tears and he looked away.

"I can't *believe* you," he said quietly.

I felt like pig shit. Poor Dean. I wished I could change things. But I just didn't love him like that. Leading him on wouldn't make things any easier on anybody.

"I have to go," I told him. "We'll talk more later, okay?" I turned to my parents who were pretending to be *very* interested in their post-apocalyptic breakfast. "Gotta go. Love you." I ate one more big forkful of my eggs while my parents hugged me and begged me to be safe. Then I marched toward Agent Hunt, who was waiting by the door. Kate was standing next to her with a determined look on her face.

"Right," I said as I walked up to them, brimming with anger and sorrow and guilt and regret. "I really, *really* need to go kill some zombies right now."

"Good," said Hunt shortly. "Because I'm going to send you on a convoy down the Parkway toward Hasting's street. George says it was completely blocked yesterday."

I looked at Kate and turned to Hunt. "So can she come?"

"We need all the volunteers we can get," Hunt said. "If you can vouch that she wasn't involved in her mother's shenanigans."

"What shenanigans?" Kate asked.

"Come on," I said, putting my arm around her waist. "Let's go kill things."

Howie

I lay on my cot in this underground cell, chained hand and foot, for hour after hour, but I wasn't bored. Hadn't I spent months in confinement? It didn't matter.

Like Milton says in *Paradise Lost.*

The mind is its own place, and in itself
Can make a heav'n of hell, a hell of heav'n.

Stella had been right when she had argued that Satan was on the side of right in *Paradise Lost*. Why should the angels subjugate themselves?

What was I doing here? Why should I feel forced to choose sides in this ridiculous battle for supremacy? Can right and wrong exist if there were no law to call some things right, and others wrong? Let them destroy each other. What did it matter to me? What had humanity ever brought besides the pain of loss, and self-hatred? Grinding misery of decades of self-denial. Unable to be truly human, yet denying myself my own potential. And now here I was again, again. Casting my neck under the same yoke, again.

Why?

Stella

I'll never forget that first day out on the streets after the fall. Soon, surprisingly soon, it would become routine. Drive through the zombies. Look for people. Pull them into the truck. But that first day, it was like a waking dream. The road from SFU is long and heavily wooded. It was devoid of zombies. I stood next to Kate and Hazel on the back of the truck, near the front of the convoy, and looked out at the city skyline past the trees. It was hard to believe that anything had changed. But then we passed some people trudging wearily up the mountain, lugging bags and looking dirty and frightened.

"That's a good sign," said Fatima Tehrani, who was on the same truck. "Some people got the emergency signal about coming to Burnaby Mountain."

"Aren't we going to stop for them?" I asked.

"They'll get picked up by one of the cars in the back and delivered to B-MOSZ."

Our truck lurched. "Here we go," shouted the driver, sticking his head out of the window. I looked around and there, at the bottom of Hastings, was chaos. There was a big pileup at the intersection of Hastings and Barnet Highway, and the entire mess was snarled with zombies. They were growling and trying to get at people trapped in vehicles and generally just being their usual selves. Cars were scattered in a mess going all the way down Hastings and as far as I could see down Barnet Highway, too.

I vaulted down from the truck and walked forward. Make way for me. The horde froze.

"Ms. Blunt, please do not run toward the infected threat!" said Baum, running up behind me and grabbing me by the shoulder.

I resisted the instinct to grab his wrist and flip him over onto his back. I'd already done that to him once before.

Make way for me.

"Agent Baum, please do not grab me when I'm controlling an entire zombie horde," I said with dignity. "Just tell people to get to work, please."

"What are you doing?" Kate asked me as everyone got out of the vehicles and filed past me. "Oh, did no one tell you?" I asked. "I'm a highly prized anti-zombie weapon who can freeze the undead with her mind."

"No, did you know that in the two fucking years we've known each other, you never got around to mentioning that?"

"Sorry about that. We'll talk later. I promise. Right now I really have to concentrate, unless you want to be that guy's lunch," I said, pointing at an old man in a dressing gown who was staring at us and drooling. Kate sidled away. "Noted."

Bit by bit we cleared a path. My head started to ache again. I wondered if my mother would be able to freeze zombies with some practice. Then it wouldn't all be on me. I also wondered when the murder-zombies would turn up again. Because they had to know I was here.

Howie

"I can feel you gettin' restless in there," said Ray. He stood outside my door, but I could hear him. If I raised my voice, he could even hear me speak back.

"Need…. Need more…" was all I could say. The urge was becoming excruciating. Why was I here? Why was I tolerating this? I was going to break these handcuffs. Break down that door. Fight my way out. I might be able to do it. I might be able to catch someone. To feast. Need. I needed it. Needed something. I couldn't bear it.

"Dad's gonna bring by some brains in a bit. That should settle you some."

"Can't… can't eat… that."

"I can't hear what you're saying but you're probably saying you won't eat that shit. Good thing it ain't up to you. You ate it before and you'll eat it again."

"No good. No good."

"Hold tight, Howie. You're in there, somewhere. Don't let this goddamn disease beat you."

I could break free. But even if I survived, even if I escaped, Stella would never trust me again. Not if I broke out. Not if I feasted. And to be exiled from her… surely that would be worse. I had to hold on. But it was hard when she wasn't near. Hard to remember.

"Weak. Too weak, Ray. I'm going to break free. And then you'll have to kill me."

"Yep, I will. But I don't think you're gonna. Look, Howie. I know I always ragged on you for your stupid hang-ups. Do you remember, after it all first happened? When we first moved in with Doc? You wouldn't go to school, you wouldn't look after Hazel, you wouldn't do nothing but sit there with your music and your damn poetry. D'you remember that?"

"Yes." Barely, but yes. Some collection of neurons could fire in a pattern that made me remember an eleven-year-old boy, trying to hide from something too big for him to live with.

"I ragged on you for that. I said you were giving up. I said you were weak. But Howie, I'm the weak one. You're... you walked into your house, and you seen what your Pop had done, and you just went and got a hammer and you dealt with it. I... I didn't do that. I ran. I hid. My brother Tommy bit me and Ruthie tried to bite me and then Mum came at me and I just ran away to the barn and I hid with the cows."

I was silent. I knew his family. They were my friends. Friends. What a strange concept.

"So my family got taken out by strangers. They might've even roamed off and bit more people, I don't know. But it shoulda been me. I shoulda dealt with 'em. But I didn't. And you, you were only eleven. But you did it."

Terrible memories were rising in my mind. Why did they bother me? Such human things were beyond me now. The genetic relationship between myself and the man I had called Papa, and the woman I had called Mama, could not explain the anguish that came with the recollection of their faces. The infant whom my father had killed, my sibling, Henry, was a larval human, barely capable of speech. Furthermore, the incident occurred so long ago that, had he lived, Henry would now be an elderly man. How could events which took place so long ago still have a hold on me?

And yet, those powerful human memories helped, somehow. They reminded me of Howie Fontaine. And I was silent, as I remembered more and more.

Yes. I remembered.

50

Stella

"Hazel," I said as we loaded some more survivors into the not-infected truck, "You're listening for those murder-zombies, right? Just… I've been using my brain freeze a lot this morning, and…"

"I'm listening," she said. "But its a big city. And hordes have built up around other minds. They're making those minds louder. It helps stop you from standing out so much. Besides," she said, wiping her mouth with her sleeve. "You're worn out. I can feel it. Yesterday you froze half the city. Today you're only doing maybe a block or two."

But I had stopped listening. I was watching Kate, who was moving further and further away from the others.

"Kate!" I shouted.

Baum turned and followed my gaze. "KATELYN!" he bellowed. "STOP!"

Kate stopped guiltily.

"I'm sorry," she said. "I have to go get Riya. I can't take it anymore. I need to go to her."

"Very well," said Baum.

Kate stopped, looking surprised.

"But you mustn't go alone. We will direct our movements in Riya's direction."

"Really?" I said. I had been expecting him to bully Kate for being her mother's daughter, not agree to use an entire convoy of people to go look for her lost girlfriend. This might be the first time I had ever not totally hated him.

Baum looked annoyed. "Enough people have lost loved ones. Whichever direction we go, we will find people who need rescuing. If the people we rescue happen to be family and friends of current survivors, it will raise morale. Katelyn has the right to search for her friend."

"Girlfriend," said Kate.

Baum just nodded shortly. "How far was her apartment from here?"

Howie

Pain. So much pain. Not physical pain. It had been so long since I had felt the injury of a broken bone or stubbed toe that I could no longer remember what those sensations felt like. But somehow, still, remembering hurt. I couldn't be Howie without suffering.

When I remembered holding baby Henry on my lap, watching my parents waltz around the room to the sound of Hazel playing on the piano, I suffered. When I remembered walking in on the remains of my father's last meal, the small, bloody leg with no body attached to it, I experienced anguish. Was my life nothing but misery? I remembered loss after human loss, the loss of my family, the loss of my friends, the loss of hope for the future. I remembered the loss of Stella, the hole she had made when she left and took my heart with her.

And why had she left? Because Howie Mullins was a weak and useless thing. Brain damaged, unable to learn quickly — Howie had been unworthy of her. Struggling along for decades trying to be human, when he could have been so much more.

I was worthy of her now. I was beyond her, even. What was the purpose of giving this up? Finally, I could learn at lightning speed, understand concepts beyond the grasp of most other humans. Finally, Stella would have to struggle to keep up with *me*.

How could I give that up?

Forget stupid Howie, and his pain, and his wretched attempt to deserve a brain like Stella's.

I was more, now.

More.

Stella

Riya lived in North Burnaby in an apartment building just off of Hastings, so we weren't far away. But we were stopped by a massive horde. It was even bigger than the one around the Costco yesterday. They pressed up against the windows of a tiny corner store, lurching and clawing. The store had iron bars over its windows, which is good because it looked like the zombies had already broken the glass.

"There must be a ton of people in that store," I said, but Hazel shook her head.

"Not many. But one of them is *really* nice. I've noticed it around before."

Okay, I admit it. I actually felt jealous. I guess after two years of constantly being told how speshul-and-purdy my brain was, it had become a core part of my identity or something. Great. Just when I think I have my faults under control, I discover a new one. I didn't need a new character arc in the middle of a fucking apocalypse.

"Nicer than mine?" I asked casually.

Hazel shrugged. "You're not the only nice mind around, you know. You're just the only one that can do… whatever it is that you do."

Some of the zombies turned and started to lurch toward us as we moved closer, but most of them ignored us — ignored *me* — and stayed focused on the stupid corner store.

I was jealous. Over *zombies*. Fuck!

"What if… what if one of those zombies is…" Kate said, reminding me that some people had real problems, like missing girlfriends who were very likely dead. I would never say it aloud, but I couldn't imagine tiny, thoughtful, people-loving Riya surviving a zombie attack, and I hadn't forgotten that one of her roommates had been 'sick' the night before the outbreak happened.

All I could do was squeeze Kate's hand and hope like hell that one of those zombies was not an adorable East Indian girl with big brown eyes.

Baum gave me the signal and I focused my brain.

Make way. Make way for me.

The snarling and reaching stopped. The horde calmed, and one by one they turned to look toward us. Toward *me*. Take that, Tasty Corner Store Brain.

I scanned their faces for Riya. If she was there, I needed to spot her before Kate did. Better Kate hear it from me first, rather than spot her girlfriend drooling blood in the crowd.

Agents hopped out of the vehicles to push aside zombies and clear a wide path to the door.

"The threat has been temporarily neutralized!" bellowed Baum into his loudspeaker. "You may emerge and we will take you to a safe location."

The door to the corner store finally creaked open, and an elderly Korean man emerged, looking very nervous. For some reason, once I saw him, I felt less jealous about the tasty-brain thing. Okay, he might have a great brain, but I didn't think Howie was going to, like, fall in love with this guy instead of me.

Then I reminded myself that since Howie was crazy and infectious, brain jealousy should be the least of my worries at the moment.

"It's okay?" asked the man.

"Yes," said Baum, gesturing to the path they had cleared. "But time is limited. Please come with us, and you will be safe."

"There is a girl," said the man, glancing behind him.

And Riya stepped out of the store.

"Riya!" Kate screamed and Riya's head snapped to the side. I got distracted, and the zombies started to look away, back to Riya and the man, and I quickly got myself back under control.

I am here. Pay attention to me. Make way.

Kate was scrambling out of the truck, and Riya started to rush over but Baum stopped her.

"Please proceed in an orderly manner," he said. "Katelyn! Wait there."

But Kate was having none of that shit. She pushed aside zombies to cut her own path straight toward Riya, and they would've had the sweetest, most touching reunion if I hadn't gone and fucked it up.

Because you see, while Kate was moving through the horde, I spotted Amy. And she was one of the dead.

51

Stella

Amy was wearing pink pyjamas which were smeared with blood. She had bed-head and a slightly surprised look on her face. The look was also unmistakably vacant, and her mouth hung agape in that zombie way.

No. NO. No no no no no no no no no.

I had texted her. I HAD TEXTED HER. I told her to be safe. I TOLD HER.

But she never texted back. And now she was standing there, one shoulder higher than the other, leaning forward, and dead. DEAD.

Worse than dead.

I made a strangled kind of high pitched noise — something between a scream and a groan. Kate, who was on her way to Riya, turned at the sound. I jumped down from the truck. I had to get closer. I had to be sure. Maybe it was another tiny, doll-like blonde girl who happened to look exactly like the friend who had listened endlessly to my boy-problems and never lost faith in the power of true love.

I pushed zombies aside and went face to face with Amy. It was definitely Amy. Kate saw her now, too, and she started to scream.

Shit. SHIT. Oh, shit. I didn't know how to handle this. I didn't know how to process it. I could hear my pulse in my ears as I stared at the thing which was totally my friend, while also hideously unlike her in every way.

Kate went up to Amy and grabbed her and shook her, but Amy's head just wobbled loosely and her jaw dropped further open. She was like a manikin of Amy — a grotesque parody of Amy. A nightmare of Amy.

And in my shock and my grief, I lost control, and the dead around me started to move, and Amy twitched, and snarled, and lunged. She went for Kate, but thank God, Kate's anti-zombie armour got in the way. Kate scrambled backwards, her face a mask of horror, and bumped into five more zombies. I raised my arm to knock Amy out — *I'm sorry, Amy, I love you, I'm sorry* — but a zombie grabbed my arm and nearly wrenched it out of its socket while another one bit me on the shoulder. Thank God for armour — the bite didn't penetrate.

I tried to put my zombie freeze back up but I couldn't control it when Amy was right in front of me, trying to kill Kate. Amy loved Kate. They'd known each other since kindergarten. And I just couldn't handle it.

People were shrieking and shouting because now the survivor truck was surrounded by zombies. I had to stop them. I had to stop them. But I was still bellowing with disbelief inside and I couldn't concentrate, I couldn't summon the right feeling, and they all just kept moving.

And then I heard Riya scream Kate's name. Shit. *Riya.*

Everything stopped. Finally, my zombie freeze must be working. The zombies had gone quiet again, and they were all turning their heads.

But they weren't looking at me.

I turned my head, too, and I saw Riya barging through the zombies, shoving them aside, with an expression of icy fury on her bespectacled face. She threw — literally threw — Amy off of Kate.

"Get the hell away from my girlfriend," she said. Kate was sobbing and covering her face, but Riya pried Kate's hands away. She pulled Kate to her feet, yanked up her riot mask, and then kissed her with desperate, passionate fervour.

I walked over and looked down at Amy.

"I'm sorry," I told her, tears streaming down my face. "I'm so sorry I didn't save you."

And I brought my disruptor down on her head.

Amy's arms flew out as the electric jolt flowed through her, and I started to sob as she spasmed and lay still.

Howie

Morton Mullins was outside the door. I heard the key turn in the lock, and he entered.

"You may lock me in, Ray," he said. There was a click as Ray turned the key.

Morton studied me from behind his glasses. Howie Mullins had worn glasses. Without them, the world was slightly blurry at a distance, as if there were two of each object, their images overlapping.

"How are you doing, son?" he enquired.

"I have felt better," I said.

"Ray tells me you suffer extreme mood swings. You alternate between remembering who you are and thinking you are something else. You are also extremely infectious. You are in the grips of a disease. You have lost track of which thoughts come from the disease, and which come from you, as a person."

"The disease and I are one. You cannot separate them."

"Perhaps not at the moment. But I hold out hope. I have brought you a meal."

"Pork, I suppose."

"Mutton, I'm afraid. As you know, I use mutton for my lab subjects and those are the supplies I have on hand. I will petition Michaella to go to our house and salvage our supplies there, so I hope I shall have pork for you soon. If the meat spoils before it can be collected, our family will have an urgent problem with food supplies."

"Your food supply is all around you."

"I have no interest in that source."

"Liar. The virus has an interest. It calls to you."

"The virus makes me aware of the brains of those around me, which is proving useful at the moment. While it does occasionally give me unsettling visions, I have no desire to act upon them." He laid the bowl down in front of me. I stared down in distaste.

"Eat up. It is better than nothing, surely." He paused. "Incidentally, do you have any suggestions for non-human sources of food in the months to come?"

I shrugged. "Hunting. Farming. Send Ray and some others to reclaim a farm or two, and salvage any surviving farming families. It will provide fresh produce for the humans, and you can eat the disgusting offal if you wish to continue in your idiocy."

He nodded, then walked to the door and spoke. "You may release me, Ray."

The door opened just enough to let Morton through, and then quickly shut again. The key turned in the lock.

I stared at the cold tissue in the bowl before me.

No. I needed more.

Stella

"But I don't even know what I did," Riya argued.

Riya's zombie-freeze had dropped quickly after she and Kate were reunited. And then, because she was all worked up over Kate, the zombies were crazy for her. But by then I had recovered my composure enough to stop the zombies again.

The agents raided the corner store for supplies while Kate and Riya and I rolled Amy up in a tarp. Baum had warned us that the only way to dispose of her body was to incinerate it, but we could think of it as a cremation and it was better than the alternative, which was rotting in the street, still wearing her pyjamas.

"We met when we were five," Kate had said to Riya and me, tears dripping from her nose. "She shared her grilled cheese sandwich with me."

We just hugged her. There was nothing we could say which would make this suck less.

Now that the convoy was rolling again and we were away from the zombie horde, we were being checked for bites.

"Looks like the armour did its job," said Fatima.

"Thank fuck," I said. "I felt a bunch of them trying to bite me."

"Is Mr. Lim okay?" Riya asked.

"Surprisingly, yes. All the zombies near you decided to go for you, I guess," said Fatima. "And then you stopped them before they got to you."

"But how?" Riya insisted. She was snuggled into Kate, who was clutching her like she was a teddy bear.

"It was the same way it happened for me the first time," I told her. "Howie was getting attacked by zombies and me just... needed them to get out of my way."

"I always thought you had a nice brain," said Hazel. "I always noticed it when I was checking on Stella at night. But I didn't know you could do that."

"Did you check on me *often?*" I asked. I suddenly thought about Dean, whether Hazel had known.

"Yes. So did Ray. We did night shifts because you would recognize us if you saw us." Hazel cocked her head as she looked at Riya. "She feels really different from you, though. The freeze was different. Kind of… cold. But… really powerful."

"More powerful than me?" I asked, trying really *really* hard not to feel displaced.

Hazel shrugged.

"I feel like I'm going insane," said Kate, rubbing her eyes. "This is all a crazy dream."

"Once Stella realized she could do it, she did it easily," said Hazel to Riya. "So you should, too."

Riya shook her head in a confused way. Her glasses magnified her dark, frightened eyes.

"I think I'd already had practice because I did it all the time anyway," I said to Hazel. "I'd been using it for years to move through crowds." I looked at Riya. "I guess slim people don't need to know that trick."

"Well, it's good news, anyway," said Fatima. "We need as many people like you as we can get."

The longer we went without being attacked by the ravaging murder-zombie types, the jumpier I got. I mean, it may also have been general nerves since I'd had to re-kill a good friend and witness the devastation that was our city. In any case, it was almost a relief when Hazel stood up and grabbed my shoulder.

I shouted a warning and other people took up the call as I followed Hazel's pointing finger. Shit, there was a fucking *pack* of them. And one of them was wearing a human skull like a *helmet*. It looked fucked *up*.

Adrenaline shot through me. I remembered how the Apex types and crazy zombie types had hesitated for a second — just a second — when I first turned on my zombie freeze.

"Riya, if you could find your way to doing your thing, now would be a really great time," I said.

"Why, what's happening?" Riya followed everyone's gaze. "Who are *they*?"

"I can buy you a second, but only a second," I shouted down to Baum.

"Then wait until they're close so we can get headshots," he called back.

Look at us, working together and not throwing insults at each other. We were growing as people.

"Riya, if those guys get into that truck, they're going to kill and eat Kate and all the rest of us," I said. "And they're way more infectious than the regular type of zombie."

"They're zombies too?" she straightened her glasses and leaned forward.

They were close. Fuck, they were really close. My heart was slamming into my chest.

"Now!" I bellowed.

MAKE WAY. MAKE WAY FOR ME, YOU FUCKING FUCKING ASSWIPES.

They slowed down. They looked confused. Guns roared, and a couple of braver agents ran up with disruptor batons.

I AM HERE, IT'S STELLA YOU FUCKING FUCKS.

Two dropped, but the other four started moving again. And now they were looking right at me. One of them dropped when Agent Mike — I didn't know his last name — swatted him with a disruptor. The other two jumped up and landed on top of the armoured Humvee on the edge of our procession, and went to jump right into my truck.

"Riya, now would be a *great* time to do something," I shouted, raising my baton in front of me.

"I'm trying!" she said tearfully.

Hazel was sitting quietly, gazing at me in a peaceful way. I dropped my freeze as the zombie with the human skull on his head and a skinny woman wearing a motorcycle helmet launched themselves at us.

Fatima swatted the guy in the body with her baton, and he collapsed, unconscious. I did the same to the girl, and then we ripped off their head-gear and hit them again in the heads.

I turned, panting, to Riya. "Okay, you really, really need to work on the zombie freezing thing."

She nodded solemnly, her big eyes staring at the disgusting human head-helmet. Fatima dropped it out of the truck with an expression of disgust on her face, and then we rolled the two bodies out of the truck.

"Good work, everyone," said Baum heartily. "Let's move on." He turned to me and looked me in the eyes.

"I know you and I have always disagreed on my attitude toward the Mullinses," he said. "But look at that," he pointed to the head-helmet, "and understand why I considered them and their formaldehyde treatment a danger to the world."

I didn't answer. There was nothing to be said. Because as much as I despised his idiotic, pompous fuckery… he was right.

By the time we rolled back into B-MOSZ, with our trucks full of people and various supplies, the survivors had all seen me do my zombie-freeze trick at least once, and they were staring at me like I was the second coming of Jesus.

"How do you do that?" a twelve-year-old girl asked me.

"I just sort of shout 'get out of my way' in my head, and they do," I said.

"Could I do it?"

"Maybe," I said, glancing at Riya. "You never know."

Hazel made a face. I guess the girl didn't feel very powerful to her.

"You never know," I said to her. "We're still figuring all this shit out."

Hunt met us at the entrance and introduced herself to the survivors. They climbed down nervously, looking around and clutching their possessions and each other. Baum led them inside and directed them to quarantine.

"Do they still need quarantine? Hazel gave them all the okay," I said.

"If I had my way, everyone would go through a twenty-four-hour quarantine," said Hunt. "Morton and his children aren't foolproof. We don't know what their efficacy rate is, and even a single missed person would be catastrophic. Right now we have such a high volume that effective quarantine is useless. I simply cannot isolate every person we bring in. But it's going to slow down to a trickle very quickly, I'm afraid. People will either get out of the city, or they'll succumb."

"Fuck."

"We're going to have to modify all of the guidelines," she continued, watching the survivors being ushered inside. "We're going to need to create higher-level defences against an intelligent threat. We're going to need a way to sustain the population, which now includes zombies who require brains for nourishment. I have about fifty different jobs that I need done, and a tenth of the people and equipment I need."

"Are… you… confiding in me?" I asked.

"You're going to be a vital part of my plan, Stella," she said. "I never expected to be left holding the reigns of something like this. I'm going to be keeping you close. You're one of my best weapons. So, yes, I'm confiding in you."

"All right," I said. "What can I do to help? I mean, besides freezing zombies."

She rubbed her temples. "Help me find about twenty more people who can do the same thing? Like helping that girl, what's her name, figure out how she did it. Also, I'm going to call a meeting for the survivors today. Give people some information and maybe a little hope. When I do, I want you up at the front with myself and the other officials. A lot of people saw you in action, today, and I think you're going to become a celebrity."

"A… what?"

"Stella, half the people in this complex owe you their lives. Yes, you will be a celebrity. Congratulations. Go and eat."

"Can I see Howie?"

"No," she said, and she walked away.

52

Stella

Kate wanted to wait with Riya in quarantine, and I promised to bring her some food from the cafeteria. When I got back with an egg salad sandwich in each hand, Doc Mullins had shown up and was frowningly inspecting the people in the quarantine area.

"Riya's been cleared," said Kate, taking a sandwich from me. Her eyes were red with crying. I looked for Riya and found her sitting next to a forlorn-looking woman.

"What superpower do you wish you had?" she was asking. I tapped her on the shoulder and offered her a sandwich. She took it and nodded at me.

"Flying. I used to dream about flying," said the woman, wiping her eyes.

"Stella," said Doc, "I'm going to ask you and this young lady, er…" he looked at Riya.

"Riya."

"You and Riya to vacate this area. I'm trying to inspect the minds of these survivors, but your presence is increasing the difficulty of my task."

"Sorry. How's Howie?"

He looked grave. "I am concerned. He appears to be struggling with his choice to return to us, and he is experiencing extreme cravings from the virus. You must be prepared for the possibility that he will lose this battle."

"No," I said fiercely. "He can fight it. I know he can."

His eyebrows twitched. "I certainly hope you are right. In the meantime, Ray believes that the more brain material we can provide, the easier it will be for him. Michaella has agreed to loan him a vehicle. He'll attempt to reach our home to get our other supplies before they defrost. My supplies here are limited." He paused. "I assume Ray will also be bringing Army back with him. I'll have to have a talk with Michaella about him eventually. She doesn't know that our dog is infected."

"What are you going to do, long-term, though, for brains?" I pushed.

"Michaella and I will be discussing that. I have several ideas which I will need to run past her at some point."

"If we can get Morton's supplies from home, it should buy us at least a month," Hunt said, walking up to us. "Considering that I'm thinking of our survival by the day at the moment, that's plenty for now." She sighed. "I had better go talk to Howie, and see if I can get any suggestions out of him."

"Can I come?"

"No."

Howie

Agent Hunt was at my door again. There's a mind I wouldn't object to feeling beneath my fingers. Let her come in. Ah, Ray is with her. Does he think he can protect her? He? When I have the power of true potential behind me?

"We need to talk about sustainability. Morton tells me you think it's possible. We have plans to section off areas of agricultural land for crops and meat supplies, but our plans only involve walls and protections against your standard hordes. What will happen now that we have Apex and those bonkers ones in the mix? I need to know what to expect."

The question was interesting. Discussing hypotheticals entertained my intellect.

"Apex won't bother your crops or your farming efforts. You are their meat. You need to be well fed. You are fortified, and you outnumber them. They will consider you a breeding ground and ignore you while they try and fail to increase their own numbers. So long as there are plenty of survivors loose on the streets — and there will be, no matter how hard you try to find them all — They will have no reason to persecute you.

"Leave them alone, and they'll mostly leave you alone. But more and more will stop trying to function as an organization, will become lost in the bliss of the hunt, and they will attack whichever mind feels best to them. So you will want to protect any transportation convoys. If you present them with easy prey, they won't say no." I stretched back on my bed. I had no reason to withhold information. But I had had enough of being chained here. I needed to escape. Go free. Allow the virus to take my body and remake it. No more of struggling with my own humanity. It was all nonsense.

I smiled at Agent Hunt to try to put her at her ease. Give her information. Be helpful.

Ray was the problem. He was watching me with an eye that told me that I had not fooled him and likely could not fool him. Well. He would be easily dealt with. I was hungry and filled with need, and Hunt was standing right there.

I snapped the chain of my handcuffs and leaped to my feet almost in one motion. Within a single bound, I was in a hair's breadth of touching Hunt, but Ray got between us and my teeth buried into his shoulder. Disgusting. I spat it out and grappled him, but Hunt was already through the door and had it slammed shut.

We were locked in.

Too bad for Ray. I might as well kill him. If he were any other person, I could have taken him as easily as Hunt, and I would be cracking into a delicious skull already.

"Ray?" Hunt was calling through the door. "I'm sorry, I can't risk him getting into the facility."

"We need Stella," he said loudly in the direction of the door. "Get Stella."

Yes, please, get Stella. What a delicious idea. Why didn't I take her when I had the chance?

"Stella is the last person we want near him," she said.

"Stella's the one who can reach him. Get her quick before he kills me and breaks outta here."

"I don't think she can possibly move quickly enough for that," I told him. I expected him to try and fight, get me pinned down. But he sat still in my grip.

"The real Howie is in there somewhere, and Stella knows how to get him out."

"The Howie you knew was a sad shade of his potential form. You fight the virus, Ray, when you should open yourself to it. See what it can make you."

"What can it make me?" he asked.

"Free. Free to be strong, to be intelligent, to be superior in every way. Do you know how good it tastes, to have a man's brains on your tongue? You've dreamed it. It's even better than dreams."

Ray's dark eyes glittered. "You think I haven't thought about it? But here's the thing, Howie. There's more important things."

"Like what? Failing high school?"

"That world's done with, Howie. It's history. But there's scared kids out there, and crops to til, and cattle to raise. I can work a farm, and I can't get sick if I get bit. I can find survivors, and I can tell a sick mind from a healthy one. They need me, now, Howie, like no one has needed me for sixty years. I'll be damned if I'm going to give up now.

"So you'll have to kill me, I guess. But I warn you. Stella's gonna bring you to your senses, and then you're going to torture yourself over this the rest of your life. I don't want that. So if you do kill me, Howie, I guess I forgive you. Because you ain't yourself right now."

"No," I said. "I'm better." I couldn't just snap his neck. That wasn't enough for the likes of us. I'd have to smash his skull. I lifted him and moved him closer to the wall. He struggled, stronger than your normal human but nothing compared to me.

And then I felt her coming closer, and her emotions were running high.

So good. She felt so good.

I paused. I realized that it would be better to leave him alive, so they'd have a reason to open the door. Let him out.

"Howie?"

Why did the sound of that voice make my world spin? What was it about this person?

"Howie, have you hurt Ray?"

"I'm alive," said Ray. "But he's planning on bashing me against the wall so if you could stop him I'd really appreciate it."

"Howie, let Ray go!" The voice was muffled, but her mind came through loud and clear. I felt my fingers involuntarily loosen and he slipped free.

"Howie, that's your brother. Your brother Ray."

"Siblings are irrelevant. Besides, he and I share no genetics beyond the common code of the human race. And the virus."

"He was part of your family for sixty years, Howie. You know him. Look at him. Howie would never hurt someone he loved."

"Howie is gone."

"No, he's not." She sounded tearful, and her brain was thrumming. "He's in there. You're just… you're just not well right now. Okay? I need you to listen to me because we're going to get you better and then you would tear yourself up for hurting your brother. So just wait, okay?"

"Open the door and let him out, then."

"Absolutely not, I forbid it," said Hunt's voice. "I don't know how we're going to get Ray out, if we do at all, but I forbid you to open that door."

"Howie? I'm going to sit on the outside of the door. You sit on the inside. Okay? We can talk like that."

I didn't move, but I heard a soft thud and a sliding noise outside the door as she sat.

"Howie, I want you to remember. Why don't you tell me about your parents?"

"My parents were simply my genetic predecessors." Nothing more. Nothing more. No point to the pain.

"So tell me about your genetic predecessors. If they don't matter to you, you won't mind talking about them."

"I…" Their faces rose up in my mind, and I felt something other than the craving. Something made my throat close up.

"No."

"Then tell me about the first time you ever saw me."

Why did I answer? Maybe because the image was already in my mind, and I had no reason to lie. "I was in Chemistry class. It was another day. One more grey link on an unending chain of days. And then I felt you. I didn't notice you at first — there were so many minds and I had learned to ignore them, block them out. But you burst through, and it was ecstasy. I wanted to go and find you, to see the mind that could make me feel that way. But I couldn't move."

"I remember that," said Ray from the corner to which he had moved. "It freaked me out like nothing else. I was in English."

"When you walked in, it was..." I swallowed, remembering. "It was like seeing a vision. You wore a low-cut top, and your hips swayed as you walked into the room. But mostly I remember your face. Your flushed cheeks. Your pursed lips. You looked dangerous, and angry, and frightened, and I was already wild for you, and I didn't know what to do." Sad, pathetic boy. But I remembered so acutely. The longing.

Her voice quavered when she spoke. "Now tell me about the first time we kissed."

My heart was pounding. I could see it. I was there. "We were in my bedroom. I had wanted to show you my regeneration powers, but you panicked at the sight of the cleaver and you knocked me down. I... I was aroused. I loved that you had fought me. I loved the way your mind felt when it was struggling with whether to believe me. I felt that if I could not win your trust..." I looked up at the ceiling and blinked a few times. "There wouldn't be any point in anything. That there had never been a point in anything until you walked in. I would have happily agreed to simply be in your presence, to bask in you, but I longed... I longed to kiss those lips. You purse them when you're angry and every time you did it I felt desperate to kiss you. Every day since I first saw you... whenever you said something that made me laugh, whenever you said anything sarcastic or clever, I felt like I would die if I couldn't have you. But I didn't really believe that you would ever agree to it. I didn't believe that I had any chance with this stunning girl with her big brown eyes and luscious lips and brilliant mind. You were a fantasy — an impossible mirage designed to break my heart. But I had to try because I wanted you so much. And then you kissed me. And I was in heaven and hell simultaneously because I had never felt so happy or so ashamed."

"Why were you ashamed?"

"Because I didn't think I deserved you. Because you still didn't really understand what I was." I felt a rush of anger. "And you still don't."

"Yes, I do."

"No, you don't."

"I didn't back then, Howie. I didn't understand how hard everything was for you. You tried so hard to be human for me that I believed it. I didn't see how much you were struggling. I didn't see how much I hurt you when I pushed you to do more than you felt capable of. I was the one who didn't deserve you, Howie. Because you took my bad with the good, and you never asked me to be anyone I'm not. I *made* you feel ashamed. I made you feel like you weren't enough. And I'm sorry."

"I did change. I changed for the better. I can be what you want now — I can learn faster than you, understand more than you. Are you happy now?"

"No. Because I don't care about that anymore. I just want you back. The real you."

"You still want to change me."

"No, Howie. I just want you to let Ray go."

"Then let me go, and I'll let Ray go. I won't harm anyone here. But I'm done with this. I need to go. I need…"

"You're giving up on yourself, Howie. I don't want you to change. But I am asking you to fight for who you are."

"Then you're asking me to change. You're asking me to be human. But I can never be human."

"Yes, Howie. I'm asking you to be human. Because you were always human. You're still human. You're the kindest, most loving, gentlest, and wisest human I know. You also have a disease. And sometimes it changes how you think, and how you feel, but it isn't *you*. And I'm sorry that I made you feel ashamed of it. Because I see now that it doesn't matter. I don't care if you're some kind of mad genius, or if you never pass a test again in your life. I don't care if you can break steel chains, or if you get blown over by strong winds. I don't care if you can orate like Orson Welles or if you never use an exclamation mark again. All I care is that you be *Howie*. I miss Howie. I miss him so much that it hurts inside. The entire world is in chaos but the thing I want most is for you to hold me again, like you used to, and kiss me in that way you used to do — the way that made me light up inside. I'll never love anyone the way I love you. I never should have let you go."

Why were tears running down my face?

"And Howie? I know that there's nothing I can do to help you get through this. It's up to you — you can break that door down and let the virus win. Or you can struggle through it and try to take control of yourself again. I can't make that choice for you. I can't make you get well. Only you can do that. But I want you to know that I'm here. And if you decide to stay.... If you decide to fight... Well... just know that I love you. And I'll be waiting when you're really ready to step outside that door."

I didn't answer.

"But right now, I just need you to send Ray out without anyone getting killed. Okay, Howie? Howie?"

I sat down on my cot. Ray moved out of the corner and went to the door.

"Let me out quick, Stella."

"No, I need Stella to step away," said Hunt's voice.

"I'm not leaving him again," said Stella.

There was some muffled conversation, and then my door clicked open. They pulled Ray out and slammed the door shut again.

And I just sat there, on the bed, and let it happen.

A mind not to be changed by place or time.
The mind is its own place, and in itself
Can make a heav'n of hell, a hell of heav'n.

Stella

"I'll stay here. I'll sleep here, even. He needs me. He needs me to remind him who he is," I told Hunt.

"You said it yourself, Stella. This is a fight he needs to have with himself."

"Ray knew he needed me. That's why he told you to get me."

"Well, I figured she could freeze him for a second so I could get out," said Ray. "But yeah, I guess that too. He's better when she's there."

"Well, as touching as that is, I need Stella to help me salvage the human race," said Agent Hunt with a touch of asperity. "Stella, you can come and check on him, but I can't have you sitting here twenty-four hours a day, and I certainly can't have you lying asleep right outside the door. I'm calling an assembly of all of our survivors, and I need you to be there too. Understood?"

I nodded. "Yeah, I guess the human race is kind of important." I turned to the door. "DON'T YOU AGREE, HOWIE?"

He didn't answer.

53

Stella

The dining hall was really damn big, and I guess Hunt and company decided that it would work well for group announcements.

"For now, anyway. We're still powering up parts of B-MOSZ. We do have an auditorium but we don't have enough people yet to fill it," said Hunt. "The cafeteria will do fine, for now."

Hunt ordered people to stack the tables in the corner and set out the chairs until the place looked like it was ready for an elementary school Christmas concert. She sent some people off as messengers to tell everyone to come to the hall for a meeting. Then she called in her other head honcho types to come stand at the front and get ready to introduce themselves as part of the official B-MOSZ leadership: Andrea Kim, Dr. Mullins, Dr. Wong — who I met last year during the unfortunate incident with Howie and the hamster — and Baum. Yes, *Baum.* You know, the guy who failed to notice that his own girlfriend was collaborating with Apex. The guy who failed to notice that Howie had been *captured* by Apex. THAT Baum.

I mean, we were getting along better today, but still.

Baum looked equally insulted to see me standing at the front. "Teenage girls belong in the audience of this meeting, not at the front with the officials," he said.

I hated this man so much that I couldn't even.

Hunt looked mildly amused. "I realize that you both have some personal history between you."

"You're talking about the time I beat him up and tied him to a chair, aren't you?" I said. Andrea Kim and Dr. Wong looked away and covered their mouths with their hands. Baum looked like he might explode and it was great.

"But," continued Hunt with unruffled calm, "I am asking both of you to put the past behind you. It's our job to try and piece together what we have so that we can survive." She pointed at me. "Agent Baum is here because until last year he was a vital part of our team. He identified the threat from Apex and tried to warn us about it. While he was mistaken in some of the particulars, he gave us the only advance warning we had about this invasion, and he deserves our respect for it." She pointed at Agent Baum. "Stella Blunt is here because she is one of our most important weapons. Many of the people in this facility already owe her their lives in one way or another, and they know it. Like it or not, she's going to become one of the primary symbols of authority around here for that reason alone. Besides, I have a feeling about her."

"You have a feeling?" Baum asked, lip curling.

"Yes. I have the feeling people will listen to her."

"You *do* know that I am pretty much universally hated wherever I go, right?" I said to Hunt.

"I wonder why," said Baum.

I pointed at him. "It is *your* fault that Howie's a… a… whatever he is. So shut up."

"Howard Mullins went voluntarily undercover. He is a casualty of war."

"Stop it, both of you," said Agent Hunt. She pointed to one end of the room. "George, stand there." She pointed to the other end of the room. "Stella, stand there. Those of us who are adults and can stand next to each other without bickering will stand between you. People are already filing in, and I don't want any visible dissension. We must present a united front. *Do you understand?"*

"Yes," I said. Baum just snorted. But we went where she pointed and we studiously ignored each other.

I scanned the faces as people filed in. They all looked… blank. You imagine that the apocalypse would be full of people screaming and sobbing and I had already seen a lot of it, but really… people can't maintain that level of emotion non-stop. So I think everyone went sort of numb. But a number of them did seem to recognize me. I saw some of them pointing at me and whispering to each other, and maybe for the first time in my life, I didn't imagine that they were saying something awful about me.

I recognized some of them, and every time it was an incredible relief. I saw Melanie and John from my kung fu club. Did they get my text? Did it save their lives? I saw Dean coming in with his Dad and Kelly, and Kate and Riya, and my parents. But for every face I recognized, I could think of many more who were missing from the crowd. The other people from my kung fu club, from high school, from my neighbourhood… Michelle, and her parents, and Amy's parents, and even asswipes like Carter Davidson would have been a welcome sight, but I didn't see any of them. Were they dead? Hiding? Somewhere outside the city? Roaming the streets and growling?

I thought of Amy and I felt like my insides were twisting.

The room echoed with the clatter of people seating themselves in the cheap fold-up chairs, and I felt awkward and on display. I glanced at Hunt because she's a class act and I'd feel comfortable imitating her anytime. She was standing in a formal but friendly way that I could only dream of adopting and nodding at people and smiling with a sort of brief, professional, how-do-you-do smile. I would have to work on that. Jesus, I was already beginning to accept the idea of myself as some kind of community leader.

That felt really weird.

When everyone was settled, Agent Hunt clapped her hands loudly and called for attention.

"I'm going to try to dig up some sound equipment so you will be able to hear me better in the future, but in the meantime, I'm going to speak as loud as I can, and I'll ask all of you to try and keep quiet so that everyone can hear me! Now, *can* everyone hear me?"

"Yes!" replied a bunch of people.

"No!" replied a few.

Hunt made an effort to talk even louder.

"For those who don't know me, my name is Michaella Hunt. I am the head of the British Columbia chapter of the Canadian Reanimation Virus Control Service. For decades, this branch of the government has operated in secret to try and control a very frightening and deadly disease. To prevent fear and panic, it was kept a secret, but an open one — we encouraged everything from zombie movies to zombie TV shows. We hoped that no one would ever need to fight a zombie — not if we were doing our job — but if they did, we wanted them to recognize the situation and know what to do."

She paused and waited for the angry mumble to die down. "A few days ago, the world suffered an organized, deliberate attack from a subversive group. The virus was deliberately released en masse across the globe. To our knowledge, every country has been affected." She paused. "That means that no one is coming to our rescue."

People were talking again, now, and they sounded frightened. Could you blame them? She let them panic for a couple of minutes and then she clapped her hands. When that didn't work, I clapped my hands, too, and roared, "HEY! LISTEN UP!"

The room fell silent. Agent Hunt nodded at me and continued.

"As you can see, we have had this facility in place for a long time. It is important that you understand — *we are prepared*. This facility is equipped with power generators, food, weapons, and other vital supplies. It is secure." She paused again, let people murmur, and then went on. "We have all suffered terrible loss in the past couple of days. But we *must* endure! Whatever your personal feelings right now, whatever your situations, you must understand — you are precious. The human race has suffered a biological attack of a kind never before seen in the history of mankind. We are few, but we can grow. We will survive, and we will rebuild. But before we can do that, we have work to do.

"I'm going to need volunteers to help go on rescue missions and salvage missions. I'm going to need people who are willing to learn how to shoot a gun, how to kill a zombie, and how to risk their lives for the sakes of others. I'm going to need people who understand machines, to help us keep our facility running. I'm going to need doctors, to keep our population healthy. I'm going to need positive, enthusiastic, *helpful* team players to help me get our society up and running again!"

The room had gone quiet.

"When we built this facility, we also made a contingency plan. I have in my hand," and she held up a thick paper document, "a detailed thirty-year plan which outlines exactly how we can get sustainable, manage the outbreak, grow, and rebuild our city. But I can't do this on my own! I need you! I need every one of you. Right now, right this instant, I need three volunteers to help me take a census of our new population. Where are my volunteers?"

Six hands shot up in the air, and she pointed to the three nearest to her. "Perfect. At the end of this meeting, I'm going to give you three pens and paper. And I want everyone else to line up in front of one of these three excellent volunteers to tell them your name, your job history, and your skill sets. If you have an idea for a job, you can do for us, great, but if not, trust me — I will find a job that will use your skill set to its best advantage. Does everyone understand?"

"Yes!" people shouted in unison. They were paying real attention now. They didn't look numb anymore.

Was that… hope?

"Now, I'm to introduce some of the other members of our head team. I want you to know that this will not be a dictatorship, and the establishment of a democracy is part of our plan, but to start, we need people who understand about the virus, and our facilities, and our thirty-year plan. This is Andrea Kim. Some of you may have met her when you arrived. Ms. Kim has been with the BC branch of CRVCS for three years. Before that, she was a member of the BC RCMP's emergency response team. Andrea?"

Agent Kim stepped forward and waved. "Hi! Most of you met me when you were being processed. I want you to know that I am here to help, and I will protect you all to the best of my ability."

Hunt nodded and then gestured to Baum. "Now, I want to introduce you to George Baum, who graduated to us after a successful career with the intelligence branch of the Canadian Border Services Agency. George?"

Baum cleared his throat and tugged on his uniform before regarding the crowd with his usual pompous demeanour. "Thank you, Agent Hunt. I want all of our citizens to know that I am dedicated to helping rebuild and protect the remains of our beautiful country. Within each of you resides the heart of Canada. We are a nation of peacekeepers. We are a nation of diverse heritages. We are the nation that invented hockey, basketball, and Trivial Pursuit. We built the Canadarm and the snowmobile. We invented medical insulin and the walkie-talkie. We are the home of Superman, Margaret Atwood, K.D. Lang, David Suzuki, and Terry Fox." His hand had wandered over his heart as he spoke, and I thought I saw tears standing in his eyes.

"While we may have lost our infrastructure, our communication systems, and our Tim Hortons Restaurants, we have not lost ourselves. I will stand by you as we rebuild with the values we hold most dear: our reputation for cooperation, peace-keeping, courtesy, and diversity."

"Thank you, George," said Hunt, interrupting when it looked like he was going to keep talking. "Now, I want to introduce you all to a young woman whom many of you have already met — Ms. Stella Blunt."

She beckoned me forward. Oh, fuck. I had to say something now?

"Talk to them," she said in my ear. "Introduce yourself. Tell them what you can do."

"Uh… hi," I said, projecting my voice as well as I could. The room was deathly silent. "I'm Stella. I'm a Biology student at SFU. Some of you met me today on the… on the outside. Uh… so… last year I discovered that I can focus my mind in a way that makes zombies freeze up. And, I figure, if I can do it, maybe some of you can do it. So maybe start practising. The goal is to kind of shout in your head and boss your way through the zombies. Anyway. If some of you come on salvage missions and stuff as volunteers, I'll probably be there too, to help out. And... yeah. Nice to meet you all."

They were all riveted. I wasn't used to this much positive attention. I couldn't handle it. I backed up, and Hunt took over again, introducing Dr. Mullins and Dr. Wong as the head scientists involved in finding a vaccine and a cure for the virus. She didn't mention their lab assistant, Leanne Wilson. She also didn't mention that Doc was also a zombie and that he had accidentally discovered the thing that made this worldwide disaster possible.

I guess that would've been a buzzkill.

Instead, she told everyone that the best way for us to get organized and save the human race was to do our paperwork and figure out where everyone belonged in the scheme of things.

I took sign-ups for weapon training — which I also signed up for of course — and salvage missions. John and Melanie from kung fu signed up, and a bunch of men and a few women. They all wanted me to promise to try and teach them how to freeze zombies, and John and Melanie wanted to talk to me about which kung fu moves were best against them.

Then Dean showed up in my line.

"I want the weapon training and I want to go out and help," he said shortly.

"You'd be good at both," I said, writing down his name. "You're athletic and shit."

He just nodded. It was so weird to see him like this... his sparkle and charm were gone.

"Dean... I'm really sorry. About everything."

"You sure picked a hell of a time to break up," he said. "I could really use you right now, you know?"

"I know. And I'm sorry."

"You sure you... I mean..."

"Yes, Dean. I'm sorry. I'm sure."

"Maybe when you've had time to adjust to everything..." he started to say, but the next person in line pushed past him and I turned and started taking the guy's name. Dean hovered for a minute or so and then

Kelly came up behind him, casting me a shy glance, and started speaking to him. He went off with her and I was relieved.

I wished that I could be there for Dean as a friend. But I knew that he wasn't ready for that, and I just didn't have anything more to give him.

All I could think about was Howie.

At this point, I figured there was a good chance that Howie would never be the same again. That he would never stop being infectious. That he wouldn't love me the way he used to.

But also, maybe… just maybe… he would.

As soon as Hunt released me from taking names, I found my parents and hugged them, and told them that I was going to spend some time talking to Howie before I went to bed. Then I went and grabbed the pillow from my room and found my way to the lower level where they had Howie stowed.

Hazel and Ray were hanging out by the door, but when they saw me they exchanged looks and moved a long way down the hall. Giving us some privacy, I guess.

I didn't announce my presence to Howie. He'd know I was there if he was awake. I just set the pillow down outside the door, sat down on it, and leaned with my back against the door.

At first, I thought he must be asleep because I didn't hear anything for a good ten or fifteen minutes. Then I felt a thump against the door. I jumped, but Howie didn't come bursting out with murder in his eyes or anything.

"Howie?" I said tentatively.

The muffled voice came from the other side of the door, and I was sure that he had sat down with his back to the door, too. "Yeah, I'm here."

"Are you sorry I came to Seattle to find you?" I needed to know.

"No," he said. "The whole time I was there… all I could think about was you."

"Really?"

"Yeah. Not always in a good way, though. I'm not the little saint that you think I am."

"You really set a trap for me? Like, you were going to kill me?"

He was quiet for a few heartbeats before he answered. "Yes. But I couldn't do it."

"Why not, Howie?"

"I don't know. I guess…" he trailed off, and I waited for approximately an eternity before he started talking again. "I remember my mother working hard on a birthday cake for me when I turned ten."

He never talked about his parents. "Yeah? What kind?" I prompted.

"Chocolate. I loved chocolate. With lots of frosting. She worked so hard, Stella. It had layers and little rosettes on it. And when the time came to cut the cake, I didn't want to do it. I didn't want to eat it. Because it looked so beautiful. It seemed like a waste. I guess it's like that. When I had you in front of me… I just couldn't make that cut."

"Was the cake good? Your mother's cake?"

"Yeah, I guess it was. But that isn't what I remember about it, you know? And maybe, if I killed you, maybe I'd remember how it tasted. But then you'd be gone, and I would never be able to just enjoy looking at the cake anymore."

I felt chilled by how casually he talked about killing me. I wanted to tell him that I'm not a fucking cake. But I had turned my back on him before because I couldn't handle his illness. I wasn't going to do it again. I wasn't going to do anything stupid, like try to go into the room or anything, but I wasn't going to turn away.

"You're still trying to decide whether or not to kill me, aren't you, Howie?"

"I go back and forth," he said. "But I think… if I were really going to do it… I would have done it when I had the chance."

"Have you always gone back and forth?" I had to know. I had known when we were dating, that the virus gave him cravings, but I had never believed that he actually wanted to kill me. If he had really always considered it an option, that seemed like really important information that I should know. It would mean that I should never be alone with him ever again, for one thing.

"I used to be afraid that I would do it by accident. But no, I never considered it a possibility… something to be desired… until I tasted freedom. And I realized that I had been torturing myself over something I couldn't control, and now I see that it's a choice I have."

"But you chose not to, Howie. You didn't kill me. You killed that man in the club, but you didn't kill me."

"I killed him to put him out of his misery. I was weak. I couldn't shake outdated notions of morality. Of empathy."

"Now that sounds like the Howie I know."

"But what am I going to do, Stella?" his voice rose in a plaintive tone that I had never heard before. "I've tasted it now. I don't know if... if I can go back to how I used to be. I can't be one of them, and I can't be one of you. And even if I could, if I decided that I could live like that... If those feelings of morality got stronger... I've eaten the brains of a lot of people, Stella. People's fathers or mothers or daughters or sons. How could I live with that, if I let the humanity come back in?"

"Why did you, Howie? What happened?"

"I went undercover. Baum told me what was happening. He thought the US government was behind it. He wanted me to get proof. But they caught me right away. I was so stupid. So stuck on morality. I wouldn't eat the human stuff. So they slipped it in. They made it sound like it's a choice, but they made sure everyone got it in the end. And... and I fought. So they locked me up. They forced it on me. And... and then I finally understood. I could see."

"And then you helped them."

"Yes. I told them what they wanted to know. Except about you. I wouldn't let them have you."

"Howie, it sounds awful, and I feel like shit that I was off living a normal life while you were going through all of that, but you don't have anything to torture yourself over. They forced it on you. You couldn't help the effect it had on you. That's just part of the disease. It's not your fault. And you need to understand — the virus makes you think things, and see things in a certain way, but that doesn't make it true. Or at least, not the whole truth. There's more to it, other things that you can't see right now, because of the virus."

"What things?" It sounded like he was crying.

"Like love, Howie."

"Love is a subjective experience which promotes pair bonding for the sake of propagation of the species."

"Yeah. It is. But Howie, just because something is subjective doesn't mean it isn't real. PAIN is a subjective experience, and that's real as hell. Or… vision. Sight. It's all a matter of reflected light and patterns on our retinas, right? Hell, we even see things upside down. But it's still *real*. It still works. I can reach out and pick up a cup because I can really see it."

Howie didn't answer.

"Do you understand, Howie? Subjective is still real. And love is real. That's why you couldn't cut your mother's cake. Because of the love she put into it. You didn't want to wreck that. And that's why you couldn't kill me, too."

He was definitely crying. I could hear him. And it was hard to understand his sobs through the door, but I was pretty sure he was saying, "But I had to cut my mother, too. I put a hammer right through her skull. I couldn't cut her cake but I splattered her brains on the wall…"

"Howie! You did that out of love, too. She was gone. I was going to do the same thing. You know that, right? I went down to Seattle to kill you. We set out to kill each other, Howie, and neither of us could do it. But if I thought you were really gone, Howie, the way your mother was? I would have done it. Because I love you."

I could hear him sobbing, and all I could do was lean against the door, knowing he was on the other side, and wish that I could hold him in my arms.

54

Howie

Torn. Torn apart. When one minute you long for goodness, and the next you long for sin, how can you know which longing is truer? If part of me believes in love, and part of me believes it is meaningless, which part do I believe? How can I know who I am when I am two people? There was the part of me that still wept for my parents, dead so many decades ago. There was the part that curled its lip in scorn and failed to understand how two near-strangers, long dead, could have any power over me. There was the part that wanted, no, *needed* to feast — that burned for it — and the part of me that was repelled by the thought and longed only to be relieved from the craving.

I lay curled on my knees, my cheek on the cool floor and my body pressed against the locked door. I leaned into Stella. She was the thing that both parts of me agreed on — that it was better to be in her presence than out of it. What I couldn't decide was whether she was my salvation or my downfall. Twenty times I thought of standing and ripping the door out of its frame. I might still be able to do it, but not for much longer. I was weakening. The math was leaving me. All I had left was the poetry.

Take me to you, imprison me, for I,

Except you enthrall me, never shall be free,
Nor ever chaste, except you ravish me.

John Donne understood. He understood craving. He understood need. He understood that goodness brings no pleasure, no reward. How can anyone choose it? How had I chosen it for so long, and why? Why? Why was I here?

Stella. She was part of it. Was it better to be lying here, against a door, feeling her mind than out in the streets and filling my need? I couldn't decide.

"I'll take over for a while, Stella," said the voice of Morton Mullins. I could feel his mind too, but vaguely. That jarring, distasteful feel of one who has been infected. How could the virus be good when it made a mind feel so bad? If the virus made us superior, shouldn't our minds feel superior too?

I grasped onto this thought like a drowning man who grabs a rope. There was something to that. I must hold onto it. Ponder it more.

"No. He needs me," said Stella.

"It is nearing midnight, and the floor is not a comfortable bed. Nor would it be wise for you to sleep here, vulnerable, while Howie is still… not himself. I will speak with him. You can return in the morning."

"But…"

"Stella, if Howie is to find himself, he must do it himself. We cannot rely on your always being with him. If he can overcome this, he must be able to maintain it outside of your presence. You understand that?"

"Yes," she said, and I felt her misery. For a moment my heart went out to her. *Stella, I don't mean to hurt you. Stella… don't cry.* Then I felt a wash of panic.

"Stella, don't leave…" If she took her mind, if I didn't have that to lean into, then what was left for me here?

"Stella needs sleep, Howie. I am here. And I have brought you something to help pass the time."

Stella's voice was thick with emotion. "I'll be back in the morning, okay, Howie? You can fight this."

I felt her move away. The heavy stone walls of the complex hid her from me as she ascended. I felt like I was falling.

"Howie," said Morton, "I can't open your door myself. Only Michaella has the key, and I have urged her to bed. But I brought something for you. Hazel took it from our house today." He cleared his throat. "You always liked Gerard Manley Hopkins, so I'll start there. Not, I'll not, carrion comfort, Despair, not fear on thee; Not untwist — slack they may be — these last strands of man/In me, or, most weary, cry I can no more. I can; Can something, hope, wish day come, not choose not to be."

Yes. Yes. I remembered.

Take me to you, imprison me, for I…

I can. Can something...

Not choose not to be….

Will ye submit your necks, and choose to bend
The supple knee? Ye will not, if I trust
To know ye right, or if ye know yourselves …

Stella, the only planet of my light,
Light of my life, and life of my desire…

My own heart let me more have pity on; let
Me live to my sad self hereafter kind,
Charitable; not live this tormented mind
With this tormented mind tormenting yet…

…Labour to kill in me this killing care:
O think I then, what paradise of joy

It is, so fair a virtue to enjoy?

...my heart lo! lapped strength, stole joy, would laugh, chéer.
Cheer whom though? the hero whose heaven-handling flung me, fóot tród
Me? or me that fought him? O which one? is it each one?...

That I may rise and stand, o'erthrow me, and bend
Your force to break, blow, burn, and make me new...

That night, that year
Of now done darkness I wretch lay wrestling with (my God!) my God.

I felt her rise in the morning. Like the sun, like tomorrow. I felt her coming to me, before she brushed her teeth or changed her clothes or ate her breakfast. It gave me strength.

Stella, the only planet of my light,
Light of my life, and life of my desire

I heard Hazel speak to her.

"We've been reading him poems all night... sometimes he recites them back to us... sometimes we start one, and he finishes it from memory. It seems to help. I think he's getting better."

"Thank God," said Stella. "He's still awake?"

"Yes. All night. I spelled off Dad a couple of hours ago."

"I can't stay long. Hunt wants me. But I wanted to check on him. Howie? How... how are you?"

I leaned against the door and stroked it, picturing her face. Remembering.

"I'm doing a bit better, Beautiful. Please be careful out there."

"Oh my God," I heard her say, her voice breaking. "He sounds like Howie. It's him."

"I need to know that you're coming back," I told her. "I… I need that right now."

Take me to you, imprison me, for I,
Except you enthrall me, never shall be free,
Nor ever chaste, except you ravish me.

"I'm coming back," she said.

"Okay. I'll still be here."

She made a sound that was both a laugh and a sob.

"Good," she said.

55

Stella

Those early days after the fall all sort of blend together in my memory. I was busy all the time. For the first time in my life, I was falling into bed without even taking some time to read. I lived practically next door to my parents but hardly ever saw them except at meals. Dad, who was one of those people who can look at a string of numbers and spot the error right away, volunteered to help with taking inventory, rationing, maintaining records, all that stuff. My mother got handed a computer and a bunch of information and was asked to put it together into nice, easy-to-digest propaganda that could be handed out to people or hung on the walls. You know, like, ten tips for adjusting to life at B-MOSZ, ten things you didn't know about fighting zombies. She also fixed a handbook of safety/security rules and regulations written by Baum which she said needed heavy editing to be readable and not terrifying.

Everyone was given some kind of job. Even kids as young as ten were given simple jobs like taking garbage bags to the incinerator or wiping the tables after meal service ended. Doctors were assigned clinic hours and scientists were recruited to Doc Mullins's lab (100% of all science was now devoted to solving the zompocalypse since carbon dioxide emissions and endangered wildlife weren't really relevant issues at the moment).

And any able-bodied person who was willing to take the risk went out on missions at least once or twice a week. And some, like me, went out there every goddamn day. The thirty-year plan included harvesting every kind of supply from canned food to condoms, clearing main roads, and slowly expanding the established "safe zone" and setting up a protected satellite farming community.

Unfortunately, the thirty-year plan was written for a boring, normal zompocalypse that only featured regular, shuffling, mindless types of zombies. It didn't say anything about ravaging brain-thirsty zombies who could run as fast as a car and then open the door when they caught up to it. It didn't say anything about a group of intelligent zombies who were intent on taking control of the world, either. So we had to kind of make up that stuff as we went along.

The last three hours of my night were always spent on the floor outside Howie's door. It was my favourite time of day, especially since I could feel more and more of his Howie-ness coming back.

I sat on one side of the door, and he sat on the other, and so, in a way, we sat side by side. And we talked. I'd tell him about my day, and he'd listen. He'd tell me about his childhood, and I'd listen. We talked in ways that we had never really talked before. He told me things he had never told me before. I learned that his first crush and best friend was named Ruth and that she was killed in the same outbreak that killed his parents. I learned that his teddy bear had actually been his baby brother's bear, which Henry had dragged everywhere with him. I learned that Howie was so wrecked after his parents' death that he spent months just sitting in bed, doing nothing, wishing he could die.

"Why didn't you tell me this stuff before?" I asked after he told me, sobbing, about how it had felt to walk into his house and see his baby brother's blood spread all over the kitchen floor.

"I didn't even like to *think* about it," he said, his husky voice thick with emotion. "Talking about it was impossible."

"So how come you can tell me now?"

He didn't answer right away, and I sat patiently and waited. I had learned to wait.

"I guess it's because I have to think about these things anyway..." he said finally. "Because... as much as it hurts... remembering brings me back. It reminds me of what matters. It reminds me that things *do* matter."

"Well... thanks for sharing them with me," I said.

"I should have done this before," he said. "I know now that I should have. But I kept it all inside. I felt like it was too big to let out, too big to even look at or think about. But now I can see that all it was doing was eating me alive."

The better Howie seemed, the more uncomfortable I felt killing ravagers on patrol. When they were dead, they looked so human and harmless, and it made me wonder if we shouldn't be trying to save them. I mentioned it to Andrea Kim, who led our patrols most days, and so she agreed to try to take one alive.

It didn't go well.

The next time one ambushed us in a warehouse, we surrounded her on all sides with our batons at the ready.

"The smart thing to do would be to surrender," said Andrea. "Or we'll kill you."

"The smart thing to do would be to eat you alive," she replied, running her lips over her teeth. She jumped in the air and almost made it over us, but Fatima managed to make contact with her ankle and she fell to the floor. And then like five of us brought our batons down simultaneously on her head and she was very, very dead.

"That did not go well," said Andrea.

I decided to talk to Howie about it.

"We tried to take a ravager alive, today," I told him. "It... didn't work well. We had to kill her after all."

"You shouldn't have tried. Taking one alive is too dangerous, Stella. Even if you chopped off her arms and legs, she'd still be contagious and there's no way she would cooperate with you."

"It's just that..." I hesitated. "Are we committing murder, Howie? I keep thinking about you, and how you were, and wondering if these ravagers... if they can be brought back, the way you're coming back. I feel like we shouldn't be killing them. They aren't like real zombies, who are dead. I killed Amy because I knew there was no better choice. But these people are alive. Maybe we should be trying to save them."

He was quiet for a long while before he answered. "We still don't know if I *can* come back from it, Beautiful."

"But you are. You're... you're more like *you* every day."

"I know. I feel more like me. Even though there are still... still flickers of the other thing. But I'm still infectious. We don't know if that will *ever* go away. And remember that *I* didn't do it to myself on purpose to begin with."

"But that girl you told me about... Cassie... they forced it on her. So now she's a ravager, right? But maybe we could bring her back. I mean, if she were here instead of in Seattle."

"Yeah, they forced it on her. But she didn't fight it, either. I told her to throw it away. And she figured out what it was. But she kept eating it." He paused, and I stayed quiet, just listening. "It's... it's really hard to come back from that, Stella. The craving... it's too strong. It even got me, and I fought it *really* hard."

"But Apex is full of people who can resist the craving, right? They're the ones that only have tiny amounts, aren't they?"

"Right. Which means that the ones who become ravagers wouldn't, or couldn't, fight the craving. It's too strong. And the only thing that could pull someone back from that is something stronger. Like the way I feel about you."

I felt a rush of emotion. Even though we talked for hours every night, we hadn't talked about *us* much. I longed to hear him tell me that he still loved me, because some part of me was terrified that he didn't, anymore. Not the way he used to. Maybe he just wanted my brains.

"How *do* you feel about me, Howie? Now, I mean."

"Oh, Stella," he said, and for some reason, the way he said that sent me back to the night of my eighteenth birthday. "Don't you know that already?"

"Not really, no," I said irritably. "I mean, the last time I saw you, you spent a lot of time trying to kill me."

"I guess I'm afraid to say what I feel because it still changes all the time and I don't know what's true. Sometimes I forget what love is. Sometimes think I just want your brains."

I winced. Howie was always honest with me now. I had never realized how much he had hidden from me, before. It was good, the being honest, but it hurt sometimes, too.

"But other times," he continued, "like now, I know that I love you. And all the time, I know that I need you."

"Well," I said, feeling a little disappointed. "I guess that's a start."

"I'm sorry. I don't know what I'll have to give you. I don't know where this is going to end. I'm still infectious. I might always be. Right now they're serving me out of disposable cups and bowls and incinerating everything my saliva has touched. But that can't go on forever."

"I thought you had this vastly superior intellect, now." I used a teasing voice, but my heart was pounding. He had to get better. He had to. "You can't even tell me what your own virus will do?"

"I can hypothesize, that's it," he said. "And I'm not as smart as I was, anyway. It's leaving me. But I think that's a good sign, in a way. I'm reverting. Morton, I mean, Dad, is injecting me with formaldehyde every three days, like he did when I was newly infected. He's hoping that will help. And I'm forcing down the brains they give me, to keep me from getting hungry. But sometimes I wonder if I can ever come fully out of it. And I don't mean just shedding the virus. I mean everything."

We were quiet for a moment as we sat, back to back with a heavy door between us, and thought about all the shitty things that had happened, and could still happen, and what those things could mean.

One thing, though, was crystal clear to me.

"Well," I said. "If that's how it is, then that's how it is. So we wait and see. But I'll be right here. Because even if you're infectious, Howie?

Even if you aren't the same? I'd still rather be sitting on this cement floor in a goddamn mountain bunker, with a door between us, than anywhere else I could be right now."

"Good," he said. "That makes two of us."

When Howie needed to be distracted from his own memories, I would talk to him about my activities on the outside. He liked to hear how things were going. I focused on the positive stuff, the same as I did when talking to my parents. Howie and my folks didn't like hearing about how I got gang-attacked by a pack of ravaging murder-zombies — it made them nervous — but they did like hearing about people I rescued, discoveries that we made.

"We found a big group of people in the rec centre in Poco," I told him one day. "They have things all set up — stockpiles of food, some weapons, even a fence with spiky things on it for the shuffling zombies to get stuck on. Most of them didn't want to come with us. They've done a lot of work to make their building secure and they're sort of proud of it now. But they were happy to know we exist, and Ray said none of their minds was especially yummy, so hopefully they'll be okay. We warned them about Apex and the ravagers and they thanked us. A couple of people with little kids came with us because we've got that preschool set up and let's face it, we're way more secure. But yeah. So now we have, like, a sister community or something. We agreed to stop by and check in on them now and then."

"They'd be safer here," said Howie.

"We'll probably find more pockets of people like that," I said. "Not everyone is going to want to live here. *I* barely want to live here. Hunt is fostering an atmosphere that's *oppressively* positive. They're talking about having community events and movie nights. Some people wanted to write an *anthem,* though Baum shut *that* down fast."

"But those pockets are what Apex was planning on," Howie said. "They weren't expecting something like B-MOSZ to be up and running.

The only reason The Service survived here is because of my family — because they couldn't infiltrate us properly."

"That reminds me," I said. "Kate's mom has officially been accepted back into your Dad's lab. Did he tell you that?"

"Yes, he did."

"Did *you* know that Kate's mom worked for The Service?"

"Yes. You understand why I couldn't say anything?"

"Yeah," I said grumpily. "I get it. I guess I'm glad I didn't know. It would have sucked to know more about Kate's mom than Kate did. That would have been a shitty secret to keep."

"Which is why I kept it."

"And are you okay with them just, like, forgiving her?"

"Yes. Apex had her tricked very nicely. She was sure that Morton — I mean, Dad — was spreading the virus. It helped that she was dating Agent Baum, who was always so suspicious of us. His suspicions fed hers, and hers fed his. I feel bad for both of them. They were duped."

"They were *idiots*," I said.

"Well," he said, and I could hear the smile in his voice. "You're biased to be on my side."

"Yeah," I said again. "I mean, he almost duped me, too, I guess. Whenever I start thinking I should apologize for jumping to conclusions and blaming him for the outbreak last year, I remember that he jumped to conclusions and assumed you were going to sell me to the U.S. government. And then I remember that he basically kidnapped you and nearly got you killed."

"He didn't kidnap me," Howie reminded me gently. "He recruited me. I went willingly."

"Would you have gone if you had known that you would end up like this?" I asked.

He was quiet for so long that I began to wonder if he had heard the question.

"I… I don't know," he said finally. "On the one hand, becoming… what I became… was my worst nightmare come true. When I agreed to go, I thought I might be killed, but I never thought that they could make me become *that*. And if I had known how likely it was, it might have scared me off. On the other hand... I think that ultimately it's a good thing I did go. Maybe it isn't good for me, personally, or you, but... thanks to me, the founder and president of Apex is dead. Their organization is in shambles. Their plan was derailed. And I was able to provide a lot of information that probably saved a lot of lives. But does that make up for the number of lives I'm responsible for ending? I don't know. I just don't know."

56

Howie

Day after day after long and lonely night, I lay on my bed and flipped through the ancient volume of collected poetry. The book, which once belonged to Morton's wife Edith, helped pull me through in the difficult months after the deaths of my family, and now it was pulling me through a different kind of crisis. I clung to it, and the words buoyed me through the waves of torment.

One day, Ray brought in a small white box along with my day's ration of brains.

"Stella's old man sent this along. It's supposed to play music. Stella thought you'd like it. Guess it's easier to transport than a stereo, and a transistor radio wouldn't do you any good."

I examined it, and the word for it rose to my mind. An iPod. God, I would miss having a functioning mind, but with every dose of pig brains or — worse — sheep brains, I could feel the vibrancy draining out of me. I was losing the power. I was losing the understanding. But I was still smart enough to figure out how an iPod worked, and I discovered hours and hours of music loaded into that tiny device. It was like a little miracle. And so my lonely nights were not so lonely anymore, now that I had Buddy Holly and Billie Holiday and John Lennon to keep me company.

Really, though, the music and the poetry were just distractions. They helped me survive the ticking of the clock which brought Stella back to my door by nine every night.

"Did Ray tell you about the farm we found?" she asked one night, without introduction or preamble, when she arrived at my door. She didn't need to announce herself. I felt her coming; I quivered with her approach, and she knew it.

I was already waiting by the door.

"Yes, he did, at some length," I told her, and I smiled to myself. I had never seen Ray so excited.

"They need more hands, Howie," he had said to me. "I don't know how to use some of the new equipment, but a lot of their stuff doesn't work now, anyway. They need someone who can help hand-milk the cows. They need someone that can't get bit to patrol the farm. They need someone who can fix fences. They need someone who can shovel muck. I can do those things. I can fling hay bales. I can clear out the zombies every morning. I can help. And I can even drive the produce back to B-MOSZ without attracting a fuck-ton of ravagers."

"You're perfect for all of that," I had told him. "I guess you'll be living there."

"Yeah. For a while, anyway. But I'll be back."

Stella was as happy for Ray as I was. "He *smiled* today, Howie, when we found that farm. No zombies in the pig barn, beef cows still in the field. Okay, some dead cows, but there's lots of live ones left. They even have chickens. It's a family-run farm, and the family was alive and well, and when they came out to greet us, Ray *smiled!*"

"Did Ray ever tell you about his mother?" I asked.

"Ray never tells anyone about anything, Howie. If he isn't making a sardonic comment, his mouth is clamped shut."

"Ray's father was killed in a tractor accident," I said, remembering as I spoke. I did this now — went off into memory, like I always had, but now I took Stella with me. "When he was, oh, I don't know, eight or nine. He was the oldest of six kids. Everyone felt so bad for his mother — left a widow with six kids under the age of ten. They assumed she'd sell the farm and move in with a relative. But she didn't. She just kept going. My Papa was her doctor, and the family lived up the road so we saw them a lot. Mrs. Kowalchuk would sometimes bring us apples or eggs, that sort of thing. And of course, since she was farming all day, she was always wearing dirty jeans, overalls. Man clothes, in my eyes, when I was a kid. It was the fifties, you know? Women wore dresses."

Stella listened quietly on her side of the door.

"I remember Mrs. Kowalchuk coming over one time when Mama wasn't home. And Pop, he jumped up and swept off his hat and offered her a cold drink and asked her to have a seat on the porch swing. And she said no to all of that and left the patty pan she had borrowed and went back up the road. And Pop asked me why I was giggling. I couldn't really explain. It just seemed funny, stout Mrs. Kowalchuk in her dirty overalls with cow pat on them and Pop treating her like she was a fancy lady. And Pop gave me this really serious look and sat me down and told me that she worked harder than any man, working that farm and raising those kids. And he told me she deserved as much or more respect than any white-dressed fancy lady who might happen to stop by. He said every woman deserved respect because they had to be stronger than men did."

"That's why you always opened doors for me and pulled out chairs," said Stella, her voice wobbling. "Because of that?"

"Yes. It wasn't because I thought you were weak. It's because that was how I was raised to treat someone strong." I paused for a moment, collected my thoughts, and went on. "When the outbreak killed Ray's family, he always said that someday he'd buy his farm back and he would turn it into a success. It was hard on him when he realized that he couldn't even pass high school, let alone get a degree in Agriculture, or even work a job that paid enough for him to save money for that farm." I paused. "It got converted into a strip mall a couple decades ago, anyway. And Ray just sort of gave up."

Stella was silent for a short while. "I'm so sorry, Howie."

"What for?" I asked curiously.

"For pushing you to go to university. I don't know what my problem was. I can't even remember why it felt so important. I didn't… I just didn't really understand how long you had tried. I didn't understand how hard everything was for you."

"I knew that," I said. "I knew you didn't understand. How could you understand? You couldn't understand how it feels to live through what we lived through and to live for as long as we lived without growing or changing much. And I *knew* that. I didn't *blame* you, Stella."

"Well, you should. Because I'm smart, and I could have understood if I had wanted to. I don't think I wanted to. I didn't want to accept what all of that really meant. I was afraid of losing you. I was trying to be practical, but I was also trying hard to keep you. And I couldn't do both so I just sort of… stuck my head in the sand, I guess."

I was nodding quietly. "I know. I knew."

"I was such an idiot," she said, and her muffled voice sounded higher pitched than usual. Her brain waves were distressed, and I knew she was crying. I felt her sadness pulse through me, and I longed to take her in my arms, kiss her, to love her. *God, I know I have done wrong but please grant me this second chance.*

"No, no," I said, rising onto my knees and pressing my face close to the door, close to her ear, as close as I could be to her mind. "No, Stella, please don't. You did nothing wrong."

"Bullshit," she said angrily, and her irritation flared through me. "I let you go and look what happened."

"What happened had to happen, Stella," I said urgently. "Stella, you need to understand. I was the first boy who ever loved you, and the first boy you ever loved. Of *course* you had doubts. And I was sick. You knew I was sick. And I was getting left behind, and it was breaking us apart. None of that was your fault. It was how things were. You needed to come to terms with my illness and you needed to know whether our love was worth all of that mess. And if that time apart from me made you decide that it *is*, well… then I'm grateful for it. Because all I want, Stella," and I could hardly breathe as I let myself think about it, "*all* I want is to be able to hold you again. To kiss you. God, I want to kiss you."

Stella made a noise that sounded like a cross between a gasp and a laugh, and I could feel her emotions rising, glowing, burning. And they were burning for me. How could I ever have believed that I could harm this woman? I knew now, I *knew*, that I would never, *could* never, damage her in any way.

"Do you really?" she asked. "You want to kiss me? Not eat me?"

"I really never wanted to eat you, Stella," I said. "I thought I did, but that's because I didn't understand myself well enough."

"You did want to eat me, though, Howie. You were pretty graphic about it. Remember that last night that we kissed? The night you ran off on me? You said you were fantasizing about my jugular."

"Stella, I didn't even scratch the surface in telling you what terrible things crossed my mind. I would see myself pulling out your innards. I would see myself cracking open your skull. I dreamed about eating your brains. I dreamed about eating you while I made love to you. It was… it was very upsetting."

"Jesus," said Stella. "Add that to the list of things you really should have told me more about at the time."

"I know. But they didn't mean anything." When I remembered those silly thoughts that used to stray across my mind back in the days before Apex, I wanted to laugh at myself. Did I really think that those thoughts were *cravings*? I knew what cravings really felt like now, and I could recognize those old intrusive thoughts for what they were — for what Morton had always told me that they were: nothing.

"I understand it better now," I tried to explain. "My black thoughts weren't wishes. They weren't desires. They were *fears.* Just like a mother might picture her baby lying blue and still in its crib, or imagine her child falling off of a chair. Those thoughts were warnings, not urges. I can see that now. I know the difference now."

"Because after… after Apex. Then you really wanted to eat me."

"I wanted brains. I *still* want them. And I wanted you. And I thought that was the same. But when it came down to it… I realized that it wasn't. So no. I never wanted to eat you. I only thought I did."

"How bad are the cravings now?" Her mind trembled with hope.

I reflected. "Not terrible. Sometimes they come on strong, like a wave, but it passes. I try to remember *what* I am craving: a person —

someone's family. And that helps. And I think about you. And that helps, too."

"Thinking about eating me?"

"No. About being with you. I think that maybe, someday, if I can just resist, if I can stay here and try hard to get better, it'll be safe to hold you again. And when I picture that, I have trouble remembering what was so tempting about… the other thing."

"Your Dad says that your virus numbers are coming down."

"Yes. But I'm still more infectious than your average zombie, Stella."

"It'll take time. The important thing is that you're getting better. And your voice is more like it used to be… not all the way, but getting closer. Flatter."

I knew it. And I hated it. "I'm going to be brain damaged again. You know that?"

"Yeah. That's okay, Howie. Really." She had told me this over and over, but she never got impatient with me. She knew that I needed to hear it, the way she needed to hear that I meant her no harm. "I don't care about your brain damage. That *never* should have been an issue. I promise it never will be again."

Except for those few precious hours spent in Stella's presence, my day was dreary and routine. These underground rooms at B-MOSZ had no windows, of course, and my cell was intended for the imprisonment of troublesome community members. Of course, there would not be much need for a jail in a post-apocalyptic world. The threat of exile was punishment enough. But this would be a place to wait until justice could be meted out, or until charges could be proven. The bare cell lit up at six every morning and went dark at ten every night. I requested, and was granted, a lamp so my books could keep me company during those times when sleep eluded me. There was a toilet which I needed rarely and a sink with which to perform my morning ablutions. The cot had a single, flat foam pillow and a thin wool blanket over hospital sheets.

It was sufficient. Compared to my cell in Seattle, it was luxurious.

Buried on the lowest level of the complex, I was far from the minds of other people. The silence was the strangest and most unnerving part. For so many years, I had been accustomed to the hum and buzz of the world around me. Sometimes it was ugly, as it had been at Apex. Sometimes it was exquisite, as when Stella was with me. But there was always something. Now there was silence.

When Hunt stopped by to question me, I felt her coming. When my father came to visit with me, I felt him coming. Stella's parents were given clearance to visit me, and so they stopped by now and then, too.

It was interesting. Isolated from the background buzz, I was able to appreciate the minds that visited me with a new level of detail. I wasn't surprised when Stella told me that her mother had managed to freeze a horde briefly. While Elaine had not yet managed to recreate the event, I suspected that many could have the ability. All it took was a level of passion and focus.

Stella had both in abundance. When she approached, it was like the sun rising in the East.

...my heart lo! lapped strength, stole joy, would laugh, chéer.

One day, I was surprised and confused to find her mind accompanied by a new one. And what a mind! Whose was it? Hunt was there too — I could feel her, like a fresh piece of paper, like a clear mountain lake. But this was another mind... it made me think of ice cream and jukeboxes. Stella's mind was like an orchestra — it made me want to close my eyes and lose myself in the power of it. This mind was like listening to Chuck Berry. It made me want to get up and dance.

"Hello, Howie. How are you this evening?" Hunt asked in her usual polite-but-efficient way.

"Fine, thank you, Agent Hunt. How are you?"

"Apprehensive," she responded promptly. "At Stella's insistence, and your father's approval, I have brought someone to meet you."

"Meet me?"

"Yes. I will not, of course, be opening the door. I am also armed with a baton."

"You don't need it," I said.

"How are your cravings?" Hunt asked.

"They are fine, thank you. I understand why you're apprehensive, but really, I'm okay."

And I was. I really was. This new mind was delightful. I would love to spend time in its presence. But the cravings were no worse. I had conquered them. I didn't want to harm this sweet, lively mind. It would be like the death of John Lennon, the death of Buddy Holly. Why would I make the music die?

"Howie?" said Stella.

"Hello, Beautiful," I said, laying my hand against the door and wishing I was touching her face.

"This is Riya… she's Kate's girlfriend."

"Ah..." I understood better now. Stella had told me about Riya.

"Hello, Howie," said Riya. Her voice was soft and gentle. You never would have known that such a lively mind lived behind it. "It's so wonderful to meet you. I've heard so much about you from Stella and Kate."

"I'm embarrassed already," I said.

"No, don't be! They were very complimentary."

"Really?" I was surprised. "Even… even Kate?"

She laughed. "Yes, even Kate."

"Well, that's a pleasant surprise."

"There's something I want to ask you," said Riya. Her mind was brimming with curiosity.

"Then please ask." My eyes roamed my barren room. "I have nothing but time."

"Tell me… what is your idea of the perfect day?"

I was startled. Of all the questions Kate's girlfriend could have asked me, I never would have expected this one.

"Uh…" It's not that I didn't have an answer. The image rose to my mind instantly. But I wasn't sure I wanted to share it.

"I'll tell you mine. I would love to travel to a new country, meet the local people, explore, try the food, and then dance with my new friends."

Her answer touched me. It also made me sad. But really, was my perfect day any more possible? Maybe perfect days were only to be dreamed, in any case.

"My perfect day… would be a day spent with Stella," I said after a moment's pause. "I would wake her up, and kiss her, and cook her breakfast. We would walk together, and talk, and laugh. We would go somewhere quiet, just the two of us. And we would read to each other and talk some more, maybe listen to music together. Just… just be." Why were there tears in my eyes? "And then I would take her in my arms and…" I stopped talking. The rest was too private to say aloud. But I thought it. Oh, I thought it all the time.

"Damn you, Howie," Stella said, her voice rough with tears. "How do you do that?"

"Yes, very touching," said Hunt. "Okay, I'm satisfied. Time to go."

"But I have more questions I want to ask Howie," protested Riya.

"Some other time. I'm a busy woman and I don't want to stand here and babysit all evening."

"So leave Riya here," said Stella. "Howie says he's safe."

"Howie is not wholly to be trusted," said Hunt. "It's bad enough that I let you spend time with him unguarded. I'm not leaving the two of you together alone with him. He has his limits and I don't want to lose my best weapons if he misjudges his own self-restraint."

A memory rose to my mind. "Agent Hunt… do you remember when you first met my father?"

"I… yes, of course I do," said Hunt. I had thrown her off balance a little with my change in topic.

"He told me that you went against orders because you were certain that the orders were unsafe. And when you were overridden, you were proved right."

"Yes…"

"He came home and told us about it and said, 'that young woman is smarter than all her superiors put together. She puts safety before all else. We need more people like that. I only hope they learn to see her worth.'"

I could feel Hunt softening, pausing. For a moment, I thought, *it would be so easy. I could fool them. I could escape.* But the thought was fleeting. This was where I wanted to be. This was who I wanted to be.

With this tormented mind tormenting yet…

"He said that?" she asked. She was touched. I could feel it.

"Yes. So I want to thank you. For working to keep people safe. It's better to be cautious. I understand."

"Thank you," she said, her voice almost hesitant. But when she spoke again, it was with her usual stern tone. "Now. I have many other things to do. Riya, come with me, please. One powerful anti-zombie brain to be left alone with the ravager at a time, please."

"But surely he can't get through that door?"

"You didn't see him bend steel or lift a person with one hand," said Hunt grimly. "I'm not certain about anything."

"It was nice to meet you, Howie," said Riya.

"Pleasure to meet you," I said. I was disappointed that she was leaving, but I had told Hunt the truth. I understood. There was also a strange feeling to Stella's mind, and I wanted to find out more. I hoped she would stay.

Of course, she stayed.

"So… what did you think of Riya?" she asked after the footsteps of the others had faded down the hall, and the door to the stairwell had banged shut.

"I liked her."

"You did?"

"Of course," I said, perplexed. "Should I not? You've told me yourself that you like her. I expected her to be likable, and she was."

"Of course I like her. She's a sweetheart. I know you couldn't see her, but she's so adorable you just want to put her in your little pocket. And she's… she's such a people person. She's like my exact opposite, and yet she's one of the few people we've found who can pull my brain freeze trick. When Mom did it, it made sense. But when Riya did it… I don't know."

"We still don't understand how some people can do that, Stella. Even Apex didn't really understand it. They went for all the best minds they could find, by default, just in case. But they didn't know for sure. There's no way to know, I suppose. You told me that Riya still can't do it on demand."

"She almost did it tonight in practice, apparently. She's been wanting to meet you for a while. This was her reward for finally getting it right." Stella paused. She felt so agitated, and it was an emotion that I couldn't place. "Ray says when she does it, it's like a cold wind that blows right through you. Or like being carried away down a river."

I was perpetually fascinated by our tendency to take a sensation for which English had no words and try to describe it using similes and metaphors. "Interesting. He always described you in terms of light."

"I guess her mind is really different from mine," said Stella. There was a hint of a question in her voice.

"Very."

"But… it's a nice mind?"

"It's a wonderful mind," I said.

And I felt her respond, and that's when I recognized the feeling. It was how I used to feel when she brought up her Drama partner. What was his name?

I stifled a laugh. "You're jealous," I said.

"How did you fucking know that?"

I didn't answer. Stella muttered something which I couldn't hear through the door but I suspect was something along the lines of, 'Stupid mind-readers'.

"Okay, so I'm a little jealous," said Stella after a minute. "A bit."

I decided that wisdom lay in silence.

"Okay, so go ahead and tell me," said Stella. "Is her brain prettier than mine?"

It was even harder not to laugh this time. Oh, my beauty. My star.

Light of my life, and life of my desire

"Is that why you wanted to bring her down here? To find out if I would love her mind more than yours?"

"No," said Stella in a tone that usually meant, 'Yes'. "I mean, not entirely. She did want to meet you. But… yeah, I guess. A bit. I wanted to know."

"Stella, your mind is… exquisite. It's a work of art, a precious thing, an experience that I would walk over hot coals to reach."

"That's not saying much, since you can't feel pain."

"My point is that I adore your mind. But it is not why I love you."

"It isn't?"

"No. At least, not entirely. I love your mind. I love to be in its presence. But so does my father. So does Hazel. So does Ray."

"Ray? He doesn't act like it."

"I don't think Ray particularly likes loving your mind. But he admits that it's pleasurable. Even Army loves it."

"Yeah, whenever I visit Hazel he drools on my shoe. Ray wants to take him with him to the farm, but Hazel wants to keep Army here. She's started taking other dogs with her on hikes since she's not scared of running into zombies in the woods."

"In any case, only one of us is in love with you, Stella. Not my father. Not Ray. Not Army. Just me."

"Thank goodness for that. Imagine if Doc had a crush on me. Awkward."

"I love *you*, Stella. All of you. I love your tough exterior. I love your passionate interior. I love your determination. I love your intelligence. I love that you have the body of a queen. I love… everything."

"Howie?"

"Yes?"

"There's something you need to know." She was full love and pain. Why? Why did my love hurt her?

"What's that?"

"You need to know… while you were gone… you know I didn't know you were missing, right?"

"I asked them not to tell you."

"Well. I uh. I dated someone else for a little while."

Oh God, the pain. I had suspected it. I knew that she probably would. I knew that she deserved to. And it shouldn't matter because whoever he was, she wasn't with him. She was here, with me. But God forgive me, I wanted to find him, the one who dared touch those lips. They were mine. She was *mine.*

"Howie? You okay?"

"Yeah," I said, and I tried to hide it, but my voice was full of pain. She wasn't mine, I reminded myself. She was hers.

"Well… anyway. I broke up with him. Before all of this. Because I realized… Howie, I realized that I couldn't love him the way I loved you. It wasn't working. I just didn't have room for him. All I wanted was you."

"Really?" I clung to this. This was what mattered. I would hold on to the sound of her voice tonight when I was plagued with thoughts of her, her arms wrapped around another. *I couldn't love him the way I loved you.* Of course she couldn't. I was hers.

"Really. I tried to forget you. I tried to move on. But I couldn't. Because when I closed my eyes, all I could see was you."

Stella

My house had never had good afternoon light, and it was dim when I turned the key and opened the door. Even though it had only been empty for a few weeks, it had an abandoned feel to it. Or maybe that was just my imagination.

It had taken us a while to expand out to my old neighbourhood, but when we did, Hunt said I could stop at my house and pick up some of our things.

I remembered how, when we moved to Vancouver, my parents made me get rid of half of my things, and it had felt like the end of the world. Now the world had actually ended, and I could only bring what I could carry out of here in one trip.

It's hard to pick the most special of special things you own, and even harder to pick for other people. I went for the photo albums, and Mom's jewelry, and a little statue Dad loved that Mom had always made fun of. The Christmas stuff was still up, so I pulled some of Dad's favourite ornaments off of the tree — like the lopsided clay star I made in grade three, and a family photo of the three of us loaded into a cheap metal snowflake from Michaels, and the cross stitch with my name that my Dad's mother had made for me when I was born. We'd probably never have a Christmas tree again, but I knew Dad would want them, anyway. After a moment's hesitation, I removed the mistletoe from over the door, too. Dad loved mistletoe. I grabbed a couple of Mom's favourite books and a couple of Dad's.

Most of the suitcase I was filling was with Mom and Dad's stuff, because my favourite things were all at my apartment, which I could visit without much trouble, since it was so close to B-MOSZ. But I did pull open my dresser drawer, and after a minute of rummaging, I found it — a delicate gold ring, with a gleaming ruby.

I put that in my pocket.

57

Stella

I don't know what made me swing by the lab that day. I was coming in, dusty and blood-spattered, after we hit a big horde on the way back to base. I had suffered through bite-check, where all the parts of me not covered by armour were invasively inspected by volunteers, and I desperately wanted to get my stiff muscles into a hot shower — even though all the showers were on ten minute timers.

But despite all of that, I needed to talk to Doc Mullins about Howie.

Because after I left him at night and crawled into my creaking, thin little bed, I fretted. I was losing track of time — the days all blended into each other — but it had been weeks, now. And Howie was better, no question. His voice was getting more and more of its usual husky drone, although when I told him about Dean — God, that had sucked — it still went all high pitched and awful, so I knew I had hurt him. But most of the time, he seemed like the old Howie. He had even told me a science joke the night before.

But as far as I knew, he was still infectious, and that scared the shit out of me. What if he, just, like, *never got better*? What if the rest of my life was going to be sitting on a cement floor and talking to the love of my life through a steel door?

I mean, I could get a chair eventually, but *still*.

They couldn't keep him there forever. They couldn't keep feeding him out of paper cups forever. I mean, among other problems, paper cups were non-renewable resource now.

I had to talk to his dad.

And so I veered off down the hall on my way into B-MOSZ and walked up to the lab.

I heard the raised voices before I got close enough to knock, and I paused.

"...A danger to every man, woman, and child in this entire facility! He's already given you all the information you're going to get from him, and we don't even know how accurate it was... it completely contradicts the story he was giving me while he was at Apex..."

"Because that wasn't *him*, George," said Hunt's voice shortly. "We've been over this."

"You don't know that! You admit yourself that he changed significantly after being fed those human brains. You don't know anything for certain."

"You forget, George, that I am quite good at discerning truth from lies," said Doc Mullins's voice in its usual intellectual monotone.

"Not good enough to clear my name when I was accused of treason!"

"My ability to detect brain waves is not admissible in court as evidence," said Doc, with a nuance of amusement in his voice.

I raised my hand and knocked loudly on the lab door.

Everyone fell silent. The door opened.

"Hello, Stella," said Doc, adjusting his glasses. "How may we help you?"

"I want to join in the argument," I said, walking in. "We're fighting about Howie, right?"

"You surmise correctly," said Doc. I shot him a glance. He *was* amused.

"Great, where can I join in?" I said.

Baum looked at me with disgust. "I was making the argument that young Howard should be released from the facility, or executed."

"Uh, no," I said. "That's not happening."

"Excuse me, I believe I am in charge of this facility," said Hunt. *She* looked amused too, and I caught her exchanging glances with Doc.

"Yeah, and I'm the only person around here who has her zombie-freezing skills under control," I said. "And everyone I pass in the halls treats me like the second coming of Christ."

Baum winced. "I wouldn't go so far as to say that. Let's make at least a Canadian comparison. You're treated like a Trudeau, I would go so far to say."

"Sure. Whatever. My point is, yeah, my opinion matters. And you're not getting rid of Howie."

"I share Stella's sentiment, although I am less essential," said Doc.

"Of course you're essential, Morton, and we're all fond of Howie," said Hunt tiredly. "At least, Howie as he was. I'm not a fan of the new, improved version."

"The old one's coming back. You'd know that if you spent more time with him," I argued.

"I'm a bit busy trying to save my little corner of the world," she said with some asperity. Doc held up his hand, and she seemed to bite her tongue.

"Michaella is severely overstretched," said Doc. "But I agree with Stella. Howie's personality is reverting very nicely to his old self. We have every reason to believe that he is a ravager no more."

"Except for this," said Baum, pointing at a small stick with two dots on it.

"He's still positive, huh?" I asked, looking at the dots.

"It's much lighter than previous tests," said Doc. "The virus load is easing. I am greatly encouraged."

"It is a daily risk to keep him here. This is supposed to be a secure facility. We have a community to protect," said Baum. "Furthermore, how do you plan to explain to *anyone* what he is? It is hard enough to convince people to coexist peacefully with infected individuals. Far too many people are beginning to notice that the Mullinses do not use armour when they go on patrol and that they take their meals privately. It is only a matter of time before it is common knowledge that they are infected, and we may have a small rebellion on our hands when the time comes. No one is going to want infected people sleeping in the same facility as their children."

"You explain that they are *infected* not *infectious,*" I said.

"Except for young Howard!"

"He won't be infectious forever!" I shouted. "He can't be! He's GOT TO GET BETTER."

"Stella..." Hunt started to say.

"NO!" I shouted, tears beginning to run down my face. "He's getting better! He'll get BETTER."

They were quiet. Baum looked almost pitying.

"You do think so, don't you?" I said to Doc pleadingly.

"I am hopeful, yes," he said. "But perhaps we should discuss worst case scenarios."

"I agree," said Baum.

"I can't stay for this," I said. "I'm out of here."

I slammed the door behind me as I stepped out into the hall. I wiped my eyes and strode back to the main corridor. I really needed that hot shower.

"Hey, Stella!" people called as I walked by. I smiled and waved as necessary.

Popularity felt *weird*.

Then a hand gripped my shoulder, and I spun around and nearly kicked the person who had grabbed me. I caught myself just in time.

It was Dean.

"You scared me!" I growled.

"Sorry," he said, holding up his hands. "I just saw you going by and I wanted to talk."

"Okay," I said reluctantly, stepping out of the way of the other people coming off patrol. "Were you out on patrol today, too?"

"Yeah. Helping inspect the future fence line. Clearing things, you know." His dark eyes glanced down at his feet.

I nodded.

"I was wondering..." he said, still staring at his shoes, "...they're doing that movie night thing tonight. Are you going?"

"No."

"Oh." He looked up again. He had dark circles under his eyes. His sparkle was gone. I ached for him. For his pain. "I thought maybe..."

"Yeah, I know they made me announce it at the meeting. Hunt likes to make me talk about trivialities in front of everyone at the weekly pep-talk. But I have something else I need to do tonight."

Like I'd give up my time with Howie to watch *Sleepless in Seattle*, which struck me as a weirdly tone-deaf choice. But then, most people hadn't *seen* Seattle on the day of the fall. To me, it was a movie about a world that no longer existed. It was historical fiction.

"How's your Dad?" I asked.

Dean shrugged half-heartedly. "Oh... he's been having a rough time, but they've got him working on the wording for the community policies and stuff, and they want him on the justice committee, so that's keeping him busy."

"Good... good," I said. I was trying to figure out how to escape the conversation. I was saved by Baum, of all people.

"Miss Blunt, can I speak with you?" he asked, marching up to us.

"Yeah, sure," I said almost eagerly. Anything to end this awkwardness with my ex.

"Okay, well... see you around, Stella," said Dean, giving me his lost-puppy-dog look. Once again I wished I could be his friend without giving him false hope. But I was keeping my distance because I knew that was kinder.

And maybe it was kinder to myself, too. Because I missed physical affection. He was an attractive guy, and he was comfortable and familiar, and it would be easy — too easy — to lay a head on his shoulder or to try and work off some of these complex emotions that we lived with every day.

But Howie was worth more to me. There was no contest. I would rather be sexually frustrated and on the other side of Howie's door than emotionally lonely and unsatisfied with Dean.

"Bye, Dean. Talk to you later. Say hi to your Dad. And Kelly."

He nodded and trudged away.

I turned to Baum. "What now?"

"First of all, you can start using a more polite tone. You are a community leader, now. The way you behave and speak to others will have an impact on the group as a whole."

I considered this. "Okay. Fair. How can I help you?"

"I am seeking your reassurance that you do not plan to enter into a romantic relationship with young Howard, should he ever be deemed releasable."

"I… you what?"

"I am extremely concerned for your welfare and the welfare of the community."

"Really? You're still on the whole zombies-shouldn't-date kick? REALLY?"

"I realize that you think I'm prejudiced," he said, looking impatient. "But I actually do have very valid reasons to be concerned. Has anyone actually *talked* to you about the risks of sexual relations with an infected individual?"

"Howie did! He was always *very* concerned for my 'welfare'."

"Considering that he entered into a romantic relationship with you, I disagree on that score. I was delighted to hear that you had begun dating a healthy human boy. However, I understand that you and your boyfriend have dissolved ties."

"Yeah, you just interrupted me talking to him, actually."

Baum looked chagrined. "I wouldn't have intruded if I'd realized that. I want you to be happy, you know. I want to encourage you to pursue more healthy relationships."

"I will pursue whatever relationships I damn well please, pardon my French," I said. "Howie is sick and needs to get better. That's all, for now. And my love life is no one's business but mine. So, respectfully, as a community leader, I am asking you to butt out."

I stormed off and Baum let me go. I have a way of freezing people, you see, and it isn't just zombies that it works on.

"I hate that after all he put you through, after all you went through *at his request,* he wants to get *rid* of you," I raged at Howie that evening. I had taken my hot shower, scarfed down a brief meal of fresh-from-the-farm steak and canned peas, changed into my PJs, and then booted it down the stairs to Howie.

"He's trying to keep people safe, Beautiful," said Howie. "He's genuinely is concerned for everyone's welfare."

"He's a pompous, moronic asshole."

"Well, no one's perfect," said Howie. "I'm less pompous, but I've cannibalized a lot more people than he has."

"At least you can joke about it now," I said.

"There's a line from Gerard Manley Hopkins — *My own heart let me more have pity on; let/Me live to my sad self hereafter kind/Charitable; not live this tormented mind.* I'm trying to do that. I can't help what happened to me, so I'm trying to think of the future."

"The future which Baum is determined to take away from you."

"He won't, though. Not if I get better. He won't like it but he'll let me stay. And that's all I want. To stay here. Near you."

"Also books, right?"

"Those too."

"Good morning, unit one hundred three five," said my father one morning as I joined my Mom and him for breakfast. "I see you have received your daily ration of morning nourishment. I, too, have received my daily ration of morning nourishment. Let us consume it within fifteen minutes as delineated by the schedule before we assume our regularly scheduled tasks."

"Dad, you invented this numbering system for keeping everyone's rations and stuff organized," I said, looking at the stamp on my hand which showed that I had received my breakfast.

"Sure. Because it makes sense, and it's efficient. It's still depressing as hell."

"The joy of being a cog in the corporate machine," said my mother. "What's happened to us, Tim? You're turning people into numbers and I'm helping write propaganda."

"Technically, it's not a corporate machine, it's a socialist machine. No currency," pointed out Dad.

"I wonder how long before that changes?" my mother mused.

"Check their damn thirty-year plan," I said, looking gloomily at my limp piece of bacon. "At least we have eggs now. I like this farming thing."

"So, where are you risking life and limb today?" Dad asked, shovelling eggs into his mouth.

"Nowhere. I'm getting my first day off in two weeks. I'm-a SLEEP. And maybe read a book."

"You're going to spend it outside Howie's door, aren't you?"

"Yeah, probably. But with a book, maybe. Or he could read to me from one of the books Hunt let him have."

"Has it ever occurred to you to, like, bring a chair?" my mother asked. "Instead of making your butt numb on the cement floor?"

"No. It would feel weird and formal. I feel closer to him when I sit on the ground."

"Well, you won't be sitting there today," said Hunt, behind me.

I turned and glared at her. "You're taking away my day off? Really? This had better be important."

"Uh, Stella, they use you to rescue people. I'm pretty sure that's always important," said Dad.

"I didn't say that I was taking away your day off," said Hunt. "As challenging as today's planned trip to UBC will be, I think our convoy will actually be safer moving past the downtown core without you on it. We don't know where Apex is, or how many Ravagers are in the area. In any case, I'm making sure that everyone is doubly well armed, I'll have Hazel monitoring for brain waves, and they have full permission to turn back if necessary. No, I am not taking away your day off."

"But you said..."

"That you won't be sitting outside Howie's door today." She had a hint of a sparkle in her eye.

"Why not?"

"Because his father tested him again this morning, and he tested negative."

I stood. "SHUT. UP."

"I'll take that to mean, 'thank you for that wonderful piece of information, Agent Hunt,'" she said with a bit of a smile. "He actually tested negative yesterday, too, but we wanted twenty-four-hour confirmation."

"So I can go in and see him?"

"Yes. With an escort. *If* he's chained. He might still have the strength to break the chain but it would still make me feel better."

"Sure. Whatever it takes. Let's go!"

I charged away from the table, leaving the remains of my breakfast behind.

"So, I'll just bus your tray then, shall I?" shouted Dad after me.

Everyone stepped out of my way. Not because I was using the force of my personality on them, but because… people just made way for me now. I had always been visible, but in the past, that made me feel like a target. Hell, even *zombies* targeted me. But that was all ancient history now. Here, in this place, I was a celebrity. People greeted me by name in the halls and thanked me for pulling them to safety. People treated me with awe.

All it took was the end of the world.

Hunt followed me at a brisk pace with a smile on her face. When we got down to Howie's door, Doc was stepping out of the room. He was smiling, too.

"Howie submitted quite willingly to being handcuffed. He tells me that he doesn't think he has the strength to snap them, but also assured me that he has no intention of trying."

"Good," said Hunt. She opened the door and looked in. "I'm sending her in, now, Howie. If you give us the slightest reason to think that you're going to hurt her, we will lock you away and throw away the key."

"I won't hurt her," said Howie. "I couldn't even hurt her when I was beside myself. There is no way that I will hurt her now that I'm myself again."

"But you don't mind being handcuffed?"

"Agent Hunt, I would submit to being hogtied and placed in an iron maiden if it meant that I could see Stella."

"Fair enough. Go on in, Stella."

I stepped into the room cautiously and looked.

He was Howie. They'd given him clean clothes, and he had tucked his button-down shirt neatly into his slacks just like he always used to do. They'd found him a pair of glasses. His hands were cuffed in front of him, and his feet were cuffed together. His foggy blue eyes were smiling at me, and his shy, dimpled grin was back. My heart thudded wildly. I hadn't seen that smile in almost a year. God. It was part of a world that had been completely lost to me, and I think that some part of me assumed that Howie and his smile had gone with it.

"Hello, Beautiful," he said in his soft, husky, bland little voice. "You're a sight for sore eyes."

I had thought that when — or if — I finally saw him again and it was safe, I would grab him and start kissing him. But it doesn't feel natural to grab someone who is cuffed hand and foot and start smooching them. Especially when you have the guy's father and your boss watching you. But I drank in every bit of Howie's *Howieness*. Like his dimple. God, I wanted to do things to that dimple.

"They said that you're testing negative, now," I said. "That's… really good news."

"Yes, it is," he said, his eyes fixed on mine. "But it's good that they're being cautious."

"Is it okay… to have me here? Are you thinking about killing me?"

"It's more than okay. And no, I'm not. I know now that I could never do it, so there's no point in thinking about it. I feel like I have the virus more under control than I ever have before. But it's going to take time for me to prove it."

He looked so healthy. He looked so calm. He looked like Howie.

"Sit down," he said, jerking his hands toward the bed. "Let's read until they get bored of watching us."

And so we took turns reading poetry to each other, leaning shoulder to shoulder, head to head. Heart to heart.

Howie

I had forgotten how sexy Stella was. I had remembered her long brown hair, which was looking longer now. I had remembered her brown eyes, and how they sparkled when she looked at me. I had remembered her hourglass figure, the body that was both soft and strong, just like Stella. But somehow, I hadn't remembered — couldn't remember — how it all looked when combined with the force of her personality. When she walked in, I wanted to fall to my knees in front of her.

But she was so hesitant, so nervous, that it broke my heart. I suppose I had expected her to march in and kiss me or something. But now I saw that I would have to earn her back, rebuild the trust that I had broken when I grabbed her and threw her on the ground.

You couldn't use force on Stella.

Any kind of push, any resistance, and she would close up. Stella was so passionate, so tender, that she guarded herself reflexively. You had to be gentle. You had to be open. You had to be trustworthy. You had to make her feel loved. And when you did, she opened like a flower to the sunshine.

But I had destroyed that, and I could see the guardedness in her eyes. Despite all of our long talks, despite everything we had been through together, her trust was yet to be earned back.

So, I resigned myself. I wouldn't get to taste those lips today. That was okay. I could be patient. I had to earn her. I had to deserve her. I had worked hard to get here, and I could work harder still.

That night, that year
Of now done darkness I wretch lay wrestling with (my God!) my God.

She was worth it. She was worth all of it. And I knew my way to her heart. So handed her a book, and I listened to her voice reading my favourite poems aloud while I dreamed of the day when I could love her again.

58

Stella

Hunt got sick of standing there and watching us read Gerard Manley Hopkins poems at each other after about an hour. I'd been hoping she'd decide everything was fine and leave us alone so we could work through the weirdness of being close to each other again, but she called me out, instead.

"If he continues to do well, we'll start trusting him unsupervised," she said. "But for now, I want..."

"Yeah, yeah, I get it," I said. "Doc! Wait!"

Howie's father had been heading for the stairwell, but he stopped and turned. "Yes, Stella?"

"I have some questions I need to ask you. Important ones. Do you have a few minutes?"

He glanced at his watch. "I need to check on some experiments. If you want to come with me, I will certainly endeavour to answer your questions."

"Great."

I followed him up to the top level and to his lab. Dr. Wong was in there, too. I looked for Kate's mom, but I didn't see her. Just as well. Talk about awkward.

"Hi, Dr. Wong."

"Call me Gordon," he said with a quick smile. "Doc, I'm about halfway through these slides, but things are looking pretty much the way we expected."

"Ah well," said Doc. "We'll collate the data and start planning the next step."

"I was hoping to speak to you privately," I said to him impatiently. He looked resigned.

"Gordon, Stella wants to speak with me and I'm going to be taking the infected ones out for swabbing anyway. Do you mind stepping out?"

"What if *she* gets bitten?" he asked.

"Stella is more than capable of incapacitating a few hamsters."

"Yeah, I guess so," he said. "I'll go take a bathroom break, then." He stretched, switched off the microscope, stood up, and left.

"So what experiment is this?" I asked Doc as he opened the first cage and pulled out a hamster.

"Thanks to some guidance from Howie, I have recreated my experiment from the seventies, but with very modest dosages of human brain tissue."

"Where did you…" I started to ask, and then I decided that I didn't want to know about it.

"If I keep the doses low enough — only once a week — I can prevent the aggression, and now we have plexiglass cages for them, so I don't have to worry about them bending bars."

"But they're infectious?"

"Yes. Very. And intelligent. He's watching you."

I looked, and the hamster was staring at me with an intensity that was definitely unnerving. I stepped back a few paces.

"Don't worry, I've got a firm grip on him. We've discontinued his dosages, the way we did with Howie, and are waiting to see what the long-term effects are." He swabbed the hamster's cheek and then dropped it back in the cage. It tried to leap out of the open door but he shut it quickly and the hamster bonked its head on the plexiglass.

"Now," he said, turning to me. "What is it you wish to discuss?"

"Is Howie completely clear? Like, not infectious at all?"

"It appears so, yes. We're a couple of weeks behind with our hamster experiment, so I cannot confirm. But it seems that he is back to normal."

"When do you think Hunt is going to feel ready to let him be free to come and go?"

He raised his eyebrows. "You would have to ask Michaella that yourself."

"Because when he is, I want him to live with me. In my room."

His eyebrows climbed further into his hairline. "Michaella will not like that. If she had the manpower for an armed guard by your bedside, she would have it. Putting Howie — with his recent history — in a room with you when you are most vulnerable will not strike her as wise."

"I know that. But what do you think? Do you think Howie would hurt me?"

"I am inclined to believe that Howie has made a full recovery. His brain waves feel like those of his siblings… mostly. They are richer than before. More complex. That may be residual intelligence, or it may simply be that he has learned more and become a little wiser. I have no reason to believe that he wishes you any harm. The fact that he refrained from hurting you when he was under the full effect of the virus indicates to me that Howie's willpower is extremely strong. He believes, and I agree, that if he didn't hurt you then, there is no risk of him hurting you now."

"Would you vouch that to Agent Hunt?"

"I've already given her my opinion. But I am a scientist, Stella. I don't work on hunches. I work on science. I plan to demonstrate it using my laboratory subjects. But that takes time."

"Have you only tested Howie's saliva?"

"Are you asking if I have tested his blood?"

"No. I want to know how dangerous it would be for Howie and me to have sex." My cheeks burned a bit, but I wasn't going to shy away from the question. I needed to know. "Using a condom, obviously," I said hurriedly when he looked surprised. "Or not even *that* kind of sex but just… you know. Contact?"

"I have never been concerned that the virus may be transmissible in that way," he said.

"What?" I was floored. "But… Howie said we couldn't have sex because you thought it might be transmissible! He said you tested with hamsters and everything. And Baum…"

"Yes, I did, with some concerning results. But if Howie told you that the virus was passed directly from the males to the females, he mislead you. Z0381E is not a sexually transmissible virus. What I told Howie, and what my experiment confirmed, was that a pregnancy would be dangerous due to the way the genome of the virus incorporates itself into the reproductive system. Sexual contact is safe, but pregnancy represents a grave concern. Happily, there are excellent contraceptive options available these days. I understand that those are being liberated from stores and warehouses along with other pharmaceuticals. As for George, well… he's a very cautious man."

"You mean… it's safe to have sex? It was *always* safe to have sex? His jizz is *fine*?"

"As long as you made every effort to prevent pregnancy, yes." He was obviously uncomfortable. He kept polishing his glasses.

I wanted to go pound Howie into the ground. Except I couldn't because the poor guy had been to hell and back, so there was no point in yelling at him for lies he told me a year ago.

"But… why…"

"Howie didn't want to take the risk of your becoming pregnant. When he was younger, accidental pregnancy was very common. And it still is, or was, despite the many advances in birth control, due to improper use. I think Howie may have had an inflated idea of risk."

I was trying hard not to be angry, but fuck.

Doc looked at me sympathetically. "Howie suffered a great deal from anxiety around the virus and its effects on him. If he was not willing to consider intercourse with you, then feel assured that it stemmed from that anxiety, and not a wish to deceive you. While I can hardly say that his recent experiences are a good thing, I do think that he may have laid some of those demons to rest. You can discuss the topic with him again if you like."

I sighed heavily. "Yeah, and I can hardly kick his ass about it now. Thanks, Doc. I have to go think some things through."

Hunt rapped on my door at seven thirty the next morning.

"Rise and shine, Stella. You haven't turned up for breakfast, and I can't have you fainting on patrol from low blood sugar. Get up, eat, and get dressed. We roll out at eight."

I opened the door to my room. "Yeah, I don't know if I'm going to go out, today."

She put a hand on one hip. "Excuse me?"

"I think might just stay home."

"Are you *ill*?"

"No. I'm wanting to draw up a contract. You have assignments for me day after day, with no regularly scheduled days off. You keep me working from eight in the morning until eight at night."

"I just gave you a day off! Stella, we're all overworked these days, and I'm sorry, but there are people out there who need our help, and you are a vital..."

"Yeah, no, I get that. I do. But I have some terms I'd like you to agree to."

"Terms? Are you looking for overtime pay and a benefits package?" she looked annoyed. "Because I haven't had a day off *yet*, Stella. I don't even know what the word means anymore."

"I know, and I sympathize, I do. But I have a few things I really need to lay down as requirements."

She closed her eyes for a few seconds. "Get dressed. Eat your breakfast. Show up for patrol. I will sit down with you and listen to your terms *after eight p.m.*"

"Aye aye, captain."

I knocked on Hunt's door after I finished my weapon training that night. I was wiped. When Hunt opened the door, she looked wiped, too.

"Come in. I hear you had a rough day out there."

"You could say that," I said, stepping into her room. "I think Ravagers laid down those metal bits on purpose to puncture our tires."

"I'm sure of it," she said. "I'm glad you managed to get everyone back up the mountain to safety. This is why we normally have a two-truck minimum, so that if one vehicle fails there is a second. I shouldn't have allowed you to go out singly. But we're stretched thin and so I risked it. I apologize."

"Don't. You made a tough call, and it didn't work out. It's okay. We caught the Ravager who set the trap, and we got the tire changed and got out before more showed up. It worked out."

"If you hadn't been there, I don't see how they could have gotten the tire changed without being attacked by a horde. Of course, that's why I allowed your truck to go alone in the first place. You gave me that extra margin of safety. But protocols are there for a reason and I won't make that mistake again. Have a seat." She gestured to the single chair at her desk and sat on the bed. "Before you get to your own demands, I've made a list of terms that I want you to agree to." She handed me a list.

I scanned the document. "Risk life and limb, stay within the confines of B-MOSZ at all times unless sent with armed guards, become proficient in at least three types of ranged weapon, try to teach people to do my brain freeze trick, set an example around the community, minimize public swearing, participate in your little group cheer community meetings, work to bolster the spirits of the people, etc etc. Yeah, I expected all of this. It's fair."

"So. What are your terms?" She asked. "Ice cream on Sundays? Two days off a week? If so, I warn you, I strike a hard bargain."

"So do I. I don't care about days off. I mean, I want them when I can get them but I trust you to tell me when that is. You care about people's emotional well-being, and I'm valuable to you. You're not going to run me into the ground, especially if I tell you that I'm cracking up."

"So what is it, then, Stella?"

"Howie. I want Howie. I want him free. I want him helping on patrols — no one better — and you could think about putting him in the kitchen too, because he's a good cook and some of your kitchen volunteers suuuuuck."

She folded her arms and frowned. "I do plan to let Howie free as soon as I feel completely comfortable that he is to be trusted."

"Yeah, well, I'm not done. He's going to be my roommate. We will be boyfriend and girlfriend and we will live together like other adults in a relationship. And no one — not you, not Agent Baum, *no one* — will make a fuss about it."

"You're making this a *condition*?"

"Yes. Because I could see this dragging on for months. First allowing Howie to come on patrol, but tied up. Then allowing him to roam, but in handcuffs. Weeks before I'm even allowed to be alone with him. And I can see you refusing to allow him alone in a room with me when I'm sleeping. Look me in the eye and tell me that you weren't planning on treating him like a criminal for a really, really long time."

She looked me in the eye, and I stared right back at her.

"I have no intention of letting Howard Mullins roam free, or sleep in your bed, for a long time. Until very recently, he was mentally and emotionally unbalanced, not to mention highly contagious. That's not something I can just allow to roam my facility."

"He was unwell, but he still came with us. He still gave us information. He may have saved lives."

"He *has* saved lives, I'm certain of it," she said. "And all of this information was good. But I can't afford to take risks right now. Our situation is precarious at best. It's ridiculous to me that you're willing to risk lives out of sheer impatience, and furthermore, that you're willing to blackmail me by making your services contingent on it."

"It isn't *sheer impatience*. It's an image thing." I pointed at her list. "If people see him going around in handcuffs, or tied up, or under guard, they will *never* trust him. He will be the enemy. Forever. And then, when he and I try to move in together, you and Baum will sit me down and tell me that I have to set an example, that I'm a leader of the community and that it would risk everyone's trust if I'm seen *fraternizing* — you *know* Baum would use that word — with the enemy. It's going to be bad enough when people learn what the Mullinses are. And they will, because it's pretty obvious — I mean, they go out on patrols without armour and they can feel the brainwaves of survivors. Oh, and we have stockpiles of brains for them. So it's not exactly going to be a secret. That's going to cause friction *guaranteed.* Add one of them under armed guard, and you're going to have *problems.*"

She blinked and raised her eyebrows.

I held up the list again and read from it.

"Ms. Blunt agrees to exhibit language and conduct in public which befits a community leader." I folded my arms. "I can see Baum applying that against me, to say that it included not hanging around with former-Ravager zombies in public, and certainly not cohabitating with them. So I want it written in there. Howie gets amnesty. I am given complete freedom to live my personal life as I choose, regardless of how that *befits a community leader,* or I don't go out on patrol at all. I want to help people, but I will not give up my life to be your political puppet, and I won't let you turn Howie into a pariah, either. It's just not happening. Okay?"

Hunt twisted her lips in thought as we sat there, staring each other down.

"You realize that I can force you, right?" she said. "You realize that we can handcuff you ourselves and march you out to a truck every morning?"

"Yes. But I don't think you would. My conditions are reasonable, and you're a reasonable person," I said.

"You're counting on my being soft."

"No, I'm counting on you not being an idiot. Your choices are to march both Howie *and* me under armed guard, in handcuffs, onto a patrol truck every morning, which wouldn't exactly make people feel relaxed, or that all was well within their new community, or lock us both up and lose me on patrols, *or* agree to my perfectly reasonable demands and save yourself a lot of headache and trouble."

Hunt rapped her fingers on her thigh.

"All right," she said. "You have a deal. But I need to add some more conditions to your contract."

59

Howie

I was listening to the iPod that Stella's father had loaned me when I felt Agent Hunt coming down the hall. I sat up, and my door clicked and flew open.

"Okay, Howie," said Hunt. "You're free."

"I'm… what?"

"Free. Free to roam the facility. Free to become a part of the community. *Not* free to leave the facility without permission, or attack or kill any of my population."

"I wouldn't do that." It was already hard to remember how I could ever have wanted that. Oh, I could feel the virus there, lurking in the back of my mind. But I was master of it, now.

That night, that year, of now done darkness

"Good. In that case, I have someone coming down to show you to your new quarters upstairs."

It was Stella. I felt her coming down the hall, and I felt her joy. I trembled at it.

my heart lo! lapped strength, stole joy, would laugh, cheer.

She stepped into my room, smiling. "Hello, stranger."

"Hello yourself," I replied. My voice was shaking. "They're really letting me go?"

"Yep. We had a talk, Agent Hunt and I. Get your books, and anything else they let you have in here."

I gathered my few meagre possessions — the books, the iPod, my change of clothes, and I followed Stella down the echoing hallway. Agent Hunt walked behind, and I could feel her concern and her suspicion. This was thanks to Stella, this miracle, because Hunt still didn't trust me.

How long had it been since I had the pleasure of walking behind Stella? Each of her steps seemed to drive my blood pressure higher. But the black thoughts didn't intrude. I didn't fear them anymore — they knew they had no power over me.

I followed her up the stairwell and into a busier hallway. It was full of life. Minds buzzed at me. People smiled at Stella as she passed. I felt their awe and respect for her.

Finally, they all see what I see. They all see how magnificent this young woman is.

It was hard to grasp that now I would be free to come and go from my room as I pleased. I could go to her door in the mornings. Perhaps kiss her goodnight at night. I could woo her again as she deserved to be wooed.

"What the fuck?" said a voice. I felt a mind near me surge with possessive rage, and I turned to see the boy from our high school, her drama partner. I saw how he looked at me, and how he looked at her, and I felt his hurt and his fury, and I knew with a sudden, sickening certainty that this was the boy Stella had dated while I lay chained to a chair. He had tasted her lips. He had held her body against his. No. It was more than that. I knew, as his pain burned through me, that he had known Stella in ways that I never had. I wanted to vomit. I wanted to hit him, attack him, this soft human thing, for daring to touch what was mine. *MINE.*

But she wasn't really mine. She was hers. And so was I.

"What's up, Dean?" asked Stella. The weariness in her voice calmed me instantly. I focused on her mind. She wasn't happy to see him. This boy, this handsome young man with the lively mind, he hadn't made her happy.

"Where the fuck did *he* come from?" he said, pointing at me. Then he looked sharply back at Stella. "This is why, isn't it? You're going back to *him*?"

"Have a good day, Dean," Stella said. Her voice was patient, but I could feel the edge to it.

"Good to see you again," I said to him gravely as we walked on.

Stella wasn't mine. But I was hers, and she knew it, and she had chosen to come back to me. It didn't matter what she had done with that boy. Because her heart had stayed with me.

"This is your new room," Stella said, leading me into a bedroom with two cots pushed up against each other to make one double bed. I walked in and looked around. It was smaller than my cell, and it was already decorated. The small metal shelf was loaded with books, including a familiar leather-bound copy of *Jane Eyre*. A large picture frame held a collage of snapshots of Stella, her family, and her friends.

"I cleared out the top drawer for you," she said, without looking at me. She opened the drawer, "So you can put your sad little heap of clothes in there."

I looked back at Agent Hunt, but she was gone. Stella looked out into the hallway and closed the door.

"I have to tell you that Hunt gave me a panic button," she said, "So if you're planning on attacking me, there'll be people with electric dildos here in seconds."

I smiled. "I will never hurt you. But… what…"

"This is my room, dingus," she said. "You're moving in with me." She raised one eyebrow. "Unless you don't want to."

I felt like I could barely breathe.

"Living… with you?"

"Yes. This *our* bed. We will sleep in it together. Again, unless you don't want to. Speak the word and Hunt will be delighted to give you your own room. This part was the hardest bit to negotiate."

I opened my mouth and no words come out.

"I feel like I need your consent, here, Howie. Again, if you don't want to…"

"I want to," I said, the words coming out in a gasping rush. "Of course I… I just never…"

"Welcome to adulthood, Howie," she said with a smirk, taking my bundle of books and clothes and putting it in the top drawer. "I checked the calendar. Today's my birthday. And you're my birthday present to myself."

"Happy birthday," I breathed. I couldn't handle this much joy. It was too good. Living… with Stella? Sleeping in her bed? So… when she undressed… and when we went to bed… my brain stalled at the concept.

"So, can I kiss you now? You know, without you trying to eat my face or something?" Her eyes were sparkling, but I could tell she was feeling hesitant. She was still remembering how I attacked her. I could barely remember it — it was more dreamlike than most of my dreams. But to her, it must still feel very real.

I stepped forward and took her in my arms. Oh, God. I had forgotten the soft feel of her warmth. I had forgotten everything. Once, I had wondered how I could live without her. Now I just wondered how I could be lucky enough to live *with* her.

"Yes, you can kiss me," I whispered. I didn't lean in. I didn't push her. The slightest resistance might throw up her defences. "Night after night, Stella, I've thought about kissing you. I love you. Please, please kiss me."

She closed the gap and our breaths mingled as our lips touched for the first time in far, far too long. At first, the kiss was soft and tentative, but I felt her breathing quicken as the kiss became harder, more insistent. She opened herself to my hunger for her and I felt her passion burning through the ravaged vestiges of my nervous system. God, I wanted her. I quaked at the taste of her. There was no bliss better than this.

After a minute she pulled away. "You're trembling," she said. "Do you need a minute?"

"No," I said, my voice raspy. "I could do this forever."

"Well, we have all day. I used my birthday as a reason to beg off of patrol today." She gave me a little push on the chest. "Have a seat."

I sat on the bed and she perched next to me. I leaned in, slowly so she would have time to stop me if she wanted to, and kissed her neck in the way that always lit her up inside.

"Oh, Howie. I missed you so fucking much," she whispered.

"I am in love with you," I breathed, taking her hands in mine.

And I felt her break open and her love flooded out of her.

"Oh God… how do you do that…?" She was crying, and I kissed each tear as it rolled down her cheeks. "I'm so sorry, Howie. I'm so sorry I hurt you. I'm so sorry I threw you away…"

I shushed her and held her tightly. "You didn't throw me away. You were right. I was destroying myself to try to become what we both thought you wanted. I was hurting myself for you. And that should never be okay. And I wasn't being honest with you. And I'm sorry. I'm sorry."

Stella pulled away, and I wanted to cling to her, to beg her to stay with me, to let me love her, but I let her go. Any force would just push her away.

She stood, wiped her face with the back of her hand, and reached into her pocket. Then she dropped to one knee and pulled out a gleaming ruby ring.

My heart felt as if it would burst.

"I don't want to marry you," she said, "because I'm only nineteen and the world is over so there really isn't much point in it. But I love you and I want you to know that I'm yours. You're mine. We're ours. Okay?"

I took the ring. I reached out and took Stella's left hand, and I slid the ring onto her ring finger.

"I'm yours," I said to her softly, "I'm yours forever."

We kissed again, and this time it went on and on. I could feel her love thrumming right through me, and it was ecstasy as she pulled off my shirt and kissed my chest until I was moaning for her, desperate for her touch, for her skin, for her warmth.

She pulled away from me again and it was like torture. She sat back with a knowing smirk on her face which just made me even more frantic to kiss her. She reached into her back pocket and pulled out a condom.

I froze.

"What… what are you…?"

"Oh, yeah, that's my other birthday present," she said waving the package. "I want to have sex. I've wanted to have sex with you for years, and today I'm going to ride you into oblivion, Howard Joseph Fontaine Mullins."

Oh God. Was this a dream?

"But… but…"

"Yeah, I talked to your Dad. You're apparently 100% *not* contagious in any way. You lied to me."

"No… if you…" She stepped back, pulled her shirt over her head and dropped her pants. I lost the ability to speak again.

"Were you just afraid?" she asked. "Even with birth control, were you really so afraid?"

I nodded.

"Afraid I would get pregnant?"

I nodded again. "And afraid to tell you what could happen if you got pregnant."

"Very bad things, I'm sure. But it's okay. You don't have to be afraid. I've been on birth control for a long time and we have an entire city's worth of pharmacies stocked with more of it. I also have *multiple* condoms, so if it's okay with you, I plan to make today a *very* good birthday." She climbed on to the bed, and I felt like I must be in a dream because surely things like this couldn't happen in real life.

"Are… are you sure?" I felt a flood of relief. Some part of me had always been certain that she would leave, that she wouldn't want to be with someone who was only capable of spawning monsters.

"I am sure that I won't get pregnant," she said. "And I am sure that I am willing to take that risk. And I am sure that I want to be with you. I want all of you, Howie. Your good and your bad. It's all mine. It's all part of you. The virus isn't something for me to overlook. It makes you strong, and it helps you find people who need saving. It helps you see through my messed-up personality and find the real me inside. And I love that. I *need* that. There is nothing, Howie," she said as she ran her hands down my stomach and to the button of my pants, "*nothing* about you that I don't love and accept. You are everything I need you to be. Okay?"

If hearts could break from relief and happiness, mine would have.

She undressed me slowly — sensually — and she watched me closely as she rolled a condom expertly into place. I could feel the heat from her skin on mine, and I couldn't stop trembling.

"Tell me," she whispered as she mounted me. "Just tell me if you want me to stop."

When we finally, oh finally, joined together, my back arched at the feeling of her around me. My hands clutched her hips as we moved together, our minds together, driving us both to ecstasy.

"Oh… Oh God, oh God, Stella…. DON'T STOP."

READ MORE FOR FREE!

Want to read more about Howie, Stella, and the other characters? Sign up for C.L. Lynch's exclusive bonus content and get *free* novellas featuring your favourite characters from the Stella Blunt series!

The novellas include *With You,* a Howie and Stella Christmas story, *Not Feast on Thee,* the tragic tale of Howie's zombification, and *The Bean Counter,* the story of how Tim and Elaine Blunt first met.

You will also receive a story about Stella's childhood, Ray's backstory and more!

Finally, you will also be sent exclusive offers to preview upcoming books for FREE.

Sign up here:

Http://www.cllynch.com/bonus

TURN THE PAGE TO READ AN EXCERPT FROM *BIOLOGY*

THE THIRD AND FINAL BOOK IN THE STELLA BLUNT TRILOGY!

Preface

One of the things about being essentially immortal is that you start to take life for granted. It can even be something you resent, as you watch the people around you grow old and die. For a long time, I felt like a rock in the stream of life. Death isn't something I fear - partially because I no longer have self-defensive instincts and partially because it is one of the many natural parts of life that I have always been denied.

For a while, I had led myself to think that I could truly rejoin life. I had pictured myself with a family, living, growing, changing. I had hope. I had joy. I had Stella. But now all of that was gone. My life had been snatched away.

Now, I was probably walking to my own death, and I didn't care. All that mattered was getting revenge. They had already taken my life in every other way.

So I would bring them their death.

1

Howie

My Stella looked stunning, even in riot gear. The heavy truck rumbled slowly down the ruined road, crushing fallen tree branches and discarded recyclables under its tires. I still wasn't used to the emptiness of the world, even though we did this day after day, week after week. The abandoned houses looked dead, and their broken windows made me think of empty eye sockets. But if Stella was sharing my gloomy thoughts, she didn't show it. She balanced effortlessly in the back of the truck, rifle in her hand, and scanned the sides of the road for any sign of true life. She looked at ease, and powerful, and tough. And I loved it.

I was supposed to be looking for survivors too, but I could do it while sitting down, looking at Stella, and simply trying to listen for a healthy mind.

Of course, Stella's mind was so overpowering that this was difficult. When I was with Stella, which was every moment I could get, the feel of her thoughts was so powerful that I had to really concentrate to notice anyone else at all. It's like trying to block out your favourite song while it plays at top volume, to try to hear someone calling you from way down the road.

If they really thought there was a good chance of finding survivors on this street, they would have sent me out without her. They don't really care if something happens to me. But this street had been canvassed several times already. There wasn't really much hope. This trip was a scavenging mission.

That's when I thought I felt it: a slight snarling of the melody. A blackness that felt as foul as Stella felt fair. I stiffened and sat up. I laid my hand on Stella's thigh and she looked down immediately.

"They're coming," I said.

Stella shouted a warning, and the soldiers in the back of the truck snapped to attention. The truck sighed to a stop.

For a moment, there was utter silence.

Then the ravagers attacked.

ABOUT THE AUTHOR

C.L. Lynch is a socially awkward introvert living in Vancouver, Canada. She wrote Chemistry, the first book in the Stella Blunt trilogy, as a reaction to reading Twilight. It started out as a joke, but she got caught up in the characters and her friends urged her to publish the book. She is now an award-winning author who is working hard on the third book of the series, Biology, while hiding from her adult responsibilities.

She loves to get emails as further distraction from adulting, so send her a line at author@cllynch.com or follow her online:

Facebook

https://www.facebook.com/cllynchauthor/

Twitter

https://twitter.com/lynchauthor

Tumblr

https://cllynchauthor.tumblr.com/

ACKNOWLEDGEMENTS

Thanks go out to all of the people who helped cheer this book to the finish line.

Christine Lynch – aka Mum - thank you for treating my writing like real work and not just a 'hobby'. Your investment, both financially and emotionally, means more than I can ever express.

Rebecca DeVoe - Howie's number one fan - without your willingness to read my raw, unedited nonsense, I don't know if I would have had the courage or the insight to turn this book into something vaguely resembling a readable story.

James Avery Fuchs - editor, poet, and extraordinary human being - you caught typos and missing words that I missed after reading the damn manuscript *three times!* Not to mention the whole past-tense debacle. Yeesh.

Amelia the Amazing - you're the best business partner and cheerleader a friend could ask for, and I value you all the more because you aren't afraid to point out my mistakes.

And all my other awesome beta-readers, including but not limited to:

Brayden Spjuth, Cat Karelis, Chris Ann Hanousek, Christine Kelley, Cynthia Loiselle, Emerson Graves, Francesca, Hannah Povey, Hank Haynes, Jeannie Chiasson, Jennifer Sheils, Jessica Green, Jodie Shackleford, Jules Ironside, Lorena González Gamero, Margaret Bak, Max Baker, Renaye Weekes, Sofia Degetau, Suzan Brooking, Tara Jake-Zettel, Tanyawriter, Wendy Rinebold, and Yasmeen Underwood… *thank you* for helping me to save this book when I was starting to think that it might be a hopeless tire fire. Your glowing praise buoyed me up, and your insightful critiques gave me insight into my readership and helped me figure out which parts of the book to keep, and which parts to prune.

Without all of you, this book would be way, way crappier. Consider yourselves heroes. You're my heroes, anyway.

89318565R00413

Made in the USA
Lexington, KY
26 May 2018